New

A Harlem numbers writer makes it through another day of conning and corruption . . . a farm boy comes of age in a Louisiana jail cell . . . "Mr. Jiveass Nigger" introduces himself . . . an old dining car waiter tells it like it really was when the trains ran on time and Blacks poured the coffee with big white grins . . . poems flower in the nightmare landscape of America, nurtured by rage, and with roots running deep and firm in Black culture . . . James Baldwin talks about the price of fame and why he split the scene . . . the voice of Malcolm X speaks its living truths from beyond the grave . . . and much, much more . . .

Black is beautiful—and here the whole fantastic spectrum of that beauty can be seen in a superbly knowledgable, wide-ranging collection—selected by the editor of the highly acclaimed previous volume, Black Voices, *also available in a Mentor edition.*

Ⓜ   Ⓢ (0451)

Recommended Reading from MENTOR and SIGNET

☐ **THE COLLECTED STORIES OF CHARLES W. CHESNUTT. Edited and with an Introduction by William L. Andrews.** This important collection contains all the stories in Chesnutt's two published volumes, *The Conjure Woman* and *The Wife of His Youth and Other Stories of the Color Line*, along with two uncollected works: the tragic "Dave's Neckliss" and "Baxter's Procrustes," his parting shot at prejudice.   (628438—$5.99)

☐ **THE AFRICAN-AMERICAN NOVEL IN THE AGE OF REACTION: THREE CLASSICS. Edited and with an Introduction by William L. Andrews.** Includes *Iola Leroy* by Frances E. W. Harper, *The Marrow of Tradition* by Charles W. Chesnutt, and *The Sport of the Gods* by Paul Laurence Dunbar—novels that remain significant as works that influenced a nation's conscience.   (628497—$5.99)

☐ **NARRATIVE OF THE LIFE OF FREDERICK DOUGLASS:** *An American Slave* **by Frederick Douglass.** Preface by William Lloyd Garrison. One of the most eloquent indictments of slavery ever recorded, revealing the inhumanity suffered by slaves in the pre-Civil War South.
                                                          (161882—$4.99)

Prices slightly higher in Canada

―――

Buy them at your local bookstore or use this convenient coupon for ordering.

PENGUIN USA
P.O. Box 999 – Dept. #17109
Bergenfield, New Jersey 07621

Please send me the books I have checked above.
I am enclosing $_____ (please add $2.00 to cover postage and handling).
Send check or money order (no cash or C.O.D.'s) or charge by Mastercard or VISA (with a $15.00 minimum). Prices and numbers are subject to change without notice.

Card #_____ Exp. Date _____
Signature_____
Name_____
Address_____
City _____ State _____ Zip Code _____

For faster service when ordering by credit card call **1-800-253-6476**

Allow a minimum of 4-6 weeks for delivery. This offer is subject to change without notice.

NEW
BLACK VOICES

An Anthology of Contemporary
Afro-American Literature

Edited, with an Introduction and
Biographical Notes, by Abraham Chapman

A MENTOR BOOK

MENTOR
Published by the Penguin Group
Penguin Books USA Inc., 375 Hudson Street,
New York, New York 10014, U.S.A.
Penguin Books Ltd, 27 Wrights Lane,
London W8 5TZ, England
Penguin Books Australia Ltd, Ringwood,
Victoria, Australia
Penguin Books Canada Ltd, 10 Alcorn Avenue,
Toronto, Ontario, Canada M4V 3B2
Penguin Books (N.Z.) Ltd, 182–190 Wairau Road,
Auckland 10, New Zealand

Penguin Books Ltd, Registered Offices:
Harmondsworth, Middlesex, England

First Mentor Printing, March, 1972
18 17 16 15 14 13 12 11

Copyright © 1972 by Abraham Chapman
All rights reserved

 REGISTERED TRADEMARK—MARCA REGISTRADA

Library of Congress Catalog Card Number: 74:181598

Printed in the United States of America

Acknowledgments and Copyright Notices

Copyrights for poems, stories, and critical articles published from manuscript for the first time in this anthology are held by their authors and all rights are reserved by their authors.

JAMES BALDWIN, "Why I left America" copyright © October 1970 by the Hollingsworth Group, Inc., reprinted by permission of *Essence* magazine.

IMAMU AMIRI BARAKA (LeROI JONES), "Ka 'Ba" and "Sacred Chant for the Return of Black Spirit and Power" from *Black Magic Poetry, 1961-1967*, copyright © 1969 by LeRoi Jones, reprinted by permission of the publisher, The Bobbs-Merrill Company, Inc. "The Legacy of Malcolm X, and the Coming of the Black Nation" from *Home: Social Essays* by LeRoi Jones copyright © 1965, 1966 by LeRoi Jones, reprinted by permission of William Morrow and Company, Inc.

GERALD W. BARRAX, "The Scuba Diver Recovers the Body of a Drowned Child," "The Old Glory" and "For a Black Poet" from *Another Kind of Rain*. copyright © 1970 by Gerald W. Barrax, reprinted by permission of University of Pittsburgh Press.

BLACK ACADEMY OF ARTS AND LETTERS, "Purposes" and "Founding Address" by C. Eric Lincoln, reprinted by permission of Black Academy of Arts and Letters, Inc.

BLACK WORLD FOUNDATION, "Program," reprinted by permission of Nathan Hare, President, Black World Foundation.

(*The following pages constitute an extension of this copyright page.*).

ISAAC J. BLACK, "Racist Psychotherapy" from *Nkombo,* Vol. 2, No. 4, copyright 1969 by BLKARTSOUTH, reprinted by permission of BLKARTSOUTH.

GWENDOLYN BROOKS, "Riot" from *Riot* copyright © 1969 by Gwendolyn Brooks, reprinted by permission of the publisher, Broadside Press, Dudley Randall, Publisher.

CECIL BROWN, "Prologue" from *The Life and Loves of Mr. Jiveass Nigger,* by Cecil Brown copyright © 1969 by Cecil Brown, reprinted by permission of Farrar, Straus, & Giroux, Inc.

F. J. BRYANT, JR., "Cathexis" copyright © 1972 by F. J. Bryant, Jr., published from manuscript by permission of the author.

ELDRIDGE CLEAVER, "Psychology: The Black Bible" from *Eldridge Cleaver: Post-Prison Writings and Speeches,* ed. by Robert Scheer. copyright © 1967, 1968, 1969, by Eldridge Cleaver, reprinted by permission of the publisher, Random House, Inc.

JOHNETTA B. COLE, "Culture: Negro, Black and Nigger" from *The Black Scholar.* Vol. 1, No. 8, copyright 1970 by *The Black Scholar,* reprinted by permission of *The Black Scholar.*

CYRUS COLTER, "Mary's Convert" copyright 1965 by *Chicago Review,* The University of Chicago Press, reprinted by permission of *Chicago Review.*

CONYUS. "The Great Santa Barbara Oil Disaster OR:" and "Confession to Malcolm" copyright © 1972 by Conyus, published from manuscript by permission of the author, and "i rode with geronimo" copyright 1970 by Conyus from *Dices or Black Bones,* Houghton Mifflin Co., reprinted by permission of the author.

JAYNE CORTEZ, "Lonely Woman" and "Suppression" from *Pisstained Stairs and The Monkey Man's Wares* copyright 1969 by Jayne Cortez and "I'm a Worker" and "The Rising" copyright © 1972 by Jayne Cortez and published from manuscript, all by permission of the author.

VICTOR HERNANDEZ CRUZ, "First Claims Poem" and "urban dream" from *Snaps* copyright © 1968, 1969 by Victor Hernandez Cruz, reprinted by permission of Random House, Inc.

JAMES CUNNINGHAM, "Hemlock for the Black Artist: Karenga Style" from *Negro Digest* magazine, January, 1968, reprinted by permission of *Black World* and the author.

TOM DENT, "For Walter Washington" and "Ray Charles at Mississippi State" from *Nkombo,* Vol. 2, No. 3, copyright 1969 by Free Southern Theatre, reprinted by permission of BLKARTSOUTH.

EMORY DOUGLAS, "On Revolutionary Culture" reprinted from *The Black Panther,* January 3, 1970.

RALPH ELLISON, "Remarks at the American Academy Conference on the Negro American, 1965" reprinted by permission from *Daedalus,* Journal of the American Academy of Arts and Sciences, Boston, Massachusetts, Vol. 95, No. 1 (Winter, 1966).

JAMES A. EMANUEL, "Whitey, Baby," "Black Man, 13th Floor," "For 'Mr. Dudley,' A Black Spy," "Panther Man" copyright © 1972 by James A. Emanuel, published from manusript by permission of the author.

MARI EVANS, "Vive Noir!" copyright 1970 by Mari Evans and reprinted from manuscript copy by permission of the author.

RONALD L. FAIR, "We Who Came After" copyright © 1969 by Ronald L. Fair, reprinted by permission of William Morris Agency and Ronald Fair.

VAL FERDINAND, "whi/te boys gone" and "Food for Thought" from *Nkombo* Vol. 2, No. 3, 1969 and "The Blues (in two parts)" and "2 B BLK" from *The Blues Merchant.* published by BLKARTSOUTH, and "BLKARTSOUTH/get on up!" from manuscript copyright 1972 by Val Ferdinand, all published by permission of the author and BLKART-SOUTH.

RONALDO FERNANDEZ, "legacy of a brother" from *Impatient Rebel* copyright 1969 by Free Southern Theatre, reprinted by permission of BLKARTSOUTH.

CALVIN FORBES, "Reading Walt Whitman" copyright 1970 by Calvin Forbes from *Survival,* Spring, 1970 (published by the Urban League of Boston) "Europe" and "Lullaby for Ann-Lucian" copyrigbt © 1972 by Calvin Forbes, published from manuscript, all by permission of the author.

ERNEST J. GAINES, "Three Men" from *Bloodline* by Ernest J. Gaines copyright © 1963, 1964, 1968 by Ernest J. Gaines and reprinted by permission of the publisher, The Dial Press.

ADDISON GAYLE, JR., "The Son of My Father" from *The Black Situation* by Addison Gayle, Jr., copyright 1970, reprinted by permission of the publisher, Horizon Press, New York.

NIKKI GIOVANNI, "My Poem" from *Black Judgement,* copyright © 1968 by Nikki Giovanni, reprinted by permission of the publisher, Broadside Press.

CARL H. GREENE, "Something Old, Something New." "The Realist" and "The Excuse" copyright © 1972 by Carl H. Greene, all published from manuscript by permission of the author.

KIRK HALL, "blackgoldblueswoman" and "today is not like they said" copyright © 1972 by Kirk Hall and published from manuscript by permission of the author.

NATHAN HARE "Algiers 1969: A Report on the Pan-African Cultural Festival" from *The Black Scholar,* Vol. 1, No. 1, 1969, reprinted by permission of *The Black Scholar.*

MICHAEL S. HARPER, "A Mother Speaks: The Algiers Motel Incident, Detroit," "Zocalo," "The Guerilla-Cong" from *Dear John, Dear Coltrane,* copyright © 1970 by University of Pittsburgh Press, reprinted by permission of University of Pittsburgh Press. "High Modes: Vision as Ritual: Confirmation" copyright © 1972 by Michael S. Harper, published from manuscript by permission of the author.

WILLIAM J. HARRIS, "My baby" and "A Daddy Poem" copyright © 1972 by William J. Harris, published from manuscript by permission of the author.

ROBERT HAYDEN. "The Dream (1863)" by Robert Hayden from *Words in the Mourning Time* copyright © 1970 by Robert Hayden, reprinted by permission of October House, Inc.

CHESTER HIMES, "Dilemma of the Negro Novelist in the U.S.A." from *Beyond the Angry Black* (Second Edition 1966) ed. by John A. Williams, copyright 1966 by John A. Williams and reprinted by permission of the publisher, Cooper Square Publishers, Inc.

EVERETT HOAGLAND, "The Anti-Semanticist" from *Black Velvet* (Revised Edition), copyright © 1970 by Everett Hoagland, reprinted by permission of the publisher, Broadside Press.

LANCE JEFFERS, "Old Love Butchered (Colorado Springs and Huachuca)," "Trellie," "I do not know the power of my hand," and "There is a nation" copyright © 1972 by Lance Jeffers and published from manuscript by permission of the author. "Afro-American Literature: The Conscience of Man" is published from manuscript, revised by the author from an earlier version printed in *The Black Scholar*, January, 1971. Copyright © 1972 by Lance Jeffers and reprinted with his permission.

NORMAN JORDAN. "I Have Seen Them," "When A Woman Gets Blue," "Be You," "The Silent Prophet," "The Poet, The Dreamer" from *Destination: Ashes* copyright © 1969 by Norman Jordan, all reprinted by permission of the author, and "July 27" copyright © 1972 by Norman Jordan and published from manuscript by permission of the author.

MAULANA RON KARENGA, "Black Art: Mute Matter Given Force and Function" from *Negro Digest* January, 1968, retitled by the author for this republication, copyright January 1968 by *Negro Digest*, reprinted by permission of *Black World* and the author.

BOB KAUFMAN, "Cocoa Morning," "Heavy Water Blues" and "Geneology" from *Golden Sardine*. copyright © 1967 by Bob Kaufman, reprinted by permission of the publisher, City Lights Books.

WILLIAM MELVIN KELLEY, "A Good Long Sidewalk" copyright © 1964 by William Melvin Kelley, from the book *Dancers on the Shore* by William Melvin Kelley, reprinted by permission of Doubleday and Company, Inc.

JOHN OLIVER KILLENS, "Foreword" from *The Cotillion* copyright © 1971 by John Oliver Killens and reprinted by permission of Trident Press/division of Simon & Schuster, Inc.

ETHERIDGE KNIGHT, "A Time to Mourn" from *Black Voices from Prison* ed. by Etheridge Knight, copyright © 1970 by Pathfinder Press, and reprinted by permission of Pathfinder Press, Inc. "A WASP Woman Visits a Black Junkie in Prison" from *Greater Works*, March 1966 and reprinted by permission of its successor, *Event* magazine of the American Lutheran Church Men. "The Warden Said to Me the Other Day," "Crazy Pigeon," "It Was a Funky Deal," and "For Langston Hughes" from *Poems from Prison* copyright © 1968 by Etheridge Knight, all reprinted by permission of the publisher, Broadside Press.

KUSH, "A Message for Langston" from *Nkombo* Vol. 2, No. 4, copyright 1969 by BLKARTSOUTH, reprinted by permission of BLKARTSOUTH.

OLIVER LAGRONE, "Suncoming," "Remnant Ghosts at Dawn," and "Lines to the Black Oak" all copyright © 1972 by Oliver LaGrone and published from manuscript by permission of the author.

DON L. LEE, "One Sided Shoot-out" from *We Walk the Way of the New World*, copyright © 1970 by Don L. Lee, "a poem to complement other poems" from *Don't Cry, Scream* copyright © 1969 by Don L. Lee, all reprinted by permission of the publisher, Broadside Press.

RICHARD A. LONG, "Black Studies: International Dimensions" from *CLA Journal* Vol. XIV (September, 1970) reprinted by permission of *CLA Journal*.

AUDRE LORDE, "Generation" and "New York City 1970" copyright © 1972 by Audre Lorde and published from manuscript copies, and "Coal" from *The First Cities*, copyright © 1968 by Audre Lorde, all by permission of the author.

K. CURTIS LYLE, "Sometimes I Go to Camarillo & Sit in the Lounge" from *Confrontation: A Journal of Third World Literature* Vol. 1, No. 1, 1970, and "Lacrimas" copyright © 1972 by K. Curtis Lyle from manuscript, both poems reprinted by permission of the author.

JAMES ALAN McPHERSON, "A Solo Song: For Doc" from *Hue and Cry* by James Alan McPherson copyright © 1968, 1969 by James Alan McPherson, reprinted by permission of Atlantic-Little, Brown and Co.

NAOMI LONG MADGETT, "Sally: Twelfth Street," "Brothers at the Bar," "Souvenir," and "The Twenty Grand" copyright © 1972 by Naomi Long Madgett, all published from manuscript by permission of the author.

CLARENCE MAJOR, "Vietnam #4" copyright © 1967 by Clarence Major, reprinted by permission of the author, "Self World" from *Swallow the Lake* copyright © 1955, 1970 by Clarence Major, reprinted by permission of Wesleyan University Press.

MALCOLM X, "Statement of Basic Aims and Objectives of the Organization of Afro-American Unity" and "Basic Unity Program" from *The Last Year of Malcolm X* ed. by George Breitman copyright © 1967 by Merit Publishers, reprinted by permission of Pathfinder Press, Inc. and Mrs. Betty Shabazz.

JOE MARTINEZ, "Rehabilitation and Treatment" from *Black Voices From Prison* ed. by Etheridge Knight, copyright © 1970 by Pathfinder Press, reprinted by permission of Pathfinder Press, Inc.

ADAM DAVID MILLER, "Some Observations on a Black Aesthetic" copyright © 1970 by Adam David Miller, from *The Black Aesthetic*; reprinted by permission of Adam David Miller and Doubleday & Co., Inc. "The Africa Thing" and "The Hungry Black Child" from *Dices or Black Bones*, Houghton Mifflin Co., copyright 1970 by Adam David Miller, reprinted by permission of the author and Houghton Mifflin Co. "the pruning" and "mulch" copyright © 1972 by Adam David Miller, published from manuscript by permission of the author.

NAYO (BARBARA MALCOLM), "Bedtime Story," "Black Woman Throws a *Tantrum*," "I watched little black boys," "easy way out" from *I Want Me a Home* copyright 1969 by Free Southern Theatre, and "First time I was sweet sixteen" from *Nkombo* Vol. 2, No. 4, copyright 1969 by BLKARTSOUTH, all reprinted by permission of BLKARTSOUTH.

LARRY NEAL, "The Middle Passage and After," "Harlem Gallery: From the Inside" from *Black Boogaloo (Notes on Black Liberation)* copyright © 1969 by Larry Neal and "Lady's Days" from manuscript of *Hoodoo Hollering Bebop Ghosts*, copyright 1972 by Larry Neal, all published by permission of the author.

TEJUMOLA OLOGBONI (ROCKIE D. TAYLOR), "Changed Mind" and "Black Henry" from *Drum Song* copyright 1969 by Rockie D. Taylor and "I Wonta Thank Ya" copyright 1972 by Rockie D. Taylor, published from manuscript, all by permission of the author.

JOHN O'NEAL, "Shades of Pharoah Sanders" from *Nkombo* Vol. 2, No. 3, copyright 1969 by Free Southern Theatre, reprinted by permission of BLKARTSOUTH.

RAYMOND R. PATTERSON, "What We Know," "Black Power," "When I Awoke," "A Word to the Wise is Enough," "Schwerner, Chaney, Goodman," and "This Age" reprinted from the *Award* book, *26 Ways of Looking at a Black Man* by Raymond R. Patterson, copyright 1969 by Raymond R. Patterson, reprinted by permission of the publisher. Universal Publishing and Distributing Corporation.

ROBERT DEANE PHARR, "The Numbers Writer" from *New York Magazine*, September 22, 1969, copyright © 1969 by Robert Deane Pharr, reprinted by permission of the Sterling Lord Agency.

N. H. PRITCHARD, "The Signs" and "Passage" from *The Matrix* by Norman H. Pritchard, Jr. Copyright © 1963, 1967, 1969, 1970 by Norman H. Pritchard, Jr. Reprinted by permission of Doubleday & Company, Inc.

DUDLEY RANDALL, "Primitives" and "The Melting Pot" from *Cities Burning,* copyright © 1968 by Dudley Randall. "Old Witherington" from *Ten: Anthology of Detroit Poets.* copyright © 1968 by South and West, Inc.' all reprinted by permission of the author and Broadside Press.

EUGENE REDMOND, "Parapoetics," "Spearo's Blues (Or: Ode to a Grecian Yearn)," and "Definition of Nature" from *Sentry of the Four Golden Pillars,* copyright 1970 by Eugene Redmond, reprinted by permission of the author.

ISHMAEL REED, "catechism of d neoamerican hoodoo church" copyright 1970 by Ishmael Reed published by permission of the author, and "Introduction" from *19 Necromancers from Now,* by Ishmael Reed, copyright © 1970 by Ishmael Reed, reprinted by permission of Doubleday & Company, Inc.

ED ROBERSON, "Four Lines of a Black Love Letter Between Teachers" from *When Thy King Is a Boy,* copyright 1970 by University of Pittsburgh Press, reprinted by permission of University of Pittsburgh Press.

SONIA SANCHEZ, "liberation / poem" and "on watching a world series game" from *We a BaddDDD People.* copyright © 1970 by Sonia Sanchez, reprinted by permission of the publisher, Broadside Press.

WALT SHEPPERD, "An Interview with Clarence Major and Victor Hernandez Cruz" from *Nickel Review,* September 12, 1969, copyright by *Nickel Review* 1969, reprinted by permission of *Nickel Review.*

STEPHANY, "What marked the river's flow," "Who collects the pain," "I have spent my life," "It is again," "Moving deep" from *Moving Deep* copyright © 1969 by Stephany, reprinted by permission of the publisher, Broadside Press, Dudley Randall, Publisher.

STERLING STUCKEY, "Through the Prism of Folklore: The Black Ethos in Slavery" from *The Massachusetts Review* Vol. IX, No. 3. Summer 1968, copyright © 1968 by The Massachusetts Review, Inc. and reprinted by permission of The Massachusetts Review, Inc.

JEANNE A. TAYLOR. "A House Divided" from *The Antioch Review,* Vol. XXVII, No. 2, Fall 1967 reprinted by permission of *The Antioch Review.*

MIKE THELWELL, "Bright an' Mownin' Star" from *The Massachusetts Review*. Vol. VIII, No. 4 1966, copyright © 1966 and reprinted by permission of The Massachustts Review, Inc.

LORENZO THOMAS. "Inauguration" copyright 1972 by Lorenzo Thomas, published from manuscript by permission of the author.

SOTERE TORREGIAN, "Poem for the Birthday of Huey P. Newton," "The Newark Public Library Reading Room" and "Travois of the Nameless" copyright 1972 by Sotère Torregian, all published from manuscript by permission of the author.

QUINCY TROUPE, "A Day in the Life of a Poet," "Impressions of Chicago," "you come to me" and "The Syntax of the Mind Grips" copyright 1972 by Quincy Troupe, all published from manuscript by permission of the author.

DARWIN T. TURNER, "The Teaching of Afro-American Literature" from *College English*, April 1970, copyright © 1970 by the National Council of Teachers of English, reprinted by permission of the publisher and Darwin T. Turner.

MARGARET WALKER, "Ballad of the Hoppy-Toad" from *Prophets for a New Day* copyright © 1970 by Margaret Walker, reprinted by permission of the publisher, Broadside Press.

VICTOR STEVEN WALKER, "The Long Sell" copyright © 1972 by Victor Steven Walker, published from manuscript by permission of the author.

RAYMOND WASHINGTON, "Vision from the Ghetto" and "Freedom Hair" from *Visions from the Ghetto*, copyright © 1969 by Free Southern Theatre and "Moonbound" from *Nkombo* Vol. 2, No. 3 copyright 1969 by Free Southern Theatre, reprinted by permission of BLKARTSOUTH.

TOM WEATHERLY, "autobiography," "your eyes are mirth," "blues for frank wootens" and "mud water shango" from *Maumau American Cantos*, copyright © 1970 by Tom Weatherly, reprinted by permission of the publisher, Corinth Books.

RON WELBURN, "Whichway," "lyrics shimmy like." "Condition Blue / Dress," "put u red-eye in," "and universals" and "tu" copyright 1972 by Ron Welburn, published from manuscript; "black is beautiful" and "it is overdue time" from *Nickel Review,* March 30, 1970, all published by permission of the author.

JAY WRIGHT, "The Neighborhood House" and "Jalapeña Gypsies" copyright 1972 by Jay Wright, published from manuscript by permission of the author.

AL YOUNG. "A Little More Traveling Music," "A Dance for Ma Rainey," "A Dance for Militant Dilettantes" and "Dance of the Infidels" from *Dancing* copyright 1969 by Al Young and reprinted by permission of Corinth Books. "The Prestidigitator (1)" and "The Prestidigitator (2)" copyright 1972 by Al Young published from manuscript by permission of the author. "Chicken Hawk's Dream" copright © 1966 by Fenian Head Centre Press, reprinted by permission of Wender & Associates, Inc. "Statement on Aesthetics. Poetics, Kinetics" copyright 1972 by Al Young, published from manuscript by permission.

TO MY DAUGHTERS
LAURA AND ANN

CONTENTS

Contents

III. CRITICISM

INTRODUCTION

This book is a companion volume to *Black Voices: An Anthology of Afro-American Literature*, not a revised edition or substitute. It begins where that book leaves off. It is a continuation into the present, an addition of new Black writing of the Sixties, especially the late Sixties, and early Seventies, to the rich and varied body of Afro-American writing which has evolved in the United States over a span of more than two centuries. It is an attempt to reflect the latest stage, a most exciting stage, in the long and meaningful development of Black self-expression and self-definition in literature and criticism. It is an invitation to explore the dynamics and diversification of the new currents in Black writing and thinking, which cannot be done with any single book alone, this or any other.

The Black literary scene is far too complex and rich in polarities, as well as individual explorations in a multitude of directions, to be properly encompassed in any one book. This volume concludes with a bibliography of all the books and collections of poetry by the eighty-four writers represented in this anthology. And even this relatively large number of writers does not include all of the interesting and vital Black writers of today. For a variety of very different reasons I could not include selections from the works of all of the writers I would have liked to. Quite a few writers who are as important and as much a part of the contemporary Black literary scene as some of the writers who are included in this book simply had to be left out. I have tried to include as many diverse literary and critical trends as possible, in keeping with the underlying principle of selection in *Black Voices*: accent on the diversity of Black sensibilities, modes of expression, and independent thinking, as part of a conscious battle against the myth of the Black monolith and the racist tendencies to squeeze the great spectrum of Black humanity into the false molds of a few Negro stereotypes.

This book consists entirely of works written or first published in the Sixties or early Seventies. The essay by Chester Himes was first published in the United States in the Sixties but appears to have been written in the Fifties. Some compilers of contemporary literature have fixed an author's age, thirty or thirty-five years, as the line of demarcation between the contemporary and the old. Many of the writers in this anthology are young, but I have not limited my selections by any arbitrary age classification. Some young writers are old in outlook and style and some writers who are old in years remain young in outlook, continue to grow and develop, and are new and revolutionary. I understand as contemporary all writers who are alive, writing and publishing, and giving voice to the times in which we live, in many different ways, by expressing their own selves and creating the imaginative worlds and structures which grow out of their inextricable involvement in our age. My only criterion was works by writers who were alive when the book was submitted to the publisher in late spring 1971. There is one exception, in the documents section—the final program of Malcolm X, a significant expression of Black thought in the Sixties which remains very much alive in various currents of contemporary Black culture. Fourteen of the eighty-four authors in this book were represented in *Black Voices;* in this collection I have added newer works by them.

This anthology includes new writing, never before published, in addition to selections from magazines and books. This is particularly true of the poetry section which grew in scope and developed with a momentum exceeding my original expectations. I wrote to a number of poets about the preparation of this anthology and asked if they had any poems in manuscript that I could see. In response I not only received poems in manuscript but names of other poets with the suggestion that I write to them and consider their work. In some instances I received poems in the mail with a note informing me that one poet or another had told them I was working on this book and that I might be interested in seeing the enclosed poems. The net result is that at least fifty-five of the poems in this volume, by twenty-two different poets, were selected from manuscript. Two of the statements in the criticism section, by Val Ferdinand (Kalamu ya Salaam) and Al Young, embodying two different views of Black literature today, were written especially for this anthology. And the short story by Victor Steven Walker is by a young writer who has never appeared in print before.

The selections of each of the writers included in this anthology are preceded by a brief biographical note. Most of the biographies include the author's year of birth, but some do not. Some writers preferred not to include this information and I have chosen in this matter to respect the wishes of the authors, and their right to privacy, rather than to strive rigidly for formal stylistic uniformity.

The Black population in the United States is concentrating increasingly in the big cities and metropolitan centers and much of the writing in this book is urban. A Census Bureau compilation made public on May 18, 1971, reported that nearly half the nation's Black population is concentrated in fifty cities, and a third of the total in fifteen cities. There are now eleven cities in the United States with Black populations of a quarter of a million or more. These cities are:

Cities	Black Population
New York City	1,666,636
Chicago	1,102,620
Detroit	660,428
Philadelphia	653,791
Washington	537,712
Los Angeles	503,606
Baltimore	420,210
Cleveland	287,841
New Orleans	267,308
Atlanta	255,051
St. Louis	254,191

There are selections in this book by writers living and writing in all of these cities with the exception of Washington and Baltimore.

I repeat, this anthology is an invitation to the students of American literature and of Afro-American expression to explore further the depths, tensions, and polarities of the new Black writing, a vital part of the contemporary literature of the United States, in other books and in the Black literary and cultural journals and periodicals. Some of the writers and poets represented in this anthology with poems and critical essays are playing a prominent part in the new Black literary movements and have compiled important collections of new

Black writing (fully listed with the works of the respective authors in the bibliography at the end of this book) which illuminate various aspects of, and approaches to, contemporary Black writing. Some of the writers not included in this anthology will be found in these other collections just as some of the writers not included in other compilations of contemporary Black writing can be found in this collection.

In point of time, the preparation and publication of *Black Voices* did not coincide with any historical end of an era in Afro-American life and literature, or even end of a decade. The selections were completed in 1967 and the introduction was written early in 1968, the year of publication. A single-volume collection of Afro-American fiction, autobiography, poetry, and literary criticism, spanning a century and a quarter of writing, each category presented in chronological progression, *Black Voices* ended with the beginnings of the new Black writing of the Sixties. The book went to press at a time of great ferment, transition, and change in Black American life and culture. It was a time of intense searching for new political and aesthetic directions, new forms and modes of expression, new approaches to language and style.

It was a seed time of diverse beginnings and internal debates in the Black communities, resurgent Black nationalism, burgeoning revolutionary impulses, a critical examination of the meaning and value of old concepts of "integration" as contrasted with the rising emphasis on self-determination and Black Power. It was a time of discussions on the relationship between racial oppression and class oppression, of explorations of the relationships between the Black movements and Black consciousness in the United States and the Third World anticolonialist aspirations and the areas of common interest of oppressed peoples and groups everywhere. It was a time of the blossoming of the dashiki and the proud cultivation of Afro hair styles, tangible and symbolic evidence of two important and simultaneous currents of feeling and thinking: the widening discontent and disillusionment in the Black communities with the way things are in the United States, with the American system and White America, and a renewed affirmation of the African origins of the Afro-American and the African, non-Western elements, in the culture created by Afro-Americans in the United States.

In the opening essay in *Soul on Ice*, published in 1968, Eldridge Cleaver expressed one important feeling of the time which continues to run strong in the newer writing in this anthology, in these words:

Nurtured by the fires of the controversy over segregation, I was soon aflame with indignation over my newly discovered social status, and inwardly I turned away from America with horror, disgust and outrage.

The Black arts movement and the Black aesthetic movement were emerging then, reflecting all of this ferment and rejection of the old, but at a much earlier stage of development than today. And older patterns of thought also prevailed. That is why, concluding my introduction to *Black Voices*, I wrote:

> This is a time of great liveliness, controversy, and creativity in the Black literary world in the United States. . . . New literary voices are being heard . . . I close this anthology reluctantly with the feeling that so much is happening and being born that it would be good to keep the book open and bring in still more of the new. But the end of this anthology is not conclusion, I hope, but further beginnings: greater appreciation of what Black writers have contributed and are contributing to the diversity of American literature, and movement towards greater inclusion of works by Negro writers in our American literature courses in the high schools and colleges.

Now the Black arts movement is in a new stage of development. Ron Welburn, one of the new Black poets and critics who is represented in the Poetry section of this anthology, explained it this way in a recent review in *The New York Times Book Review* (February 14, 1971):

> The black-arts movement has reached a new level of commitment and sophistication; its focus is no longer protest against white America, but an embracement and celebration of the black experience.

And to appreciate fully what it means to celebrate Blackness and the Black experience it is well to recall how George Lamming, the Black West Indian novelist, defined Black quite some time ago as "synonymous with originating in Africa." Celebration of Blackness includes celebration of the African roots of the Afro-American and Ron Welburn's poems and others in this anthology are interesting revelations of how this African consciousness and memory are embodied in Black American writing today. Black American relationships to Africa, past and present, the African contexts of Black culture, and aspects of pan-Africanism today, are discussed in selections by Richard A. Long and Nathan Hare in the criticism section of this book.

Another historical question which is very much alive today in the new Black reexamination of the past is the whole question of the true nature of the slave experience in the United States and the nature of the very rich and important culture created by the slaves. This vital historical and cultural problem is discussed in the article by Sterling Stuckey in the criticism section.

In this anthology I have included both early and later expressions of the Black arts movement, including an early critical essay and later poems by Imamu Amiri Baraka (LeRoi Jones), a leading force and moving spirit in the Black arts movement. I have paid special attention in this anthology to one of the Black arts movements, BLKARTSOUTH, as a concrete example of this movement. Most of the anthologies which reflect the new Black arts movements have concentrated largely or exclusively on the Black arts movements in the North. In view of the continuing importance of the South as a region of Black habitation with its particular flavors and life styles, and in view of the fact that a Black arts movement has developed in the South, I conclude the poetry section of this anthology with a collection of poems by poets of the BLKARTSOUTH movement under the group heading "BLKARTSOUTH POETS," and I include in the criticism section a statement by Val Ferdinand (Kalamu ya Salaam) on the BLKARTSOUTH movement written especially for this anthology. In these poems we see one of the characteristic features manifest in writing of the Black arts movement all over the country, the political message, the didactic poem, the revolutionary "rap" poem. Examples of this type of poetry are included in this anthology, and not only by the BLKARTSOUTH poets, along with very different kinds of poetry.

Less critical attention has been devoted to the fact that the Black arts movement itself has been an arena of intense internal struggle and debate. Many have stressed message and statement over and beyond any considerations of craftsmanship while others have criticized poor writing very sharply and have championed standards of artistic excellence and craftsmanship as a must for true Black art. The poet Stanley Crouch, one of the latter, in an article entitled "Toward a Purer Black Poetry Esthetic" published in *Journal of Black Poetry* (Fall 1968) wrote:

One of the major problems in Black Writing today is that most of the people who pass themselves off as writers either cannot write, are capitalizing on something that has moved from true feeling to a name-calling fad masked as "Revolutionary Black Nationalism," or, *they have no respect for the craft* (many times both aforementioned viruses spread through these people's work). No. I am not talking about the use and following of european standards of writing or european standards of art in general: I'm talking about the use of esthetic standards that are Black in nature and have proved themselves valid in the Afro-Asian East and the American Black West. For instance, Benin sculpture could not be as beautiful as it is if the artists involved were only interested in showing themselves to others as hiply "conscious." John Coltrane's music would not be what it is had he not spent many hours perfecting his ability to project the purest things he felt. John's way of saying it was that one has to keep cleaning the mirror, keep pushing towards the crux of things. Same thing: Milford Graves, Cecil Taylor, Ornette Coleman, Henry Grimes. The one thing they all have in common is WORK (Cecil has been known to practice ten hours a day over a long period of time). . . . It is because of this, and because of what I know *true* Black Art to be, that I believe that we should strive to leave a literature as rich as the music we've produced, a literature that will sit next to Duke Ellington, Bird, Bud, Trane, Ornette, Billie and the droves of others who've made Black Music the most moving and beautiful thing to have happened in the west for the last seventy years, have made it that *true* Black Art I just spoke of.

Today we are also witnessing a further "new breed" of Black writers who accept their Blackness thoroughly, organically, and naturally, and have gone beyond some of the original premises of the Black arts movement of the Sixties. They reject any prescribed definition of Blackness, they oppose dogmatism and attempts at the institutionalization of Blackness in any particular movement or organization which will try to tell the Black writer how he should write or what he may write about. They stress the importance of the individuality and originality of the Black artist. Al Young, one of these writers who is represented in the fiction, poetry, and criticism sections of this anthology, declared in an interview published in the *San Francisco Sunday Examiner & Chronicle* (May 3, 1970):

Until recently Black writers were almost required to write something that was overtly angry, something that said, "Charley, Whitey, I'm gonna cut your throat." It gave the white reader a titillation, it sold, and publishers were pushing it because it did sell. It's reached the point now, though, where the public is no longer excited by clenched fists, by pseudo-black anger—I say "pseudo" because of the way Madison Avenue has been exploiting it.

In the Seventies there's going to be a rich flowering of Black genius, unlike anything that has been seen before. There are young writers coming up who are not so much interested in frightening the Man, meaning Mr. Charley, but in expressing themselves deeply as human beings—writers like Ishmael Reed and Cecil Brown and Paul Lofty and William Anderson—writers interested in bringing out the enormous variety of feeling and thought in the Black community, which you weren't allowed to see in the Sixties when Black Anger was the only thing fashionable.

Ishmael Reed is represented in both the poetry and criticism sections of this anthology and Cecil Brown in the fiction section. And in the criticism section of this anthology the polemic of James Cunningham with Maulana Ron Karenga and the interview with Clarence Major and Victor Hernandez Cruz reflect other aspects of contemporary Black critical thinking in opposition to any set or rigid definition of Black writing. Thus in the criticism section, I have tried to present the views of the proponents and opponents of the Black aesthetic, the critical views of Ralph Ellison and Chester Himes, the present thinking of James Baldwin, and newer currents of critical thinking of the Seventies.

This book, like *Black Voices*, is designed both for the general reader and the student of the full spectrum of the literature of the United States. It is conceived as part of the far from finished struggle to establish and consolidate the inclusion of Afro-American literature in the English curriculum of all the schools and colleges in our country. Not a single token writer or single school or trend, but the variety of Black literature. First, because of the validity and distinctiveness of this literature as literature and also because of its special significance, value, and relevance as an antidote to the very long pathological history and continuing symptoms of racism in American culture.

The sheer quantity of Black writing published in the last four or five years, including writings of the past which had been out of print for years or had not been published during the long, long chain of time when Black writing suffered so acutely from the impacts of racism on publishing and the literature courses taught in the high schools and colleges, is phenomenal. The entire thrust of the Black consciousness movements has resulted in far greater exposure of Black writing in the general American publishing world, university presses, magazines, and periodicals. But in some strange dialectic this has been related to a very different phenomenon: the growth and development of numerous Black political and cultural periodicals and journals, Black publishing houses, theaters, and Black arts centers. *Black World* (formerly *Negro Digest*) has developed under the editorship of Hoyt W. Fuller into a central, national vehicle for new Black writing and forum for literary and cultural discussion and debate. *The Black Scholar* has emerged as an important new journal of Black studies and research. There are selections from both of these publications in this book and the program of *The Black Scholar* is presented in the documents section. Many additional new journals and periodicals have been born in the last few years, some regional, some with a particular political point of view, and many devoted to literature and the arts or opening their pages to new writing.

Symptomatic of the profound changes that have taken place in the latter years of the Sixties, in terms of the audience that the Black writers can reach and the new climate for Black culture, as compared with the Harlem Renaissance of the Twenties and right through the early years of the Sixties, are facts like these: In 1926 Langston Hughes and other writers and artists of the Harlem Renaissance tried to establish a Black "magazine of the arts." It was called *Fire* and a first issue was published. It was panned by the Negro press in New York, ignored by the white critics, couldn't reach an audience, and died aborning. In contrast, *The Journal of Black Poetry*, edited by Joe Goncalves in San Francisco, was born in 1965, has maintained publication continuously with fourteen issues, to date, and has increased its size and number of pages. Volumes of verse have been published by independent Black publishing houses, within the past few years, in Chicago, Detroit, Cleveland, Cincinnati, Milwaukee, Madison, Wisconsin, and East St. Louis, Illinois, in the Midwest; New York, Newark, Philadelphia, and Pittsburgh, in the East; New Orleans, Nashville, and Tougaloo, Mississippi, in the South; and San Francisco, Berkeley, Los Angeles, and Compton, California, in the West.

Three of these publishing houses, Broadside Press in Detroit, Jihad Productions in Newark, and Third World Press in Chicago, are by now reaching out quite extensively. Broadside Press, created, edited, and directed by the poet Dudley Randall, is the oldest and has published more titles than any of the other new Black publishing houses. In its latest publication it lists thirty-six books of poetry, including three anthologies and forty-six Broadsides of single poems. It also produces Broadside Voices, a series of cassette tapes by poets reading their own books that have been published by Broadside Press, has initiated a series of Broadside posters with single poems, and has issued its first record, "Rappin' and Readin'," by Don L. Lee. Quite a few of the poems in this anthology are reprinted from Broadside Press publications.

In a special article written for the anthology *Black Expression* on the Black poetry movement today, Dudley Randall observed:

When two of the Broadside poets were asked for poems for a new little magazine, they refused, saying they preferred not to appear in a white publication . . . The younger poets no longer plead, or ask for rights from the white man. Instead of searching themselves for faults which engender the contempt of the white man, and, after regarding his wars, his hypocritical religion, his exploitation, his dehumanization, they dub him—"the Beast." They no longer pity themselves . . . Instead, they say, "I am black and beautiful." They reject whiteness and white standards. They call themselves blacks, rejecting the word Negro, which they say was given to them by white men. Some poets have taken African names. Le Graham is now Ahmed Alhamisi, Rolland Snellings is Asaka Muhammad Toure.

This intensified pride in blackness has made the new poets indifferent to a white audience. [Randall then lists a series of Black publications which he describes as] periodicals where they can publish for a black audience without white censorship . . . Writing for a black audience out of black experience, the poets seek to make their work relevant and to direct their audience to black consciousness, black unity, and black power. This may be called didacticism or propaganda, but they are indifferent to labels put upon it. They consider such labels as part of white standards, and they reject white standards. . . . In spite of my emphasis on the black consciousness of the poets, I do not wish to leave the impression of a monolithic sameness. There are all shades of opinion and militancy among the poets. Some are proudly black, and others would prefer to be colorless. In fact, just as the two Broadside poets refused their poems to a white magazine, recently two Negro poets declined to submit their poems to a black periodical.

Most of the new journals and publishing houses are part of what Hoyt W. Fuller, a leading force in the Black aesthetic movement, describes as "the revolution in black literature" now going on. In one of the two articles by him in Addison

Gayle, Jr.'s critical anthology *The Black Aesthetic,* Fuller writes:

> There is a revolution in black literature in America. It is nationalist in direction, and it is pro-black. That means, in effect, that it is deliberately moving outside the sphere of traditional Western forms, limitations, and presumptions. It is seeking new forms, new limits, new shapes, and much of it now admittedly is crude, reflecting the uncertainty, the searching quality of its movement. But, though troubled and seeking, it is very, very vital.
>
> The creators of the new black literature are deeply concerned with image and myth. They are about the business of destroying those images and myths that have crippled and degraded black people, and the institution of new images and myths that will liberate them.

One of the new literary journals, *Nommo,* is published by the Organization of Black American Culture's (OBAC) Writers' Workshop in Chicago. Its direction was defined in the following "Statement of Purposes" of OBAC Writers' Workshop:

> The Writers' Workshop of the Organization of Black American Culture (OBAC) is a community-oriented unit with the general aim of seeking out and encouraging the literary talent within the Black Community. Beyond that, the Workshop strives toward the conscious development and articulation of a Black Aesthetic, and the following goals are inherent in this larger one:
>
> *The encouragement of the highest quality of literary expression reflecting the Black Experience
>
> *The establishment and definition of the standards by which that creative writing which reflects the Black Experience is to be judged and evaluated
>
> *The encouragement of the growth and development of Black critics who are fully qualified to judge and to evaluate Black literature on its own terms while, at the same time, cognizant of the "traditional" values and standards of Western literature and fully competent to articulate the essential differences between the two literatures.

A number of the OBAC poets have had their poetry collections published by Third World Press which is also based in Chicago. The latest circular of Third World Press lists twenty-two titles. Its editors have issued the following "Statement of Purpose":

The third world is a liberating concept for people of color, non-europeans—for Black people. That world has an ethos —a black aesthetic if u will—and it is the intent of Third World Press to capture that ethos, that black energy. We attempt to give an initial exposure to black writers. We publish black (poetry, historical notes, essays, short stories, and hopefully novellas) for Africans here (most often referred to as "negroes") and Africans abroad. And because we publish black—profit it's not our thing/not our thing.

Today we witness Black poets who have established national literary reputations on the basis of the works they have published in the Black magazines and publishing houses, in readings to Black audiences, and appearances in Black cultural programs on the educational television network. Don L. Lee, Dudley Randall, Mari Evans, Nikki Giovanni, Sonia Sanchez, Etheridge Knight, and other writers represented in this anthology won their recognition with works they published in Black periodicals or the editions of the Black publishing houses. It was only after they had received recognition in the Black literary world that the works of these writers and others began to appear in the anthologies and, in some instances, in books of their own published by general or major American publishers. This is a clear indication of the influence and importance of the Black cultural organs.

These independent Black publishing ventures are cultural manifestations of the larger movement of Black nationalism which is a strong force today and one of the important contexts of the new Black writing. To understand many facets of contemporary Black literature it is necessary to comprehend the ideological premises of Black nationalism. In the criticism section of this anthology the selections by Maulana Ron Karenga, a leader and ideologist of the movement of Black cultural nationalism, Imamu Amiri Baraka, Addison Gayle, Jr., and Val Ferdinand are all different expressions of present-day Black nationalist thinking. Professor James Turner, now director of the Afro-American studies program at Cornell University, has been explaining and summarizing the premises of contemporary Black nationalism and its historical roots in various Black publications. In an article entitled "The Sociology of Black Nationalism" in *The Black Scholar* (December, 1969) he wrote:

The movement of black nationalist ideas is dominated by the collective consciousness of its adherents as members of a minority group, which is subordinated to another and more powerful group within the total political and social order.

The ideological preoccupations of black nationalism revolve around this central problem, the black man's predicament of having been forced by historical circumstances into a state of dependence upon the white society considered the master society and the dominant culture. The essential theme of black nationalism can be seen as a counter-movement away from subordination to independence, from alienation through refutation, to self-affirmation. . . . The theme of disgrace and subjugation is the point of departure of the whole ideological expression of black nationalism, which derives from the political and cultural uprooting of black people in general through colonial conquest and enslavement. The overwhelming sentiment that dominates in this connection is the belief that the group is being denied a "true" and unadulterated experience of its humanity as a result of being forced into a social system whose cultural values preclude an honorable accommodation. The black nationalist recognizes himself as belonging to an outgroup, an alien in relation to the white society which controls the total universe in which he moves. This sentiment of belonging no longer to oneself but to another goes together with an awareness of being black, which becomes translated in social terms into a caste and class consciousness. The association between race and servitude is a constant theme in Afro-American literature. The economic exploitation and social discrimination which define persons of African descent as a social category gives many of its members an avid sense of race consciousness as a consequence of mutual humiliation.

In a later article, in *Black World* (January, 1971), Turner presents a picture of the Black nationalist movement today and defines its objectives. He observes:

Unlike the civil rights movement, which focussed on the struggle for legal equality and integration, Black Nationalism addresses itself to the cultural and psychological malaise of the oppression Blacks have had to endure. Nationalism has taken many forms among Africans in America. Some of the most recent varieties are Religio-Nationalism, represented by the Nation of Islam; Cultural Nationalism of Ron Karenga and Amiri Baraka; Marxist Revolutionary Nationalism of the Black Panther Party; Economic Nationalism of the Black Capitalism Advocates; Political Nationalism of the Republic of New Africa; and Pan-African Nationalism of Brother Malcolm X. As a political orientation the basic proposition shared by all variants of Black Nationalism (though advocating different social blueprints at times) is that all things created and occupied by Blacks should be controlled by Black people, and that the purpose of every effort should be toward achieving self-determination (variously defined) and a relatively self-sufficient Black community.

Moving to definitions, Turner asserts:

Thus, Black Nationalism can be objectively defined as:

(1) The desire of Black people to determine their own destiny through formation, preservation, and control of their own political, social, economic, and cultural institutions.

(2) The determination of Black people to unite as a group, as a people in common community, opposing white supremacy by striving for independence from white control.

(3) The resistance of Black people to subordinate status and the demand for political freedom, social justice, and economic equality.

(4) The development of ethnic self-interest, racial pride, group consciousness, and opposition to and rejection of the dominant ideas of white-defined society perceived to be incompatible with this objective.

(5) The re-evaluation of self and of the Black man's relationship with the social system in general.

Quite a few of the selections in this anthology reveal how contemporary Black writers see and feel the realities and problems which are of preeminent concern to Black people and to the Black nationalist movement. In addition to the fiction, poetry, and criticism sections I have added a documents section, as the final category in this anthology, in place of the autobiography section included in *Black Voices*. It opens with the program developed by Malcolm X for his Organization of Afro-American Unity, his ultimate thinking on political and cultural questions at the time of his assassination on February 21, 1965. The importance of Malcolm X and his thinking in the development of the Black movements of today is fundamental and the views of Malcolm X embodied in this program, which have had great impact on the thinking of Black writers, have not been readily accessible. It is presented as source material for the understanding of important currents of contemporary Black thinking. In addition I have included the programs and objectives of a number of new Black cultural institutions which have been established in the past few years.

In the criticism section of this anthology I present the Black Panther Party's program "On Revolutionary Culture" as formulated by Emory Douglas, the party's minister of culture. It contrasts sharply with the program of Black cultural nationalism of Ron Karenga which has been the target of vigorous polemics in the Black Panther Party press. The ideology of the Black Panther Party increasingly came into conflict with those forces in the Black nationalist movement who conceive their anti-integrationist position as opposition to any Black alliances or coalitions with whites. It was on this question, as well as opposition to the way the Black Panther Party was being led and its criticism of cultural nationalism, that Stokely Carmichael resigned in July 1969 as prime minister and as a member of the Black Panther Party in a controversy with Eldridge Cleaver which is a revealing part of the political and cultural history of the times reflected in the writings in this book. In his letter of resignation Carmichael condemned the tactics and rhetoric of the party as "dividing black revolutionaries and the black community" and declared:

The party has become dogmatic in its newly acquired ideology and thinks that it has the only correct position. All those who disagree with the party line, in part or completely, are lumped into the same category and labeled cultural nationalists, pork chop nationalists, reactionary pigs, etc. . . .

The alliances being formed by the party are alliances which I cannot politically agree with, because the history of Africans living in the United States has shown that any premature alliance with white radicals has led to complete subversion of the blacks by the whites, through their direct or indirect control of the black organization.

Eldridge Cleaver replied in "An Open Letter to Stokely Carmichael" and wrote:

You have never been able to distinguish the history of the Black Panther Party from the history of the organization of which you were once the chairman—the Student Non-Violent Coordinating Committee. It is understandable that you can have such fears of black organizations being controlled, or partly controlled, by whites, because most of your years in SNCC were spent under precisely those conditions. But the Black Panther Party has never been in that situation. Because we have never had to wrest control of our organization out of the hands of whites, we have not been shackled with the type of paranoid fear that was developed by you cats in SNCC. Therefore we are able to sit down with whites and hammer out solutions to our common problems without trembling in our boots about whether or not we might get taken over in the process. . . .

In February 1968, at the Free Huey Birthday Rally in Oakland, California . . . you took the occasion to denounce the coalition that the Black Panther Party had made with the white Peace and Freedom Party. What you called for instead was a Black United Front that would unite all the forces in the black community from left to right, close ranks against the whites, and all go skipping off to freedom. Within the ranks of your Black United Front you wanted to include the Cultural Nationalists, the Black Capitalists, and the Professional Uncle Toms. . . .

The enemies of black people have learned something from history even if you haven't, and they are discovering new ways to divide us faster than we are discovering new ways to unite. One thing they know, and we know, that seems to escape you, is that there is not going to be any revolution or black liberation in the United States as long as revolutionary blacks, whites, Mexicans, Puerto Ricans, Indians, Chinese and Eskimos are unwilling or unable to unite into some functional machinery that can cope with the situation. Your talk and fears about premature coalition are absurd, because no coalition against oppression by forces possessing revolutionary integrity can ever be premature. If anything, it is too late, because the forces of counterrevolution are sweeping the world, and this is happening precisely because in the past people have been united on a basis that perpetuates disunity among races and ignores basic revolutionary principles and analyses. . . .

You speak about an "undying love for black people." An undying love for black people that denies the humanity of other people is doomed. It was an undying love of white people for each other which led them to deny the humanity of colored people and which has stripped white people of humanity itself.

I do not quote Eldridge Cleaver's letter as the political statement of an organization but as the outlook of an important new writer who came forward in the late Sixties, in the same manner that I include the views of Ralph Ellison, James Baldwin, and others on more than literature in the criticism section. *Soul on Ice* is undoubtedly one of the important Black books of the period, not only for what it says but the way it says it, for its style and tone and searching of the inner self, and Eldridge Cleaver's more recent fiction is beginning to find its way into the literary anthologies. At the present time the Black Panther Party has suffered severe blows and been torn apart. But the entire phenomenon of the rise of the Black Panther movement, which captured the imagination of Black people and America as a whole, transcends the membership and the ideological conflicts within a particular organization. This is clear from the poems in this anthology and other writings by Black writers inspired by the Black Panther movement as a symbolic expression of the spirit of resistance and militancy in Black America today.

The whole question of how to end oppression, how to achieve freedom, is not an isolated or narrow political question in Black American life. It is very prominent in the thinking and feelings of the people and is part of the marrow of Black literature, in the same way that Irish freedom has been part of the marrow of Irish literature. Eldridge Cleaver is not alone among contemporary Black writers in the feeling that there is a natural common interest between Black people and all oppressed groups and forces opposed to oppression and repression. Quite a few Black writers today are thoroughly separatist in their convictions and feelings. Others have different views and feelings which are evident in poetry and fiction as well as in essays. This is another aspect of the diversity and conflict of ideas in Black literature today.

The poetry section embraces the largest number of writers in this anthology. It opens with more recent poems by four of the best known and widely recognized poets, Gwendolyn Brooks, Margaret Walker, Robert Hayden, and Imamu Amiri Baraka, who are represented more extensively in *Black Voices,* then presents poems by forty-two additional poets in alphabetical order and concludes with a group of eight "BLKARTSOUTH Poets." Because of the selection principle of concentrating on living writers in this book, I did not include any poems by Langston Hughes who died in 1967. The poems that he wrote in the Sixties, included in his posthumously published book *The Panther and the Lash* are, however, an important part of Afro-American expression of the Sixties, and he is present in this book in the felt evidence of his influence on the work of some of the younger poets and in some of the poems in this anthology devoted to Langston Hughes.

There are many reasons for the prominent place of poetry in Black literature. Poetry is both the oldest form of expression in Afro-American literature and the medium of literary expression which by its nature is both intensely personal and very often the quickest to capture and express the feeling of the immediate moment, of time as it is unfolding, of the contemporary in the throes of its transitions.

There are, of course, many different styles and forms of Black poetry. But much of contemporary Black poetry is not structured metrically, in the traditional measured feet of English poetry, but rhythmically, in musical beats, very frequently the rhythms and beats of modern jazz, a music of African origins. Jazz is not only a form of expression emulated and drawn upon by Black poets but frequently an important subject of poems and stories. The jazz artist most frequently cited and eulogized in verse by contemporary Black poets is John Coltrane. Many Americans still do not appreciate the artistic richness, complexity, and highly individualized modes of expression of modern jazz and as a result remain deaf to some of the distinctive music of significant contemporary Black poets. Listening to John Coltrane, Charlie Parker, Yusef Lateef, the Modern Jazz Quartet, Cecil Taylor, and other jazz artists referred to by the Black writers is one way to open the ear and the senses to some of the distinctive music of Black poetry.

A basic source for modern jazz and Black poetry is the blues, a unique form of Black music. The blues is not only a musical form, it is a way of viewing life, a way of feeling, a way of creating a structure out of chaos and mustering strength for survival in a brutal world.

Ralph Ellison has written:

> The blues is an impulse to keep the painful details and episodes of a brutal experience alive in one's aching consciousness, to finger its jagged grain, and to transcend it, not by the consolation of philosophy but by squeezing from it a near-tragic, near-comic lyricism. As a form, the blues is an autobiographical chronicle of personal catastrophe expressed lyrically.

Richard Wright has written:

> Yet the most astonishing aspect of the blues is that, though replete with a sense of defeat and down-heartedness, they are not intrinsically pessimistic; their burden of woe and melancholy is dialectically redeemed through sheer force of sensuality, into an almost exultant affirmation of life, of love, of sex, of movement, of hope. No matter how repressive was the American environment, the Negro never lost faith in or doubted his deeply endemic capacity to live. All blues are a lusty, lyrical realism charged with taut sensibility. (Was this hope that sprang always Phoenix-like from the ashes of frustration something that the Negro absorbed from the oppressive yet optimistic American environment in which he lived and had his being?)

And in one of the tales of Simple by Langston Hughes, Simple puts it this way:

"I do not know why so many young folks these days and times do not like the blues," said Simple. "They like Rock and Roll, and Rock and Roll ain't nothing much but a whole lot of blues with sometimes a Boogie beat mixed in. Rock and Roll is seventy-two-and-one-half percent blues. But it don't have so many different kinds of expressions as does the blues! The blues can be real sad, else real mad, else real glad, and funny, too, all at the same time. I ought to know. Me, I growed up with the blues. Facts is, I heard so many blues when I were a child until my shadow is blue."

Echoes, variations, and transformations of the blues can be felt and heard quite frequently in contemporary Black poetry. And many of the Black poets today make their poetry in and out of the strong, sharp, juicy, uninhibited, everyday language of the people. Don L. Lee, one of many Black poets and critics who have written about the uses of language in contemporary Black poetry, says in his latest book, a volume of criticism entitled *Dynamite Voices: Black Poets of the 1960's:*

The language of the new writers seemed to move in the direction of actual music. The poets were actually defining and legitimizing their own communicative medium. Their language as a whole was not formal Anglo-Saxon English. It carried its own syntax, not conventional by Western standards, and often referred to as non-communicative, obscene, profane. In short, it was the language of the street, charged to heighten the sensitivity of the reader. . . . Many of the words and sounds of the street could not be found in Webster. By Black language we mean a language which is not recorded in a dictionary—a language as changeable as Blacks who left the South. For instance, the most used and overused word found among the new poets is *mothafucka.* None of its several meanings denotes copulating with one's mother.

Lee goes on to cite four examples with four different connotations of the word, depending on the context, and adds:

Keep in mind that in the Black world the use of the word *muthafucka,* as in the white world, is the sign of an uncultured, ill-mannered nigger. However, the word has many meanings. And it is not synonymous with western "motherfucker," which means exactly what it says—*to lay yr momma.*

While Webster may not be helpful for Black language, Clarence Major's most recent book, *Dictionary of Afro-American Slang,* will be, and in it he offers the following definition: "Motherfucker: any male; the connotation is not necessarily negative."

Dudley Randall, in his introduction to Sonia Sanchez's book of poems *We A BaddDDD People*, writes:

> This tiny woman with the infant's face attacks the demons of this world with the fury of a sparrow defending her fledglings in the nest. She hurls obscenities at things that are obscene.

The Black aesthetic, a relatively new term in the critical vocabulary, celebrates and seeks to give the fullest possible expression to the original styles of life, rhythms, images, sensibilities, musical patterns, and forms of language usage and idiom which Black people have developed as part of the total Black experience in Africa and the Western world.

Black aesthetic, on its most literal level of meaning, is an aesthetic of African origin which has evolved further and changed in its own ways, in the course of interaction with other cultures and aesthetics, as Black people inhabited large stretches of the world outside of Africa.

W. E. B. DuBois, who was a pioneer in so many areas of Black studies, illuminated the whole process of African-Western cultural interaction in his analysis of the spirituals in *The Souls of Black Folk* (1903). He traced the development of the slave songs to three stages of development, noting:

> The first is African music, the second Afro-American, while the third is a blending of Negro music with the music heard in the foster land. The result is still distinctively Negro and the method of blending original, but the elements are both Negro and Caucasian. One might go further and find a fourth step in this development, where the songs of white America have been distinctively influenced by the slave songs. . . .

In essence, *cultural interaction and blending in such a way that the original styles and character of Black people are not lost.* And this is the difference between cultural interaction and cultural genocide.

Contemporary Black nationalism, as we have already seen, is unquestionably one of the important contexts of the genesis of the Black aesthetic movement. But there is also a much older, and international, context from which the Black aesthetic concepts in the United States today derive a significant part of their substance and content, a context as old as the involvement of Africa in the history, development and enrichment of the Western world: the context of Africans and their descendants in the Western world repudiating and struggling against the colonialist and racist assumptions, structures, and values of white superiority in Western culture, Western theories which the Black scholar and revolutionary thinker Frantz Fanon designated as "the doctrine of cultural hierarchy." Fanon viewed the "doctrine of cultural hierarchy" as an important organic component of colonialism and racism which have traditionally negated, derogated, "inferiorized," and sought to destroy the cultural values, ways of life, and self-respect of all colonized and oppressed peoples.

For a classical formulation of this doctrine, reminding us how deeply theories of white cultural superiority are ingrained in the rational and liberal traditions of Western thinking, suffice it to recall the view of David Hume, in his *Philosophical Works*, in 1748:

> I am apt to suspect the negroes, and in general all the other species of men (for there are four or five different kinds) to be naturally inferior to the whites. There never was a civilized nation of any other complexion than white, nor even any individual eminent either in action or speculation. No ingenious manufactures amongst them, no arts, no sciences. On the other hand, the most rude and barbarous of the whites, such as the ancient Germans, the present Tartars, have still something eminent about them, in their valour, form of government, or some other particular. Such a uniform and constant difference could not happen in so many countries and ages, if nature had not made an original distinction betwixt these breeds of men. . . . In Jamaica indeed they talk of one negro as a man of parts and learning; but 'tis likely he is admired for very slender accomplishments, like a parrot, who speaks a few words plainly.

Africans and their descendents in other continents have been struggling against such attitudes since their initial encounters with white racism. Much of this significant struggle still remains to be written, but I should like to cite, as an example, a long-forgotten missionary pamphlet published in Philadelphia in 1800: *The Black Prince*. It is a popular account of the conversion of an African prince who was brought to England in the year 1791 for a Christian education and it reveals, in part, how his African pride and values had to be broken before he could be converted to Christian humility, as the following passage illustrates:

He [Naimbana] was present once in the House of Commons during a debate on the slave trade. He there heard a gentleman, who spoke in favour of the trade, say some things very degrading to the character of his countrymen. He was so enraged at this, that on coming out of the House, he cried out with great vehemence, "I will kill that fellow wherever I meet him, for he has told lies of my country." He was put in mind of the Christian duty of forgiving his enemies, on which he answered nearly in the following words:—"If a man should rob me of my money, I can forgive him; if a man should shoot at me, I can forgive him; if a man should sell me and all my family to a slave ship, so that we should pass all the rest of our lives in slavery in the West Indies, I can forgive him; but," added he with much emotion, "if a man takes away the character of the people of my country, I never can forgive him." Being asked why he would not extend his forgiveness to one who took away the character of the people of his country, he answered,—"If a man should try to kill me, or should sell my family for slaves, he would do an injury to as many as he might kill or sell, but if any one takes away the character of black people, that man injures black people all over the world; and when he has once taken away their character, there is nothing which he may not do to black people ever after. That man, for instance, will beat black men, and say, "O, it is only a black man, why should I not beat him!" That man will make slaves of black people; for when he has taken away their character he will say, "O, they are only black people, why should not I make them slaves." That man will take away all the people of Africa, if he can catch them, and if you ask him, but why do you take away all these people, he will say, "O, they are only black people, they are not like white people, why should not I take them?" That is the reason why I cannot forgive the man who takes away the character of the people of my country.

Some of the concepts of the Black aesthetic are contemporary variations of this very old battle to prevent white people from robbing Black people of their cultural character.

In addition, the proponents of the Black aesthetic are also drawing upon a more recent international context of Black thinking: the negritude movement which emerged and developed in the Thirties, Forties, and Fifties in the French-speaking Carribean, the West Indies, Africa, and among Africans studying in France. A study of the speeches and discussions at the two great international conferences of Negro artists and writers organized by the negritude movement in 1956 and 1959, and published in the journal *Présence Africaine*, shows that a number of concepts now being stressed in the

Black aesthetic movement had already come to the fore at that time. Richard Wright participated in both of these conferences and was associated with the movement during the years that he lived in Paris.

At the First International Conference of Negro Artists and Writers in Paris, in 1956, Richard Wright delivered a paper, which has not received the attention it deserves, in which he declared:

> I have spent most of my adult life and most of my waking hours brooding upon the destiny of the race to which I belong by accident of birth and by accident of history. . . . First of all, my position is a split one. I'm black. I'm a man of the West. These hard facts condition, to some degree, my outlook. I see and understand the West; but I also see and understand the non- or anti-Western point of view. How is this possible? This double vision of mine stems from my being a product of Western civilization and from my racial identity which is organically born of my being a product of that civilization. Being a Negro living in a white Western Christian society, I've never been allowed to blend, in a natural and healthy manner, with the culture and civilization of the West. This contradiction of being both Western and a man of color creates a distance, so to speak, between me and my environment. . . . Me and my environment are one, but that oneness has in it, at its very heart, a schism. I regard my position as natural, though others, that is Western whites, would have to make a most strenuous effort of imagination to grasp it. . . .
>
> Since I'm detached from, because of racial conditions, the West, why do I bother to call myself Western at all? What is it that prompts me to make an identification with the West despite the contradiction involved? The fact is that I really have no choice in the matter. Historical forces more powerful than I am have shaped me as a Westerner. I have not consciously elected to be a Westerner; I have been made into a Westerner. Long before I had the freedom to choose I was molded a Westerner. It began in childhood. And the process continues.
>
> Hence, standing shoulder to shoulder with the Western white man, speaking his tongue, sharing his culture, participating in the common efforts of the Western community, I say to that white man: "I'm Western, just as Western as you are, maybe more; but I don't completely agree with you." . . . My point of view is a Western one, but a Western one that conflicts at several vital points with the outlook of the West!

He addressed these words to Black writers and artists from Africa, the United States, the Caribbean regions and South

America, Black writers who write in English, French, Spanish, and Portuguese, who are parts of diverse national literatures and cultures, and are fully as conversant with Western culture as white Western writers. But despite differences of geography and language and immediate environmental conditions, the bond that united them was their Black experience everywhere in the Western world, the racial differentiation they experienced everywhere in the West, the barriers everywhere in the West which did not allow the Black man, in the words of Richard Wright, "to blend, in a natural and healthy manner, with the culture and civilization of the West."

It was at this conference that Frantz Fanon delivered the paper in which he formulated his views on the "doctrine of cultural hierarchy."

Léopold Sédar Senghor, the poet who is now president of Senegal and a leading theoretician and founder of the initial negritude movement, delivered a paper at this conference in which he stressed that "image and rhythm . . . are the two fundamental features of African Negro style," thus defining his view of the two fundamental and distinctive features in which the African aesthetic, a term used by spokesmen of the negritude movement before the term Black aesthetic was used in the United States, was different from the European aesthetic. Senghor also declared in his paper:

> The spirit of African Negro civilization, consciously or not, animates the best Negro artists and writers of today, whether they come from Africa or America.

At this conference the West Indian novelist George Lamming delivered an interesting paper on "The Negro Writer and His World" in which he said:

> To speak of the situation of the Negro writer is to speak, therefore, of a problem of Man, and, more precisely, of a contemporary situation which surrounds us with an urgency that is probably unprecedented. It is to speak, in a sense, of the universal sense of separation and abandonment, frustration and loss, and above else, of some direct inner experience of something missing. . . . There are, I would suggest, three kinds of worlds to which the writer bears in some way a responsibility, worlds which are distinct, and yet very deeply related. There is first of all the world of the private and hidden self. . . . But that private world of the writer is modified, even made possible, by the world in which he moves among other men. Much as he may wish that through the presence of the others that one's own presence is given mean-

ing. What, then, is the relation of a writer to a society in which, for reasons which have nothing to do with his work, he is regarded as different? When that difference carries consequences of injustice, his relation is not different from that of any other who shares a similar misfortune. An identical suffering holds them together in attack or defense with those who are part of his misfortune; and since this misfortune of difference enters his private world, one expects his work as a writer to be, in part, a witness to that misfortune.

And it was at this conference too that Aimé Césaire, the poet from Martinique who originally coined the word negritude, declared:

We have wondered what is the common denominator of an assembly that can unite men as different as Africans of native Africa, and North Americans, as men from the West Indies and from Madagascar.

To my way of thinking the answer is obvious and may be briefly stated in the words: colonial situation. . . . I think it is very true that culture must be national. It is, however, self-evident that national cultures, however differentiated they may be, are grouped by affinities. Moreover, these great cultural relationships, these great cultural families, have a name: they are called *civilisations*. In other words, if it is an undoubted fact that there is a French national culture, an Italian, English, Spanish, German, Russian, etc., national culture, it is no less evident that all these cultures, alongside genuine differences, show a certain number of striking similarities so that, though we can speak of national cultures peculiar to each of the countries mentioned above, we can equally well speak of a European civilisation.

In the same way we can speak of a large family of African cultures which collectively deserve the name of Negro-African culture and which individually reveal the different cultures proper to each country of Africa. And we know that the hazards of history have caused the domain of this civilisation, the locus of this civilisation, to exceed widely the boundaries of Africa. It is in this sense, therefore, that we may say that there are, if not centres, at least fringes of this Negro-African civilisation in Brazil and in the West Indies, in Haiti and the French Antilles and even in the United States. . . .

All who have met here are united by a double solidarity; on the one hand, a *horizontal solidarity*, that is, a solidarity created for us by the colonial, semi-colonial or para-colonial situation imposed upon us from without; and on the other, a vertical solidarity, a *solidarity in time*, due to the fact that we started from an original unity, the unity of African civilisation, which has become diversified into a whole series of cultures all of which, in varying degrees, owe something to that civilisation.

The Second Congress of Negro Writers and Artists met in Rome in 1959. Its slogan was: The Unity of Negro African Cultures. This congress, like the first conference of 1956, was organized by the Society of African Culture and *Présence Africaine*, the magazine of the negritude movement which was established in Paris in 1947, remains very much alive today, and repeatedly reminds its readers of its origins in these words:

> Since 1941, in Paris, Africans, Madagascans, and West Indians in Paris have been preoccupied with affirming the "presence" or ethos of the black communities of the world, of defending the originality of their way of life and the dignity of their cultures.

Alioune Diop, the Senegalese intellectual who founded *Présence Africaine*, declared in the opening speech of the second congress:

> One of our tasks is imposed by the need for our peoples to escape assimiliation, to de-westernise themselves so as not to stifle their own genius. This de-westernising tendency, readily observable in our countries, from Madagascar to Haiti, from Timbuctoo to Johannesburg, from Nigeria to Kenya, is aimed both at institutions, hierarchies and authorities, and at means of expression, ethical references and historical values. We are determined to retain the gifts of the West, on condition that they are used according to our own genius and our own circumstances. . . . That is why, reasonably and legitimately, we take as our mission to work, each in his own field, toward freeing the mental disciplines and the arts from those shackles with which the compromised demands of Western hegemony have their universal application. To de-westernise in order to universalise, such is our desire. To universalise, it is necessary that all should participate in the creative work of mankind. . . . Our artists and our writers intend therefore to use a language, a type of aesthetics perceptibly different from those of the West.

Clearly the present day American movement for a Black aesthetic is no random phenomenon. It has roots in a much older and bigger international context which has long been combating the racism in Western culture and seeking to define the distinctive qualities of Negro or Black aesthetic. In the United States, for decades, the Negro cultural movements of the past were more hopeful that Negro culture would be able to express itself freely and fully within a context of integration and cultural pluralism and diversity. Long before the angry Black American poets of today made their appearance on the scene, earlier Black poets in the Carribean had come to other conclusions reacting to the assimilationism and Frenchification of the Black middle class. Aimé Césaire, in one of his poems in his *Soleil cou-coupé* collection, called out:

> Europe
> I give my suport to all that powders the sky with its insolence
> to all that is loyal and fraternal to all that has the courage
>   to be eternally
> new to all that can give its heart to fire to all that has the
>   strength to
> burst from an inexhaustible sap to all that is calm and sure
> to all that is not you
> Europe
> pompous name for excrement

And Leon Damas, the Black poet from Guiana, in a poem written in the 1930s, cried out:

> I feel ridiculous
> in their shoes, in their dress suits,
> in their starched shirts, in their hard collars,
> in their monocles and bowler hats.

And later in the poem he went on:

> I feel ridiculous
> with their theories which they season
> according to their needs and their passions.
>
> I feel ridiculous
> among them, an accomplice, among them a pimp,
> among them a murderer, my hands terrifyingly red
> with the blood of their civilisation.

The soil that breeds these attitudes, as Frantz Fanon, who disagreed with many of the ideas of the negritude movement, pointed out in his paper at the Second Congress of Negro Writers and Artists in 1959, was Western racism. Fanon said:

> The Negro, never so much a Negro as since he has been dominated by the whites, when he decides to prove that he

has a culture and to behave like a cultured person, comes to realize that history points out a well-defined path to him: he must demonstrate that a Negro culture exists.

And it is only too true that those who are most responsible for this racialization of thought, or at least for the first movement toward that thought, are and remain those Europeans who have never ceased to set up white culture to fill the gap left by the absence of other cultures. Colonialism did not dream of wasting its time in denying the existence of one national culture after another. The concept of negritude, for example, was the emotional if not the logical antithesis of that insult which the white man flung at humanity. This rush of negritude against the white man's contempt showed itself in certain spheres to be the one idea capable of lifting interdictions and anathemas . . . The Negroes who live in the United States and Central or Latin America in fact experience the need to attach themselves to a cultural matrix. Their problem is not fundamentally different from that of the Africans. The whites of America did not mete out to them any different treatment from that of the whites who ruled over the Africans. We have seen that the whites were used to putting all Negroes in the same bag.

The Black aesthetic movement in the United States is a contemporary American development of this fundamental antiracist current of feeling and thinking inherent in negritude.

For years we have been reading postmortems on negritude, partly because of the sharp criticism of many of its tenets by some important African writers and Black writers in the West, but the postmortems have repeatedly proved to be premature. The strong current of antiracist feeling and thinking in negritude will not disappear or die so long as white racism exists. The new wave of negritude in the Black aesthetic movement in the United States, of unprecedented intensity and scope, is evidence of the stubborn persistence of racism in our country, of the movement toward "two societies, one black, one white—separate and unequal" which the Kerner Commission Report of 1968 warned about, of the failures of integration and desegregation in our country.

The general American literary periodicals began to take cognizance recently of the term "Black aesthetic," in a limited and haphazard way, in condescending and piqued tones, tending to equate it with the single anthology *Black Fire*, which is only one expression of a far more diverse movement. A review article by Jack Richardson in *The New York Review* (December 19, 1968) even went so far as to say that "madness" is "a reasonably accurate descriptive term for much of what is happening in Negro literature and in the criticism surrounding it." How pathetically simple, to dismiss the revolt by Black writers against racist criteria in Western and American culture and literary criticism as unworthy of rational analysis or debate. The fact is that the negritude and Black aesthetic movements have raised fundamental questions of literary theory which Western literary criticism and literary theory have not grappled with properly and have failed to answer.

Black literature illuminates, in the most profound human ways, how it feels and what it is like to live in a racist society, articulates the cultural richness and diversity distilled from the Black experience in the United States, expresses the anxieties and aspirations of modern man and contemporary urban life, and probes the vast complexities of the human soul. For these reasons it deserves to be read widely and to be studied in our schools. This book is offered in the hope that it will stimulate further exploration of contemporary Black writing.

ABRAHAM CHAPMAN

The University of Wisconsin—Stevens Point

1.

Fiction

JOHN OLIVER KILLENS (1916–   )

From his first novel Youngblood *(1954), to his fourth,* The Cotillion, or One Good Bull Is Half the Herd, *published in 1971, the work of John Oliver Killens is evidence of complex literary development and changes. Born in Macon, Georgia, Killens lived and was educated both in the South and the North. He has written material for television and motion pictures, including the film* Odds Against Tomorrow *starring Harry Belafonte, as well as articles, essays, and fiction. He has been an influential force in the development of contemporary Black writing as a critic, teacher of creative writing, and director of literary workshops. He was a teaching fellow in creative writing at Fisk University, chairman of the Workshop of the Harlem Writers' Guild, and at present heads the Black Culture Seminar and Creative Writers Workshop, as adjunct professor, at Columbia University. Following is the "Foreword" to his latest novel,* The Cotillion, *not an external foreword by the author about his novel, but the first-person introductory statement of the fictional narrator of the novel, an entity unto itself, revealing a Black narrative stance of the Seventies.*

The Cotillion

Foreword

To Whom It May Concern
(and to all you all who ought to be)

My name is Ben Ali Lumumba, and I'm free, Black and twenty-three. Okay, Lumumba is my given name. Dig. The name I gave myself, that is. My slave name was—well to hell with that. I'm a writer, understand. And I just finished the novel that I'm forewording to you, dear readers. I used to write my novels as I lived them from Rio all the way to Zanzibar. In the oral tradition of my African ancestors. I wrote my novels with my laughter and my tears, with my blood and sweat and years of wondering as I wandered (thanks to Langston) carousing, reading, brawling, learning, looking, drinking, fornicating, from Tashkent to Johannesburg, with all races and religions. I did not discriminate. Right now though, I should state, categorically, I have a tendency to boast and brag, or, in other words, exaggerate, and sometimes I'm a liar, like most men who have been to sea. I was a seaman, see?

Yeah, and like I can lie with the best of them. Which ought to put me in good stead as a writer, right? One has to lie sometimes to get closer to the truth. Check that out. Okay, so after all those years of the seven seas and far-off places in my blood, I was a salty sonofabitch, and I didn't mind dying if dying was all. And here I am back in the Apple, New York City, and my land legs are still a little wobbly, but all that is over now, and I have settled here in this place a few blocks from where my mother birthed me. Dig. I decided to be a writer. What else could I do, sentenced as I was (by me) to dry land for the rest of my young life's duration? I mean, I'd had it, for a time, with that traveling-is-broadening shit. Now I was ready to zero in. Focus, baby. I bought me a typewriter months (or was it years?) ago, brought it to my crib and began to write my first book. Then I started on my second book, after I gave up on my first one. Temporarily. My first book was entitled *All the Way to*

Timbuktu, but I laid it aside momentarily till I could learn much more intelligence about the international scene, where things are never ever what they seem. My second book is the one I have just finished, the one I'm introducing with this hellfire introduction to whomsoever it may concern. Dig it.

This book is kind of halfly autobiographical and halfly fiction, all based on facts as I have gathered them. I got my log together, baby, from the natural source, the horse's mouth and his hinder parts. Also from the lips of the sweetest girl on this terrible wonderful earth. Dig it, and like I went to one of them downtown white workshops for a couple of months and got all screwed up with angles of narration, points of view, objectivity, universality, composition, author-intrusion, sentence structure, syntax, first person, second person. I got so screwed up I couldn't unwind myself, for days. I said, to hell with all that! I'm the first, second and third person my own damn self. And I will intrude, protrude, obtrude or exclude my point of view any time it suits my disposition. Dig that. I read all the books on writing. Egri, John Howard Lawson, Percy Lubbeck, McHugh, Reynolds. You name it. I know all about the dialectical approach, character development, cause-and-effect and orchestration, the obligatory scene, crisis, climax, denouement, and resolution. I was uptight with the craft shit. Can you dig it?

I decided to write my book in Afro-Americanese. Black rhythm, baby. Yeah, we got rhythm, brothers, sisters. Black idiom, Black nuances, Black style. Black truths. Black exaggerations. Oh I can use the big Anglo-Saxon words with the best of them, and I used them every now and then for the benefit of those brothers and sisters of the middle-class persuasion who are unduly impressed with the king and queen's faggoty unimaginative English. Nevertheless and basically, this is a Black comedy. I mean a Black black comedy. Dig it. And I meant to do myself some signifying. I meant to let it all hang out.

But now, on with the story. And Black blessings to you all. Right on—

BEN ALI LUMUMBA
son of
Harlem, U.S.A.

P.S. But the story is not about me, not really about me, but about a fox named Yoruba.

B.A.L.

ROBERT DEANE PHARR

A man in his fifties when his first novel, The Book of Numbers, *was published in 1969, Robert Deane Pharr exemplifies the difficulties Black Americans with literary talent have so frequently found in attaining publication and conditions to devote time to writing. Pharr, who attended four Negro colleges in the South in the 1930s, worked as a waiter most of his life in resort hotels and later at the Columbia University Faculty Club in New York. In a letter to the editor, he writes: "I am the son of a hardshell Baptist minister and school teacher. Born accidently on purpose in Richmond, Va., but raised in New Haven, Conn. Graduated from New Haven High School and later received my B.A. from Virginia Union University in Richmond, Va.* The Book of Numbers *was my first novel and it met with critical success. My second book is due in October of 1971 and is titled* S-R-O. *It is about life in a ghetto hotel. My editor calls it 'a junky hotel.' I live in New York City and am currently at work on a novel which might well be called 'All you ever wanted to know about sex and drugs but were afraid to ask a Black Man.'" The following short story was published in* New York *Magazine, September 22, 1969.*

The Numbers Writer

Freddy woke up and yawned. It was ten o'clock. He reached under his pillow and took out a huge bankroll. He spat on his thumb and forefinger before he began to count it. The sound was loud, the act opulent and possessive. It was a habit acquired long before he had had any real money to count.

After counting his money he cocked his head to one side and figured rapidly. He had made over $110 yesterday. He counted off $500 and put it into his pants pocket. The rest of the money he put into his pillowcase.

A little later he started to dress, putting on clean clothes from the skin out. He went out of his room and walked down the hall toward the front door of the apartment. He passed the front room, making believe he did not see his landlady watching TV. He didn't feel like listening to her tonight. The old woman was a black phonograph record. Always the same. Nothing but numbers. The dizzy old bitch actually believed he could tell her what tomorrow's number was going to be if he wasn't so mean.

In the street he hailed a taxi and told the driver to take him to Greene's Bar on Seventh Avenue. As he entered the plush lounge, Freddy changed. It was not that Freddy ever looked as if he lacked confidence, but now he exuded a certain arrogance—something predatory. He was on his home ground. This was different from Edgecombe Avenue. This was Harlem, and Freddy was in the action. Anywhere on 125th Street and from 125th to 135th on Seventh. As Freddy made his way to the rear, all but one of the 12 people standing at the bar stopped him to give him money and to quietly tell him the number they wanted to play for tomorrow.

When Freddy reached the end of the bar, where he could see and be seen by everyone who entered, he ordered a Chivas Regal and mentally chided himself for not having eaten breakfast.

A beautiful girl entered the bar. She was about 22, with olive skin and luxurious hair which she wore at shoulder length. She had that same confident, arrogant way of moving that Freddy had.

She came directly to Freddy. "Where the hell you getting all these freakish numbers from lately?" she said. "Eight-eight-five. Who'da thought two eights were coming out today?"

Freddy didn't smile. He didn't like to talk about numbers. It seemed like black people could talk about something else some of the time.

"There's no such thing as a freakish number," he said. "All numbers are the same."

Freddy had a warm voice. It wasn't a hustler's voice. At least it wasn't the kind of voice a hustler is expected to have. His voice was a sort of lullaby. Most women liked it.

It was the voice and not the words that made the girl smile. "You trying to get an attitude with me?" she asked.

"No. But every day a number comes out. Three digits. No fix. Pick what you like, what's there to talk about?"

"You *have* got an attitude," the girl said. "Well, here's my five dollars, and wish me luck."

"Same thing? Seven-oh-four? And hell, I wish everybody luck. How'm I gonna get my percentage if people don't hit?"

She laughed companionably, showing large white teeth. "You get yours whether we chumps hit or not. I saw you wheeling that fine joint Saturday."

"It ain't mine," Freddy said quickly. "It's my uncle's."

"All you numbers cats are alike. Scared as hell of the man. Don't you know a black man's got as much right to own a Cadillac as a whitey?"

"You tell that to the man! You realize I'm paying the fuzz three bills a week? And what you think they'd be asking if they thought I was really making it?"

Her eyes widened. "Three hundred dollars a week? Why that don't leave you nothing!"

"It leaves me enough to move you off 132nd Street. A fox like you is supposed to be living in the Lenox Terrace at least, if not better. Why you keep ducking and dodging me?"

She smiled good-humoredly. "You got three girlfriends you admit to, and I'm too young and good-looking to get lye thrown in my face. Dig it?"

"I don't dig no lye-tossing women. So you ain't got nothing to worry about."

"Listen, Freddy. When a woman's got a man who keeps her in a fine pad in Jersey she'll do anything to keep him. You hear me? Anything!"

"I made a hell of a mistake when I bought that house in Jersey. It's a lemon. And it was a bigger mistake to let that black bitch live in it. She's the evilest and sometime-iest woman I ever shacked up with."

"Black is beautiful, so they tell me."

"Black women are the meanest there is. If I had any sense I'd get me a gray chick or somebody who's half white like you."

"You got my money?"

Freddy and the girl both turned to look at the man. He was very black and muscular, but he was shorter than Freddy, who was over six feet. And he was old. Forty. Maybe 45, even. Freddy was slightly disconcerted because he prided himself on being able to spot anyone entering Greene's before they spotted him. "Tomorrow," he said briefly. It was a dismissal, but he didn't turn his back.

"Uh-uh. Tomorrow's too late." And then suddenly there was a snub-nosed .38 in the man's hand.

"Wasting me won't get you your $810," Freddy said.

"That's right, Obie," the girl said quickly and stepped between Freddy and Obie.

Freddy pushed her aside. "Nigger," he said softly, "I eats pistols."

Obie sort of wavered in silence. The girl rubbed her elbow where she had struck it when Freddy had shoved her up against the bar.

"You ain't got no heart, Obie," Freddy said heavily. "You is nothing."

"I'm gonna give you until tomorrow morning," Obie said.

"You ain't gonna give me nothing, faggot!" Freddy said. "You get paid when I get paid off, and not until. Maybe it's an overlook. Maybe they lost my slips. Maybe you don't get paid off for three or four days." He pulled out his roll and then put it back in his pocket. "I'm carrying over five bills here, and I was gonna give you three of them until my man paid off, but now you can just suck air." Hardly seeming to move, he suddenly jerked the gun out of Obie's hand and flicked it open and saw that it wasn't loaded. "I ought to kick your ass," he said softly and dropped the gun on the floor.

"Get this nigger," the girl murmured. She looked at Obie. "And don't ever come around me anymore. I don't care how much bread you got."

Obie turned and hurried out of the bar.

The girl laughed quietly. "You got heart, Freddy. How you know that thing wasn't loaded?"

Freddy grunted. "When the hell does anybody know a piece ain't loaded?" he said. "But I know Obie. All chumps are the same. And Obie ain't crazy. He's stupid, but he ain't crazy. And none of these square chumps is ever gonna do anything that'll prevent them from being able to show up on whitey's job tomorrow morning. That's why hustling's so great in Harlem."

It had all happened so quickly that no one else in the bar was aware of it. For the first time Freddy took a sip of his drink. Then he put his arm around the girl. "Thanks, babee," he muttered.

"You going to pay Obie? You shouldn't. I know I wouldn't."

"He hit for $1.50," Freddy said slowly. "I got me a good hustle. I write over $200 worth of numbers a day, which gives me a cool 40 bucks. You think I'd chance my good rep for a lousy $810?"

"People would still play with you when they found out what happened."

"Don't bet on that. Chumps like to deal with a winner, if you know what I mean. I'm a stone hustler. I'm down with it, dig? And he threatened me, even if it was with a empty pistol. The way the squares'll be telling it is that I crapped in my pants. I should have hurt Obie."

A man came up to put his numbers in, and after that someone came up to Freddy every five minutes. Never once did Freddy write down a number. Like all big-time Harlem numbers writers, he had a photographic memory. He had to; after all, a man could get more time for carrying a slip with numbers written on it than for being caught with a packet of heroin.

For almost two hours Freddy would continue to take bets. Then he would leave and go to his room to write them down. Then he would go to another bar for another two hours, following the same routine. Then he would go out to still another bar and remain there until closing time.

At midnight Freddy did not have to look at his watch to know what time it was. It was as if his mind was too choked to memorize another number.

He glanced at the girl and wondered. That business with Obie had put him on a sexual edge, but he had to take care of business now. Some other time. She was beautiful, she was down with it and she was nobody's whore. At least by Harlem's standards she wasn't. She had three or four old guys who each kicked in 20 or 25 bucks a week. She lived in a cheap room on 132nd Street between Seventh and Lenox. She was probably the only girl born in that block who wasn't a junkie.

Freddy guessed that she liked the way she lived. No jealous young studs, and she was so pretty mostly everything was free. Drinks, even meals. Her only real expenses were her clothes. All in all, Freddy figured he didn't care. But she had got in front of that gun, and she was boss.

He finished his drink, touched her arm lightly and said, "Take care." Then he walked out of the bar.

He took a cab to Edgecombe Avenue. When he entered his room he went to the dresser and began to write down all the numbers and bets he had collected. In 15 minutes he was through. Then he took all the money he had received in Greene's and put it in a drawer, and out of the same drawer he took a small pistol and put it in his pocket. The same pocket in which he kept his bankroll. If a cop went in that pocket, Freddy wanted him to find that $500. He wasn't about to take any bust on a Sullivan charge.

After that Freddy went out to the second bar, returning in two hours to write down the action. When he got back the third time he wrote down his numbers quicker than before, although he had just as many to record as the other times. But now he was in his stride, and he had lots more hustling to do. He had to go downtown to a Bickford's, then hustle the whiteys and black gals who prowled Times Square. After that he had his block to cover. That was the block on 141st Street between Seventh and Eighth, where he had been raised. Here he would go from tenement to tenement. Both sides of the street. It wasn't much of a hustle. Mostly welfare chumps. It was like charity, but the chumps didn't trust anybody but him. About ten o'clock he would be through and have time for a nap.

He left the room and was all the way to the lobby when he remembered that he had two 25-cent hits to pay off in Bickford's. He went back up to his room, cursing all the way. Not because he had to come back, but because he had forgotten. You're not supposed to forget in the numbers business. If you forgot you got dead.

When he walked in the Bickford's restaurant the two winners were already there, sitting at different tables. One was white, the other black. Freddy went to the counter and got eggs and coffee and took them to the table where the white winner was sitting.

"You had the right one," Freddy said in greeting.

"Two, three dollars I play on all my regular numbers, but only a quarter on six-three-eight," the white man said. His name was Jack and he worked in the hotel around the corner. "Hell! My old lady dreams it. I tell her she's nuts. I only played it so it wouldn't come out. A quarter, like insurance I plays it. But the damn thing hadda come out. How you like that?"

Freddy reached in his inside coat pocket and took out a folded sheaf of bills and handed it to Jack underneath the table. "Go in the toilet and count it," he said.

Jack's eyes protruded and he laughed. "I know you got my 135 here. Colored people is all I trust. Now if you was white it'd be different."

"Yeah," Freddy said tonelessly. He hated to see a white

man win anything, and he wondered why he took the risk of messing with whiteys.

Jack kept the money in his lap as he counted off five five-dollar bills which he handed back to Freddy. "Put it in your pocket," he said and then got up and left the restaurant.

Freddy looked across the room at Joe, the black winner. Joe came over to him and sat down. Freddy took one $135 packet from another pocket and gave it to Joe under the table. Joe got up and went to the lavatory. He stayed almost five minutes. When he came back he said, "How much I owe you?"

Freddy stared at him. It wasn't really a look of contempt, but Joe got the message just the same. All over the United States where numbers are played by black men it is obligatory to tip a numbers writer $2 on every five-cent hit. Joe had hit for a quarter, so he owed Freddy $10, and he knew it. He grinned sheepishly and handed it over. Freddy didn't thank him.

From Bickford's Freddy went to 141st Street and after that went back to Edgecombe Avenue. There was a woman standing in front of his building. Freddy grunted a hello. She was a woman Freddy wasn't even supposed to know. Not a dap guy like Freddy. The woman was strictly from the jungle. Evil. Her dark face was razor-scarred. Alcohol had made her thick lips loose and juicy. She carried a greasy shopping bag, just like the other hags around 116th Street who collected soda bottles out of trash cans until they had enough to buy a pint of wine. What hair showed from beneath the dirty scarf on her head was uncombed. She was a 60-year-old slut. The slag of Harlem.

"Why so early?" Freddy asked.

The woman spoke with just a trace of a West Indian accent. "I got a funeral to go to."

"I almost got wasted this morning. Last night, I mean."

The woman sniffed. "Black men! Not a domn one of you is worth a domn."

"To you black Harlem bitches only white is right."

"We been taught the hard way," the woman said.

"You bring me my 900?" Freddy asked as they walked to his room. And when the woman didn't answer he grunted, "Yeah, I know. I'm just wasting my breath asking you. But do you realize this guy put a gun in my ribs?"

"Black men!" the woman snorted. "Fifty, sixty dollars a day you make in commissions! Percentage on hits! Tips! And you don't got $810?"

"What the hell's that got to do with it?" Freddy yelled hoarsely. "Those damn wops in Jersey take all and send nothing back! You're gonna tell me to keep today's take and the money tomorrow and the day after that. And then I'm supposed to have enough to pay the hit. Nothing whitey takes outa Harlem ever comes back. The money you take to Jersey every day is gone forever!"

"Blacks!" the pickup woman said.

"Women that ain't worth a damn, a Cadillac I'm scared to drive and a money-sucking house in Jersey I stays in one night a week. And for all this I gotta get in front of a gun for whitey!"

"You black men had it all, and what did you do? You bragged, you wouldn't pay off, you played the fool. Not one bullet was fired, but you let the white man take it all. Yet and still a black brother will shoot his black brother writer if he don't get paid instantly. Every day God sends, a black man gets killed over numbers." The pickup woman bored her hatred into Freddy's eyes.

"This is my last day and not a domned black man can do a domned thing about it. I ought to say nigger, but I'll never use that word."

"What you quitting for?"

"Puerto Rican. From now on the Spanish will do all the handling." Then the woman actually spat on the floor. "Black men! White folks don't even trust you to run their errands anymore. Spanish is the house Negroes now, you just a field hand!" She had almost been raving, but suddenly she calmed and became strictly business. "Give me your slips. Keep today's receipts towards that $1.50 hit."

Freddy went to the dresser and wrote down all the bets he had received since the last time he left the room. Finally he was through. He put all the work in a large envelope. The woman held up her shopping bag and Freddy dropped the envelope into it. The woman went out of the room. Freddy sighed and undressed.

At two o'clock he woke up and was out of the house in 15 minutes. He took a cab to a bar on St. Nicholas Avenue. And as he entered this bar he assumed a walk and air that was more arrogant and predatory than when he was in Greene's or any of the other places he had been since ten o'clock the previous night. Now it was the single action. This was his. All his! He was no field hand now.

As Freddy walked in the bar people began to crowd around him to place their single-action bets.

The daily number in Harlem comes out in single digits. One at a time. That is, at three o'clock the first digit comes out. In playing single action, people bet on what that digit will be. It can be anything from a zero to a nine. There are 10 choices, but players only get paid eight-to-one odds if they win.

There are many people in Harlem who will only play the single action, for in single action the man who takes your bets remains right there in the bar with you. He pays off instantly, and you don't have to go looking for him. In a way it's like going to the race track. Only it doesn't cost as much.

There's fun and conversation to be had while the single action is on. There is a carnival spirit and excitement every afternoon in a single-action bar. When Freddy had taken the last bet on what the first digit would be he went to the last booth in the bar and sat down. In a few moments the telephone rang and Freddy got up to answer it. When he came out of the booth he said, "It's a seven."

The bar threw up a concerted exclamation of anguish and joy. Everyone who had bet on a seven to lead crowded around Freddy to be paid. Then came the business of new bets on what the second digit would be.

At four o'clock. Freddy received another phone call. The second digit was a zero. Again Freddy paid off the lucky ones, including one man who had bet $12 on a zero.

At quarter after five the phone rang again. The third digit was another zero. Of the more than 50 people in the bar, not one had played a zero for the last digit. So although Freddy had shown a loss all afternoon he wound up with a $70 profit. Freddy's phenomenal memory flashed back over all the numbers he had written since last night. In all, eight people had played 700, and since the writer automatically receives 10 percent of all winnings, Freddy had over $100 coming to him from the hits. And then there would be the tips on top of that. Not a bad day.

He gave the bartender $10 for a drink of Chivas Regal and told him to keep the change. He took the drink to the last booth and sat down.

At exactly six o'clock a Ford sedan with three white men in it stopped in front of the bar. The man in the back seat got out and came into the bar. He went directly to Freddy. Freddy had five $10 bills laid out on the table. The plain-clothesmen picked them up and walked back out of the bar.

When he got in the car the detective in the driver's seat asked. "What'd he say?"

"Nothing. He never says nothing."

"Then maybe we ought to raise it. What's $50 a day between three?"

"For Christ sake! You gotta leave him something," the man sitting next to him said. He was very young to be a detective.

"He ain't supposed to have nothing," the driver said. "He don't work. If he wants something for hisself, let him get out and work for it like we do."

CYRUS COLTER (1910–   )

Born in Noblesville, Indiana, but long a resident of Chicago, Cyrus Colter began writing fiction late in his life, in 1960, as a weekend break from his work as an Illinois Commerce Commissioner. His stories have appeared in Chicago Review, Prairie Schooner, Epoch, *and other literary journals, and in* The Best Short Stories by Negro Writers *(1967), edited by Langston Hughes. In 1970 Colter won the Iowa School of Letters Award for Short Fiction, an award recently established by the School of Letters at the University of Iowa to foster the art of the short story.* The Beach Umbrella, *his award-winning collection of short stories, was published by University of Iowa Press in 1970. Novelist Vance Bourjaily, one of the judges for the award, described Colter as "what a writer is and always has been—a man with stories to tell, a milieu to reveal and people he cares about." In 1971 his collection of short stories received two additional literary awards in the Midwest: a prize from the Friends of Literature, in Chicago, and the Patron Saints Award of the Society of Midland Authors. The following story was published in* Chicago Review, *Vol. 17, No. 2 & 3, 1964, and is reprinted by permission of* Chicago Review.

Mary's Convert

Forty-third Street, near the "el," the street of rib joints and taverns, was more cluttered and overrun than usual. It was the heat. It lay on the sidewalk like an electric blanket and scores of restless people were in motion. Driven from their baking kitchenettes, they looked uprooted and a little dazed, as some stood at the curb and moped, or turned in at a corner door for beer.

Jerome stood wiry tall and casual at the newsstand, inspecting the headlines and the cover girls; he looked young even for a teen-ager, and wore skin-tight, hep cat pants.

"Whutaaya want, boy?—a comic book?" the dirty man selling newspapers said.

Jerome made no reply, but watched as an old Cadillac with a roasting radiator crept by, and two clowning loafers shouted obscenities across the street at each other. Then he resumed with the headlines.

"These here papers are for *sale,*" the newsman insisted, joking. "This ain't no library."

Jerome paused and gave him an unruffled look. Finally he said, "Okay, gim'me a comic book."

The newsman's black horny hand reached up for a book. Jerome's shirt was open at the throat but despite the heat, the long sleeves were buttoned at the wrists. He extracted a tightly-folded dollar bill from his pants watch pocket.

"Ten," the newsman said, taking the dollar bill and handing over the comic book. He gave back ninety cents change, and Jerome checked the two quarters and four dimes in his palm before sticking them in his watch pocket. Then he hesitated, his young, brown face expressionless, and viewed the newsman. "Seen the Red Lion 'round here this afternoon?" he asked.

The grimy newsman stiffened. He stood staring at Jerome. "Whut'd you say?" he scowled.

"Seen the Red Lion 'round?" Jerome repeated.

"You git outa my face," the newsman whispered. "—you little bastard, you. You ain't sixteen!"

"What's it to you?" Jerome's face was all flat nose, so spreading flat that there were only slits for nostrils. He watched the newsman with a level gaze. "You know Tommy," he said, ". . . you take care o' him all right."

"I ain't even talkin' to you." The newsman turned his sweaty back. "Go on, *beat it!*"

Jerome studied him. "Okay . . . ole *Red Lion*," he said. Then he sauntered off, leaving the newsman glowering.

Along 43rd Street, the few people still left in the hot, mangy, brick and stone kitchenette buildings were hanging out of their windows in hope of a breath of air. They were mostly frowzy women, of all shapes and colors, who would often yell down at their children or passing friends on the sidewalk where the pigeons were liberal with droppings and floss. Jerome was in no hurry as he walked. The hell with the Lion . . . who was he trying to kid; not him. He'd wait and see Tommy that evening; no problem. Tommy'd go to the Lion for him; Tommy was great people; swell, big-hearted—had given him his first fix. That was last spring, almost five months now. It seemed longer. They'd had many a one together since then. But Tommy always said any guy with sense could kick the habit, whenever he wanted to—and that a guy with sense always knew when he'd better *start* kicking too. Tommy was smart; never got puff-headed about anything—more like a brother, a big brother. And religious too—real religious; belonged to the Church of God in Christ.

Jerome opened the comic book as he walked and, casually turning the pages, scanned the cartoons. He hadn't meant to buy it—had let the Red Lion rush him, and still hadn't done any business with him; only got chased away. He approached the corner of 43rd and Calumet. Then he saw her. She was a young, brown-skinned woman—and wore flowing white robes. She was passing out leaflets and darted from one passer-by to the next, gesticulating, exhorting, thrusting her literature at them. Her head was draped to the shoulders in the same heavy, white fabric of her robes and despite the 95-degree heat no part of her body was visible except occasionally her feet, in high-heeled shoes, and her hands and face. But what Jerome could see of her face attracted him. There were gaudy rhinestone rings on her fingers and when she turned to face him he could see huge golden earrings dangling back up under her white head covering.

She jumped at him, shooting out a leaflet. "Young man, have you talked with Jesus today?" She blocked his path.

He said nothing and tried to step around her.

"Young man! Have you talked with Him?—just once today?" She pushed the leaflet at his chest.

Jerome was cowed. "No'm," he said.

"Then read this! Read it." She shook the leaflet at him.

Slow anger gathered in his face. "I don't want it, lady." He side-stepped toward the curb.

Suddenly she snatched the comic book from his hand and, breathing in his face, dropped it to the sidewalk.

His first impulse was to swing at her. But he stood motionless.

Then someone behind him gripped his arm. As he spun around, a squinty-eyed black man, his face deeply pitted, grinned and pointed at the woman. "Don't pay her no mind," he sniggered. "That's Sanctified Mary." He turned to her. "Whut's th' matter, Mary? You off the stuff again? Kicked it, eh?—fuh a week or two—an' took up Jesus." He laughed.

Mary was sullen, silent.

"She's savin' souls *now*," the man said to Jerome, "but jus' ask her t' pull up that Kluxer sheet an' show you her arm. Go on—ask her."

Jerome looked at him, and then at Mary, but said nothing.

Suddenly the man leapt forward and seized her by the wrist, and yanked her to him.

She went raving wild. "You son of a bitch, you!" she screamed, fighting and clawing him. "Take your filthy hands offa me, Jug Smith!" Her leaflets scattered to the sidewalk.

The man struggled and tugged her around in front of Jerome and with his free hand slid her robe sleeve up her arm to the shoulder. "Look!" he breathed. "Look here! Whut's Jesus gotta say 'bout *that?*" Near the elbow on the inside of her arm were a dozen purple-dotted needle scars. "Y'see?" Jug panted. "She's a mainliner. Y'*see?* Now you git t'hell outa here," he grinned at her, "an' leave this kid alone." He turned her loose.

She was incoherent. "*I'll kill you!*" she finally shrieked, lunging at him. Still grinning, he grabbed both her arms and held her off.

Someone yelled from across the street. "You-all better cut out all that 'who struck John' over there, Jug! See that squad car?—up in fronta the drug store."

Jug looked up toward the drug store and laughed. But he turned Mary loose again and trotted across the street.

She was ready to cry. Jerome stood by, helpless. Soon he stooped down and picked up a few of the scattered leaflets, glancing at one. There was much fine print, but the caption in bold type read: KEEP LOOKING UP—JESUS NEVER FAILS.

He offered her the leaflets, which she finally took grudgingly, still whispering curses to herself at Jug Smith.

"Don't worry 'bout that guy," Jerome said. "He ain't nothing but a hoodlum."

She still fought tears. "He made me forget m'self—and say all those bad words!" she whimpered, "and I been tryin' so hard . . . to do what Jesus wants. *So* hard."

Jerome began inching away. The heat from the pavement was coming through the soles of his shoes and his shirt was sticky.

Mary came alive. "Young man!"—she shoved a wrinkled leaflet at him—"put this in your pocket an' read it when you get home! An' keep on reading it. HE never fails."

Jerome took the leaflet and stuffed it in his shirt pocket, and then continued down the street, leaving his comic book lying on the sidewalk.

About an hour later he was home, climbing the creaking stairs of the apartment building where he lived with his uncle and aunt. He was bored. He'd kill some time till Tommy got off from work at 5:30 . . . but he couldn't get Sanctified Mary off his mind; imagine *her* a hop-head; some nut; a real screw-ball; not a bad looking chick, though; if she just didn't wear all that mad get-up—robes! Jug Smith had identified them with the Klan. Kluxer sheets he called them; she wasn't a day over twenty-three or -four; how could she put on all that hot crap in August and go out in the boiling sun and pass out leaflets about Jesus? He didn't get it; it didn't make *any* kind of sense; he'd tell Tommy. Tommy was religious.

He took out his key and let himself in. The blinds were all the way down, and he stumbled against a chair as he groped for the light switch. No one was home and the place was suffocating, with the windows shut tight and the sun outside on the west wall. But he knew not to open a window—his Aunt Bertha would raise hell for him "acting like a fool and letting in all that street heat." He went into the kitchen, opened the refrigerator and took out a cold bottle of milk. He uncapped the bottle, upped it and swilled almost half before he slumped in a kitchen chair, still holding the bottle, and sat staring at the sooty vacant wall, thinking of old fine Mary wearing her sharp high heels under the robes! and all that fake jewelry on both hands! that didn't look very religious to *him;* maybe she'd just forget to take the rings off whenever she'd switch over from sinning; and she could sin a while too, he bet—once you got her in a groovey mood;

and a mainliner!—she was all mixed up; needed help; Tommy should see her; *she* hadn't kicked it; it *wasn't* all that easy, probably; she sure looked sexy, though—even in the funky robes.

He got up and put the milk back in the refrigerator. He stretched and yawned. His face rippled like rubber around his pancake-flat nose—and his boredom deepened. Then he remembered the leaflet in his shirt pocket and took it out to examine it. Soon he was sprawled in the chair again, reading:

KEEP LOOKING UP—JESUS NEVER FAILS

Elder Griffin, the great preacher and spiritual leader, asks: Have you talked with Jesus today? If you have not, or without success, then come to the Temple at 4178 Calumet, and pray with me. Only a small silver offering is asked. Open 8 AM to 10 PM, daily and Sundays.

The Elder says: Come to me if you are troubled and almost beat down to the ground. Are you sick, unhappy, disgusted with life? Does bad luck seem to follow you wherever you go? Then come to the Temple. I am here to help you see the mysteries of God's work—His mercy, and your salvation. I can do these things only through His will. *I* am nothing— Jesus is all. But to receive His Comfort and blessings, you must get right with God.

May I ask you the most important question in your whole life? It is this: Are you prepared to meet God? Your joy or your sorrow for all eternity depends upon this one question. If you are not, then you must make a start now. You must prepare! The Word of God tells us that because we are sinners we are condemned to die. "For the wages of sin is death." Romans 6:23. "Sin bringeth forth death." James 1:15. What does it mean to be a sinner condemned to die? It means separation from God, the Father, for all eternity. As you read this, won't you hear the voice of Jesus as He beckons you to come? "Ho, everyone that thirsteth, come ye to the waters." Isa. 55:1. "Incline your ear and come unto Me. Hear, and your soul shall live." Isa. 55:3.

Jerome read to the end and sat deep in thought. Finally he gave the leaflet a methodical fold and put it back in his shirt pocket. Soon he got up and wandered into the living room. That stuff sounded like Aunt Bertha; she was nutty on religion too, but she was older. It was okay for older people to be so religious if they wanted to, but Mary . . . what could she see in an old bastard like Griffin? . . . *Elder* Griffin! . . . Ah, but maybe he wasn't so old; maybe he was a young stud; hip to the tip—with a line for all the chicks; he'd love to see the Elder once; a real weird deal, this was; he'd talk to Tommy about it. Finally he strolled out the front door of the apartment and down into the hot street again. Maybe if he went back down on 43rd, he'd run into Mary again.

When he reached 43rd and Calumet, Mary was nowhere to be seen. He stood in the doorway of a sweltering fish shack and listened to the juke box pouring out the blues—"Just a dre-e-e-e-eam ah had on mah mind! . . ." Finally he went in and sat at the counter and bought a grape pop. Maybe Mary was up on King Drive with her handbills by now, he thought, swigging the pop; or else she'd gone on home—to get out of those steamy robes; and take a bath; she'd probably had enough of Jesus and Elder Griffin for one day—in all that heat; she was just climbing in the tub now, maybe—buck naked. He wondered if she knew the Red Lion—when she had been sinning, that is; all the mainliners at one time or another knew the Lion; couldn't she get mad easy!—flipped her lid on the street there when Jug got after her . . . and made her backslide; Aunt Bertha always said there was nothing in the world worse than a backslider—because they never had any religion in the first place; but she didn't know Mary; that was okay too; she'd hate Mary; Aunt Bertha was always talking about how she didn't want anything to do with any "low-down people"—whiskey-heads, and bad women, and all that; and hop-heads! Lord!—she'd skin him alive if she knew about him and Tommy and all the fixes they'd had together; maybe he ought to put Tommy down—and kick the habit; he could kick it if he wanted to; maybe Tommy couldn't though, no matter what he said; Mary hadn't. He sat at the counter with the sweating bottle of pop in his hand, wishing he knew Mary better, wishing he knew where to find her; she probably wouldn't have any time for somebody sixteen years old, though. But before very long he finished the pop, got up, and sauntered out of the fish shack into the street again.

It was quarter to five when he stood in the vestibule of a run-down apartment building on 48th Street bending forward to scan the stacks of penciled names over the mail boxes. He had just come from the Temple, a large bare room with a few folding chairs over a pool hall, where a woman, also in white robes, had given him Mary's ("Sister Mary Bivens's") address. Looking now at the names over one of the mail boxes, he saw that Mary lived, apparently with many relatives, on the third floor. There was no doorbell to ring, so he went up. When he reached the third floor, right side, he knocked. Inside he could hear noisy children. Soon the door was opened by a little black girl, with a tooth out in front. She appraised him.

"Miss Mary home?" he asked. He was shy.

The child viewed him with misgiving, and called back into the apartment. "Mama! A man wants to see Aunt Mary!" Now three more children came galloping to the door.

Finally a woman wearing worn-out bedroom slippers appeared. She was sweating. "My sister's 'sleep," she said. "Whatayou want?"

"Oh, I just wanted to see her." Jerome was offhand. "I was talkin' with her today—down on 43rd Street—and just thought I'd drop by. I can see her some other time."

"Are you from Elder Griffin's?" Her curtness softened some.

"I just came over from the Temple—yes'm." Jerome was quick.

"Are you one of Mary's converts?"

". . . Yes'm . . ."

The woman studied him. ". . . Okay," she finally said, "come on in. I'll see if she'll come out." She stepped aside to let him in. "She's awful tired," she said, shuffling from the room.

Jerome stood in the middle of the bare floor. The children had lost interest in him now and were romping again. A pair of large oval portraits under glass hung on the wall over the sofa. They were apparently of grandparents, and were enlarged and touched-up in a blurry pastel-tint; the old man had a gray kinky beard, and wore a shirt fastened at the neck with a brass collar button but no collar or tie; the woman looked like a New Orleans creole, with her hair severely parted in the middle and her dress padded and built-up at the shoulders. But nothing in the room reminded him of Mary. Wouldn't she be surprised to see *him!*—she'd remember him all right. But she might be mad at him for seeing her disgraced right there on the street in front of him.

Mary's sister came back in the room. "Come on—in here," she summoned. He followed her into Mary's humid bedroom. Mary sat barefooted on the side of the bed in a dressing gown. She did look tired. On a chair in front of her was a tiny, whirring electric fan. As they entered, she quickly pulled the sheet around her and let it drape down to hide her feet. She still wore the rhinestone rings on her fingers.

"Well . . ." She gave him a weary smile.

"Hello, Miss Mary." His voice was weak and bashful.

"Uh-huh, I knew it." She spoke with conviction. "You been thinking about what I told you—I can see it. You been talkin' to Jesus, like I told you." She smiled. "Ain't that right?"

"Yes'm." Jerome grinned and looked at the floor.

"Let me talk to him, Dillie." She was abrupt with her sister who stood in the doorway. Dillie left the room with a long face.

"What's your name, son?" Mary said.

"Jerome."

"Jerome what?"

"Jerome Williams."

"Uh-huh, and why'd you come here, Jerome?"

He hesitated—stumped. Then he thought of the leaflet. He fumbled in his shirt pocket, pulled it out, and stood holding it, saying nothing.

"My sister said you just come over from the Temple," Mary said. Then she saw the leaflet—"What's that you got there?"

"It's what you was passing out today," Jerome said.

"Well, bless your heart! Ain't that nice. Do you understand what Elder Griffin was gettin' at?" She pulled up the bed sheet to swing her legs around onto the bed, as Jerome coolly glimpsed her bare knees before she could cover them. His quiet breath came faster. "That's why you came," she said, "you don't understand it all, do you?" She pointed at the leaflet in his hand. "Sit down there," she nodded toward a straight-back chair at the side of the dresser.

Reluctantly he backed away from the bed and sat down. The window was up and the sharp cries of playing children reached up from the sidewalks below.

"Jerome . . . y'know what?"

"No'm."

"I want you to go out tomorrow—with me—and pass out literature."

He looked at her. ". . . okay," he finally said.

"You been getting the message all right . . . or you wouldn't be here. I told you—Jesus never fails."

Jerome shifted his feet.

"Now, what is there about it you don't seem to understand?" Unconsciously she wiggled her toes under the peak of the sheet.

He was too distracted to answer.

"Here, gim'me that," she said, and stretched from the bed toward him, took the leaflet, and then lay back again. She began to read: "What does it mean to be a sinner, condemned to die? It means separation from God, the Father, for all eternity." She stopped and looked at him. "Jerome, that's terrible . . . but it's true. D'you see the Elder's message there?"

Jerome hesitated. "I think so."

She took another passage. "The Word of God tells us that because we are sinners we are condemned to die. For the wages of sin is death. Romans 6:23. Sin bringeth forth death. James 1:15." She raised herself up now and stared out the window into space. ". . . Ah, we all understand *that*," she mused aloud.

Her dressing gown had fallen away from one shoulder, revealing an untidy brassiere strap. He sensed she hadn't bathed yet. But her face looked clean, and free of make-up. He recognized the break in the line of one eyebrow as scar tissue, put there by men's fists. She held the leaflet in her lap, still gazing off in space. Suddenly he noticed that the left sleeve of her dressing gown had worked up, exposing her forearm, and again he saw the needle scars.

She quickly caught him staring. "What's th' matter with you, Jerome? What you looking at?"

His eyes swept up to her face.

"You were lookin' at my *arms!*" she suddenly cried, thrusting both arms out straight. The dark purple dots glared. Jerome, flustered, shook his head no. "Yes, you were too!" Her eyes blazed. "Is that what you come here for?—outa curiosity—to make fun of me?" She hurled back the bed sheet and sprang out of bed, the dressing gown parting and showing her thighs.

"Aw, no, Miss Mary!" He cringed in his chair as she stood over him. "I didn't come here for that, Miss Mary!"

"You damned little liar, you!" She began shaking him. "An' coming in here with my literature stuck in your pocket! Now, what'd you come here for? *Tell* me!" She gave him a savage shaking.

Jerome trying to fend off her hands could smell the sweaty perfume on her body and underwear. "I come here to see *you*, Miss Mary."

She stepped back from him. "Don't lie to me, boy! Don't you lie, now!—Did Jug Smith tell you t' come here!—to pester me some more, to make it harder for me?—because I won't have nothing to do with dogs like him no more! *Did he?*"

"No'm! I *told* you!" Jerome pleaded.

She seemed not to hear him. "Nobody don't know, or care, about what I'm goin' through! Nobody!"

"You're wrong about me, Miss Mary."

"No, I ain't either!" She stood over him again and glared. Then slowly he began unbuttoning the left sleeve of his shirt. He turned the inside of his arm up and pushed the sleeve above the elbow. There sat a welter of purple-dotted needle scars.

". . . Oh!" Mary gasped, and turned her back. She would not look at him and sank on the bed. "You poor boy, you! You poor boy!" Soon she was crying.

Jerome sat and watched her.

"I'm so sorry!" she moaned, crying in the bed sheet she held to her eyes. "I'm *so* sorry!"

Jerome was confident now. Tommy should see him, he thought. He got up boldly and went to the bed and sat down beside her. The shouts of the children in the street below overcame the faint whirr of the little electric fan, as it fluttered the bed sheet against her leg. He put his arm around her waist. "I didn't mean to make you cry, Miss Mary."

"You came here for help," she looked at him through tear-wet lashes, "and I acted awful . . . cussed you out. . . . Oh, forgive me, baby—you're only a baby."

He held her tighter now. Soon he pressed his lips hard against the side of her face. They sat silently. She seemed to relax.

She looked at him again. ". . . You're only a baby," she repeated, softly like a mother, and stroked his forehead, and then his flat nose, with her sensitive fingers. He could smell the musky-sweetish perfume and was racked with impatience. Suddenly he seized her and, moaning softly, crushed her mouth open with his lips.

Then she viewed him sadly. ". . . And you've started your bad ways so young," she said. "You shouldn't be like me—weak. I'm weak—*so* weak."

He felt the tornado inside him. But he kept his arm around her waist and waited.

Finally she gazed in his vacant face. "Go close the door, Jerome," she said, ". . . and throw the lock."

He sprang at the door, eased it shut, and threw the lock. Hanging on the nail was her long white robe.

ERNEST J. GAINES (1933–   )

*Born on a Louisiana plantation, where he worked in the
fields during his childhood, Ernest J. Gaines moved to California at the age of fifteen. He graduated from San Francisco
State College in 1957. The following year he won a Wallace
Stegner Creative Writing Fellowship for study at Stanford
University and in 1959 he received the Joseph Henry Jackson
Literary Award. Gaines has published three novels and a
volume of collected short stories,* Bloodline *(1968). His
stories have been reprinted in* Southern Writing in the Sixties,
The Best Short Stories by Negro Writers, *and many other
anthologies. The following story is from his book* Bloodline.

Three Men

Two of them was sitting in the office when I came in there.
One was sitting in a chair behind the desk, the other one
was sitting on the end of the desk. They looked at me,
but when they saw I was just a nigger they went back to
talking like I wasn't even there. They talked like that two or
three more minutes before the one behind the desk looked at
me again. That was T. J. I didn't know who the other one
was.

"Yeah, what you want?" T. J. said.

They sat inside a little railed-in office. I went closer to the
gate. It was one of them little gates that swung in and out.

"I come to turn myself in," I said.

"Turn yourself in for what?"

"I had a fight with somebody. I think I hurt him."

T. J. and the other policeman looked at me like I was

crazy. I guess they had never heard of a nigger doing that before.

"You Procter Lewis?" T. J. said.

"Yes, sir."

"Come in here."

I pushed the little gate open and went in. I made sure it didn't swing back too hard and make noise. I stopped a little way from the desk. T. J. and the other policeman was watching me all the time.

"Give me some papers," T. J. said. He was looking up at me like he was still trying to figure out if I was crazy. If I wasn't crazy, then I was a smart aleck.

I got my wallet out my pocket. I could feel T. J. and the other policeman looking at me all the time. I wasn't supposed to get any papers out, myself, I was supposed to give him the wallet and let him take what he wanted. I held the wallet out to him and he jerked it out of my hand. Then he started going through everything I had in there, the money and all. After he looked at everything, he handed them to the other policeman. The other one looked at them, too; then he laid them on the desk. T. J. picked up the phone and started talking to somebody. All the time he was talking to the other person, he was looking up at me. He had a hard time making the other person believe I had turned myself in. When he hung up the phone, he told the policeman on the desk to get my records. He called the other policeman "Paul." Paul slid away from the desk and went to the file cabinet against the wall. T. J. still looked at me. His eyes was the color of ashes. I looked down at the floor, but I could still feel him looking at me. Paul came back with the records and handed them to him. I looked up again and saw them looking over the records together. Paul was standing behind T. J., looking over his shoulder.

"So you think you hurt him, huh?" T. J. asked, looking up at me again.

I didn't say anything to him. He was a mean, evil sonofabitch. He was big and red and he didn't waste time kicking your ass if you gave him the wrong answers. You had to weigh every word he said to you. Sometimes you answered, other times you kept your mouth shut. This time I passed my tongue over my lips and kept quiet.

It was about four o'clock in the morning, but it must've been seventy-five in there. T. J. and the other policeman had on short-sleeve khaki shirts. I had on a white shirt, but it was all dirty and torn. My sleeves was rolled up to the elbows, and both of my elbows was skinned and bruised.

"Didn't I bring you in here one time, myself?" Paul said.

"Yes, sir, once, I think," I said. I had been there two or three times, but I wasn't go'n say it if he didn't. I had been in couple other jails two or three times, too, but I wasn't go'n say anything about them either. If they hadn't put it on my record that was they hard luck.

"A fist fight," Paul said. "Pretty good with your fists, ain't you?"

"I protect myself," I said.

It was quiet in there for a second or two. I knowed why; I hadn't answered the right way.

"You protect yourself, what?" T. J. said.

"I protect myself, *sir*," I said.

They still looked at me. But I could tell Paul wasn't anything like T. J. He wasn't mean at all, he just had to play mean because T. J. was there. Couple Sundays ago I had played baseball with a boy who looked just like Paul. But he had brown eyes; Paul had blue eyes.

"You'll be sorry you didn't use your fists this time," T. J. said. "Take everything out your pockets."

I did what he said.

"Where's your knife?" he asked.

"I never car' a knife," I said.

"You never car' a knife, what, boy?" T. J. said.

"I never car' a knife, *sir*," I said.

He looked at me hard again. He didn't think I was crazy for turning myself in, he thought I was a smart aleck. I could tell from his big, fat, red face he wanted to hit me with his fist.

He nodded to Paul and Paul came toward me. I moved back some.

"I'm not going to hurt you," Paul said.

I stopped, but I could still feel myself shaking. Paul started patting me down. He found a pack of cigarettes in my shirt pocket. I could see in his face he didn't want take them out, but he took them out, anyhow.

"Thought I told you empty your pockets?" T. J. said.

"I didn't know—"

"Paul, if you can't make that boy shut up, I can," T. J. said.

"He'll be quiet," Paul said, looking at me. He was telling me with his eyes to be quiet or I was go'n get myself in a lot of trouble.

"You got one more time to butt in," T. J. said. "One more time now."

I was getting a swimming in the head, and I looked down at the floor. I hoped they would hurry up and lock me up so I could have a little peace.

"Why'd you turn yourself in?" T. J. asked.

I kept my head down. I didn't answer him.

"Paul, can't you make that boy talk?" T. J. said. "Or do I have to get up and do it?"

"He'll talk," Paul said.

"I figured y'all was go'n catch me sooner or later—sir."

"That's not the reason you turned yourself in," T. J. said.

I kept my head down.

"Look up when I talk to you," T. J. said.

I raised my head. I felt weak and shaky. My clothes was wet and sticking to my body, but my mouth felt dry as dust. My eyes wanted to look down again, but I forced myself to look at T. J.'s big red face.

"You figured if you turned yourself in, Roger Medlow was go'n get you out, now, didn't you?"

I didn't say anything—but that's exactly what I was figuring on.

"Sure," he said. He looked at me a long time. He knowed how I was feeling; he knowed I was weak and almost ready to fall. That's why he was making me stand there like that. "What you think we ought to do with niggers like you?" he said. "Come on now—what you think we ought to do with you?"

I didn't answer him.

"Well?" he said.

"I don't know," I said. "Sir."

"I'll tell you," he said. "See, if I was gov'nor, I'd run every damned one of you off in that river out there. Man, woman and child. You know that?"

I was quiet, looking at him. But I made sure I didn't show in my face what I was thinking. I could've been killed for what I was thinking then.

"Well, what you think of that?" he said.

"That's up to the gov'nor, sir," I said.

"Yeah," he said. "That's right. That's right. I think I'll write him a little telegram and tell him 'bout my idea. Can save this state a hell of a lot trouble."

Now he just sat there looking at me again. He wanted to hit me in the mouth with his fist. Not just hit me, he wanted to beat me. But he had to have a good excuse. And what excuse could he have when I had already turned myself in.

"Put him in there with Munford," he said to Paul.

We went out. We had to walk down a hall to the cell block. The niggers' cell block was on the second floor. We had to go up some concrete steps to get there. Paul turned on the lights and a woman hollered at him to turn them off. "What's this supposed to be—Christmas?" she said. "A person can't sleep in this joint." The women was locked up on one end of the block and the men was at the other end. If you had a mirror or a piece of shiny tin, you could stick it out the cell and fix it so you could see the other end of the block.

The guard opened the cell door and let me in, then he locked it back. I looked at him through the bars.

"When will y'all ever learn?" he said, shaking his head.

He said it like he meant it, like he was sorry for me. He kept reminding me of that boy I had played baseball with. They called that other boy Lloyd, and he used to show up just about every Sunday to play baseball with us. He used to play the outfield so he could do a lot of running. He used to buy Cokes for everybody after the game. He was the only white boy out there.

"Here's a pack of cigarettes and some matches," Paul said. "Might not be your brand, but I doubt if you'll mind it too much in there."

I took the cigarettes from him.

"You can say 'Thanks,' " he said.

"Thanks," I said.

"And you can say 'sir' sometimes," he said.

"Sir," I said.

He looked at me like he felt sorry for me, like he felt sorry for everybody. He didn't look like a policeman at all.

"Let me give you a word of warning," he said. "Don't push T. J. Don't push him, now."

"I won't."

"It doesn't take much to get him started—don't push him."

I nodded.

"Y'all go'n turn out them goddamn lights?" the woman hollered from the other end of the block.

"Take it easy," Paul said to me and left.

After the lights went out, I stood at the cell door till my eyes got used to the dark. Then I climbed up on my bunk. Two other people was in the cell. Somebody on the bunk under mine, somebody on the lower bunk 'cross from me. The upper bunk 'cross from me was empty.

"Cigarette?" the person below me said.

He said it very low, but I could tell he was talking to me and not to the man 'cross from us. I shook a cigarette out the pack and dropped it on the bunk. I could hear the man scratching the match to light the cigarette. He cupped his hands close to his face, because I didn't see too much light. I could tell from the way he let that smoke out he had wanted a cigarette very bad.

"What you in for?" he said, real quiet.

"A fight," I said.

"First time?"

"No, I been in before."

He didn't say any more and I didn't, either. I didn't feel like talking, anyhow. I looked up at the window on my left, and I could see a few stars. I felt lonely and I felt like crying. But I couldn't cry. Once you started that in here you was done for. Everybody and his brother would run over you.

The man on the other bunk got up to take a leak. The toilet was up by the head of my bunk. After the man had zipped up his pants, he just stood there looking at me. I tightened my fist to swing at him if he tried any funny stuff.

"Well, hello there," he said.

"Get your ass back over there, Hattie," the man below me said. He spoke in that quiet voice again. "Hattie is a woman," he said to me. "Don't see how come they didn't put him with the rest of them whores."

"Don't let it worry your mind," Hattie said.

"Caught him playing with this man dick," the man below me said. "At this old flea-bitten show back of town there. Up front—front row—there he is playing with this man dick. Bitch."

"Is that any worse than choking somebody half to death?" Hattie said.

The man below me was quiet. Hattie went back to his bunk.

"Oh, these old crampy, stuffy, old ill-smelling beds," he said, slapping the mattress level with the palm of his hand. "How do they expect you to sleep." He laid down. "What are you in for, honey?" he asked me. "You look awful young."

"Fighting," I said.

"You poor, poor thing," Hattie said. "If I can help you in any way, don't hesitate to ask."

"Shit," the man below me said. I heard him turning over so he could go to sleep.

"The world has given up on the likes of you," Hattie said. "You jungle beast."

"Bitch, why don't you just shut up," the man said.

"Why don't both of y'all shut up," somebody said from another cell.

It was quiet after that.

I looked up at the window and I could see the stars going out in the sky. My eyes felt tired and my head started spinning, and I wasn't here any more, I was at the Seven Spots. And she was there in red, and she had two big dimples in her jaws. Then she got up and danced with him, and every time she turned my way she looked over his shoulder at me and smiled. And when she turned her back to me, she rolled her big ass real slow and easy—just for me, just for me. Grinning Boy was sitting at the table with me, saying: "Poison, poison—nothing but poison. Look at that; just look at that." I was looking, but I wasn't thinking about what he was saying. When she went back to that table to sit down, I went there and asked her to dance. That nigger sitting there just looked at me, rolling his big white eyes like I was supposed to break out of the joint. I didn't pay him no mind, I was looking at that woman. And I was looking down at them two big pretty brown things poking that dress way out. They looked so soft and warm and waiting. I wanted to touch them right there in front of that ugly nigger. She shook her head, because he was sitting there, but little bit later when she went back in the kitchen, I went back there, too. Grinning Boy tried to stop me, saying, "Poison, poison, poison," but I didn't pay him no mind. When I came back in the kitchen, she was standing at the counter ordering a chicken sandwich. The lady back of the counter had to fry the chicken, so she had to wait a while. When she saw me, she started smiling. Them two big dimples came in her jaws. I smiled back at her.

"She go'n take a while," I said. "Let's step out in the cool till she get done."

She looked over her shoulder and didn't see the nigger peeping, and we went outside. There was people talking out there, but I didn't care, I had to touch her.

"What's your name?" I said.

"Clara."

"Let's go somewhere, Clara."

"I can't. I'm with somebody," she said.

"That nigger?" I said. "You call him somebody?"

She just looked at me with that little smile on her face—

them two big dimples in her jaws. I looked little farther down, and I could see how them two warm, brown things was waiting for somebody to tear that dress open so they could get free.

"You must be the prettiest woman in the world," I said. "You like me?"

"Lord, yes."

"I want you to like me," she said.

"Then what's keeping us from going?" I said. "Hell away with that nigger."

"My name is Clara Johnson," she said. "It's in the book. Call me tomorrow after four."

She turned to go back inside, but just then that big sweaty nigger bust out the door. He passed by her like she wasn't even there.

"No, Bayou," she said. "No."

But he wasn't listening to a thing. Before I knowed it, he had cracked me on the chin and I was down on my back. He raised his foot to kick me in the stomach, and I rolled and rolled till I was out of the way. Then I jumped back up.

"I don't want fight you, Bayou," I said. "I don't want fight you, now."

"You fight or you fly, nigger," somebody else said. "If you run, we go'n catch you."

Bayou didn't say nothing. He just came in swinging. I backed away from him.

"I wasn't doing nothing but talking to her," I said.

He rushed in and knocked me on a bunch of people. They picked me clear off the ground and throwed me back on him. He hit me again, this time a glancing blow on the shoulder. I moved back from him, holding the shoulder with the other hand.

"I don't want fight you, "I told him. "I was just talking to her."

But trying to talk to Bayou was like trying to talk to a mule. He came in swinging wild and high, and I went under his arm and rammed my fist in his stomach. But it felt like ramming your fist into a hundred-pound sack of flour. He stopped about a half a second, then he was right back on me again. I hit him in the face this time, and I saw the blood splash out of his mouth. I was still backing away from him, hoping he would quit, but the nigger kept coming on me. He had to, because all his friends and that woman was there. But he didn't know how to fight, and every time he moved in I hit him in the face. Then I saw him going for his knife.

"Watch it, now, Bayou," I said. "I don't have a knife. Let's keep this fair."

But he didn't hear a thing I was saying; he was listening to the others who was sicking him on. He kept moving in on me. He had both of his arms 'way out—that blade in his right hand. From the way he was holding it, he didn't have nothing but killing on his mind.

I kept moving back, moving back. Then my foot touched a bottle and I stooped down and picked it up. I broke it against the corner of the building, but I never took my eyes off Bayou. He started circling me with the knife, and I moved round him with the bottle. He made a slash at me, and I jumped back. He was all opened and I could've gotten him then, but I was still hoping for him to change his mind.

"Let's stop it, Bayou," I kept saying to him. "Let's stop it, now."

But he kept on circling me with the knife, and I kept on going round him with the bottle. I didn't look at his face any more. I kept my eyes on that knife. It was a Texas jack with a pearl handle, and that blade must've been five inches long.

"Stop it, Bayou," I said. "Stop it, stop it."

He slashed at me, and I jumped back. He slashed at me again, and I jumped back again. Then he acted like a fool and ran on me, and all I did was stick the bottle out. I felt it go in his clothes and in his stomach and I felt the hot, sticky blood on my hand and I saw his face all twisted and sweaty. I felt his hands brush against mine when he throwed both of his hands up to his stomach. I started running. I was running toward the car, and Grinning Boy was running there, too. He got there before me and jumped in on the driving side, but I pushed him out the way and got under the ste'r'n' wheel. I could hear that gang coming after me, and I shot that Ford out of there a hundred miles an hour. Some of them ran up the road to cut me off, but when they saw I wasn't stopping they jumped out of the way. Now, it was nobody but me, that Ford and that gravel road. Grinning Boy was sitting over there crying, but I wasn't paying him no mind. I wanted to get as much road between me and Seven Spots as I could.

After I had gone a good piece, I slammed on the brakes and told Grinning Boy to get out. He wouldn't get out. I opened the door and pushed on him, but he held the ste'r'n' wheel. He was crying and holding the wheel with both hands. I hit him and pushed on him and hit him and pushed on him, but he wouldn't turn it loose. If they was go'n kill me, I didn't want them to kill him, too, but he couldn't see that. I shot away from there with the door still opened, and after we had gone a little piece, Grinning Boy reached out and got it and slammed it again.

I came out on the pave road and drove three or four miles 'long the river. Then I turned down a dirt road and parked the car under a big pecan tree. It was one of these old plantation quarters, and the place was quiet as a graveyard. It was pretty bright, though, because the moon and the stars was out. The dust in that long, old road was white as snow. I lit a cigarette and tried to think. Grinning Boy was sitting over there crying. He was crying real quiet with his head hanging down on his chest. Every now and then I could hear him sniffing.

"I'm turning myself in," I said.

I had been thinking and thinking and I couldn't think of nothing else to do. I knowed Bayou was dead or hurt pretty bad, and I knowed either that gang or the law was go'n get me, anyhow. I backed the car out on the pave road and drove to Bayonne. I told Grinning Boy to let my uncle know I was in trouble. My uncle would go to Roger Medlow—and I was hoping Roger Medlow would get me off like he had done once before. He owned the plantation where I lived.

"Hey," somebody was calling and shaking me. "Hey, there, now; wake up."

I opened my eyes and looked at this old man standing by the head of my bunk. I'm sure if I had woke up anywhere else and found him that close to me I would've jumped back screaming. He must've been sixty; he had reddish-brown eyes, and a stubby gray beard. 'Cross his right jaw, from his cheekbone to his mouth, was a big shiny scar where somebody had gotten him with a razor. He was wearing a derby hat, and he had it cocked a little to the back of his head.

"They coming," he said.

"Who?"

"Breakfast."

"I'm not hungry."

"You better eat. Never can tell when you go'n eat again in this joint."

His breath didn't smell too good either, and he was standing so close to me, I could smell his breath every time he breathed in and out. I figured he was the one they called Munford. Just before they brought me down here last night, I heard T. J. tell Paul to put me in there with Munford. Since he had called the other one Hattie, I figured he was Munford.

"Been having yourself a nice little nightmare," he said. "Twisting and turning there like you wanted to fall off. You can have this bunk of mine tonight if you want."

I looked at the freak laying on the other bunk. He looked back at me with a sad little smile on his face.

"I'll stay here," I said.

The freak stopped smiling, but he still looked sad—like a sad woman. He knowed why I didn't want get down there. I didn't want no part of him.

Out on the cell block, the nigger trustee was singing. He went from one cell to the other one singing, "Come and get it, it's hot. What a lovely, lovely day, isn't it? Yes, indeed," he answered himself. "Yes, indeed . . . Come and get it, my children, come and get it. Unc' Toby won't feel right if y'all don't eat his lovely food."

He stopped before the cell with his little shiny pushcart. A white guard was with him. The guard opened the cell door and Unc' Toby gave each one of us a cup of coffee and two baloney sandwiches. Then the guard shut the cell again and him and Unc' Toby went on up the block. Unc' Toby was singing again.

"Toby used to have a little stand," Munford said to me. "He think he still got it. He kinda loose up here," he said, tapping his head with the hand that held the sandwiches.

"They ought to send him to Jackson if he's crazy."

"They like keeping him here," Munford said. "Part of the scheme of things."

"You want this?" I asked.

"No, eat it," he said.

I got back on my bunk. I ate one of the sandwiches and drank some of the coffee. The coffee was nothing but brown water. It didn't have any kind of taste—not even bitter taste. I drank about half and poured the rest in the toilet.

The freak, Hattie, sat on his bunk, nibbling at his food. He wrapped one slice of bread round the slice of baloney and ate that, then he did the same thing with the other sandwich. The two extra slices of bread, he dipped down in his coffee and ate it like that. All the time he was eating, he was looking at me like a sad woman looks at you.

Munford stood between the two rows of bunks, eating and drinking his coffee. He pressed both of the sandwiches together and ate them like they was just one. Nobody said anything all the time we was eating. Even when I poured out the coffee, nobody said anything. The freak just looked at me like a sad woman. But Munford didn't look at me at all—he was looking up at the window all the time. When he got through eating, he wiped his mouth and throwed his cup on his bunk.

"Another one of them smokes," he said to me.

The way he said it, it sounded like he would've took it if I didn't give it to him. I got out the pack of cigarettes and gived him one. He lit it and took a big draw. I was laying back against the wall, looking up at the window; but I could tell that Munford was looking at me.

"Killed somebody, huh?" Munford said, in his quiet, calm voice.

"I cut him pretty bad," I said, still looking up at the window.

"He's dead," Munford said.

I wouldn't take my eyes off the window. My throat got tight, and my heart started beating so loud, I'm sure both Munford and that freak could hear it.

"That's bad," Munford said.

"And so young," Hattie said. I didn't have to look at the freak to know he was crying. "And so much of his life still before him—my Lord."

"You got people?" Munford asked.

"Uncle," I said.

"You notified him?"

"I think he knows."

"You got a lawyer?"

"No."

"No money?"

"No."

"That's bad," he said.

"Maybe his uncle can do something," Hattie said. "Poor thing." Then I heard him blowing his nose.

I looked at the bars in the window. I wanted them to leave me alone so I could think.

"So young, too," Hattie said. "My Lord, my Lord."

"Oh shut up," Munford said. "I don't know why they didn't lock you up with the rest of them whores."

"Is it too much to have some feeling of sympathy?" Hattie said, and blowed his nose again.

"Morris David is a good lawyer," Munford said. "Get him if you can. Best for colored round here."

I nodded, but I didn't look at Munford. I felt bad and I wanted them to leave me alone.

"Was he a local boy?" Munford asked.

"I don't know," I said.

"Where was it?"

I didn't answer him.

"Best to talk 'bout it," Munford said. "Keeping it in just make it worse."

"Seven Spots," I said.

"That's a rough joint," Munford said.

"They're all rough joints," Hattie said. "That's all you have—rough joints. No decent places for someone like him."

"Who's your uncle?" Munford asked.

"Martin Baptiste. Medlow plantation."

"Martin Baptiste?" Munford said.

I could tell from the way he said it, he knowed my uncle. I looked at him now. He was looking back at me with his left eye half shut. I could tell from his face he didn't like my uncle.

"You same as out already," he said.

He didn't like my uncle at all, and now he was studying me to see how much I was like him.

"Medlow can get you out of here just by snapping his fingers," he said. "Big men like that run little towns like these."

"I killed somebody," I said.

"You killed another old nigger," Munford said. "A nigger ain't nobody."

He drawed on the cigarette, and I looked at the big scar on the side of his face. He took the cigarette from his mouth and patted the scar with the tip of one of his fingers.

"Bunch of them jumped on me one night," he said. "One caught me with a straight razor. Had the flesh hanging so much, I coulda ripped it off with my hands if I wanted to. Ah, but before I went down you shoulda seen what I did the bunch of 'em." He stopped and thought a while. He even laughed a little to himself. "I been in this joint so much, everybody from the judge on down know me. 'How's it going, Munford?' 'Well, you back with us again, huh, Munt?' 'Look, y'all, old Munt's back with us again, just like he said he'd be.' They all know me. All know me. I'll get out little later on. What time is it getting to be—'leven? I'll give 'em till twelve and tell 'em I want to get out. They'll let me out. Got in Saturday night. They always keep me from Saturday till Monday. If it rain, they keep me till Tuesday—don't want me get out and catch cold, you know. Next Saturday, I'm right back. Can't stay out of here to save my soul."

"Places like these are built for people like you," Hattie said. "Not for decent people."

"Been going in and out of these jails here, I don't know how long," Munford said. "Forty, fifty years. Started out just like you—kilt a boy just like you did last night. Kilt him and got off—got off scot-free. My pappy worked for a white man who got me off. At first I didn't know why he had done it—I didn't think; all I knowed was I was free, and free is how I wanted to be. Then I got in trouble again, and again they got me off. I kept on getting in trouble, and they kept on getting me off. Didn't wake up till I got to be nearly old as I'm is now. Then I realized they kept getting me off because they needed a Munford Bazille. They need me to prove they human—just like they need that thing over there. They need us. Because without us, they don't know what they is—they don't know what they is out there. With us around, they can see us and they know what they ain't. They ain't us. Do you see? Do you see how they think?"

I didn't know what he was talking about. It was hot in the cell and he had started sweating. His face was wet, except for that big scar. It was just laying there smooth and shiny.

"But I got news for them. They us. I never tell them that, but inside I know it. They us, just like we is ourselves. Cut any of them open and you see if you don't find Munford Bazille or Hattie Brown there. You know what I mean?"

"I guess so."

"No, you don't know what I mean," he said. "What I mean is not one of them out there is a man. Not one. They think they men. They think they men 'cause they got me and him in here who ain't men. But I got news for them—cut them open; go 'head and cut one open—you see if you don't find Munford Bazille or Hattie Brown. Not a man one of them. 'Cause face don't make a man—black or white. Face don't make him and fucking don't make him and fighting don't make him—neither killing. None of this prove you a man. 'Cause animals can fuck, can kill, can fight—you know that?"

I looked at him, but I didn't answer him. I didn't feel like answering.

"Well?" he said.

"Yeah."

"Then answer me when I ask you a question. I don't like talking to myself."

He stopped and looked at me a while.

"You know what I'm getting at?"

"No," I said.

"To hell if you don't," he said. "Don't let Medlow get you out of here so you can kill again."

"You got out," I said.

"Yeah," he said, "and I'm still coming back here and I'm still getting out. Next Saturday I'm go'n hit another nigger in the head, and Saturday night they go'n bring me here, and Monday they go'n let me out again. And Saturday after that I'm go'n hit me another nigger in the head—'cause I'll hit a nigger in the head quick as I'll look at one."

"You're just an animal out the black jungle," Hattie said. "Because you have to hit somebody in the head every Saturday night don't mean he has to do the same."

"He'll do it," Munford said, looking at me, not at Hattie. "He'll do it 'cause he know Medlow'll get him out. Won't you?"

I didn't answer him. Munford nodded his head.

"Yeah, he'll do it. They'll see to that."

He looked at me like he was mad at me, then he looked up at the bars in the window. He frowned and rubbed his hand over his chin, and I could hear the gritty sound his beard made. He studied the bars a long time, like he was thinking about something 'way off; then I saw how his face changed: his eyes twinkled and he grinned to himself. He turned to look at Hattie laying on the bunk.

"Look here," he said. "I got a few coppers and a few minutes—what you say me and you giving it a little whirl?"

"My God, man," Hattie said. He said it the way a young girl would've said it if you had asked her to pull down her drawers. He even opened his eyes wide the same way a young girl would've done it. "Do you think I could possibly ever sink so low?" he said.

"Well, that's what you do on the outside," Munford said.

"What I do on the outside is absolutely no concern of yours, let me assure you," the freak said. "And furthermore, I have friends that I associate with."

"And them 'sociating friends you got there—what they got Munford don't have?" Munford said.

"For one thing, manners," Hattie said. "Of all the nerve." Munford grinned at him and looked at me.

"You know what make 'em like that?" he asked.

"No."

He nodded his head. "Then I'll tell you. It start in the cradle when they send that preacher there to christen you. At the same time he's doing that mumbo-jumbo stuff, he's low'ing his mouth to your little nipper to suck out your manhood. I know, he tried it on me. Here, I'm laying in his arms in my little white blanket and he suppose to be christening me. My mammy there, my pappy there; uncle, aunt, grandmammy, grandpappy; my nan-nane, my pa-ran—all of them standing there with they head bowed. This preacher going, 'Mumbo-jumbo, mumbo-jumbo,' but all the time he's low'ing his mouth toward my little private. Nobody else don't see him, but I catch him, and I haul 'way back and hit him right smack in the eye. I ain't no more than three months old but I give him a good one. 'Get your goddamn mouth away from my little pecker, you no-teef, rotten, eggsucking sonofabitch. Get away from here, you sister-jumper, God-calling, pulpit-spitting, mother-huncher. Get away from here, you chicken-eating, catfish-eating, gin-drinking sonofabitch. Get away, goddamn it, get away . . .' "

I thought Munford was just being funny, but he was serious as he could ever get. He had worked himself up so much, he had to stop and catch his breath.

"That's what I told him," he said. "That's what I told him. . . . But they don't stop there, they stay after you. If they miss you in the cradle, they catch you some other time. And when they catch you, they draw it out of you or they make you a beast—make you use it in a brutish way. You use it on a woman without caring for her, you use it on children, you use it on other men, you use it on yourself. Then when you get so disgusted with everything round you, you kill. And if your back is strong, like your back is strong, they get you out so you can kill again." He stopped and looked at me and nodded his head. "Yeah, that's what they do with you—exactly. . . . But not everybody end up like that. Some of them make it. Not many—but some of them do make it."

"Going to the pen?" I said.

"Yeah—the pen is one way," he said. "But you don't go to the pen for the nigger you killed. Not for him—he ain't worth it. They told you that from the cradle—a nigger ain't worth a good gray mule. Don't mention a white mule: fifty niggers ain't worth a good white mule. So you don't go to the pen for killing the nigger, you go for yourself. You go to sweat out all the crud you got in your system. You go, saying, 'Go fuck yourself, Roger Medlow, I want to be a man, and by God I will be a man. For once in my life I will be a man.' "

"And a month after you been in the pen, Medlow tell them to kill you for being a smart aleck. How much of a man you is then?"

"At least you been a man a month—where if you let him

get you out you won't be a man a second. He won't 'low it."

"I'll take that chance," I said.

He looked at me a long time now. His reddish-brown eyes was sad and mean. He felt sorry for me, and at the same time he wanted to hit me with his fist.

"You don't look like that whitemouth uncle of yours," he said. "And you look much brighter than I did at your age. But I guess every man must live his own life. I just wish I had mine to live all over again."

He looked up at the window like he had given up on me. After a while, he looked back at Hattie on the bunk.

"You not thinking 'bout what I asked you?" he said.

Hattie looked up at him just like a woman looks at a man she can't stand.

"Munford, if you dropped dead this second, I doubt if I would shed a tear."

"Put all that together, I take it you mean no," Munford said.

Hattie rolled his eyes at Munford the way a woman rolls her eyes at a man she can't stand.

"Well, I better get out of here," Munford said. He passed his hand over his chin. It sounded like passing your hand over sandpaper. "Go home and take me a shave and might go out and do little fishing," he said. "Too hot to pick cotton."

He looked at me again.

"I guess I'll be back next week or the week after—but I suppose you'll be gone to Medlow by then."

"If he come for me—yes."

"He'll come for you," Munford said. "How old you is—twenty?"

"Nineteen."

"Yeah, he'll come and take you back. And next year you'll kill another old nigger. 'Cause they grow niggers just to be killed, and they grow people like you to kill 'em. That's all part of the—the culture. And every man got to play his part in the culture, or the culture don't go on. But I'll tell you this; if you was kin to anybody else except that Martin Baptiste, I'd stay in here long enough to make you go to Angola. 'Cause I'd break your back 'fore I let you walk out of this cell with Medlow. But with Martin Baptiste blood in you, you'll never be worth a goddamn no matter what I did. With that, I bid you adieu."

He tipped his derby to me, then he went to the door and called for the guard. The guard came and let him out. The people on the block told him good-bye and said they would see him when they got out. Munford waved at them and followed the guard toward the door.

"That Munford," Hattie said. "Thank God we're not all like that." He looked up at me. "I hope you didn't listen to half of that nonsense."

I didn't answer the freak—I didn't want have nothing to do with him. I looked up at the window. The sky was darkish blue and I could tell it was hot out there. I had always hated the hot sun, but I wished I was out there now. I wouldn't even mind picking cotton, much as I hated picking cotton.

I got out my other sandwich: nothing but two slices of light bread and a thin slice of baloney sausage. If I wasn't hungry, I wouldn't 'a' ate it at all. I tried to think about what everybody was doing at home. But hard as I tried, all I could think about was here. Maybe it was best if I didn't think about outside. That could run you crazy. I had heard about people going crazy in jail. I tried to remember how it was when I was in jail before. It wasn't like this if I could remember. Before, it was just a brawl—a fight. I had never stayed in more than a couple weeks. I had been in about a half dozen times, but never more than a week or two. This time it was different, though. Munford said Roger Medlow was go'n get me out, but suppose Munford was wrong. Suppose I had to go up? Suppose I had to go to the pen?

Hattie started singing. He was singing a spiritual and he was singing it in a high-pitched voice like a woman. I wanted to tell him to shut up, but I didn't want have nothing to do with that freak. I could feel him looking at me; a second later he had quit singing.

"That Munford," he said. "I hope you didn't believe everything he said about me."

I was quiet. I didn't want to talk to Hattie. He saw it and kept his mouth shut.

If Medlow was go'n get me out of here, why hadn't he done so? If all he had to do was snap his fingers, what was keeping him from snapping them? Maybe he wasn't go'n do anything for me. I wasn't one of them Uncle Tom-ing niggers like my uncle, and maybe he was go'n let me go up this time.

I couldn't make it in the pen. Locked up—caged. Walking round all day with shackles on my legs. No woman, no pussy—I'd die in there. I'd die in a year. Not five years—one year. If Roger Medlow came, I was leaving. That's how old people is: they always want you to do something they never did when they was young. If he had his life to live all over—how come he didn't do it then? Don't tell me to do it when he didn't do it. If that's part of the culture, then I'm part of the culture, because I sure ain't for the pen.

That black sonofabitch—that coward. I hope he didn't have religion. I hope his ass burn in hell till eternity.

Look how life can change on you—just look. Yesterday this time I was poon-tanging like a dog. Today—that black sonofabitch—behind these bars maybe for the rest of my life. And look at me, look at me. Strong. A man. A damn good man. A hard dick—a pile of muscles. But look at me—locked in here like a caged animal.

Maybe that's what Munford was talking about. You spend much time in here like he done spent, you can't be nothing but a' animal.

I wish somebody could do something for me. I can make a phone call, can't I? But call who? That ass-hole uncle of mine? I'm sure Grinning Boy already told him where I'm at. I wonder if Grinning Boy got in touch with Marie. I suppose this finish it. Hell, why should she stick her neck out for me. I was treating her like a dog, anyhow. I'm sorry, baby; I'm sorry. No, I'm not sorry; I'd do the same thing tomorrow if I was out of here. Maybe I'm a' animal already. I don't care who she is, I'd do it with her and don't give a damn. Hell, let me stop whining; I ain't no goddamn animal. I'm a man, and I got to act and think like a man.

I got to think, I got to think. My daddy is somewhere up North—but where? I got more people scattered around, but no use going to them. I'm the black sheep of this family—and they don't care if I live or die. They'd be glad if I died so they'd be rid of me for good.

That black sonofabitch—I swear to God. Big as he was, he had to go for a knife. I hope he rot in hell. I hope he burn—goddamn it—till eternity come and go.

Let me see, let me see, who can I call? I don't know a soul with a dime. Them white people out there got it, but what do they care 'bout me, a nigger. Now, if I was a' Uncle Tom-ing nigger—oh, yes, they'd come then. They'd come running. But like I'm is, I'm fucked. Done for.

Five years, five years—that's what they give you. Five years for killing a nigger like that. Five years out of my life. Five years for a rotten, no good sonofabitch who didn't have no business being born in the first place. Five years . . .

Maybe I ought to call Medlow myself. . . . But suppose he

come, then what? Me and Medlow never got along. I couldn't
never bow and say, "Yes sir," and scratch my head. But I'd
have to do it now. He'd have me by the nuts and he'd know
it; and I'd have to kiss his ass if he told me to.

Oh Lord, have mercy. . . . They get you, don't they. They
let you run and run, then they get you. They stick a no-good,
trashy nigger up there, and they get you. And they twist your
nuts and twist them till you don't care no more.

I got to stop this, I got to stop it. My head'll go to hurting
after while and I won't be able to think anything out.

"Oh, you're so beautiful when you're meditating," Hattie
said. "And what were you meditating about?"

I didn't answer him—I didn't want have nothing to do
with that freak.

"How long you're going to be in here, is that it?" he said.
"Sometimes they let you sit for days and days. In your case
they might let you sit here a week before they say anything to
you. What do they care—they're inhuman."

I got a cigarette out of the pack and lit it.

"I smoke, too," Hattie said.

I didn't answer that freak. He came over and got the pack
out of my shirt pocket. His fingers went down in my pocket
just like a woman's fingers go in your pocket.

"May I?" he said.

I didn't say nothing to him. He lit his cigarette and laid
the pack on my chest just like a woman'd do it.

"Really, I'm not all that awful," he said. "Munford has
poisoned your mind with all sorts of notions. Let go—relax.
You need friends at a time like this."

I stuffed the pack of cigarettes in my pocket and looked
up at the window.

"These are very good," the freak said. "Very, very good.
Well, maybe you'll feel like talking a little later on. It's always good to let go. I'm understanding; I'll be here."

He went back to his bunk and laid down.

Toward three o'clock, they let the women out of the cells
to walk around. Some of the women came down the block
and talked to the men through the bars. Some of them even
laughed and joked. Three-thirty, the guard locked them up
and let the men out. From the way the guard looked at me, I
knowed I wasn't going anywhere. I didn't want to go anywhere, either, because I didn't want people asking me a pile
of questions. Hattie went out to stretch, but few minutes
later he came and laid back down. He was grumbling about
some man on the block trying to get fresh with him.

"Some of them think you'll stoop to anything," he said.

I looked out of the window at the sky. I couldn't see too much, but I liked what I could see. I liked the sun, too. I hadn't ever liked the sun before, but I liked it now. I felt my throat getting tight, and I turned my head.

Toward four o'clock, Unc' Toby came on the block with dinner. For dinner, we had stew, mashed potatoes, lettuce and tomatoes. The stew was too soupy; the mashed potatoes was too soupy; the lettuce and tomatoes was too soggy. Dessert was three or four dried-up prunes with black water poured over them. After Unc' Toby served us, the guard locked up the cell. By the time we finished eating, they was back there again to pick up the trays.

I laid on my bunk, looking up at the window. How long I had been there? No more than about twelve hours. Twelve hours—but it felt like three days, already.

They knowed how to get a man down. Because they had me now. No matter which way I went—plantation or pen—they had me. That's why Medlow wasn't in any hurry to get me out. You don't have to be in any hurry when you already know you got a man by the nuts.

Look at the way they did Jack. Jack was a man, a good man. Look what they did him. Let a fifteen-cents Cajun bond him out of jail—a no-teeth, dirty, overall-wearing Cajun get him out. Then they broke him. Broke him down to nothing—to a grinning, bowing fool. . . . We loved Jack. Jack could do anything. Work, play ball, run women—anything. They knowed we loved him, that's why they did him that. Broke him—broke him the way you break a wild horse. . . . Now everybody laughs at him. Gamble with him and cheat him. He know you cheating him, but he don't care—just don't care any more . . .

Where is my father? Why my mamma had to die? Why they brought me here and left me to struggle like this? I used to love my mamma so much. Her skin was light brown; her hair was silky. I used to watch her powdering her face in the glass. I used to always cry when she went out—and be glad when she came back because she always brought me candy. But you gone for good now, Mama; and I got nothing in this world but me.

A man in the other cell started singing. I listened to him and looked up at the window. The sky had changed some more. It was lighter blue now—gray-blue almost.

The sun went down, a star came out. For a while it was the only star; then some more came to join it. I watched all of them. Then I watched just a few, then just one. I shut my eyes and opened them and tried to find the star again. I couldn't find it. I wasn't too sure which one it was. I could've pretended and choosed either one, but I didn't want to lie to myself. I don't believe in lying to myself. I don't believe in lying to nobody else, either. I believe in being straight with a man. And I want a man to be straight with me. I wouldn't 'a' picked up that bottle for nothing if that nigger hadn't pulled his knife. Not for nothing. Because I don't believe in that kind of stuff. I believe in straight stuff. But a man got to protect himself. . . . But with stars I wasn't go'n cheat. If I didn't know where the one was I was looking at at first, I wasn't go'n say I did. I picked out another one, one that wasn't too much in a cluster. I measured it off from the bars in the window, then I shut my eyes. When I opened them, I found the star right away. And I didn't have to cheat, either.

The lights went out on the block. I got up and took a leak and got back on my bunk. I got in the same place I was before and looked for the star. I found it right away. It was easier to find now because the lights was out. I got tired looking at it after a while and looked at another one. The other one was much more smaller and much more in a cluster. But I got tired of it after a while, too.

I thought about Munford. He said if they didn't get you in the cradle, they got you later. If they didn't suck all the manhood out of you in the cradle, they made you use it on people you didn't love. I never messed with a woman I didn't love. I always loved all these women I ever messed with. . . . No, I didn't love them. Because I didn't love her last night—I just wanted to fuck her. And I don't think I ever loved Marie, either. Marie just had the best pussy in the world. She had the best—still got the best. And that's why I went to her, the only reason I went. Because God knows she don't have any kind a face to make you come at her . . .

Maybe I ain't never loved nobody. Maybe I ain't never loved nobody since my mama died. Because I loved her, I know I loved her. But the rest—no, I never loved the rest. They don't let you love them. Some kind of way they keep you from loving them . . .

I have to stop thinking. That's how you go crazy—thinking. But what else can you do in a place like this—what? I wish I knowed somebody. I wish I knowed a good person. I would be good if I knowed a good person. I swear to God I would be good.

All of a sudden the lights came on, and I heard them

bringing in somebody who was crying. They was coming toward the cell where I was; the person was crying all the way. Then the cell door opened and they throwed him in there and they locked the door again. I didn't look up—I wouldn't raise my head for nothing. I could tell nobody else was looking up, either. Then the footsteps faded away and the lights went out again.

I raised my head and looked at the person they had throwed in there. He was nothing but a little boy—fourteen or fifteen. He had on a white shirt and a pair of dark pants. Hattie helped him up off the floor and laid him on the bunk under me. Then he sat on the bunk 'side the boy. The boy was still crying.

"Shhh now, shhh now," Hattie was saying. It was just like a woman saying it. It made me sick a' the stomach. "Shhh now, shhh now," he kept on saying.

I swung to the floor and looked at the boy. Hattie was sitting on the bunk, passing his hand over the boy's face.

"What happened?" I asked him.

He was crying too much to answer me.

"They beat you?" I asked him.

He couldn't answer.

"A cigarette?" I said.

"No—no—sir," he said.

I lit one, anyhow, and stuck it in his mouth. He tried to smoke it and started coughing. I took it out.

"Shhh now," Hattie said, patting his face. "Just look at his clothes. The bunch of animals. Not one of them is a man. A bunch of pigs—dogs—philistines."

"You hurt?" I asked the boy.

"Sure, he's hurt," Hattie said. "Just look at his clothes, how they beat him. The bunch of dogs."

I went to the door to call the guard. But I stopped; I told myself to keep out of this. He ain't the first one they ever beat and he won't be the last one, and getting in it will just bring you a dose of the same medicine. I turned around and looked at the boy. Hattie was holding the boy in his arms and whispering to him. I hated what Hattie was doing much as I hated what the law had done.

"Leave him alone," I said to Hattie.

"The child needs somebody," he said. "You're going to look after him?"

"What happened?" I asked the boy.

"They beat me," he said.

"They didn't beat you for nothing, boy."

He was quiet now. Hattie was patting the side of his face and his hair.

"What they beat you for?" I asked him.

"I took something."

"What you took?"

"I took some cakes. I was hungry."

"You got no business stealing," I said.

"Some people got no business killing, but it don't keep them from killing," Hattie said.

He started rocking the boy in his arms the way a woman rocks a child.

"Why don't you leave him alone?" I said.

He wouldn't answer me. He kept on.

"You hear me, whore?"

"I might be a whore, but I'm not a merciless killer," he said.

I started to crack him side the head, but I changed my mind. I had already raised my fist to hit him, but I changed my mind. I started walking. I was smoking the cigarette and walking. I walked, I walked, I walked. Then I stood at the head of the bunk and look up at the window at the stars. Where was the one I was looking at a while back? I smoked on the cigarette and looked for it—but where was it? I threw the cigarette in the toilet and lit another one. I smoked and walked some more. The rest of the place was quiet. Nobody had said a word since the guards throwed that little boy in the cell. Like a bunch of roaches, like a bunch of mices, they had crawled in they holes and pulled the cover over they head.

All of a sudden I wanted to scream. I wanted to scream to the top of my voice. I wanted to get them bars in my hands and I wanted to shake, I wanted to shake that door down. I wanted to let all these people out. But would they follow me—would they? Y'all go'n follow me? I screamed inside. Y'all go'n follow me?

I ran to my bunk and bit down in the cover. I bit harder, harder, harder. I could taste the dry sweat, the dry piss, the dry vomit. I bit harder, harder, harder . . .

I got on the bunk. I looked out at the stars. A million little white, cool stars was out there. I felt my throat hurting. I felt the water running down my face. But I gripped my mouth tight so I wouldn't make a sound. I didn't make a sound, but I cried. I cried and cried and cried.

I knowed I was going to the pen now. I knowed I was going, I knowed I was going. Even if Medlow came to get me, I wasn't leaving with him. I was go'n do like Munford said. I was going there and I was go'n sweat it and I was go'n take it. I didn't want to have to pull cover over my head every time a white man did something to a black boy—I wanted to stand. Because they never let you stand if they got you out. They didn't let Jack stand—and I had never heard of them letting anybody else stand, either.

I felt good. I laid there feeling good. I felt so good I wanted to sing. I sat up on the bunk and lit a cigarette. I had never smoked a cigarette like I smoked that one. I drawed deep, deep, till my chest got big. It felt good. It felt good deep down in me. I jumped to the floor feeling good.

"You want a cigarette?" I asked the boy.

I spoke to him like I had been talking to him just a few minutes ago, but it was over an hour. He was laying in Hattie's arms quiet like he was half asleep.

"No, sir," he said.

I had already shook the cigarette out of the pack.

"Here," I said.

"No, sir," he said.

"Get up from there and go to your own bunk," I said to Hattie.

"And who do you think you are to be giving orders?"

I grabbed two handsful of his shirt and jerked him up and slammed him 'cross the cell. He hit against that bunk and started crying—just laying there, holding his side and crying like a woman. After a while he picked himself up and got on that bunk.

"Philistine," he said. "Dog—brute."

When I saw he wasn't go'n act a fool and try to hit me, I turned my back on him.

"Here," I said to the boy.

"I don't smoke—please, sir."

"You big enough to steal?" I said. "You'll smoke it or you'll eat it." I lit it and pushed it in his mouth. "Smoke it."

He smoked and puffed it out. I sat down on the bunk 'side him. The freak was sitting on the bunk 'cross from us, holding his side and crying.

"Hold that smoke in," I said to the boy.

He held it in and started coughing. When he stopped coughing I told him to draw again. He drawed and held it, then he let it out. I knowed he wasn't doing it right, but this was his first time, and I let him slide.

"If Medlow come to get me, I'm not going," I said to the

boy. "That means T. J. and his boys coming, too. They go'n beat me because they think I'm a smart aleck trying to show them up. Now you listen to me, and listen good. Every time they come for me I want you to start praying. I want you to pray till they bring me back in this cell. And I don't want you praying like a woman, I want you to pray like a man. You don't even have to get on your knees; you can lay on your bunk and pray. Pray quiet and to yourself. You hear me?"

He didn't know what I was talking about, but he said, "Yes, sir," anyhow.

"I don't believe in God," I said. "But I want you to believe. I want you to believe He can hear you. That's the only way I'll be able to take those beatings—with you praying. You understand what I'm saying?"

"Yes, sir."

"You sure, now?"

"Yes, sir."

I drawed on the cigarette and looked at him. Deep in me I felt some kind of love for this little boy.

"You got a daddy?" I asked him.

"Yes, sir."

"A mama?"

"Yes, sir."

"Then how come you stealing?"

" 'Cause I was hungry."

"Don't they look after you?"

"No, sir."

"You been in here before?"

"Yes, sir."

"You like it in here?"

"No, sir. I was hungry."

"Let's wash your back," I said.

We got up and went to the facebowl. I helped him off with his shirt. His back was cut from where they had beat him.

"You know Munford Bazille?" I asked him.

"Yes, sir. He don't live too far from us. He kin to you?"

"No, he's not kin to me. You like him?"

"No, sir, I don't like him. He stay in fights all the time, and they always got him in jail."

"That's how you go'n end up."

"No, sir, not me. 'Cause I ain't coming back here no more."

"I better not ever catch you in here again," I said. "Hold onto that bunk—this might hurt."

"What you go'n do?"

"Wash them bruises."

"Don't mash too hard."

"Shut up," I told him, "and hold on."

I wet my handkerchief and dabbed at the bruises. Every time I touched his back, he flinched. But I didn't let that stop me. I washed his back good and clean. When I got through, I told him to go back to his bunk and lay down. Then I rinched out his shirt and spread it out on the foot of my bunk. I took off my own shirt and rinched it out because it was filthy.

I lit a cigarette and looked up at the window. I had talked big, but what was I going to do when Medlow came? Was I going to change my mind and go with him? And if I didn't go with Medlow, I surely had to go with T. J. and his boys. Was I going to be able to take the beatings night after night? I had seen what T. J. could do to your back. I had seen it on this kid and I had seen it on other people. Was I going to be able to take it?

I don't know, I thought to myself. I'll just have to wait and see.

RONALD L. FAIR (1932–   )

Born in Chicago, Ronald L. Fair began writing somewhere between the ages of twelve and sixteen because of "my anger with the life I knew and inability of anyone I knew to explain why things were the way they were." He was educated in Chicago high schools, spent two years at a local business college, and for eleven years, from 1955 to 1966, was a court reporter, working as a stenographer. It was during this time that his first two novels were written and published. In 1967 he taught at Columbia College in Chicago and subsequently was a visiting teacher at Northwestern University. He was visiting professor in the English department of Wesleyan University for the 1970–71 academic year. His third book of fiction, World of Nothing, consisting of two novellas, was published in 1970. His stories have appeared in a variety of anthologies. The narrative that follows has had a strange publication history. A truncated version, entitled "Thank God It Snowed," was published in The American Scholar, *winter of 1969–70, but was erroneously classified as an article, presumably in the belief that it was an autobiographical sketch. The "I" in the narrative is in fact a first-person fictional narrator, and Mr. Fair's title for this narrative, as it stands, is "We Who Came After." The text is reprinted from the anthology* 19 Necromancers from Now *where it is entitled "Part One of a Two-Part Prologue." Ultimately it will appear as the prologue to Ronald Fair's third novel,* We Can't Breathe, *forthcoming from Harper & Row.*

We Who Came After

This is a narrative of what it was like for those of us born in the Thirties. Our parents had come from Mississippi, Louisiana, Tennessee, Georgia, Alabama and many other southern states where the whites were so perverse and inhuman in their treatment of blacks, but mostly they came from Mississippi. They came to the big cities armed only with glorious fantasies about a new and better world, hoping to find the dignity that had been denied them, hoping to find the self-respect that had been cut out of them. They came north, and we were the children born in the place they had escaped to—Chicago.

You know, we were so young that we didn't know we were supposed to be poor. We were so young and excited with the life we knew that we had not yet learned we were the ones who were supposed to be deprived. We were even so young that sometimes we forgot we were supposed to be hungry, because we were just too busy living.

I can remember one spring, after the snow had finally seeped into the earth, and the mud in the vacant lots had become dirt again, how we would move over those lots cautiously, like the old rag man, our eyes sparkling with enthusiasm, our minds pulsating with the thrill of finds we

surely knew would be there because there had been a whole
winter of snow covering up the treasures that grownups had
discarded—unknowingly, to our advantage. Things that we
needed because they were treasures and were of value to
us.

There would be razor blades, some broken in half, some
whole, all rusty; a new metal.

"Careful, Sam. Don't cut yourself, man. If you do, man,
your whole hand'll rot off."

A bottle! God, a bottle like we had never seen.

"I bet some ole rich white lady came along here and threw
it away."

"Naw."

"I bet she did. Bet it was full of some rich perfume or
somethin. Let's see if we can find the top?"

"Here's a top."

"Naw. Too big."

"I bet she kept the top."

"Ain't no rich lady been by here."

"She was."

"She wasn't."

"Well, I don't care. I know what I'm gonna do with it
anyway so it don't matter. I'm gonna take it home to mama.
She'll like it. She ain't never had no bottle like this before."

Maybe we would find a bullet, half of a scissors, the
standard, big-name pop bottles which we would hoard to be
returned to the school store or the grocery store or the drugstore only one or two at a time because the store owners
never seemed to like giving up the deposit and the fewer
the bottles, the less they would grumble. And always, reminding us of the problems of the grownups, there would be the
wine bottles. Having the wine bottles available to us at that
time, when we were very young, when we were young enough
for vacant lots and alleys to be places of joy, was really a
blessing because we could smash them against the side of the
brick buildings that helped protect our lot. Sometimes we
smashed them with such force that little slivers of glass sprang
back in our direction. We dodged them, laughingly, saying,
"Ain't no wine bottle fast enough to catch me."

The thought of the slivers of glass striking back at us
excited us no end, and we moved closer to the wall and
smashed them with even more force. Once, though, a wine
bottle got even with me as a fragment of it ripped through
my trousers and imbedded itself in my thigh. But I did not cry

out. I just went on smashing the damn things against the wall because I hated them.

I didn't cry until later in the day when, safely hidden behind the locked bathroom door of our apartment, I dug it out with one of my mother's needles. I could not have let the others know that I hadn't moved quickly enough to dodge the glass. Many years later I learned that each of us at one time or another had lost the battle with the flying glass. But those admissions came many years later when we were secure in our manhood.

Sometime we'd spend as many as twenty or thirty minutes breaking wine bottles and then return to treasure searching. And just as we'd begin to tire of it, someone would find a dime-store ring, or a part of a *watch*, and we would return to our game with charged enthusiasm. Tin cans we stocked at the edge of the lot. There would be time for them later on. The rusty cans were treasures for those even smaller than us because their sides were weak, and when they slammed their heels down into them, fitting the cans to their shoes, the cans gave way easily, and off they'd go down the alley, just like us, fitted with a pair of heels that sometimes sent sparks flying and always sounded the message of children on the move.

There was a cardboard box that we had avoided, partly out of fear and partly because we were saving it for later.

One of the boys raised it, then reached in and came out yelling. "Look. A basket."

"Quick, get the band off it and you got the first loop of the year."

"Here, you can use my stick, but remember, I get the first turn after you."

And he would be gone from the lot for a while, the stick in his hand, the loop spinning along at his side, stick tapping it gently on its way, again, again, again.

But the rest of us were still there; glass everywhere, rusty nails, more cans, a gas can!

"Hey, maybe Mr. Branch'll buy it from us?"

"Naw. He's got enough gas cans."

"Don't gas stations always need new cans for kerosene, though? Huh? Don't they?"

"Naw, you dummy. They sell it in bottles."

"I know that. But sometimes people don't have bottles and still wanta buy kerosene."

"They use bottles."

"Hey," somebody would say, "let's go kill rats."

A unanimous roar of approval would go up and we

would begin searching for sticks and bricks. Once sufficiently armed, we would leave our land of treasures and move down the alley toward one of the very best games we knew.

Each of us had relatives who had either been bitten by rats or frightened out of their wits by them. There was the story of the friend who used to live in the neighborhood but whose parents moved out when his baby sister had her right ear eaten away by one of them. There was also the story we whispered among ourselves about one of the group whose grandmother was said to have cooked her very best stew from rats she trapped in her pantry.

Almost from infancy we had been fighting them; in our sleep, fighting the noise they made in the walls as they chewed their way through the plaster to get at what few provisions we had; in our alleys, our Black Boulevards, fighting to get them out of the garbage and into their holes so we could play a game of stick ball with no fear of being bitten while standing on second or third base. Outside of the white insurance men who made their rounds daily collecting quarters and half dollars for the burial policies our parents paid for over and over, making the insurance companies richer and ending with our parents in their old age having almost enough money to pay the price of a pine-box funeral, outside of those strange little white peddlers who came into the neighborhood every week and trapped our mothers with flashy dresses, petticoats, slips and shoes supposedly half-priced ("No-money-down, lady." But the records were kept by the salesmen in their payment books, and the payments never ended.), outside of the white men from the telephone company who came far too often to take away someone's telephone, outside of these *strangers* who moved among us with all the arrogance and authority of giants, we hated the rats most.

We didn't always win against them, but we kept fighting because we knew if we didn't continue killing them they would soon make the alleys unsafe even for us. Once a new boy moved into the neighborhood with a BB gun, and with the large supply of ammunition he had, we killed two hundred rats in one day. We made bows and used umbrella staves for arrows and got so good with them that we only missed about two-thirds of the time.

But the best way to kill them was with bricks and clubs. We'd walk quietly down the alley, our little platoon advancing on the army of rats, plowing, in the summertime, through mounds of junk piled against the fences (always there because the garbage trucks came through so seldom), until we reached a mound that gave off sounds of their activity. We would surround it, leaving only the fence as their escape route, look at each other, nervous, excited, our blood blasting away inside of our temples, then one of us would poke a stick into the pile of garbage, and, with our anxiety mounting, we would wait for them to react.

The rats had already sensed our presence and had grown silent, waiting for the danger to pass. The stick would go in again and then, quickly, they would frantically dig their way farther into the garbage. They would not come out. Another stick, and finally a gray thing, its teeth sparkling like daggers in the early morning sun, would spring from the pile and charge one of us with all the rage and hostility of the killer it was. A brick would miss him, but a club would catch him in mid-air just as he was about to dig his teeth into someone's leg. His insides would explode out of him and blood would shoot into the air like a spurt from a fountain. Another one was out. A brick would stun him and then the clubs would beat him to death. Two others began climbing the fence and we left the fence stained with their blood. And then, as often happened, the biggest and oldest of them dashed between us and quickly disappeared into another pile of garbage. Including his tail, he was at least two feet long and as fat as any cat in the neighborhood, and even though we chased him, and spread the pile he had hidden in all over the alley, he was able to escape by squeezing through a small hole in the fence. It seemed to us we had been trying to kill that one rat for years, but there were so many that were two feet long that we could never be sure.

We were often victorious, but once in a while the rats would get the better of us; a child would be bitten by one of them. Sometimes we would club the rat away from his leg. Sometimes we would all run home crying, afraid of them all over again and thankful that it was someone else who had felt the needle-like teeth, and sometimes we would carry our crying friend home to his mother, hoping that he would not have to go through the torture of the shots.

Then, after our parents finally let us out again, we would group around a light pole on the street, or a fire hydrant, propping our feet on it pretending to be grown-up waiting for the news from the hospital about our wounded comrade.

But sometimes, even in the midst of the hunt, we would hear the call of the merchants, or the youth on the corner selling papers:

"Chi-cog-oo De-feen-da."

"I got em green. I got em ripe."

"Ice . . . Ice man."

"Waa-ta-mel-lons."

"Egg man . . . Chickens."

"I got em green. I got em ripe."

It would be a hot summer day. It was always another hot summer day with the heat seeming to rise up from the side-walks, from the tarred streets, from foods fermenting in the garbage, from the grassless yards and weed-filled vacant lots.

Now it was later in the day. Window shades would go up. People would come out on their porches, stretch, survey the hot, drab ugliness they had seen for years and return to their sweltering apartments that trapped the heat and held it until, finally, chilling winds from the lake worked their way beyond the white people who lived where it was cool all the way west to where we lived. Women would put cards in their kitchen windows that informed the ice man of just how many pounds of ice they wanted. Other children who had not yet done their chores would be seen emptying the pan of water that held the remnants of twenty-five or fifty pounds of ice over the banister down into the back yard.

But no matter how hot it was, we were determined to stay outdoors as long as we could until the voices of our mothers began calling us to lunch and then supper—or, in the case of some of us, until we felt our sisters or brothers might have prepared supper of black-eyed peas and cornbread. And for some, it was only the bread.

This was all a long, long time ago, you see, before the days of shopping centers and supermarkets. For those of us who lived in that neighborhood, it was even before the age of refrigerators. It was the age of the icebox!

So at the sound of our distinguished merchants, our musical alley-merchants, we would forget about the rats and run through our alleys seeking out the men who brought the merchandise to our doors.

The excitement of the arrival of the merchants gave us another game as we ran through the debris in much the same way as one might run through shallow water at the beach. It wasn't so bad in winter, but in the summer one had to fight the gnats and flies and mosquitoes and rats and cats and dogs. The flies would take wing as we passed through their feeding ground and the noise was so horrendous that it was like a low-flying airplane. I sometimes think we were the breeding place of flies and rats for the entire city.

In school we had read stories about children in the country, but they had nothing on us. They could run through their tall grass, playing where nature was kindest, and we could run through our garbage, and since we had all been immunized naturally, we were totally unaffected by those little microscopic fellows that so terrified the white people who had clean alleys—alleys that were even paved! We could run through our tall garbage-grass where mother nature, in a negative sort of way, was kind to us too.

And when we heard the deep voice of Sampson calling "Ice . . . Ice man," we would run even faster because he was the man we all wanted to be like. We'd cut through yards, across streets, in front of traffic, through other alleys until we found him. We'd meet the ice truck and ride through our Black Boulevards as honored guests, snatching little chips of ice whenever Sampson would cut off a block with the ice pick. We all shared the same admiration for the giant in our lives. And I guess worshiping him as we did was a bit strange when one realizes that Sampson had to work harder than anyone else. Sometimes he'd let us help. He'd say, "Y'all gotta work for your ride." Four or five of us would scramble into the truck and push and strain for what seemed like an hour just to get it close enough to the edge of the truck so he could lean in, snag the block of ice with his tongs—one hundred pounds of ice—run his pick down the seams, tick-tick-tick, and a fifty-pound block would slide over to the side of the truck. He'd swing his tongs again, clamp them down on the ice and sling it over his shoulder like it was only a loaf of bread, all so effortlessly that his breathing didn't alter in the slightest.

His muscles would rise up like swells and little beads of perspiration, giving the effect of liquid silver, rolled over those black swells. He could do anything with his muscles. He used to make his biceps dance while we provided the musical accompaniment with our clapping hands.

Sampson also let us take our punching exercises on his muscular abdomen. He'd line us up and let us hit him in the stomach as hard as we could. And with each earth-shattering blow he'd rear back and laugh his deep warm laugh.

But one day when we were trying to crash his abdominal wall one of the smaller guys wanted to have his turn. He stepped up, took careful aim and swung as hard as he could. Sampson had already started laughing long before the blow landed, but his loud, husky laugh changed to a soprano's scream as he grabbed his groin and fell to the ground.

We were shocked, so shocked that we could not move for all of one minute. We just knew that even his testicles were made of solid muscle.

"I got Sampson. I knocked Sampson down!" the little guy screamed as he ran down the alley, the victory just too overwhelming for his young years.

Sampson remained our hero, though, even though he no longer let us take punching exercises on his abdomen. I think, as I look back now on those years, that the warmest feeling of my childhood there in that strange city that I still call home, surely must have been the coolness of sitting inside an ice truck on a hot summer day as Sampson allowed us to think we were helping him.

Sometimes the summer afternoons were not as exciting as we would have wanted them to be, but the mornings were always filled with excitement. We'd leave Sampson and head on to other alleys, following the sounds of the people we wanted to see.

"Watermelon. Get your sweet, red, ripe watermelons here."

"Fish. Fish man. I got your catfish—whitefish."

"Rags. Rag man."

"I got perch, blue gills, carp. Fish man."

"Fresh eggs. Chickens. Young chickens. You got the skillet I got the chickens. Egg man."

And then the one with the grand stock and the old horse-drawn cart, drawn by a horse that knew the route so well that he would wander just far enough ahead to a place where his master would probably make a sale and then stop.

"Vegetable man. Vegetable man. Got your pretty green vegetables. I got your string beans. I got em green. I got em ripe. I got your greens, lady. I got your black-eyed peas. My greens is good, lady. My greens so good they sweet, lady."

Then a woman would call to him, "Vegetable man."

"Yes, ma'am," he would answer, ready to sing the chorus that went along with the impending sale.

"Got any okra?"

"Do I got okra? Yes, ma'am. I sure do got okra," he would answer. "I got the best okra in Chicago. My okra's as good as okra from heaven."

And the woman, knowing what was to come, would try to stop him. "Oh, shut yo mouf up man and bring it on up here then."

Yes, ma'am, I sure will."

"Act like a woman's got all day t' stand here talking t' you."

But he was not to be outdone. Walking up the stairs he

would stop on each landing and sing the lines that went with the purchase: "Lady says she wants okra. Do I got okra? I got the best okra in the world. Vegetable man. Here's your vegetable man. I got em green. I got em ripe. I got fresh greens and cabbage and carrots. I got em green. I got em ripe."

And while he was gone from his truck the bravest of the lot would snatch a bunch of carrots and we would all dash away giggling.

Running, we could still hear his words, although they were becoming soft as snow as we crossed another street into another alley: "I got em green. I got em ripe. I got em green. I got em ripe."

Finally we'd stop in a vacant lot and play a game we had invented. I don't have any idea who started it. An old broom or mop handle was all we needed. Then we would put tar on the end of it. In the summer the tar on the street melted and all we had to do was dig it up with the stick or a piece of glass or sometimes on very hot days, with our fingers. The tar furnished the necessary weight at the tip. (Besides that, it was good to chew.)

Then two boys would stand at either end of the vacant lot facing each other. We had never even so much as heard of the act of javelin throwing, but we were mastering it. However, our game was not just throwing the stick. That would have been too simple and we would have lost interest immediately. The real challenge was that we had to catch the stick in flight. No one person was any better or worse at this game than another. Now that I think about it, I realize how unusual we were. There was no need to compete because we loved each other so much. There was only the need to excel like everyone else and be part of our strange black world where excellence was only average.

When we tired of this game we went on to kick the can, or stickball, or racing! And when it was too hot for that, we would sit under someone's porch and play root the peg, or just sit around under a tree talking about the world as we knew it and how we were determined not to take what our parents had taken from white people, how *we* were going to fight.

Sometimes we left the neighborhood. The beach was several miles east of us. When the heat had become totally unbearable, we would start the long walk over 63rd Street to the lake. If we were very lucky and had saved a little money, we could ride the streetcar back. That way we didn't have to fight the white boys again. But most of the time there was no money so we walked back over the same street we had come earlier that day and sometimes we didn't even have to fight. Sometimes.

A few years before we were able to go to the beach by ourselves, back in the time when our parents took us on some festive occasion like Memorial Day or the Fourth of July, we had been forced to remain on the other side of the cyclone fence that separated us from the whites. But now we were older and when the police approached us to tell us to get back to "our" side of the fence, we took to the water.

Finally they gave up, confident that we were, as the man in charge put it, "just a bunch of crazy niggers." And that year we showed him just how crazy we were when we tore the fence down!

The charges were destruction of government property. But by now there were so many of us, and we were represented by a lawyer who seemed to enjoy representing Negroes who had no money ("a dirty commie bastard," one of the policemen whispered of him), that the charges were dropped and the fence was gone forever.

But there were cool times, too. There were the rains that came in the spring and the fall. The rain.

Sometimes it rained so hard that the sewers plugged up within three minutes. We would be outside, playing in a vacant lot, and before we could reach cover we were soaked, and the lot, weeds worn down and away by our persistent feet, was turned to mud. The rain fell like heavy hands on a drum, and the mud thinned, and colored the rain.

We ran. We ran to shelter. Not so much because we were afraid of getting wet, but because none of us wanted to go through that painful experience of having our parents look at us and accuse us of not having enough sense to come in out of it. We ran. And no matter how fast we ran, we could never keep time with the rapid cadence of the thousands, of the millions of raindrops. The rain came on us like a great mysterious, cleansing thing that cleared the air of all dust and brightened and re-colored things with a kind of gentle rendering that lasted for days; that sometimes lasted long enough for us to forget how dirty things had been before it came with the sweet breezes from the lake.

The sewers were totally ineffective, and we were delighted, because it meant that we had pools of water for sailing our popsicle-stick boats, the tarred streets and curbs refusing to let the water escape. Those of us who were truly adventurous wandered into the vacant lots and sailed our tiny cruisers on much more lavish waters.

Strange, now that I look back on the rain of my childhood, that I never think of it as being an unpleasant experience to be wet with rain. Oh, we sang songs about chasing the rain away, and we had little sayings that were passed on from generation to generation; some of them had probably come to us from as far back as the superstitious people hundreds of years before. When there was a flash of lightning that streaked across the sky a child would say, "The devil's beatin his wife." And when the deafening explosion of thunder followed, another child would reply, "Yeah, man, but she's fightin back." And strange, too, that I think of it as being always a blessing that cooled the city. But I cannot forget the icy rain that fell in the fall and winter, chilling us through our heavy wool jackets and two sweaters, and a shirt and even through our long underwear. We laughed at each other, mocking the one who shivered the most and then ultimately praising him. "Man, this cat keeps himself warm by shivering. Must be the warmest cat outside today."

Those fall rains were a prelude to the heavy gray cloud that would be with us for months to come. There would be snow after them, but the snow would be transformed almost immediately as it worked its way through the perpetual grit-cloud that hovered over our city, so that the grayness of the outside would blend with the grayness of our worlds inside where we spent the winter months keeping our roaches and rats fat so that they could go on producing their newborns along with us come the spring.

I remember that spring I became aware of the necessity of rain. I remember that spring I realized that had the rain not come, had it not washed down the buildings, had it not methodically worn away the industrial waste from the trees and shrubbery, had it not washed the millions of tiny particles away in swirling whirlpools that only little children can appreciate, had it not, as it fell through the almost invisible powder that formed a poisonous gas working on our lungs, brightened, had it not given us pure air to breathe, we would have been asphyxiated by our misery. The spring rains would go on for about two months, and during that time we were distracted from the unpleasantness inside by the brightness and beauty the rain created outside. (Even weeds growing six feet high in a vacant lot can be beautiful when there is nothing else growing.) The rains would continue and we would try to soak them into our souls because soon the heat of summer would be with us, and with it would come the extreme depression of that gray grit-cloud that tried to remind us of our place in society.

But of all the seasons, winter was the most impressive. It was always beautiful in the winter. Everything was clean and smelled even better than it did after a spring rain. The temperature was often zero or below, and with holes in our shoes and no rubbers, our feet were always wet and cold, but it was a good time of year. Most of us carried pieces of newspaper in our pockets and when the paper in our shoes became too wet we would step inside someone's doorway and change the expendable linings. There was snow everywhere and the half dozen or so sleds on the block were enough to accommodate the thirty or forty children.

Snowplows never came through our neighborhood. It was good they didn't because the snow was a wedge against a reality we were glad not to face. I thank God it snowed as much as it did when we were young. I thank God we were freed from everything that was familiar.

Sometimes it seemed to snow for days; as if the elements had contrived to free us by transforming ugliness into beauty. There were other parts of the city that hated to see the snow come, and their snowplows worked almost daily trying to set the calendar back. But we prayed for it in our neighborhood. There were no landscaped gardens for us. There had been no year of fun on the golf course. There was no grass to be covered up, only broken glass and pages of old newspapers dancing in the wind with the leaves from the big cottonwoods that were always shedding something. There were no rose bushes that had to be protected against the subzero temperature, only weeds that were more than strong enough to fend for themselves. There was really not much beauty at all, only a gray, dirty, sad world we had lived in for nine months and we were delighted to see it changed.

In the alleys the snow packed down hard on the mounds of garbage and provided us with hills for sliding. It leveled the uneven sidewalks. It even painted the buildings and filled the holes in the streets and in yards and laid lawns, for once, over all the neighborhood. It was clean. It was pure. It was good.   .

With the coming of the snow, life became gentler as sounds became muffled. The snow was so special that all the children in the neighborhood respected its holiness and played more quietly.

Sampson would still come through three days a week, but

he didn't sell much ice now. Who needed ice when every window sill was a refrigerator? The other four days of the week he would deliver coal. But there was one very cold winter when he figured out a way to sell both at the same time. He built wooden platforms on both sides of his truck and he lined them with ice and then covered the ice with canvas so it didn't get coal dust on it. And then, inside the truck, he dumped two or three tons of coal. He still didn't sell much ice, but at least he was able to travel the alleys in good conscience that year.

When we were very young we ate the snow. As we grew a little older, we washed girls' faces in it. And as we became of age, we rolled it up in little balls and threw them at shiny new cars driven by white people passing through our neighborhood on the their way to work.

It was indeed beautiful in the winter. I remember one year the snow was so high that as we ran down the wavy path that led in front of the buildings we had to jump up to see over the top. And it was always clean! An empty wine bottle was swallowed up by it, and tucked away so we wouldn't have to see it for a while. Old Jesse, who was always vomiting his insides up early in the morning so that we'd see it on the way to school, was temporarily forgotten because the snow covered over his chili-mack and sweetened the air again. Inside the doorways of the buildings the urine smell was still there, but not outside in the gangways like it was the rest of the year. Outside it smelled like it did everywhere else in the city; like it smelled where people had jobs and money. Outside it was like a dream and it was a pleasure to get soaked with it; chilled and shivering until we could stand it no longer. And even then we didn't want to go in, for inside was a reality that no climatic conditions could change. Even on Christmas day with snow everywhere and a few toys under the trees and the radio playing Christmas music, and people saying "God bless you" everywhere in the world, even on *Christmas day* when it grew late and we stepped inside our dungeons we realized that those God-bless-yous were not meant for us.

ETHERIDGE KNIGHT (1933–   )

*Known and acclaimed primarily as a poet (see his poems in
the poetry section pp. 276–79), Etheridge Knight began writing
poetry and short stories while incarcerated in Indiana State
Prison. Born in Mississippi, Knight grew up in Indianapolis
and was given a twenty-year prison sentence in 1960. He has
written: "I died in Korea from a shrapnel wound and nar-
cotics resurrected me. I died in 1960 from a prison sentence
and poetry brought me back to life." He was released on
parole at the end of 1968 and has produced a remarkable
book,* Black Voices in Prison *(Pathfinder Press, 1970), which
he describes as "a collection of testaments, essays, short
stories, poems, and articles, most of which are by and about
black men who are imprisoned" in Indiana State Prison. In
this preface to this book he says that "the whole experience
of the black man in America can be summed up in one word:
prison." He also says: "Prison is the ultimate in oppression."
The book includes poems and prose by Knight, and the following story is the concluding work in* Black Voices in Prison.

A Time to Mourn

He stepped out of the darkness and hypnotic noise of the
prison Tag Shop into a sea of sunshine spilling like foam-
tipped waves off the high slaty-gray walls and washing the
asphalt street and Industry Buildings in sheets of heat. He
pulled his cap down over his eyes and followed the deputy
warden's messenger across the street and down a spotless
sidewalk that cut a surgical path through the neatly mowed
lawn, which lay like a green carpet crisscrossed by white
walks and dotted with great circular beds of flowers and

whirring lawn sprinklers. He heard lazy shouts floating in the oppressive air and the sharp smack of a baseball being slammed; to his left, he saw a few men shagging flies out on the baseball field whose bare dirt diamond looked like an open palm against the green carpet; above the outfield, atop the wall, he saw a guard watching the players, squatting on his heels, his rifle across his lap.

He followed the messenger past a wire-enclosed brick powerhouse that hummed and bristled and clacked with activity, and whose twin smokestacks, piercing the sky like devil's horns, dominated the entire prison. After nodding curtly to a group of men lounging on a coal pile that flanked the powerhouse, he heard someone call: "What's up, Big Joe?" He ignored the question and glanced at the slick-haired messenger who walked imperiously ahead, his heels clicking against the sidewalk. He quickened his pace. The same question rose in his throat, but he quickly swallowed it, and slowed down his steps. He was Big Joe Noonan; he didn't question finks who worked for the deputy. He raised his cap, ran his hand over his kinky black hair, now speckled with gray, then settled the cap back on his head and lifted his chin. He was a lifer; he would wait and see.

The buzzer sounded outside the deputy's office, and he rose from the bench and walked over to the guard stationed at the deputy's door. Turning his back and raising his arms, he stood silently as the guard's hands moved swiftly over him: under his arms, down the center of his back, over his buttocks, between his legs, and down to his socks. Then the guard tapped him lightly on the shoulder and he turned and walked into the deputy's office.

His face remained unchanged when he saw the prison chaplain sitting behind the deputy's desk. So, this is the pitch, he thought. Why haven't you been to church lately, Joe? . . . well, listen to his speech, smile nice, then go back to work. . . . He moved to the front of the desk and looked down into the bright eyes of the chaplain. I'm here, Reverend Dickerson . . . no sweat . . . I'll listen, no trouble . . . just rattle it off and let me get back to work . . . Aloud he said, "You sent for me, sir?"

"Yes, Joe." The chaplain waved to a straight-backed chair. "Sit down. I won't beat around the bush, Joe. I'm afraid that I have some bad news for you. The warden received a telegram today that your uncle has died. As you know, it's my job to have to inform you men of such things. And I'm truly sorry, Joe. I see from your record here that your uncle is listed as your only living relative? . . ."

His eyes dropped from the chaplain's face to the shiny desk top. Dead . . . the old man dead . . . my only living relative? Ha! dead as a fish . . . look out the window . . . my only relative . . . what about my daughter they gave her away she's twenty-two now I wouldn't know her if I saw her, she wouldn't see me anyway, I killed her mother and I killedher-motherandIkilledhermother and . . . no sweat look out the window no trouble . . . Uncle Jake dead . . . no sweat no trouble . . . listen and go back to work. . . . He unfolded his arms and slowly rubbed his hands up and down his trouser legs. Then he folded his arms again across his chest.

"As you also know, Joe, it is our policy to allow a man to attend the funeral of a member of his immediate family, that is, if he can afford the expenses for himself and an accompanying guard. . . ."

Uncle Jake. Dead . . . I wonder if they shaved off his gray mustache . . . I wonder if he wet the bed . . . I wonder if he was scared like I was scared of the Chair and the smell of Lysol and I killed her mother and they are dead Uncle Jake and Marta are dead. . . .

". . . But, unfortunately, since your uncle resided outside the state, the usual policy does not apply. However, you will be permitted to send a message of sympathy, and flowers if you like. . . ."

I should say something I should do something I should . . . flowers I should send the dead . . . and Marta liked flowers red ones and yellow ones and redandwhite and yellow . . . no sweat . . . no trouble. . . . He kept his eyes on the shiny desk top and his arms folded across his chest.

"I know this is hard news, Joe," the chaplain was saying. "Perhaps you'd like to sit and talk for awhile about your uncle."

He shoved his chair back and rose. "No, thank you, sir," he said. "But I appreciate you telling me about my uncle."

"I'm sorry, Joe."

"Thank you, sir," Joe said, turning to go.

"Oh yes, Joe, one more thing. If you want to, you can go from here directly to your cell. Perhaps you'd like to be by yourself for awhile."

"If it's all the same, sir, I'd rather go back to work."

He watched the chaplain flush and heard him say: "Suit yourself, suit yourself." Then he walked out of the deputy's office and once more followed the slick-haired messenger down the spotless sidewalk.

Uncle Jake dead and Marta dead and this slick-haired fink prancing in front of me like a woman and Marta was a woman soft and warm . . . and my daughter is a woman now . . . and Marta mourn for Uncle Jake and Reverend Dickerson mourn alone a little . . . a time to be born and a time to die and a time to mourn and a time to danceanddance and Marta danced and danced with anybody and Marta died and Uncle Jake is dead . . . Uncle Jake didn't like the visiting room and didn't visit but once a year and twenty years is time and time is time . . . time to plant Uncle Jake and Marta planted flowers yellow and white and red . . . red red like her lips and I weeped for Marta and Uncle Jake is dead and Marta danced and I weeped dancing red laughing and I criedredbloodcryingred and Marta diedcryingredcrying . . . no sweat, no trouble . . . and . . .

He turned the corner by the powerhouse and quickly stepped off the sidewalk. Four guards, their white caps gleaming in the sun, were hustling a young convict down the walk, towards the deputy's office. As they passed Joe, he saw the young man's face lifted to the sky, his black skin glistened with sweat, and blood oozed from a gash above his eye, his lips were pulled tightly over his teeth as he struggled to free himself. Joe leaned his back against the fence enclosing the powerhouse, his fingers entwined in the wire mesh. He watched the five men scuffle by silently except for their hard breathing and the scraping of their shoe soles on the concrete. For a moment his eyes locked with those of the convict, then the young man was hustled around the corner and out of sight.

As Joe stepped back onto the sidewalk he became aware of the convicts who had risen from the coal pile and were now lined up along the fence, their fingers hooked through the wire. "That kid's doing hard time . . ." "Yeah, he's got a lot to learn." "I bet he'll wear out 'fore the Hole do." "Say, did you see that lump he put on ol' Fat Ass . . ." He fell into step behind the messenger and the voices faded away.

Uncle Jake is dead and the kid is dead and got a lot to learn . . . and Marta got a lot to learn . . . and I fought 'em too twenty years ago and I died in the Hole and the Hole is still there and the kid is dead and Marta is dead red like blood and flowers flowing from the kid's head and Marta's chest . . . and twenty years the damn kid will learn that he is

dead like Marta and me and UncleJakedeadweepingredblood-
crying . . . slow down kid no sweat no trouble . . .

"The chaplain told me about your uncle, Joe. Are you
sure you don't want me to take you to the cellhouse?" They
were at the door of the Tag Shop, and the messenger leaned
against the door, looking up at Joe with an unspoken question
deep in his eyes. "Nobody's in the cellhouse now; it's quiet
there, and everything . . ."

"No, kid, thanks anyway."

The slick-haired messenger threw up his hand and moved
off. "Maybe sometimes, Joe. See ya."

Joe stepped inside the dim Tag Shop, into the rhythmic,
pulsating intensity of a hundred machines. After checking in
with the shop guard, he went to his locker and hung up his
cap; then he went to his stamping press and flipped on the
switch. Settling himself on his stool, he picked up a stack
of license plates and began to feed them, one by one, into
the hungry machine. Into the right side, out the left. No
sweat, no trouble.

WILLIAM MELVIN KELLEY (1937–   )

*Born in New York City, William Melvin Kelley graduated
from the Fieldston School and then went on to Harvard University where he studied under Archibald MacLeish and John
Hawkes. His first novel,* A Different Drummer *(1962), won
the Richard and Hinda Rosenthal Foundation Award of the
National Institute of Arts and Letters. Since then he has published three additional novels and a volume of collected short
stories; he has received a number of literary prizes, grants,
and honors. He lived in Rome for a year, has taught at the
New School, has been a Bread Loaf Scholar and author-in-
residence at the State University of New York in Geneseo.
The following story is from* Dancers on the Shore *(1964),
his collection of short stories.*

A Good Long Sidewalk

The barbershop was warm enough to make Carlyle Bedlow sleepy, and smelled of fragrant shaving soap. A fat man sat in the great chair, his stomach swelling beneath the striped cloth. Standing behind him in a white, hair-linted tunic which buttoned along one shoulder, Garland, the barber, clacked his scissors. Garland's hair was well kept, his sideburns cut off just where his wire eye-glasses passed back to his ears. "Hello, Carlyle. How you doing?" He looked over the tops of his glasses. "So you decided to let me make a living, huh?"

"Yes, sir." Carlyle smiled. He liked Garland.

"Taking advantage of Bronx misery?"

"Sir?"

"I mean when folks is having trouble getting their cars dug out, you making money shoveling Bronx snow."

"Oh. Yes, sir." Garland was always teasing him because Carlyle's family had moved recently from Harlem to this neighborhood in the Bronx. He maintained Carlyle thought the Bronx was full of hicks.

"Okay. You're next. I'll take some of that snow money from you." He returned to the fat man's head.

Carlyle leaned his shovel in the corner, stamped his feet, took off his jacket, sat down in a wire-backed chair and picked up a comic book. He had already read it, and put it down to watch the barber shave the fat man's neck with the electric clippers.

The fat man, who had been talking when Carlyle came in, continued: "Can't see why he'd want to do that, can you, Garland? But ain't that just like a nigger!" He was very dark. The skin under his chin was heavily pocked and scarred.

"And just like a white woman too!"

"Man, these cats marry some colored girl when they starting out, just singing in joints and dives. She supports him while he's trying to get ahead. But then he gets a hit record, or a job at the Waldorf and—bingo!—he drops her quick, gets a divorce, and marries some white bitch."

"White chicks know where it's at. They laying in wait for him. When he makes it, they'll cut in on a good thing every time. Anyway, it won't last a year. And you can quote me on that." Garland finished cutting great patches of hair from the man's head and started to shape the back.

A short, light-skinned Negro opened the door and leaned in. "Hello, Garland." He did not close the door and cold wind blasted in around him.

"Say, man, how you doing? You after the boy there. All right?" He continued to work, hardly looking at the head in front of him; he could cut hair blindfolded.

The short man nodded and closed the door behind him. He removed his coat, put his gloves carefully into a pocket, sat down, and stretched. Only then did he take off his hat. His hair was straight and black; he did not seem to need a haircut. "I read in *The Amsterdam* how Mister Cool and his white sweetie finally got shackled."

"Yes, sir. We just talking about that." Garland reached behind him, touched a switch and from an aluminum box, lather billowed into his palm. "Ain't that just like a Negro!"

"And like a white bitch too!" the fat man added. "Don't trim the sideburns, Garland. Just around the ears. I'll trim the sideburns myself."

Garland nodded. "Man, I seen the same thing happen a thousand times. A Negro making more money than a white man starting to act foolish like a white man. Even though he should know better. I guess it ain't really that Negro's fault. All his life he been poor and a nobody." Garland put the lather behind the fat man's ears. "So as soon as he gets some money it's bound to mess up his mind."

"Don't touch the sideburns, Garland." The fat man shifted under the striped sheet. "Yeah, I think you right. And them white bitches is waiting to ambush him."

The short man folded his thin arms across his chest. "Well, don't all a colored man's problems begin with Mister Charlie and Miss Mary?"

"Mostly when Miss Mary wants to make time with her nigger chauffeur or handyman and Mister Charlie finds out about it. He don't blame Miss Mary for it, that's sure." The fat man leaned forward.

Garland stopped shaving, reflecting. "Mostly when you find some white woman being nice to you, nicer than she ought to be. Then watch out!" He started to shave behind the fat man's ears. "Them white women know where it's at."

The short man nodded. "Yeah, but I can't see why no colored man'd want to marry no white chick on purpose like Mister Cool did. Not when there's so many fine spade chicks around."

Garland agreed. "I like my women the way I like my coffee: hot, strong, and black!"

The fat man jerked his head. "I guess he thinks he taking a step up. Now he thinks he better than all the other boots standing on the corner. He's got himself a white recording contract with a big white company, and a booking at a fine, white night club, and a white Cadillac and an apartment on Park Avenue painted all white and a white bitch too. Why, man, he almost white himself . . . except for one thing: he still a nigger!"

They all laughed, slapping their thighs.

It seemed much colder with his hair cut short, his neck shaved clean. Carlyle trudged flat-footed, planting his feet firmly so as not to slip, up the middle of the carless street, through the shadows cast by the snow-clogged trees. He wished he could go home, take off his wet shoes, listen to records, and read the paper that each night his father carried home tucked under his arm. He knew too that the later it got, the angrier his father would be; his father liked to eat as soon as he came home. Besides, his father would want him or his little brother to clear their own driveway and Carlyle had not asked to take the shovel. He decided then, walking along the rutted street, he would not waste his time with small jobs; he would look for a long snow-banked walk of a house set way back from the street.

This is what he finally found, down a solitary side street lit faintly by a single street lamp at the middle of the block; the house, set back on a short hill that surely, in the spring and summer, would be a thick lawn, perhaps bordered with flowers. Snow clung to the empty, blackened branches of a hedge concealing a grotesque iron fence. The house too was grotesque, painted gray, its gables hung with dagger-like icicles.

He hesitated a moment, looking up at the house; there did not seem to be any light burning, and he did not want to wade twenty or thirty feet through shin-deep snow only to find no one at home. Going farther on up the sidewalk, he found a lighted window down the side near the back and he returned to the gate and started up the drifted walk.

The porch was wood and clunked hollow when he stamped the snow from his feet. He climbed the steps gingerly and peered at the names on the door-bell. If there was a man's name, he still might not find work—women living alone or old couples more usually needed someone to clean snow. There was a woman's name—Elizabeth Reuben—and a man's too, but his, which was typed, had been recently crossed out. Carlyle rang the bell.

No longer walking, his feet got cold very quickly and when, after what seemed a long while, the door opened—and then only a crack—he was hopping from one foot to the other.

"Yes? What is it?" He could see a nose and one eye, could hear a woman's voice.

"Miz Reuben?" He slurred the 'miss' or 'missus' so as not to insult her either way.

"Yes."

"Would you like to have your walk shoveled?" He moved closer and spoke to the nose and eye.

There was a pause while she looked him over, up and down, and inspected the shovel he held in his hand. "No. I'm sorry. I don't think so."

"Well, uh . . ." There was nothing else to say. He thanked her and turned away.

"Wait!" It sounded almost like a scream. And then softer: "Young man, wait."

He turned back and found the door swung wide. The nose and eye had grown to a small, plumpish, white woman of about forty in a pale blue wool dress. She was not exactly what he would have called pretty, but she was by no means a hag. She was just uninteresting looking. Her hair was a dull brown combed into a style that did her no good; her eyes were flat and gray like cardboard. "On second thought, young man, I think it would be nice to have my walk cleaned off. I'm expecting some visitors and it will make it easier for them . . . to find me." She smiled at him. "But come inside; you must be frozen solid walking around in all this snow and cold."

"That's all right, ma'am. I'll start right away." He took a step back and lifted his shovel.

"You do as I say and come in the house this very moment." She was still smiling, but there was enough of a mother's tone in her voice to make him walk past her through the door, which she closed behind him. "Rest your coat and shovel there and follow me. I'm taking you into the kitchen to put something warm into your stomach."

He did as she ordered and walked behind her down the hall, lit by a low-watt bulb in a yellowing shade.

The first thing he noticed was that the kitchen smelled of leaking gas. There was a huge pile of rags and bits of cloth on the table in the center of the room. There were more rags on the window sill and stuffed at the bottom of the back door.

She saw him looking at them. "It's an old house. It gets very drafty." She smiled nervously, wringing her hands. "Now, are you old enough to drink coffee? Or would you rather have hot chocolate?"

He had remained on his feet. She bustled to the table and swept the rags onto the floor with her arm. "Sit down, please." He did. "Now, what would you rather have?"

"Hot chocolate, please."

"Hot chocolate? Good. That's better for you." She headed toward the stove, almost running; it was big and old-fashioned with a shelf for salt and pepper above the burners. "What's your name, dear?"

"Carlyle, ma'am. Carlyle Bedlow."

"Carlyle? Did you know you were named after a famous man?"

"No, ma'am. I was just named after my father. His name's—"

She was laughing, shrilly, unhappily. He had said something funny but did not know what it was. It made him uneasy.

"What, dear? You started to say something. I interrupted you."

"Nothing, ma'am." He was wondering now what he had said, and why she was being so nice, giving him hot chocolate. Maybe she was giving him the hot chocolate so she could talk to him about things he did not understand and laugh at his ignorance. It was just like the men in the barbershop said: Most of a colored man's trouble began with white people. They were always laughing and making fun of Negroes . . .

"Do you like your hot chocolate sweet, Carlyle? I can put some sugar in it for you." Behind her voice he could her the milk sizzling around the edges of the saucepan, could hear the gas feeding the flame.

"Yes, ma'am. I like it sweet."

The milk sizzled louder still as she poured it across the hot sides into his cup. She brought it and sat across from him on the edge of her chair, waiting for him to taste it. He did so and found it good; with his mind's eye, he followed it down his throat and into his stomach.

"Is it good?" Her gray eyes darted across his face.

"Yes, ma'am."

She smiled and seemed pleased. That puzzled him. If she had him in to laugh at him, why was she so anxious to get him warm, why did she want him to like the hot chocolate? There had to be some other reason, but just then the chocolate was too good to think about it. He took a big swallow.

"Well now, let's get down to business. I've never had to hire anybody to do this before. I used to do it myself when I was younger and . . . then . . . there was a man here who'd do it for me . . . but he's not here any more." She trailed off, caught herself. "How much do you usually get for a stoop and a walk that long?" She smiled at him again. It was a fleeting smile which warmed only the corners of her mouth and left her eyes sad. "I've been very nice to you. I should think you'd charge me less than usual."

So that was it! She wanted him to do her walk for practically nothing! White people were always trying to cheat Negroes. He had heard his father say that, cursing the Jews in Harlem. He just stared at her, hating her.

She waited an instant for him to answer then started to figure out loud. "Well, let's see. That's a long walk and there's the sidewalk and the stoop and the steps and it's very cold and I probably can't get anyone else . . . It's a question of too little supply and a great deal of demand." She was talking above him again. "I'd say I'd be getting off well if I gave you five dollars." She stopped and looked across at him, helplessly. "Does that sound fair? I really don't know."

He continued to stare, but now because he could hardly believe what she said. At the most, he would have charged only three dollars, and had expected her to offer one.

She filled in the silence. "Yes, five. That sounds right."

He finished his chocolate with a gulp. "But, ma'am, I wouldn't-a charged you but three. Really!"

"Three? That doesn't sound like enough." She bolted from the table and advanced on him. "Well, I'll give you the extra two for being honest. Perhaps you can come back and do something else for me." She swooped on him, hugged, and kissed him. The kiss left a wet, cold spot on his cheek. He lurched away, surprised, knocking the cup and saucer from the table. The saucer broke in two; the cup bounced, rolled, lopsided and crazy, under the table.

"No, ma'am." He jumped to his feet. "I'm sorry, ma'am."

"That's all right. It's all right. I'm sor—That's all right about the saucer." She scrambled to her knees and began to pick up the pieces and the cup. Once she had them in her lap, she sat, staring away at nothing, shaking her head.

Now he knew for certain what she was up to; he remembered what Garland had said: When you find some white woman being nicer than she ought to be, then watch out! She wanted to make time with him. He started from the kitchen. Maybe he could leave before it was too late.

"Wait, young man." She stood up. "I'll pay you now and you won't have to come inside when you're through." She pushed by him and hurried down the shadowy hallway. He followed her as before, but kept his distance.

Her purse was hanging on a peg on the coat-rack, next to his own jacket. She took them both down, handed him his jacket, averting her eyes, and fumbled in her purse, produced a wallet, unzipped it, pulled out a bill and handed it to him.

"But it's a five, ma'am." He could not understand why she wanted to pay him that much now that he was not going to make time with her.

She looked at him for the first time, her eyes wet. "I told you I'd pay you five, didn't I?"

"Yes, ma'am."

"All right. Do a good job. And remember, don't come back."

"Yes, ma'am."

"You let yourself out." She started to the back of the house even before he had finished buttoning his jacket. By the time he opened the door she was far down the hall, and, as he closed it behind him and stepped into the dark, twinkling cold, he could hear her in the kitchen. She was tearing rags.

The next evening the white woman was in the newspaper. A boy trying to deliver a package had found her in the gas-filled kitchen, slumped over a table piled high with rags. Carlyle's father, who saw it first, mentioned it at dinner. "Had a suicide a couple blocks from here." He told who and where.

Carlyle sat staring at his plate.

His father went on: "White folks! Man, if they had to be colored for a day, they'd all kill they-selves. We wouldn't have no race problem then. White folks don't know what hard life is. What's wrong, Junior?"

"She was a nice lady."

His parents and his little brother looked at him.

"You know her, Junior?" His mother put down her fork.

"She was a nice lady, Mama. I shoveled her walk yesterday. She give me five dollars."

"Oh, Junior." His mother sighed.

"Five dollars?" His father leaned forward. "Crazy, huh?"

"Have some respect!" His mother turned on his father angrily.

Carlyle looked at his mother. "Are white people all bad? There's some good ones, ain't there, Mama?"

"Of course, Junior." His mother smiled. "What made you think—"

"Sure, there is, Junior." His father was smiling too. "The dead ones is good."

MIKE THELWELL (1938–   )

Born in Jamaica, West Indies, Mike Thelwell came to the United States in 1959 to attend Howard University. He worked with the Student Nonviolent Coordinating Committee and was director of the Washington office of the Mississippi Freedom Democratic Party. His stories have been published in Negro Digest, Short Story International, Story *magazine, and* The Best Short Stories *by Negro Writers, compiled by Langston Hughes. He teaches at the University of Massachusetts and has contributed fiction and articles to* The Massachusetts Review. *The following story is reprinted from the Review, Vol. VIII, No. 4, Autumn 1966.*

Bright an' Mownin' Star

Traveling south from Memphis on Highway 49, one crosses over the last rolling hill and the Mississippi Delta stretches before you like the sea, an unbroken monotony of land so flat as to appear unnatural. So pervasive is this low-ceilinged, almost total flatness that one loses all other dimensions of space and vision. An endless succession of cotton and soybean fields surround the road.

A few weather-grayed shacks, stark, skeletal and abrasively ugly perch in a precarious oasis hacked out in the narrow, neutral strip between the road and the encroaching fields. Contemptuous of weather, time and gravity, they stand apparently empty, long-abandoned and sheltering nothing but the wind. Then some appear, no different in point of squalor and decrepitude from the others, except that people stand before them.

At one point a single huge tree, off in a cotton field a distance, breaks the horizon. It is the first tree of any size that has appeared. This tree is an oak that bears small, gnarled acorns so bitter that there is no animal that will eat them. Its wood is very hard, but is knotty, faulted, and with a grain so treacherous and erratic that it cannot easily be worked. It is used for nothing more durable than a weapon. In this region they are called blackjacks, from the sootlike darkness of the bark, and find utility mainly in conversation as a metaphor of hardness, "tougher'n a blackjack oak."

This one is unusual beyond its mere presence and size, having both name and history. Its appearance, too, is unusual. The trunk and lower limbs are fire-charred to a dull black. These limbs are leafless and dead, but the topmost branches in the center of the tree continue to grow. In a strange inharmony the living oak flourishes out of the cinders of its own corpse. White folk call this tree the Nigger Jack, while Negroes speak of it hardly at all, save on those Sundays when the tree becomes the central symbol in some hell-fire sermon, for it is widely known that the flames that burned the oak roasted the bodies of slaves judged dangerous beyond redemption or control.

Once, it is said, some young black men from the county, returned from defeating the Kaiser, resolved to fell and burn the tree. On the night before this event was to take place, a huge and fiery cross was seen to shine at the base of the tree, burning through the night and into the next day.

For many years—the space of three generations—the land around this tree has lain fallow, producing annually only a tangled transient jungle of rabbit grass and myriad nameless weeds, for no Negro could be found who might be bribed, persuaded, or coerced into working there.

Lowe Junior grunted deep in his chest as the heavy, broad-bladed chopping hoe hit into the dry black earth. He jerked it up, sighted on the next clump of wire-grass and weeds, and drove the hoe-blade into the furrow just beyond the weeds, and with the same smooth motion pulled the blade towards his body and slightly upwards, neatly grubbing out the intruder in a little cloud of dust, without touching the flanking cotton plants.

"Sho do seem like the grass growin' faster'n the cotton." He leaned on the hoe handle and inspected the grubbed-up weed. "Hit be greener an' fatter'n the cotton evrahtime. Heah hit is, middle o' June, an hit ain't sca'cely to mah knee yet." He ran his glance over the rows of stunted plants, already turning a dull brownish green, then squinted down the row he was chopping, estimating the work left. He saw much "grass" wrestling its way around and between the cotton. "Finish dishyer after dinner," he said, noting that the sun had already cleared the tip of the blackjack oak which stood some ten rows into the middle of the field. Dragging his hoe he started towards the tree's shade.

Lowe Junior was tall, a gaunt, slightly-stooped figure as he shambled with the foot-dragging, slightly pigeon-toed, stiff-backed gait that a man develops straddling new-turned furrows while holding down the jerking, bucking handle of a bull-tongue plow. His boots and the dragging hoe raised a fine powder of dust around his knees. When he reached the tree he leaned his tool against the trunk and stretched himself. He moved his shoulders, feeling the pull of the overalls where the straps had worn into his flesh during the morning's work. Holding the small of his back, he arched his middle forward to ease the numb, cramping ache that hardly seemed to leave the muscles in his back. Then he straightened up and stood for a while looking out over his cotton.

Then Lowe Junior turned to the tree and took a pail which hung from one of the broken stubs. He touched the blackened trunk, running his hands over the rough cinders. "Thet fiah oney toughed yo' up, thass all . . . an there ain't nothin' wrong with thet." There was something familiar, almost affectionate, in his voice and action. When he first started working this section, he had carefully avoided the tree, sitting on the hot earth in the rows to eat and rest. But he had become accustomed to the tree now, was grateful for its shade, and he found himself accepting it as the only other living thing he encountered during the day. After all, he assured himself, "Hit cain't be no harm to no tree, fo' a certain fack."

He eased himself down ponderously, almost painfully, like a man too old or too fat, and began to eat. In the pail were butter beans boiled with country peppers, wild onions, and slabs of salted fatback. This stew was tepid, almost perceptibly warm from the midday heat. The coating of pork grease that had floated to the top had not congealed. Lowe Junior briefly debated making a small fire but decided against taking the time. He ate quickly, stirring the stew and scooping it into his mouth with a thin square of cornbread, biting into the gravy-soaked bread, then chewing and swallowing rapidly. Finishing his meal he drank deeply from a kerosene tin filled with water and covered with burlap (wet in the morning but now bone dry), which stood among the roots of the tree.

He stretched himself again, yawned, belched, spat, and braced himself firmly against the tree. He lay there limply, his eyes closed as though to shut out the rows and rows of small, drying-out plants that represented the work of his hands, every day, from can see to can't, since early in the spring.

"Ef hit would jes' rain some . . . seems like the mo' a man strain, hits the harder times git. Li'l rain now, an' the cotton be right up, but soon'll be too late." Weariness spread in him and the effort even of thinking was too great. He just lay there inert, more passive even than the tree, which at least stood. Even if by some miracle this cotton in the section he was "halfing" for Mr. Riley Peterson survived the drought, rains coming in August or September would turn the dust into mud and rot whatever cotton was ripening in the bolls— or else wash it into the mud.

A sudden panic came upon Lowe Junior, stretched beneath the tree. He could hardly feel his body, which was just a numbness. He felt that he could not rise, could not even begin, for his body would not obey him. For a brief moment he was terrified of making the effort lest he fail. Then he sat up suddenly, almost falling over forward from the violence of his effort. "Better study out whut t' do. No profit to layin' here scarin' m'se'f. Quarter section be a lot o' farmin' fo' a man. Sho ain't be able to keep t' grass outen the cotton by myse'f."

This was a problem for him, had been ever since he had asked Mr. Peterson to give him this quarter section. He was young but a good worker; still Mr. Peterson might not have given it to him had it not been for the fact that no other tenant would take it. Lowe Junior did not want to ask for help with the chopping because, in "halfing," the cost of the seed, fertilizer, ginning, and any hired help came out of the tenant's half. Already most of his half belonged to Mr. J. D. Odum, the merchant in Sunflower who had "furnished" him. He knew that he would have to have help with the picking, and did not want to hire any help before then, when he would at least have an idea of the crop's potential. "Man can en' up with nothin' thet way," he muttered. "Hit'll happen anyways, tho'. Figured to put in eight mebbe even nine bale fo' my share come the crop . . . now be the grace o' the good Gawd ef ah makes fo' . . . man doan feel much even t' keep on . . . Lawd, hit be better t' die, than t' live so hard." He found little comfort in those grim lines from the old Blues to which his grandmother was so partial. She was always incanting that song as though it had a special meaning for her.

After his father died, and his mother went off to the north to find work, it was the old woman, pious and accepting, who had told him the old stories, raised him in the Church, and interpreted for him the ways of their world. He remembered her story of how God had put two boxes into the world, one big and the other small. The first Negro and the first white man had seen the boxes at the same time and run towards them, but the Negro arrived first and greedily appropriated for himself the larger box. Unfortunately this box contained a plough, a hoe, a cop-axe, and a mule, while the smaller box contained a pen, paper, and a ledger book. "An' thass why," the old woman would conclude, her face serious, "the Nigger been aworkin' evah since, an' the white man he reckon up the crop; he be sittin' theah at crop time, jes' afigurin' an' areckonin'; he say

> Noughts a nought,
> Figgers a figger,
> All fo' us folks,
> None fo' the Nigger.

He had been fifteen before he even began to doubt the authenticity of this explanation. Now the old lady was ailing and very old. But she had not lost her faith in the ultimate justice of the Lord or her stoic acceptance of whatever He sent. It was a joke among the neighbors that when the good sisters of the Church went in to see the old lady, now failing in sight and almost bedridden, her answer to the question, "How yo' keepin', Miz Culvah?" invariably was "Porely, thank d' Lawd." Lowe Junior chuckled, got up, dusted off his clothes, and went out into the sun.

That evening he stopped work early, just as the sun was setting, and started home, trudging slowly over the flat dusty road past fields, a few as parched and poor as his own, and large ones where elaborate machinery hurled silvery sprays over rows of tall lush plants. A wind swept the fine cool spray into the road. He felt the pleasant tickling points of coldness on his face and saw the grayish dust coating his overalls turn dark with the moisture. Minute grains of mud formed on his skin. He looked into the dazzling spray and saw a band of color where the setting sun made a rainbow.

> D' Lawd give Noah d' rainbow sign,
> No mo' watah, d' flah nex' time.

"Thass whut the ol' woman would say, an tell evrahbody thet she seen d' Lawd's sign. Be jes' sun an' watah, tho'." He did not look at the green fields. Looking straight ahead into the dust of the road, he increased his pace. He wanted only to get home.

Just where the dust road meets the highway, at the very edge of a huge field, was the shack. Tin-roofed with gray clapboard sides painted only with the stain of time and weather, it had two small rooms. As Lowe Junior came up the road, it seemed to be tossed and balanced on a sea of brown stalks, the remains of last year's bean crop which came up to the back door.

In the front, the small bare yard was shaded by a pecan tree already in blossom. Small lots, well-kept and tidy, grew okra, butter-bean and collard green plants on both sides of the yard. Lowe Junior walked around the shack to a stand-pipe in back of the stoop. He washed the dust from his head and arms, filled his pail and drank. The water was brown, tepid, and rusty-tasting. He sprinkled the okra and bean plants, then entered the shack. The fire was out, and the huge pot hanging over the fire, from which he had taken his dinner that morning, had not been touched.

"Mam, Mam," he called softly, "Yo' awright?" There was no answer, and he went into the old woman's room. The room was stifling-hot as the tin roof radiated the day's heat. The air was heavy with the smell of stale urine, old flesh, and night sweat. The old lady lay against the wall, partially covered by an old quilt. A ray of sunlight beamed through a small knothole and lighted up the lined and creasing skin pattern on one side of her face. A single fly buzzed noisily around her open mouth and lighted on the tuft of straggling white hairs on her chin. Her eyes stared at a framed picture of the bleeding heart of Jesus, violent red and surrounded by a wreath of murderous-looking thorns and a hopeful glow, which hung on the opposite wall above the motto, "The Blood of Jesus Saves."

Lowe Junior searched his pockets slowly, almost absently, for two coins to place over her eyes. His gaze never left her face and, as he looked, the ray of sunlight gradually diminished, seeming to withdraw reluctantly from the face, finally leaving it to shadow.

Failing to find any coins, he straightened the limbs, pulled the quilt over the face, and went to tell the neighbors.

When he returned, the thick purple Delta darkness had descended with a tropical suddenness. He added more beans, fatback and water to the stew, and started the fire. Then he lit a kerosene lantern and took it into the yard to a spot beneath the pecan tree. He hung the lantern on a branch and began to dig.

The neighbors found him still digging when they began to arrive in the little yard. The first small group of women was led by Sister Beulah, a big, imposing, very black woman with a reputation for fierce holiness. She stood out from the worn and subdued group not only because of the crisp whiteness of her robe and bandanna but in her purposeful, almost aggressive manner. She led the women to the side of the hole.

"Sho sorry t' heah 'bout Sistah Culvah, but as you knows . . . ," she began.

"She inside," Lowe Junior said without looking up, "an' ah thanks yo' all fo' comin'."

Interrupted in mid-benediction, Beulah stood with her mouth open. She had failed to officiate at buryings in the community only twice in the past twenty years, and then only because she had been holding revivals at the other end of the state. She had never quite forgiven the families of the deceased for not awaiting her return. She resented Lowe Junior's thanks, the first she had ever received for doing what she thought of as an indispensable service. May as well thank the grave.

"Thet boy sho actin' funny," she murmured, and swept into the shack to take charge of preparations.

More neighbors straggled into the yard. Another lantern was brought and hung in the tree, widening the chancy and uncertain perimeter of light in the otherwise enveloping blackness of the Delta night. Each man arriving offered to help Lowe Junior with the digging. Some had even brought tools, but Lowe Junior stonily refused all offers.

"Ah be finished time the box git heah," he answered without looking at the men. "Sho do thank yo', tho'."

So the men sat and smoked, speaking only in murmurs and infrequently. The women passed out steaming plates of stew and tins of coffee bitter with chicory. Lowe Junior declined all food. The plates in the shack were emptied and rotated until all were fed. After a muttered consultation, one of the men approached Lowe Junior. He was old, his hair very white against his skin. He was very neat and careful of himself, moving with great dignity. His faded overalls were clean and shiny from the iron. He stood quietly at the side of the hole until Lowe Junior stopped work and looked up at him. Then he spoke, but so softly that the other men could not make out his words. The yard was very silent.

"Brothah Culvah. The peoples ain't easy in min'. They come to he'p yo' an heah yo' takin' no he'p." Lowe Junior said nothing.

"In time o' grief, praise Jesus, folks, they wants t', an' mo'n thet, they needs, t' he'p . . . they come t' pay respeck t' the daid an' share the burden an' sarrow o' d' livin'. Thass how hits allus bin . . . Son, when folks offer comfort an' he'p, a man mus' accep' hit, 'caus hit's mebbe all they got."

Lowe Junior looked at the old man.

"Yo' unnerstan' what ah'm asayin', son?" he asked gently. "The peoples doan feel like as if they got anythang t' do heah, anythang thet they needs t' be adoin'."

Lowe Junior looked into the darkness. His voice was low and without inflection. "Hit aint no he'p to give, ain't no sarrow t' share. Hits jes' thet the ol' woman was ol', an now she daid. Ain't no sarrow in thet."

They became aware of a sound. It came from the shack and at first did not seem to intrude or in any way challenge the dark silence. It began as a deep sonorous hum, close in pitch to the sound of silence. Then it grew, cadenced and inflected, gathering power and volume until it filled the yard and was present, physical and real. The men picked up the moan and it became a hymn.

hhhmmmmmmmmMMMAY THE CIRCLE . . . BE UN-
BROKEN BYE AN BYE, LAWD . . . BYE
ANNNN BYE

"Peoples can sang," Lowe Junior said. "Praise Jesus, they can allus do thet."

The old man walked away silent. He sat on the stoop ignoring the questioning looks of the others. He hunched over, his frail body gently rocking back and forth, as though moved against his will by the throbbing cadences of the singing. He sat there in isolation, his eyes looking into the darkness as at his own approaching end, his face etched with lines of a private and unnamable old man's sorrow. Deep and low in his chest he began to hum the dirge melody.

Lowe Junior chopped viciously at the earth. The people intoned the old and troubled music that they were born to, which, along with a capacity to endure, was their only legacy from the generations that had gone before, the music that gathered around them, close, warm and personal as the physical throbbing of their natural life.

When the hole was to Lowe Junior's chin, the Haskell boys came into the yard carrying the coffin. It was of green pitchpine, the boards rough-planed so that all depressions on the surface of the boards were sticky with sap. The men also brought two boxes so that the coffin would not rest on the ground. The Haskells stood by the hole, wiping their gummy hands on their overalls.

"Yo' reckon hit'll be awright?" Ben Haskell asked.

"Sholey. Sho, hit'll be jes fine. Yo' done real good; hits a coffin, ain't hit?" Lowe Junior still had not looked at the coffin, which was surrounded by the neighbor men. The Haskells stood silent, looking at him.

" 'Sides, ol' woman . . . allus was right partial t' scent o' pine. Yassuh, hit'll be right fine," Lowe Junior said. Ben Haskell smiled, a diffident embarrassed stretching of his mouth. "Yo' said cedar, but see, quick as yo' needed hit, pine wuz all we could git."

"Thass right," his brother assented.

Leastwise, Lowe Junior thought, Mist' Odum wouldn' give yo' all cedar fo' credit. He repeated softly, "Yo' done good, real good." The Haskells beamed, relieved, and expressed again their sympathy before moving away.

The yard was now full, some twenty persons stood, hunkered, or sat around. Set on the boxes in the center of the group, the raw white coffin dominated the scene like an altar, filling the air with the pungent odor of crude turpentine.

Lowe Junior walked around the coffin and approached the steps of the shack. The neighbors' eyes followed him. Sister

Beulah met him at the door. He saw the faces of the other women peering down at him from behind her. All conversation ceased.

"Brothah Culvah, this yer ah'm agonna say ain't strickly mah business. Some would say hit rightly ain't *none* o' mah concern atall." She paused, looking at Lowe Junior and the men in the yard. Nothing was said, and she continued. "But lookin' at hit anothah way, hit what ah'm gonna say, *is* mah business. Hits bin troublin' mah min', an hits lotsa othah folks heah, what ah *knows* feel d' same way." When she paused again, there was a faint assenting Ahmen from the people.

"So ah'm agonna say hit . . . Now, yo' all knows me, bin apreachin' an aservin' the Lawd in these parts fo' thutty year, an live heah thutty year befo' thet." Murmurs of "Thass right" came from the group.

"Yas, thass the Lawd's truth, an ah knows Sistah Culvah, Miss Alice we used t' call her, from the fust come off t' plantation, an' nobody evah had a word o' bad to say 'bout her, praise Jesus. Yas, an' ah know yo' po' mothah, an yo' se'f, Brothah Culvah, from evah since." The murmurs from the neighbors were stronger now. Encouraged, Sister Beulah continued. She was now speaking louder than anyone had spoken in the yard all evening.

"She wuz a good woman, a go-o-d woman, she knowed Jesus an' she wuz saved. Hits true, towards the las' when she wuz porely an' gittin' up in age, she couldn' git to meetin' to praise her Gawd, but yo' all knows she *lo-oved* the Church." She took a deep breath. "Now, ah knows thet back then, in slavery times, when the ol' folks could' do no bettah, an' had to hol' buryin's an' Chris'nin' an' evrah-thang at night. But, thank Jesus, them days is gone. They's gone. Hit ain't fittin' an' hit aint right an' propah t' hol' no buryin' at night, leas' hit ain't bin done herebouts. The body o' the good sistah, now called t' Glorah, ain't even bin churched. Yo' knows thet ain't right. Ah knows thet, effen she could have somepin t' say, she'd want hit done right at the las'! Ah *kno-o-ows* in mah heart she would."

"Yas, yas, ahah, praise Jesus." The neighbors agreed.

"An Brothah Culvah, yo' a young man, yo' a Gawd-fearin' man, an' ah knows yo' wants t' do right. Cause . . . yo' know hit says . . . the longes' road mus' ha' some endin', but a good name endureth fo'evah." On this dramatic and veiled note of warning the huge white-draped woman ended.

Everyone was quiet, but there was a faint expectant shuffling of feet as the people looked at Lowe Junior.

" 'Tain't no call t' fret yo'se'f," he said. "Ol' woman wuz ol' an now she gone. Ah be aburyin' her tonight." There was a quickly-stifled murmur from the people. No one spoke, and Lowe Junior continued more softly.

" 'Tain't thet whut yo' say ain't got right to hit, Sta' Beulah, 'cause hit do. But hits no law say thet effen yo' buryin' t' do, hit cain't be done in the night."

"Yas, Brothah Culvah, effen yo' *got* t' do hit. Doan seem like t' me hits no hurry . . ." Beulah said.

"Yas'm, hit is a hurry. See, ah feel like ah should take care o' this thang personal. Ol' woman raise me from when ah wuz young, ah wants t' take care o' the buryin' personal."

"Whut's wrong with t'morrow? Yo' answer me thet."

"Me no tellin' jes' where ah'll be t'morrow," Lowe Junior said, lifting one end of the coffin and asking Ben Haskell to help with the other end. They took it into the shack to receive the body.

"Hey, Lowe, yo' sho nuff fixin' t' leave?" Ben could not keep the excitement out of his voice.

"Thass right." Lowe Junior's first knowledge of his decision had come when he heard himself telling Beulah, a moment before.

"Yo' mean yo' ain't even gon' stay t' make yo' crop?"

"Any one o' yo' all wants t' work hit is welcome t' my share. Ah'll sign a paper so Mist' Peterson an Mist' Odum'll know." Temptation and fear struggled in Ben's eyes, and finally he said only, "Ah'll tell d' other'ns . . . but supposin' no one wants t' take hit?"

"Yo' mean 'bout Mist' Peterson . . . well, he got mo' cotton. Fack is, he got 'bout all theah is."

"Lawd's truth," Ben agreed, and went quickly to share the news with the men in the yard. There the women were grouped around Sister Beulah who was threatening to go home. After what she judged to be sufficient entreaty to mollify her hurt dignity, she agreed to remain and conduct the burial, but only because "hits mah bounden duty to see to hit thet the pore daid woman gits a propah Christian service." She led the women into the shack to put the old lady into the coffin.

After everyone had taken a last look at the corpse, Ben Haskell nailed the lid on and the coffin was brought out and placed on the boxes. During the singing of "Leaning on the Everlasting Arms," two of the women began to cry. Lowe Junior stood a short distance off under the shadow of the pecan tree and looked out over the darkness. He took no part in the singing until the lines of "Amazing Grace,"

> Ah wunst wuz lost but now ah'm Found,
> Wuz blind but now ah See.

In a loud but totally uninflected voice, he repeated "Wuz blind but now ah See."

This unexpected voice, coming as it were from behind her, distracted Sister Beulah who had begun to "line out" the succeeding lines for the benefit of any backsliders who might have forgotten them. She stopped, turned, and glared at Lowe Junior, then continued in the joyful and triumphant voice of one whose seat in the Kingdom is secure beyond all challenge.

"*'Twuz Grace thet taught mah heart t' feah,*" she exulted; "*An' Grace mah feah relieved.*" Her face was illuminated, radiant with the security of grace.

When the coffin was being lowered and was a quarter of the way down, the rope under the head slipped, and it thudded into the hole, almost upright. The people stood in momentary shocked silence. Sister Beulah at the head of the grave raised her massive white-sleeved arms to the sky as though appealing for divine vindication of this sacrilege, the result of Lowe Junior's stubbornness. Lowe Junior quickly lay flat on the edge of the grave, and shoved the high end of the coffin with all his strength. He grunted with the effort and the box slid into place with a heavy thump, followed by the rattle of dirt and pebbles from the sides.

At that moment the sky lightened. They all looked up and saw the risen moon peering from behind a wall of dark clouds that had not been there when the sun set.

"Glorah, Glorah!" a man shouted hoarsely, and the ritual resumed. Sister Beulah had thought to preach her famous "Dead Bones Arisin" sermon, capped with a few well-chosen words on the certain doom of impious children, but recent events had lessened her zeal. Almost perfunctorily she recounted the joys and glories of Salvation and the rewards awaiting the departed sister. Then they piled dirt on the coffin, patted down the pile, and departed.

Lowe Junior sat on the steps. Barely acknowledging the final murmured consolations, he watched the neighbors leave. He realized that he was not alone when the old man approached the stoop.

"Ah heah yo' is leavin', Brothah Culvah. Done any thankin' on wheah yo' goin' an' whut yo' gonna be doin'?"

Lowe Junior did not answer. He in no way acknowledged the old man's presence.

"Thass awright, yo' doan have t' answer 'cause ah knows—yo' ain't! Jes' like ah wuz when ah wuz 'bout yo' age. An ah lef' too, din' know wheah ah wuz agoin' nor whut ah wuz lookin' fo'. Effen yo' doan know whut yo' seekin', Brothah Culvah, yo' cain't know when yo' find hit."

Now Lowe Junior was looking at the man; he seemed interested in what he was saying. It was the first interest he had shown in anyone else that evening.

"See, Brothah Culvah, ah travelled aroun' some when ah wuz yowr age, an heah ah is now. Ah never foun' no bettah place nowheahs." He shook his head. "Fo' usses, theah wuzn't none, leastways not thet ah could fin'."

"But as leas' yo' looked," Lowe Junior said.

"Thass why ah'm asayin' t' yo' whut ah is. 'Cause ah did. Brothah Culvah, yo' a good worker, yo' knows farmin' an cotton, but whut else do yo' know? Ah disbelieves thet yo' even bin so far as Memphis."

"Well," Lowe Junior said, "t'morrow thet won' be true. But ah 'preciates yo' kin'ness."

The old man hobbled into the darkness, shrouded in his own knowledge.

Lowe Junior sat on the steps and watched him leave, until finally he was alone. He went to the tree, blew the lamp out, and sat in the darkness. . . . When the sun came up next morning he had not moved. The astringent pitchpine smell still hovered in the still air. Lowe Junior saw that the morning sky was covered by a heavy metallic-gray cloud that had come swirling up from the Gulf in the dark. He entered the shack and looked about him for something to take. In the old woman's room he found nothing. He returned, picked up his hoe, turned around in the small room, saw nothing else that he wanted, and started to leave. On the steps he changed his mind and reentered the house. In the old woman's room he took the picture of the Sacred Heart from the frame. Then from a small wooden box he took a Bible which he held by the covers and shook. Three crumpled bills fluttered to the floor. He gave the book a final shake, tossed it into the box, then picked up the bills and carefully wrapped them in the picture. He placed the package in the long deep side-pocket of his overalls. He picked up his hoe from the steps and started out. At the dirt road he turned, not towards the highway, but east towards his section. Soon he could see the top of the oak in the thin dawning light.

"Sho nevah put no stock in all thet talk 'bout thet tree," he mused. "Burned like thet on the sides an so green t' the top, hit allus did put me in min' o' Moses an the burnin' bush. But ah wager a daid houn', ain't no Nigger agoin' t' work thisyer lan' now."

He stood for awhile looking at the tree, at the lean runted plants. "Sho do feels like ah knows yo' evrah one, evrah row and clump o' grass like hit wuz the face o' mah own han' or mah own name."

He strode up to the tree, set his feet, and swung the hoe against the trunk with all the strength of his back. The hickory handle snapped with a crack like a rifle in the early morning. The blade went whirring into the cotton-rows. He felt the shock of the blow sting the palm of his hands, and shivver up into his shoulders. He stepped away from the tree and hurled the broken handle as far as he could into the field.

"Theah," he grunted, "yo' got the las' o' me thet yo' is gonna git—the natural las'."

He started back towards the highway at a dead run. There were tears in his eyes and his breath was gusty. He tired and slowed to a walk. He saw the first raindrops hitting heavy into the thick dust of the road, raising sudden explosions of dust and craters of dampness where they struck. Before he reached the cabin, torrents of water were lashing the face of the Delta. When he reached the highway, he turned once to look at the mean little house, gray and forlorn in the storm. He saw a pool already spreading around the roots of the pecan tree.

The dry earth gave off an acrid smell as the water dampened it. "Be nuff now fo' evrah one, white an black," Lowe Junior thought and laughed. "Sho doan mattah now effen they takes ovah mah fiel'. Hit be all washed out, evrah natural one."

The rain swept down with increased violence. He was completely drenched, streamlets ran down his face, washing away the dust. "Ah nevah seed the like. Sho now, be hongry folk heah this year. Even white folk be hongry in the Delta this winter." He walked steadily down the highway stretching into the distance.

AL YOUNG (1939–   )

Poet, novelist, and teacher of creative writing, Al Young sent the following autobiographical note in response to a query from the editor: "Born under Gemini at the outset of World War Two. Grew up in Southern & Midwestern U.S. Educated at the U. of Michigan & U. of California at Berkeley. For some time earned a precarious living as a musician & FM disc jockey, but have also worked in less glamorous fields. From late 1966 thru 1969 taught writing for the San Francisco Museum of Art's Teen Workshop Project, & served as instructor & linguistic consultant for the Neighborhood Youth Corps. Founded & edited the irregular review Loveletter in the late 1960s. Presently teaching creative writing at Stanford University & working on the novel Who Is Angelina? Recipient: Stegner Fellowship in Creative Writing, 1966; Joseph Henry Jackson Award, 1969; Natural Arts Council awards for writing & editing, 1969 & 1970. Books: Dancing, poems (Corinth Books, N.Y., 1969); Snakes, a novel (Holt, Rinehart & Winston, N.Y., 1970—Sidgwick & Jackson, London, 1971); The Song Turning Back Into Itself, poems (Holt, Rinehart & Winston, N.Y., 1971)." The following story was first published in Stanford Short Stories 1968.

Chicken Hawk's Dream

Chicken Hawk stayed high pretty much all the time and he was nineteen years old limping down academic corridors trying to make it to twelfth grade.

Unlike his good sidekick Wine, whose big reason for putting up with school was to please his mother, Chicken Hawk just loved the public school system and all the advantages that came with it. He could go on boarding at home, didnt have to work, and could mess over a whole year and not feel he'd lost anything.

He sat behind me in Homeroom Study Hall, sport shirt, creased pants, shiny black pointy-toed stetsons, jacket, processed hair. He'd look around him on lean days and say, "Say, man, why dont you buy this joint off me so I can be straight for lunch, I'd really appreciate it."

One morning he showed up acting funnier than usual. Turns out he was half-smashed and half-drunk because he'd smoked some dope when he got up that morning, then on the way to school he'd met up with Wine, so the two of them did up a fifth of Nature Boy, a brand of sweet wine well known around Detroit. Wine wasnt called Wine for nothing. Between the Thunderbird and Nature Boy he didnt know what to do with himself. He was a jokey kind of lad who drank heavily as a matter of form—his form. "I like to juice on general principle," is the way he put it.

That morning Chicken Hawk eased up to me during a class break. "Man, I had this dream, the grooviest dream I had in a long time, you wanna know how it went?"

By that time I thought I could anticipate anything Chicken Hawk would come up with, but for him to relate a private dream was something else, something new. "What you dream, man?"

"Dreamed I was walkin round New York, you know, walkin round all the places where Bird walked and seen all the shit he seen and all thru this dream I'm playin the background music to my own dream, dig, and it's on alto sax, man, and I'm cookin away somethin terrible and what surprise me is I can do the fingerin and all that jive—I can blow that horn, I know I can blow it in real life, I *know* I can! You know somebody got a horn I can borrow, I'll show everybody what I can do."

"Drew's got an alto and he live up the street from me. Maybe you could get your chops together on his horn. It dont belong to him tho, it's his brother's and Drew dont hardly touch it, he too busy woodsheddin his drums. I'll ask him if you can come over after school and play some."

"Aw, baby, yeah, nice, that's beautiful, Al, that sure would be beautiful if you could arrange all that. Think maybe Drew'd lemme borrow it for a few days?"

"Well, I dont know about all that, you could ask him."

"Yeah, unh-hunh, know what tune I wanna blow first?

Listen to this . . ."—and he broke off into whistling something off a very old LP.

Wellsir—Drew said OK, to bring Chicken Hawk on over and we'd see what he could do. "But if you ask me the dude aint nothin but another pot head with a lotta nerve. On the other hand he might just up and shake all of us up."

Six of us, mostly from band, went over to Drew's house after school to find out what Chicken Hawk could do with a saxophone. As we went stomping thru the snow, old Wine was passing the bottle—"Just a little taste, fellas, to brace ourself against the cold, dig it?"

Drew's mother, a gym teacher, took one look at us at the front door and said, "Now I know all you hoodlums is friendsa Drew's but you are not comin up in here trackin mud all over my nice rugs, so go on round the back way and wipe your feet before you go down in the basement, and I mean wipe em good!"

We got down there where Drew had his drums set up and Drew got out his brother's old horn. "Be careful with it, Chicken Hawk, it aint mine and Bruh gon need it when he get back from out the Service."

We all sat around to watch.

Chicken Hawk, tall, cool, took the horn and said, "Uh, show me how you hold this thing, just show me that, show me how you hold it and I'll do the rest."

"Show him how to hold it, Butter."

One of the reed players, a lightskin fellow named Butter, leaned over Chicken Hawk and showed him where to place his fingers on the keys. Chicken Hawk looked at Butter as tho he were insane. "Look here, gimme a little credit for knowin somethin about the thing will you, you aint got to treat me like I'm some little baby."

"Then go ahead and blow it, baby!"

"Damn, I shoulda turned on first, I'd do more better if I was high. Anybody got a joint they can lay on me?"

Everybody started getting mad and restless. Drew said, "Mister Chicken Hawk, sir, please blow somethin on the instrument and shut up!"

"Shit, you dudes dont think I can blow this thing but I mo show you."

"Then kindly show us."

Poor Chicken Hawk, he finally took a deep breath and huffed and puffed but not a sound could he make. "You sure this old raggedy horn work?"

"Dont worry about that, man," Drew told him, "just go head and play somethin. You know—*play?*"

Chicken Hawk slobbered all over the mouthpiece and blew on it and worked the keys until we could all hear them clicking but still no sound. He wiped his lips on his coat sleeve and called his boy Wine over. "Now, Wine, you see me playin on this thing, dont you?"

"Yes, I am quite aware of that, C.H."

"You see me scufflin with it and it still dont make a sound?"

"Yes, I aint heard anything, C.H., my man."

"Then, Wine, would you say—would you say just offhand that it could be that Drew's brother's horn aint no damn good?"

Old Wine looked around the room at each of us and rubbed his hands together and grinned. "Well, uh, now I'd say it's a possibility, but I dont know about that. Would you care for a little taste to loosen you up?"

Chicken Hawk screwed his face up, blew into the instrument and pumped keys until he turned colors but all that came out were some feeble little squeaks and pitiful honks. "Well gentlemen," he announced, "Ive had it with this axe. It dont work. It's too beat-up to work. It just aint no more good. I can blow it all right, O yeah—I could play music on it all right but how you expect me to get into anything on a jive horn?"

Drew took the saxophone and carefully packed it back inside its case. Wine passed Chicken Hawk the Nature Boy and we all started talking about something else. There were no jokes about what had just happened, no See-Now-What-I-Tell-You.

Drew got to showing us new things he'd worked out on drums for a Rock & Roll dance he'd be playing that weekend. He loved to think up new beats. After everyone got absorbed in what Drew was doing, Chicken Hawk and Wine, well-juiced, eased quietly up the back steps.

I saw Chicken Hawk on 12th Street in Detroit. He was out of his mind standing smack on the corner in the wind watching the light turn green, yellow, red, back to green, scratching his chin, and he smiled at me.

"Hey, Chicken Hawk!"

"Hey now, what's goin on?"

"You got it."

"And dont I know it, I'm takin off for New York next week."

"What you gon do in New York?"

"See if I can get me a band together and cut some albums and stuff."

"Well—well, that's great, man, I hope you make it. Keep pushin."

"Gotta go get my instrument out of the pawnshop first, mmmm—you know how it is."

"Yeah, well, all right, take care yourself, man."

JAMES ALAN McPHERSON (1943–   )

Born in Savannah, Georgia, James Alan McPherson grew up in that city, attended Morgan State College in Baltimore, and graduated from Morris Brown College in Atlanta in 1965. In that year he was awarded the combined Reader's Digest-United Negro College Fund prize for literature. He went on to Harvard Law school, which he graduated in 1968, and continued to write short stories during his law studies. He won an Atlantic award for the best new story of 1968 to appear in that magazine. He received an award from Atlantic to write a volume of short stories which was subsequently entitled Hue and Cry and published in hardcover in 1969 and in paperback in 1970. This is his only published book to date. After graduating from Harvard he went into journalism for a while, has taught English at the University of Iowa, and is a contributing editor to The Atlantic. Ralph Ellison has hailed McPherson as "a writer of insight, sympathy, and humor and one of the most gifted young Americans I've had the privilege to read." The following story is from McPherson's book Hue and Cry.

A Solo Song: For Doc

So you want to know this business, youngblood? So you want to be a Waiter's Waiter? The Commissary gives you a book with all the rules and tells you to learn them. And you do, and think that is all there is to it. A big, thick black book. Poor youngblood.

Look at me. *I* am a Waiter's Waiter. I know all the moves, all the pretty, fine moves that big book will never teach you. *I* built this railroad with my moves; and so did Sheik Beasley and Uncle T. Boone and Danny Jackson, and so did Doc Craft. That book they made you learn came from our moves and from our heads. There was a time when six of us, big men, danced at the same time in that little Pantry without touching and shouted orders to the sweating paddies in the kitchen. There was a time when they *had* to respect us because our sweat and our moves supported them. We knew the service and the paddies, even the green dishwashers, knew that we did and didn't give us the crap they pull on you.

Do you know how to sneak a Blackplate to a nasty cracker? Do you know how to rub asses with five other men in the Pantry getting their orders together and still know that you are a man, just like them? Do you know how to bullshit while you work and keep the paddies in their places with your bullshit? Do you know how to breathe down the back of an old lady's dress to hustle a bigger tip?

No. You are summer stuff, youngblood. I am old, my moves are not so good any more, but I know this business. The Commissary hires you for the summer because they don't want to let anyone get as old as me on them. I'm sixty-three, but they can't fire me: I'm in the Union. They can't lay me off for fucking up: I know this business too well. And so they hire you, youngblood, for the summer when the tourists come, and in September you go away with some tips in your pocket to buy pussy and they wait all winter for me to die. I am dying, youngblood, and so is this business. Both of us will die together. There'll always be summer stuff like you, but the big men, the big trains, are dying every day and everybody can see it. And nobody but us who are dying with them gives a damn.

Look at the big picture at the end of the car, youngblood. That's the man who built this road. He's in your history books. He's probably in that big black bible you read. He was a great man. He hated people. He didn't want to feed them but the government said he had to. He didn't want to hire me, but he needed me to feed the people. I know this, youngblood, and that is why that book is written for you and that is why I have never read it. That is why you get nervous and jump up to polish the pepper and salt shakers when the word comes down the line that an inspector is getting on at the next stop. That is why you warm the toast covers for every cheap old lady who wants to get coffee and toast and good service for sixty-five cents and a dime tip. You know that he needs you only for the summer and that hundreds of youngbloods like you want to work this summer to buy that pussy in Chicago and Portland and Seattle. The man uses you, but he doesn't need you. But me he needs for the winter, when you are gone, and to teach you something in the summer about this business you can't get from that big black book. He needs me and he knows it and I know it. That is why I am sitting here when there are tables to be cleaned and linen to be changed and silver to be washed and polished. He needs me to die. That is why I am taking my time. I know it. And I will take his service with me when I die, just like the Sheik did and like Percy Fields did, and like Doc.

Who are they? Why do I keep talking about them? Let me think about it. I guess it is because they were the last of the Old School, like me. We made this road. We got a million miles of walking up and down these cars under our feet. Doc Craft was the Old School, like me. He was a Waiter's Waiter. He danced down these aisles with us and swung his tray with the roll of the train, never spilling in all his trips a single cup of coffee. He could carry his tray on two fingers, or on one and a half if he wanted, and he knew all the tricks about hustling tips there are to know. He could work anybody. The girls at the Northland in Chicago knew Doc, and the girls at the Haverville in Seattle, and the girls at the Step-Inn in Portland and all the girls in Winnipeg knew Doc Craft.

But wait. It is just 1:30 and the first call for dinner is not until 5:00. You want to kill some time; you want to hear about the Old School and how it was in my day. If you look in that black book you would see that you should be polishing silver now. Look out the window; this is

North Dakota, this is Jerry's territory. Jerry, the Unexpected Inspector. Shouldn't you polish the shakers or clean out the Pantry or squeeze oranges, or maybe change the linen on the tables? Jerry Ewald is sly. The train may stop in the middle of this wheatfield and Jerry may get on. He lives by that book. He knows where to look for dirt and mistakes. Jerry Ewald, the Unexpected Inspector. He knows where to look; he knows how to get you. He got Doc.

Now you want to know about him, about the Old School. You have even put aside your book of rules. But see how you keep your finger in the pages as if the book was more important than what I tell you. That's a bad move, and it tells on you. You will be a waiter. But you will never be a Waiter's Waiter. The Old School died with Doc, and the very last of it is dying with me. What happened to Doc? Take your finger out of the pages, youngblood, and I will tell you about a kind of life these rails will never carry again.

When your father was a boy playing with himself behind the barn, Doc was already a man and knew what the thing was for. But he got tired of using it when he wasn't much older than you, and he set his mind on making money. He had no skills. He was black. He got hungry. On Christmas Day in 1916, the story goes, he wandered into the Chicago stockyards and over to a dining car waiting to be connected up to the main train for the Chicago-to-San Francisco run. He looked up through the kitchen door at the chef storing supplies for the kitchen and said: "I'm hungry."

"What do you want *me* to do about it?" the Swede chef said.

"I'll work," said Doc.

That Swede was Chips Magnusson, fresh off the boat and lucky to be working himself. He did not know yet that he should save all extra work for other Swedes fresh off the boat. He later learned this by living. But at that time he considered a moment, bit into one of the fresh apples stocked for apple pie, chewed considerably, spit out the seeds and then waved the black on board the big train. "You can eat all you want," he told Doc. "But you work all I tell you."

He put Doc to rolling dough for the apple pies and the train began rolling for Doc. It never stopped. He fell in love with the feel of the wheels under his feet clicking against the track and he got the rhythm of the wheels in him and learned, like all of us, how to roll with them and move with them. After that first trip Doc was never at home on the ground. He worked everything in the kitchen from putting out dough to second cook, in six years. And then, when the Commissary saw that he was good and would soon be going for one of the chef's spots they saved for the Swedes, they put him out of the kitchen and told him to learn this waiter business; and told him to learn how to bullshit on the other side of the Pantry. He was almost thirty, youngblood, when he crossed over to the black side of the Pantry. I wasn't there when he made his first trip as a waiter, but from what they tell me of that trip I know that he was broke in by good men. Pantryman was Shiek Beasley, who stayed high all the time and let the waiters steal anything they wanted as long as they didn't bother his reefers. Danny Jackson, who was black and knew Shakespeare before the world said he could work with it, was second man. Len Dickey was third, Reverend Hendricks was fourth, and Uncle T. Boone, who even in those early days could not straighten his back, ran fifth. Doc started in as sixth waiter, the "mule." They pulled some shit on him at first because they didn't want somebody fresh out of a paddy kitchen on the crew. They messed with his orders, stole his plates, picked up his tips on the sly, and made him do all the dirty work. But when they saw that he could take the shit without getting hot and when they saw that he was set on being a waiter, even though he was older than most of them, they settled down and began to teach him this business and all the words and moves and slickness that made it a good business.

His real name was Leroy Johnson, I think, but when Danny Jackson saw how cool and neat he was in his moves, and how he handled the plates, he began to call him "the Doctor." Then the Sheik, coming down from his high one day after missing the lunch and dinner service, saw how Doc had taken over his station and collected fat tips from his tables by telling the passengers that the Sheik had had to get off back along the line because of a heart attack. The Sheik liked that because he saw that Doc understood crackers and how they liked nothing better than knowing that a nigger had died on the job, giving them service. The Sheik was impressed. And he was not an easy man to impress because he knew too much about life and had to stay high most of the time. And when Doc would not split the tips with him, the Sheik got mad at first and called Doc a barrel of motherfuckers and some other words you would not recognize. But he was impressed. And later that night, in the crew car when the others were gambling and drinking and bullshitting about the women they had working the corners for them, the Sheik came over to Doc's bunk and said: "You're a crafty mother-fucker."

"Yeah?" says Doc.

"Yeah," says the Sheik, who did not say much. "You're a crafty motherfucker but I like you." Then he got into the first waiter's bunk and lit up again. But Reverend Hendricks, who always read his Bible before going to sleep and who always listened to anything the Sheik said because he knew the Sheik only said something when it was important, heard what was said and remembered it. After he put his Bible back in his locker, he walked over to Doc's bunk and looked down at him. "Mister Doctor Craft," the Reverend said. "Young-blood Doctor Craft."

"Yeah?" says Doc.

"Yeah, says Reverend Hendricks. "That's who you are." And that's who he was from then on.

II

I came to the road away from the war. This was after '41, when people at home were looking for Japs under their beds every night. I did not want to fight because there was no money in it and I didn't want to go overseas to work in a kitchen. The big war was on and a lot of soldiers crossed the country to get to it, and as long as a black man fed them on trains he did not have to go to that war. I could have got a job in a Chicago factory, but there was more money on the road and it was safer. And after a while it got into your blood so that you couldn't leave it for anything. The road got into my blood the way it got into everybody's; the way going to the war got in the blood of redneck farm boys and the crazy Polacks from Chicago. It was all right for them to go to the war. They were young and stupid. And they died that way. I played it smart. I was almost thirty-five and I didn't want to go. But I took *them* and fed them and gave them good times on their way to the war, and for that I did not have to go. The soldiers had plenty of money and were afraid not to spend it all before they got to the ships on the Coast. And we gave them ways to spend it on the trains.

Now in those days there was plenty of money going around and everybody stole from everybody. The kitchen stole food from the company and the company knew it and wouldn't pay good wages. There were no rules in those days, there was no black book to go by and nobody said what you couldn't eat or steal. The paddy cooks used to toss boxes of steaks off the train in the Chicago yards for people at the restaurants there who paid them, cash. These were the days when ordinary people had to have red stamps or blue stamps to get powdered eggs and white lard to mix with red powder to make their own butter.

The stewards stole from the company and from the waiters; the waiters stole from the stewards and the company and from each other. I stole. Doc stole. Even Reverend Hendricks put his Bible far back in his locker and stole with us. You didn't want a man on your crew who didn't steal. He made it bad for everybody. And if the steward saw that he was a dummy and would never get to stealing, he wrote him up for something and got him off the crew so as not to slow down the rest of us. We had a redneck cracker steward from Alabama by the name of Casper who used to say: *"Jesus Christ! I ain't got time to hate you niggers, I'm making so much money."* He used to keep all his cash at home under his bed in a cardboard box because he was afraid to put it in the bank.

Doc and Sheik Beasley and me were on the same crew together all during the war. Even in those days, as young as we were, we knew how to be Old Heads. We organized for the soldiers. We had to wear skullcaps all the time because the crackers said our hair was poison and didn't want any of it to fall in their food. The Sheik didn't mind wearing one. He kept reefers in his and used to sell them to the soldiers for double what he paid for them in Chicago and three times what he paid the Chinamen in Seattle. That's why we called him the Sheik. After every meal the Sheik would get in the linen closet and light up. Sometimes he wouldn't come out for days. Nobody gave a damn, though; we were all too busy stealing and working. And there was more for us to get as long as he didn't come out.

Doc used to sell bootlegged booze to the soldiers; that was his specialty. He had redcaps in the Chicago stations telling the soldiers who to ask for on the train. He was an open operator and had to give the steward a cut, but he still made a pile of money. That's why that old cracker always kept us together on his crew. We were the three best moneymakers he ever had. That's something you should learn, youngblood. They can't love you for being you. They only love you if you make money for them. All that talk these days about integration and brotherhood, that's a lot of bullshit. The man will love you as long as he can make money with you. I made money. And old Casper had to love me in the open although I knew he called me a nigger at home when he had put that money in his big cardboard box. I know he loved me on the road in the wartime because I used to bring in the biggest moneymakers. I used to handle the girls.

Look out that window. See all that grass and wheat? Look at that big farm boy cutting it. Look at that burnt cracker on that tractor. He probably has a wife who married him because she didn't know what else to do. Back during wartime the girls in this part of the country knew what to do. They got on the trains at night.

You can look out that window all day and run around all the stations when we stop, but you'll never see a black man in any of these towns. You know why, youngblood? These farmers hate you. They still remember when their girls came out of these towns and got on the trains at night. They've been running black men and dark Indians out of these towns for years. They hate anything dark that's not that way because of the sun. Right now there are big farm girls with hair under their arms on the corners in San Francisco, Chicago, Seattle and Minneapolis who got started on these cars back during wartime. The farmers still remember that and they hate you and me for it. But it wasn't for me they got on. Nobody wants a stiff, smelly farm girl when there are sporting women to be got for a dollar in the cities. It was for the soldiers they got on. It was just business to me. But they hate you and me anyway.

I got off in one of these towns once, a long time after the war, just to get a drink while the train changed engines. Everybody looked at me and by the time I got to a bar there were ten people on my trail. I was drinking a fast one when the sheriff came in the bar.

"What are you doing here?" he asks me.

"Just getting a shot," I say.

He spit on the floor. "How long you plan to be here?"

"I don't know," I say, just to be nasty.

"There ain't no jobs here," he says.

"I wasn't looking," I say.

"We don't want you here."

"I don't give a good goddamn," I say.

He pulled his gun on me. "All right, coon, back on the train," he says.

"Wait a minute," I tell him. "Let me finish my drink."

He knocked my glass over with his gun. "You're finished *now*," he says. "Pull your ass out of here *now!*"

I didn't argue.

I was the night man. After dinner it was my job to pull the cloths off the tables and put paddings on. Then I cut out the lights and locked both doors. There was a big farm girl from Minot named Hilda who could take on eight or ten soldiers in one night, white soldiers. These white boys don't know how to last. I would stand by the door and when the soldiers came back from the club car they would pay me and I would let them in. Some of the girls could make as much as one hundred dollars in one night. And I always made twice as much. Soldiers don't care what they do with their money. They just have to spend it.

We never bothered with the girls ourselves. It was just business as far as we were concerned. But there was one dummy we had with us once, a boy from the South named Willie Joe something who handled the dice. He was really hot for one of these farm girls. He used to buy her good whiskey and he hated to see her go in the car at night to wait for the soldiers. He was a real dummy. One time I heard her tell him: "It's all right. They can have my body. I know I'm black inside. *Jesus*, I'm so black inside I wisht I was black all over!"

And this dummy Willie Joe said: "Baby, *don't you ever change!*"

I knew we had to get rid of him before he started trouble. So we had the steward bump him off the crew as soon as we could find a good man to handle the gambling. That old redneck Casper was glad to do it. He saw what was going on.

But you want to hear about Doc, you say, so you can get back to your reading. What can I tell you? The road got into his blood? He liked being a waiter? You won't understand this, but he did. There were no Civil Rights or marches or riots for something better in those days. In those days a man found something he liked to do and liked it from then on because he couldn't help himself. What did he like about the road? He liked what I liked: the money, owning the car, running it, telling the soldiers what to do, hustling a bigger tip from some old maid by looking under her dress and laughing at her, having all the girls at the Haverville Hotel waiting for us to come in for stopover, the power we had to beat them up or lay them if we wanted. He liked running free and not being married to some bitch who would spend his money when he was out of town or give it to some stud. He liked getting drunk with the boys up at Andy's, setting up the house and then passing out from drinking too much, knowing that the boys would get him home.

I ran with that one crew all during wartime and they, Doc, the Sheik and Reverend Hendricks, had taken me under their wings. I was still a youngblood then, and Doc liked me a lot. But he never said that much to me; he was not a talker. The Sheik had taught him the value of silence in things that really matter. We roomed together in Chicago at Mrs. Wright's place in those days. Mrs. Wright didn't allow women in the rooms and Doc liked that, because after being out for a week and after stopping over in those hotels along the way, you get tired of women and bullshit and need your privacy. We weren't like you. We didn't need a woman every time we got hard. We knew when we had to have it and when we didn't. And we didn't spend all our money on it, either. You youngbloods think the way to get a woman is to let her see how you handle your money. That's stupid. The way to get a woman is to let her see how you handle other women. But you'll never believe that until it's too late to do you any good.

Doc knew how to handle women. I can remember a time in a Winnipeg hotel how he ran a bitch out of his room because he had enough of it and did not need her any more. I was in the next room and heard everything.

"Come on, Doc," the bitch said. "Come on honey, let's do it one more time."

"Hell no," Doc said. "I'm tired and I don't want to any more."

"How can you say you're tired?" the bitch said. "How can you say you're tired when you didn't go but two times?"

"I'm tired of it," Doc said, "because I'm tired of you. And I'm tired of you because I'm tired of it and bitches like you in all the towns I been in. You drain a man. And I know if I beat you, you'll still come back when I hit you again. *That's* why I'm tired. I'm tired of having things around I don't care about."

"What *do* you care about, Doc?" the bitch said.

"I don't know," Doc said, "I guess I care about moving and being somewhere else when I want to be. I guess I care about going out, and coming in to wait for the time to go out again."

"You crazy, Doc," the bitch said.

"Yeah?" Doc said. "I guess I'm crazy all right."

Later that bitch knocked on my door and I did it for

her because she was just a bitch and I knew Doc wouldn't want her again. I don't think he ever wanted a bitch again. I never saw him with one after that time. He was just a little over fifty then and could have still done whatever he wanted with women.

The war ended. The farm boys who got back from the war did not spend money on their way home. They did not want to spend any more money on women, and the girls did not get on at night any more. Some of them went into the cities and turned pro. Some of them stayed in the towns and married the farm boys who got back from the war. Things changed on the road. The Commissary started putting that book of rules together and told us to stop stealing. They were losing money on passengers now because of the airplanes and they began to really tighten up and started sending inspectors down along the line to check on us. They started sending in spotters, too. One of them caught that red-neck Casper writing out a check for two dollars less than he had charged the spotter. The Commissary got him in on the rug for it. I wasn't there, but they told me he said to the General Superintendent: "Why are you getting on me, a white man, for a lousy son-of-a-bitching two bucks? There's niggers out there been stealing for *years!*"

"Who?" the General Superintendent asked.

And Casper couldn't say anything because he had that cardboard box full of money still under his bed and knew he would have to tell how he got it if any of us was brought in. So he said nothing.

"Who?" the General Superintendent asked him again.

"Why, all them nigger waiters steal, *everybody knows that!*"

"And the cooks, what about them?" the Superintendent said.

"They're white," said Casper.

They never got the story out of him and he was fired. He used the money to open a restaurant someplace in Indiana and I heard later that he started a branch of the Klan in his town. One day he showed up at the station and told Doc, Reverend Hendricks and me: "I'll see you boys get *yours.* Damn if I'm takin' the rap for you niggers."

We just laughed in his face because we knew he could do nothing to us through the Commissary. But just to be safe we stopped stealing so much. But they did get the Sheik, though. One day an inspector got on in the mountains just outside of Whitefish and grabbed him right out of that linen closet. The Sheik had been smoking in there all day and he was high and laughing when they pulled him off the train.

That was the year we got in the Union. The crackers and Swedes finally let us in after we paid off. We really stopped stealing and got organized and there wasn't a damn thing the company could do about it, although it tried like hell to buy us out. And to get back at us, they put their heads together and began to make up that big book of rules you keep your finger in. Still, *we* knew the service and they had to write the book the way we gave the service and at first there was nothing for the Old School men to learn. We got seniority through the Union, and as long as we gave the service and didn't steal, they couldn't touch us. So they began changing the rules, and sending us notes about the service. Little changes at first, like how the initials on the doily should always face the customer, and how the silver should be taken off the tables between meals. But we were getting old and set in our old service, and it got harder and harder learning all those little changes. And we had to learn new stuff all the time because there was no telling when an inspector would get on and catch us giving bad service. It was hard as hell. It was hard because we knew that the company was out to break up the Old School. The Sheik was gone, and we knew that Reverend Hendricks or Uncle T. or Danny Jackson would go soon because they stood for the Old School, just like the Sheik. But what bothered us most was knowing that they would go for Doc first, before anyone else, because he loved the road so much.

Doc was over sixty-five then and had taken to drinking hard when we were off. But he never touched a drop when we were on the road. I used to wonder whether he drank because being a Waiter's Waiter was getting hard or because he had to do something until his next trip. I could never figure it. When we had our layovers he would spend all his time in Andy's, setting up the house. He had no wife, no relatives, not even a hobby. He just drank. Pretty soon the slicksters at Andy's got to using him for a good thing. They commenced putting the touch on him because they saw he was getting old and knew he didn't have far to go, and they would never have to pay him back. Those of us who were close to him tried to pull his coat, but it didn't help. He didn't talk about himself much, he didn't talk much about anything that wasn't related to the road; but when I tried to hip him once about the hustlers and how they were closing in on him, he just took another shot and said:

"I don't need no money. Nobody's jiving me. I'm jiving them. You know I can still pull in a hundred in tips in one trip. I *know* this business."

"Yeah, I know, Doc," I said. "But how many more trips can you make before you have to stop?"

"I ain't never gonna stop. Trips are all I know and I'll be making them as long as these trains haul people."

"That's just it," I said. "They don't *want* to haul people any more. The planes do that. The big roads want freight now. Look how they hired youngbloods just for the busy seasons just so they won't get any seniority in the winter. Look how all the Old School waiters are dropping out. They got the Sheik, Percy Fields just lucked up and died before they got to *him*, they almost got Reverend Hendricks. Even *Uncle T.* is going to retire! And they'll get us too."

"Not me," said Doc. "I know my moves. This old fox can still dance with a tray and handle four tables at the same time. I can still bait a queer and make the old ladies tip big. There's no waiter better than me and I know it."

"Sure, Doc," I said. "I know it too. But please save your money. Don't be a dummy. There'll come a day when you just can't get up to go out and they'll put you on the ground for good."

Doc looked at me like he had been shot. "Who taught you the moves when you were just a raggedy-ass waiter?"

"You did, Doc," I said.

"Who's always the first man down in the yard at train-time?" He threw down another shot. "Who's there sitting in the car every tenth morning while you other old heads are still at home pulling on your longjohns?"

I couldn't say anything. He was right and we both knew it.

"I have to go out," he told me. "Going out is my whole life, I wait for that tenth morning. I ain't never missed a trip and I don't mean to."

What could I say to him, youngblood? What can I say to you? He had to go out, not for the money; it was in his blood. You have to go out too, but it's for the money you go. You hate going out and you love coming in. He loved going out and he hated coming in. Would *you* listen if I told you to stop spending your money on pussy in Chicago? Would he listen if I told him to save *his* money? To stop setting up the bar at Andy's? No. Old men are just as bad as young men when it comes to money. They can't think.

They always try to buy what they should have for free. And what they buy, after they have it, is nothing.

They called Doc into the Commissary and the doctors told him he had lumbago and a bad heart and was weak from drinking too much, and they wanted him to get down for his own good. He wouldn't do it. Tesdale, the General Superintendent, called him in and told him that he had enough years in the service to pull down a big pension and that the company would pay for a retirement party for him, since he was the oldest waiter working, and invite all the Old School waiters to see him off, if he would come down. Doc said no. He knew that the Union had to back him. He knew that he could ride as long as he made the trains on time and as long as he knew the service. And he knew that he could not leave the road.

The company called in its lawyers to go over the Union contract. I wasn't there, but Len Dickey was in on the meeting because of his office in the Union. He told me about it later. Those fat company lawyers took the contract apart and went through all their books. They took the seniority clause apart word by word, trying to figure a way to get at Doc. But they had written it airtight back in the days when the company *needed* waiters, and there was nothing in it about compulsory retirement. Not a word. The paddies in the Union must have figured that waiters didn't *need* a new contract when they let us in, and they had let us come in under the old one thinking that all waiters would die on the job, or drink themselves to death when they were still young, or die from buying too much pussy, or just quit when they had put in enough time to draw a pension. But *nothing* in the whole contract could help them get rid of Doc Craft. They were sweating, they were working so hard. And all the time Tesdale, the General Superintendent, was calling them sons-of-bitches for not earning their money. But there was nothing the company lawyers could do but turn the pages of their big books and sweat and promise Tesdale that they would find some way if he gave them more time.

The word went out from the Commissary: "Get Doc." The stewards got it from the assistant superintendents: "Get Doc." Since they could not get him to retire, they were determined to catch him giving bad service. He had more seniority than most other waiters, so they couldn't bump him off our crew. In fact, all the waiters with more seniority than Doc were on the crew with him. There were four of us from the the Old School: me, Doc, Uncle T. Boone, and Danny

Jackson. Reverend Hendricks wasn't running regular any more; he was spending all his Sundays preaching in his Church on the South Side because he knew what was coming and wanted to have something steady going for him in Chicago when his time came. Fifth and sixth men on that crew were two hardheads who had read the book. The steward was Crouse, and he really didn't want to put the screws to Doc but he couldn't help himself. Everybody wants to work. So Crouse started in to riding Doc, sometimes about moving too fast, sometimes about not moving fast enough. I was on the crew, I saw it all. Crouse would seat four singles at the same table, on Doc's station, and Doc had to take care of all four different orders at the same time. He was seventy-three, but that didn't stop him, knowing this business the way he did. It just slowed him down some. But Crouse got on him even for that and would chew him out in front of the passengers, hoping that he'd start cursing and bother the passengers so that they would complain to the company. It never worked, though. Doc just played it cool. He'd look into Crouse's eyes and know what was going on. And then he'd lay on his good service, the only service he knew, and the passengers would see how good he was with all that age on his back and they would get mad at the steward, and leave Doc a bigger tip when they left.

The Commissary sent out spotters to catch him giving bad service. These were pale-white little men in glasses who never looked you in the eye, but who always felt the plate to see if it was warm. And there were the old maids, who like that kind of work, who would order shrimp or crabmeat cocktails or celery and olive plates because they knew how the rules said these things had to be made. And when they came, when Doc brought them out, they would look to see if the oyster fork was stuck into the thing, and look out the window a long time.

"Ain't no use trying to fight it," Uncle T. Boone told Doc in the crew car one night, "the black waiter is *doomed*. Look at all the good restaurants, the class restaurants in Chicago. *You* can't work in them. Them white waiters got those jobs sewed up fine."

"I can be a waiter anywhere," says Doc. "I know the business and I like it and I can do it anywhere."

"The black waiter is doomed," Uncle T. says again. "The whites is taking over the service in the good places. And when they run you off of here, you won't have no place to go."

"They won't run me off of here," says Doc. "As long as I give the right service they can't touch me."

"You're a goddamn *fool!*" says Uncle T. "You're a nigger and you ain't got no right except what the Union says you have. And that ain't worth a damn because when the Commissary finally gets you, those niggers won't lift a finger to help you."

"Leave off him," I say to Boone. "If anybody ought to be put off it's you. You ain't had your back straight for thirty years. You even make the crackers sick the way you keep bowing and folding your hands and saying, 'Thank you, Mr. Boss.' Fifty years ago that would of got you a bigger tip," I say, "but now it ain't worth a shit. And every time you do it the crackers hate you. And every time I see you serving with that skullcap on *I* hate you. The Union said we didn't have to wear them *eighteen years ago!* Why can't you take it off?"

Boone just sat on his bunk with his skullcap in his lap, leaning against his big belly. He knew I was telling the truth and he knew he wouldn't change. But he said: "That's the trouble with the Negro waiter today. He ain't got no humility. And as long as he don't have humility, he keeps losing the good jobs."

Doc had climbed into the first waiter's bunk in his longjohns and I got in the second waiter's bunk under him and lay there. I could hear him breathing. It had a hard sound. He wasn't well and all of us knew it.

"Doc?" I said in the dark.

"Yeah?"

"Don't mind Boone, Doc. He's a dead man. He just don't know it."

"We all are," Doc said.

"Not you," I said.

"What's the use? He's right. They'll get me in the end."

"But they ain't done it yet."

"They'll get me. And they know it and I know it. I can even see it in old Crouse's eyes. He knows they're gonna get me."

"Why don't you get a woman?"

He was quiet. "What can I do with a woman now, that I ain't already done too much?"

I thought for a while. "If you're on the ground, being with one might not make it so bad."

"I hate women," he said.

"You ever try fishing?"

"No."

"You want to?"

"No," he said.

"You can't keep *drinking*."

He did not answer.

"Maybe you could work in town. In the Commissary."

I could hear the big wheels rolling and clicking along the tracks and I knew by the smooth way we were moving that we were almost out of the Dakota flatlands. Doc wasn't talking. "Would you like that?" I thought he was asleep. "Doc, would you like that?"

"Hell no," he said.

"You have to try *something!*"

He was quiet again. "I know," he finally said.

III

Jerry Ewald, the Unexpected Inspector, got on in Winachee that next day after lunch and we knew that he had the word from the Commissary. He was cool about it: he laughed with the steward and the waiters about the old days and his hard gray eyes and shining glasses kept looking over our faces as if to see if we knew why he had got on. The two hardheads were in the crew car stealing a nap on company time. Jerry noticed this and could have caught them, but he was after bigger game. We all knew that, and we kept talking to him about the days of the big trains and looking at his white hair and not into the eyes behind his glasses because we knew what was there. Jerry sat down on the first waiter's station and said to Crouse: "Now I'll have some lunch. Steward, let the headwaiter bring me a menu."

Crouse stood next to the table where Jerry sat, and looked at Doc, who had been waiting between the tables with his tray under his arm. The way the rules say. Crouse looked sad because he knew what was coming. Then Jerry looked directly at Doc and said: "Headwaiter Doctor Craft, bring me a menu."

Doc said nothing and he did not smile. He brought the menu. Danny Jackson and I moved back into the hall to watch. There was nothing we could do to help Doc and we knew it. He was the Waiter's Waiter, out there by himself, hustling the biggest tip he would ever get in his life. Or losing it.

"Goddamn," Danny said to me. "Now let's sit on the ground and talk about how *kings* are gonna get fucked."

"Maybe not," I said. But I did not believe it myself because Jerry is the kind of man who lies in bed all night, scheming. I knew he had a plan.

Doc passed us on his way to the kitchen for water and I wanted to say something to him. But what was the use? He brought the water to Jerry. Jerry looked him in the eye. "Now, Headwaiter," he said. "I'll have a bowl of onion soup, a cold roast beef sandwich on white, rare, and a glass of iced tea."

"Write it down," said Doc. He was playing it right. He knew that the new rules had stopped waiters from taking verbal orders.

"Don't be so professional, Doc," Jerry said. "It's me, one of the *boys*."

"You have to write it out," said Doc, "it's in the black book."

Jerry clicked his pen and wrote the order out on the check. And handed it to Doc. Uncle T. followed Doc back into the Pantry.

"He's gonna get you, Doc," Uncle T. said. "I knew it all along. You know why? The Negro waiter ain't got no more humility."

"Shut the fuck up, Boone!" I told him.

"You'll see," Boone went on. "You'll see I'm right. There ain't a thing Doc can do about it, either. We're gonna lose all the good jobs."

We watched Jerry at the table. He saw us watching and smiled with his gray eyes. Then he poured some of the water from the glass on the linen cloth and picked up the silver sugar bowl and placed it right on the wet spot. Doc was still in the Pantry. Jerry turned the silver sugar bowl around and around on the linen. He pressed down on it some as he turned. But when he picked it up again, there was no dark ring on the wet cloth. We had polished the silver early that morning, according to the book, and there was not a dirty piece of silver to be found in the whole car. Jerry was drinking the rest of the water when Doc brought out the polished silver soup tureen, underlined with a doily and a breakfast plate, with a shining soup bowl underlined with a doily and a breakfast plate, and a bread-and-butter plate with six crackers; not four or five or seven, but six, the number the Commissary had written in the black book. He swung down the aisle of the car between the two rows of white tables and you could not help but be proud of the way he moved with the roll of the train and the way that tray was like a part of his arm. It was good service. He placed everything neat, with all company initials showing, right where things should go.

"Shall I serve up the soup?" he asked Jerry.

"Please," said Jerry.

Doc handled that silver soup ladle like one of those Chicago Jew tailors handles a needle. He ladled up three good-sized spoonfuls from the tureen and then laid the wet spoon on an extra bread-and-butter plate on the side of the table, so he would not stain the cloth. Then he put a napkin over the wet spot Jerry had made and changed the ashtray for a prayer-card because every good waiter knows that nobody wants to eat a good meal looking at an ashtray.

"You know about the spoon plate, I see," Jerry said to Doc.

"I'm a waiter," said Doc. "I know."

"You're a damn good waiter," said Jerry.

Doc looked Jerry square in the eye. "I know," he said slowly.

Jerry ate a little of the soup and opened all six of the cracker packages. Then he stopped eating and began to look out the window. We were passing through his territory, Washington State, the country he loved because he was the only company inspector in the state and knew that once he got through Montana he would be the only man the waiters feared. He smiled and then waved for Doc to bring out the roast beef sandwich.

But Doc was into his service now and cleared the table completely. Then he got the silver crumb knife from the Pantry and gathered all the cracker crumbs, even the ones Jerry had managed to get in between the salt and pepper shakers.

"You want the tea with your sandwich, or later?" he asked Jerry.

"Now is fine," said Jerry, smiling.

"You're doing good," I said to Doc when he passed us on his way to the Pantry. "He can't touch you or nothing."

He did not say anything.

Uncle T. Boone looked at Doc like he wanted to say something too, but he just frowned and shuffled out to stand next to Jerry. You could see that Jerry hated him. But Jerry knew how to smile at everybody, and so he smiled at Uncle T. while Uncle T. bent over the table with his hands together like he was praying, and moved his head up and bowed it down.

Doc brought out the roast beef, proper service. The crock

of mustard was on a breakfast plate, underlined with a doily, initials facing Jerry. The lid was on the mustard and it was clean, like it says in the book, and the little silver service spoon was clean and polished on a bread-and-butter plate. He set it down. And then he served the tea. You think you know the service, youngblood, all of you do. But you don't. Anybody can serve, but not everybody can become a part of the service. When Doc poured that pot of hot tea into that glass of crushed ice, it was like he was pouring it through his own fingers; it was like he and the tray and the pot and the glass and all of it was the same body. It was a beautiful move. It was fine service. The iced tea glass sat in a shell dish, and the iced tea spoon lay straight in front of Jerry. The lemon wedge Doc put in a shell dish half-full of crushed ice with an oyster fork stuck into its skin. Not in the meat, mind you, but squarely under the skin of that lemon, and the whole thing lay in a pretty curve on top of that crushed ice.

Doc stood back and waited. Jerry had been watching his service and was impressed. He mixed the sugar in his glass and sipped. Danny Jackson and I were down the aisle in the hall. Uncle T. stood behind Jerry, bending over, his arms folded, waiting. And Doc stood next to the table, his tray under his arm looking straight ahead and calm because he had given good service and knew it. Jerry sipped again.

"Good tea," he said. "Very good tea."

Doc was silent.

Jerry took the lemon wedge off the oyster fork and squeezed it into the glass, and stirred, and sipped again. "*Very* good," he said. Then he drained the glass. Doc reached over to pick it up for more ice but Jerry kept his hand on the glass. "Very good service, Doc," he said. "But you served the lemon wrong."

Everybody was quiet. Uncle T. folded his hands in the praying position.

"How's that?" said Doc.

"The service was wrong," Jerry said. He was not smiling now.

"How could it be? I been giving that same service for years, right down to the crushed ice for the lemon wedge."

"That's just it, Doc," Jerry said. "The lemon wedge. You served it wrong."

"Yeah?" said Doc.

"Yes," said Jerry, his jaws tight. "Haven't you seen the new rule?"

Doc's face went loose. He knew now that they had got him.

"Haven't you *seen* it?" Jerry asked again.

Doc shook his head.

Jerry smiled that hard, gray smile of his, the kind of smile that says: "I have always been the boss and I am smiling this way because I know it and can afford to give you something." "Steward Crouse," he said. "Steward Crouse, go get the black bible for the headwaiter."

Crouse looked beaten too. He was sixty-three and waiting for his pension. He got the bible.

Jerry took it and turned directly to the very last page. He knew where to look. "Now, Headwaiter," he said, *"listen* to this." And he read aloud: "Memorandum Number 22416. From: Douglass A. Tesdale, General Superintendent of Dining Cars. To: Waiters, Stewards, Chefs of Dining Cars. Attention: As of 7/9/65 the proper service for iced tea will be (a) Fresh brewed tea in teapot, poured over crushed ice at table; iced tea glass set in shell dish (b) Additional ice to be immediately available upon request after first glass of tea (c) Fresh lemon wedge will be served on bread-and-butter plate, no doily, with tines of oyster fork stuck into *meat* of lemon." Jerry paused.

"Now you know, Headwaiter," he said.

"Yeah," said Doc.

"But why didn't you know before?"

No answer.

"This notice came out last week."

"I didn't check the book yet," said Doc.

"But that's a rule. Always check the book before each trip. *You* know that, Headwaiter."

"Yeah," said Doc.

"Then that's *two* rules you missed."

Doc was quiet.

"Two rules you didn't read," Jerry said. "You're slowing down, Doc."

"I know," Doc mumbled.

"You want some time off to rest?"

Again Doc said nothing.

"I think you need some time on the ground to rest up, don't you?"

Doc put his tray on the table and sat down in the seat across from Jerry. This was the first time we had ever seen a waiter sit down with a customer, even an inspector. Uncle T.

behind Jerry's back, began waving his hands, trying to tell Doc to get up. Doc did not look at him.

"You *are* tired, aren't you?" said Jerry.

"I'm just resting my feet," Doc said.

"Get up, Headwaiter," Jerry said. "You'll have plenty of time to do that. I'm writing you up."

But Doc did not move and just continued to sit there. And all Danny and I could do was watch him from the back of the car. For the first time I saw that his hair was almost gone and his legs were skinny in the baggy white uniform. I don't think Jerry expected Doc to move. I don't think he really cared. But then Uncle T. moved around the table and stood next to Doc, trying to apologize for him to Jerry with his eyes and bowed head. Doc looked at Uncle T. and then got up and went back to the crew car. He left his tray on the table. It stayed there all that evening because none of us, not even Crouse or Jerry or Uncle T., would touch it. And Jerry didn't try to make any of us take it back to the Pantry. He understood at least that much. The steward closed down Doc's tables during dinner service, all three settings of it. And Jerry got off the train someplace along the way, quiet, like he had got on.

After closing down the car we went back to the crew quarters and Doc was lying on his bunk with his hands behind his head and his eyes open. He looked old. No one knew what to say until Boone went over to his bunk and said: "I feel bad for you, Doc, but all of us are gonna get it in the end. The railroad waiter is *doomed*."

Doc did not even notice Boone.

"I could of told you about the lemon but he would of got you on something else. It wasn't no use. Any of it."

"Shut the fuck up, Boone!" Danny said. "The one thing that really hurts is that a crawling son-of-a-bitch like you will be riding when all the good men are gone. Dummies like you and these two hardheads will be working your asses off reading that damn bible and never know a goddamn thing about being a waiter. *That* hurts like a *motherfucker!*"

"It ain't my fault if the colored waiter is doomed," said Boone. "It's your fault for letting go your humility and letting the whites take over the good jobs."

Danny grabbed the skullcap off Boone's head and took it into the bathroom and flushed it down the toilet. In a minute it was half a mile away and soaked in old piss on the tracks. Boone did not try to fight, he just sat on his bunk and mumbled. He had other skullcaps. No one said anything to Doc, because that's the way real men show that they care. You don't talk. Talking makes it worse.

IV

What else is there to tell you, youngblood? They made him retire. He didn't try to fight it. He was beaten and he knew it; not by the service, but by a book. *That book,* that *bible* you keep your finger stuck in. That's not a good way for a man to go. He should die in the service. He should die doing the things he likes. But not by a book.

All of us Old School men will be beaten by it. Danny Jackson is gone now, and Reverend Hendricks put in for his pension and took up preaching, full-time. But Uncle T. Boone is still riding. They'll get *me* soon enough, with that book. But it will never get you because you'll never be a waiter, or at least a Waiter's Waiter. You read too much.

Doc got a good pension and he took it directly to Andy's. And none of the boys who knew about it knew how to refuse a drink on Doc. But none of us knew how to drink with him knowing that we would be going out again in a few days, and he was on the ground. So a lot of us, even the drunks and hustlers who usually hang around Andy's, avoided him whenever we could. There was nothing to talk about any more.

He died five months after he was put on the ground. He was seventy-three and it was winter. He froze to death wandering around the Chicago yards early one morning. He had been drunk, and was still steaming when the yard crew found him. Only the few of us left in the Old School know what he was doing there.

I am sixty-three now. And I haven't decided if I should take my pension when they ask me to go or continue to ride. I *want* to keep riding, but I know that if I do, Jerry Ewald or Harry Silk or Jack Tate will get me one of these days. I could get down if I wanted: I have a hobby and I am too old to get drunk by myself. I couldn't drink with you, youngblood. We have nothing to talk about. And after a while you would get mad at me for talking anyway, and keeping you from your pussy. You are tired already. I can see it in your eyes and in the way you play with the pages of your rule book.

I know it. And I wonder why I should keep talking to you when you could never see what I see or understand what I understand or know the real difference between my school and yours. I wonder why I have kept talking this long when all the time I have seen that you can hardly wait to hit the city to get off this thing and spend your money. You have a good story. But you will never remember it. Because all this time you have had pussy in your mind, and your fingers in the pages of that black bible.

JEANNE A. TAYLOR (1934–   )

Born and brought up in Los Angeles, Jeanne A. Taylor began writing when she was still in junior high school and became editor of her school paper and yearbook. She graduated from Los Angeles City College in 1954 and has been a social worker-probation officer, working with the Department of Employment and Division of Highways. She became a member of the famous Writers' Workshop in Watts in May 1966 and served as secretary of its council. In the anthology From the Ashes: Voices of Watts, *edited by Budd Schulberg, she is represented with three prose selections. The Antioch Review devoted its Fall 1967 issue to works by the members of The Watts Writers' Workshop assembled after the selection for the* From the Ashes *anthology had been completed. The following is one of two short stories by Mrs. Taylor in that* Watts *issue of* The Antioch Review.

A House Divided

Asa Brown hated his counterparts who lived on the Eastside. Afro-Americans, the delta immigrants called themselves now. They deserved to stay right where they were. The majority of them were too stupid and too lazy to get out anyway. Real black men were found across town in the tracts of two- and three-bedroom stucco houses. Where the lawns are impeccably cut, fertilized, and watered; early morning traffic is the new Ford and Chevrolet car pools of husbands who work in the high rise civil service buildings downtown or in the suburban aircraft plants; brown-skinned "white collar" mothers take their children to the nursery or the Eastside-stranded grandparent baby-sitters each morning; Saturday nights, couples play whist or listen to Willie Bobo and Cannonball Adderly at a Sunset Strip or pier front club; holidays are spent barbecuing and drinking Scotch; and the only police visits are the result of the disturbing the peace complaints filed by the aged whitey who is asking $30,000 for his $16,000 house and finally has it in escrow.

These are Asa Brown's people.

Asa Brown Investments was located on the northwest side of Sample Street. The heart of Los Angeles' Eastside. The office was sandwiched between Stein's Second Hand Store and an unoccupied store front whose former tenants had been The Lasting Church of God in Christ. The Lasting Church hadn't lasted very long. Six months after the store front was leased, it had become vacant again. The rumor had circulated up and down Sample Street that the Reverend Mister Smallwood, the Lasting Church's Jehovah, had disappeared with his honey-hued pianist and all of his congregation's $2500.

"No better for 'em," Asa said, when Dock the bartender at JoJo's told Asa about it. Asa emptied the shot glass of Jim Beam, tapped the bar with his manicured forefinger, and smiled as Dock refilled the glass. "No better for 'em. If they can't see nothing but hand clapping and tambourine banging. No better for 'em."

Asa had grown up on Mott Avenue. Three blocks from where Sample Street crossed Fifth Place. His widowed mother still lived in the thirty-five-year-old whitewashed frame, surrounded by a steel mesh fence. Asa pleaded, nagged, and finally played the buffoon in his attempt to get the old woman to move west of Main Street.

"Listen, Mattie Brown," Asa would say, planting a kiss on her ebony satin brow, "west is where it is. And when did Auntie Mattie ever get left out of the action?" But the widow remained steadfast in her refusal to move. She grew roses, daisies, and marigolds around the border of the front lawn next to the fence. In the back yard she cultivated a garden of mustards and collards, sweet corn, and tomatoes. She knitted afghans for her grandchildren's beds, crocheted table cloths and doilies for her daughter-in-law, and filled Asa's freezer with home made yeast rolls and chicken pies. But she would not leave the house on Mott Avenue.

Asa's patience finally diminished. One night when he and his wife Callie were splitting a tall can of Schlitz and looking at "Duel in the Sun" on the late show, Asa's nasal voice suddenly filled the room. "Hell, if the old lady don't want to move, let her stay there. She owns the place. She gets income from that other roach-infested four-unit rental even if it is the county that foots the bill. I help her with the taxes. If she wants to stay around all those Mississippi coons, let her!"

Callie tore her hazel eyes away from the color splash on the television screen. A pink blush rose in her octaroon cheeks. She stared momentarily at Asa then returned to the handsome face of Gregory Peck.

The next day Asa closed the office early. At four-fifteen he sent home the pretty tawny high school senior who worked as his part-time secretary. The office usually stayed open until six-thirty, late enough to catch the hod carriers and longshoremen who might be working overtime. The more overtime the more green to invest in Asa Brown Investments: the service station over on Central and Clymar; the all-"blood"-run supermarket at Sample and Germaine Streets; the proposed Afro-American Progressive Credit Union. Asa watched the student close the door and start down the street toward the mid-city bus stop. He walked to the paned wall at the front of the two-desked office and followed her until the gold lambs wool sweater, the maiden hips swaying in the beige knit skirt, and the jaunty white kid boots were out of sight. Asa smiled. He didn't mind paying the girl a full salary when she didn't make all her hours. She was one of his people. He sure as hell wouldn't have one of the new breed of nappy-haired, bangle-wearing nationalists sitting behind his mahogany stenographer's desk.

It took five minutes to walk from the office to JoJo's. Jo-Jo's was a landmark. As much a part of Sample Street as the empty cigarette packs and squashed beer cans gutter. As enduring as the Jewish pawn shops, the Jewish clothing stores, and the syndicate-owned, "blood"-run liquor stores. Asa slipped onto a stool at the far end of the bar beneath the Hamm's bear smiling out of his winter wonderland. Dock waved from the cash register, picked up the familiar bottle of bourbon and a shot glass, and started towards his friend. Dock and Asa went way back together. They had gotten drunk for the first time out of the same fifth of wine that Asa slipped out of the Chink grocery down the street from the high school. They were fifteen years old and as Eastside as the youngsters who now sported tee shirts with Malcolm X's spectacled image.

Asa shook his head and pointed to the Hamm's bear.

Dock shrugged. "What's the matter? You sick? You ain't had nothing but beer all week!"

Asa waited until he had taken the foam from the glass before he spoke. "You know this Lottie Stevens you been investing for? Well, things are looking bad. She's got over $5,000 in and . . . hell, I've gotta fold."

Asa put the beer glass down and thought of his mother. An ancient lioness at sixty. Bent from scrubbing Mister Charlie's floor; numb after taking the crap his father dished out. Asa had been glad when the old man died and the gray face and snow hair were out of view forever. Lottie Stevens was probably like his mother. She had to be to think like Asa Brown people. Migrated to Los Angeles, from Louisiana or Texas, before the Japs ever thought of dropping a bomb at Pearl Harbor. Before niggers began writing home about the bread they made at North American and Lockheed. Asa emptied the glass of lager. He couldn't waste sympathy on Lottie Stevens. He had never even seen her. She didn't even have sense enough to tend to her own business. Dock of all pople took care of it for her. Dock was still chitlins and black-eyed peas; twenty-five-dollar suits and turned-up-toed shoes; Saturday night broads, black as tar and ugly as sin. Coons, all of them. The Jews were getting fat off of them every day. It seemed fitting that one of their own ought to be in on the take too. Yes, Asa Brown had done all right. Callie had an account at Robinson's and Haggarty's. Her shoes came from Wetherby Kyser. Callie drove the Barracuda to her job at city hall. He drove the old Chevy when he made the east of Main Street trip to the office each morning, and he sported the new thick cut hair. Just another one of the brothers. The last time he and Callie went to Vegas they had stayed at The Flamingo and gambled at the plush casinos of The Dunes, The Alladin, and Caesar's Palace. The sidewalks of the strip belonged to Mister and Missus Asa Brown. The pale-skinned whiteys with their fat paunches and starved-for-glamour's-sake women could no longer hoard it for themselves. Yes, they left gaudy downtown Vegas to the poor whiteys and the niggers whose Vegas experience was a once in a lifetime dream.

Asa shook his head. He didn't have time to cry about Lottie Stevens or any of the others. The supermarket hadn't brought in the loot he anticipated. Coons still did their shopping at the rebuilt Safeways and Ralphs that they had leveled during the riots. It just went to show how dumb a nigger was. When Texaco showered credit cards onto the populace, the service station's business dropped. The niggers went for that sucker bait. He had hired two Muslims as mechanics in the station's body shop. But on a windy rain-promising-sky day late in November, the grease monkeys forgot Elijah Mohammed's teaching and got loaded on a half gallon of Gallo port. They messed up two cars. The word got around. The body and fender shop had been closed ever since. There was never any sweat though. When Callie had the miscarriage she wouldn't go to any other hospital but Cedars, and it had cost him nearly $1,000. Adjusting the books was simple; a new advertising expenditure for the market was created. The week of their fourth wedding anniversary party he gave Callie a blue mutation mink stole. So the study of economic conditions in the community was initiated, and business analyst A. Bowen was added to the payroll and placed on the books under miscellaneous necessities. That was the breaks.

Asa looked down the bar at Dock. Dock was making a couple of gin and tonics for two business-suited whiteys. Fuzz. Asa could spot them a mile away. Why had Dock put up for this Lottie Stevens? She probably belonged to the scrubbing floors, little-Charlie's-nanny sect like his mother. Put in over $5,000. Every penny her black hands had ever saved.

"Hey, Dock," Asa called, "I'll take that bourbon after all."

Seeing Mattie Brown's whitewashed frame house always did something to Asa. He sure as hell couldn't live in the house on Mott Avenue again. Not if his life depended on it and there wasn't a fat chance of that. Still it was home. Mattie was bent over the ironing board, listening to Mahalia Jackson's thunder voice singing "Precious Lord Take My Hand." Mattie glided the iron back and forth over a starched white dress for Asa's baby girl.

"Mama, I told you, you don't have to iron perma-prest. That's what it means, permanently-pressed."

Mattie looked up. "Them little dresses don' look right, with no starch in 'em. Sit down. I jus' took a sweet potato pie out of the stove. I'll make you a cup of hot tea."

Asa shook his head. But it didn't do any good. He'd have to eat even if he wasn't hungry. When he got home he was going to raise Cain with Callie. He'd told her when the kids slept over, not to leave their clothes. His Mama's back was too painful to be bending over an ironing board. His Mama ironed everything, even the dish towels.

While Asa sat at the oak table near the kitchen, half of the sweet potato pie in his stomach, the remaining portion tempting from the pyrex dish in front of him, he could hear Mattie putting gumbo into an empty half-gallon pickle jar. The smell of crab paws and large pink shrimp, okra, and tomatoes filled his nostrils. Callie at least appreciated receiving Mattie's New Orleans dishes.

"Mama, the business is finished," Asa muttered, his mouth full of pie. Mattie dropped the ladle with which she had been spooning the gumbo. Asa looked into the kitchen. The pupils of Mattie's eyes moved crazily back and forth and her thin dark lips trembled in her equally dark face. Asa thought of Lottie Stevens.

"Don't worry, Mama. I got something else going. Your son is going to be one of the new mayor's field deputies. It's a seventeen-thousand-a-year job. Think about it, Auntie Mattie. Seventeen thousand bucks a year."

"You mean you done sold us out for a white man at City Hall?"

Asa washed down the last of the pie with the cold tea. He brushed the flakey crumbs from the side of his mouth and thought about Lottie Stevens.

"Where's your savings, Mama?"

"Asa, I ask you somethin' first. I don' care how old you git. Answer me first."

"I ain't sold out to nobody. I'll be right down here in this area. Sample Street always been my home, ain't it? I'll be right here serving my people jest like always. Making Los Angeles a better place to live, like always." Conning Mattie was hard. She knew a lie a yard away. Asa's head was starting to hurt. "Where's your savings, Mama? You raised that bastard-in-Beverly-Hills' children for that money."

Mattie picked up the ladle and finished filling the pickle jar. "It's in the bank. Where you think it was?"

Mattie Brown died the day after the investors were notified of the demise of Asa Brown Investments. Asa had never been able to cry even as a kid when his father beat him with a cat-o-nine tails. The passing of his mother was the deepest wound he had ever sustained. But there were no tears. He grieved and thought about Lottie Stevens. The night of the rosary for Mattie, family and friends gathered in the flower-wreathed living room on Mott Avenue after returning from the mortuary. Neighbor women moved in and out of the kitchen, pouring coffee, refilling the dishes on the table with fried chicken, potao salad, cake, and cookies. Black hands pumped Asa's arm until it ached. Teary-eyed brown women hugged his neck, planting kisses on his moist cheeks, community expressions of sympathy for the loss of his mother, the failure of his business, and nigger bewilderment at another example of God's inexplicable will. Dock stood by the front door never taking his angry eyes from Asa's face, and Asa thought of Lottie Stevens.

Asa went through Mattie's papers ten times. He found the deed for the house on Mott Avenue; the rent subsidy agreement with the county for the units north of Sample and Germaine Streets; a yellow scotch-tape-mended paper attesting to the fact that one Mattie Marie St. Amant had married Asa Joseph Brown in the city of New Orleans at the Church of the Blessed Sacrament on January 30th, 1932. The birth certificate of Asa Joseph Anthony Brown, Junior, born July 10th, 1930, was attached to the marriage certificate with a rusted paper clip. Asa wanted Mattie's bank book and he couldn't find it. Asa could feel Callie's eyes on his back again as he went through the papers for the last time. That's what he had told her when he had opened the box again after dinner the night before. "Listen, Callie, if Mama was Lottie Stevens, I took her life as sure as if I had smothered her in her bed." Callie was holding the evening paper in her hands. She threw it into the den next to Asa's feet. But Asa was already opening a paper-filled manila envelope.

"So what if Auntie Mattie was Lottie Stevens?" Callie said, anger reddening her yellow skin.

Asa looked up. "Well, I guess I'll buy that stained glass window she always wanted for St. Gregory's."

"Have you seen Dock? Have you asked him about Lottie Stevens?" Callie wiped the tears from her eyes. "That window would cost over $1500. All the savings we've got left."

Asa looked blankly at Callie. He'd heard that Dock was dabbling in politics. Someone else was taking his place at JoJo's. Asa picked up the marriage certificate and read it over again for the eleventh time.

Callie really flipped when Asa told her that the mayor had given the field deputy job to an Eastside nigger who owned a cleaning shop on Sample Street. "Some unfavorable community sentiment just now, with your business holdings going sour," the mayor said. Asa tried to explain to Callie that being the mayor's economic board representative paid less but in time he'd be back on top again. Callie pursed her pink lips and spat in his face. Asa slapped her good. Later he apologized. Sure, if he had known the field deputy job would fall through he wouldn't have donated the window to St. Gregory's. But the Mattie Brown-Lottie Stevens-filled days and nights had ceased. Asa knew that if he had to do it over again, St. Gregory's would get Mattie Brown's window.

Asa walked up Sample Street. Past the loan shops, the small dirty-floored groceries, the beauty shops, and the second-hand stores. Past the old Asa Brown Investment office. Large white letters outlined in red paint decorated the windows now: LOOK TO HIM WHO SAVES. THE MACEDONIA BAPTIST CHURCH. REVEREND B. B. BLAKELY, PASTOR. Asa laughed. When he opened his next office it would be further down on Sample Street. Maybe near the furniture store or the new Woolworth's.

JoJo's was empty except for Dock and a woman who was sitting at the bar drinking a glass of sherry. Dock nodded as Asa pointed to the Hamm's bear.

"Come on down here," Dock called.

Asa took a seat next to the woman. She was wrapped in a heavy black coat and he noticed that her hands shook when she reached for the sherry. Gray wool escaped the confines of a faded blue bandana tied around her head. Dock put the bottle of beer on the bar.

"This is my Auntie, Asa," Dock said.

Asa turned and looked into a pair of faded brown eyes. The pupils changed to blue-black and he was looking at his Mama again. Mattie Brown smiled.

"Auntie Lottie, this is Asa Brown," Dock said.

A chill seized Asa and tears slid down his cheeks. Mattie Brown's glazed eyes bore into him.

"Lottie Stevens?" Asa muttered.

"Lottie Stevens," Dock said.

Asa put a half dollar on the bar and hurried out to Sample Street. He had to get home. Back to Asa Brown people. It just went to show you what happened when you started thinking like a coon. Damn it! You acted like 'em too.

CECIL BROWN

*A young critic, playwright, and professor at the University of
California, Berkeley, Cecil Brown has published in the* Parti-
san Review *and* Kenyon Review *and has won attention with
his first novel* The Life and Loves of Mr. Jiveass Nigger. *In
the course of the novel the first person narrator has occasion
to explain what he means by jive in a brief dialogue with a
friend that runs like this:*

> "What you mean by jive, man, you mean he told lies like
> you?
> "Reb, everything is a lie. Life is a lie. But people don't
> know that, see. Only smart people like me know that.
> "You jiveass nigger, Reb said, laughing.
> "No, I'm telling the truth.
> "You jiveass nigger, get away from here.
> "Well, shit I guess you right, Reb. I am jiving because jiving
> is the truth, and I'm the living truth."

Following is the self-contained "Prologue" to The Life and
Loves of Mr. Jiveass Nigger *revealing another Black narrative
stance of the Seventies.*

The Life and Loves of Mr. Jiveass Nigger

Prologue

A Prismatic Account of Some Important
Matters

One   The Spirit of the Father

I must swear 'fo God this is the cussinges' man ever born,
he must've been cussing when he came into this world, when

his mother, Miss Lillybelle Washington, gave birth to this heathen the first thing he said must've been a cuss word, he probably cussed out the midwife and his mother and anybody else who happened to be in sight, cussed them out for bringin' him into the world, he is that kind of man, you know. . . . There ain't a soul in this communitiy he ain't cussed out, hardly a dog or cat either. But the Lord is gonna visit this nigger, you watch and see, he's gonna visit this nigger. When I met him, when I first laid eyes on this nigger he was cussing, out in the street cussing with my brothers, and I said to myself, why is that nigger always using cusswords? So I thought it was just youth, just being young, and I was foolish enough to up and marry that fool. He tole me after we got married he was gonna stop cussing, and you know the stranges' thing is that he did. And three months later, he cuss old man Lennon into a blue streak. Old man Lennon ain't never bother no body, that old man been walking around this town for forty years picking up junk in his wheelbarrow and taking it home to see what use he could fine out of it, and he happened to come by the house and this nigger of mine claimed the man picked up his hammer. Lord God Almighty, did he cuss that poor man out. I can't stand no cussing man, I don't like no cussing man, Lord gib me any kind of man, a short, square-headed man, a ugly man, any kind of man, but don't give me no cussing man. I got experience to prove this: that there ain't but one thing a cussing man is good for and that is cussing. There is one thing about a cussing man that you can bet your bottom dollar on and that is he will cuss, and if he don't cuss, grits ain't grocery, eggs ain't poultry, and Mona Lisa was a man. But the Lord gonna visit that nigger, the Lord, or somebody, gonna visit him, because you can't go through life cussing out everybody, everything you see, you just can't do that, and get away with it. Or am I a fool? That nigger cussed out God himself, yes he did. I was telling him he should go to church, you know once in a while, not all the time, just once in a while, and that nigger broke bad and said that the Lord could kiss his black ass. But the Lord ain't gonna kiss no nigger's black ass, or if he do kiss it then that nigger knows something I don't know and wanna find out about pretty quick. My grandmother, Dennier Saint Marie, she's dead and gone now, she tole me when I was nothing but a five-year-old. Tole me to never marry a cussing man. One of her boyfriends, she had aplenty, she had three children by black men and three by white men, and some by an Indian too (we got all kinds of blood in us), one of her boyfriends, who use to wear that straw hat that put you in the mind of a tap dancer, he had just come into the gate and we was all sitting on the porch, it was a Sunday afternoon, and there was some white and red roses in the garden and we had picked some red roses and pinned them to our clothes in honor of the fact that our mother was alive, it was Easter Sunday you know and Gramma had a white one for her blouse, and this boyfriend of hers came bursting into the gate, just cussing like a nigger, I mean he was *talking*, but every few words was a cuss word, and Gramma just turned politely to him and said would you excuse yourself, there's some ladies present, and he said you never heard shit before, everybody shits, and Gramma said you better get your filthy ass out of this garden. And when he left, she turned to me (it seems like she was speaking only to me even though there were about twelve people present) and said, honey don't ever marry a cussing man, because a cussing man ain't good for nothing but one thing—and that's cussing. Now those was some words I should have heeded, but I didn't heed them, I went right out and the first man I looked at good I married (because I loved him) and he turned out to be a cussing man. I don't care what my sons be, I don't care really what they do, just so they don't grow up cussing everything they lay eyes on. I can't stand no cussing man. When I hear a man cussing, my insides go to pieces. That's one thing about white men. They shor don't cuss like niggers. Of course, a poor white peck will cuss. A poor white peck will cuss worse'n a nigger. I am talking about white men who ain't poor like them pecks. I guess a nigger man cuss because he is so poor and ain't nothin' but a nigger. But a nigger should learn not to cuss, he should learn not to cuss too much. To tell you the truth, there ain't nothin' wrong with cussing, I do a little bit myself, but there is somethin' wrong with a nigger cussing *all the time*. There is somethin' wrong with that kind of nigger, somethin' done gone wrong deep down inside of that nigger, if everything he says is a blasphemous cuss word, if every time he opens his mouth it's a cocksucker, motherfucker-down-the-ditch-up-the-ditch-longheaded-sonofa-bitch, or if he is always saying, I wish I was dead, I'm gonna be glad when I die (like some niggers I know), and things like this, then there is something deep down wrong with that nigger and he oughta go to church and testify. But this man won't testify, he above testifying, he rather cuss, I guess cussing is his way of testifying. I can understand that, I just hope God understands it.

When George's mother married his father she was fifteen and a very fine woman. She was probably one of the finest women in the world. George's father was a young, strong black man when he married the woman, but he had one fault which the woman grew to resent very strongly, and that was that he cursed. It was true too that he cursed all the time. It was also a contagious thing. If you were around George's father you would be cursing too without even really knowing it. George tried not to curse. He tried very hard, and he was very good at it. He could talk whole sentences without cursing once, and then he could hold a conversation with almost anybody (that is to say, any adult) without cursing, and finally he was able to talk a whole day without saying a curse word—or at least he thought he could; that is to say, it seemed so to *him*. Once, however, in the classroom, Ellen accused him of calling her a curse name, which for the life of him he could not remember having said. He turned to Reb for verification, and Reb slowly shook his head affirmatively, indicating that indeed he had spoken a curse word. He could not believe that he was that unconscious of himself. And yet there was Reb looking disappointed and sad because he had to tell the truth. But no! he had not cursed, it was his father speaking through him, speaking through him unconsciously. He began to hate his father who was buried deep inside of him and who was a nigger and cursed all the time. He began to hate the unconscious part of himself. He tried to be conscious of every single thing that he did; he wanted to be conscious of every single reaction he had on people, and when he thought that people reacted to something in him which he himself did not recognize or know he became uncomfortable.

And worst of all his father wanted George to become a lawyer or doctor, and George knew he wanted this, so that when George was five or six and went to visit him in prison, George said to him, I think I'll be a lawyer or doctor or something like that. His father's thin black face yielded a white set of teeth. But did George Washington become a lawyer or doctor, or something like that? No, he became a hustler, a jiveass, a jazz player who could never quite get the kind of versatility to match the humming in his head, a well-read hanger-on, a poet without the appropriate metaphors. Yeh, didn't he head straight for Harlem when he graduated from high school, throwing away a scholarship to a good Negro college only a hundred and fifty miles away, threw it away because he thought the college was inferior to his innate ability and would hence hamper his growth? But what did he do instead? Did he attend a better college in the North? No. He just sat around thinking that if he had gone to Princeton, like his friend Randall, he'd have done extremely well, because Randall was not so bright and he did all right. Sat around and even invented a myth of himself at Princeton, calling the myth Paul Winthrop, Jr. Paul Winthrop, Jr., was the most well-read Princetonian to walk the campus in many years, especially knowledgeable on English literature of the period 1590–1600.

And the myth of Julius Makewell, the original nigger—ex-gorilla (who actually came on that way). SCENE: *an attractive blonde like the one right out of the Dodge Rebellion television commercial, sitting in a fire-red Fiat. Enter from the left wing (125th Street),* JULIUS: *hair not combed in weeks, standing twisted on his head in a million different directions, eyes weird and red from wine.*

JIVEASS NIGGER ALIAS GEORGE WASHINGTON ALIAS JULIUS
    MAKEWELL: Hey, gimme a ride.
GIRL: Where you going?
JULIUS: Where you going? Uptown Downtown Eastside
    Westside?
GIRL: Uh . . . okay, sure . . . if you promise not to . . .
    (*Cut to:* GIRL's *bedroom. A big large bed with impressive wooden frame. Poster of Eldridge Cleaver on one wall and Martin Luther King on another. Both* JULIUS *and* GIRL *sit on bed.*)
GIRL: So that's it. That's all you want, huh? Is that why you
    say you're coldblooded? You mean, you want to just . . .
    as you said, screw me, just like that, huh? Without even
    having any idea of what I'm like at all. Just walk right in
    and stick it in, huh? Is that the kind of person you are, is
    it?
JULIUS (*sheepish*): Yes.
GIRL (*exasperated*): You mean, you don't even wanna know
    my name? You don't even care who I am at all?! You
    mean you can do that—walk right off the street and into
    bed??
JULIUS (*painfully*): Yes.
GIRL: Jesus Christ, what kind of person are you?

JULIUS (*seriously attempting an explanation*): I've been this way . . . (*He glances at the* GIRL's *legs, which are opened and uncovered by her micro-mini*) . . . been this way all my life. (*Turns to the audience, and in an aside*): Yeah, I guess this is what it means to be a Negro.

GIRL (*very sympathetic*): It must be a terrible way to be!

JULIUS: I just have to do it. (*His hands caress the* GIRL's *most available thigh and then move farther up.*)

GIRL: Oh, I understand . . . (*Panting with excitement*) . . . but you don't think you could wait . . . until . . . I mean, we've only known each other ten minutes . . .

JULIUS (*caressing* GIRL): I've always been this way. I—I just can't help it.

GIRL: Well, is that all you want?

JULIUS: This is all I want.

GIRL: Just my body?

JULIUS (*sheepish*): Uh, yes.

GIRL: You don't even want to know my name?!

JULIUS: We went through this once—NO!

GIRL (*thoughtfully*): Well, if *that's* the way you want it, okay. (*Begins panting again as she takes off clothes.*) Sure you . . . don't wanna know my name.

JULIUS: No. This is a one-day stand. I'll never see you again.

GIRL: Okay . . . if this is what you want . . . (*Undresses.*)
(*Fade into darkness.*)

And you don't go to sleep afterwards, and you think about the TV, the radio, the ring, the watch, and the $32.89 in her handbag, but what can she really complain about. 'Cause I ain't got shit in this world. Yo' daddy got it all, baby!

And anything else he could grab onto. Any other myth of the self. And lying to himself, successfully selling overpriced encyclopedias to illiterate black people in the slum tenements of Brooklyn and Harlem and hustling and flimflamming a 250-pound woman preacher in Harlem for all she was worth. Lies. Yeh, yeh. Why? Why? Why?

Two   A Brief History

Let us backtrack a moment. The most salient characteristic of George Washington's early childhood (and, indeed, his early youth) was his *individuality*. This talent of his, the almost fanatical ability to remain *different* against all odds, was apparent even at birth: young George Washington was born on the Fourth of July in the year of Our Lord nineteen hundred and forty-four in his father's bed, which had been recently vacated by George's grandfather, who had to flee the county for having (allegedly) whipped a fellow—Josh Smith, to be exact—with a slab because the said Josh had accused George's grandfather of having fathered a child by Josh's poor wife. George was assisted in entering this world by his grandmother, a squatty little woman with very definite strains of Indian blood, who will swear to this day that when George Washington came out of the womb he was grinning. No one knew what he was grinning about. Except, of course, George himself. His grandmother claimed he was the blackest baby she'd ever seen come into the world, and later on, when George was older, she went on to offer the opinion that he was the *blackest child she'd ever seen period*. There is some truth in this, for the child was extremely dark, and it was this unusual hue that led many members of the family to think that he was destined to become, as it were, the black sheep of the family. But the most amazing change occurred to George when he was in the last of his fifth year: his skin began to get lighter, until, at age twelve, he possessed the finest shade of brown complexion imaginable, and it was this complexion that he kept for the balance of his days. No one really understood why the change took place at the time that it did, or really what it signified. It is, however, a small matter, and besides it is only his mother and grandmother who still insist that George Washington was once *really* black. His mother, furthermore, is very pleased with the brown hue of her first-born.

When George was only two, his father, Jake, who, incidentally, was the one who earmarked him with the name George, went off to prison, in very much the same fashion as some young fathers were at that time going off to war—that is to say, reluctantly. With the exception of brief visits, George did not see his father for a great number of years, but he was not without a father figure. Quite to the contrary, young Washington lived in a household that was abounding with male models: his four uncles, ranging from age seventeen to twenty-eight, who shared the house with the rest of the family (twelve or thirteen or fourteen, depending on whether you counted Buckcaesar or Siren as dogs or humans), were very excellent models, indeed. Illiterate, generous, intuitive, simple, and hopelessly backwards, they were probably some of the finest men in the whole world. From them little

Washington learned at an exceptionally early age how to swear, talk about women, talk *to* women, how to farm, hunt, fish, avoid unnecessary work, how to relax, how to tell when a white cracker is trying his best to get something for nothing (which is most of the time), and how to look at a nappy head woman and tell if the sap's running. Like all true students, George outgrew his teachers and became something his uncles never dreamed of: he became literate, which is to say, he became a voracious reader of any piece of printed matter he could lay hands on. Because he was such a lover of reading, and being the only one in the household who could read (with the exception of his mother), it was his task and pleasure to read any bit of mail, be it a letter from Aunt Mabel in Philly or third-class advertisement sheets, aloud for all to hear, in very much the fashion of the town crier. He was much appreciated by the family for his learning and gentlemanly bearing, and was much loved by all. And thus he spent his early years until the age of twelve, at which point he was (un)fortunately seduced by a wayward and voluptuous aunt. After this initial loss of innocence, the boy took to laying out with women, and to heavy usage of rot-gut liquor, cigarettes, and reefers. When he was only eight, his teacher once asked the class who the father of our country was, and of course George was quick to shout out his name—proudly. In a brief five years, however, all this optimism was shot to hell, for George's most favorite expression of his philosophical view of life was summed up in a conscious parody of Ecclesiastes' famous dictum: "I have seen all the works that are done under the sun; and, behold, all *is* jive and vexation of the spirit." Many a night he lay his gun down on an oak, and stared up at the stars and, wondering what it all meant, lost his consciousness in a spiritual transcendence that would leave him shivering and scratching about, two hours later, for his soul. Upon recovering, he would chant, "Jive, it's all jive."

In high school, George had a sidekick named Reb. Reb was mean and slick, which was why George liked him. The last thing George saw of Reb was the back of his straw hat. The two of them were sitting in the principal's office, waiting for the baldheaded sonabitch to peep his head in the door. Reb had a mallet and George had a piece of pine slab. Reb's fine straw hat was cocked to the side, and sweat was trickling down his brown forehead. George was a little scared too. After Reb leveled on that nigger principal's head with that mallet, he broke out and ran. The last thing George saw was the back of his straw hat. Then, five years later, George came back to Royaltown to visit. He had been up in Harlem flim-flamming a colored woman preacher out of $935 and thought he would take a little vacation. He wanted to see his family again and where he grew up. So here he was back home. He went to the high school to see his brother play basketball. The place had not changed. He saw an extremely attractive girl sitting watching his little brother shoot some perfect shots into the basket and he went over to the girl and as it turned out she was Reb's wife and she said Reb was in the army in Vietnam, that he was a sergeant, had been decorated, and that he didn't want to kill any more Vietnamese people but that he didn't have any choice but as soon as he could get out of it he was going to, which was in June. And George thought that the girl was extremely attractive and Reb was very fine and then he thought of Reb in a foxhole somewhere in that lonely country and he was sad but then he said to the girl that he had grown up with her husband and that she shouldn't worry because Reb was going to survive because he was a beautiful, jiveass nigger. George did not believe the girl understood his last phrase. Three days after that he was in Copenhagen.

And in final desperation you fling yourself on a plane and land in a city named Copenhagen. You want to know why it is that you tell so many lies. Do other people lie like this? Is there any motherfucker in this despiteful world who ever told himself the truth? You want to know. And so, your story opens:

VICTOR STEVEN WALKER (1947–   )

The work of Victor Steven Walker, a still unpublished writer, was called to my attention by a teacher of creative writing at the University of Illinois while Mr. Walker was a student

*there. In response to a request for biographical information
he wrote: "I was born Victor Steven Walker on July 19, 1947,
in Chicago, Illinois. I graduated from the University of Illinois
in 1969 with a major in Psychology. After graduation I taught
for a year in the Chicago public schools where I am currently
employed. This is my first publication." The following story
is published from manuscript.*

The Long Sell

He walked up to the room and stood for a minute staring
at the number, then turned the key and let the door swing
back. A faint smell of warmness pushed over his face. With
his free hand he switched the light on and walked over to
the double-bed dropping the suitcase. Brown leather, a mass
of buckles and straps bulging around the middle. The bed,
massive, groaned up a small mushroom of dust from a flesh
pink spread sagging—an old woman her legs spread. He
stood for a minute, the sweat dribbling down his forehead, his
coat gaping and his stomach weighing over the buckle, trying
to catch his breath. Removing his straw hat, he reached back
and pulled out a white handkerchief and mopped his brow
then ran it over the sweat band and tossed it down in the
chair. Moving to the window he raised it to the top and
leaned on the sill. Nothing. Unbuttoning the collar he fell
back on the bed his lids dropping shut.

He awoke later, how much he didn't know; his mouth open,
a string of saliva running down his chin, he let his eyes roll
slowly over the ceiling. It felt as if his suitcase was on his
chest. He looked down and patted himself then pushed
through the humidity to the edge of the bed. He had left the
door unlocked. Drawing himself up he walked over to the
door and closed it fastening the chain. He did not bother
with the transom. Walking back to the bed, he stood for a
moment staring down at the suitcase. Hot enough for you old
girl? he laughed and began unfastening his valise, his hands
fanning across the bag like a keyboard pushing buttons and
latches. Finally unhitching the straps the valise seemed to
sigh like a woman who has just slipped off her girdle. Flipping
the lid back she opened up silk and ruffles filled with brushes,
lotions, crèmes and toiletries. He stepped back putting his

hands on his hips. Whew! Bending back over he reached into the liner pouch and pulled out a picture of a young man in uniform and set it on the dresser. He undid his suspenders, walked over to the bathroom and turned on the faucet which struggled with a monkey wrench before the water splashed into the bowl. Rolling up his sleeves he cupped his hands and rushed the water on his face several times blowing through his mouth. Then with one wet hand he began to massage the back of his neck screwing it into the air. When he had finished he pulled his jacket on and stared a moment at the photograph. To Mama with love. He checked his keys put on his hat walked to the door and out.

Drifting out from the hotel lobby, he looked left then turned up the avenue. It was still early and the heat waved out before his eyes. He turned and crossed between the cars. There was no traffic and few pedestrians. He looked down at the pavement which began to heat the soles of his shoes. Emerging on the edge of a park he turned down one of the shaded paths. A woman passed with a baby buggy and he nodded politely as she passed. Further down a couple leisured hand in hand.

Veering over to a bench he sat sorry that he hadn't brought his valise. It would have been an ideal place to set up. A few pigeons pecked about the bench. Digging into his breast pocket he pulled out a stick of Spearamint unwrapped it and put it into his mouth. A young woman approached and sat on the other end of the bench. He smiled down at her, but she didn't seem to notice. Turning back he flipped the gum wrapper across the walk and stretched his legs crossing them in the path.

He sat for a while watching the passers-by pass by. A sailor sat down on the bench between he and the young lady. For a minute he watched the sailor's profile from the corner of his eye. There was something familiar about the face, what he couldn't put his finger on, but the day was hot and so pushing the straw hat down over his eyes he fell asleep.

Say, you got a match? He looked up into the dark crown then removed the hat. Yeh, I think so he mumbled digging into his pockets. At least I should have. He looked over into the boy-young face only to see himself reflected in the sunglasses.

Here they are he said drawing them from his pocket and handing them to the young man, his eyes never leaving the face but following the movement of the cigarette to the mouth, the light-up and slow, deep first suck on the cigarette.

The young head tilted back slowly blowing a stream of smoke through the air and stared out over the path.

She was married.

Huh? He didn't quite understand what the sailor was talking about.

The young sailor kept staring at something across the path. She was married, pop. He turned the dark glasses on the old man. You know. She was married. Had a ring and everything. He handed the matches back.

The old man kept staring at himself reflected double in the glasses then suddenly blinking he understood. Oh you mean the young lady. He looked down the bench. It was empty. He smiled slowly, I see now.

The sailor dragged on the cigarette and his young face seemed to harden, the smoke rushing from his nose. You wouldn't be starin at me would you, pop, the voice biting into the old man's ear. I guess I was. No harm though. You just kinda reminded me of somebody. I got a boy your age. In the army. The sailor stared out for a moment, then took off his sunglasses, massaging his temples. He looked back at the old man, his eyes small and red. Sorry.

Aw that's alright. You tied up down in San Diego? The sailor nodded. Yeh I don't live here either. I'm a salesman, beauty supplies. He grinned slyly, Avon calling.

Hey, let me show you a picture of my boy, his hand fumbling into his back pocket. He brought forth a fat brown wallet and began thumbing through the plastic cases. Here it is. He handed it to the sailor.

Nice looking kid. The salesman took it back. Yeh, looks just like his ma. He stared for a minute almost frowning then looked up at the sailor. Heck he's oldern that now. This picture musta been taken seven, eight years ago. He tucked it back into the wallet and put it into his coat pocket. He must be as old as you. How old are you, if you don't mind my askin. Twenty? Twenty-one?

The sailor let the cigarette drop crushing it with his toe. Twenty-two.

My boy exactly said the old man, or leastways in September. His mind shaded over with autumn memories and he found himself walking toward a red coupe that blocked the driveway. He walked back putting his foot on the running-board and peered in. Jesus if this ain't a car. The screen door slammed. A tidy younger man with a small black bag approached mopping his brow and nodded. Jonas.

He didn't look up, letting his eyes drift over the wood

paneled dashboard instead. The young man tossed the bag through the car window and stood for a second. She's ill Jonas.

He looked up then straightened. Its the boy. She took it hard when he up and joined "Sam." He looked back at the car. This must a set you back some. The man reached out grabbing him by the arm. Jonas will you listen. Its not only that; she's really sick. She needs someone to look after her.

Don't you think I know that. Hell, you think I been workin all these years for nothin. You an your fancy car.

You aren't married to that job you know. He moved into the car and started the engine, Jonas standing alongside.

I'll look after her, don't chu worry.

Like your son.

The young man rose spreading his legs and stretching, the salesman craning his neck and catching the sun hitting off the glasses. Say why don't I buy you a beer. The sailor looked a bit cautiously at the salesman. I mean its the least we civilians can do for our fighting men. The sailor looked down, his head eclipsing the sun throwing shadow over the old salesman. Sure pop. As long as you can buy it I can drink it. The old man looked up for a minute and smiled then slapping the dress white thigh he grinned, Let's go.

Two beers. He looked over at the sailor. That alright with you son? The sailor nodded, Suits me fine, pop, I ain't fancy. The old man laughed. I like you, navy; you're alright. Pulling out his handkerchief he took off his straw and mopped his head, leaving his hat on the counter. Whew! Fella could clean up sellin air conditioners. He paused. I'm a salesman you know.

You told me.

He looked disappointed. Did I? Well I guess I must have. I spose I told you I sell cosmetics too. Well I don't, not really. You know what I really peddle? He looked around the bar his voice sliding into a whisper: dope.

The sailor turned around almost falling off the seat. The salesman laughed. But first you got to get their attention. His hand reached up and slapped the sailor on the back. You should of seen yourself, kid. I thought you were going to fall off the stool. His hand dropped from around the sailor, his voice easing out of the laughter. That's the whole trick, navy, getting people to take notice. He turned and slid his hand around the glass which was now sitting before him bringing it to his pink lips and thirsting it down, his adam's apple slowly working up and down. The sailor sat quietly looking into his beer his finger running gently around the lip of the glass, the muscles in his jaw tightening. Maybe you're right.

The salesman put down the glass. Damn right, I'm right. I'm a lot oldern you navy and I know. He looked in the mirror across the bar. See that bimbo over there in the booth. He grabbed the sailor's sleeve. Don't turn around. Look in the mirror. The sailor looked.

She's sitting and waiting for some trick to come along and buy her a drink. He squeezed the boy's arm. And you know she don't want no drink really. He reached back over and poured down the rest of the beer signaling the bartender. Whisky. He looked over at the sailor who nodded. Make that two.

The salesman turned back toward the reflection. She don't want no drink don't you know. The sailor ogled the mirror scooping a thick patch of foam from the empty glass with his finger and licking it. She don't want no drink. She don't even want the trick that comes in an' buys it. The bartender brought the whiskies setting them on the bar.

The salesman looked up at the broad expanse of white shirt and fat face that sweated profusely, but not on the starched white collar, the sleeves rolled over the elbow and one red striped towel thrown over the shoulder. He looked up at the small pinched eyes. Well Sam—

My name ain't Sam said the bartender reaching under the counter and bringing out a toothpick putting it between his teeth.

The saleman smiled. Sure it is. All bartenders are named Sam.

I ain't. His face massively silent. A fat stone.

Trouble is you're defensive, Sam. The fat face did not seem to change expression. I was just kiddin an' you took er serious. The sailor did not look at the bartender but stared at the mirror.

The salesman smiled. Hell, man we're all too damn defensive. Scairt someone's gonna put one over on us, make a fool of us. He looked over at the sailor throwing his arm around his shoulder. It's just like I was tellin navy here. I'm a salesman: Jonas P. Putnam. He reached into his coat and brought out a small card handing it to the bartender who stared at it for a moment and dropped it on the counter. The salesman looked down. You can keep that; I got plenty.

Anyway you can see I'm a salesman. He paused groping

through the fat face. What I'm tryin to say is that I come in contact with a lot of people and I know.

What? said the bartender, his little mouth opening round and funny in his massive face.

I know you're lonely, Sam. Lonely and scared just like me just like everybody. Hell, you wouldn't believe some of the people I meet on the road. Two days ago I sold a complete beauty kit to a fifty year old woman who lived out in The Valley by herself. You hear me, Sam? By herself! A fifty, sixty year old woman and you know what she says to me? She says, Mr. Putnam do you have any of those blonde wigs, just to try on mind you. Krist! Putnam shook his head and tossed the whisky into his mouth. I tell you Sam if I seen one I seen a hunnerd, lonely an cryin out and nobody to hearum. You're a bartender, you tell me. Ain't it so.

The fat face seemed to open like a melon, the seed-black eyes staring past the room. Yeh, its so. A customer slapped the counter and like a finger snapping brought the bartender back, his eyes blinking. I—I got customers. Can't you see. I got no time to chat. He turned to leave then looked back, My name ain't Sam either.

For a minute Putnam remained in the same attitude staring at the row of bottles that underlined the mirror, his eyes running slowly over them, his head unmoving. He brought the glass to his lips and drank slowly, his eyes spreading over the entire row. How many you figure they got?

Huh?

Bottles. How many bottles you spose they got navy? He looked over at the sailor. They're all alike navy, every last one of them. He fumbled in his pocket pulling out a bill and ordered another round.

I just oughta walk over there and order her a drink, that's what I oughta do, pop. His tongue flicked out over his lips. I bet she's good, you know? I bet she's darn good.

Don't be no trick, navy. Don't lettum ever make you no trick. Once they think you needum they'll walk all over you.

She ain't gonna walk all over me, pop. We're just gonna have a nice little chat, you know, kind of sociable like—like we're havin—then maybe . . . He looked over at Putnam.

Then maybe what? You think that's all there is to it? Wham-bam thank you ma'am. Well, it ain't. He raised the jigger to his lips gulping down the whiskey, his ring finger catching the light. It ain't that simple. Believe me navy it ain't that simple at all.

Here let me buy you another round. Scotch? The sailor

nodded, but it was clearly at the woman reflected in the mirror that had turned slightly and was looking at his reflection to which he nodded. I dunno, pop; I think you gotta take whatever you can get when you can get it.

I suppose that's what I thought at your age. That's what my boy thinks now. But it ain't true. None of it. His voice loosened becoming warm and funky with whisky, rolling over the sailor's face. You don't take a goddamn thing in this world, not a goddamn thing. You look up one day and you're fifty-seven and you haven't got a thing, nothing. All them things you took, you thought you took, you look up and there's nothing. Nothing but this big hole you been tossin things down. You wake and all there is is this hole.

Maybe so. He tilted the glass back looking into the mirror. Maybe so, pop, but like I say you got to take what you can get. He grinned. Someways even a hole's a profit.

But Putnam was not listening. Somewhere in the back of his mind a screen door shut cracking the air like a rifle. He stepped into the Nash clutching and shifting into first, the frame house receding in the rear-view. You're away from home too often. You don't need to be, I need you more at home now. He pulled a mint from his pocket and tossed it into his mouth. The woman sat on the bed her deep eyes and scalloped cheeks hollowing him out and drawing in the room. What do you expect, that I quit? After thirty-four years you all of a sudden expect me to up and quit cause you start feelin a little lonely. He began rumaging through the closet. It ain't as if you were the first woman to have a son grow up on you, my mama had seven. You seen my blue tie? Its on the second hook on the right. What? The second hook. He came out of the closet pulling the tie under the collar and walked across the room. Look in a few more years I'll be able to retire (he kissed her on the forehead) then we can be together all the time, but not now. He let the car idle then shifted and slowed onto the highway. It ain't like I'm being hard, just practical.

He looked at the sailor, the smooth-firm face smiling into the mirror. Maybe you're right. The sailor turned. About takin it while you can. He pulled a bill from his pocket and layed it on the bar. I think the john calls he said, patting the boy on the back. Hold the fort. The sailor nodded and smiled into the mirror.

It was small. He stared straight ahead unzippering his pants, the fluorescent light washing across the porcelain and white brick tile. He could see the little red car parked in the driveway. Don't tell me you're leavin already, Mr. Putnam. He edged slowly up the brick drive. I declare, you gotta be the fastest salesman I know. And after all the business I give you. The least you could do is sit and chat awhile. You act like you was married to your job or somethin. When he had reached the screen door he was completely spent, his knees unsteady and his stomach falling to his bowels. His eyes turned back on the car, the grill grinning from the driveway. You will be back and sell me some more of your wares won't you, Mister Putnam? He had wanted then to yell out Dee, Dee, just like now. And now he stood looking at the screen door wanting to yell out: Dee I'm home, I'm home. No more road Dee, no more road, I'm home.

The urinal flushed. Putnam stood for a moment looking across at the tiles. A sign to the left: no loitering. Zippering his pants he walked over to the door and out.

The sailor had gone. Of course. Putnam walked down the bar and sat on the stool. It was still warm. He looked into the mirror. You know navy, I got a boy just about your age.

JOE MARTINEZ

The following parable is reprinted from Black Voices in Prison *(see p. 120)—the remarkable collection of writing, autobiographical testaments, and other forms of expression by inmates of Indiana State Prison, compiled by the Black poet Etheridge Knight. The only biographical information available about Joe Martinez is the fact that he is a Black prisoner at Indiana State Prison.*

Rehabilitation and Treatment

The convict strolled into the prison administration building to get assistance and counseling for his personal problems. Just inside the main door were several other doors, proclaiming: *Parole, Counselor, Chaplain, Doctor, Teacher, Correction,* and *Therapist.*

The convict chose the door marked *Correction,* inside of

which were two other doors: *Custody* and *Treatment*. He chose *Treatment*, and was confronted with two more doors, *Juvenile* and *Adult*. He chose the proper door and again was faced with two doors: *Previous Offender* and *First Offender*. Once more he walked through the proper door, and, again, two doors: *Democrat* and *Republican*. He was a Democrat; and so he hurried through the appropriate door and ran smack into two more doors; *Black* and *White*. He was black; and so he walked through that door—and fell nine stories to the street.

2.

Poetry

GWENDOLYN BROOKS (1917–   )

*Widely acclaimed as a major American poet of our times,
Gwendolyn Brooks (Blakely) is poet laureate of the state of
Illinois; she was awarded the Pulitzer Prize for poetry in 1950
and numerous other honors and awards. A particularly meaningful tribute to her was the publication in 1971 of* To Gwen,
With Love *(Johnson Publishing Company), a book of photographs, portraits, poems, and literary contributions by more
than fifty Black American writers and artists "to celebrate the
existence of the extraordinary woman named Gwendolyn
Brooks," as Hoyt W. Fuller, managing editor of* Black World,
explained. The following poem is the first poem of Riot,
*a poem in three parts arising from the disturbances in Chicago
after the assassination of Martin Luther King in 1968, published by Broadside Press (Detroit) in 1969.*

Riot

A riot is the language of the unheard.
—MARTIN LUTHER KING

John Cabot, out of Wilma, once a Wycliffe,
all whitebluerose below his golden hair,
wrapped richly in right linen and right wool,
almost forgot his Jaguar and Lake Bluff;
almost forgot Grandtully (which is The
Best Thing That Ever Happened To Scotch);
  almost

forgot the sculpture at the Richard Gray
and Distelheim; the kidney pie at Maxim's,
the Grenadine de Boeuf at Maison Henri.

Because the Negroes were coming down the
    street.

Because the Poor were sweaty and unpretty
(not like Two Dainty Negroes in Winnetka)
and they were coming toward him in rough ranks.
In seas. In windsweep. They were black and loud.
And not detainable. And not discreet.

Gross. Gross. *"Que tu es grossier!"* John Cabot
itched instantly beneath the nourished white
that told his story of glory to the World.
"Don't let It touch me! the blackness! Lord!" he
    whispered
to any handy angel in the sky.

But, in a thrilling announcement, on It drove
and breathed on him: and touched him. In that
    breath
the fume of pig foot, chitterling and cheap chili,
malign, mocked John. And, in terrific touch, old
averted doubt jerked forward decently,
cried "Cabot! John! You are a desperate man,
and the desperate die expensively today."

John Cabot went down in the smoke and fire
and broken glass and blood, and he cried "Lord!
Forgive these nigguhs that know not what
    they do."

MARGARET WALKER (1915–   )

*Margaret Walker, who was born in Birmingham, Alabama,
and grew up in New Orleans, declared in one of her early*

poems: "My roots are deep in southern life; deeper than John Brown or Nat Turner or Robert Lee" and cried out: "O Southland, sorrow home, melody beating in my bone and blood!" In her poetry and in her Houghton Mifflin Literary Award novel Jubilee (1966), *Margaret Walker has given literary expression to the Black experience in the South in historic depth and has creatively drawn upon the rich resources of Black folklore and folk idiom. She graduated from Northwestern University and received an M.A. and later her Ph.D. in creative writing from the University of Iowa Writers' Workshop. Her first volume of poems,* For My People, *was the 1942 selection in the Yale University Series of Younger Poets. She has taught English at Livingstone College (Salisbury, North Carolina) and West Virginia State College, and since 1949 has been a member of the English department at Jackson State College in Jackson, Mississippi. The following poem is from her latest collection of poetry,* Prophets for a New Day, *published by Broadside Press in 1970.*

Ballad of the Hoppy-Toad

Ain't been on Market Street for nothing
With my regular washing load
When the Saturday crowd went stomping
Down the Johnny-jumping road,

Seen Sally Jones come running
With a razor at her throat,
Seen Deacon's daughter lurching
Like a drunken alley goat.

But the biggest for my money,
And the saddest for my throw
Was the night I seen the goopher man
Throw dust around my door.

Come sneaking round my doorway
In a stovepipe hat and coat;
Come sneaking round my doorway
To drop the evil note.

I run down to Sis Avery's
And told her what I seen
"Root-worker's out to git me
What you reckon that there mean?"

Sis Avery she done told me,
"Now honey go on back
I knows just what will hex him
And that old goopher sack."

Now I done burned the candles
Till I seen the face of Jim
And I done been to Church and prayed
But can't git rid of him.

Don't want to burn his picture
Don't want to dig his grave
Just want to have my peace of mind
And make that dog behave.

Was running through the fields one day
Sis Avery's chopping corn
Big horse come stomping after me
I knowed then I was gone.

Sis Avery grabbed that horse's mane
And not one minute late
Cause trembling down behind her
I seen my ugly fate.

She hollered to that horse to "Whoa!
I gotcha hoppy-toad."
And yonder come the goopher man
A-running down the road.

She hollered to that horse to "Whoa"
And what you wanta think?
Great-God-a-mighty, that there horse
Begun to sweat and shrink.

He shrunk up to a teeny horse
He shrunk up to a toad
And yonder come the goopher man
Still running down the road.

She hollered to that horse to "Whoa"
She said, "I'm killing him.
Now you just watch this hoppy-toad
And you'll be rid of Jim."

The goopher man was hollering
"Don't kill that hoppy-toad."
Sis Avery she said "Honey,
You bout to lose your load."

That hoppy-toad was dying
Right there in the road
And goopher man was screaming
"Don't kill that hoppy-toad."

The hoppy-toad shook one more time
And then he up and died
Old goopher man fell dying, too.
"O hoppy-toad," he cried.

ROBERT HAYDEN (1913–   )

*Born in Detroit, Robert Hayden did his undergraduate work
at Wayne State University and received his M.A. from the
University of Michigan where he subsequently taught English
for two years. For many years he was a member of the
English Department at Fisk University in Nashville, Tennessee, and he is now professor of English at the University of
Michigan. His poems have appeared in* Poetry, Atlantic, *and
many other periodicals; he has won several prizes and fellowships including the Avery Hopwood Award from the University of Michigan in 1938 and in 1942 and The Grand
Prize for Poetry at The First World Festival of Negro Arts
held in Dakar, Senegal, in 1965. He is poetry editor of the
Baha'i magazine* World Order. *The biographical note in*
Kaleidoscope, *the anthology of poetry edited by Robert Hay-*

*den, asserts: "Hayden is interested in Negro history and folk-
lore and has written poems using materials from these sources.
Opposed to the chauvinistic and the doctrinaire, he sees no
reason why a Negro poet should be limited to 'racial utter-
ance' or to having his writing judged by standards different
from those applied to the work of other poets." The following
poem is from his latest volume of verse,* Words in the Mourning Time, *published in 1970 by October House.*

The Dream

(1863)

That evening Sinda thought she heard the drums
and hobbled from her cabin to the yard.
The quarters now were lonely-still in willow dusk
after the morning's ragged jubilo,
    when laughing crying singing the folks went off
with Marse Lincum's soldier boys.
But Sinda hiding would not follow them: those
Buckras with their ornery
    funning, cussed commands, oh they were not were not
the hosts the dream had promised her.

and hope when these few lines reaches your hand they will
fine you well. I am tired some but it is war you know and
ole jeff Davis muss be ketch an hung to a sour apple tree like
it says in the song I seen some akshun but that is what i listed
for not to see the sights ha ha More of our peeples coming
every day. the Kernul calls them contrybans and has them
work aroun the Camp and learning to be soljurs. How is the
wether home. Its warm this evening but theres been lots of
rain

How many times that dream had come to her—
more vision than a dream—
    the great big soldiers marching out of gunburst,
their faces those of Cal and Joe
    and Charlie sold to the ricefields oh sold away
a-many and a-many a long year ago.
Fevered, gasping, Sinda listened, knew this was
the ending of her dream and prayed

that death, grown fretful and impatient, nagging her,
would wait a little longer, would let her see.

and we been marching sleeping too in cold rain and mirey
mud a heap a times. Tell Mama Thanks for The Bible an not
worry so. Did brother fix the roof yet like he promised? this
mus of been a real nice place befor the fighting uglied it all
up the judas trees is blosommed out so pretty same as if this
hurt and truble wasnt going on. Almos like somthing you
mite dream about i take it for a sign The Lord remembers
Us Theres talk we will be moving into Battle very soon agin

Trembling tottering Hep me, Jesus Sinda crossed
the wavering yard, reached
a redbud tree in bloom, could go no farther, clung
to the bole and clinging fell
to her knees. She tried to stand, could not so much
as lift her head, tried to hold
the bannering sounds, heard only the whipoorwills
in tenuous moonlight; struggled to rise
and make her way to the road to welcome Joe and Cal
and Charlie, fought with brittle strength to rise.

So pray for me that if the Bullit with my name rote on it
get me it will not get me in retreet i do not think them kine
of thots so much no need in Dying till you die I all ways
figger, course if the hardtack and the bullybeef do not kill me
nuthing can i guess. Tell Joe I hav shure seen me some ficety
gals down here in Dixieland & i mite jus go ahead an jump
over the broomstick with one and bring her home, well I muss
close with Love to all & hope to see you soon Yrs Cal

IMAMU AMIRI BARAKA (LeROI JONES)
(1934–   )

*Poet, playwright, novelist, essayist, social critic, music critic,
anthologist, editor, and director of Spirit House, a Black
community organization in Newark, LeRoi Jones, or Imamu
Amiri Baraka as he now prefers to be known, is a leading*

*figure of the nationalist Black arts movement. His poems,
plays, stories, and essays have reached a very wide audience
and have been extensively anthologized. The following two
poems are from his third volume of verse,* Black
Magic *(Collected Poetry, 1961–1967), published in 1969 by Bobbs-
Merrill. One of his essays appears in the criticism section
(see pp. 457–67).*

(see pp. 457–67)

Ka 'Ba

A closed window looks down
on a dirty courtyard, and black people
call across or scream across or walk across
defying physics in the stream of their will

Our world is full of sound
Our world is more lovely than anyone's
tho we suffer, and kill each other
and sometimes fail to walk the air

We are beautiful people
with african imaginations
full of masks and dances and swelling chants
with african eyes, and noses, and arms,
though we sprawl in gray chains in a place
full of winters, when what we want is sun.

We have been captured,
brothers. And we labor
to make our getaway, into
the ancient image, into a new

correspondence with ourselves
and our black family. We need magic
now we need the spells, to raise up
return, destroy, and create. What will be

the sacred words?

Sacred Chant for the Return of Black Spirit and Power

Ohhh break love with white things.
Ohhh, Ohhh break break break let it roll down.

Let it kill, let it kill, let the thing you are destroy
let it murder, and dance, and kill. Ohhh OhhhOhhh break
the white thing. Let it dangle dead. Let it rot like nature needs.

MMMMMMMMMMM

MMMMMMMMMM ... OOOOOOOOOO ... Death Fiddle
                                      Claw life
                                      from space
Time

                                      Cries inside
                                      bleeds the
                                      word

The sacred Word

Evilout. Evilin. Evil Evil
White evil, god good, break love. Evil Scream.

Work smoke-blood steams out thick bushes.
We lay high and meditating on white evil.
We are destroying it. They die in the streets.
Look they clutch their throats. Aggggg. Stab him.
Agggggg.
MMMMMMMM
OOOOOOOO

Death music reach us.
Bring us back our strength.

To turn their evil backwards
is to
live.

GERALD W. BARRAX (1933–)

Born in Atalla, Alabama, Gerald W. Barrax grew up in Pittsburgh and graduated from Duquesne University. He has been a radio mechanic, postal clerk and mail carrier. He went on for the master of arts degree, and now teaches in the English department at North Carolina Central University in Durham. His poems have appeared in the Journal of Black Poetry, Poetry *magazine, and other periodicals and in Robert Hayden's anthology* Kaleidoscope: Poems by American Negro Poets *and Paul Carrol's anthology* The Young American Poets. *He won the Bishop Carroll Scholarship for Creative Writing and a gold medal award from the Catholic Poetry Society of America. He says that sometimes he speaks as "a vulnerable mortal and sometimes as a vulnerable Black American" and that Blackness and death "are implicit in all my responses to people and the world I live in and in everything I write." The following poems are from* Another Kind of Rain, *his first volume of verse, published by University of Pittsburgh Press in 1970.*

The Scuba Diver Recovers the Body of a Drowned Child

Maria, she said. No city river
Should take a name like that.
You should have been an island child and dived or fallen
Into water that liquified sunlight. Once,
    in the Bahamas, Maria, I saw
a school of fish frightened by the shadow of a plane.

There aren't enough Marias
Even in the Caribbean with all its light
To give one of you to this waste and muck.
Did you die in the taste of mills and factories? And
    when the shadow passed
over the clear water I was swimming among them.

How much of your life was there to see
To make you almost forget to breathe?
It was here, waiting for you. Scenes
Passing out of all our lives into yours. Bright
    sun. The painted fish
swimming in and out of the coral around me.

Your mother said . God . here under the river .
You were a beautiful girl she said.
All our lives have passed. Your black world blacker
Here where the sun never reaches. Next
    summer the sands will be whiter   I will go down deeper
without my mask   and come up and let the air suck my lungs
    out

when we go up   Maria
she will arrange your hair
and the wind will dry it
sun warms you
she said you were beautiful
she will know

The Old Gory

1 (red)

Nice of you, white
of you to reserve some of the red
land for the savage
whose fondness for your hair was really a compliment second only
to his knowing in-
stinc-tive-ly
Eve's tempter's tongue.
    Amazing the things that creep

under your beds.
Now it's yellow reds.
The color of the land never changes
neither do the tongues
whether splitting truth
(with or with out treaties)
or chemical fire licking
tenderly   lovingly   the round snub-nosed faces
of the evil menace.
   Big of you to reserve the red
land for the children.
You giveth and you taketh away.
   Curious how you never noticed
the stripes of your bunting
matched and bled
the same colors as your white sheets
and the slave's back and ragged scrotum
and the wet soil under the bodies of black soldiers.
   It was red.
   The same as yours.
   It's the color of the land that never changes.
Funny now
that you should ask why.

2 (white)

"The Bible is a book of race"
he said the white race he
said also that Jews are not
and the afterthought that Blacks
are not nearly human enough was un
necessary he smiled. The slave
traders, ships' captains, and plantation
owners smiled too knowing their good
books as well as he reading in comfort
that God was on their side every time
they laughed away some thing pretending to be
human

The dust of the earth was Robin Hood flour.

So now I've heard it after all
these years fall into place
and I can stop worrying how to tell

Christ from the Klansman
and why
you seem to dwell
so much
on your s*st*rs

3 (blue)

you made me blue
with the color of your fidelity   not true
as my blues blue

                              . because you didnt listen
when black was blue was black was Blue/
s.
in what name do you color truth
                              now
that Black is the space between people   ?

For a Black Poet

BLAM! BLAM! BLAM! POW! BLAM! POW!
RATTTTTTTAT! BLACK IS BEAUTIFUL, WHI
TY! RAATTTTTTTAT! POW! THERE GO A HON
KIE! GIT'M. POEM! POW! BLAM! BANG!
BANG! RATATAT! BLAM! COME ON, POEM! GET
THAT WHI-TE BEAST! BLAM! BLAM! POW!
ZAP! BANG! RAAATTTTTTTATAT! BLAM! BLAM!

How many fell for you, Brother?
How many did you leave
in the alley ballsmashed
headkicked in by your heavy feet?

The things we make as men
are guns triggered more efficiently than poems
and knives / and targets for the fires.

Men make revolutions
Poems will bring us to resurrection

There is prophecy in fire
and a beauty you can not see

a sound you cannot hear
below the exploding level of your poems
                              dress to kill
                              shoot to kill
                              love to kill
                              if you will
                              but write to bring back the dead

And you are beautiful, Brother
not because you say so but because
black is the beauty of night a Black woman
   the way a woman knows her beauty
      whose blackness falls
      softly from the spaces between stars
      who confirms our terror at her beauty in silence
and whose deepest blackness is the matrix
for the pendant worlds that hang
                              spinning from her ears.

And Black , like the swan
the shadow of itself who knows the secret
in the middle of its beauty is doubled silence
rarer than the white rush of lust
that led Leda's swan children
slouching thru their cycles of destruction.

The black panther.
His soft walk of lithe strong paces
a way of knowing   the hunter
                                   the hunted

        the beautiful) (silent (terrible beauty) quiet (terror
from   fear) the
panicked   (fear
beast / 's   (fear
crash / ing   (fear
bel / low   (fear and
ug / ly   fear

Beautiful as
a Black poempoetperson should be who
   knows what beauty lurks in the lives of men who
   know what Shadow falls between promise and praise.

The things that make us men.

Your child's questioning black fingers
touching you
is the poem
and more terror and beauty
because of the Shadow between you
than all your words.

The way blackness absorbs   swallows everything
and you Brother bring back up only upper cases
undigested at that

                        while beaten far below the level
                              of your voice
                            your life's deepest meanings lie
                              fallow.

What I mean is the way some things scream
at you   when synesthesia destroys   sometimes the beholder
                                      and the beauty

and the sense of beauty is not truth
and no longer hurts
and frightens instead of making us
feel its terror.

F. J. BRYANT, JR. (1942–   )

*Born in Philadelphia, where he still resides, F. J. Bryant, Jr.
graduated from Lincoln University in Pennsylvania and is
now a caseworker at the Montgomery Mental Health Center.
His poems have appeared in the* Journal of Black Poetry,
Negro Digest, Nickel Review, *and other periodicals; in
Clarence Major's anthology* The New Black Poetry; *in the
LeRoi Jones–Larry Neal anthology* Black Fire; *and in* To
Gwen, With Love. *He is expecting publication of his first
book of poems,* While Silence Sleeps, *by Windfall Press in
the latter part of 1971. The following poem is published from
manuscript.*

Cathexis

No thing . . .
  no-thing . . .
    nothing.
scratchy army coat, a hat, faint, on the bed end.
fire escape, itchin' chicken pox, pot,
looked in, splashed eyes, lying on couch,
blind,
hurt.

open eyes, walk to door, Mom stuttered,
raining . . .
initialed ring slips, rolls, drops, floats
on stream gurgling along curb into sewer,
gray,
hurt.

Tina, pretty Tina Miles.

venetian blinds, slat raised, David passes,
books under arm. people happy, Christmas tree,
angel hair, people happy, venetian blind, raised
slat, pale lamppost light, muddy brown snow
slushy dark, two gun holster, football helmet,
gray-silk scarf, taken, don't know
who,
hurt.

wide steps, funny smell, lady in white, needle,
funny mark on my arm. room, little
chairs and tables, glass, clay,
paint, paper, funny smell, teacher, cot room,
funny smell, graham crackers, warm milk,
uncle's dark house, riding in car, treetops
whiz, green fence, high, playground.
climb trees, funny smell, the tree top, looking
down, sandy brown color ground, falling,
arm,
hurt.

nurse pulling, arm hurting, screaming for mom,
cast itching, lost; ruler, pencil, twig,
itching,
hurt.

school, 1st grade, cast, abc's tacked on blackboard,
Mrs Hardwood, Geo. Washington's wet pants,
running, running, kissing, running.

Alberta, pretty Alberta Briggs.

school, 2nd grade, Mrs Cotton cried on Mother's Day,
we sang M-O-T-H-E-R, she cried, we
sang,
hurt.

school, 3rd grade, don't remember, why? . . .
school, 4th grade, Mrs Hall, many rulers across
my palm, long stick across backside, for my own good,
sticks,
hurt.

Mrs Land was sexy.

played war, army, baseball.
school, new school, 5th grade, played "chink" with
Leander Wilson, ring worm, Carolyn in my class, told,
talking, high hat biscuits, Sybil, pretty Sybil,
moved,
hurt.

school, new school, 6th grade, new family,
basketball, Venesa, pretty Venesa's light brown eyes,
Ivory Cohen, Stanley, big fat Joyce, big fat Joyce's
big fat family, Billie Smith's pretty sister, Catherine.
cold, safety patrol, Jewish holiday's empty school,
pretty Lois with the big eyes, Darlene, pretty skin.
"Jenny Juice."
Mike called me nigger . . .
I didn't know . . .
nigger,
hurt.

Lois' mother said not to come anymore.
Darlene's father frowned, moved away.

at corner fish store they talk different when I
walk in. playground fun, dances, *Night Owl,*
big chested Mary Jenkins, basketball, cat
family fights, mike called me,
nigger,
hurt.

CONYUS

*A new poetic voice from San Francisco, with a group of
poems in Adam David Miller's poetry anthology* Dices or
Black Bones: Black Voices of the Seventies, *Conyus has
written in response to my request for biographical data: "as
far as biographical info i would only want what is below:
9/25/70 Conyus is in San Francisco. He is living, studying,
and listening to the bells. (there was a beautiful sunset, the
day he wrote this)." All of the following poems are from
manuscript with the exception of "I Rode with Geronimo"
which appeared in* Dices or Black Bones. *In the poem cycle
"The Great Santa Barbara Oil Disaster OR:" the persona in
the poems is one of a group of prisoners sent out to clean
up the beaches around Santa Barabara after the oil disaster.*

The Great Santa Barbara Oil Disaster OR:

#1

we ride down the coast hwy through the rain
to a beach that sits in a rocky cove
    hidden from the eye.

i sit far in the rear of the bus
where the shadows pass warmly
    over the metal walls

looking through steamed windows
   at the disheveled scenery.

a mexican girl stands in the muddy debris
of her home rummaging through the mud;
   the river passed suddenly two days
ago & shifted the geography.

the clouds mount overhead,
   prostituting themselves
in small squalls & we turn left

off the freeway into the spent community
   of carpinteria like a funeral procession
on a saturday in the march winds.

beyond the border of the thin sidewalks
   sit the bleached out houses on paper stilts
with their blinds moving in pale blue motion.

we walk beneath the dingy sky
single file to the beach,
   everything around us is a bloody womb.

#2

all day we work behind the sea breaker
   in the black sand, shoveling straw
into the mouth of the skip loader,
   while the cat skinner rides high
in the seat with a hole for his eye.

in the window of an opulent club
   a servant appears to sway
in the breeze like a feather
coolly emerging from his dream.

i sit on a concrete wall
   swinging my legs over the ice plants,
touching the crushed sandwich beneath my work shirt.

after lunch we return with rakes & hip boots,
throwing sand upon the oily rocks
   & wading through the tide
that dissolves the tracks of feet.

i turn my back to the ocean
& pull the rain jacket tight,
    looking over my shoulder at the horizon.
in the distance, someone is singing a song
    that i can hardly hear.

#3

the children come to the beach
with their dogs barking happily
at a safe distance.

they watch us rake the debris
with magnetism in huge piles
for the cat skinner.

sunlight filters the surf
about our feet with blood
& birds & invincible powers.

the children run into the ocean
with granite blocks of ice,
    & symmetrically the night descends.

#4

the women
of santa barbara
watch us carry
the drift wood
across the clover field,
then go home to husbands
& kill babies
in the morning
with a small pill
while we sleep.

#5

green frogs croak in the rain pond;
dawn drizzling through the mist.

a white gull
floats face upward
in the greasy water.

i watch the tide
push the gull
against the rocks
in my silence.

#6

pearl crack
the dawn is leaking,
quiet patterns
on the street.

cool winds
their thin flagellation,
fragilely
soars across my face.

the sun set
on   the ocean
&   there   wasn't
any confusion.

#7

the citizens of santa barbara
brought rags for us to wipe

our oily black hands on.
i found a red one

& wore it around my neck,
this is called love.

#8

crickets
            in
the vacant field

sing loudly
when the sky
devours the land
in its blackness

of caskets
&

beautiful
cadillacs.

#9

(poem to the girl seen walking
below my window at 4:00 a.m.)

    i see you there
walking on the freshly
cut grass
        uncertain
about your decision
to either
      drown
the shadow or melt
the ambivalent
         rose.

#10

—for kiyono

all
night
i
touched
your
breast
kissed
your
thighs
letting
the
long
black
hair
cover
me
thickly
&
when
i
awoke
alone

with
only
a
love
stain
on
the
sheet
i
fell
in
love
with
dreaming

#11

all these men
were standing

at various levels
of confession shouting

at each other
about incarceration

for many years   for many years
for many thousand
of years

hiding and laughing
hiding and laughing
hiding and laughing

the hatred
the hatred
the explosion

beneath breast
laughing
coughing
away their
lives

#12

wensday.
the rain
fell heavily
& the beach
is specked
with piles
of straw & drift wood.

in the afternoon
we throw cans
of gasoline
onto the piles
& watch them
evaporate
like the happiest
years of your life.

#13

we pick up the sky
& move the ocean
like a giant anaconda's
head;
  they sit on the beach
watching us . . .

we place a hot badger's claw
in the cool ashes;
  they watch & move their lips slowly.

we part the sand
& bury ourselves
in a canal of lilies;
  they turn to face each other
  in awe, pretending they don't see us.

#14

beneath the houses
the shadows escape
till
  dawn
comes walking with death

on her arm
putting out lights
that burn too low

#15

the chinese girl
　　　　　served us
in cellophane gloves
　　　　　　the paper
tasting food at 7:00 a.m.
across the glossy counter.
　　　　　　the sky
was just beginning
to show traces of Aurora
　　　　　in
the east
　　　　& a continent
lowered its battled head.

　　　　　later,
on the beach
　　　　　cleaning oil
from the spume
　　　　　& beach furniture,
i ate the apple
she had given me
& thought of her
　　　　　in that
　　　　　　christian
white uniform.

thought
that she probably
felt
　　　that she was ugly
because she wasn't white
　　　　　　　& had
slanted eyes
　　　　　　& so
i took
another bowl of corn flakes
& told her that
　　　　　i didn't
want the meat.

do you think
                she understood
that i
loved her ?

#16

the 1st. night   we arrived
the girls   in the
                    dormitory
across from us
                    paraded before
their window in
bras & panties
                being friendly.

   the people
came   to watch us work
   & some said,
"my! don't they look almost human?"

sometimes the
children's ball
bounded in our area
   & we smiled.
(everyone laughed alot the first day.)

   the sun/set

& we watched its dying legions

instruct the children to play
beyond the ring of flowers
& watch the red flags
                    be
cause the sky would
fall if they harbored
ambitions in our minds.

& so
we didn't laugh
anymore, or smile
                    at all
from then on
                we just worked

slowly with our
heads keeping low
& our eyes on the ground
   so the sky wouldn't fall
& the people wouldn't know.

#17

damp mist in the cool monday dawn
we board the bus with packs on our backs
in silence for a strategic location,

heading north out of santa barbara
in the wake of working nine to five/ers;

passing through small towns
where old men sit in bleached overalls
beneath dusty hats & nondescript daughters

& we pass like a shadow
of death
       to them.

#18

in morgan hill
stitting next to
the fence post
with gray clouds
clipping the mountains
reminded me of freedom
& i thought that i was flying
& i thought that i was free

#19

they unpacked us here
in dimly lit rooms
with dust & wax on the mantel,

some of us get stored in cardboard
& others in canvas
until next year
when xmas comes again
or the Great Santa Barbara Oil Disaster/ OR:

i rode with geronimo

i rode with Geronimo
i took Custer's scalp

i am the Scottsboro boys
i went with Robeson to Europe

i am the hand reaching/for bread and soup in the 30's
i was the peasant—shot down by Franco

i was the back held taut for slave whips
i suffocated in the bow of your slave ship
i died ———— (with Emmet Till
at the bottom of the Mississippi)

i fried in the ovens of Buchenwald
i'm the lament
of ten millions Jews
echoed throughout concentration camps

i'm the soldier of a thousand wars
fighting around the world dying   lonely
on foreign soils   forgotten

i'm Garcia Lorca
pointing defiant fingers at Spanish brigades
& dancing wildly with Gypsies to the music
of flamenco guitars and lonely ballads

i am President Kennedy
bleeding in the arms of his country
wondering   what happen/

i'm Bessie Smith, Billie Holiday
winging blues to Christ
him
on his cross
nodding his head

i am the soul of the people
i'm the scapegoat of my country————
i'm the bleeding lamb of the world

i'm the wino eyes red reeking reeling
in the doorway of some decayed tenement
clutching his liquid fantasy

i am my Black brothers
searching high atop coconut palms
for manhood   lost in a shuffle
of white egret feathers

i am my mother
being raped in the corn fields of Georgia
Topsy is my sister,
Stepin Fetchit my brother
Uncle Tom & Aunt Jemima my kin ————

Trujillo killed my father/
i picked cotton to send lily white
girls through college

i am Harlem
black bottom of an ivory   top
Watts
burning hair of a mangy scalp

i'm the riot running through the streets
throwing bricks   setting fires   looting stores
taken lives————
given lives————

i am the wail the wind brings to you at night————
the increase in your stocks
your hemorrhoid problem
the reason you hate yourself
i force you to the suburbs
i make you sweat

i'm the tired body of Malcolm
resting————
thirsty blood oozing
from the loopholes of America

in the night dreams
of a young Negro child
ending certainly before the early sunrise

i am the ghost of Charlie Parker
riding the junky nod
to heaven & preaching hell
with monotones of alto sweetness
                    i'm the phantom
                    of a thousand lynchings
                    motionless
                    waiting in the draperies
                    like a senile butler
to appear in a third rate mystery & murder my oppressors.

Confession to Malcolm

i killed you Malcolm,
the first time i got locked
inside my shit yellow complexion
& laughed at all my black brothers
who walked through life with glassy do's
& morphine eyes.

i killed you that time
i let sonny boy get his
ass kicked by some white boys
in the junior high school toilet,
while i ran outside to even the odds.

i killed you when shirley
my half sister by my mother's
other husband called me a
bastard black shit-yellow ass
nigger child in front of my other
half sister & brother,
& i cried instead of reciting poetry.

i killed you when augie
went to hustling up on 12th
street for bobo & mother
thought she was at the library.

i murdered you at ford's
when i went to work for this
old honkie foreman who told me
that my father was a good boy
who had worked hard until the
day he died at his job for
thirty years & hoped i could
do as well.

i lynched you in hudson's dept. store
that xmas when the white clerk talked
to my mother like she was a piece of
black trash because she touched some
costume jewelry to her tired breast
& tarnished the copper, ivory.

i killed you when i reached
for a jar of conk o lean
bleaching out dreams in my veins
with another spoon of shit,
angry because i couldnt join
the elite crowd with a pair of
triple-a cancellation knob toes
& have a coming out party.

i murdered you when they
tied emmet till to the bottom
of the mississippi & shot medgar in the night;
martin is dead, bird's throat cut, trane,
billie, eric gone in the night. another
moat filled with the bodies of black genius.

and then there was pee wee
who died in his mother's stomach,
black & lonely like so many nigger children
whose mothers have to sit in lines at
the county hospital while the hemmorage
fills up her stomach with the lethal liquid.

i killed you the first time
i let them rape me in the cane field
or laid atop some lumpy mattress
with my thighs spread for $10.00
& a bag of funky chitterlings.

i killed you in college
with a quo-vadis strung tight
around my head like a brain tumor,
performing tricks on the football field
like a lion unleashed in the roman pits.

i murdered you Malcolm
when i let jimmy baldwin
get fucked in the ass by giovanni
to substantiate white religion,

i killed you when
i sanctioned rochester to act
like a fool nigger or lightin to do
imitations of butterfly mcqueen on his knees.

i killed you in bohemian quarters
throughout the world, selling black
for a quick fuck or some folksy job
in a dirty coffee house.

i killed you
when i continued to live
in this denatured racist democracy laugh
the first time i laid foot on this soil
not of my own free will & forgot swahili,
yoruba, bantu, pig latin, the dozens. . . .

i killed you Malcolm
from that first day
i killed you.

JAYNE CORTEZ

"Born in Arizona—Raised in Watts—Now residing in New York City U.S.A." is all that Jayne Cortez prefers to have said about her in the way of biographical information. Her poems have appeared in Negro Digest, Journal of Black Poetry, *and other literary magazines. Since the publication, in 1969, of her first volume of verse,* Pisstained Stairs and The Monkey Man's Wares, *she has begun to receive critical recognition as a new poet interesting for the ways in which she blends Black musical forms and the blues into her poetry. "I'm a Worker" and "The Rising" are new poems published from manuscript; the other two poems are reprinted from* Pisstained Stairs and The Monkey Man's Wares.

Lonely Woman

A wasted flow of water hiding
   Sliding
down the face
of a lone-ly one

This black woman's
oblong tears
render
softly felt wetness
warm like sperm
to melt
the calling—calling
flesh

Is there any reason
for this not so
dry—Dry season

Cutting tongue of fear
please
won't you hear
the stretch marks
of Loneliness
bent—in this
cold woman's tear
Night Raining
in
The Woman's Quarters
Listening to
Crickets
small—weak
dark like me
—sit—
Stripped——nude
from the trembling cadence of fire
Lit——
in Ornette's horn

Crickets that cry

Come—weep—with—us
come—weep—with us
come weep with us
Lone-ly wo-man

Lonely Woman
come weep with us

I'm A Worker
(to all my sisters in the garment industry)

My legs swollen from pressing pedals
my hands stiff from pushing cloth
I have a craving for food that's why
I have to piece work my ass off

You want some honey
you want some gunnie
I'm looking for that thing called survival money

Yes in the mornings on the buses &
in the evenings coming home
you'll hear me talk about the foreman the
floorlady the bossman & the bossman's ho
cause they all gettin rich off me & my veins varicose
believe me that's all I've got to show

If I had some honey
If I had some gunnie
think I'd have that thing called survival money

I'm so tired of this 8 to 4
sittin standin waitin for the bell to ring daytime
nighttime sometime shit with these broken
needles broken threads & taxes I
don't know what to do
why don't I collect unemployment?
that's right I paid 20 years worth of dues
but get this
if I quit?
the motha fuckin social security truant officer nazi's
don't want to get up off my long earned fufu

I got some honey
I got some gunnie
but god damn I can't find no survival money

I think I'll kill me a machine &
see if I can't get a raise that way
cause this minute to minute agony
just ain't gon bring in no sufficient pay
I got the landlord   gas   lights   the union   telephone
department store   subways   buses   & 4 human beings to feed
so tell me   tell me   tell me
do you think a revolution is what I need

Suppression

I lay paralyzed
with moorish fingers pressed firmly against my head
hypnotizing my temples as I attempt to scream
but cannot move
Held firm
firm as a baby's head pulled from darkness
a thin hair between giant tweezers

I left my body
I left the cry in the air to become spectator to my dream
The cry in the air was my body
The great pussy pinching throb between my thighs in the nest
   of pleasure
was my body
the pregnant volcano pressing my belly near eruption
was my body

I rose from this my body to see me on fire
and the fire burnt my eyes & I could not see
The fire cracked my eardrums & I could not hear
The fire charred my tongue & I could not speak
The fire consumed my brain and I could not think
The fire brushed ashes onto my forehead so I could not be
   blessed
as I threw myself upon me to purify me with myself by fire

In this heated passion
I wanted to wrap myself in the calling tunnel of darkness
to produce the flood that flashed from your rod
through quivering succulent lips
and at that moment
my body merged with myself
transferring the cry in the night to where you lay listening.

The Rising

Horns protruded from the
holes of a skeleton

gripping my bed as i
closed my eyes to the men
falling naked from heaven
my teeth waxed with candles
the stars burning my lips
a metronome conducting
orchestras of bone people
skeletons fighting skeletons
against my body sweet among skulls
I ran through ribs & my
legs were sawed off I
spat between rotted out seed pits &
my own seeds became knots on my forehead
I shot without looking & the moon
stuck out its tongue as I sucked
peyote & knelt for the wedding between
fire & the fluid of my sorrow
in combat with myself
a refugee without feet
a virgin in a cathedral of hanging flesh
I the new flag to a revolution
the failure of death
blackly tuning the sun for the reign of
the rising sphinx

VICTOR HERNANDEZ CRUZ (1949–   )

*Born in a small village in Puerto Rico, the writer moved with
his family to the United States when he was four years old.
He lived in New York City for many years until he recently
became a member of the faculty of the English department at
the University of California at Berkeley. He writes out of the
Black and Puerto Rican experiences in the United States in
his own individual way. His poems have appeared in* Umbra,
of which he was an editor, Journal of Black Poetry, New York
Review of Books, Evergreen Review, Ramparts, *and other*

periodicals and in Black Fire *and other anthologies of contemporary Black writing. He is presently working on a novel. The following poems are from his first volume of poetry,* Snaps, *published by Random House in 1969.*

First Claims Poem

who i break my head against
who i jump on
who i fall into   who i am

who i am   a skull   eyes looking for trouble
to leave the shapes you got the same i cannot do that to crush & twist them i will

a skull   eyes   black hair   a final word
a lip opening unusual a third open a
cut the taste of blood a finger kissing
slowly an eye   an open window where i
live   black burlap   malcolm   x hanging on
the wall burning candle the sound of a
high-pitched conga drum Ishmael's book is
still to be read mongo coming out from the
speakers   conga going up walls   there is
still time   there is still hope   there is time
i think to fail again & again&again & again
there is time for all this   there is time for Ish's
book there is time to win a prize there is
time   it is time for those who will win
the awards   i have time & in time i will
fail

who i break my head against
who i jump on
who i fall into   who i am

it is time to deserve
who i deserve
what do i deserve

if i do not deserve anything on this earth
if not a drop of things here is mine

i deserve
i deserve
        with all the hand clappings
        all the space from here to the moon.

urban dream

1

there was fire & the people were yelling. running crazing.
screaming & falling. moving up side down. there was fire.
fires. & more fires. & walls caving to the ground. & mercy
mercy. death. bodies falling down. under bottles flying in
the air. garbage cans going up against windows. a car
singing brightly a blue flame. a snatch. a snag. sounds of
bombs. & other things blowing up.
times square
electrified. burned. smashed. stomped
hey over here
hey you. where you going.
no walking. no running. no standing.
STOP
you crazy. running. stick
this stick up your eyes. pull your heart out.
hey.

2

after noise. comes silence. after brightness (or great big
flames) comes darkness. goes with whispering. (even soft
music can be heard) even lips smacking. foots stepping all
over bones & ashes, all over blood & broken lips that left their
head somewhere else, all over livers, & bright white skulls with
hair on them. standing over a river watching hamburgers
floating by. steak with teeth in them.
flags. & chairs. & beds. & golf sets. & mickey mouse
broken in half.
governors & mayors step out the show. they split.

3

dancing arrives.
like in planes. like in cars.

yes. yes. yeah. mucho boogaloo. mucho.
& sections of land sail away. & suicide rises. idiots jumping
into fires. the brothers five sing the blues as they sink.
kids blow their brains out, first take glue, & then shoot their
skull caps off, with elephant guns.

& someone sings & someone laughs. & nobody knows.
& chant to gods.
& chant to gods.

JAMES A. EMANUEL (1931–   )

*Born and reared in Alliance, Nebraska, James A. Emanuel
worked on ranches and farms as a teen-ager, attended Howard
University (B.A.), Northwestern University (M.A.), and
Columbia University (Ph.D.) and is now associate professor
of English at The College of the City of New York. He first
published his poems in college publications and in* Ebony
Rhythm *(1948); in 1958 his work began to appear in* Phylon,
Negro Digest, The Midwest Quarterly, The New York Times,
Freedomways, *and other periodicals. He has published a book-
length critical study,* Langston Hughes *(1967), essays and book
reviews, two volumes of poetry and is coeditor of the anthology* Dark Symphony: Negro Literature in America. *His
work has been anthologized in about thirty-five collections
and textbooks in the United States, England, and France. He
is general editor of the forthcoming Broadside Critic Series
on Black Poets. The following poems were selected from
manuscript, prior to the publication of his latest collection
of poetry,* Panther Man, *published in 1970 by Broadside Press
in Detroit.*

Whitey, Baby

WhatCHU care
what I feel

when I think blk
pull down the shades / on my mind
turn my back t yr hand
putcha outa my room
digya outa my life?

WhatCHU know
bout stayin in the dark
cause ya cant blieve nothin
nobody says / bout good things
ya gonna get
xcep somethin Mama made?

WhatCHU know
bout Daddy comin home fired
cause crackers tricked m
out s job,
and broodin in s broken chair
takin a hour takin off s coat?

Gonna show / you / KNOW
by shakin yr hair
sadlike, wearin tighter pants
on trips,
puttin a button where yr heart is.

Who ya gonna TELL, baby,
when ya feel / I dont care
anymore?

What THEY care
whatchu feel?

Black Man, 13th Floor

Hotel Ameridemocratogrando
12 floors below me, 12 above
stops nothin at my life
(this 13th floor
this legacy from black charioteers
swung low, stolen away
riding middle passage

between the breathing floors
ashcakers brought to bed on clay
massa's thirteeners
seedsmen of me)

lyin here waitin stoppin nothin
but when them little sissy operators
leap past 12 my mind whips out a pistol shot
"THIRTEEN!"
earcrackin every massa bound for 25
upsnatchin all thirteeners clustered black below—

Hotel Ameridemocratogrando
crowdin m in with me
bettin on my life squeezin out
crawlin through some other stinkin
middle passage—

makin brotherbreathin cool
the floor of me
gather it up
13th entire
ashcakers together
and move us away
from the crash

For "Mr. Dudley," a Black Spy

Harlem dud,
pulpit spoiler of the Word,
shapeshifter faking cards,
credentials slicking up whatever role
Master Whitey Big
kicked on you: painter,
preacher, plumber,
butt-hustler reeking,

I saw you
hear you lisping cute
for Adam, tricking Clayton
fooling Powell, fronting cameras
that choked that big white collar round your neck,

you strangling,
spit missing Bimini.

I saw you
know you mixing Judas paint
with Judas praise when you pushed in
that startled woman's door,
with "Mr. Dudley" on your card
and in your peeling mind already Judas pipes
installed to plumb, to bug the private hearts,
to taptape fireside bedside table talk—
her family Black but not your kind,
below their Afroes
cheekless for your kiss.

I saw you
remember you mixing in, slick-
fingering the campus Blacks,
taptapping on Columbia shoulders,
systemshakers not startled by you,
uncle, old jitterbug slobbering young jive,
sidling sleeve-tugger, lisping
for inside dope, hustling Harlem filter tips
and names to trade on.

For you, "Dudley,"
and your beardless, baubled clan,
these loathings
to suck on.

Panther Man

Wouldnt think
t look at m
he was so damn bad
they had t sneak up on m,
shoot m in his head
in his bed
sleepin
Afroed up 3 inches
smilin gunpowder.

Hey, Mister Panther!
Get up
and fight that cracker-back,
back m gainst the wall
of YOUR room
where YOU sleep
with YOUR dreams
and take down his goddam name
take down his goddam number
give m a motel napkin
to hold the blood
where YOUR bullet
grabbed m,
tell m YOUR name
YOUR race
make m write it down
in HIS blood
for HIS momma to remember,
back m out yr door
and make m come in RIGHT—
in daylight
with ALL his pukey buddies
behind guns cursin Black men,
makin gut noises
wakin up the WORLD.

Tell m, Panther!
Get up out yr dead bed;
if THATS the way he is
even yr GHOST
can take m.

MARI EVANS

*Born in Toledo, Ohio, Mari Evans lives in Indianapolis where
she has been writer-in-residence and instructor in Black litera-*

*ture at Indiana University-Purdue University, Indianapolis;
she is also producer/director/writer of "The Black Experience," a weekly presentation of WTTV Channel 4. The show
draws its materials and participants from the Black community and has been described by Mari Evans as "an exploration of the psychodynamics of the Black revolution."
She has lectured and read her poetry at numerous colleges and
universities in the United States and served as a consultant
in the Discovery Grant Program of the National Endowment
of the Arts in 1969 and 1970. Her poems have appeared in
forty or more anthologies and textbooks, including works in
Italian, German, Swedish, French, and Dutch. The following
poem was selected from manuscript prior to the publication
of her collection of poems* I Am a Black Woman *in 1970 by
William Morrow.*

Vive Noir!

i
   am going to rise
   en masse
   from Inner City

              sick
                 of newyork ghettos
             chicago tenements
          l a's slums

weary
      of exhausted lands
      sagging privies
      saying yessuh yessah
      yesSIR
      in an assortment
      of geographical dialects i
have seen my last
broken down plantation
even from a
distance
      i
will load all my goods
in '50 Chevy pickups '53
Fords fly United and '66
caddys i

have packed in
the old man and the old lady and
wiped the children's noses
            I'm tired
            of hand me downs
                shut me ups
                pin me ins
                    keep me outs
                        messing me over have
                    just had it
                    baby
                    from
                    you . . .
i'm
gonna spread out
over America
                intrude
my proud blackness
all
    over the place
                i have wrested wheat fields
                from the forests

                turned rivers
                from their courses

                leveled mountains
                at a word
                festooned the land with
                bridges
                            gemlike
                        on filaments of steel
                                moved
                glistening towersofBabel in place
                        like blocks
                sweated a whole
                civilization
                    . . . for you
                now
                        i'm
                gonna breathe fire
                through flaming nostrils BURN
                        a place for

                    me

in the skyscrapers and the
schoolrooms on the green
lawns and the white
beaches
        i'm
gonna wear the robes and
sit on the benches
make the rules and make
the arrests say
who can and who
can't
                baby you don't stand
                a
                chance
i'm
    gonna put black angels
    in all the books and a black
    Christchild in Mary's arms i'm
    gonna make black bunnies black
    fairies black santas black
    nursery rhymes and
                        black
    ice cream
            i'm
gonna make it a
    crime
        to be anything BUT black
        pass the coppertone

gonna make white
a twentyfourhour
lifetime
J.O.B.
        an' when all the coppertone's gone . . . . ?

CALVIN FORBES

*In a letter to the editor Calvin Forbes writes about himself:
"I was born in Newark, N.J., and raised there though I have*

*been in California and Hawaii and now live in Boston. I have
been to several schools: Rutgers, The New School, Stanford.
At present I teach Afro-American and African Literature at
Emerson College in Boston." He has published poems in* The
Yale Review, The American Scholar, *and other periodicals.
Two of the following poems are published from manuscript;
"Reading Walt Whitman" appeared in* Survival, *published by
the Urban League of Boston, Spring, 1970.*

Reading Walt Whitman

I found his wool face, I went away
A crook; there were lines I followed
When his song like a whistle led me.

Daily my wooden words fell, a parade
Of sticks, a broom bent over a thief's
Head. But then along came Langston

The proper shepherd who sat on history
Missing our music, dividing me; after
His death I rewrote, I robbed, and hid

In a foxhole until my lines were wood
On top, and soft underneath the bark.
Good Langston sat too long to lift me.

Europe

is endowed with the first move
Initiative enough to enhance to
A minimal edge; then element
Enters the game and many lovers
End in a draw. In almost every

Battle play positional with their
King. The traditional pawn breaks

Castles, achieves early equality
And wins but his heart is empty.

For the apex is the assault: drive
The enemy queen to a bad beginning
And later their romantic rook
Is shunted. Black commands the
Salient lines, the projected angle.

Resignation is justified only if
Followed by your mate. Europe hangs
On to the ghost. The blacks cross
Themselves and win. Can you see how?

Lullaby for Ann-Lucian

My mother sliced the south for us
She divided a poison from the flesh.
And every bite made the farmer laugh.

But your golden parents are oceanic
Touching lands my mother never knew.
A lighthouse keeps you off the rocks.

Shine: though the fruit is foreign
Leave the rind. And don't swallow
The seeds, or you'll wake up a crow.

When an enemy of the harvest arrives
The country children use sling shots.
They recognize his color and his greed.

NIKKI GIOVANNI (1943–   )

Nikki Giovanni was born in Knoxville, Tennessee, majored in history at Fisk University in Nashville, and "dropped out of a Masters Program at the University of Pennsylvania," as she noted in an autobiographical note in The New Black Poetry. *She now teaches creative writing at Rutgers University. Her individual poems have appeared in* Black Dialogue, Journal of Black Poetry, Negro Digest, *and many other publications. She has read her poetry on the educational television program "Soul" and her poems have appeared in many anthologies and have won a wide contemporary audience. The following poem is from* Black Judgement (1968), *the first of three collections of her poetry published by Broadside Press.*

My Poem

i am 25 years old
black female poet
wrote a poem asking
nigger can you kill
if they kill me
it won't stop
the revolution

i have been robbed
it looked like they knew
that i was to be hit
they took my tv
my two rings
my piece of african print
and my two guns

if they take my life
it won't stop
the revolution

my phone is tapped
my mail is opened
they've caused me to turn
on all my old friends
and all my new lovers
if i hate all black
people
and all negroes
it won't stop
the revolution

i'm afraid to tell
my roommate where i'm going
and scared to tell
people if i'm coming
if i sit here
for the rest
of my life
it won't stop
the revolution

if i never write
another poem
or short story
if i flunk out
of grad school
if my car is reclaimed
and my record player
won't play
and if i never see
a peaceful day
or do a meaningful
black thing
it won't stop
the revolution

the revolution
is in the streets
and if i stay on
the 5th floor
it will go on

if i never do
anything
it will go on

CARL H. GREENE (1945–   )

*In a letter to the editor, in December, 1970, the author writes:
"Carl H. Greene, twenty-five, was born in and presently lives
in Philadelphia. He has attended the Indiana Institute of
Technology, Lincoln University, Pa., and the University of
Pennsylvania as an English major. His works have appeared
in: A Galaxy of Black Writing, Ed.—Baird Shurman; Voices
of the Revolution, Ed.—Edith Kaplan; The Best in Poetry,
Ed.—Barbara Fisher. He has received the Cyclo-Flame poetry
award, for 1970, and his works may be found in various
poetry magazines across the country." The following poems
are published from manuscript.*

Something Old, Something New

a neon sign blinked red,
and it was an old bed,
in an old hotel.
n'd i wondered how much
sex,
n'd how many sexes
the bed had borne,
n'd the mattress sagged,
n'd she lay close against
me on virgin sheets,
n'd it was her first
time too.

The Realist

i know the limitations of my body,
and the unintellectual grasp of
people, places and things
for, i stopped dreaming at 10,
& my imigination is a cynical
self-possession of hungry fears
n'd aching thoughts.
so,
it really doesn't matter if i
win or lose in life today,
I've tried.

The Excuse

boys forget about women
when they go off to war,
men don't.
i've been married close to
10 years,
n'd been out here,
close to 9 months with guns
ringing in my ears.
(the front is hell n'd a little more).
tonight they go'n to send us into
a town about 20 miles back for
r & r.
lord, i've committed a lot of
sins, but i've got an extremely
good excuse.

KIRK HALL (1944–   )

Born in Montclair, New Jersey, Kirk Hall now lives in Pittsburgh. He received a B.A. in sociology at Virginia Union University in Richmond in 1967. His poems have been published in Journal of Black Poetry, *in* Connections, *the publication of Oduduwa Production in Pittsburgh, and in the anthologies* Black Fire *and* Spectrum in Black. *The following poems are published from manuscript.*

blackgoldblueswoman

Black Gold, blackgold . . . aint no oil
blackgold . . . b-l-a-c-k-g-o-l-d
moving moving moving to me away from me
all around me for me
can i watch you
pardon me if i stare . . . or
touch you if I dare . . . . .

Blackgold blueswoman
winking your eye strutting down the way
smiling at the brother
check him out . . . . check him out
check him out quick
                        there aint too many
Blackgoldblueswoman
doing an old freshdance in the middle of the floor
we watching you
gettin' down right there (aint no records playing)
aint no records playing, blueswoman

. . . but don't stop
we all want to dance to your tune
BLACKGOLDBLUESWOMAN

today is not like they said. . . .

bleeding hearts talk of happy days
and gymshoes with candydolls gone
with tomorrow's heat and sticky
handprints on new fourth-hand dress
of handmade happiness switching downtown

tired feet walk through streets
of encampment where garbage stops up
worn soles but fails to keep out the
stoneheat of endless sidewalk
because home is nowhere

and deaf ears hear firetrucks
flying past the corner and feet
running to see and thoughts saying
o please don't let it be me
and don't we all know feel see
that the best we do is not good enough
and misery is for the
dying

MICHAEL S. HARPER (1938–   )

*For the past decade Michael S. Harper, who studied creative
writing at the famous Iowa University Writers' Workshop,
has been publishing poems in* Poetry, Poetry Northwest,
Southern Review, Quarterly Review of Literature, Negro Di-

gest, December, *and other magazines. His first volume of verse,* Dear John, Dear Coltrane, *was published in 1970 by University of Pittsburgh Press. Born in Brooklyn, New York, he spent many years in California where he worked as a postal clerk and teacher. Harper has been poet-in-residence at Lewis and Clark College and visiting lecturer in literature at Reed College (both in Portland, Ore.), associate professor of English and consultant in Black studies at California State College at Hayward and for the academic year 1970–71 was a fellow at The Center for Advanced Study of the University of Illinois. He is now associate professor of English at Brown University. Three of the following poems are from his book* Dear John, Dear Coltrane, *and* "High Modes: Vision as Ritual: Confirmation" *was selected from the manuscript of his second volume of verse,* History Is Your Own Heartbeat, *prior to its publication by University of Illinois Press.*

A Mother Speaks:
The Algiers Motel Incident, Detroit

It's too dark to see black
in the windows of Woodward
or Virginia Park.
The undertaker
pushed his body back
into place
with plastic and gum
but it wouldn't
hold water.
When I looked
for marks
or lineament
or fine stitching
I was led away
without seeing
this plastic
face they'd built
that was not my son's.
They tied the eye
torn out
by shotgun

into place
and his shattered
arm cut away
with his buttocks
that remained.
My son's gone
by white hands
though he said
to his last word—
"Oh I'm so sorry,
officer, I broke your gun."

High Modes: Vision as Ritual: Confirmation

Black Man Go Back To The Old Country
Black Man Go Back To The Old Country
Black Man Go Back To The Old Country
Black Man Go Back To The Old Country

And you went back home for the images,
the brushwork packing the mud
into the human form; and the ritual:
Black Man Go Back To The Old Country.

We danced, the chocolate trees and samba
leaves wetting the paintbrush, and babies
came in whispering of one, oneness,
otherness, forming each man in his music,
one to one: and we touch, *contact-high,*
high modes, *contact-high,* and the images,
contact-high, man to man, came back.
Black Man Go Back To The Old Country.

The grooves turned in a human face,
Lady Day, blue and green, modally,
and we touched, *contact-high,* high modes:
Black Man Go Back To The Old Country.

Bird was a mode from the old country;
Bud Powell bowed in modality, blow Bud;
Louis Armstrong touched the old country,

and brought it back, around corners;
Miles is a mode; Coltrane is, power,
Black Man Go Back To The Old Country
Black Man Go Back To The Old Country
Black Man Go Back To The Old Country.

And we go back to the well: Africa,
the first mode, and man, modally,
touched the land of the continent,
modality: we are one; a man is another
man's face, modality, in continuum,
from man, to man, *contact-high,* to man,
contact-high, to man, high modes, oneness,
contact-high, man to man, *contact-high:*

Black Man Go Back To The Old Country
Black Man Go Back To The Old Country
Black Man Go Back To The Old Country
Black Man Go Back To The Old Country

for Oliver Lee Jackson

Zocalo

We stand pinned
to the electric mural
of Mexican history
and listen to a paid guide
explain fresco technique
and the vision of Diego Rivera:
Cortes, crippled with disease,
his Indian woman and son,
sailor raping an Indian
in frocks of priesthood.

In the center the Mexican
eagle peels the serpent
and cools his thirst on desert cactus;
Hidalgo forced into Independence,
that bald creole iconoclast
lost east of Guadalajara;
near him, Montezuma
passively meets Cortes,

salutes the Gods,
dies, the mistake of his people;
corn mixes with chickens and goats,
housepets, muskets and cactus wine.

To your left Rockefeller,
Morgan, the atomic bomb,
Wall Street, the pipeline to the Vatican;
below, the Mexican people pay
for the chosen friar
and the dignity of retreat
to the hills above the central valley.

Then comes Juarez—our guide's
voice rings with full-blooded pride
at the full-blooded Indian
busting the military;
he disbands the church,
opens his arms, and gives
the land to the people.
Our guide is speaking in Spanish:
"You see, my friends, we want the land
that Santa Anna gave you for ten
million pesos; we want Texas, Arizona
and the rest of the west;
take the painting, absorb it—
then give us back our land."

The Guerrilla-Cong

He looks back at me
from LIFE—
Geronimo run down
by black cavalry
in Mexico,
an illiterate Eskimo woman
called Kim,
Charlie Cong;
he looks like a child,
which he is,
though he isn't;
he has fought

361 battles over three years;
He is on CBS
having lost his identity
having lost his genitals
having lost our war.

WILLIAM J. HARRIS (1942–   )

*In a letter to the editor, William J. Harris writes: "I was born
and reared in Yellow Springs, Ohio—one of the few towns in
the Midwest to which I would want to return. In Wilberforce,
Ohio, I attended Central State University, a predominantly
black school. At present I am a graduate student at Stanford
University, near San Francisco, reluctantly finishing up my
class work and preparing to plunge into my thesis on LeRoi
Jones. My work has appeared in* The Antioch Review, The
Beloit Poetry Journal, Into 2, Nine Black Poets, Black Out
Loud, Natural Process, A Galaxy of Black Writing, *and other
places." The following poems are published from manuscript.*

My baby
loves flowers

She has them
everywhere

Our apartment
(barely big enough
for the two of us)
has turned into
a horticultural center

—matched nowhere
in the known world

Last night
my baby
wore a garland
of daisies
in her long
brown hair

that crown
made my baby
look like
the queen of spring

an 1890's Goddess

a Gibson girl
come home
to her man
across time

a real knockout
for the eyes
of stately
downtown
Saturday night
Palo Alto.

This morning
searching the
kitchen for food,
I see   my baby
has placed the daisies
in water
in a little spice bottle
on the window sill

so they might be flowers
a little longer

My baby
loves flowers

A Daddy Poem

My father is a hand-
some guy.

Looks like
a cross between
Clark Gable & Ernest Hemingway.
If you don't believe me,
I got proof:
Once a white woman
(at one of those
          parties)
said, to my father,
"You're good looking
for a colored man."

EVERETT HOAGLAND (1942–   )

Originally from Philadelphia, Everett Hoagland graduated from Lincoln University in Pennsylvania in 1964, with a creative writing award. He now lives in Pomona, California, and teaches African-American poetry at Scripps College for the Claremont Black Studies Center. His work has appeared in Negro Digest, The Nickel Review, Ra, *and other periodicals, and in* The New Black Poetry. *He has presented public readings of his works on both the east and west coasts. The following poem is from* Black Velvet, *his collection of poetry published in 1970 by Broadside Press (Detroit).*

The Anti-Semanticist

honeystain ...
the rhetoricians of blackness
matter me not
we are black
and you are beautiful

it matters me not whether
your breasts are american pumpkins or
african gourds
they are full and you are beautiful

it matters me not be your belly
black or brown
it is soft and you are beautiful

it matters me not be your buttocks
bourgeoise or "grass roots"
they are good
and you are beautiful

it matters me not if your bread loaf
thighs
are negro or afro-american
they are round and so ripe
and you are so beautiful

it matters not whether it is
Victoria Falls within your orgasms
instead of Niagara

there is little definition i need
indeed
it matters only that there is
black power
in your loving

this i know

you are beautiful
you are beatiful beyond reference
you are the night interpreted
you are
you

LANCE JEFFERS (1919–   )

*Poet, critic, and author of fiction, Lance Jeffers has sent the
following biographical note to the editor: "Lance Jeffers,
reared in Nebraska and California, teaches the writing of
poetry and the writing of the novel at California State College
at Long Beach. He is a* cum laude *graduate of Columbia, received a master's degree from Columbia University, and has
done advanced graduate work at the University of Toronto.
He has published short stories in* The Best American Short
Stories, 1948, Quarto, Dasein, *and* A Galaxy of Black Writing; *poetry in* Phylon, Tamarack Review, Burning Spear,
Dasein, Black Voices, Freedomways, Black Fire, Nine Black
Poets, The New Black Poetry, Watts Poets, Beyond the
Blues, A Galaxy of Black Writing, Survive, Afroamerican
Literature, *and other anthologies; and an essay in* The Black
Seventies. *A volume of his poetry,* My Blackness Is The
Beauty of This Land, *has been published by Broadside Press
in Detroit. An excerpt from his novel* Witherspoon *was
published in* A Galaxy of Black Writing, *and he was granted
a full-time leave during the spring semester, 1971, by California State College at Long Beach to complete a second
novel. He lives with his wife Trellie (who teaches in the Black
Studies Department at California State College at Long Beach)
and their three daughters in Compton, California." In September, 1971, Jeffers left California with his family to serve as
Chairman of the Department of English at Bowie State College in Bowie, Maryland. The following poems are published
from manuscript.*

Old Love Butchered (Colorado Springs and Huachuca)

This purple cloud of grief within my heart,
this sweeter-still than black-thigh woolly night,
this mute life nesting old-age in an oak,
this hill-creased path of beaten grass—

these eyes upon the ground, and humpbacked child,
this old foredoomed and grisly tearwrench love,
live yet awhile in rawveined tenderness,
yet live a time in rawveined tenderness.

Trellie

From the old slave shack I chose my lady,
from the harsh garden of the South,
from slaves bending between the rows of cotton,
from Charlie James whose soul was African
    in the unredeeming Southern sun,
from song of slaves who stuffed the sky
    like chitlins down their throats,
from woman dark who leaned back and
    wombed out the grandeur of her song in poetry
    as long and deep as prehistoric night,
in song as causeful as the fiery center of the earth,
in love as muscular as thighs of darkskinned god
    who cradled Africa at his chest,
in love as nippled as milk that flows from Nile to sea,
from the old slave shack I chose my lady:

She lies here frank beside me in the night, she
    is the greatness of the slaves without their fear,
she is the anger of this day and elegant pride that
    touched black child who walked three miles
    to school and saw white child's bus leave her
    trampling in the dust:

She has a beauty that I aspire,
She has a grandeur that I require,
some other rapture that my song must lyre,
some woolier head to batter the entombment of my fire,
to lay my stunted heart upon the pyre
　　and blow upon my godliness till
　　it come down my mouth,
　　the soul of my grandfather's sire
as he stood harried in slavery.

And as I lie beside her in the night, I foresee
　　America's birth in death while
　　tyranny grinds its knife to seek my veins and outraged eye;
foresee myself in prison camp,
hooking guillotine's blade to my neckflesh when morning
　　comes,
and she engrieved within my breast to weep my death,

what more marrowed sorrow could there be?
What tear large as blackness' pyramid will lodge my eye
　　and drop when my life's blood prepares to leave her and
　　　　sink beneath
　　the soil?
But this black South will run the reindeer down
　　from frozen North
　　to bring Trellie's love to me within my grave,
bring her love to all my whiter crimes and grudging heart,
to all my assassination of myself,
to my unyielding hatred of tyranny:
our children's conquering will grow like elephant tusks
　　from earth I drench in blood:
ten thousand children will redwood from my genes
　　to mount the earth in my black people's time!

I do not know the power of my hand

I do not know the power of my hand,
my hand is withered, coldcreamed,
fledgling, weak, and cold,
shivering, sonorous, diseased,
the power of my hand is held at bay,
lowered into the vale of dishonesty, my hand,
and suffering,

but if I knew the power of my hand,
the masculinity and grandeur of my hand,
saw the blackness of my hand revolve beneath the coldcream,
saw the hair upon my hand spring like redwood warts
    against the sky's raw face,
saw the muscles of my hand caress a piano's dark fingers
    like a god who couples with the fire of earth's deep core
    and brings forth infants who are impervious to hell:

if I were to know the power of my hand
    to psalm a whole black nation with my song,
to sing a world to woolen sleep beneath my strings,
to rouse flamenco to the sky's sweet sombre-down
    and blues a vest of life upon my grandsire's corpse,

if I were to know the power of my hand
to genius the human race to peace
    and pluck the wicked eggs from out its genes,
to write a script that only beauty's eye could read
and all that could not read would coffins ride:

for I am humanity cupped in hand,
and all the vulgared song will turn to rye,
and all the symphonied wrongs are cursed to die,
and all despair that's realmed to ply
    its deathy trade on sorrow's wharf
will drown, a human race of angels ride the tide!

There is a nation

There is a nation in my brawny scrotal sac,
a nation in my spine,
a nation in my graveled throat,
a nation in the succored egg that climbs my womby well,
there is a nation in my crimes against myself,
    my sombre settling ancient quarrels within my groin,
ah, some nation crawls, back broken, out my lungs and
    dives into my bowels to anguish-die.

And when my spirituals lay like future tension in my skull,
    when blues hobbled skinny and broken-legged to my
    janitor's room,

when the cement of a San Francisco playground ripped my
    armflesh
    and a stepfather's hostile face was in my clime,
a nation bore my semen unbeknown to my peak
for a nation lay silent-surly also in his janitor's heart and time,
his janitor's time,
a nation lay silent-surly in his time.

The nation was born when I was niggered in a wheatfield town
and lonely as I was, I spat bread,
a nation was born when I was sliced into a dozen bloody books
    that wrote their Teddy Wilson song
    on supercilious ground,
a nation was born when white swans were my ikon,
a nation was born in hatred and in the illness of a scruffy love,
a nation was born when I beheld an ocean broader
    than Pacific between the swans and Africa that survives
    in me: between the swans and Africa that survives in me.

A nation was born, a nation was born,
a nation long and black and sick, a nation strongly whole,
a nation Africa'd of laughter,
a nation Africa'd of song,
a nation sombre in its bleeding, a nation cunning in its strong,
a nation subtle to survive, a nation lion, a nation lamb,
a nation conquering on its knees,
a nation blackrosed, festivaled, orange-breasted, serene,
a nation waging war with genitals and wit,
a nation granite, nation winged, a nation, yes,
a nation in my soul.

NORMAN JORDAN (1938–   )

*Poet and playwright Norman Jordan was born in Ansted, West
Virginia, and has lived in Cleveland for the past twenty-one
years. His plays have been staged in San Diego, Cleveland,*

and New York. His poems have appeared in Cricket, Journal
of Black Poetry, Black World, Confrontation, *and other
periodicals and in the anthologies* Black Fire, The New Black
Poetry, Right On!, *and* Black Out Loud. *He has received a
United Nations playwright's award and participated in the
1967 UN International Playwright's Workshop. He is currently writer-in-residence and first recipient of the Harriet Eels
Performing Arts Fellowship at Karamu House, a metropolitan
center for the arts and multiracial communication. (With a
multiracial program that does not exclude anybody, Karamu
House, located in Cleveland's inner city for fifty-six years,
now has a Black center of gravity and a Black perspective.)
Mr. Jordan's first volume of poetry,* Destination: Ashes, *was
published in 1969 by Vibration Press in Cleveland, is currently in its fifth printing and will be published anew by Third
World Press in Chicago. His second collection of poetry,*
Above Maya, *is now at the printer's. All but one of the poems
that follow are from* Destination: Ashes; *the poem "July 27,"
is published from manuscript.*

I Have Seen Them

I have seen them trying. . . .
to sober up
to be heard
to listen
to live—
Lord Knows, I have seen them.

I have seen them waiting. . . .
for relief
for a job
for winter to pass
for life—
Yes Lord, I have seen them.

I have seen them crying. . . .
because it's too late
because they can't feed their babies
because they are tired of maybe
because they are afraid—

Dear Lord yes, I have seen them
Praying. . . .
for miracles.

When A Woman Gets Blue

No man knows
How empty a woman feels
When she gets blue.
When her man is gone
and troubles call,
No man knows.
When a woman's been trying,
when a

When a woman's been trying
When a woman's been suffering,
No man knows.
When a woman is alone,
When a woman feels un-needed
No man knows.
When all the world seems cold
And a woman cries
No man knows.
When a woman's heart aches
And her lips are silent
No man knows.
No man knows
The lonely hurt
When a woman gets blue.

Be You

It's getting
to be a thing
Man   Man
the dead empty
eyes   eyes
each time around

the same dead
empty eyes
    (It's hard to
    hip a fool
    cause he thinks
    he's already hip)
Trane was
heavy   heavy
because Trane did
his thing
Trane was in Tune
with Trane
and *His* God
and *his* people
Too many good poets
are killing themselves
trying to be
like LeRoi
Jones   Jones
can take care of Jones
Don Lee raps for Don Lee
Larry Neal and Bill Russell
create from Larry Neal and Bill Russell

      (and we are all
      blessed because
      they do)

Write *your* poem
Sing *your* song
Paint *your* picture
Be your own Black self

BE YOU

The Silent Prophet

    Trane
    must have
    died
    a thousand
    times
    trying to tell
    us

what it was
all about
but we were
so busy
dancing
we couldn't hear
his music.

July 27,

Overheard
a brother saying
to a sister:
"With love
and a few other
minor things
we can
have down here
what's going on up there."
Unzipping his pants,
she asked,
"Up where?"

The Poet the Dreamer

With time
and space
in
his hip-pocket

The Poet
hops and skips
to the edge
of God's eye
and pees on
last year's
dead flowers.

BOB KAUFMAN

An associate of Lawrence Ferlinghetti and Allen Ginsberg in the "Beat" movement, Bob Kaufman was first published in Beatitude Magazine *in San Francisco in the late 1950s. His broadsides, "The Abomunist Manifesto," "Second April," and "Does the Secret Mind Whisper" were first published separately by City Lights and then included in his first book,* Solitudes Crowded With Loneliness, *published by New Directions in 1965. This book was translated and published in France in a large pocketbook edition and received high critical acclaim from the leading French revues. For years his work was better known and more highly esteemed in Europe than in the United States. The following poems are from his second collection of poetry,* Golden Sardine, *published in 1967 by City Lights Books.*

Cocoa Morning

Variations on a theme by morning,
Two lady birds move in the distance.
Gray jail looming, bathed in sunlight.
Violin tongues whispering.

Drummer, hummer, on the floor,
Dreaming of wild beats, softer still,
Yet free of violent city noise,
Please, sweet morning,
Stay here forever.

Heavy Water Blues

The radio is teaching my goldfish Jujitsu
I am in love with a skindiver who sleeps underwater,
My neighbors are drunken linguists, & I speak butterfly,
Consolidated Edison is threatening to cut off my brain,
The postman keeps putting sex in my mailbox,
My mirror died, & can't tell if i still reflect,
I put my eyes on a diet, my tears are gaining too much weight.

I crossed the desert in a taxicab
only to be locked in a pyramid
With the face of a dog
on my breath

I went to a masquerade
Disguised as myself
Not one of my friends
Recognized

I dreamed I went to John Mitchell's poetry party
in my maidenform brain

Put the silver in the barbeque pit
The Chinese are attacking with nuclear
Restaurants

The radio is teaching my goldfish Jujitsu
My old lady has taken up skin diving & sleeps underwater
I am hanging out with a drunken linguist, who can speak
    butterfly
And represents the caterpillar industry down in Washington
    D. C.

I never understand other peoples' desires or hopes,
until they coincide with my own, then we clash.

I have definite proof that the culture of the caveman,
disappeared due to his inability to produce one magazine,
that could be delivered by a kid on a bicycle.

When reading all those thick books on the life of god,
it should be noted that they were all written by men.

It is perfectly all right to cast the first stone,
if you have some more in your pocket.

Television, america's ultimate relief, from the indian
   disturbance.

I hope that when machines finally take over,
they won't build men that break down,
as soon as they're paid for.

i shall refuse to go to the moon,
unless i'm inoculated, against
the dangers of indiscriminate love.

After riding across the desert in a taxicab,
he discovered himself locked in a pyramid
with the face of a dog on his breath.

The search for the end of the circle,
constant occupation of squares.

Why don't they stop throwing symbols,
the air is cluttered enough with echoes.

Just when i cleaned the manger for the wisemen,
the shrews from across the street showed up.

The voice of the radio shouted, get up
do something to someone, but me & my son
laughed in our furnished room.

Geneology

Great-Grandfathers, blessed by great-grandmothers,
Shaped recently cooled buried stars, downed moons.

Creating hawk-beaked hatchets, phallic pikes, fire,
To tear out stubborn determined cells, clinging to
Other great-grandfathers, other great-grandmothers.

Proudly survived fathers, goaded by proud mothers,
Rolled lead drippings into skull piercing eternities.

Sent to stamp death on final presences, life forms,
Of other survived fathers, other proud mothers.

Sons, grandsons, daughters, granddaughters, bastards
Rolling the atmosphere into sinister nuclear spheres,

Insane combustions, to melt the bones, ivory teeth,
Of other sons, grandsons, daughters, granddaughters,
Bastards.

Here, Adam, take back your God damn rib.

ETHERIDGE KNIGHT (1933–　　　)

*A biographical note on Etheridge Knight appears in the fiction
section (see p. 120). Gwendolyn Brooks wrote the preface to
his first book of verse,* Poems from Prison *(1968), and declared: "This poetry is a major announcement." The poems
that follow are from that volume, published by Broadside
Press (Detroit), with the exception of "A WASP Woman
Visits a Black Junkie in Prison," which was published in*
Greater Works *(March, 1966), the predecessor of* Event, *the
magazine published by the American Lutheran Church Men.*

The Warden Said to Me the Other Day

The warden said to me the other day
(innocently, I think), "Say, etheridge,
why come the black boys don't run off
like the white boys do?"
I lowered my jaw and scratched my head
and said (innocently, I think), "Well, suh,
I ain't for sure, but I reckon it's cause
we ain't got no wheres to run to."

Crazy Pigeon

Crazy pigeon strutting outside my cell—
Go strut on a branch or a steeple bell.
Why coo so softly in this concrete hell?

Fly away, dumb bird. Go winging off free.
Stop coo coo cooing, stop taunting me.
Find your pretty mate and let me be.

Like mine yours might be stone cold in her grave—
And mine too was pretty as a mourning dove.
Dumb prancing pigeon, mourning for your love.

A WASP Woman Visits a Black Junkie in Prison

After explanations and regulations, he
Walked warily in.
Black hair covered his chin, subscribing to
Villainous ideal.
"This can not be real," he thought, "this is a
Classical mistake;

This is a cake baked with embarrassing icing;
Somebody's got,
Likely as not, a big fat tongue in cheek!
What have I to do
With a prim blue and proper-blooded lady?
Christ in deed has risen
When a Junkie in prison visits with a Wasp woman.

"Hold your stupid face, man,
Learn a little grace, man; drop a notch the sacred shield.
She might have good reason,
Like: 'I was in prison and ye visited me not,'—or
    some such.
So sweep clear
Anachronistic fear, fight the fog,
And use no hot words."

After the seating
And the greeting, they fished for a denominator,
Common or uncommon;
And could only summon up the fact that both were
    human.

"Be at ease, man!
Try to please, man!—the lady is as lost as you:
'You got children, Ma'am?' " he said aloud
The thrust broke the dam, and their lines wiggled in
    the water.
She offered no pills
To cure his many ills, no compact sermons, but small
And funny talk:
"My baby began to walk . . . simply cannot keep his
    room clean. . . ."
Her chatter sparked no resurrection and truly
No shackles were shaken
But after she had taken her leave, he walked softly,
And for hours used no hot words.

It Was A Funky Deal

It was a funky deal.
The only thing real was red,
Red blood around his red, red beard.

It was a funky deal.

In the beginning was the word,
And in the end the deed.
Judas did it to Jesus
For the same Herd.   Same reason.
You made them mad, Malcolm. Same reason.

It was a funky deal.

You rocked too many boats, man.
Pulled too many coats, man.
Saw through the jive.
You reached the wild guys
Like me.   You and Bird.   (And that
Lil LeRoi cat.)

It was a funky deal.

For Langston Hughes

Gone   Gone
  Another weaver of black dreams has gone
we sat in June Bug's pad with the shades drawn
and the air thick with holy smoke. and we heard
the Lady sing Langston before we knew his name.
and when Black Bodies stopped swinging June
Bug, TG and I went out and swung on some white cats.
now I don't think the Mythmaker meant for us to do *that*
but we didn't know what else to do.

Gone   Gone
  Another weaver of black dreams has gone

OLIVER LaGRONE

Poet, sculptor, and teacher, Oliver LaGrone was born in Mc-Alester, Oklahoma, grew up in that state, and has been living and working in Detroit since 1940. He received his college and specialized training in fine arts and sociology at Howard University, the University of New Mexico, Cranbrook Art Academy, and Wayne State University. He has had one-man sculpture shows in New Mexico, Michigan, Ohio, and Illinois. He turned seriously to the writing of poetry during the depression years and has published two volumes of verse. He teaches Afro-American history and culture in the Detroit public schools. For the 1970-71 academic year he was visiting lecturer in Art and Afro-American History and Culture at Pennsylvania State University's Capitol Campus at Middletown. His poems and articles have appeared in Negro Digest, Negro History Bulletin, Saturday Review, New York Times Book Review, UAW-CIO Monthly, *many other periodicals and a number of anthologies. His poem "The Limited" was awarded first prize in the annual poetry contest of the Michigan Poetry Society in 1966. Oliver LaGrone visited five West Coast countries in Africa in 1970 and is now finishing a book on African art. The following poems are published from manuscript and two of the poems grew out of his journey in Africa.*

Suncoming

Fireblade
Flame scimitar's cutting edge
Of copper-molten red
peeped

Climbed up the Nights
    skyline
Surrounded by followed
Over up was led in Court
    procession
Cloud changings burnt-orange
Yellow shed took on new hues
As east into her eye we
    sped
Cloud ranges zig-zag higher zones
With heavy childlike charcoaled
Scrawls laterals angry erratic dark
Till brazen full-seething
    stark
Naked horizon-free
The glowed fireball
    alone
Majestic center of radiant fury
    Giver and taker supreme
    Dispelled them all
        sounded
The hammered cymbals
    call
The burning blast our eyes bedazzled
Withering turned in pain away
From look at splendors pure array
So quickly turning African night
To cloudless blazing tropic
    day

Remnant Ghosts at Dawn

Vultures waft circles
In lazy Afric skies
Graced wings glide down
The hungry eyes
Vigilings . . .

The deflate lizard swells
And quick away
Stops
Head lifts and jerks

In sharp alerts
To right and left
Looking listening . . .
No walk or hall
No trench or wall
Can make it stay
(Not one to be a captive
or at bay.)

In mouth of portugals
Old cannon sunning
The scaly lounger ploys
His never ending play
No sentry's stomp
Or flintlock sound
Now sends him
Scurrying away
A vagrant with a mission . . .

Brass cannon cankered
The reptile lazing
The vulture at scavage
And the gate—guard gone
Ghosts and remnants
Of the bitter chapter
Of other days when the
Slavers craze was
Lust for the prize
In the black-gold pawn . . .
Where history stands
Frozen for new eyes
At break of another dawn . . .

Lines to the Black Oak

(For Paul Robeson)

Sing!
Great dark oak
Across the forest wide
Harp for those muted voices

Whose echo rose and died
Haven for wing-borne dream
Life
That when wrathed by storms
Nests in your mast-like
Wrestling song
(Your harbinger)
To still alarms
Then wield again
The pinioned arms . . .

Dark citadel
Reared below the distant stars
With outstretched fingers
Reaching for the boon
Free harmonies above
The mournful cry
(The prostrate moan)
Of dog-bay at the moon . . .
While deep within
The earth's outpouring spring
Still greater hands
Are spread to root and feed
Out of the all-vast mother-hoard
To bring
The acorn destiny of the
Father's seed.

DON L. LEE (1942–   )

*Identified as a Chicago poet for the city in which he has lived
since his college days, Don L. Lee, born in Little Rock, Arkansas, has won wide recognition as a poet of the new Black
consciousness. He is a staff member of the Museum of African-
American History in Chicago and has taught Afro-American
literature and history at Columbia College and at Roosevelt*

*University. He was writer-in-residence at Cornell University
where he also taught Black literature.*

Gwendolyn Brooks, in an introduction to Don't Cry,
Scream, *the third of Don Lee's four books of poetry, hailed
him as "a further pioneer and a positive prophet" of Black
poetry. She wrote: "Don Lee has no patience with black
writers who do not direct their blackness toward black audiences." And he has written: "The black writer learns from his
people . . . Black artists are culture stabilizers, bringing back
old values, and introducing new ones." The first of the following two poems is from* We Walk the Way of the New
World, *his latest collection of poetry published in 1970 by
Broadside Press in Detroit, and the second is from* Don't Cry,
Scream, *published in 1969 by Broadside Press.*

One Sided Shoot-out

(for brothers fred hampton & mark clark, murdered 12/4/69 by chicago police at 4:30 AM while they slept)

only a few will really understand:
it won't be yr/mommas or yr/brothers & sisters or even me,
we all think that we do   but we don't.
it's not *new*   and
under all the rhetoric the seriousness is still not serious.
the national rap deliberately continues, "wipe them niggers
    out."
(no talk do it, no talk do it, no talk do it, notalk notalknotalk
    do it)

& we.
running circleround getting caught in our own cobwebs,
in the same old clothes, same old words, just new adjectives.
we will order new buttons & posters with: "remember fred"
    & "rite-on mark."
& yr/pictures will be beautiful & manly with the deeplook/
    the accusing look
to remind us
to remind us that suicide is not black.

the questions will be asked & the answers will be the new
cliches.
but maybe,
just maybe we'll finally realize that "revolution" to the real-
world
is international 24hours a day and that 4:30AM is like
12:00 noon,
it's just darker.
but the evil can be seen if u look in the right direction.

were the street lights out?
did they darken their faces in combat?
did they remove their shoes to *creep* softer?
could u not see the whi-te of their eyes,
the whi-te of their deathfaces?
didn't yr/look-out man see them coming, coming, coming?
or did they turn into ghostdust and join the night's fog?

it was mean.
& we continue to call them "pigs" and "muthafuckas"
forgetting what all
black children learn very early: "sticks & stones may break
my bones but names can
never hurt me."
it was murder.
& we meet to hear the speeches/ the same, the duplicators.
they say that which is expected of them.
to be instructive or constructive is to be unpopular (like: the
leaders only
sleep when there is a watchingeye)
but they say the right things at the right time, it's like a
stageshow:
only the entertainers have changed.
we remember bobby hutton. the same, the duplicators.

the seeing eye should always see.
the night doesn't stop the stars
& our enemies scope the ways of blackness in three bad shifts
a day.
in the AM their music becomes deadlier.
this is a game of dirt.

only blackpeople play it fair.

a poem to complement other poems

change.
life if u were a match i wd light u into something beautiful.
    change.
change.
for the better into a realreal together thing. change, from
    a make believe
nothing on corn meal and water. change.
change. from the last drop to the first, maxwellhouse did.
    change.
change was a programmer for IBM, thought him was a brown
    computor. change.
colored is something written on southern out-
    houses. change.
grayhound did, i mean they got rest rooms on buses.
    change.

change.
change nigger.
saw a nigger hippy, him wanted to be different. changed.
saw a nigger liberal, him wanted to be different.
    changed.
saw a nigger conservative, him wanted to be different.
    changed.
niggers don't u know that niggers are different. change.
a doublechange. nigger wanted a double zero in front of his
    name; a license to kill,
niggers are licensed to be killed. change. a negro: something
    pigs eat.
change. i say change into a realblack righteous aim. like i
    don't play
saxophone but that doesn't mean i don't dig 'trane.'
    change.

change.
hear u coming but yr/steps are too loud. change. even a lamp
    post changes nigger.
change, stop being an instant yes machine. change.
niggers don't change they just grow. that's a change;
    bigger & better niggers.

change, into a necessary blackself.
change, like a gas meter gets higher.
change, like a blues song talking about a righteous tomorrow.
change, like a tax bill getting higher.
change, like a good sister getting better.
change, like knowing wood will burn. change.
know the realenemy.
change,
change nigger: standing on the corner, thought him was
                              cool. him still
                    standing there. it's winter time, him cool.

change,
know the realenemy.
change: him wanted to be a TV star. him is. ten o'clock news.
            wanted, wanted. nigger stole some lemon & lime
            popsicles,
            thought them were diamonds.
change nigger change.
know the realenemy.
change: is u is or is u aint. change. now now change. for the
            better change.
            read a change. live a change. read a blackpoem.
            change. be the realpeople.
            change. blackpoems
will change:

know the realenemy. change. know the realenemy. change
    yr/enemy change know the real
change know the realenemy change, change, know the
    realenemy, the realenemy, the real
realenemy change your the enemies/   change your change
    your change your enemy change
your enemy. know the realenemy, the world's enemy.
    know them know them know them the
realenemy change your enemy change your change
    change change your enemy change change
change change your change change change
your
mind nigger.

AUDRE LORDE (1934–   )

*A New York poet, Audre Lorde has appeared in numerous
periodicals and anthologies, has published two volumes of
verse, and presently teaches in the Arts and Languages Division of John Jay College of Criminal Justice, The City University of New York. She has taught creative writing at City
College, a course in the Black experience at Lehman College,
and has been poet-in-residence at Tougaloo College in Mississippi under a National Endowment for the Arts grant.*

*In a statement accompanying her poems in Sixes and Sevens,
Paul Breman's anthology published in London in 1962, Audre
Lorde wrote: "I am a Negro woman and a poet—all three
things stand outside the realm of choice. . . . I was not born
on a farm or in a forest, but in the centre of the largest city in
the world—a member of the human race hemmed in by stone,
away from the earth and sunlight. But what is in my blood
and skin of richness, of brown earth and noonsun, and the
strength to love them, comes the roundabout journey from
Africa through sun islands to a stony coast, and these are the
gifts through which I sing, through which I see. This is the
knowledge of sun, and of how to love even where there is no
sunlight." The following poems are from her published work,
but "Generation" appears here in a version newly revised by
the poet since its initial publication.*

Generation

How the young attempt and are broken
differs from age to age.
We were brown free girls
love singing beneath our skins

sun in our hair in our eyes
sun our fortune
and the wind had made us golden
made us gay.

In a season of limited power
we wept out our promises
and these are the children we try now
for temptations that wear our face.
But who comes back from our latched cities of falsehood
to warn them the road to nowhere
is slippery with our blood
to warn them
they need not drink the rivers to get home
for we have purchased bridges
with our mothers' bloody gold
and now we are more than kin
who have come to share
not only blood
but the bloodiness of failure.

How the young are tempted
and betrayed into slaughter
or conformity
is a turn of the mirror
Times question only.

New York City 1970

How do you spell change brother like frayed slogan underwear
with the emptied can of yesterday's meanings
with yesterdays' names?
And what does the we-bird see with
who has lost its I's?

There is nothing beautiful left in the streets of this city.
I have come to believe in death and renewal by fire.
Past questioning the necessities of blood
Or why it must be mine or my children's time
that will see this grim city quake to be reborn
blackened again but this time with a sense of purpose;
Tired of the past tense forever—of the assertions and

repetition of the ego trips through an incomplete self
where two years again proud rang for promise but now
it is time for fruit and all the agonies are barren;—
only the children are growing;
And how else can the self become whole
save by making self into its own new religion?
I am bound like a true believer
to this city's death by accretion and slow ritual
and I submit to its coming penance for a trial as new steel is
    tried
I submit my children likewise to its death throes and agony
and they are not even the city's past lovers.
But I submit them to the harshness to the cold to the
    brutalizations which if survived
will teach them strength or an understanding of how strength is
gotten and will not be forgotten; It will be their city, then;
I submit them loving them above all others save myself
to the fire to the rage to the ritual scarifications
To be tried as the steel is tried
and the throes of the city shall try them
as the blood-splash of a king victim
tries the hand of a destroyer.

I hide behind tenements and subways in fluorescent alleys
watching as flames walk the streets of this empire's altar
raging through the veins of a sacrificial stenchpot
smeared against the east coast of a continent's insanity
which was conceived in the psychic twilight of murderers
and pilgrims now rank with money and nightmare
and too many useless people
who will not move over nor die who cannot bend
even before the winds of their own preservation
even under the weight of their own hates
who cannot amend nor conceive nor even learn to share
their own visions;
who bomb my children to mortar in churches
and work plastic offal and the excess flesh of their enemies
into barren fantastic temples where obscene priests
finger and worship each other in secret;
who think they are praying when they squat
to shit money-pebbles shaped like their parents' brains
who exist to go into dust to exist again
grosser and more swollen
and without ever relinquishing
space or breath or energy from their private hoard.

Keeper and inmate, they prance up and down
the dream corridors of this madhouse
lecturing the world on utility and sex and their fantasies
of god and insecticide and the joy of plastic sin.

I do not need to make war nor peace
with these ill-born and murderous deacons
who bare psychic asses to the moon
and each others' probing subway rush hour fingers
who refuse to recognize their role in this covenant we live upon
and so have come to fear and despise even their own children
But I condemn myself and my loves past and present
and the blessed enthusiasms of all my children
to this city without reason or future
without hope
but to be tried as the new steel is tried
before trusted to the slaughter.

I walk down the withering limbs of my last discarded house
and there is nothing worth salvage left in this city
but the faint reedy voices like echoes
of once beautiful children.

Coal

I

Is the total black, being spoken
From the earth's inside.
There are many kinds of open.
How a diamond comes into a knot of flame
How a sound comes into a word, colored
By who pays what for speaking.

Some words are open
Like a diamond on glass windows
Singing out within the crash of passing sun
Then there are words like stapled wagers
In a perforated book—buy and sign and tear apart—
And come whatever wills all chances
The stub remains
An ill-pulled tooth with a ragged edge.
Some words live in my throat

Breeding like adders. Others know sun
Seeking like gypsies over my tongue
To explode through my lips
Like young sparrows bursting from shell.
Some words
Bedevil me.

Love is a word another kind of open—
As a diamond comes into a knot of flame
I am black because I come from the earth's inside
Take my word for jewel in your open light.

K. CURTIS LYLE (1944–   )

A member of the original Watts Writers' Workshop and currently in the Black studies program at Washington University in St. Louis, K. Curtis Lyle has provided the following biographical note to the editor: "Born in Los Angeles, California, May 13, 1944. I've lived there all my life and still call it home. Began serious writing in the 10th grade at Manual Arts High School. I've written two plays which I had performed in Seattle, Washington, in 1968; Wichita *and* The Processes of Allusion. *Plays were performed by a group I helped put together called the Surgical Theatre. Have been writing mostly poetry since then. My influences are: Artaud, Octavio Paz, Cesar Vallejo, Aime Cesaire, Jean Joseph Rabearivelo, and Felix T'chikaya U' Tamsi. I am currently Writer-in-Residence at Washington University of St. Louis." The poem "Sometimes I Go to Camarillo & Sit in the Lounge" is reprinted from the first issue of* Confrontation: A Journal of Third World Literature, *and "Lacrimas" is published from manuscript.*

Sometimes I Go to Camarillo & Sit in the Lounge

Sometimes   I stare into an awning of spirit
and the prose of her son
burning my eye into a vacuum
of frozen blisters

Sometimes   my face hanging its tongue
half-way between mechanized jawbones
and ancient skull caps

Sometimes   I-am-viewing the world as
yellow trumpets of starving blues
against a piece of body that used
to hold some Vietnamese mother's breast
or the ultra-high-frequency screams
of some stupid marine with his cold
fingers stumbling down past waistbands
and ending the milk of the life of some
heroic woman

Sometimes   the nature of my sickness
a driving sunflower rain of stone
and seeds onto centipedes
the choral of my brutality
pulling fifty legs from a body
maiming it for life

Sometimes   deep in the animated suspension
of my alconarcotic dreams
I am wishing for an act of holiness
and cleansing

I-am-wishing for an hour of napalm
on ALL Junior Chambers-of-Commerce
Sometimes
I go to Camarillo and sit in the lounge
fascinated
       by
incurable tics   on vacant schizoid cheeks
       I
sit and watch   spastic foam in the trenches
of madmen's mouths
the emptiness   of alienated sound   somehow
passionately colloquial like
truncated elegance   or   reams

                 of   poetic potential rolling across
            asylum   floors for the dead heart
                 of   emasculates
they (the inmates)   propped in gutters of cafeteria
their (funky)   bowels running thru America's
                              kitchen ascending minds transcending
                              the walls of room 305
they (the inmates)   a love conversation of sweet mangoes
                              to a nation of malarial armies
they (the inmates)   a continuous poem of bird-caged heads
                              battering-rammed against the
                              immobile word of corporate prophets
Sometimes   I-am-reading short stories
                              of Nelson Algren
                                        or
                              Pietro Di Donato
                                        and
                              ignoring whole epochs
                                        of
                              my history
my limbs   painting the gray factories
                                        of
                              the world reds blues purple-blacks—
                              crazy colors for the fleshy segment
                                        of
                              my memory bank
my life   l o n g i n g   l o n g i n g
                              for the women of Dahomey . . . and . . .
                              their strong thighs . . . blacker . . .
                              than anthracite warmer than fresh
                              French bread
Sometimes   late morning's motioning birds
                              pressing tired headlines of bitter skies
                              into my forehead
                                        puritas
                              water flowing beneath a burning bridge
                                        of
                              snowflakes
                                        and
                              the nobility of my dead grandfather's ash
deeper

                              deeper still
                                        till
                              lost in the interior
                                        of

himself

> God himself
> an irrepressible soul-blowing
> nuclear heroes
>   into
> the rivers of time
>   and
> space

Lacrimas or there is a need to scream

> a torrent
> of cobalt bullets
> smashed into the heart
> of the lone ranger, heavily
> damaging his dreams
> and a fine marching chord
> from amon ra
> garroted machiavelli's mother, anonymously
> dragging her voice to the other side
> of her eardrum
> and pushing her pupil
> to the northeast corner
> of her eyeball
> and as we close our mouths
> over these violent tears
> we understand that misery
> is a real language
> and whether our ageless tears
> are soft or loud
> introjected into our body
> they put us closer to the universe
> than a cannabis plant being fertilized
> by a soundless crystal
> of cocaine

NAOMI LONG MADGETT (1923–   )

Prominent in the Detroit group of poets, Naomi Long Madgett was born in Norfolk, Virginia, and grew up in New Jersey and St. Louis, Missouri. She has published three volumes of poetry, has been widely anthologized, and is the author of two textbooks. In 1965 she was the first recipient of the $10,000 Mott Fellowship in English at Oakland University. She is a member of the National Writers Club, the Detroit Women Writers, and the Michigan State Council for the Arts (Literature Committee). She taught English in a Detroit high school for more than a decade, has been on the English faculty at Eastern Michigan University, and is currently teaching at the University of Michigan. The following poems are published from manuscript.

Sally: Twelfth Street

I mix my men and booze
(And anything I choose)
With undiscriminating ease.

The Sunday preacher merges with my gin
Smoothly as gambling man. (Well, any sin
Defiles some Eden of its own.)

What dregs remain in bottles I can swill
With equal fervor (wine or whiskey) till
Gullet rebels.

What elixir, what gall
In men and alcohol!
What zero,—and yet all in all!

Brothers at the Bar

Rat-fink
Buddy
Before you

Palomine

Baby
Olefriend
do me in

throw your arm
around my shoulder
Wrap my soul
in the bearhug of
reassurance

Trust me

Baby

i'm for YOU

I love *you* like a brother
too

Souvenir

This is not what I meant to keep.
I thought of bitter-bright rememberings,
Pressed petals of forgetmenots
Or once-bold daffodils.

Not
This hardness—
Not
These brittle stalks of
Weeds.

The Twenty Grand
(Saturday Night on the Block)

Nobody else can have as much fun as
While being so oblivious to
Or waste as much energy on

Nobody can be kinder, more forgiving than
Have so much soul and spirit as
Drown so much anger and frustration in
Or trade so much of love and wisdom for

But
Saturday night is ending
And Sunday morning's patience getting weary

And it is time now
It is time
It is time
It is time
Now

CLARENCE MAJOR (1936–   )

From Atlanta by way of Chicago and other places, Clarence Major now lives and works in New York City. His widely acclaimed The New Black Poetry *(1969) is an important pioneer anthology of contemporary Black poetry. He has been publishing poems, fiction, and articles in a wide variety of publications for the past fifteen years.* All-Night Visitors, *his first novel, was published in 1969, and his second novel,* No, *is scheduled for 1972. Three privately printed collections of his poems were published between 1954 and 1965, and in 1970 his latest book of verse,* Swallow the Lake, *a National Council of the Arts Selection, was published by Wesleyan University Press. His latest book is* A Dictionary of Afro-American Slang *(International Publishers, 1970). Clarence Major has been an associate editor of* Umbra *and* Journal of Black Poetry *and has edited or participated in the editing of a number of other literary journals. The following poems are from his published work.*

Vietnam #4

a cat said
on the corner

the other day
dig man

how come so many
of us
niggers

are dying over there
in that white
man's war

they say more of us
are dying

than them peckerwoods
& it just
             don't make sense

unless it's true
that the honkeys

are trying to kill us out
with the same stone

they killing them other cats
with

you know, he said
two birds with one stone

Self World

can redwhite & blue I enter
               some self, the self

                    of some-
                    body
;myself ?   in pure flesh & mind love
                    all of me   ?
Sounds silly
                    but read again, & enter yourself, to
see as I see

            MY 3 YEAR OLD BLACK EYES
            TRAGIC, BEAUTIFUL PAIN
            LOOKING FROM THOSE YEARS
such a photo

                        define this trembling nation, the
sacred "untouchable
                        insanity. (Concessions

A coldturkey promise, myself. Some face, image
                        can this image, red white & blue
enter
            these monsters, they use deodorant,
and brush their teeth.
                                    And do not know
anything, even as I explain
                            myself. Or
language, how it is our beauty
            true in
            MY 3 YEAR OLD BLACK EYES
            TRAGIC, BEAUTIFUL PAIN
            LOOKING FROM THOSE YEARS
same as   now

ADAM DAVID MILLER

*Poet, teacher, critic, and editor of the interesting poetry an-
thology* Dices or Black Bones: Black Voices of the Seventies
(Houghton Mifflin, 1970), Adam David Miller was born and

spent his life through high school in Orangeburg, South Caro-
lina. He now teaches Afro literature and composition at
Laney College in Oakland, California. In 1964 he helped
found The Aldridge Players/West, a San Francisco Afro
drama group and since then has served variously as produc-
tion coordinator, actor, and director. He is San Francisco Bay
Area correspondent for Black Theatre. *He is a founding editor*
of The Graduate Student Journal, *a magazine of opinion at*
the University of California at Berkeley, where he received his
M.A. in English. Two of the following poems appeared in
print in Dices or Black Bones *and "the pruning" and "mulch"*
are published from manuscript.

The Africa Thing

What is Africa to thee?

Let's shuffle

Paint that horn
on backwards—
Knock me some skin   Blow! O

They say home
is a place
in the mind
where you
can rest
when you're tired
not where
your great great
great grandfather
had his farm

Africa?

Africa   beble be
is that old man   ba
in the pickin field   bo
making that strange high sound   bibob
and all the people following   blaaba
Africa is a sound   ba ba

Africa   buddi di oooooo
is the touch   rock a diooooo
of that old woman
your mother could not stand   do oo do o
but did respect
who caught you as you fell
and held you
and rocked you

Fat black bucks in a wine barrel   boom
boom
What is Africa to thee   bam
thou thoo thum   boom
I smell the sweat of an english scum   boom boom

—Mamma, Mamma, but he *does*
It's *not* just his breath
He stink
Hushsssh, chile
Somebody'll hear you
Say *smell.*

Africa
is the look
of Tweebie Mae
Snapping her
head around
before she took off
      Caint ketch me
in the soft dark
You caught her

Africa
is all them roots
and conjurs
and spells
wails and chants
(say blues and hollers)
and all them stories
about Stackalee
and John Henry
and Bodidly
and the camp meetings
where the wrestling

and head and head
the foot races
the jumping
the throwing

We brought all that down
to dance at birth
when you're sick
take a wife
lose your luck
when you die

and singing in the woods
    in the fields
  when you walk
and singing on the levies
    on the chain gang
    in jail
singing and dancing when you pray
and dancing by the light of the moon
until you drop.

Africa is the singing
of these lines
of me
of you
of love
singing.

The Hungry Black Child

    lord
    forgive me
    if i twist the sunset
    but when evening twist my belly
    i see red
    walking the field the woods
    the houses on my street
    white
    burning burning

the pruning

cutting back
wherever the weather
and life permits

when the weight
of the new growth
faces the dead in me

a new grower
my memory
of last year's harvest
dimmed

will i
be able to see
beyond the prickly pile
and the open gashes

mulch

clipped
separated
piled up

left under the sun
to rot

inert mass
you make heat
that would destroy you

and from
this apparent destruction
create new green

LARRY NEAL (1937–   )

Poet, critic and editor, Larry Neal coedited the anthology
Black Fire *with Imamu Amiri Baraka (LeRoi Jones). He was
born in Atlanta, Georgia, grew up in Philadelphia, received a
B.A. from Lincoln University, in Pennsylvania, and did gradu-
ate work at the University of Pennsylvania. He is now living
in New York City and is a member of the faculty at The
College of the City of New York. Formerly arts editor of*
Liberator, *Larry Neal is an editor of* The Cricket, *a magazine
on Black music, and a contributing editor of the* Journal of
Black Poetry. *A collection of his poetry,* Black Boogaloo
(Notes on Black Liberation), *was published in 1969 by
Journal of Black Poetry Press. In a preface to this book
Imamu Amiri Baraka wrote: "Black Boogaloo is the new
consciousness. The New Learning. Black, because that is the
culture and race that spawned it. But, for sure, it is for any-
body. Anybody, who can feel. Any human longing for spirit
Needing Needing Spirit Food." He was awarded a Guggen-
heim fellowship (1971–72) for studies in contemporary Afro-
American culture. Two of the following poems are from* Black
Boogaloo, *his first volume of poetry, and "Lady's Days" is a
revised version of an earlier poem from the manuscript of*
Hoodoo Hollering Bebop Ghosts, *his second collection of
poems, to be published by Random House.*

The Middle Passage and After

Decked, stacked, pillaged from
their homes
packed bodies on bodies rock in the belly
of death.
sea blood, sea blood churns
production for the West's dying

machine; commodities for profit—
stuffed empires with spices;
moved history closer to our truth—
death's prophecy—in the sea their
screams and the salt smell on our
faces pressed against one another,
hands push stiffward, push for air room.

Our nightmares are tight compacted
whitenesses, smotherings of babies,
jammed into drunken limits.
our souls are open skies and children
zooming across green places;
open clearings, rhythms bursting
sea-shell prisons; are things heard
in between tropical blasts of wind;
are ancestor-wisdom making itself
known in every black face born or about to be.

Harlem Gallery: From the Inside

The bars on Eighth Avenue in Harlem
glow real yellow, hard against formica
tables; they speak of wandering ghosts
and Harlem saints; the words lay slick
on greasy floors: rain wet butt in the junkie's
mouth, damp notebook in the number-runner's hand.
no heads turn as the deal goes down—we wait.

The Harlem rain explodes, flooding the avenues
rats float up out of the sewers. Do we need the
Miracles or a miracle?

Listen baby, to the mean scar-faced sister,
between you and her and me and you there are no
distances. short reach of the .38, a sudden burning
in the breast, a huge migraine hammering where your brain
used to be. then its over, no distance between the needle
and the rope. instant time, my man, history is one quick
fuck; you no sooner in then you come, a quick fuck.

uptight against the sound, but everything ain't all right.
nitty-gritty would-be warriors snap fingers, ghosts booga-

loo against the haze, Malcolm eyes in the yellow glow
blood on black hands. compacted rooms of gloom, Garvey's
flesh in the rat's teeth. Lady Day at 100 centre street,
Charlie Parker dying in the penthouse of an aristocratic
bitch. Carlos Cook, Ras, Shine, Langston, the Barefoot
Prophet. Ira Kemp, the Signifying Monkey, Bud Powell.
Trane, Prez, Chano Pozo, Eloise Moore—all
falling faces in the Harlem rain
asphalt memory of blood and pain.

Lady's Days

Birds follow the sun/rain coming on/we drive South/
    me and Billie/drive South where birds go
    follow sun/ but tonight/rain
Short pushing toward Baltimore/me and Billie/rain
    or was it D.C./or the hick towns of squares
    and yokels/come/come to hear the Lady sing
Rain nights/ the car/ the towns lingering blues in her
    voice/south where birds go/lingering blue
    in her voice south where birds go/come
    to hear the Lady sing/I rember the
Faces/ the soft and the hard/faces raining hard /faces
    scarred/they wailed for the song and moaned
    digging the gardenia bit she had going/scars
    digging the gardenia thing that she was
    was into/Lady's days
Song turning soft in her mouth/digging as the mouth turned
    softly in the song/ they dug you
    They dug you yeah/heavy smoke moaning/the
Room shifting under red lights/heavy smell of alcohol
    and moan/smells/spot lights/spot lights
    for the Lady/raining gardenias and sorrows
Faces/the pain rides them/more pain/their pain/ the pain
    rides them/ghosts ride them/your voice rides
    them/shifting under red spot lights/smoke
One night between sets I asked you what it meant/the pain
    raining/and the moans of scars and gardenias/
    is that the way it is Billie/I asked you/
    remember baby when I asked you that
Slow power of the blues you said/rember please
    you said/you said/that it had to

be that way/there was no reason you said
no reason for towns faces moans
Against the rain/uptight/the steady pull of death
can't help you sweetheart/you said
remembering the time in Philly/the cops
crashing the hotel room looking for the
scag/looking for a piece of your ass
O baby
That's how some towns were you said/hitting the city
limits/stiff memories/ we had good times
though/ the morning sessions after the gigs
Now slow rain/towns lingering blue/smoke as solitude
faces/ days as wailing song/under red spot
lights/your head against my shoulder Lester
plays his solo/rain/hotel rooms/ scag/the
light dreams/ the car cuts night/ now the
warm woman and the voice hovering over us
Road house stop/the john for the niggers/ a special john
for the Lady/ for Billie beautiful/ the raped
child/rain
Rape lingering after the bath at the end of the night
the rape child/ and they would worship
at your body/ the Lady/rape lingering/
They walked home/drunk/smelling of your flesh/as you/
lay bleeding/under red spots

TEJUMOLA OLOGBONI (ROCKIE D. TAYLOR) (1945–)

An artist and a poet, Rockie D. Taylor was born in Salina Kansas, stayed there until he was eleven years old, and has been living in the "inner core" in Milwaukee since his family moved there in 1956. He studied at the University of Wisconsin-Milwaukee, where he received his bachelor's degree and later a degree in art education, and pursued further graduate study in fine arts and African cultural studies at Indiana University. He is now lecturer and Black poet-in-

residence in the Afro-American Studies Department at the University of Wisconsin-Milwaukee. He is a member of the Black Poetic Messengers, which provides a center for analysis and criticism of Black creative writing in Milwaukee; he was one of the founders of the Gallery Toward the Black Aesthetic in Milwaukee, a community-based organization "working toward the establishment of the Black Aesthetic that will cover all forms of expression." In 1969 he published Drum Song, *his first collection of poetry, which opens with the following introductory poem by Gwendolyn Brooks:*

> Rockie Taylor sharpens,
> clarifies the blur—
> for himself and for us.
>
> His real lyricism has
> a literal sharpness
> that makes it contemporary,
> and emphasizes
> its Black pertinence.
>
> He speaks to
> Black people
> in an affectionate
> but definite
> voice. And Black people
> listen and
> respond.

Two of the following poems are from Drum Song, *and "I Wonta Thank You" is published from manuscript.*

Changed Mind
(or the day i woke up)

> if I speek good english
> and take a
> baf
> evry day
> Then I'll be
> accepted by that
> Grea
> T
> Whi

Te
race

george
washington
Ameri
can so pure
never told
a
Black ly

Li
n
coln
so hu
man he done free
d a
inslaved
race

mc arthur said (in history books)
"We shall return
an I said
Amer
I
ca is a bitch
us is a bitch

I'd hear the star spangled etc. & etc.
my soul would burn
tears came
to
my
eyes

I said we Amer
I
can
s are kool

was walken down
the street
one
day
singen Amer

I
ca in step with
the beat.
red, WHITE, and
stars on blue, etc., etc.
runnen thru my cloroxed mine

when a cop
stop
ped me, wanted some
I.D.
said
"What nationality are
U

I said proud
ly
Amer
I
CAN

he said "NO you can'
T

NIGGER

Black Henry

When Henry was a baby
Folks'd tell his momma, "My, but
Your son is BLACK
       his momma just smiled
       like she knew something
       they didn't

When Henry went to school
It was always, "Git back
Too big,
Too BLACK
smut colored Henry
       but he still kinda
       held his head up tho'
       with the beginnins of a smile

like he knew something
they didn't

When Henry was a boy
"How 'bout a movie?"
He'd ask the girls
"Uh-uh I'm busy
Ol BLACK Henry" they'd say
as he was walking away
blue BLACK Henry
   he still kinda
   held his head up tho'
   with the beginnins of a smile
   like he knew something
   they didn't

Then something happened
Came a man
Named X
  and Rap
  and Stoke taught blk/ppl how to love
           themselves

Now when you see Henry
Comin down the street
  the folks he'd meet would say
   after he walked away
"AIN'T THAT BLACKMUTHAFUKKA BEAUTIFUL"
   he'd kinda
   hold his head up
   with the beginnins of a smile
   like he know something
   they *know*

I Wonta Thank Ya . . . .

GOD
you aint
made life no
easy thang
but I wonta

thank ya
for my
Black Woman

scoldin me
soothin me
soft voice
warm wind
huggin me
holdin me
my Queen
showin me
how to be the King
I used to
be

When I couldnt give her
nuthin
she returned a smile
when I done wrong
she forgave me more
    than all your
pale angels
And when I couldnt
believe
in
you,
I could believe
in my
Black Woman

They put my
sweet sable woman
through
the hardness
of hell. . . . . .
but to look
in her
soft
brown
eyes
ain't nobody could tell

lovin me
movin me

evening star
ebony shadows
night bird
cricket song
soft grass
warm wind
dark
deep
skin
like the
summernight
sky

M
M
Mmm
good
wooly
hair
small warm
round breasts
inviting
thighs
and arms
flat smooth belly
like the grasslands
and the rythm
of Africa in her fluid hips
full fine lips
like ripe purple plums
that grow only
at the
top
of the tree

oooweee!
my
Black Woman

even when she call me
baby
make me feel like a
Man
rubs my work-weary back
like no other woman can

God
you aint
made life no
easy thang,

but I wonta
thank ya
for
my
Black
Woman

RAYMOND R. PATTERSON (1929–)

A native New Yorker who lives and teaches in that city, Raymond R. Patterson attended Lincoln University in Pennsylvania and received his M.A. in English from New York University. When he was an undergraduate, in 1950, he received first prize for poetry in a competition sponsored by the University of Pennsylvania Press. His poems have appeared in many magazines and anthologies, and he has given readings of his poetry throughout the state of New York. His first volume of poetry, 26 Ways of Looking at a Black Man, *was published in 1969 by Award Books. The following poems are from this book.*

What We Know

There is enough
Grief-
Energy in
The blackness

Of the whitest Negro
To incinerate
America.

Black Power

I stepped from black to black.
It was so simply done—
Like walking out of shadow
And going forth in sun—
And I will not look back.

But if you ask me how
That day was, what I saw,
These memories linger now:
An easing at the core,
A clearer sense of what
I am, a keener taste
For life; the urge to touch
My shining hands and face—
And marvel at how much
They please me in each case.

Still one of Nature's creatures;
Yet my own self; content
With all my inner features,
The knowledge I was meant
To give them liberty.

What passed was slavery—
Of giving hatred back,
Of hating to be free
Of what turned black in me
Through tortured history.

What sense can words convey
Of what it was I saw?
. . . The weather of that day,
The pain I knew before
Without once looking back
I stepped from black to black?

When I Awoke

When I awoke, she said:
Lie still, do not move.
They are all dead, she said.

Who?
I said.

The world,
She said.

I had better go,
I said.

Why?
She said. What good will it do?

I have to see,
I said.

"A Word to the Wise Is Enough."

—Benjamin Franklin

A word to the violent has never been sufficient.
They have a hard speech that shatters conversation.
Practically speaking, a word to the violent is wasted.
Words fall dumb between mind and tribal mind until we
    come
To the scarred roots of our native idiom,
Where language does what it means.

Witness the education of J. H. Meredith
In Mississippi:
While he tortured his proud mind with words
To argue his manhood,
Our Nation got a different message in blood
Sent directly by violent people.

Later there were words and more words.
(Was he being rhetorical?) He was heard to cry out,
Under the burden of them, "Is any help coming!"
—Face down on an American road,
A shotgun's answer buried in his back.
—Schooled by hard knocks, you might say.

And for what
Have we our native philosophers
If not to listen to in times of crisis?
Their clear, indigenous spirit built
A commonwealth of proper respect,
If not a community of love—and coined in patriot's creed!
"Speak softly and carry a big stick"? No. Not that trap.
Rather, let words lie
Silent. Be automatic.
Wipe the blood from your lips, Negro.
Arrange your speech
Carefully, in a clip.

Schwerner, Chaney, Goodman

Behind you, now,
Your final pain,
Your dreams,
The search in darks
Toward friendless hands,
The violent men you could have saved,
Your loved and fumbling nation.

Before us, now,
Your deeds to do again.
The darkness around this world engraved:
Three lives
In deathless constellation.

This Age

What year is this? Who can truthfully say?
Have we reached the middle or the end

Of the Twentieth Century?
Choose a date. But let's not pretend.
No more lying almanacs, please; no more
Bogus calendars or phony electronic clocks!
The universe is shot full of holes! Space
Has sprung its locks! Are we on a subway
Or a seesaw? Whose face haunts the sky?
Is it too late to die?

O the earth grinds! Time winds and unwinds
Against the living grain. What is that muffled
Thump like something falling again and again?
Why are we here? A different place? A different
Age? These broken instruments again?

All night we lie on the floor
Aware, yet cold in our catastrophe of stars—
The tired droop of your furious head
Echoing my rage. Are we already dead?
Would you believe the years? Should we debate again?
We are missing! Those constellations are our fallen tears.
Why were they shed? And who can put them back and
    strum the spheres
That we may turn to singing and to bed?

N. H. PRITCHARD (1939–   )

*An experimental and original poet, frequently employing the
concretist style which appeals to the eye as well as to the
ear, N. H. Pritchard is highly regarded by critics and readers
of the new poetry. He was born in New York City and
graduated with honors in art history from Washington Square
College, New York University. At this college he was a contributor to the literary magazine and president of the Fine
Arts Society. He pursued graduate studies in art history at
The Institute of Fine Arts and Columbia University. Cur-*

*rently he is teaching a poetry workshop at The New School
for Social Research in New York and is poet-in-residence at
Friends Seminary. His poems have appeared in many magazines, including* Umbra, Negro Digest, Liberator, The East
Village Other, Poetry Northwest, *and in several anthologies.
He reads his poems on the record albums* Destinations: Four
Contemporary American Poets, *and* New Jazz Poets. *His
first volume of poetry,* The Matrix: Poems 1960–1970, *was
published in 1970 by Doubleday, and the following two poems
are from that book.*

The Signs

```
        in
          a
           cove
              where
hhhhhhhhhhhhhhhhhhhhhhhhh hhhhhhhhhhhhhhhhhhhhhhhhhhhhh
     uuuuuuuuuuuuuuuuuuuuuuuu
              uuuuuuuuuuggggggggggggggggggggggg ggggggggggggggggg
        waves
      geeeeeeeeeeeeeeeeeeeee eee
            bowed
                about
                     the
                        sea
and
and
and
and
and              the lone mast lost its sail
and
and              the sky's root fell upon the land
and
and              a nigh replaced the sky with time
and
and              a lie disgraced the why with brine
and
and
and
and
and

              they took advantage of the signs
              they took advantage of the signs
```

PASSAGE
PASSAGE
PASSAGE
PASSAGE
PASSAGE
PASSAGE
PASSAGE
PASSAGE
PASSAGE
PASSAGE
PASSAGE
PASSAGE
PASSAGE
PASSAGE
PASSAGE
PASSAGE   In silence there regard the dim
PASSAGE
PASSAGE   he who with shoeless strode
PASSAGE
PASSAGE   the dust of waisted jeers
PASSAGE
PASSAGE   see you him too
PASSAGE
PASSAGE   and there another just as near
PASSAGE
PASSAGE   and some taunted them with treacherous eyes
PASSAGE
PASSAGE   though bowed they to hoom passed
PASSAGE
PASSAGE
PASSAGE
PASSAGE
PASSAGE
PASSAGE
PASSAGE
PASSAGE
PASSAGE
PASSAGE
PASSAGE
PASSAGE
PASSAGE
PASSAGE

DUDLEY RANDALL (1914–   )

Founder, editor, and guiding spirit of Broadside Press in Detroit, the leading Black poetry publishing press in the United States, Dudley Randall has been an active force in the development of comtemporary Black poetry. Gwendolyn Brooks dedicated her last book of poetry, Riot: *"For Dudley Randall, a giant of our time." He was born in Washington, D.C., received his B.A. in English from Wayne University in Detroit, his master's degree in library science from the University of Michigan in 1951, and has been earning his livelihood as a librarian in Detroit.*

Coauthor with Margaret Danner of Poem Counterpoem *and coeditor with Margaret Burroughs of the anthology* For Malcolm: Poems on the Life and Death of Malcolm X, *Mr. Randall has published two collections of his poetry, and his third volume of verse is to be published by Third World Press in Chicago. His poems have appeared in many periodicals and anthologies and have been translated into French, Italian, and Dutch. In the summer of 1966 Randall visited Paris, Prague, and the Soviet Union with a delegation of Afro-American artists. In 1970 he visited Ghana, Togo, and Dahomey in Africa. Two of the following poems are from* Cities Burning *(1968), the first collection of his poetry, and "Old Witherington" was published in* Ten: An Anthology of Detroit Poets, *published in 1968 by South and West, Inc.*

Primitives

Paintings with stiff
homuncules, flat in iron
draperies, with distorted

bodies against spaceless
landscapes.

Poems of old
poets in stiff
metres whose harsh
syllables
drag like
dogs with
crushed
backs.

We go back to
them, spurn difficult
grace and
symmetry,
paint tri-faced
monsters,
write lines that
do not sing, or
even croak, but that
bump,
jolt, and are hacked
off in the mid-
dle, as if by these dis-
tortions, this
magic, we can
exorcise
horror, which we
have seen and fear to
see again:

hate deified,
fears and
guilt conquering,
turning cities to
gas, powder and a
little rubble.

The Melting Pot

There is a magic melting pot
where any girl or man

can step in Czech or Greek or Scot,
step out American.

Johann and Jan and Jean and Juan,
Giovanni and Ivan
step in and then step out again
all freshly christened John.

Sam, watching, said, "Why, I was here
even before they came,"
and stepped in too, but was tossed out
before he passed the brim.

And every time Sam tried that pot
they threw him out again.
"Keep out. This is our private pot.
We don't want your black stain."

At last, thrown out a thousand times,
Sam said, "I don't give a damn.
Shove your old pot. You can like it or not,
but I'll be just what I am."

Old Witherington

Old Witherington had drunk too much again.
The children changed their play and packed around him
To jeer his latest brawl. Their parents followed.

Prune-black, with bloodshot eyes and one white tooth,
He tottered in the night with legs spread wide
Waving a hatchet. "Come on, come on," he piped,
"And I'll baptize these bricks with bloody kindling.
I may be old and drunk, but not afraid
To die. I've died before. A million times
I've died and gone to hell. I live in hell.
If I die now I die, and put an end
To all this loneliness. Nobody cares
Enough to even fight me now, except
This crazy bastard here." And with these words
He cursed the little children, cursed his neighbors,
Cursed his father, mother, and his wife,

Himself, and God, and all the rest of the world,
All but his grinning adversary, who, crouched,
Danced tenderly around him with a jag-toothed bottle,
As if the world compressed to one old man
Who was the sun, and he sole faithful planet.

EUGENE REDMOND

*Poet, critic, editor, and educator, Eugene Redmond was born
in St. Louis, Missouri, and grew up across the Mississippi in
East St. Louis, Illinois. He was educated at Southern Illinois
University and Washington University in St. Louis, where he
received his M.A. in English literature. For two years he
served as senior consultant to Katherine Dunham's Performing Arts Training Center at Southern Illinois University and
was formerly director of language workshops and poet-in-
residence at Southern Illinois University's Experiment in
Higher Education. Eugene Redmond was writer-in-residence
at Oberlin College in 1969–70 and is now poet-in-residence
in ethnic studies at Sacramento State College, California. His
poems have appeared in a variety of magazines and in
Tambourine, Today's Negro Voices, The New Black Poetry,
and other anthologies. The following poems are from Sentry
of the Four Golden Pillars, a privately printed collection of
his poems published in 1970.*

Parapoetics

(For my former students and writing
friends in East St. Louis, Illinois)

Poetry is an *applied science:*
  Re-wrapped corner rap;

Rootly-eloquented cellular, soulular sermons.
Grit reincarnations of
Lady Day
Bird
& Otis;
Silk songs pitched on 'round and rhythmic rumps;
Carved halos (for heroes) and asserted maleness:
Sounds and sights of fire-tongues
Leaping from lips of flame-stricken buildings in the night.

Directions: apply poetry as needed.
Envision.
Visualize.
Violate!
Wring minds.
Shout!
Right words.
Rite!!
Cohabitate.
Gestate.
Pregnate your vocabulary.
Dig, a parapoet!

Parenthesis: Replace winter with spring, move Mississippi
to New York, Oberlin (Ohio) to East St. Louis, Harlem
to the summer whitehouse. Carve candles and flintstones
for flashlights.

Carry your poems.
Grit teeth. Bear labor-love pains.
Have twins and triplets.
Furtilize poem-farms with after-birth,
Before birth and dung [rearrange old words];
Study/strike tradition.

Caution to parapoets:
Carry the weight of your own poem.
... it's a *heavy lode.*

Spearo's Blues (Or: Ode to a Grecian Yearn)
(A soliloquy in seven parts)

I

I can't hear myself think in America no more!
With the spectre of Vietnams at our own front door!

II

The dark'nin threat from within is dissent.
But that ain't what Tom Jefferson meant.
(*Ceasar wouldn't've dug it at all, yall!*)

III

That's why I'm shooting for "Mars" by A.D. 2000.
(Aside: I may get back to D.C. before then if
the light years are limp and long.)

IV

With the muse on my mailing list,
Green lights and bouquets from Barry,
Dick's (groping-gripping) gracious silence,
(Alas, though I hear his thoughts through a
bug in his floor: *"I remember when I was an
unemployed skitzoid."*),
Ky Kentucky Fried and in the Colonial Casket,
Cleaver neatly collected and exiled in paperback,
Me neo-naked in taled tunic
(*a real Ulyssean cock!*),
The Parthenon's a stone's throw
From Pillars of Pennsylvania Avenue.

V

The mouth's the message: Think later.
Besides, you're in quick-draw country.
(cf., Barry's Law.)

VI

(Aside: Anyway, cultureless America's a long
Way from Athens (Ohio) or Olympus. *It's the I.Q.
that counts.*)

VII

And now, yellow Americans,
Tradition is what this country needs.
What? what? (cupping the ear)

Finis

Observor: "I hear the wail of a tenor-troubled anglo-sax.
And from among the dung, a silent tongue is rung:
'Bring hue and crew
Take cue from Agnew
And do this in remembrance of Joe McCarthy!' "

Definition of Nature

In this stoned and
Steely park,
Love is an asphalt
Fact:
            flowers
            birds
            trees
            rushing or creeping brooks
are framed on walls and tv tubes.

But each night when the city shrinks,
            the stars roof us,
And any bush becomes
            our Bantu wonderland.

ISHMAEL REED (1938–   )

Ishmael Reed is very much of an original, in fiction and poetry. He has published two highly acclaimed novels, The Free Lance Pallbearers *(1967) and* Yellow Back Radio Broke-Down *(1969), a collection of poetry, and has edited* 19 Necromancers from Now: An Anthology of Original American Writing for the 1970s *(1970). He was born in Chattanooga, Tennessee, has lived in New York City, attended the University of Buffalo, and is currently a lecturer in American literature at the University of California at Berkeley. He also appears in the criticism section of this anthology. The following poem appeared in* Umbra's Blackworks 1970–71 *and is the title poem of his first collection of poetry published in 1970 in London in Paul Breman's Heritage series.*

catechism of d neoamerican hoodoo church

a little red wagon for d black bureaucrat
who in d winter of 1967 when i refused to
deform d works of ellison & wright—his betters—
to accomodate a viewpoint this clerk thot irresistible,
did not hire me for d teaching job
which he invitd me to take
in d first place.

this is for u insect w/ no antennae, goofy
papers piling on yr desk—for u & others. where
do u fugitives frm d file cabinet of death get
off in yr attempt to control d artist?
keep yr programming to those computers u love so
much, for he who meddles w/ nigro-mancers
courts his demise!

1

our pens are free
do not move by decree. accept no memos
frm jackbootd demogs who wd exile our minds.
dare tell d artist his role. issue demands on
cultural revolution. 2 words frm china where an
ol woman sends bold painters to pick grasshoppers
at 3 in d a.m. w/ no tea, no cigarettes & no
beer. cause ol women like landscapes or portraits
of their husbands face. done 50 yrs ago. standing
on a hill. a god, a majesty, d first chairman.
o, we who hv no dreams permit us to say yr name
all day. we are junk beneath yr feet,
mosquito noises to yr ears, we crawl on our
bellies & roll over 3 times for u. u are
definitely sho nuff d i my man.

2

is this how artists shd greet u?
isnt yr apartment by d river enough? d
trees in d park? palisades by moonlight is
choice i hear. arent u satisfid? do u
want to be minister of culture? (minister, a
jive title frm a dead church!) dressd in a
business suit w/ medals on yr chest! hving
painters fetch yr short, writers doing yr taxes,
musicians entertaining yr mistresses, sculptors
polishing yr silverware. do u desire 4 names
instead of 2?

3

i do not write solicitd
manuscripts—oswald spengler said
to joseph goebbels when askd to make a
lie taste like sweet milk.

because they wrote d way they saw it, said
their prayers wrong, forgot to put on their number in d
a.m., got tore dwn in d streets & cut d fool:
men changd their names to islam & hung up d phone on them.
meatheaded philosophers left rank tongues of ugly mouth on
their tables. only new/ ark kept us warm that summer. but
now they will pick up d tab. those dear dead beats who put
our souls to d wall. tried us in absentia before

some grand karate who hd no style. plumes on garveys hat
he was.

4

word of my mysteries is getting around, do not cm
said d dean / invite canceld to speak in our chapel
at delaware state. We hv checkd yr background, u make
d crucifixes melt. d governor cant replace them.
stop   stop   outlandish customer.

5

i am becoming spooky & afar you all. i
stir in my humfo, taking notes. a black cat
superstars on my shoulder. a johnny root dwells
in my purse. on d one wall: bobs picture
of marie laveaus tomb in st louis #2. it is
all washed out w/ x . . . s, & dead flowers &
fuck wallace signs. on d other wall:
d pastd scarab on grandpops chest, he was
a nigro-mancer frm chattanooga. so i got it
honest. i floor them w/ my gris gris. what
more do i want ask d flatfoots who patrol d beat
of my time. d whole pie? o no u small fry
spirits. d chefs hat, d kitchen, d right
to help make a menu that will end 2 thousand yrs
of bad news.

6

muhammed? a rewrite man for d wrong daily
news. messenger for cons of d pharaohs court.
perry mason to moses d murderer & thief. pr man
for d prophets of SET. as for poets? chapt
26 my friends—check it out. it is all there in
icewater clear.

ghandi? middleclass lawyer stuck on himself.
freed d brahmins so they cd sip tea & hate cows.
lenins pants didnt fit too good,
people couldnt smoke in front of him, on d
train to petrograd he gv them passes to go
to d head.

d new houngans are to d left of buck rogers,
ok buck up w/ yr hands. where did u stash
our galaxies?

7

bulletin

              to d one who put our
art on a line. now odd shapes will nibble u.
its our turn to put u thru changes. to drop
dour walter winchells on u like, i predict
that tomorrow yr hands will be stiff. to d
one who gaggd a poet. hants will eat yr
cornflakes. golfballs will swell in yr jaws at noon.
horrid masks will gape thru yr window at dusk. it will
be an all day spectacular. look out now,
it is already beginning. to d one who strongarmd
a painter. hear d noise climbing yr steps? u will
be its horse. how does that grab u? how come u
pull d sheets over yr head? & last & least o cactus
for brains. u muggd a playwright, berkeley cal.
spring 68. we hv yr photos. lots of them. what
was that u just spat/up
a lizard or a spider?

8

spelling out my business i hv gone
indoors. raking d coals over my liver,
listening to my stories w/yng widow
brown, talking up a trash in bars (if
i feel up to it). doing all those things put down
in that odor of hog doodoo printd as
a poem in black fire. i caught d whiff of yr
stink thou sow w/ mud for thots. d next
round is on me. black halloween on d rocks.
straight no chaser.

down d hatch d spooks will fly / some
will thrive & some will die / by these
rattles in our hands / mighty spirits
will shake d land.

so excuse me while i do d sooner toomer.
jean that is. im gone schooner to a meta

physical country. behind d eyes. im gone be.
a rootarmd ravenheaded longbeard im gone be.
a zigaboo jazzer teaching mountain
lions of passion how to truck.

9

goodhomefolks gave me ishmael. how
did they know he was d 'afflictd one'?
carrying a gag in his breast pocket. giving
d scene a scent of snowd under w/ bedevilment.
i am d mad mad scientist in love w/ d dark.
d villagers dont understand me. here they come
with their torches. there goes a rock
thru d window. i hv time for a few more hobbies:
making d cab drivers dream of wotan
cutting out pictures of paper murderers
like d ol woman w/ d yng face
or is it d yng woman w/ d ol face?
take yr pick. put it to my chest.
watch it bend. its all a big punchline
i share w/ u. to keep u in stitches.
& ull be so wise when their showstopper
comes:
>   this is how yr ears shd feel
>   this is what u shd eat
>   this is who u shd sleep w/
>   this is how u shd talk
>   this is how u shd write
>   this is how u shd paint
>   these dances are d best
>   these films are d best
>   this is how u shd groom yrself
>   these are d new gods we made for u
u are a bucket of feces before them.
we know what is best for u. bend down
& kiss some wood.
make love to leather. if u
dont u will be offd

10

& d cannd laughter will fade &
d dirty chickens will fly his coop
for he was just a geek u see.
o houngans of america—post this on yr
temples.

DO YR ART D WAY U WANT
ANYWAY U WANT
ANY WANGOL U WANT
ITS UP TO U / WHAT WILL WORK
FOR U.

so sez d neoamerican hoodoo
church of free spirits who
need no
monarch
no gunghoguru
no busybody ray frm d heddahopper planet
of wide black hats & stickpins. he was
just a 666* frm a late late show &
only d clucks threw pennies

ED ROBERSON

Poems by Ed Roberson, a lecturer in the English department at the University of Pittsburgh, have been published in New Directions 22, Atlantic, and other periodicals. He has been an advertising manager, a tankman in an aquazoo, and a research assistant in biology. He won the grand prize in the Atlantic poetry contest in 1962. The following poem is from When Thy King Is A Boy, his first volume of verse, published in 1970 by University of Pittsburgh Press.

Four Lines of a Black Love Letter Between Teachers

bored. confused actually. have started several letters.
usually about   4 in the morning wch is to say something

*false prophet of the apocalypse

about my tenantcy in the house of sleep/black.
evicted. universal. wch is to say 'There's a certain
                                     amount of traveling
wch is to say   in a dream deferred.'
i taught Langston Hughes today. Same In Blues.
and my soul/*stoppt before the mirror at my body sleeping in
    the whiteness of the moon* . . . .

brought it back.saved   newspaper then lost it
waking up.about the confrontation hate
the loss of meaning in that word) between the black
students and the president   of the campus the folks made him
look like a fool. he is   retreating into his power bag
more jab about in loco parentis do you dig it tsk tsk

there is something about music in this letter. mmm how you
do me this heh way. but the lecture was music   you know
i got so many bags i can only read they faces
from inside.run out   of labels even fore
i run me out of words   wch is to say
/descriptions   there's that refrain again
wch of the wch ways to gone   and say . . . /black

a classical problem lawd
i/s here by mysef
got no company.what i got
/i
already got.what i know
i know
why i bother with puttin it down.nuthin
nobody else know   wch is to say.
all you all/you people why you want it down   this way
i was about to attend a sinkin.when yall showed up with the
hole . . . mmmiss you baby

you ask was it all right. i said yes wch is to say.
i didn't say (to you no.no is not
a pill.quinine nor enovid.yes is.for me.
tastes weird as anything else
about us. put a hair
on my hope maybe my chest. but thas oright.
been loving other men's sons lately
buying toys for students' sons on my way to dinner
don't take much to get an A from me.
hey hey you there baby at the end of this line

let me be yo sidetrack till yo mainline come
i can do more switchin than yo mainline
done now   students about presumption.'A certain
amount of nothing
in a dream deferred.'

1 Ibid.,
2 vid., next refrain.
3 ad int./cf., today is a ♀ . sine loco(:op.cit.,
4 i.e.,i am   watering an irish rose.   ooop pop a dop bop

i've lost the letter of this act.
with a pun as multiple as that.
"theys liable to be confusion."
to write   a love letter for someone else
to you the one i love
is a love   in a where someworld sometime else
done now
so signed if this is the night, who else but but
is it   black
but look/here look here one more
thing.every new love adds   to the meaning of love any lingering love old love has to catch up even to linger. so you're
going to have his black baby

SONIA SANCHEZ (1935–   )

*Poet and playwright, Sonia Sanchez was born in Birmingham,
Alabama, lived in New York City, studied at New York
University and Hunter College, was associated with the
Black arts movement in Harlem, and has taught at San
Francisco State College. She is married to Etheridge Knight,
whose work appears in the fiction and poetry sections of this
anthology. Her plays have appeared in the special Black
theater issue of* The Drama Review *and in* New Plays from
the Black Theatre *edited by Ed Bullins. Her poems have
appeared in many magazines and anthologies, and three col-*

lections of her poetry have been published by Broadside Press.

In the introduction to We A BaddDDD People, *Sonia Sanchez's second collection of poetry, Dudley Randall writes: "This tiny woman with the infant's face attacks the demons of this world with the fury of a sparrow defending her fledglings in the nest. She hurls obscenities at things that are obscene. She writes directly, ignoring metaphors, similes, ambiguity, and other poetic devices. But her bare passionate speech can be very effective." The following two poems are from* We A BaddDDD People *published in 1970.*

liberation / poem

blues ain't culture
     they sounds of
oppression
    against the white man's
shit /
  game he's run on us all
these blue / yrs.
      blues is struggle
        strangulation
of our people
     cuz we cudn't off the
white motha / fucka
      soc° / king it to us
but. now.
    when i hear billie's soft
soul / ful / sighs
     of "am i blue"
        i say
no. sweet / billie.
     no mo.
no mo
  blue / trains running on this track
    they all been de / railed.
am i blue?
    sweet / baby / blue /
       billie.
 no. i'm blk/
   & ready.

on watching a world series game

O say can u see
on the baseball diamond
all the fans
                clappen for they nigger/players
yeh.
            there ain't nothing like a
            nigger playen in the noon/day
            sun for us fun/loving/spectators.
                                    sometimes
they seem even human.
                    (that is to say
                            every now and then.)
hooray. hurrah. hooray.
                        my. that nigger's
tough on that mound.
                    can't git no
batters past him.
                wonder where he
was found
            makes u wonder if
it's still a wite man's game.
                        WHO that flexing
his wite muscles.
                oh god yes. another wite hero
to save us from total blk/ness.
                        Carl YASTRZEMSKI
yastruski.   YASTROOSKI.
    ya - fuck - it.   yeh.
                            it's america's
most famous past time
                    and the name
    of the game
                        ain't baseball.

STEPHANY

In 1969 Broadside Press published a collection of love poems,
Moving Deep, *by an unknown poet called Stephany. Introduc-*
ing the poems, without any biographical information, Dudley
Randall wrote: "When I made arrangements to meet Stephany
(Margaret Burroughs had let me use the kitchen of her
Museum of African American History as my office while I
was in Chicago), her poetry had led me to expect an older,
more sophisticated person. I was amazed to meet a freckled-
faced girl in baggy Levis with her shirt tails hanging out,
and to learn that she was not yet twenty-one, and had written
some of these poems while still in her teens." The poems are
untitled and are simply numbered in sequence from 1 to 32.
The following poems are from Moving Deep *and are desig-*
nated with their numbers in the book.

16

What marked the river's flow
lies solid now
ice beneath the snow.

The warmth is past,
frozen to the plastic mold
of yesterday, yet

not a sun has cast
a shadow long
or a moon revealed

one movement of
the constant flight
away.

19

Who collects the pain
screamed
into
the blue black sky

The sorrow of
the afternoon
is marked by more
than falling leaves,

is strained into
a tear,
thundering against
the rain.

23

I have spent my life
thus far
drifting in valleys
of greenness

through valleys
of pain.

Appears before me
now a plain
a desert plain

I want to be
a flower
again.

26

It is again
now that there
is you

painless and
without a name
the days

each in the
name of you
in joy

they come and come

My soul
is round
with you,

Life is again
with
you.

27

Moving deep
more and
more
in me

the thought
   of you
      comes and comes

in me
this joy,
the thought
of you.

LORENZO THOMAS

One of the younger poets represented in the anthology Black
Fire, *Lorenzo Thomas lives in Jamaica in New York City.
He has published his poems in* Liberator *and other periodicals
and was co-editor of* Omnivore. *In response to a request for
biographical information from the editor, he writes: "I
attended Queens College in New York; have published in
several places including* Massachusetts Review, Art & Literature, C, Floating Bear, Angel Hair, *etc. Currently concerned
with translations and transformations of ancient and Third
World literature. During the period when the poems you have
were written, I was closely connected with the* Umbra *group
in New York." The following poem is published from manuscript.*

Inauguration

The land was there before us
Was the land. Then things
Began happening fast. Because
The bombs us have always work
Sometimes it makes me think
God must be one of us. Because
Us has saved the world. Us gave it
A particular set of regulations
Based on 1) undisputable acumen.
2) carnivorous fortunes, delicately
Referred to here as "bull market"
And (of course) other irrational factors
Deadly smoke thick over the icecaps,
Our man in Saigon Lima Tokyo etc etc

SOTÈRE TORREGIAN' (1941—

A surrealist poet, Sotère Torregian' has provided the following biographical information: "Born June 25, 1941. Of Afro ancestry, Black and Arab, from the island of Sicily in the Mediterranean. Raised 'riding supermart cars' in ghetto Newark, where was first one in family to attend college in that city, Rutgers University. Surrealist inspiration from 1962 on—as well as African poets of 'The Negritude School.' Affiliated with 'New York Group' of poets and painters. Taught poetry in New York City. Works appeared in Italy, France, England, and South America. In 1967 recipient of Frank O'Hara Prize for Poetry from Poet's Foundation, New York. Is married, father of two children, and now resides in California where, under the chairmanship of Dr. Saint-Clair Drake, is consultant and instructor in African and Afro-American Literature at Stanford University, Black Studies Program. Currently working on textbook of Third World Literature. Anthologies: The Young American Poets *(Follett, 1969). Books:* The Wounded Mattress *(Oyez, Berkeley) and* The Golden Palomino Bites the Clock *(Angel Hair, New York). Journals:* Paris Review, Art and Literature, *and others." The following poems are published from manuscript.*

Poem for the Birthday of Huey P. Newton

This birthday card
Comes into your cell
It is a birthday card you cannot see
It is signed by the nameless
It is signed by dreams

The endless dreams of man of the Primal Peoples
By their fires tonight
It is signed by Chaka
It is signed by Atibon Legba
It is signed by the blood of Sharpesville
The skull of Baccaville is coughing
It is signed Always in our embrace by Niccolo Sacco
And Bartolomeo Vanzetti
It is signed by all the Unknown Soldiers hidden
Under the sidewalks on which we walk
It is signed by our glass hands
It is signed by all the watercolors of the world's children
It is signed
By the birds
And the Dolomites that make music
It is signed by the Apollo Club of Harlem
And the songs that are not ours
And we wish were ours
It is signed by the Dome of the Rock at
Jerusalem
It is signed in peacock
By Billy Holliday
It is signed in my lost hours
It is signed in hunger gazing at luxury
And the stars that fall from that sky
It is signed by the painters of The Lascaux Caves
It is signed by rivers wearing smiles of snow

It is the Birthday Card of the World

The Newark Public Library Reading Room

I have a new home. A roaring Sparring Partner like a sunspot
Orifice for the gray membrane theodicy & lexicon
    of my laughing years.
It is the Public Library of the Skull
Where everyday round the clock poor old vagabond-eccentrics
and alcoholics enter
The vagabonds jest with the librarians tell them their
    jokes lives and troubles
O Harlequinade

And the librarians grow hysterical up their left sleeves
Until I can see a zigzag shape grinning and I know
These winos are the real harlequins!
An old waif in breadline clothes and tattered hat reads at a
    table
Back issues of Better Homes & Gardens
And from a strange periodical called "Gourmet" he
  righteously scribbles
Down frighteningly vast tracts on scrap paper and paper bags
As if the world depended on it.
I must get away from these harlequins.

It is in this smudged lapidarium that I look for my Chantarelle

You are between the resemblance and the divine image
It is my blood that flows down the unchartered street of
Dreams where in the monotone cleft
You are motionless between the resemblance and the divine
  image unreconciled
There remaining I find the eternal scansion with which
  Eratosthenes
Measured the earth and the lips of the heavens

Travois of the Nameless

Note: "Travois" is the name given by the French to the method whereby the North American Plains Indians were wont to
carry their earthly belongings tied to the poles of their (dis-
mantled) teepees and attach the same to their horses in their
migrations across the plains.

6 : o' clock our passageway
In fine pains of the Third World
I pass by on my way home the bank exhibiting its trophies
                 overlaid silver Iago smile
Exposing the African mother with mammalian breasts
            like pulling a diseased rabbit out
   of its proud windows
O the world without its rest   Travois of the nameless

With their miseries ;
Sandwich man giving out his last ration card
to me ghost city in the fog

             I stand on the verge of making
Handing a suicide note to the candyshop
& its drooling passersby my map of words clientel
of old ladies who come one by one out of the throng
Ah, Third World !
Third World ! my epithalium

I can go no further than the frontiers of my nose

Ah the world without its rest   the world without its rest
My Sybarite we must replenish
the world without its rest
             come home to you from the gorge of the penumbra

Forever I approach you,
the world without its rest
saturated with wickerwork into which flows
the smell of the eyes   of
my immortal disguise

Your Rainbow House of Wines & Spirits

QUINCY TROUPE (1943–)

*One of the original members of the Watts Writers' Workshop,
Quincy Troupe edited the anthology* Watts Poets and Writers
*published by the House of Respect in 1968. Born in New
York City, he was raised in St. Louis, Missouri, and attended
Grambling College in Louisiana and Los Angeles City College.
He has been writer-in-residence at Ohio University, taught
Third World and Black literature there, and founded Con-
frontation: A journal of Third World Literature published
by the Black Studies Institute of Ohio University in Athens.
He is now a member of the faculty of Richmond College,
Staten Island, and lives in New York. His poems have ap-
peared in many periodicals, in* New Directions 22, *and in a
number of anthologies. His book* Embryo: Poems 1967–1971
will be published by Barlenmir House in April, 1972, in hard

cover and paperback. The following poems are published from manuscript.

A Day in the Life of a Poet

Woke up crying the blues:
bore witness to the sadness of the day;
the peaceful man from Atlanta
was slaughtered yester/day.
Got myself together
drank in the sweetness of sun/shine,
wrote three poems to the peace/full lamb
from Atlanta; made love
to a raging Black woman
drank wine
got high: saw angels
leading the lamb to heaven?
the blues gonna get me
gonna get me for sure!
went to the beach/to forget
if only eye can
about the gentle soul from Georgia;
ate clam chowder soup and fish sandwiches;
made love in the sand
to this same beautiful woman:
drank in all her sweetness:
lost future child in the sand,
saw the bloody sun falling
behind weeping purple clouds;
tears fell in rivers for this gentle lamb
whom eye cant forget.
The bloody star sinking
into the purple grave: blackness falls.
Go out into the decay of day;
copped three keys;
the key of happiness,
the key of creative joy,
the key of sadness.
Came back and watched the gloom on the tube
at her house; which was disrupted.
Kissed her: went home by the route
of the mad spacedways: dropped tears in my lap

for the lamb in Atlanta.
Home at last.
Two letters under the door;
a love letter from the past
grips at the roots of memory:
at last another poem published!
good news during a bad news weekend;
lights out;
drink of grapes;
severed sight close's
another day
in the life.

Impressions/of Chicago; For Howlin' Wolf

1.

the wind/blade cutting in
& out swinging in over the lake
slicing white foam from the tips
of delicate fingers
that danced & weaved
under the sunken light/night;
this wind/blade was so sharp & cold
it'd cut a four-legged mosquito into fours
while a hungry lion slept on the wings of some chittlins
slept within the blues of a poem that was forming

we came in the sulphuric night drinkin' old crow
while a buzzard licked its beak atop the head of richard nixon
while gluttonous daly ate hundreds of pigs that were his ego
while daddy-o played bop on the box
came to the bituminous breath of chicago
howling with three million voices of pain

& this is the music;
the kids of chicago have eyes that are older
                    than the deepest pain in the world
& they run with feet bared over south/side streets
shimmering with a billion shivers of glass
razors that never seem to cut their feet;
they dance in & out of the traffic,
the friday night smells of fish

the scoobedoo sounds
of bo didely

2.

these streets belong to the dues payers
to the blues players drinkin whiskey on satdaynight
muddy waters & the wolfman howlin smokestack lightnin
how many more years down in the bottom
no place to go moanin' for my baby
a spoonful of evil
back door man
all night long how many more years
down in the bottom built for comfort

you come to me

you come to me
during the cool hours
of the day bringing
the sun; if you come
at midnight, or at two
in the morning, you come
always bringing the sun;
the taste of your sweetness
permeates my lips and my hair
with the lingering sweetness of Harlem
with the lingering sweetness of Africa
with the lingering sweetness of freedom;
woman, eye want to see
your breast brown and bared,
your nippled eyes staring,
aroused-hard and lovely;
woman, eye want to see
the windows of your suffering
washed clean of this terrible pain
we endure together;
woman, eye want to see
your song filled with joy,
feel the beauty of your laughter;
woman, black beautiful woman,
eye want to see

your black graceful body
covered with the sweat of our love
with your dancer's steps to music
moving rhythmically, panther like
across the african veldt;
woman, eye want to see you
naked, always in your natural beauty;
woman, eye want to see you
proud; in your native land

The Syntax of the Mind Grips

the syntax of the mind grips
the geography of letters
the symbol burns then leaves
the ocean bleeds pearls/washes the shore
where the darkness crawls in all alone
and sits like a panther with luminous eyes
watches us make love with the trees
the beautiful woman in the grass
curls her pulling legs
around my shoulders
the old maid weeps in the window
covers her face with her blue veined
withered white hands and with
her fingernails painted red
gouges out her war-shattered eyes
while the mirror breaks in the bathroom
falls like razors to the floor
where a junkie is sprawled
with a death needle in his arm
a child cuts his feet in the streets
screams for the old maid
who makes the flags
who is weeping in the window
but the stars have fallen from the flags
and she does not hear anything
but her own weeping
because the flag has become a garrote
that is choking the breath/love of a people
whose hero is the armless legless brainless
vegetable who sits upon his bloodied stump

in a wheel/chair, in a veterans
hospital in washington;
he cannot speak for the blood
that he has swallowed;
he cannot see for the death
his eyes have seen;
he cannot hear for the screams
his ears have heard; but he feels
the pain drenched sorrow of the old maid
who is weeping because the stars
have fallen from the flag
and because of the love scene
in the grass beneath her window

TOM WEATHERLY (1942–   )

*The essential biographical information about Tom Weatherly
is embodied in his poem "autobiography" which opens the
following selection of his poems. He has published in* Noose,
The Saint, Simbolo Oscuro, 3C 147, Utter & The World. *The
following poems are from* Maumau American Cantos, *his first
collection of poetry, published in 1970 by Corinth Books.*

autobiography

tomcat born on railroad
avenue, scottsboro, alabama
to big tom & lucy belle
weatherly, november 3, 1942

dad in european theatre
mom & i living
wif his mom & dad

after the war dad & mom & lil sis & i
moved to the mountain
street home. grade & high school
at george washington carver, split
off to morehouse college at the end of
eleventh grade.

two & half years at morehouse
semester at alabama a & m
then parris island
& dante's inferno, another semester
at normal, alabama made q frat sic
wif bundle of sticks in hand.
indefinitely suspended from a & m
for publishing The Saint on campus
without permission.
                    had a vision
entered a.m.e. ministry
assistant pastor of saint pauls scottsboro
& next year pastor of church great grandad
pastored (bishop i.h. bonner had feel for tradition).
had a division:left god mother hooded youth &
the country for new york, lived on streets,
parks, hitchd the states.
                            dishwasher at hip bagel,
waiter in the mountains, cook at lion's head,
proofreading, copyediting, baking, bellhopping,
camp counselor, dealing, fuckd up in the head.
rantd in the saint marks poetry project, ranting
now in afro-hispanic poets workshop east harlem.
HOLDER OF THE DOUBLE MOJO HAND &
13TH DEGREE GRIS-GRIS BLACK BELT.

                                    your eyes are mirth

            your eyes are mirth
            trauma. i am he,
            born out of the laughter
            of your sleep. your
            sleep closed to me
            traps me inside it. waking
            in the morning of joy.

i am ignorant and stretch
my shape . . .

and you awakening
pull me close.

blues for franks wooten

House of the Lifting of the Head

let me open mama your 3 corner box.
yes open mama your 3 corner box.
i have a black snake baby his tongues hot.

you shake round those curves baby dont quite make
the grade.
you shake round those curves baby dont make the grade.
man come home tired dont want no lemonade.

we been blowing spit bubbles baby in each others mouf.
we been blowing spit bubbles baby in each others mouf.
burst all them bubbles mama norf cold like the souf.

let me be your woodpecker mama tom do like no pecker
would.
let me be your woodpecker mama tom tom do like no
pecker would.
open your front door baby black dark come home for
good.

mud water shango

a big muddy daddy my daddys gris-gris to the world.
i'm a big muddy daddy daddys gris-gris to the world.
got a mojo chop for sweet black belt girl.

daddys a river & my mamas shore is black.
daddys a river mamas shore is black.
flood coming mama you cant keep it back.

lightning in my eyes mama thunder in your soul.
theres lightning in my eyes mama thunder in your soul.
i'm a river hip daddy mama dig a muddy hole.

RON WELBURN (1944-   )

*A poet and jazz musician with a rapidly growing reputation
as a jazz critic and literary critic, Ron Welburn was born in
Bryn Mawr, Pennsylvania, and grew up in Philadelphia. He
has written about himself: I began shaping my socio-aesthetic
interests while in high school, becoming familiar with available jazz music, also playing the cornet and alto saxophone.
I entered Lincoln University [in Pennsylvania] in 1964. My
foremost intentions in life are 1. explore the aesthetic value
of human feelings; 2. advance the stature of Afro-American
culture through literature and music."*

*He was poet laureate at Lincoln University (1966–68)
and received his M.A. in creative writing at the University
of Arizona. He has taught literature in Afro-American studies
at Syracuse University. He was a contributing editor of* Nickel
Review *and published poems, a feature column of jazz criticism, and frequent book reviews in this lively literary publication. He has also published widely in other periodicals and
anthologies. He contributed an essay to* The Black Aesthetic
*(1971), the anthology of Black criticism. Six of the following
poems are published from manuscript; "black is beautiful" and
"it is overdue time" first appeared in* Nickel Review.

Whichway

land of Pharoah
everywhichway Egypt is

is not to be Babylon; or
do we side with Moses
or Pharoah?
do we wander or build
civilizations, to leave
behind us & before our children
his face & body of simba?*
we we everywhichway turn on
Moses on Pharoah?
do we E
gypt our thing?

---

black is beautiful
green earth
red clay hearts of the babylon
center
black is red & green
black is brown & yellow
is colors dancing their resilience
in the sun
black is eclipse so beautiful
in the covering of the faces with hands
by children is eclipse
so fine
so black it is green and brown
as earthsong oldbop dance to
the popcorn hallelujia
is beautiful black is
into redclay earth & leaves & grass
black is beautiful barefoot sundays
color is life summarily
snow is occasional beauty
in its season
this is the turning season and
joyspring comes around the corner
black is spring green & redearth
though groundhog sees his shadow.

*(Swahili) lion—*Ed.*

it is overdue time
to mojo* the demons
to mojo them with ju-ju*
to place their likeness on their porches
with darts in the throat
there will be no blood from the throat
they have sucked themselves dry of us
now it is time for mojo
it is time for ju-ju
it is time to salute Legba* with the talking drum
time to entice Damballah* with the saxophone
it is time now for jihad and rhythm dance
                     of the loa's ride
time for waving cane, knives
for the majic of ju-ju.

lyrics shimmy like
fertility serpents at damballah's
breasts
twisting lyric horns and piano
and piano and drums
spoken word of gods in the jungle
network of cities in the jungle
streetpaths and extinguished lights
in cities chained and unchained
moving and preparing the movement
of satellites
like new ark is and the crescent

*Note: In response to a query from the editor the poet provided the
following definitions for the words with asterisks in this poem:
mojo—(Afro-American) a use of magic powers for influence
ju-ju—(Yoruba) a god that can take image form; possesses magical
powers for influence
Legba—in the voudoun of Haiti, the ruler of roads, streets and pathways; the first to be invoked at a voodoo ceremony
Damballah—in the voudoun of Haiti, the loa (god) of fertility.

hanging its rhythm over the houses
of renegade believers with other names
afraid of the serpent
afraid of the lyric piano and drums
do not be   we are not to
be unlyrical
we shimmy fertility ridden by our loas
and in our warring jungles
even brick walls will sing.

Condition Blue/ Dress

condition blue/ dress
blue-like upper horn's
bent neck in the light
a condition of blue
a dressed up lyric like horn
you are
plenty sound night
plenty coups
plenty condition blues.

---

put u red-eye in
redrink stain on our fingers'
tips from the blood
we have arranged for murders
to take shape with drums and happenstance
in the mind twisting in
red-irons of wine
we would spew on all our competitors
and all our crooning enemies
singing the blues
making the god the devilblue
casting lots over otis redding
and ma rainey
we are victims of
the defecations that rule the arc

of the sunarm sweeping
over our heads and disappearing
into the cloak of the earth
we will drink red-wine until
our intestines treat our eyes like
the python and the ground fowl
and one day a ghost will stand
above us and the crowd
screaming over his (fake) guitar
and what we will do with
our horns broken and our wine gone
will betray your disbelief.

---

and universals
are not that world
wide men can dig em
but are classics in their
own style/ bagthing
that like dilsey's endurance alone
is universal in our hands
the call for
universals
comes only out of pale places
as an insipid word for conquest
and exploitation: our plotted fates
in a charlatan gypsy's crystal ball
like a masque over divisions
in africa
in asia
in latino
we are the ones they ask
to be universal.

---

        tu
        cson's of blackmens/
        brothers south
        and west

still cut n shoot each
other n stab sideways
under the watchful
swineye of jack the
guvnur—one-eyed-jack
that is—the cyclops of
scotts eye u dale eye me one
eyes tu
csons of blackmens/
in an open boat of gin
routed like odysses.

JAY WRIGHT (1935–   )

*Jay Wright was born in Albuquerque, New Mexico, and spent
his early youth in California. He completed his undergraduate
studies at the University of California at Berkeley, his M.A.
at Rutgers University (1966), and had a writing fellowship
at Princeton in 1970–71. He writes, in a letter to the editor:
"I have published in:* New American Review, The Nation,
New Republic, Yale Review, Evergreen Review, Negro
Digest *(now* Black World), Umbra, For Malcolm, Black Fire,
The Outsider, Poetry Northwest, Hiram Poetry Review,
American Weave, Religious Humanism, Poetry Review *(London),* Union Seminary Quarterly, Soulscript, New Negro
Poets: USA, Hanging Loose, 31 New American Poets *and*
Natural Process. *My book of poems,* The Homecoming
Singer, *will be published by Corinth Books next fall. I am,
at the moment, a Hodder fellow in playwriting, Committee
on Humanistic Studies, Princeton University." The following
poems are published from manuscript.*

The Neighborhood House

1

So many people lie in this alley
we call it the neighborhood house.
If you lift your eyes,
the roofs are lined with young black boys,
threatening indifferently to jump.

2

It looks bombed-out here.
Bricks jut up like stubbled old men
bending over fragments of glass
as if they were gravestones.
Children run in the wired-in area,
spit in the familiar camp.
In the dark, among the rubble,
you might see a black girl, spread out,
her arms moving like butterfly wings
against the stiff caress of a boy.
Or maybe it's an old man,
impaled on a pole, cursing the wind.
When sirens rake up the streets,
widows and wives sing laments.
So familiar.

3

So like judgment.
Then through the silent house,
a youth comes to indict us.
He tells us of his great, great grandfather,
who stood under a saint and a gesture,
listening to fourteen strange letters,
his bones splitting at the roots.
He sings you a rhumba strung
with Mandingo, Bantu, Yoruba, Dahomeyan names,
dropping like pearls he recovered.
He stands in this filthy garden,
chanting up moon-fed pools

and the din of forests.
Tense drums beat in his eyes:
Yelofe, Bakongo, Banguila, Kumbá, Kongué.
"What does it matter?" he says,
and turns from you.
"I have a name,
an interminable name,
made from interminable names.
It is my name,
free and mine,
foreign and yours,
indifferent as the air,
and I live in the neighborhood house."

4

This is our neighborhood house,
drumming for echoes in an indifferent city.
A house nurturing epic poets
who may sing no more,
or sing
red songs
like savannas,
like fighting rings,
like the bed
of a woman just delivered.

> Nicolás Guillén, *Casa de Vecindad*
> *Deportes*
> *El Apellido*

Jalapeña Gypsies

When you come out of that
clean bus station in Jalapa,
and walk west toward the Tecajetes,
three gypsies flutter from the gardens,
and come at you
like flowers floating up
in the stiff summer wind.
The heavy one approaches first,
while her sisters stand

as though they expect nothing good from you,
as though they can see in your eyes
how afraid they make you.
She speaks, easily and surely,
"Put something in your hand
and I can tell you something
good about your life."
You look at her half-whispering breasts,
at the virgin and the pagan medals
dangling there, and you stop
in that voice, really afraid
that she does know you.

You listen/
you aren't there/ for a moment/
you go back to your bus/
gray and empty in those hills/
pink and yellow buds steeped in mud/
the green shaded into green into brown
into soft orange against blue/

> How can you move
> in this womb,
> and feel the city's sting?
> How can you sit
> in the droning bus,
> and not sleep in innocence?

Behind you,
a little girl,
playing with dolls and dishes,
watches the slow movement of colors.
"Me encanta esa.
Tu crees en las cosas . . . ?
No, ya estoy sorda."*
What makes her silent
is in the gypsy's fingers
going over your forehead,
in the quick step of her tongue
in your life/
                    in your life/
in a sculptor's eyes

*Note: The three Spanish lines in the poem, in English translation,
mean: "That enchants me. Do you believe in the things . . . ? No,
already I am mute."—*Ed.*

as he tells you
that the night
is feminine and diabolical.

> And Percy would always
> make it at night,
> high on speed, or gin,
> or sounds,
> clinched with legs
> he wouldn't release,
> until he would,
> as though the night
> and his woman
> would run off together,
> laughing, not ever in the act,
> not satisfied.

Can you believe a gypsy?
Can you believe any woman
who would leave you,
or make you sit silent
under whispering leaves?
But what is there
in your life
that you would protect
against her?
All you can remember
is the motion
of your obscure fingers,
scurrying over other bodies,
warped by the very warmth
of your insatiable touch.
All you feel is
the radiation of your own touch.

> You want to touch the gypsy,
> as your hand comes up
> like a magnet toward her lips
> and down her neck/
> your hand/ like water
> running over her body/
> and she is not so strange/
> only a traveler
> inviting you behind
> that clean bus station/
> with lips parting

like a flower budding/
with harsh teeth in your neck/
a harsh grind in love/
she knows you have left
enchanting gardens before/
she knows you will recognize yourself
in any prophecy that she makes/
she knows you don't want to see
danger in moping trees/
or a child's silence/
or the intoxicated loving
of black men in closed
sweaty rooms/

You are the traveler
she waits for,
the one who will touch
a city in darkness,
and leave before dawn
shows you its other face.
You are always looking
for gypsies, and signs in rainy forests,
and love in rooms
that you can shuffle
like a deck of cards
and cast away.
You are always
in the beginning
of some prophecy
that you will not believe
to save your life.

You travel in cities
that travel in you,
lost in the ache
of knowing none.

AL YOUNG (1939–   )

A biographical note on Al Young appears in the fiction section (see p. 146), and his statement on poetics appears in the criticism section (see pp. 553–54). "The Prestidigitator (1)" and "The Prestidigitator (2)" are published from manuscript, and the other poems are from Dancing, *his first collection of poetry, published in 1969 by Corinth Books.*

A Little More Traveling Music

A country kid in Mississippi I drew water
   from the well
& watched our sun set itself down behind
   the thickets,
hurried from galvanized baths to hear music
over the radio—Colored music, rhythmic & electrifying,
more Black in fact than politics & flit guns.

Mama had a knack for snapping juicy fruit gum
& for keeping track of the generations of chilrens
she had raised, reared & no doubt forwarded,
rising thankfully every half past daybreak
to administer duties the poor must look after
if theyre to see their way another day, to eat, to live.

•

I lived & upnorth in cities sweltered & froze,
   got jammed up & trafficked
in everybody's sun going down but took up with the
   moon

as I lit about getting it all down up there
   where couldnt nobody knock it out.

Picking up slowly on the gists of melodies, most noises
   softened.
I went on to school & to college too, woke up cold
& went my way finally, classless, reading all poems,
   some books & listening to heartbeats.

Well on my way to committing to memory the ABC
   reality,
I still couldn't forget all that motherly music,
those unwatered songs of my babe-in-the-wood days
until, committed to the power of the human voice,
I turned to poetry & to singing by choice,
reading everyone always & listening, listening for a
   silence deep enough
to make out the sound of my own background music.

A Dance for Ma Rainey

I'm going to be just like you, Ma
Rainey this monday morning
clouds puffing up out of my head
like those balloons
that float above the faces of white people
in the funny papers

I'm going to hover in the corners
of the world, Ma
& sing from the bottom of hell
up to the tops of high heaven
& send out scratchless waves of yellow
& brown & that basic black honey
misery

I'm going to cry so sweet
& so low
& so dangerous,
Ma,
that the message is going to reach you
back in 1922

where you shimmer
snaggle-toothed
perfumed &
powdered
in your bauble beads
hair pressed & tied back
throbbing with that sick pain
I know
& hide so well
that pain that blues
jives the world with
aching to be heard
that downness
that bottomlessness
first felt by some stolen delta nigger
swamped under with redblooded american agony;
reduced to the sheer shit
of existence
that bred
& battered us all,
Ma,
the beautiful people
our beautiful brave black people
who no longer need to jazz
or sing to themselves in murderous vibrations
or play the veins of their strong tender arms
with needles
to prove that we're still here

A Dance for Militant Dilettantes

No one's going to read
or take you seriously,
a hip friend advises,
until you start coming down on them
like the black poet you truly are
& ink in lots of black in your poems
soul is not enough
you need real color
shining out of real skin
nappy snaggly afro hair
baby grow up & dig on *that*!

You got to learn to put in about
stone black fists
coming up against white jaws
& red blood splashing
down those fabled wine & urine-
stained hallways
black bombs blasting out real white estate
the sky itself black with what's to come:
final holocaust
the settling up

Dont nobody want no nice nigger no more
these honkies man that put out
these books & things
they want an angry splib
a furious nigrah
they dont want no bourgeois woogie
they want them a militant nigger
in a fiji haircut
fresh out of some secret boot camp
with a bad book in one hand
& a molotov cocktail in the other
subject to turn up at one of their conferences
or soirees
& shake the shit out of them

Dance of the Infidels

in memory of Bud Powell

The smooth smell of Manhattan taxis,
Parisian taxis, it doesnt matter, it's
the feeling that modern man is all youve
laid him out to be in those tinglings & rushes;
the simple touch of your ringed fingers
against a functioning piano.

                          The winds of Brooklyn
still mean a lot to me. The way certain chicks
formed themselves & their whole lives around
a few notes, an attitude more than anything.
I know about the being out of touch, bumming

nickels & dimes worth of this & that off
him & her here & there—everything but
hither & yon.

Genius does not grow on trees.

I owe
you a million love dollars & so much more than
thank-you for re-writing the touch & taste & smell
of the world for me those city years when I could
very well have fasted on into oblivion.

Ive just
been playing the record you made in Paris with Art
Blakey & Lee Morgan. The european audience
is applauding madly. I think of what Ive heard
of Buttercup's flowering on the Left Bank & days
you had no one to speak to. Wayne Shorter is
beautifying the background of sunlight with
children playing in it & shiny convertibles
& sedans parked along the block as I blow.

Grass
grows. Negroes. Women walk. The world, in case
youre losing touch again, keeps wanting the same
old thing.

You gave me some of it; beauty I sought
before I was even aware how much I needed it.

I know
this world is terrible & that one must, above all,
hold onto the heart & the hearts of others.

I love *you*

The Prestidigitator [1]

A prestidigitator makes things disappear,
vanish, not unlike a well-paid bookkeeper
or tax consultant or champion consumer

The poet is a prestidigitator, he makes
your old skins disappear & re-clothes you
in sturdy raiment of thought, feeling, soul

dream & happenstance. Consider him villain of
the earthbound, a two-fisted cowboy with
pencil in one hand & eraser in the other

dotting the horizon of your heart with cool
imaginary trees but rubbing out more than he
leaves in for space so light can get thru

The Prestidigitator [2]

I draw hats on rabbits, sew women back together, let fly from my pockets flocks of
vibratory hummingbirds. The things Ive got

up my sleeve would activiate the most listless
of landscapes (the cracked-earth heart of a bigot,
say) with pigeons that boogaloo, with flags that

light up stabbed into the brain. Most of all it's
enslaving mumbo-jumbo that I'd wipe away, a trick
done by walking thru mirrors to the other side

BLKARTSOUTH POETS

BLKARTSOUTH is a southern Black arts organization based
in New Orleans. It began in 1968 as a workshop within the
structure of the Free Southern Theater, the radical Black
theater in the South. The program, objectives, and history

of BLKARTSOUTH *are explained by Val Ferdinand, its director, in a statement in the criticism section (see pp. 467–73). A documentary record of the Free Southern Theater and its work is embodied in the book* The Free Southern Theater *by the Free Southern Theater (1969) edited by Thomas C. Dent, Richard Schechner, and Gilbert Moses. The writing workshop of the Free Southern Theater produced the literary publication* NKOMBO *in which the work of the* BLKARTSOUTH *writers was published. The Free Southern Theater no longer exists and* NKOMBO, *which encountered hard times and did not appear in 1970, resumed publication in 1971 edited and published as a joint venture of Tom Dent and Val Ferdinand. In response to my requests for biographical information on the following poets, Val Ferdinand wrote, in the letter accompanying the statement published in the criticism section of this book: "Could you use it instead of a bunch of individual biographies? We haven't been able to track down everybody and, too, we like to try to push* BLKARTSOUTH *instead of particular individuals." The poems by the individual poets that follow are grouped together as the expression of a contemporary Black arts movement in the South. The poems that follow were first published in 1969 issues of* NKOMBO *or in the following individual volumes of poetry published by* BLKARTSOUTH *in 1969:* The Blues Merchant *by V. Ferdinand III (Val Ferdinand),* The Impatient Rebel *by Renaldo Fernandez,* I Want Me a Home *by NAYO (Barbara Malcolm),* Visions From the Ghetto *by Raymond Washington.*

ISAAC J. BLACK

Racist Psychotherapy

If not a so-called Negro bought a bottle/
played the numbers/ spent 80 percent
of his annual net on a white-on-white Cadillac/

if we stuck by our women/cooled the b.s.
in barbershops/if we stopped crowding
those welfare centers while hiding John
under the bed/if we worked from dawn to dusk/
joined the NAACP and became lifetime members/
if we stopped hanging out on streetcorners/
crooning anywhere/grabbing pocketbooks/
showing our teeth/if we kept our neighborhoods
clean and peaceful/let the mailman pass through
once and awhile/if we wore white shirts
with dark ties/stopped making babies/noise/
if we denounced Rap and Stokely/stopped
turning tricks/becoming potheads/if we
took the academic course/went to Harvard/
stopped shouting that whitey did this or that/
didn't marry their daughters/play house
on the side/think it would make a difference?

TOM DENT

For Walter Washington

We blk blues singers
we blken the chords
with shots of blue. . . .
we blk blues singers
we are you pleadin
I gave you all my love
please don't abuse it
we are you cryin
I tried my best
but it wasn't worth it
we are you wishin
the rain smell would
drive away the sweaty mad dreams of

last night
we are you watchin
all the half-empty
half-caught
days of yr life
pass before yr face
we are you
listenin to the field slide of my voice
the wolf wail of my guitar
open up
the strained/face
you-knew-it-all-the-time
stopped/time
of yr moments
we are you
comin down off
                    the
                         speed
                              of
                                all
                                   that
back home
where life lay
open
ready.

New Orleans is an easy town
to dance the blues in:
everybody
tune yr mind
guitar.

Ray Charles at Mississippi State

I hear people waiting for the riot to begin in their hearts ...

I hear white boys rustling through seatsocks and yearbooks
and sliderules and long green farms their fathers own, rustlin
their feet on the sawdust floor of the livestock building waiting
for the riot to begin ...

I hear white girls smoothing the wrinkles of long cotton
dresses, waiting for his voice to echo the long, cool rape ...

I hear the clatter of that Black boy's mind countin and recountin the black votes in Isaquena County ten years hence, waiting for the band to get set and the lights to dim . . .

I hear the cymbals of clashing musics, one of the radio like a steady drone, the other echoing the shattered, unrepaired windows of a small Baptist church, unseen, but deep at the end of a long dirt road miles from the highway . . .

I hear the clang of sounds of battling lives—one life whispering "tell me, tell me you'all love us," the other shocked, and deadened, but still staggering out from under B-Sweet leaden armpits to spit, "we don't love you, we don't love you" and stronger: "our blues ain't your plaything" . . .

I hear the band ripping 'em off, the certain rhythm rocking slowly like waves washing all night against a boat tied to shore . . .

Then Rev. Charles comes on, rocking from side to side like a black mechanical music machine and sings: "calm down noise, it's all gon end too soon. Listen to the Blues."

Those who could did.

VAL FERDINAND (KALAMU YA SALAAM)

whi/te boys gone
to the moon
plantin flags & stuff
why you boys goin
to the moon
dont yall think

yall done fucked up enuf
without messing
wit somebody else's world

in the beginning
it was africa
you just wanted to see
you said
& once having seen
commenced to fucking up

open up them china gates

& let's hunt tigers in india

you whi/te boys sho nuff likes
what ever anybody else has
all ways got to be
digging in somebody's bag
always got to be plantin flags & stuff

whi/te boys done gone
to the moon
just like they come here
talking bout it's a
great adventure & we is
the first ones here
& plantin flags

whi/te boys gone to the moon
whi/te boys done gone to the moon
sho hope them lil brothers up there
dont show um how
to plant corn

The Blues (in two parts)

I

Our best singers
can't really sing

you take like otis redding
that nigger never could sing
in fact i believe he only knew
maybe two notes at the most
& a couple of
phrases/no melody
strictly atonal stuff
i mean like what does
yes are am mean
or even na-na-na
what's da matter baby
mr. redding you is singing
like you is in a hurry or
something, maybe you
got to go to the bathroom
& now you take that
lil ugly no singing nigger
james brown
now he can dance his
ass off, ain't no
doubt bout that
but he can't sing
not a lick &
talkin bout a
lickin stick
somebody need to
beat him all upside
his haid w/h his own
damn lickin stick
& that band
he got, they don't know
nothin but one song
that's how come
they got to have
two drummers
them two dudes is suppose
to be among the best
we got/black
people we gon have to do better
or shut our mouth
cause i mean
what is mother popcorn and
for sho dud-dum de-de de-dum-dum
ain't no song

II

The blues
is not song
it is singing
no voice
is needed
only the knowledge
the blues is not
not notes
it is feeling
it is not death
it is being
it is not submission
it is existing
you take the ing
it is the ing of th-ings
whether it be
laugh-ing or dy-ing
swing-ing or hang-ing
from a tree
sometimes it be
hurting so bad
when you is singing
or feeling the blues
till you just have to
drop the g trying
to e-eeeee-eeeeee-aassssse
on in

2 B BLK

WHERE/FROM/HERE
R WHAT ELSE THEN R WE TLKING BOUT
2 B BLK
IS MAYBE BULLETS
AND GUNS & COCKTAILS
BUT IS ALSO
MAYBE US BEING
STRONG SOMETIMES ALONE
SOMETIMES TOGETHER

WHERE EVER WE ARE
2 B BLK
WE MUST BE READY TO TEAR DOWN
WALLS OF SHIT &
LET OUR MINDS RUN THRU THE RUBBLE
OF WHAT IS LEFT
2 B BLK
IS TO B MANY THINGS
CAN BE MANY THINGS
SHOULD BE MANY THINGS
BUT 2 B BLK BROS & SISTERS
WE MUST BE READY
IN MY HOUSE TO B BLK
IS TO DO BLK
WHICH IS SIMPLY
TO LIVE & CONTROL YOUR LIVES
2 LIV & CONTROL YR LIVES
DO BLK DO BLK DO BLK DO BLK DO BLK

Food for Thought

what is a blk poem &/or what is it
that we writing

blk poetics is
motion stood still
notes played twice
molotov rose buds
& nigger tomorrows
it do not necessarily be like
anything you heard before &
yet it will still sound familiar
good blk poets can fly
propelled by the sounds
of a funky poem/at heart
blk poems is sung when
sung if really sung poems
are/become song
& song is what we (blk people)
do best
nothing is concrete, blk lives are in a constant state of flux
life styles(patterns) change so quickly that less you be in it

you can hardly be of it
you can get next to blk people if you rap with them right
poems may be writ in english but they is done up in blk &
recited in time, coinciding with the hip beats & funky rhythms
of sweet blk lives
blk people have done it to the english language, they have
niggerized it
we are finding that blk poetry has to do mostly with rhythm,
images, & sound
1. rhythm/blk dancing, poems got to dance too, leastwise
move & pat your foot, but you can't read the rhythms, them
is something you got to ride/be/hear/feel; our poetic
rhythms are breakaways from iambs & are moving into
booagloos, funky butts & popcorns
2. images/most good images come from blues, blues singers
were our 1st heavy poets & image just means saying it in
your own way like it is for others, images can/should connect
one consciousness with another's, blk folk are good at
sharing feelings
3. sound/how you sound, every poet his own sound so
to be recognized any/everywhere whenever he do his do/
sound is the ultimate expression of creativity, every good
artifact sounds(sings, swings, says something
we must consider ameer baraka(leroi jones) the "bird" of
blk poetics, it was he who helped us break those old milk
wagon rhythms down & helped us to get into brown tranes
of cascading rhythms, he showed us images like up against
the wall & jitterbugs & love of self & his sound, when
he read cats just shake their head & go "damn."
we the young birds of blk poetics throw our songs brilliant
against the beautiful black sky of an emerging peoplehood
& with the love of us (you/me/we=us) in our hearts we
pronounce blk poetry to be here & now the baddest words
writ/spoken in the english language
PEACE&LIBERATION

RENALDO FERNANDEZ

legacy of a brother

markings on a shitter wall
crude markings
carved with crude tools
yeah, markings on a shitter wall
WILLIE WAS HERE IN 59
but willie died in 63
fighting vc
and his body was never found
NOW all that remains are
crude markings
yeah, crude markings on a shitter wall
WILLIE WAS HERE IN 59
please
        don't let um paint
            that WALL

KUSH

A Message for Langston

Well Langston
nothin much has changed.

White folks gone to the moon
but we still down in the
ghetto lookin for a nickle
to shoot pool.

We've got more poets now
they talkin bout bein
blk & proud & beautiful
but maybe it comes
too easy
in yr day blk & beautiful
was harder to say.

you should see the way
the white folks givin us money
wonder what Simple would say—
Yr prediction bout Baldwin
came true
the train passed him by
last summer.

Coltrane's gone &
Willie Mays is getting old.
Blk life's still
festering
like an open sore
nobody knows how long
before its gonna explode.

I hope where you are
they have
gin & tonic. . . .
if the deal
goes down soon
better save me some.

NAYO (BARBARA MALCOLM)

Bedtime Story

Hey Mama, what's revolution?
    It's war, son
War where soldiers fight huh?
    Yeah baby soldiers fightin and killin 'n' dyin
We gonna have a war gainst whitefolks huh?
    Yeah baby I guess so
But why we haf to have a war Mama?
    Cause the white devils tricked us
                tricked us in to be slaves
Are we slaves now Mama?
    Yeah—might as well be
But I don't wanta be a slave Mama
    I know son—I know we won't be
    much long—go to sleep now honey
Cause of the revolution huh Mama
    Yeah son, cause of the revolution
              now hush chile and go to sleep

Hey Mama when we gonna have the revolution?
    soon son—soon as we can
But—Mama we ain't got no army
    Boy did I tell you to go to sleep
    we'll make a army alright, don't you worry
Will it take long time to make a army Mama?
    Naw son, I hope not
Who's gonna be in the army Mama?"
    Oh I guess ya Daddy and ya uncles
    and a whole lot o' black folks
    and boy hush and go to sleep

And me Mama—kin I be in the army when I git big?
      Boy you ain't gonna be fit for no army
      and nothin else if you don't shut your
      mouth and go t'sleep. Soldiers
      haf to be strong, ya can't be strong
      if ya stay wake all night
      Now here—take ya gun and the
      nation's flag—sleep wit it and
      dream bout it—you satisfied
Yes mam—g'night Mama
      Night son.

Black Woman Throws a *Tantrum*

            I want me a home
            Man do you hear me
            I want me a home
            you understand.
            You done stood and let that cracker
            take my home
            Now I want me a home, nigger
            I wants a land that's mine.

            I hardly remember my home
            been so long
            you stood idle
            Now you git off ya ass
            and make me a home
            Make me a land that's mine
                  so I can set a spell
                  and breathe fresh air
                  and ease my mind
                  live—
                  and love—
                  and be buried
                  in a land that's mine

I watched little black boys
  playing soldiers
  with guns and tanks
   and U.S. flags
  shooting at Vietnamese, Japs, Indians
   and even Mau Maus

First time I was sweet sixteen
  marriage license, zircon ring—all legit
  he was captain of the football team
   and hero of all the chicks
  and I was hot stuff cause I caught him
then after graduation
  the military, stockade, dishonorable discharge
  job after job and all that
  he was still captain of the football team
   and hero of all the chicks
  and I got tired of being the football
so, picked up my two babies and split

But I was scared, you see, insecure
  I needed a cat to pay the bills
  and along come this big shouldered honey
  told me his shoulders were big enough—
  swept me right into his "protective" arms.
Never saw a cat work 40 hours a week
plus overtime and never have a cent
Never saw so many cut-off and
shut-off men in my life
Everything got mighty quiet
the radio wouldn't sizzle (electricity cut off)
meat wouldn't sizzle (gas was off)
babies wouldn't cry (they were too sick)
not even a drip from the water faucet
and him—he didn't have a word to say

too quiet for me—so I up and split
five babies by now

Welfare check was better than that
    didn't need no no-good man no how
    I'd make it on my own
    be independent
    cept it's hard to sleep in a cold bed
    and ain't no sedative for lonliness
so when this beau-ti-ful cat comes rapping
    tongue like it was pure silk
    I was gone again—nose wide open—
    and oops—knocked up again
    Haven't seen him for a couple of weeks
    not since I happened to be
    where he happened to be
    'cept he wasn't alone.
Maybe he'll come home after while
I hope so—I won't hit him with the frying pan.

Anyway meanwhile I was just sitting here—
    thinking—rocking—and getting big—
    I'm really a good woman—
        fit to be loved.

---

easy way out
    to hate the white man
    I hate you, I hate you, I hate you
            Whiteman
        for all the terrible deeds against my people
        for having all the money, for holding guns
        on me, for raping my mama, for
        kicking my papa in the nuts.
    I hate you, I hate you, I hate you
            Whiteman
      I will spend all my time hating you
      I will pull all kinds of tricks on you
      I will steal from you, I will even get
        back at you by bedding with you.

Easy way out:
          Hating whitey
          Forgetting to love self.

JOHN O'NEAL

Shades of Pharoah Sanders Blues for My Baby
(subtitle: Saphire—a poem in knegro dilect, or Simple Revisited)

Baby,
I just want you to
tell me this one thing
How I'm gon be true to you
when you so busy
being true to someone else?
See what it is I'm saying?
I tells you I loves you
places noone abouve you and
and you smiles
and says
"be patient while
I makes up my mind"
so I grins
and when you turns away
takes my aching head in one hand
and my aching heart in the other
and goes way to sing some blues
to keep from crying.
Just about then
some sweet young thing
comes along and
switches herself in front of me
and I jumps to see
if the lights shining in her eyes

shine like yours used to be
and what happens?
Boom! You got a attitude
How patient is I'm supposed to be?
Damn! Niggers getting to be more complicated than white
    folks.
Lord knows
I wisht I had the master plan
try hard as I can
I just caint understand
how I'm sposed be true
to you
when you s o o o o o busy
being true to somebody else.

> "...... the creator has a master plan
>   peace and happiness for every man ..."

RAYMOND WASHINGTON

Vision from the Ghetto

I saw
wet clothes hanging from a clothes line dripping with
blood.
God shake hands with the devil and call him his best
friend; for he said without him he would not have had a job.
A middle aged man call his father mother.
A dog buying wedding license for a woman.
Freedom with every smell of cocaine; every shot of heroin;
and with every draw of marajuana
Two soldiers from different countries fighting; they
both were throwing spit balls; one threw and knocked the
other one unconscious, the battle had been lost & won.
Space reach out to reach man.
Prostitute crowned miss universe

Life in a glass bottle
Women sitting at a table signing peace treaties, on tissue paper.
A horse in the United Nations debating for freedom, equality, justice for all men.
Man pregnant with ideas of love and understanding instead of hate & war.
Sane people in an insane asylum.
The moon lying down to rest and the sun rise to go to work.
The body of a dead animal smell of fragrance.
The earth quiver in pain, perspire, and throwup; it then cried tears fell in term of inches. Oh what a sick world.
Black people by the tens, thousands, millions, in pairs in twos hammering off the chains of oppression and brushing away the dust of humiliation from their garments.
A nude dressed in luxurious clothes.
White body, hollow no conscious, heart, no feeling, infested with maggots.
An ant share a grain with five others; I saw a woman steal food from five others.
Millions of sperms refuse to fertilize the ova.
The jungle come to the city and the city go to the jungle.
Civilization in terms of dollars.
Inhumanity preach the funeral of humanity.
A babe try to crawl back up the womb of its mother.
All, but I really didn't see, what am I, and what will I be. what will happen to me.

Freedom Hair

unrestricted/unrestrained/uncomprimising
untamed/not straightened/natural/protesting
kinky/nappy/Revolutionary hair/Black folks
hair
Don't want to be arrested/subdued/controlled
checked/restricted/restrained/or corraled/black
folks hair/freedom hair
Every grain not the same/exault itself to
the sky/giving freedom cry/hair/Black
folks hair/freedom hair
unrestricted/unrestrained/uncomprimising

untamed/not straightened/natural/protesting
kinky/nappy/Revolutionary hair/Black folks
hair.

Moon bound

Go to the moon/white folks going to the moon/going to
the moon going to the moon/white folks going to the moon

Pockets stuffed/full of trinkets & beads/cases of ten high/
looking for something to steal/plant the American flag on
the moon/America

owns the moon/The American moon
Black folks going to the moon/Blackfolks/going to the
moon whether they like it or not/they going anyway/if
moon fit for human habitation/send niggers to the moon

white folks going need chauffeurs/maids/shoeshine
boys/babysitters/& toms/Black folks going to the moon/
Black

folks on a white moon/yeh/Blackfolks on a white moon
imagine black on white

Every thing/everybody/going to the moon/Sears &
Roebuck/on the moon/New York stock exchange/
Rockefeller foundation/General Motors/going to the moon/
the American moon/white folks moon

The moon needs a G. Washington/T. Jefferson/B. Franklin
might even need a Custer/go to your local space agency/
put in your application/be something/if you never was
nothing/which you never was/this is your chance/be
something/if you lucky/there may be need for Lincoln.

Help build some Jamestown on the moon/there's moon
cotton/moon niggers pick moon cotton/moon beans/moon
niggers plant moon beans/moon stones/moon niggers dig
moon stones/white folks charging to see moon rays

if the moon/isn't fit for Human habitation/black folks
going to the moon/no, ands & buts/about it/Black folks going

on the moon/Stokely on the moon/Muhammad Ali on the
moon/Rap on the moon/undesirables on the moon/if you
wake up one morning/and find your neighbors
gone/look toward the moon/look up at the moon
Toms left stranded on the moon/singing blue moon/you
left us stranded alone/yeh/white folks/going send blackfolks
to the moon/whether they like it or not/Black folks going to
the moon

3.

Criticism

CHESTER HIMES (1909–   )

*There is a growing feeling among contemporary Black writers
that Chester Himes is a major writer of the older generation
who has never received the recognition he deserves in the
United States. John A. Williams, in the course of an interview
with and commentary on Himes in the first issue of* Amistad,
*expressed the belief that "Himes is perhaps the single greatest
naturalistic American writer living today. Of course, no one in
the literary establishment is going to admit that; they haven't
and they won't." Ishmael Reed (see page 329) dedicated his
anthology of writing for the 1970s,* 19 Necromancers from
Now, *to "The Great Mojo Bojo Chester Himes."*

*Born in Jefferson City, Missouri, Himes lived in Mississippi
as a boy and later lived in Harlem for many years and attended Ohio University in Athens (1926–29). He began his
long and prolific writing career with short stories about prison
life, while serving time in an Ohio jail, which he published in*
Abbott's Monthly *in 1932, a magazine issued by the man who
founded* The Chicago Defender. *His first story in a national
magazine was published in* Esquire *in 1934. Since then he has
published more than fifteen novels. He has lived in France as
an expatriate for many years. At least nine of his novels were
first published in France in French translation, without publication in English for many years, and at least one of his
novels is still available only in French. A number of his novels
are Harlem detective stories and he reached a mass American
audience with the recent film based on his novel* Cotton Comes
to Harlem, *one of his books first published in French. The
critical essay that follows may have been written some time
before it appeared in print because of the difficulties that
Himes encountered for many years in getting published in the*

United States. It was published in the United States in 1966 in the anthology Beyond the Angry Black *edited by John A. Williams.*

In his Amistad *interview Himes answered Williams' question on how he views the function of the American Black writer now as follows: "Well, I think the only function of the black writer in America now is just to produce works of literature about whatever he wants to write about, without any form of repression or any hesitation about what he wishes to write about, without any restraint whatever. He should just produce his work as best he can, as long as it comes out, and put it on the American market to be published, and I believe now it will be (which it wouldn't have been ten years ago). All right, now, what will come out of this ten years from now? No one knows. But at least the world will be more informed about the black Americans' subconscious. And it is conceivable, since black people are creative people, that they might form on the strength of these creations an entirely new literature that will be more valuable than the output of the white community. Because we are a creative people, as everyone knows, and if we lend ourselves to the creation of literature like we did to the creation of jazz and dancing and so forth, there's no telling what the impact will be."*

Dilemma of the Negro Novelist in the U.S.A.

Any discussion of the Negro novelists in the U.S.A. must first examine the reasons why all novelists, whatever their race and nationality, write. The obvious answer, the one that first comes to mind, is that we write to express and perpetuate our intellectual and emotional experiences, our observations and conclusions. We write to relate to others the process of our thoughts, the creations of our imaginings. That is the pat answer.

We have a greater motive, a nobler aim; we are impelled by a higher cause. We write not only to express our experiences, our intellectual processes, but to interpret the meaning contained in them. We search for the meaning of life in the realities of our experiences, in the realities of our dreams, our hopes, our memories. Beauty finds reality in the emotion it produces, but that emotion must be articulated before we can understand it. Anger and hatred require expression as do love and charity.

The essential necessity of humanity is to find justification for existence. Man cannot live without some knowledge of the purpose of life. If he can find no purpose in life he creates one in the inevitability of death. We are maintained at our level of nobility by our incessant search for ourselves.

The writer seeks an interpretation of the whole of life from the sum of his experiences. When his experiences have been so brutalized, restricted, degraded, when his very soul has been so pulverized by oppression, his summations can not avoid bitterness, fear, hatred, protest; he is inclined to reveal only dwarfed, beaten personalities and life that is bereft of all meaning. But his logic will tell him that humanity can not accept the fact of existence without meaning. He must find the meaning regardless of the quality of his experiences. Then begins his slow, tortured progress toward truth.

The Negro writer, more than any other, is faced with this necessity. He must discover from his experiences the truth of his oppressed existence in terms that will provide some meaning to his life. Why he is here; why he continues to live. In fact, this writer's subject matter is in reality a Negro's search for truth.

From the start the American Negro writer is beset by conflicts. He is in conflict with himself, with his environment, with his public. The personal conflict will be the hardest. He must decide at the outset the extent of his honesty. He will find it no easy thing to reveal the truth of his experience or even to discover it. He will derive no pleasure from the recounting of his hurts. He will encounter more agony by his explorations into his own personality than most non-Negroes realize. For him to delineate the degrading effects of oppression will be like inflicting a wound upon himself. He will have begun an intellectual crusade that will take him through the horrors of the damned. And this must be his reward for his integrity: he will be reviled by the Negroes and whites alike. Most of all, he will find no valid interpretation of his experiences in terms of human values until the truth be known.

If he does not discover this truth, his life will be forever veiled in mystery, not only to whites but to himself; and he will be heir to all the weird interpretations of his personality.

The urge to submit to the pattern prescribed by oppression will be powerful. The appeal to retrench, equivocate, compromise, will be issued by friend and foe alike. The temptations to accede will be tempting, the rewards coercive. The oppressor pays, and sometimes well, for the submission of the oppressed.

To the American Negro writer's mind will come readily a number of rationalizations. He may say to himself: "I must free myself of all race consciousness before I can understand the true nature of human experiences, for it is not the Negro problem at all, but the human problem." Or he may attempt to return to African culture, not as a source but as an escape, and say: "This is my culture; I have no other culture." But he will find that he can not accomplish this departure because he is an American. He will realize in the end that he possesses this heritage of slavery; he is a product of this American culture; his thoughts and emotions and reactions have been fashioned by his American environment. He will discover that he can not free himself of race consciousness because he can not free himself of race; that is his motive in attempting to run away. But, to paraphrase a statement of Joe Louis', "He may run, but he can't hide."

Once the writer's inner conflict has been resolved and he has elected the course of honesty, he will begin his search for truth. But the conflict will not cease. He immediately enters into conflict with his environment. Various factors of American life and American culture will be raised to stay his pen. The most immediate of these various conflicts is with the publisher. From a strictly commercial point of view, most publishers consider honest novels by Negro writers on Negro subjects bad ventures. If there is nothing to alleviate the bitter truth, no glossing over of the harsh facts, compromising on the vital issues, most publishers feel that the book will not sell. And the average publisher today will not publish a novel he thinks will not sell.

However, should the Negro find a publisher guided by neither profit nor prejudice (a very rare publisher indeed), he may run into the barrier of preconception. Many truly liberal white people are strongly opinionated on the racial theme, and consider as false or overdrawn any conception that does not agree with their own. Ofttimes these people feel that their experiences *with* Negroes (unfortunately not *as* Negroes) establish them as authorities on the subject. But quite often their opinions are derived from other Negroes who have attained financial success or material security, in fact fame and great esteem, through a trenchant sort of dishonesty, an elaborate and highly convincing technique of modern uncletomism. It is unfortunate that so many white people who take an active and sympathetic interest in the solution of the American racial dilemma become indoctrinated first by such Negroes. Instead of receiving a true picture of Negroes' personalities, they are presented with comforting illusions. Should the publisher be of this group, he concludes that the honest Negro writer is psychotic, that his evaluations are based on personal experiences which are in no way typical of his race. This publisher does not realize that his own reasoning is self-contradictory; that any American Negro's racial experience, be they psychotic or not, are typical of all Negroes' racial experiences for the simple reason that the source is not the Negro but oppression.

Then there is, of course, the publisher with such a high content of racial bias as to reject violently any work that does not present the Negro as a happy contented soul. But there will be no conflict between the Negro writer and this publisher; it will never begin.

Once the writer's work is past the printer, his inner conflict having been resolved and his publisher convinced, there begins a whole turbulent sea of conflict between the novelist and his public.

If this novelist, because he has prepared an honest and revealing work on Negro life anticipates the support and encouragement of middle-class Negro people, he is doomed to disappointment. He must be prepared for the hatred and antagonism of many of his own people, for attacks from his leaders, the clergy and the press; he must be ready to have his name reviled at every level, intellectual or otherwise. This is not hard to understand. The American Negro seeks to hide his beaten, battered soul, his dwarfed personality, his scars of oppression. He does not want it known that he has been so badly injured for fear he will be taken out of the game. The American Negro's highest ambition is to be included in the stream of American life, to be permitted to "play the game" as any other American, and he is opposed to anything he thinks will aid in his exclusion. The American Negro, we must remember, is an American; the face may be the face of Africa, but the heart has the beat of Wall Street.

But Negroes will themselves oppress other Negroes, given the opportunity, in as vile a manner as anyone else. The Negro writer must be able to foresee this reaction. The antagonism and opposition of the white American, he has already expected. These oppressors who have brutally ravaged the personality of a race, dare their victims to reveal the scars thus inflicted. The scars of those assaulted personalities are not only reminders, but affronts.

It is in this guilt which now we all know of and understand, that keeps the oppressor outraged and unrelenting. It is his fear that he will have to resolve a condition which is as much his heritage as slavery is our own. The guilt, revolving in this fear is a condition the oppressor dare not aggravate. Yet, he can not permit or accept it, a fact which traps the white oppressor in his own greatest contradiction. The oppressor can not look upon the effects of his oppression without being aware of this contradiciton; he doesn't want to be confronted with this evil, but neither can he escape or resolve it. He will go to any extent, from the bestial to the ridiculous, to avoid confrontation with this issue.

As Horace Cayton wrote, in *Race Conflict in Modern Society:*

"To relieve himself of his guilt, to justify his hate, and to expel his fear, white men have erected an elaborate facade of justifications and rationalizations. The Negro is a primitive, dangerous person who must be kept in subordination. Negroes do not have the same high sensibilities as do whites and do not mind exploitation and rejection. Negroes are passive children of nature and are incapable of participating in and enjoying the higher aspects of the general American culture. Negroes would rather be by themselves. Negroes are eaten with tuberculosis and syphilis. But all these rationalizations do not quell the gnawing knowledge that they, Americans who believe in freedom, believe in the dignity of the human personality, are actively or passively perpetuating a society which defiles all that is human in other human beings."

We already know that attacks upon the honest American Negro novelist will emanate from the white race. However, the tragedy is that among white liberal groups are people who, themselves, are guiltless of any desire to oppress, but suffer the same guilt as do the active oppressors. Because of this they abhor with equal intensity the true revelations of Negroes' personalities. There are, of course, truly thoughtful, sincere, sympathetic white people who will shudder in protest at the statement that all American Negroes hate all American whites.

Of course, Negroes hate white people, far more actively than white people hate Negroes. What sort of idiocy is it that reasons American Negroes don't hate American whites? Can you abuse, enslave, persecute, segregate and generally oppress a people, and have them love you for it? Are white people expected not to hate *their* oppressors? Could any people be expected to escape the natural reaction to oppression? Let us be sensible. To hate white people is one of the first emotions an American Negro develops when he becomes old enough to learn what his status is in American society. He must, of necessity, hate white people. He would not be—and it would not be human if he did not—develop a hatred for his oppressors. At some time in the lives of every American Negro there has been this hatred for white people; there are no exceptions. It could not possibly be otherwise.

To the Negro writer who would plumb the depth of the Negro personality, there is no question of whether Negroes hate white people—but how does this hatred affect the Negro's personality? How much of himself is destroyed by this necessity to hate those who oppress him? Certainly hate is a destructive emotion. In the case of the Negro, hate is doubly destructive. The American Negro experiences two forms of hate. He hates first his oppressor, and then because he lives in constant fear of this hatred being discovered, he hates himself—because of this fear.

Yes, hate is an ugly word. It is an ugly emotion. It would be wonderful to say there is no hate; to say, we do not hate. But to merely speak the words would not make it so; it would not help us, who are Negroes, rid ourselves of hate. It would not help you, who are not Negroes, rid yourselves of hate. And it would not aid in the removal of the causes for which we hate. The question the Negro writer must answer is: how does the fear he feels as a Negro in white American society affect his, the Negro personality?

There can be no understanding of Negro life, of Negroes' compulsions, reactions and actions; there can be no understanding of the sexual impulses, of Negro crime, of Negro marital relations, of our spiritual entreaties, our ambitions and our defeats, until this fear has been revealed at work behind the false fronted facades of our ghettoes; until others have experienced with us to the same extent the impact of fear upon our personalities. It is no longer enough to say the Negro is a victim of a stupid myth. We must know the truth and what it does to us.

If this plumbing for the truth reveals within the Negro personality, homicidal mania, lust for white women, a pathetic sense of inferiority, paradoxical anti-Semitism, arrogance, uncle tomism, hate and fear and self-hate, this then is the effect of oppression on the human personality. These are the daily horrors, the daily realities, the daily experiences of an oppressed minority.

And if it appears that the honest American Negro writer is trying to convince his audience that the whole Negro race in America, as a result of centuries of oppression, is sick at soul, the conclusion is unavoidable. It could not conceivably be otherwise.

The dilemma of the Negro writer lies not so much in what he must reveal, but in the reactions of his audience, in the intellectual limitations of the reader which so often confine men to habit and withhold from them the nobler instruments of reason and conscience. There should be no indictment of the writer who reveals this truth, but of the conditions that have produced it.

Himes' logic has noted that American Negroes *have* written honest books and that they have been published and read. That is evidence that the dominant white group in America is not entirely given over to an irrevocable course of oppression.

There is an indomitable quality within the human spirit that can not be destroyed; a face deep within the human personality that is impregnable to all assaults. This quality, this force, exists deep within the Negro also; he is human. They rest so deeply that prejudice, oppression, lynchings, riots, time or weariness can never corrode or destroy them. During the three hundred years Negroes have lived in America as slaves and near subhumans, the whole moral fibre and personality of those Negroes now living would be a total waste; we would be drooling idiots, dangerous maniacs, raving beasts —if it were not for that quality and force within all humans that cries: "I will live!"

There is no other explanation of how so many Negroes have been able to break through the restrictions of oppression, retain their integrity, and attain eminence, and make valuable contributions to our whole culture. The Negro writer must not only reveal the truth, but also reveal and underline these higher qualities of humanity.

My definition of this quality within the human spirit that can not be destroyed is a single word: *Growth*. Growth is the surviving influence in all lives. The tree will send up its trunk in thick profusion from land burned black by atom bombs. Children will grow from poverty and filth and oppression and develop honor, develop integrity, contribute to all mankind.

It is a long way, a hard way from the hatred of the faces to the hatred of evil, a longer way still to the brotherhood of men. Once on the road, however, the Negro will discover

that he is not alone. The white people whom he will encounter along the way may not appear to be accompanying
him. But all, black and white, will be growing. When the
American Negro writer has discovered that nothing ever becomes permanent but change, he will have rounded out his
knowledge of the truth. And he will have performed his
service as an artist.

RALPH ELLISON (1914–   )

The author of Invisible Man, *one of the most widely acclaimed American novels of the twentieth century, participated
in the Conference of The American Academy of Arts and
Sciences on the Negro American, May 14–15, 1965. Ralph
Ellison did not present a formal paper but he participated in
the discussions and expressed his views a number of times
during the conference proceedings. Assembled here are his
various remarks at the conference, sometimes with the question of another participant in the conference which Ellison
answered, as they appear in the transcript of the conference
proceedings in* Daedalus, Journal of the American Academy
of Arts and Sciences, Vol. 95, No. 1, Winter 1966. *Space
separates the remarks he made at different times during the
proceedings.*

*Further views of Ralph Ellison on the Negro in American
culture and literature and expressions of his literary attitudes,
extending beyond his volume of collected essays* Shadow and
Art *(1964), are embodied in interviews with him published
in* Harper's *magazine, March 1967;* The Atlantic, *December
1970; and his article "What America Would Be Like Without
Blacks" in the special issue of* Time *magazine, April 6, 1970.
Ellison is a member of the National Institute of Arts and
Letters; has taught at Bard College, Rutgers University, and
other schools; and is presently Albert Schweitzer professor in
the humanities at New York University.*

Remarks at The American Academy of Arts and Sciences Conference on the Negro American, 1965*

ELLISON: One thing that is not quite clear to me is the implication that Negroes have come together and decided that we want to lose our identity as quickly as possible. Where does that idea come from? I have encountered it in a number of places recently. One place (which almost frightened the pants off me) was in *Commentary*, where Mr. Nathan Glazer makes this assumption and follows it up with the rather frightening picture that all other immigrant and minority groups and some cultural groups in this country have somehow worked out an accommodation which respects the group identities of other peoples, but that Negroes are running wild, that we recognize no limit, and that we would like a total homogenization of the society. It is easy enough to see why Mr. Glazer would get off on that, because (as one of our participants also made very clear) he feels that Negroes have no culture.

I am not being defensive about this; I am trying to get at the logic of the assertion. If one assumes that a group, which has existed within this complicated society as long as ours, has failed to develop cultural patterns, views, structures, or whatever other sociological terms one may want to use, then it is quite logical to assume that they would want to get rid of that inhuman condition as quickly as possible. But I, as a novelist looking at Negro life in terms of its ceremonies, its rituals, and its rather complicated assertions and denials of identity, feel that there are many, many things we would fight to preserve.

*Participants in the Conference who addressed questions or remarks to Mr. Ellison included: Stephen R. Graubard, editor of *Daedalus*, the publication of the American Academy of Arts and Sciences; Talcott Parsons, Professor of Sociology at Harvard University; Everett Cherrington Hughes, Professor of Sociology at Brandeis University; John B. Turner, Profesor of Social Work at the School of Applied Social Sciences of Western Reserve University; Max Lerner, Professor of American Civilization at Brandeis University; Martin Kilson, Lecturer on Government and Research Associate of the Center for International Affairs at Harvard University; and Thomas F. Pettigrew, Associate Professor of Social Psychology at Harvard University.—Ed.

There is something else which could be thought about along this line. There are great areas of this society which are available to Negroes who have a little consciousness. The contacts which exist are not limited to the roles which they might have. The human consciousness is there. Contacts are being made. Judgments are being rendered. Choices are being made. I know that in the life styles of any number of groups in the nation, there are many things which Negroes would certainly reject, not because they hold them in contempt, but because they do not satisfy our way of doing things and our feeling about things. Sociologists often assert that there is a Negro thing—a timbre of a voice, a style, a rhythm—in all of its positive and negative implications, the expression of a certain kind of American uniqueness. (I am not talking about Negritude. The Negro sociologists fall biggest for that.) If there is this uniqueness, why on earth would it not in some way be precious to the people who maintain it?

I would like to suggest what the fighting is about. For one thing, the oversimplified and very often unfortunate slogans which are advanced in the civil rights movement act as slogans always do. Why do we demand that terrible, encyclopedic nuances be found in the slogans of the civil rights movement? No slogans have ever had that kind of complexity. They would not be slogans if they did. The other thing is that part of the struggle (which I have known now for some fifteen years) has always been not to get away from the Negro community, but to have the right to discover what one wanted on the outside and what one could conveniently get rid of on the inside. That seems to me very American. I think it is one of the assumptions which is implicit in a pluralistic society, and I see no particular reason for people to be upset by the possibility that we are actually going to achieve it.

ELLISON: From reading American literature and from studying American culture, I feel that subcultures are basically American, regardless of where they come from, whether they are Jewish or Negro, whether they are urban or rural. Once we recognize that, we can get into the area of making distinctions. One concept that I wish we would get rid of is the concept of a main stream of American culture—which is an exact mirroring of segregation and second-class citizenship. I do not think that America works that way at all. I would remind us that before there was a United States, a nation, or a form of a state, there were Negroes in the colonies. The interaction among the diversified cultural groups helped to shape whatever it is we are who call ourselves Americans. This, I think, is a very important distinction to make.

I may have been only a busboy in a club in Oklahoma City, but I knew much more about some of the things that occurred there than some of the *nouveau riche* oilmen who were members of the club. When I worked for Jewish businessmen in Oklahoma City, I learned certain things, not because I embraced the religion and not because of my blood components, but because I was in cultural contact with a group of people who were very expressive. This is America, as far as I know. I know no way of defining this reality out of existence.

Once we recognize this, where do we go from there? I find that if I am going to write something, I can very often tell where it comes from, in terms of both the traditions of the particular literary form and the traditions of the people around me. Someone should pay some attention to how the folk stories which are told about Negroes in one meeting might be told about Jews in another. There is a basic unity of the experience, despite all the other stuff. The whole problem about whether there is a Negro culture might be cleared up if we said that there were many idioms of American culture, including, certainly, a Negro idiom of American culture in the South. We can trace it in many, many ways. We can trace it in terms of speech idioms, in terms of manners, in terms of dress, in terms of cuisine, and so on. But it is American, and it has existed a long time. It has refinements and crudities. It has all the aspects of a cultural reality.

GRAUBARD: Mr. Ellison, would you tell us just a little about what you are hoping to do?

ELLISON: I must confess that I am utterly intimidated by trying to project what is to come. Nonetheless, I shall try to work from the basis of what I think I know about how Negroes actually function in this sociey. Of course, we function in many, many different ways, but I would like to reexamine our relationship to the total culture. I would like to examine some of the assumptions which we bring to this intricate relationship. I would also like to point out that each minority group, including Negroes, tries to impose its sense of the total experience upon everyone else. This is nothing to be frightened of. It is something which can be very, very creative for all of us. I think Mr. Lerner was saying pretty much the same thing when he described the Jewish experience.

I think that we all owe something to the total experience. I think that each of us has no special grasp upon reality, but that each of us lives a special part of it. It is owed to the rest. We all must learn from it. We all must be able to partake of it if we would. One of the great things about this country—one of the things which, I think, is a working assumption, although we deny it—is that any American can become, at least in a symbolic way, a member of any other group. This is how we actually work. I learned to walk in a certain way because I admired Milton Lewinson, who ran a clothing store in Oklahoma City. It was not just that I liked his walk. I liked his principles. He happened to be a Jew. But I know that that much of Milton Lewinson is Ralph Ellison. I know other people from whom I have taken certain attitudes of thought, interest in certain foods, certain literature, certain myths, and so on.

I think that this is the kind of society toward which we are working, a society in which there will be no stigma attached to taking advantage of this experience, no fear that to do so is to lose status. The feeling that I have about my own group is that it represents certain human values which are unique not in a Negritude sort of way, but in an American way. Because the group has survived, because it has maintained its sense of itself through all these years, it can be of benefit to the total society, the total culture.

PARSONS: Do you apply that general doctrine even across the sex line?

ELLISON: Yes.

HUGHES: You are not saying, then, that one cannot understand a group unless he is a member of it.

ELLISON: I do not say that at all. I think that it is like the old argument about whether a white man can play jazz. If he has a talent and has respect enough for the complexity of the music and the culture and is willing to discipline himself to it, of course, he can. Any American can learn what is going on in the rest of the culture. I think that there are certain things which are accrued over so many years and which are so subtle that no outsider can take them on. But if there is anything viable about expression and cultural or artistic form, then it is available to all the people who will pay their dues.

One of the problems with Negroes—one of my own problems—is that, for all I know about this society, so much of it is not immediately available to me. I am not asking for integration; I am talking about something else. It is that there are certain patterns—certain ways of doing things—which Negroes who wait on tables or who work as domestics in the South will know even today. But it is not so easy to know these things here and now. These things should be known not simply on the domestic level, but in terms of business. I know, for instance, Percy James, who ran a cola bottling works in Oklahoma City, years and years ago when I was a boy. For certain definite reasons, he could not expand his business. I do not know whether prejudice was the basic reason, but part of it was sheer lack of financing ability—knowing how to capitalize, knowing how to join with a bigger group without being sucked in. There are many parts of this complex American society which Negroes have been kept away from. Even most of our novelists do not give enough of a report of how life is actually lived in the country for a Negro to pick up a novel and get some clues. The constrictions and the exclusiveness very often have gotten into our perception of social complexity. I hope that this conference is a beginning step in breaking down this kind of thing.

TURNER: I know that we are not giving you enough time in which to present your main thesis, Mr. Ellison, but I am really not sure what your central theme is. It seems to me that there is enough ambiguity in what you are saying for it to be interpreted in different ways. On the one hand, you seemed to be talking about a socialization process which ought to be going on. On the other hand, you seemed to be saying that an individual depends upon some sort of subculture. I do not think you can be saying both of these things, and I think you really ought to be saying one of them.

ELLISON: I defend the subculture, because I have to work out of it, because it is precious to me, because I believe it is a vital contributing part of the total culture. I do not think I want to deny that. If I did, then I would have to throw away my typewriter and become a sociologist. I also believe that the subculture and the larger culture are interrelated. I wish that we would dispense with this idea that we are begging to get *in* somewhere. The main stream is in oneself. The main stream of American literature is in me, even though I am a Negro, because I possess more of Mark Twain than many white writers do.

LERNER: I want to ask Mr. Ellison a question which has to do with the African movements. In your picture of American Negro life as you have been working in it and living in it, Mr. Ellison, to what extent have these identity revolutions in Africa had an impact not just on the civil rights movement, but on the sense of selfhood of the Negro American?

ELLISON: Let me put it this way. Africa has always figured somewhere in the American Negro's sense of himself—certainly since I have been in the world. The Garvey movement reached Oklahoma, and a few people sold their farms and went off. (One newsdealer in Harlem never tired of telling me that but for that Marcus Garvey, he would have inherited a farm rich with oil wells.) For the most part, however, the Garvey movement was laughed at. I think the same thing is happening now. The assertion that the emerging nations of Africa have given all the stimulus to American Negroes seems very questionable when we examine how Negroes are actually operating, what their values are, what the techniques of protest are, and so on. When I see pictures of the march in Selma, I remember photographs which appeared in a crisis around 1919, when Negroes marched up Fifth Avenue carrying signs: "Am I not a man and a brother?" And when I think of that, I think back to abolitionist times. I think that what is going on now is coming out of an American Negro tradition and an accumulated discipline which go back many, many years.

Despite the Black Muslims, the stimulus is not to get away and not to find or to construct an African life style, but to become more a part of the American society. The problem for all of us—and I guess this is why I am not communicating with Mr. Turner—is that Negroes have a style of life which we have not been able to separate from segregation. But within the group, we act out, we make certain assertions, we have certain choices, and we have various social structurings which determine to a great extent how we act and what we desire. This is what we live. When we try to articulate it, when we try to define it, all we have is sociology. And the sociology is loaded. The concepts which are brought to bear are usually based on those of white, middle-class, Protestant values and life style. I know this has been said before, but I am saying it as one who looks at life through the disciplines of fiction and through the disciplines of the humanities as they come to focus in great literature.

What is going to happen now, I suspect, is that, as the society becomes more open, Negroes are going to become very arrogant. They are going to say, "This is all right, but it is not good enough." A friend, who is a critic of jazz, said recently, "No one ever thinks of the possibility that Duke Ellington might well have been a first-rate classical composer, but that he was looking for something better." This is a shocking thing from one point of view, but not from another. For example, if I went back into the church, I would go back into a shouting Negro church. I am a fairly sophisticated man, but I think that more would be communicated to me through that form of communion than through some other.

ELLISON: Mr. Pettigrew, is there any possibility that, in answering your questions about Africa, people were put on the defensive? That is, everybody seems to feel that he has to have a "homeland." In this country, no one is free not to have a homeland. Over and over again, this idea gets into the literature. One has to have some place to feel proud of. Well, I am proud of Abbeville, South Carolina, and Oklahoma City. That is enough for me.

KILSON: I am not sure that is enough for many people.

ELLISON: In my experience, by raising the possibility of Africa as a "homeland," we give Africa an importance on the symbolic level that it does not have in the actual thinking of people. Does that make any sense?

JAMES BALDWIN (1924–   )

*With his essays, novels and short stories, plays, and literary
and social criticism, James Baldwin established his reputation
as an outstanding figure in modern American literature. He
was born and grew up in New York City, lived in Europe for
a number of years, returned to the United States in 1957,
and in 1970 left America and went into exile in Paris. Ida
Lewis, editor-in-chief of* Essence *magazine, interviewed him
in Paris and then published the following conversation with
him—the fullest illumination of Baldwin's reasons for going
into exile—in* Essence *(October, 1970).*

Why I Left America

Conversation: Ida Lewis and James Baldwin

*James Baldwin is probably the most widely quoted black
writer in the past decade. He is the author of numerous
works, all of which have won critical acclaim. Among these
are his novels:* Go Tell It on the Mountain, *his first work;*
Giovanni's Room, *which was set in Paris, and* Another Country, *his first critical and commercial success. His latest:* Tell
Me How Long the Train's Been Gone. *He also wrote a number of personal essays that were collected in book form;*
Notes of a Native Son, *was his first collection, followed by*
Nobody Knows My Name, *which brought him literary prominence. The third volume,* The Fire Next Time, *was regarded
as one of the most brilliant essays written on black protest.
Two plays,* Blues for Mister Charlie *and* The Amen Corner
were performed on the American stage.

From boy-preacher in Harlem store-front churches to famed essayist and novelist, Baldwin is now an expatriate in Paris. Why expatriate? What is he about now? While we were in Paris, Essence *stopped to visit him and this is what he told us.*

IDA: Jimmy, I'm here to probe, to find out what the new James Baldwin is all about?

JIMMY: Okay. I won't duck anything.

IDA: I am curious about why you are in Paris and not New York. Haven't you been this route before?

JIMMY: It's a difficult question to answer. But for exercise, let's begin back in 1948 when I first left America. Why in the world, I've been asked, did you go to a white country? When I first heard that question it threw me. But the answer is obvious; there were no black countries in 1948. Whether there are black countries today is another question, which we won't go into now. But you know I didn't *come* to Paris in '48, I simply *left* America. I would have gone to Tokyo, I would have gone to Israel, I would have *gone* anywhere. I was getting out of America.

So I found myself in Paris. I arrived here with $40, scared to death, not knowing what I was going to do, but knowing that whatever was going to happen here would not be worse than what was certainly going to happen in America. Here I was in danger of death; but in America it was not a danger, it was a certainty. Not just physical death, I mean *real* death.

IDA: Would you explain this death you speak about?

JIMMY: The death of working in the post office for 37 years; of being a civil servant for a hostile government. The death of going under and watching your family go under.

IDA: These kinds of deaths were still part of black life when you returned to the States in '57. Why did you return?

JIMMY: I went back in '57 because I got terribly tired. It was during the Algerian war. My friends were Algerians and Africans. They are the people who befriended me when I arrived here broke. In a sense, we saved each other, we lived together. So when the war began, my friends began to disappear one by one. What was happening was obvious. When hotels were raided, I was let alone, but my friends were taken away. My green American passport saved me.

I got tired and I began to be ashamed, sitting in cafés in Paris and explaining Little Rock and Tennessee. I thought it was easier to go home. It was impossible to sit there and listen to Frenchmen talk about my Algerian friends in the terms that had always been used to describe us, you know, "You rape our women. You carry knives."

IDA: In a sense, all of us became Algerians.

JIMMY: Yes, in another language, but it was the same thing. So I went home. The rest, as we say, is history.

IDA: You became the famous James Baldwin, writer and black spokesman.

JIMMY: Yes, I played two roles. I never wanted to be a spokesman, but I suppose it's something that had to happen. But that is over now. And I discovered that the time I needed to stop and start again, the necessary kind of rest to get myself together, was not possible in America because the pressures were too great. So, I had to leave once more.

IDA: Could you be more specific?

JIMMY: Because of what I had become in the minds of the public, I ceased to belong to me. Once you are in the public limelight, you must somehow find a way to deal with that mystery. You have to realize you've been paid for, and you can't goof. I kept leaving for a short time—to do this, to do that—but to save myself I finally had to leave for good.

IDA: Can you recall that moment of decision?

JIMMY: One makes decisions in funny ways; you make a decision without knowing you've made it. I suppose my decision was made when Malcolm X was killed, when Martin Luther King was killed, when Medgar Evers and John and Bobby and Fred Hampton were killed. I loved Medgar. I loved Martin and Malcolm. We all worked together and kept the faith together. Now they are all dead. When you think about it, it is incredible. I'm the last witness—everybody else is dead. I couldn't stay in America, I had to leave.

IDA: What was buried in those graveyards?

JIMMY: That dialogue is gone. With those great men, the possibility of a certain kind of dialogue in America has ended. Maybe the possibility of it was never real, but the hope certainly was. Now, the Western world, which has always stood on very shaky foundations, is coalescing according to the principle under which it was organized, and that principle is white supremacy. From England to Sacramento, Ronald Reagan and Enoch Powell are the same person.

IDA: The other reasons?

JIMMY: I was invited to Israel and I'd planned to take my first trip to Africa after that. But when the time came, I had so many things on my mind I didn't dare go to Africa. After I visited Israel, I understood the theology of Judaism—and its mythology—better than I had before. I understood the great blackmail which has been imposed on the world not by the Jew but by the Christian. We fell for it, and the Jews fell for it. Let me put it this way. When I was in Israel I thought I liked Israel. I liked the people. But to me it was obvious why the Western world created the state of Israel, which is not really a Jewish state. The West needed a handle in the Middle East. And they created the state as a European pawn. It is tragic that the Jews should allow themselves to be used in this fashion, because no one cares what happens to the Jews. No one cares what is happening to the Arabs. But they do care about the oil. That part of the world is a crucial matter if you intend to rule the world.

I'm not anti-Semitic at all, but I am anti-Zionist. I don't believe they had the right, after 3,000 years, to reclaim the land with Western bombs and guns on biblical injunction. When I was in Israel it was as though I was in the middle of *The Fire Next Time*. I didn't dare go from Israel to Africa, so I went to Turkey, just across the road, and stayed there until I finished *Another Country*.

IDA: You sound as if you had been in spiritual trouble.

JIMMY: I was. It was very useful for me to go to a place like Istanbul at that point of my life, because it was so far out of the way from what I called home and the pressures. It's a funny thing, becoming famous. If you're an actor or dancer, it is what you expect. But if you're a writer, you don't expect what happened to me. You expect to be photographed all over the place but you don't expect the shit, the constant demands, the people's expectations. During my Istanbul stay I learned a lot about dealing with people who are neither Western nor Eastern. In a way, Turkey is a satellite on the Russian border. That's something to watch. You learn about the brutality and the power of the Western world. You're living with people whom nobody cares about, who are bounced like a tennis ball between the great powers. Not that I wasn't previously aware of the cynicism of power politics and foreign aid, but it was a revelation to see it functioning every day in that sort of a theatre.

IDA: The Turks are poor people. It seems to me that they, too, are victims of many of the same prejudices that affect black men. Did you find any comparisons?

JIMMY: It's a very curious comparison. I would say, no, because of the fact that the American black man is now the strangest creature in history, due to his long apprenticeship in the West. For example, the people of Istanbul have never seen New York. *West Side Story* is an event for them. They know nothing about what the black man has gone through in America. They still think of America as a promised land.

The American black man knows something which nobody else in the world knows. To have been where we were, to have paid the price we have paid, to have survived, and to have shaken up the world the way we have is a rare journey. No one else has made it but us. There is a reason that people are listening to James Brown, Nina Simone, and Aretha Franklin all over the world, and not to somebody from Moscow, Turkey, or England. And the reason is not in our crotch but in our heart, our soul. It's something the world denied and lied about, energy they labeled savage, inferior, and insignificant. But it has been proven that no matter what they labeled it, they cannot do without it.

The peoples of Turkey, Greece, even the peoples in Jamaica have not gone through the fire. They don't know that the dream which was America is over. I know that. What we have allowed to happen to our country is shameful. I'm ashamed of Nixon. I wouldn't hire him to become keeper of the gate in Central Park. There's no excuse for a man like Nixon to be put in charge of a country like the United States.

IDA: But don't we need all thinking and able-bodied Americans to change what has happened? We can't run away.

JIMMY: Okay, you're right. But it's like this: I believe that I've got a master stone in which I see something and I have to find a way of chiseling out what I see. I left America, finally, because I knew I could not do it there.

It doesn't matter where I do it as long as I do it. I don't believe in nations any more. Those passports, those borders are as outworn and useless as war. No one can afford them anymore. We're such a conglomorate of things. Look at the American black man, all the bloods in a single stream. Look at the history of anybody you might know. He may have been born in Yugoslavia, raised in Germany, exiled to Casablanca, killed in Spain. That's our century. It will take the human race a long time to get over this stuff.

IDA: That leaves blacks in a strange situation.

JIMMY: It certainly does. Because what has happened is that the party's over. All the pretenses of the Western world have been exposed. There is no way to convince me or any other black person in the world, to say nothing of people who are neither black nor white, that America is anything but an outlaw nation. It doesn't make any difference what one says about the Declaration of Independence, the Bill of Rights, the Magna Carta, when arms are being sold to South Africa, and the Vietnamese are being killed on their own soil by American bombs. The name of the game in America is banks and power. And one does not have to investigate too far to discover that the Western economy has been built on the backs of non-white peoples.

IDA: But to leave one's country, Jimmy, is traumatic.

JIMMY: I fought leaving for a long time. I didn't want to go. I had been based in New York for quite a while, my family and friends are there. It is my country and I'm not 24 years old any more. It was not so easy to pack up and leave. What probably convinced me that I had to leave was my encounter with Hollywood.

IDA: You went to Hollywood to write a screenplay on the life of Malcolm X?

JIMMY: Yes. I never wanted to go to Hollywood. And I would never have gone had it not been for Malcolm. When I was asked to write the screenplay on my friend's life, part of me knew that it really could not be done. But I didn't believe I had the right to turn down a possible opportunity to reveal Malcolm on-screen. I knew the odds were against me, but sometimes you take outside chances. It's better than thinking for the rest of your life that perhaps it could have been done.

Believe me, my Hollywood journey was a revelation. It was incredible to find yourself in a situation where the people who perpetrated his murder attempted to dictate his love, grief, and suffering to you. I believed Malcolm trusted me and that held me there. I tried to go down with the deal. I went the route. And when that battle was over, and I realized there was no hope—that they were speaking Hindustani and I was speaking Spanish—I was through. Day followed day and week followed week, and nothing, nothing, nothing, would penetrate. Not because they were wicked but because they couldn't hear. If they could hear, they wouldn't be white. Malcolm understood this. He said that white is a state of mind—a fatal state of mind. There I was in Hollywood. The things I was asked to write in the name of Malcolm, the advice I was given about the life and death of a friend of mine was not to be believed. So I left. I split to save my life. Ida, you once said that I was an actor. I'm an actor, but I'm also very determined.

IDA: Let's turn to another subject—your family.

JIMMY: I'd love to because my family saved me. If it hadn't been for my family, all those brothers and sisters, I'd be a very different person today. Let me explain. I was the older brother. And when I was growing up I didn't like all those brothers and sisters. No kid likes to be the oldest. You get spanked for what they do. But when they turn to you for help —what can you do? You can't drop the kid on his head down the steps. There he is, right?

So when I say that they saved me I mean that they kept me so busy caring for them, keeping them from the rats, roaches, falling plaster, and all the banality of poverty that I had no time to go jumping off the roof, or to become a junkie or an alcoholic. It's either/or in the ghetto. And I was one of the lucky ones. The welfare of my family has always driven me, always controlled me. I wanted to become rich and famous simply so no one could evict my family again.

IDA: So keeping your family from being thrown into the street was your inspiration.

JIMMY: That's really the key to my will to succeed. I was simply a frightened young man who had a family to save.

IDA: Have you remained close to your family?

JIMMY: The greatest things in my life are my brothers and sisters, and my nieces and nephews. We're all friends. They continue, in their own way, to save me. They are my life.

IDA: After you left America the last time you ended up in Istanbul. What could take a black American to Turkey?

JIMMY: There are several reasons why I went to Istanbul. One was that I had a friend there, a Turkish actor who worked with me at The Actors Studio in '58. He's memorable to me because at one point in the play version of *Giovanni*, someone had to spit on the cross, and no Christian actor was willing to do it. But my friend is a Moslem, so he loved it. Then he had to go away to Turkey to do his military service and I said, "Someday I'll visit you in Turkey." But I never really thought I would.

IDA: But wars will go on and on and on. . . .

JIMMY: Unhappily, we have yet to realize that nobody can go to war anymore and win. It's impossible. It's a dirty habit that mankind has got to give up.

But what is important to us as blacks is to realize that the kinds of wars perpetrated today are quite different from those of the past. Before Vietnam, the European wars were family affairs. Hitler's Germany was no big deal until people feared that he might take over all of Europe. He had murdered millions with the people's consent. Nobody cared. Nobody. Only when Europe itself was endangered by the madman it had created did it become moral. But right from the start Vietnam has been a racist war in which all the West is implicated. It was never a family affair. America's in the vanguard but the war reveals where the West is really based. That's a crisis. I see it as the beginning of the end.

IDA: Why have you chosen France as your refuge?

JIMMY: Laziness. Habit. I speak French; I became famous here. The French are a very special sort. They will leave you alone, let you do your thing. And all I want is to be left alone to do my gig. I couldn't, after all, pick Tokyo or Rome or Barcelona or London. They don't know me as Paris does, or vice versa. Paris was actually the only place for me to come.

IDA: Have you changed much over the last 10 years? What kind of person are you now?

JIMMY: I could say that I'm sadder, but I'm not. I'm much more myself than I've ever been. I'm freer. I've lost so much, but I've gained a lot. I cannot claim that I'm a happy man. I'm terrified, but I'm not unhappy. I've lived long enough to know what I have to do—and what I will not do.

IDA: What won't you do, Jimmy?

JIMMY: I will never sell you . . . even when you want me to. You follow me. You created me. You're stuck with me for life.

IDA: Let's talk about the meaning of being black today. What does it mean to you?

JIMMY: I think that it is probably the luckiest thing that could have happened to me or to anyone who's black. I was walking with my brother David in London a couple weeks ago, and we were sort of walking fast because there were a lot of people around us. We were trying to get some place where we could sit down and have a quiet drink and talk without having to go through all that. I said, "Davy, I wouldn't dare look back. If I looked back, I'd shake." And then, we both realized that if you are not afraid to look back, it means that nothing you are facing can frighten you.

What it means to me? Nobody can do anything if you really know that you're black. And I know where I've been. I know what the world has tried to do to me as a black man. When I say me, that means millions of people. I know that it's not easy to live in a world that's determined to murder you. Because they're not trying to mistreat you, or despise you, or rebuke you or scorn you. They're trying to kill you. Not only to kill you, but kill your mother and your father, your brothers and your children. That's their intention. That's what it means to keep the Negro in his place. I have seen the game, and if you lose it, you're in trouble, not me. And the secret about the white world is out. Everybody knows it.

All that brotherly love was bullshit. All those missionaries were murderers. That old cross was bloodied with my blood. And all that money in all those banks was made by me for them. So, for me what it means to be black is what one has been forced to see through, all the pretentions and all the artifacts of the world that calls itself white. One sees a certain poverty, a poverty one would not have believed. And it doesn't make any difference what they do now.

The terrible thing about being white is that whatever you do is irrelevant. Play your games, dance your waltzes, shoot your guns, fly your helicopters, murder your natives. It's all been done. It may take another thousand years, another twenty years, another thirty years, but I've already worn you out. Whitey, you can't make it because I've got nothing to lose. What has happened is, I've stepped outside your terms. As long as it is important to be white or black in one's own head, then you had us. Nobody gives a damn any more. Western civilization's had to be defended by the people who are defending it. By the time you sank to the level of such mediocrities as presidents, whom I will not name, I'm sorry, you've had it. Civilization depends on Mr. Nixon and Mr. Agnew? We can forget about that civilization. There's not a living soul who wants to become Richard Nixon. There never will be in the entire history of the world.

IDA: What about the new black pride?

JIMMY: It's not new. Black pride, baby, is what got my father through. Drove him mad, too, and finally killed him. There's nothing new about it, and people who think it's new are making a mistake. Black pride is in all those cotton fields, all those spirituals, all those Uncle Tom bits, all that we had to go through to get through. There's something dangerous in the notion that it is new, because we can fall into the European trap, too. After all, I've been treated as badly by black people as I have by white people. And I'm not about to accept another kind of cultural dictatorship. I won't accept it from Governor Wallace, and I won't accept it from anybody else, either. I am an artist. No one will tell me what to do. You can shoot me and throw me off a tower, but you cannot tell we what to write or how to write it. Because I won't go. Most people talking about black pride and black power don't know what they're talking about. I've lived long enough to know people who were at one time so white they wouldn't talk to me. And now they're so black they won't talk to me. I kid you not.

IDA: What about all the new blacks?

JIMMY: Maybe they'll be white next week. They go with the winds, like a water wheel. I've lived nearly half a century. No dreary young S.O.B. is going to tell me what to do. Oh, nonononono. Of course, it is inevitable. On a certain level it's even healthy. But I'm somewhere else. Now, for the first time in my life, I suppose because I've paid for it, I really do know something else.

I trust myself more than ever before. And I suppose it's only because I had to accept something about the role I play, which I didn't want to accept. But now it's all right.

IDA: Well, how do you see yourself?

JIMMY: I'm a witness. That's my responsibility. I write it all down.

IDA: What's the difference between a witness and an observer?

JIMMY: An observer has no passion. It doesn't mean I saw it. It means that I was there. I don't have to observe the life and death of Martin Luther King. I am a witness to it. Follow me?

RICHARD A. LONG

The contemporary Black arts and Black studies movements are devoting attention to the African roots of Black cultures. This important question was the theme of Richard A. Long's presidential address to the 1970 convention of the College Language Association. Professor Long is director of the Center for African and African-American Studies at Atlanta University and is also a part-time visiting professor in the Afro-American Studies Department at Harvard University. A frequent contributor to the CLA Journal and other publications, he is coeditor of the anthology Négritude: Essays and Studies. *A student of art and other branches of the humanities, in addition to literature, Professor Long has made more than ten trips to Europe (he received the* docteur ès lettres *from the University of Poitiers) and has traveled extensively in North and West Africa, the West Indies, South America, and Mexico.*

Black Studies: International Dimensions*

The Black Studies movement, so recent a phenomenon in American education, is a dynamic and complicated affair. It is taking myriad forms in response to the great variety of pressures which have impelled its translation from student demand to curricular innovation. There is, in keeping with the traditions of American education, little conscious uniformity in the picture we view from college to college, but several distinct typologies are emerging. There is much discussion of aims and methods, and much paper is being consumed.

The dangers always present in human inquiry and human endeavor have naturally enough been present in Black Studies from the start. Such dangers as dogmatism, provincialism, and ritualism are quite manifest, not to speak of charlatanism, that eternal response of cupidity to financial opportunity. Arrogance, whose progenitor is ignorance and insecurity, is seldom absent from a discussion of Black Studies.

The Black Studies movement grows out of a specialization of the general student protest movement which broke upon a startled nation a few short years ago. Student protest is an important part of the history of the twentieth century in some countries of the world. To the United States, to which things are supposed to come early if not first—lunar exploration,

*President's address delivered at The College Language Association's Thirtieth Annual Convention, Royal Coach Motor Hotel, Atlanta, Georgia, Thursday morning, April 9, 1970.

atomic submarines, actors as governors have indeed come first here—to the United States, student protest came late. It is useful to remember that fact. Who were protesting? None other than the pampered and privileged progeny of the Great American Middle Class, and they were manifesting disenchantment with that Great Middle Class Institution, the University.

In the midst of these protesters emerged a somewhat anomolous group. Black students who had been benevolently earmarked for individual rescue and who, to all intents and purposes, if not in fact, were enjoying the privileges of the pampered. Black students, too, were saying that something was wrong with the University.

The notion that something was wrong with the University did not originate with the recent protest generation. Something has always been wrong with the University. I can recall that an entire unit of the Freshman English course I took over twenty-five years ago was devoted to ritual denunciation of the University, as exemplified in thoughtful essays. The University was whoring after strange gods, they all seemed to say: technology, athletics, materialism. With the passing of time the gods have become stranger and their pursuit more lascivious. A few years ago a resolution of the monster by semantics was attempted and there was talk of the multiversity. Such is the hard hand of fate that the publicist who launched the term became the first victim of the newly-named animal, much as M. Guillotine is said to have been the first victim of his slicing apparatus.

Nevertheless the New Protest movement found tatters and tears when none had previously been noted in the Great Halls of learning, and curiously, once exposed to view, no one could deny the reality of some of these distressful signs of poverty among opulence. Black students caught up in the mood of protest soon found that their priorities were different from those of white students and there was accordingly a division of protest along classic American lines.

The University has always made the claim—essentially a pun—that its perspective was universal. In point of fact, the American University like its distant European cousin, was simply the vehicle for the transmission of a limited portion of the experience of humanity. This was historically inevitable. The offense to order and to sense was the easy assurance that this limited portion was universal, was indeed Man. The blight of this kind of thinking is no where more manifest than in a series currently being shown about, entitled *Civilization* when in point of fact, it is "selected moments" in the history of Europe.

From the awakened perspective of Black students something was definitely wrong with the claim of the University to universality when it in fact dealt with Black man only as an adjunct to white man or as a topic in social pathology. One short year ago, the most famous American university could not point to a single course in its catalog which dealt positively or affirmatively with the Black experience as a topic worthy of study in its own right.

Today, a great variety of things are going on in the name of Black Studies, and it is not part of my purpose to deplore any of them here, for this is first of all a long-overdue period of trial and error. Pleas for quality and for traditional values come oddly indeed from lips which never deplored the teaching of hotel management or the awarding of college credit for swimming. The catalog of any American college is a cause for wonder and the addition of Black Studies to such catalogs will modify their surreal aspect only in the direction of sobriety.

I do not mean that a blanket approval of Black Studies programs presently in action or proposed can be made, anymore than a blanket approval of educational programs generally. In fact, I am convinced that, in the spirit of democracy, we must not be shocked to find all levels of quality and seriousness in Black Studies programs. While hoping for the best, we must be prepared to find something less, more often than not. It is not on the individual character of Black Studies programs that we must take our stand, but on the ground that the experience of Black people must be presented in positive and distinct frames within the current curriculum. Evolution may well lead to a really universalist perspective in which there may be required no special Black Studies framework, but that will be in the remote future.

The greatest danger I perceive now in the generality of Black Studies discussions and proposals is the provincialism of circumscribing the study of the Black man to the study of the Black man in the United States. In other words, a kind of American hegemony or imperialism, but Black, if you please, now seems ready for manipulation. There is an obvious reason for it. Most newly-begotten experts in blackness know nothing about any other Black people in the world, and indeed little about Black people in the United States. There is a more subtle reason in the unconscious arrogance with which all but the most cultivated Americans approach anything beyond their shores. Far from being exempt from this attitude,

Black Americans are conspicuous for the easy assurance with which they wear this American mantle. They are instant experts on the correct Black response to any and everything, and yet Black Americans constitute merely a respectable percentage of the Blacks of the world. The Blacks of the world, I would hasten to add, are far less numerous than the non-Blacks, a fact that has recently gotten lost in some woodpile.

I am aware that there is a great deal of rhetoric about Third World and Black World perspectives. And two circumstances seem to favor such rhetoric. The first is the immediate access which the dominant American media give Americans—even Black ones—to the ears of the world. Consequently many brothers around the world believe things are happening here which have not yet happened. The second favoring circumstance is that Black intellectuals around the world, who owe a great deal to such Black Americans as W. E. B. DuBois, Alain Locke, Marcus Garvey, and Langston Hughes, are predisposed to find new signals, if not new leadership, coming from this branch of the diaspora. Neither of these favoring circumstances will long mask the incapacity Black Americans are prone to manifest in dealing with and understanding their Black brothers. This very incapacity is an index of how deeply encoded the American values are in the Black American psyche. Black commonality is most frequently preached by those who are most imbued with the individualistic ethic.

But where do we really stand on the international dimensions of Black Studies? The common experiences of the Black people of the world have seldom until now invited the attention of any save a few, anthropologists for the most part. Historians, linguists, sociologists, and psychologists have preferred to define and study isolated groups of Black people asserting blandly that no important external links exist. Black people were either cultural isolates or cultural adjuncts of non-Blacks. On the other hand there have always been sensational generalizations positing a unity of separate traits: low intelligence, criminality, musicality, sexuality. The former stance has been the "scholarly" one, with some scholars not hesitating to work the second in.

One does not have to take a position on the importance of the common experience of Black people to insist upon examining the question with something other than the optic of bland or furious assertion. It is further a reasonable proposition that the common experiences of Black people are at least as important as their diverse experiences. It is on this premise that we propose two principles in teaching and research; one the diachronic principle of the African continuum; the other, the synchronic principle of the African extension. Here we are following in the steps of DuBois who demonstrated in his life work both as scholar and activist, a continuing dedication to all people of African descent. His Pan-Africanism was scholarly as well as political.

The principle of the African continuum is, that historically radiating from the Black Core, the Black peoples of the world have carried with them modes of dealing with and symbolizing experience, modes discovered and refined through milennia in Africa itself, and that these tactical and symbolic modes constitute a viable nexus of Black culture, one of the major traditions of humanity. The principle of the African extension is that the cultural legacy of the Black Core brought into contact with a second culture, whether in the New World or Africa, can be perceived meaningfully as a model of interaction, only when compared with other such models, and hence that the study of the Afro-American family, for example, is incomplete to the extent that it takes no account of the Afro-Brazilian family and so on.

That Black Studies should be international in its orientation and scope is not only required by the nature of the inquiry itself, but is also in the general tradition of internationalism to which thinking men always have subscribed in theory, no matter how weak their practice. It is the ideal of *humanitas*. To approach Black internationalism, as some would do, as a separatist enterprise, is a romantic indulgence fraught with the usual outcomes that beset such religious enterprises—the development of cult and ritual and catechism. The role of the University is to call for open teaching and research, with the provision that each student construct his own ideology, his own religion of blackness, if you will.

What are the immediate implications for CLA in the light of the foregoing? I think that CLA must steadfastly support the development and growth of Black Studies in the University; that it must deal charitably but firmly both with the scoffers and the exploiters; that it must insist upon a really international or Pan-African dimension in such studies. Specifically in the study of language, literature, and folklore, CLA members must extend their range of inquiry and analysis to include the principles of the African continuum and the African extension. It must, of course, carefully scrutinize generalizations in this domain, directly condemning the casual and the adventitious. The road ahead for Black Studies, like life itself, will be no crystal stair. There will be tacks in it, and places with the stairs torn out. But you and I will, because we must, keep climbing.

NATHAN HARE

Publisher of The Black Scholar *and president of* The Black World Foundation *(see program in documents section, pp. 578–80), Nathan Hare began life on a sharecropper's farm near Slick, Oklahoma. He is the author of* The Black Anglo Saxons *(now in its second printing). He has published articles extensively in such periodicals as* Newsweek, Negro Digest *(*Black World*),* Saturday Review, The Times of London, Trans-Action *and* Social Education.

Introducing an interview with Dr. Hare on Black studies, in May, 1970, College and University Business, *noted: "Dr. Nathan Hare was the first coordinator to be hired for a black studies program—and the first to be fired. He was appointed to the post at San Francisco State College in the spring of 1968 'to appease' (his words) the Black Students Union. By fall, the black students and Dr. Hare were embarked on a five-month strike to press their demand for an autonomous black studies department. It was Mr. Hare who coined the phrases 'Third World Liberation Front' and 'ethnic studies.' Mr. Hare had previously gained some notoriety for his part in student unrest at Howard University (where he taught sociology to Stokely Carmichael and Claude Brown, among others), from which he was subsequently fired. (A court later upheld his contention that he was fired unjustly.) He received his B.A. at Langston University, a Negro college in Langston, Okla., and his Ph.D. from University of Chicago. In addition to teaching, Dr. Hare has been a professional boxer—and a successful one." He is on the Advisory Council of the National Conference on Black Power. The following article appeared in the first issue of* The Black Scholar, *November, 1969.*

Algiers 1969: A Report on the Pan-African Cultural Festival

There was a battle in Algiers in late July, with lighter skirmishes both old and new, and emerging signs of struggle which now lurk ready to boomerang around the world in the years (and months) to come. The troops came together, African generals and footsoldiers in the war of words and politics that splashed against the calm waters of the Mediterranean Sea—in the First Pan African Cultural Festival—from everywhere in greater numbers than ever before; from San Francisco to Senegal, from Dakar to the District of Columbia.

The conflict was over which course a potentially unified Africa could take toward national and continental liberation, particularly the role of culture in the struggle for liberation and in social and economic development. Which, in the context of things, revolves in some presently intransigent way around the relationship of black and white revolutionaries. Though antagonists centered their fire on the question of culture, the battle was recognized all around as "98 per cent political," and clearly hinged at last in long and passionate debate, private and public, over the future direction of the struggle for liberation on the continent and, indeed, the entire world.

Hundreds of delegates came from thirty-one independent African countries and representatives from six movements for African liberation, from Palestine to Angola-Mozambique and the Congo-Brazzaville. And there were Black Panthers and "black cubs" and old lions from the American contingent. Secretly exiled Eldridge Cleaver chose this occasion to reveal his whereabouts, and expatriated Stokely Carmichael came with his South African-exiled wife, Miriam Makeba. Kathleen had her baby during the Festival, and there was Panther Minister of Culture, Emory Douglass, international jazz artists, such as Nina Simone and Archie Shepp, and Julia Hervre (the late Richard Wright's daughter now living in Paris).

LeRoi Jones (whose passport had been held up) could not get over, but there were: the serious and quietly charismatic young poet, Don L. Lee; Carmichael lieutenants, Courtland Cox and Charlie Cobb; Panther Chief of Staff, David Hilliard, who had to return to the United States before the festival was over to take care of a crisis with Chicago police; and the compassionate black Parisian poet, Ted Joans. There were many young black Americans who had not been invited, but who had cared enough to piece together their own fare; including Oakland's Harriet Smith, who, as of this writing, is still in Africa traveling and lecturing.

Hoyt Fuller of *Negro Digest* was there. He had been also in attendance at the Dakar Festival of 1966 and seemed particularly struck by the contrast in the type of black Americans at the two festivals. Dakar had collected the most well-known artists and entertainers, the Duke Ellingtons and the like; Algiers had attracted the new breed young militant whether those of fame, those on the rise, or those yet to begin the making of their names. Students, of course, also came, notably from San Francisco State College, and others around the world (including Stokely's chief aide now studying sociology in Europe whose name oddly slips me at the moment though I got to know and like him well enough before I left to give him my favorite dashiki) and ex-patriated young Americans from Paris, some of whose names I never knew. Like their African counterparts, they had journeyed in search of new hopes for freedom to a most appropriate place. Algiers, Algeria—most famous in recent times for the revolutionary overthrow of a major oppressive power.

Algiers, the adopted home of the late black Martinique psychiatrist, Frantz Fanon, stands mysteriously like a quaint and complex ant hill—almost inhuman in its architectural and natural beauty—overlooking the Mediterranean at the apex of the continent of Africa, the "cradle of civilization." On the first night of the Festival, its streets were filled with multi-colored balloons floating against the background of a gaily illuminated sky, as twenty African countries came through in a parade. Guinea was the most applauded, but there was fellowship and entertainment for all, from Guinean ballet to restrained dancing in the streets.

The next day saw a somewhat different Algiers, and what has been achieved since the revolution, not all of it yet so good. The air of celebration continued, but daylight revealed, in at least one major section, project housing tenements as dilapidated as any in the United States. Esso service stations appeared, and Shell, and Hertz, and Pepsi Cola (and company); and the French colonialists slipping back in predatory droves.

Some say that the weakening of cultural resistance has increased Algerian susceptibility to the re-entry of the French and American imperialists. And so, there are signs of Algerian resistance again on the ready: revolutionary graffiti in large people's scrawl on buildings, walls and fences, and, particularly, the old pre-revolutionary symbol of resistance, the *haik* (or veil) worn by so many of the women. Most of the men, by contrast, dress in European attire, but they also are infused with revolutionary fervor. Besides,

> In the colonialist program it was the woman who was given the historic mission of shaking up the Algerian man. Converting the woman, winning her over to the foreign values, wrenching her free from her status, was at the same time achieving a real power over the man and attaining a practical, effective means of destructuring Algerian culture.[1]

With the onslaught of resistance, the woman returns to her traditional values, retreating into the irrevocable sanctuary of her old society's values, reversing her role in the colonialist program.

And yet, Algerian leaders today seem rather more concerned with the pitfalls of cultural attachment on the part of oppressed peoples. They lambasted the ultradevotion of many black intellectuals to jazz music and black art and other forms of "folkloric prestige," and denounced African intellectuals who are likewise so fascinated, who fail to visualize a certain solution for the present, and hold on to the "reactionary theory of negritude and the excessive cult of a revolutionary past. If Africans must lean on their past, this is not to regret a lost paradise but to recover it in order to assert it fully today."[2]

This was conspicuously a view shared by Libyans and

[1]Frantz Fanon, *A Dying Colonialism*, tr. by Haakon Chevalier, New York: Grove Press, 1967, p. 39.
[2]"Quand tous les africains se donnent la main," *Algerie Actualite*, semaine du 20 au 26 juillet 1969, p. 22.

other Arabic and "white African" nations[8] Even the most universal-minded black leaders and intellectuals seemed much less afraid of any dire effects of black African nationalism, though a debate raged throughout the symposium and the Festival between the more revolutionary black Africans and the proponents of "Negritude"—more about that later.

The revolutionary leader from Angola-Mozambique, for example, was unequivocal. He spoke in a calm but emotional voice, without benefit of any notes, saying that the liberal colonizer always comes over, at just the moment when oppressed black nations are achieving a takeoff in revolutionary consciousness, to introduce the duality of white-black collaboration,[4] thus prolonging the debate and dividing the forces of the oppressed.[5]

The representative from Mozambique went on to concede that these endeavors on the part of the liberal colonizer are all all right on the surface, in theory, but that a revolutionary needs a singularity of purpose and has not enough time to wrestle with the problems of assimiliating his struggle. However, he also emphasized that culture must be built around struggle. He was one of the most applauded speakers in the conference, though he was not alone. From the Vice President of the Revolutionary Council of Congo-Brazzaville also came the view that

> African culture is a culture of combat, a culture which is forged in affronting the same problems, in having the same cares. It is necessary for us to surpass that which is congealed. We believe in and want to march forward toward modernism.

But the most persistent assertion that revolution is technical and economic, and must encompass and connect itself very closely with scientific rationality and economic and scientific discoveries, came from the Algerian delegation, echoed once

[8]Fanon has written of the latent revival of racial feelings between black and white Africa. "Africa is divided into Black and White, and the names that are substituted—Africa South of the Sahara, Africa North of the Sahara—do not manage to hide this latent racism." See *The Wretched of the Earth*, New York: Grove Press, Evergreen Edition (tr. by Constance Farrington), p. 161.

[4]In this regard, he corroborates the observation of a Marxist Tunisian, Albert Memmi, "The Colonizer who Refused," *The Colonizer and the Colonized*, New York: Orion Press, 1965.

[5]Stokely Carmichael also has written recently on the way liberal oppressors tend to "represent the liaison between . . . the oppressed and the oppressor." See the pamphlet on *The Pitfalls of Liberalism*, undated but current.

or twice by a Russian delegation which was, of course, not an official participant in the symposium. The Algerian leaders went so far as to say that technique opposes culture and that whole civilizations have been sterilized by their failure to appreciate that one simple fact. While struggling for liberation, a people must "not give up self but it must listen to the world."

The black delegates such as the one from Dahomey spiritedly offered a similar appreciation of the ideal of progress, fearing that there otherwise might result a "freezing of action and ideology."[6] The most applauded speaker of the entire symposium, he held on the one hand that "there can be no people without a culture," but in the selfsame breath also insisted that "there is no society which does not change."

On the propellor of progress, Africa is priming itself for change, some cultural, some scientific and otherwise. One hundred and twenty delegates representing more than twenty-five countries met one day and held a symposium to study peaceful uses of atomic energy for the economic development of their countries, particularly in the area of agriculture. They further planned a ceremony for laying the first stone of a "regional nuclear center."[7]

Swinging the pendulum, white (or Arab) Africans, while expressing apprehensions that revolutionary black Africans might get entrapped by cultural nationalism, also recognized progressive uses of culture as an instrument for liberation instead of a crutch—and more about that later. For the moment, Libya, which spends 27% of its budget on education (the highest in the world) has, since independence, set up many cultural centers, about sixty centers now (libraries, theaters, several theatrical troupes and institutes for music, including folk troupes and folk studies toward developing national folk art). The purpose of such cultural centers, in the words of the Libyan delegate, is "to raise national consciousness."

Conflicts over culture similarly gripped black Americans and was ostensibly at the heart of the Stokely-Eldridge split, which

[6]See A Dictionary of the Social Sciences, Free Press of Glencoe, 1964, pp. 544–45, for a discussion of the relationship between the growth of belief in the idea of progress and revolutionary advances in scientific inquiry. See also Frantz Fanon, "The Algerian War and Man's Liberation," in Toward the African Revolution, tr. by Haakon Chevalier, New York: Grove Press, 1967, pp. 144–49.
[7]El moudjahid, 29 juillet, 1969, p. 1.

troubled them so much more. Some had come to the Festival in part to help resolve or at least to understand that cleavage first hand. Only two or three of them, out of the dozens there, regularly attended the symposium at the Palace of Nations— for one thing the taxi fare was eight dollars round trip—unless you had unlikely access to a car. However, the Panthers, who had a car, did not attend the symposia, concentrating instead on a back-to-the-people campaign with the Algerian populace through "Afro-American Cultural Center" programs and the press while Stokely courted the African revolutionaries and Festival delegates.

I got the impression that both succeeded rather well in what they were trying to do, that they were trying to attain fundamentally the same objectives—the liberation for our people—but along routes that were worlds apart. They appeared, therefore, to have divided up and made a pact at least on their turf. I never saw Stokely at the Afro-American Center and I never saw Eldridge at the Palace of Nations. Even at the registration center, I noted that the Panthers and most of their aides were housed in the Hotel Alletti while what Panthers call the "cultural nationalists" (a term now too loaded to have clear meaning) were in the Hotel St. George.

Within hours after my arrival, I was seated at an outdoor dining table when Eldridge appeared and greeted me. Though I knew Kathleen, I had never actually met Eldridge before. He told of the Afro-American Cultural Center and invited me to drop by. I would of course be pleased to do so. Eldridge then left my table; and, when I finally got up to go, I saw him and Stokely sitting in a very private and serious huddle. They appeared as old friends—or better yet, as estranged spouses—in a deliberately subdued quarrel. I said hello to Stokely as I passed by, having known him as a student at Howard University in the days of the passive resistance movement, and soon fell into conversation with some other black Americans. Some while later Stokely came up and invited me to the table where Makeba and a portion of their entourage were seated. I asked him what he was up to these days and he responded in a way that most black Americans over there found convincing, especially as they grew alienated from the Panthers, largely because of the prominence and arrogance of the whites in the Panther operations. This included the Afro-American Cultural Center, which some black Americans eventually came to call "the Panther Lair." The other black Americans complained of Panther hostility and distance, and the Panthers complained that the black Americans did not frequent the Center, usually overflowing with Algerian enthusiasts from the street. The relationship of black Americans and the Panthers was changing for the better in the last days of the Festival, but it had started too late to do much good.

Like most black Americans, I, too, had come with some hope of unifying those two forces within our struggle, though being more familiar than most with the deep and far-reaching sources of the split, some of which will be explored later, I was considerably less optimistic. But I, too, had some missing links to connect and was pleased to have, in any case, an essential firsthand communication. Though revolutionaries not accustomed to the search for a middle ground, most black Americans seemed totally caught off guard and, when their repeated efforts merely to get the two together for a subsequent talk continued to fall through, became quite naturally dismayed. They expressed strong fears of a coming "blood bath" within the movement. Some soon discovered and complained that there is "no middle ground anymore."

The search for ground (or "land") is just what separates Eldridge, a "Marxist-Leninist" who stresses class above color, from Stokely, who believes the matter one of "both class and color" and hopes to obtain a land base for black Americans by helping to get Nkrumah back to Ghana. This land-base would then have the same relationship to black Americans as Israel now has to American Jews. In contrast to Eldridge, Stokely chooses the Palestine liberation movement over Israel, Africa over the Third World, and Peking over Moscow. It is not easy to subsume such far-reaching matters under the umbrella of culture alone.

And so, it was inevitable that all factions of the black American contingent, like the African delegation, would relate to culture in an ambivalent way. One instance took place at a panel discussion put on by the Panthers at the Afro-American Cultural Center. I was to have been a participant but was away from the hotel all day attending the Festival symposium and missed the message left there for me. Later I did obtain a complete tape of the panel discussion, which was kicked off by Emory Douglas, Minister of Culture for the Black Panther Party. Emory early asserted that the only culture worth keeping is a revolutionary culture and denounced "cultural nationalism" as a bourgeois concept. The Panthers were popular with the young Algerians who seemed considerably to admire black Americans in general. We soon learned to say "pouvoir noir" (black power) to taxi-drivers, who could tell, from our skin color and French, that we were black Americans. Thus we could avoid otherwise frequent overcharging, or even obtain a long free ride.

Anyway, Eldridge Cleaver spoke, and the dialogue began. He began by telling of a call that morning from Black Panther Chairman Bobby Seale about harassment and persecution of fellow Panthers back home, invited dialogue and sat down.

Then a young Algerian stood and engaged Eldridge in a long debate. He was careful to point out that he had not come to denigrate the Black Panthers but wanted to raise, for clarification, "some questions of principles." It was his view that the Panthers should shun participation in "the world of publicity" and the "cult of personality." He further was disturbed by Panther program item #6—which reads: "We want all black men to be exempt from military service"—on grounds that it excluded other persons in the United States who may oppose the war. Cleaver defended on grounds that, though they knew that persons and categories other than blacks are oppressed in the United States, the Panther program was being addressed specifically to blacks, that "we not only have to attack and fight against capitalism but also against the specific policy of racism they used against us." The young Algerian then cautioned against falling into "the trap that's been set for us" by the oppressors. Then the interpreter, Julia Hervre, daughter of the later Richard Wright, spoke "just for once" on her own.

> I want to talk to you about Malcolm X, about a trip he made to Ghana and about an interview he gave to the Algerian ambassador to Ghana, who asked him to explain the situation in the United States, which he did. The Ambassador then asked him this question: 'You see, Malcolm, I suffered; you see, Malcolm, I struggled; and I was hurt. But after having struggled and waged the battle, you still looked at me as a white man. Where, Malcolm, do I stand in your theory of black revolution?' [applause] 'You see, Ambassador,' Malcolm replied—and this has never been published but should in actual fact be published—he replied, 'I've been on this continent now for three or four months and it is the first time that I have no longer used a very narrow terminology of black nationalism.' And that is why we today of the Black Panther Party who wish to be spiritual heirs to Malcolm X, no longer use the narrow term 'black nationalism.'

The Algerian spokesman then ended the exchange by saying that his group supports the struggle of the black people in the

United States, of all people there "struggling against the capitalist system," commended the courage of the Black Panthers against police oppression, and explained again that the questions had only been raised to "clarify what the real situation in that country is and the programs of the black organizations represented" on the round-table panel.

The questions he raised and the panelists' commentary reflected the current groping among revolutionaries and other oppressed persons in America and around the world for a solution to their plight. And it was also apparent that there exists no ideological clarity on anybody's part.

Had it not been for the strictly formalized structure and policies of the symposia held by the Organization of African Unity, which was sponsoring the Festival, the exchanges in the Palace of Nations most surely would have been more spirited and, frequently I am afraid, considerably less friendly. There the roots of conflict stretch farther back through the years and, to some extent, had generational overtones, or at least reflected the anachronisms of at least two eras, fired by further division between conformist and revolutionist.

The crucial debate in the Palace of Nations was that of the future, if any, of Negritude.[8] In Algeria the debate was kicked off by leading Negritude theoretician, Leopold Senghor, who, rising above the confines of Negritude itself, as well as its fellow traveler, Arabity, contended that "Africanity" is the thing which "cuts across the Festival . . . the perennial dialogue between Arabo-Berber and Negro-Africans, it is the symbiosis of two complementary ethnicities." He supported his view with laudatory accounts of how ancient Africa gave birth to the first human beings, its high civilizations, and harked back to the classical monuments of ancient Egypt.

He was not long in coming under attack. Sékou Touré, who believes that the class war has been weakened by some efforts to set forth the idea of cultural pluralism, warned fellow African leaders of whatever rank, who would lead their people to a just combat, never to permit the "false concepts of Negritude" to guide them.[9] The pitfalls of Negritude were once analyzed at length by the late Frantz Fanon, and he was much alive in the debate in Algiers, where he is highly revered

[8]For a discussion of the conflict over Negritude in the early years of the Organization of African Unity, see B. Bourtros-Ghali, "La personalité africaine," *L'Organization de l'Unité Africaine*, Paris: Librairie Armand Colin, 1969, pp. 28–64.
[9]*El moudjahid*, 23 juillet 1969, p. 2.

indeed, with a college, a street and other entities now bearing his name. Cab drivers and waiters can quote and cling to his words. There was a long feature story on him and a photo in the daily paper during the festival.

Fanon, recognizing stages in the development of the revolutionary intellectual, placed Negritude in the second stage, as a reaction against the first stage of revolution, and which typically hampered the revolutionary's leap into the third, the stage of actual combat. Negritude, on the contrary, permitted an escape into excessive glorification of the past and the traditional, both in terms of values and in costumes worn and general way of life; so that one found difficulty in incorporating the techniques of the present and the future or in turning them effectively against the oppressor. At that point in the confrontation, Negritude contrarily becomes a literature of mysticism. Fanon's point of view was echoed by many black African delegates to the Algerian Festival.[10]

Stanislas Adotevi, the delegate from Dahomey, established a "theory of melanism" on grounds that there is no culture separated from life, that the battle for culture is the battle for political life.[11] Fanon too, for his part, had pointed out in his early work that a "true culture" of oppressed peoples "could not come to life" under oppressed conditions, that the fetters would have to be withdrawn before the true attainments of a culture could be known.[12]

Those critical of Negritude looked to culture as an ideological weapon, pointing to the failure of Negritude up to now in the seizure of African consciousness. The concept, in their view, amounted to a collaboration with colonialism, leaving the matter of oppression and liberation in the realm of mystification, hostile therefore to even the cultural development of Africa. From Tanzania came the view that it is "impossible to develop an African culture without freedom."[13]

A Haitian poet now living in Cuba also took up the cry against Negritude, praising the delegates from the Congo-Brazzaville, Guinea, Algeria and the various revolutionary movements for taking similar stands. He summarized the search for identity in the formula: "We make the revolution,

---

[10]See "On National Culture," *The Wretched of the Earth,* tr. by Constance Farrington, New York: Grove Press, Evergreen Edition, 1968, pp. 206–248.

[11]*El moudjahid,* 27–28 julliet 1969, p. 7.

[12]*Black Skin, White Mask,* tr. by Charles Lam Markham, New York: Grove Press, 1967, p. 187.

[13]Cf. Fanon, *Ibid.*

therefore we exist." And he pointed to his fatherland, Haiti, as well as a number of African countries, for examples of Negritude-oriented dictators who themselves were enemies of liberation. "Negritude also will be revolutionary," he concluded, "or it will not be."[14]

There was conflict, however, in the minds of some revolutionary African leaders who wished not to discard the glories of their people's troubled past yet longed to move ahead into a new generation of black men on the rise. The solution for them, as in the case of the vice-president of the Revolutionary Council of the Congo-Brazzaville, was "to take the best" from both their own past and the modern world and "leave the rest behind."

After all was said and done by the younger critics of Negritude, the Minister of Education and Culture of Senegal angrily rebutted the attacks. He freely admitted his fears that the "cultural" symposium might run the risk of becoming a "political forum." He admitted as well that "we Africans must move beyond the stage where we go on stating that our culture does exist" and observed that "some aspects of the culture under question will change as objective conditions change." But he was adamant no less in his tenacious allegation that there is indeed a "geography of Negritude" in that ". . . Negroes are distinguished by certain particularities and values by which they live wherever they are found." He was applauded when he offered support for Palestine and said that Negritude does not prevent Libyans, Algerians, and others from participating in African Unity.

An exception was made for a representative of the Palestinian Movement (Al Fat'h) who, though not a member of the Organization of African Unity, was allowed to speak. He was greeted by heavy applause when he came to the stand. He held that there are only two worlds—colonialism and tyranny as against the forces of freedom. To him Africa is more than a continent; in fact, it is on the same political map with Palestine. He charged that Britain and Zionist forces have united against his people exactly as the imperialists have done in Rhodesia and South Africa. On another occasion he had suggested that Russia too, because of the white alliance, is in concert with and happy over the state of Israel. Britain, in his analysis, is protecting Ian Smith just as the United States

[14]*El moudjahid*, 29 juillet 1969, p. 3. See Mohamed Aziz Lahbabi, *Liberté ou liberation?*, Paris: Aubier, 1956, for an analysis of the frequent conflicts between liberty and liberation.

is protecting Israel, because economic relationships with South Africa and Israel led to close relationships in all aspects.[15]

African brothers, our story, Palestine, is your story in Africa. They came to our country as the white racists came to yours; and we tried, as you have tried, to live with them in the same state, under the emblem of law and peace. But they want, as the white minority in Africa, to establish a purely racist regime to our detriment.

This kindled the revolutionary sentiments among the African delegates as they returned to cultural considerations. A number of them had already endorsed the necessity for armed struggle; and the delegate from Tanzania was only one of those to win applause when he remarked that "freedom will only be won by the gun and the bullet."

The flames of revolution were hotter still in the hearts of the Pan African Movement for Youth. Early in the Festival, the youth had been rather suspicious of their revolutionary elders and took pains at once to see "that solutions [coming out of the Festival] conform to the aspirations of the youth." They watched impatiently the too-ready acceptance of neo-colonialist domination and imperialist aggression on Africa's immense land and riches. And they spoke of a new resistance on the rise to "parry and thrust" against colonial conspiracies "on the military, political and economic plane rather more than on the cultural."

In the end their Executive Committee held a press conference and "condemned the attempt at secession in Africa and congratulated those governments working for national unity and socio-economic promotion of their people."[16] They also saluted armed struggle for national liberation wherever it is occurring, denounced aid given by NATO and other imperialist powers to preserve the status quo, and urged moral pressure from African states and progressive peoples around the world against imperialist powers to force them to halt imperialistic aid to oppressive governments.

Support was reiterated for the peoples of Angola, Guinee-Bissao and Isles of Cape Verde, Mozambique, Naibie, South Africa, Zimbabwe and the United Arab Republic. They

---

[15]The issue of Zionist aggression was raised in O.A.U. affairs (by Gamal Abdel Nasser, the Conference of Casablanca) as early as 1961. Bourtros-Ghali, op. cit., pp. 83, 84.
[16]*El Moudjahid*, 31 juillet 1969, p. 1.

saluted the revolutionary and liberal movements in the Sudan and bestowed condemnation on attempts to overthrow progressive regimes in Africa, notably in the Sudan and in Guinea. The youth also supported the Latin American struggles and showed solidarity with the popular resistance to interference in the internal affairs of their states by imperialist powers.

In the Middle East: they reiterated solidarity and support to the Palestine Revolution, Al-Fat'h, and urged the withdrawal of "Zionist occupying troops." And they applauded, of course, the revolutionary provisional government of South Vietnam, which they recognized as a new phase in the struggle against "neo-colonialist U.S. aggression." Finally, the Executive Committee affirmed the necessity for intensifying its action, in the immediate formation of young African cadres and formed a commission to develop and build a concrete program toward that vital end.

It was left only to Algerian President Boumedienne to say that:

> The world has discovered that despite the tragedies of slavery, exile, transportation or depersonalization, Africa succeeded in preserving its dignity, its spirit, its sensitivity . . .

As of this writing, however, the unfortunate fact remains that all of that has not been quiet enough.

The first Pan-African Cultural Festival showed Africa on the verge of finding at last whatever else is needed. The people there began, in the ten days of the Festival, to tackle the problems they face, but they failed to find a common solution as the symposium committees broke down in heated discussions far into the night.

For one thing, the African people, on the continent and in America, are still suffering from the influence and intervention of western liberals and thus have only feebly begun the clarification of the uses and misuses of culture in the struggle for liberation. Before there is clarity, before there is a true and effective ideology, there has to be extensive and serious debate. But there also cannot be any fundamental discussion of culture—it was clear from the Festival—unless economic, social, political and other topics also have become clear. When once this is done, Africa may no longer stand darkly honored as simply the "cradle of civilization," but the cradle of freedom, perhaps—and brotherhood and peace—as well.

STERLING STUCKEY (1932–   )

*The significance of the rich Black culture created by the
slaves is being explored anew by contemporary Black critics
and scholars. Sterling Stuckey, represented in* Black Voices
*with a critical study of Frank London Brown, has published
articles in* Freedomways, Negro Digest, *and other periodicals
and has served as a consultant in American history to En-
cyclopaedia Brittanica Films. He has studied and taught at
Northwestern University, is a fellow of the Institute of the
Black World (see program in documents section, pp. 575–78),
and is chairman of the Afro-American Curriculum Committee
at Northwestern. The following article appeared in* The Massachusetts Review, *Vol. IX, No. 3, Summer 1968.*

Through the Prism of Folklore: The Black
Ethos in Slavery

It is not excessive to advance the view that some historians,
because they have been so preoccupied with demonstrating
the absence of significant slave revolts, conspiracies, and "day
to day" resistance among slaves, have presented information
on slave behavior and thought which is incomplete indeed.
They have, in short, devoted very little attention to trying to
get "inside" slaves to discover what bondsmen thought about
their condition. Small wonder we have been saddled with so
many stereotypical treatments of slave thought and behavior.[1]

---

[1]Historians who have provided stereotypical treatments of slave thought
and personality are Ulrich B. Phillips, *American Negro Slavery* (New
York, 1918); Samuel Eliot Morrison, and Henry Steele Commager,
The Growth of the American Republic (New York, 1950); and Stanley
Elkins, *Slavery: A Problem in American Institutional and Intellectual
Life* (Chicago, 1959).

Though we do not know enough about the institution of slavery or the slave experience to state with great precision how slaves felt about their condition, it is reasonably clear that slavery, however draconic and well supervised, was not the hermetically sealed monolith—destructive to the majority of slave personalities—that some historians would have us believe. The works of Herbert Aptheker, Kenneth Stampp, Richard Wade, and the Bauers, allowing for differences in approach and purpose, indicate that slavery, despite its brutality, was not so "closed" that it robbed most of the slaves of their humanity.[2]

It should, nevertheless, be asserted at the outset that blacks could not have survived the grim experience of slavery unscathed. Those historians who, for example, point to the dependency complex which slavery engendered in many Afro-Americans, offer us an important insight into one of the most harmful effects of that institution upon its victims. That slavery caused not a few bondsmen to question their worth as human beings—this much, I believe, we can posit with certitude. We can also safely assume that such self-doubt would rend one's sense of humanity, establishing an uneasy balance between affirming and negating aspects of one's being. What is at issue is not whether American slavery was harmful to slaves but whether, in their struggle to control self-lacerating tendencies, the scales were tipped toward a despair so consuming that most slaves, in time, became reduced to the level of "Sambos."[3]

My thesis, which rests on an examination of folk songs and tales, is that slaves were able to fashion a life style and set of values—an ethos—which prevented them from being imprisoned altogether by the definitions which the larger society sought to impose. This ethos was an amalgam of Africanisms and New World elements which helped slaves, in Guy Johnson's words, "feel their way along the course of American

---

[2] See Herbert Aptheker, *American Negro Slave Revolts;* Kenneth M. Stampp, *The Peculiar Institution* (New York, 1956); Richard Wade, *Slavery in the Cities* (New York, 1964); and Alice and Raymond Bauer, "Day to Day Resistance to Slavery," *Journal of Negro History*, XXVII No. 4, October, 1942.
[3] I am here concerned with the Stanley Elkins version of "Sambo," that is, the inference that the overwhelming majority of slaves, as a result of their struggle to survive under the brutal system of American slavery, became so callous and indifferent to their status that they gave survival primacy over all other considerations. See Chapters III through VI of *Slavery* for a discussion of the process by which blacks allegedly were reduced to the "good humor of everlasting childhood." (p. 132).

slavery, enabling them to endure. . . ."[4] As Sterling Brown, that wise student of Afro-American culture, has remarked, the values expressed in folklore acted as a "wellspring to which slaves" trapped in the wasteland of American slavery "could return in times of doubt to be refreshed."[5] In short, I shall contend that the process of dehumanization was not nearly as pervasive as Stanley Elkins would have us believe; that a very large number of slaves, guided by this ethos, were able to maintain their essential humanity. I make this contention because folklore, in its natural setting, is of, by and for those who create and respond to it, depending for its survival upon the accuracy with which it speaks to needs and reflects sentiments. I therefore consider it safe to assume that the attitudes of a very large number of slaves are represented by the themes of folklore.[6]

II

Frederick Douglass, commenting on slave songs, remarked his utter astonishment, on coming to the North, "to find persons who could speak of the singing among slaves as evidence of their contentment and happiness."[7] The young DuBois, among the first knowledgeable critics of the spirituals, found white Americans as late as 1903 still telling Afro-Americans that "life was joyous to the black slave, careless and happy." "I can easily believe this of some," he wrote, "of many. But not all the past South, though it rose from the dead, can gainsay the heart-touching witness of these songs."

[4] I am indebted to Guy Johnson of the University of North Carolina for suggesting the use of the term "ethos" in this piece, and for helpful commentary on the original paper which was read before the Association for the Study of Negro Life and History at Greensboro, North Carolina, on October 13, 1967.

[5] Professor Brown made this remark in a paper delivered before The Amistad Society in Chicago, Spring, 1964. Distinguished poet, literary critic, folklorist, and teacher, Brown has long contended that an awareness of Negro folklore is essential to an understanding of slave personality and thought.

[6] I subscribe to Alan Lomax's observation that folk songs "can be taken as the signposts of persistent patterns of community feeling and can throw light into many dark corners of our past and our present." His view that Afro-American music, despite its regional peculiarities, "expresses the same feelings and speaks the same basic language everywhere" is also accepted as a working principle in this paper. For an extended treatment of these points of view, see Alan Lomax, *Folk Songs of North America* (New York, 1960), Introduction, p. xx.

[7] Frederic Douglass, *Narrative of the Life of Frederick Douglass* (Cambridge, Massachusetts: The Belknap Press, 1960), p. 38. Originally published in 1845.

They are the music of an unhappy people, of the children of disappointment; they tell of death and suffering and unvoiced longing toward a truer world, of misty wanderings and hidden ways.[8]

Though few historians have been interested in such wanderings and ways, Frederick Douglass probably referring to the spirituals, said the songs of slaves represented the sorrows of the slave's heart, serving to relieve the slave "only as an aching heart is relieved by its tears." "I have often sung," he continued, "to drown my sorrow, but seldom to express my happiness. Crying for joy, and singing for joy, were alike uncommon to me while in the jaws of slavery."[9]

Sterling Brown, who has much to tell us about the poetry and meaning of these songs, has observed: "As the best expression of the slave's deepest thoughts and yearnings, they (the spirituals) speak with convincing finality against the legend of contented slavery."[10] Rejecting the formulation that the spirituals are mainly otherworldly, Brown states that though the creators of the spirituals looked toward heaven and "found their triumphs there, they did not blink their eyes to trouble here." The spirituals, in his view, "never tell of joy in the 'good old days'. . . . The only joy in the spirituals is in dreams of escape."[11]

Rather than being essentially otherworldly, these songs, in Brown's opinion, "tell of this life, of 'rollin' through an unfriendly world!" To substantiate this view, he points to numerous lines from spirituals: "Oh, bye and bye, bye and bye, I'm going to lay down this heavy load"; "My way is cloudy"; "Oh, stand the storm, it won't be long, we'll anchor by and by"; "Lord help me from sinking down"; and "Don't know what my mother wants to stay here fuh, Dis ole world ain't been no friend to huh."[12] To those scholars who "would have us believe that when the Negro sang of freedom, he meant

---

[8]John Hope Franklin (ed.), *Souls of Black Folk* in *Three Negro Classics* (New York, 1965), p. 380. Originally published in 1903.
[9]Douglass, *Narrative*, p. 38. Douglass' view adumbrated John and Alan Lomax's theroy that the songs of the folk singer are deeply rooted "in his life and have functioned there as enzymes to assist in the digestion of hardship, solitude, violence (and) hunger." John A. and Alan Lomax, *Our Singing Country* (New York: The Macmillan Co., 1941), Preface, p. xiii.
[10]Sterling Brown, "Negro Folk Expression," *Phylon*, October, 1953, p. 47.
[11]Brown, "Folk Expression," p. 48.
[12]*Ibid.*, p 407.

only what the whites meant, namely freedom from sin," Brown rejoins:

> Free individualistic whites on the make in a prospering civilization, nursing the American dream, could well have felt their only bondage to be that of sin, and freedom to be religious salvation. But with the drudgery, the hardships, the auction block, the slave-mart, the shackles, and the lash so literally present in the Negro's experience, it is hard to imagine why for the Negro they would remain figurative. The scholars certainly did not make this clear, but rather take refuge in such dicta as: "the slave never contemplated his low condition."[13]

"Are we to believe," asks Brown, "that the slave singing 'I been rebuked, I been scorned, done had a hard time sho's you bawn.' referred to his being outside the true religion?" A reading of additional spirituals indicates that they contained distinctions in meaning which placed them outside the confines of the "true religion." Sometimes, in these songs, we hear slaves relating to divinities on terms more West African than American. The easy intimacy and argumentation, which come out of a West African frame of reference, can be heard in "Hold the Wind."[14]

> When I get to heaven, gwine be at ease,
> Me and my God *gonna do as we please.*
>
> Gonna chatter with the Father, argue with the Son,
> *Tell um 'bout the world I just come from.*[15] (Italics added.)

If there is a tie with heaven in those lines from "Hold the Wind," there is also a clear indication of dislike for the restrictions imposed by slavery. And at least one high heavenly authority might have a few questions to answer. *Tell um 'bout the world I just come from* makes it abundantly clear that some slaves—even when released from the burdens of the world—would keep alive painful memories of their oppression.

[13]*Ibid.,* p. 48.
[14]Addressing himself to the slave's posture toward God, and the attitudes toward the gods which the slave's African ancestors had, Lomax has written: "The West African lives with his gods on terms of intimacy. He appeals to them, reviles them, tricks them, laughs at their follies. In this spirit the Negro slave humanized the stern religion of his masters by adopting the figures of the Bible as his intimates." Lomax, *Folk Songs of North America,* p. 463.
[15]Quoted from Lomax, *Folk Songs of North America,* p. 475.

If slaves could argue with the son of God, then surely, when on their knees in prayer, they would not hesitate to speak to God of the treatment being received at the hands of their oppressors.

> Talk about me much as you please, (2)
> Chillun, talk about me much as you please,
> Gonna talk about you when I get on my knees.[26]

That slaves could spend time complaining about treatment received from other slaves is conceivable, but that this was their only complaint, or even the principal one, is hardly conceivable. To be sure, there is a certain ambiguity in the use of the word "chillun" in this context. The reference appears to apply to slaveholders.

The spiritual *Samson,* as Vincent Harding has pointed out, probably contained much more (for some slaves) than mere biblical implications. Some who sang these lines from *Samson,* Harding suggests, might well have meant tearing down the edifice of slavery. If so, it was the ante-bellum equivalent of today's "burn baby burn."

> He said, 'An' if I had-'n my way,'
> He said, 'An' if I had-'n my way,'
> He said, 'An' if I had-'n my way,
> I'd tear the build-in' down!'
>
> He said, 'And now I got my way, (3)
> And I'll tear this buildin' down."[27]

Both Harriet Tubman and Frederick Douglass have reported that some of the spirituals carried double meanings. Whether most of the slaves who sang those spirituals could decode them is another matter. Harold Courlander has made a persuasive case against widespread understanding of any given "loaded" song,[18] but it seems to me that he fails to

[16]Quoted from Brown, Sterling A., Davis, Arthur P., and Lee, Ulysses, *The Negro Caravan* (New York: The Dryden Press, 1941), p. 436.
[17]Vincent Harding, *Black Radicalism in America.* An unpublished work which Dr. Harding recently completed.
[18]See Harold Courlander, *Negro Folk Music, U.S.A.* (New York: Columbia University Press, 1963), pp. 42, 43. If a great many slaves did not consider Harriet Tubman the "Moses" of her people, it is unlikely that most failed to grasp the relationship between themselves and the Israelites, Egypt and the South, and Pharaoh and slavemasters in such lines as: "Didn't my Lord deliver Daniel / And why not every man"; "Oh Mary don't you weep, don't you moan / Pharaoh's army got drowned / Oh Mary don't you weep; and "Go down Moses / Way down in Egypt-land / Tell old Pharaoh / To let my people go."

recognize sufficiently a further aspect of the subject: slaves, as their folktales make eminently clear, used irony repeatedly, especially with animal stories. Their symbolic world was rich. Indeed, the various masks which many put on were not unrelated to this symbolic process. It seems logical to infer that it would occur to more than a few to seize upon some songs, even though created originally for religious purposes, assign another meaning to certain words, and use these songs for a variety of purposes and situations.

At times slave bards created great poetry as well as great music. One genius among the slaves couched his (and their) desire for freedom in a magnificent line of verse. After God's powerful voice had "Rung through Heaven and down in Hell," he sang, "My dungeon shook and my chains, they fell."[19]

In some spirituals, Alan Lomax has written, Afro-Americans turned sharp irony and "healing laughter" toward heaven, again like their West African ancestors, relating on terms of intimacy with God. In one, the slaves have God engaged in a dialogue with Adam:

> 'Stole my apples, I believe.'
> 'No, marse Lord, I spec it was Eve.'
>
> Of this tale there is no mo'
> Eve et the apple and Adam de co'.[20]

Douglass informs us that slaves also sang ironic seculars about the institution of slavery. He reports having heard them sing: "We raise de wheat, dey gib us de corn; We sift de meal, dey gib us de huss; We peel de meat, dey gib us de skin; An dat's de way dey take us in."[21] Slaves would often stand back and see the tragicomic aspects of their situation, sometimes admiring the swiftness of blacks:

> Run, nigger, run, de patrollers will ketch you,
> Run, nigger run, its almost day.
> Dat nigger run, dat nigger flew;
> Dat nigger tore his shirt in two.[22]

And there is:

> My ole mistiss promise me
> W'en she died, she'd set me free,

[19]Quoted from Lomax, *Folk Songs of North America*, p. 471.
[20]*Ibid.*, p .476.
[21]Frederick Douglass, *The Life and Times of Frederick Douglass* (New York: Collier Books, 1962), p. 146.
[22]Brown, "Folk Expression," p. 51.

> She lived so long dat 'er head got bal'
> An' she give out'n de notion a-dyin' at all.[23]

In the ante-bellum days, work songs were of crucial import
to slaves. As they cleared and cultivated land, piled levees
along rivers, piled loads on steamboats, screwed cotton bales
into the holds of ships, and cut roads and railroads through
forests, mountain and flat, slaves sang while the white man,
armed and standing in the shade, shouted his orders.[24]
Through the sense of timing and coordination which characterized work songs well sung, especially by the leaders,
slaves sometimes quite literally created works of art. These
songs not only militated against injuries but enabled the
bondsmen to get difficult jobs done more easily by not having
to concentrate on the dead level of their work. "In a very real
sense the chants of Negro labor," writes Alan Lomax, "may
be considered the most profoundly American of all our folk
songs, for they were created by our people as they tore at
American rock and earth and reshaped it with their bare
hands, while rivers of sweat ran down and darkened the
dust."

> Long summer day makes a white man lazy,
>   Long summer day.
> Long summer day makes a nigger run away, sir,
>   Long summer day.[25]

Other slaves sang lines indicating their distaste for slave labor:

> Ol' massa an' ol' missis,
> Sittin' in the parlour,
> Jus' fig'in' an' a-plannin'
> How to work a nigger harder.[26]

And there are these bitter lines, the meaning of which is clear:

> Missus in the big house,
> Mammy in the yard,
> Missus holdin' her white hands,
> Mammy workin' hard (3)
> Missus holdin' her white hands,
> Mammy workin' hard.
> Old Marse ridin' all time,

[23]Brown, Caravan, p. 447.
[24]Lomax, Folk Songs of North America, p. 514.
[25]Ibid., p. 515.
[26]Ibid., p. 527.

> Niggers workin' round,
> Marse sleepin' day time,
> Niggers diggin' in the ground (3)
> Marse sleepin' day time,
> Niggers diggin' in the ground.[27]

Courlander tells us that the substance of the work songs "ranges from the humorous to the sad, from the gentle to the biting, and from the tolerant to the unforgiving." The statement in a given song can be metaphoric, tangent or direct, the meaning personal or impersonal. "As throughout Negro singing generally, there is an incidence of social criticism, ridicule, gossip, and protest."[28] Pride in their strength rang with the downward thrust of axe—

> When I was young and in my prime, (hah!)
> Sunk my axe deep every time, (hah!)

Blacks later found their greatest symbol of manhood in John Henry, descendant of Trickster John of slave folk tales:

> A man ain't nothing but a man,
> But before I'll let that steam driver beat me down
> I'll die with my hammer in my hand.[29]

Though Frances Kemble, an appreciative and sensitive listener to work songs, felt that "one or two barbaric chants would make the fortune of an opera," she was on one occasion "displeased not a little" by a self-deprecating song, one which "embodied the opinion that 'twenty-six black girls not make mulatto yellow girl,' and as I told them I did not

[27]Courlander, *Negro Folk Music*, p. 117.
[28]*Ibid.*, p. 89
[29]Brown, "Folk Expression," p. 54. Steel-driving John Henry is obviously in the tradition of the axe-wielding blacks of the ante-bellum period. The ballad of John Henry helped spawn John Henry work songs:

Dis ole hammer—hunh
Ring like silver—hunh (3)
Shine like gold, baby—hunh
Shine like gold—hunh

Dis ole hammer—hunh
Killt John Henry—hunh (3)
Twont kill me baby, hunh
Twon't kill me. (Quoted from Brown, "Folk Expression," p. 57.)

like it, they have since omitted it."[80] What is pivotal here is not the presence of self-laceration in folklore, but its extent and meaning. While folklore contained some self-hatred, on balance it gives no indication whatever that blacks, as a group, liked or were indifferent to slavery, which is the issue.[81]

To be sure, only the most fugitive of songs sung by slaves contained direct attacks upon the system. Two of these were associated with slave rebellions. The first, possibly written by ex-slave Denmark Vesey himself, was sung by slaves on at least one island off the coast of Charleston, S. C., and at meetings convened by Vesey in Charleston. Though obviously not a folksong, it was sung by the folk.

> Hail! all hail! ye Afric clan,
> Hail! ye oppressed, ye Afric band,
> Who toil and sweat in slavery bound
> And when your health and strength are gone
> Are left to hunger and to mourn,
> Let independence be your aim,
> Ever mindful what 'tis worth.
> Pledge your bodies for the prize,
> Pile them even to the skies![82]

The second, a popular song derived from a concrete reality, bears the marks of a conscious authority:

> You mought be rich as cream
> And drive you coach and four-horse team,

[80]Frances Anne Kemble, *Journal of a Residence on a Georgia Plantation, 1838–1839* (New York: Alfred Knopf), pp. 260–61. Miss Kemble heard slaves use the epithet "nigger": "And I assure you no contemptuous intonation ever equalled the prepotenza (arrogance) of the despotic insolence of this address of these poor wretches to each other." Kemble, *Journal*, p. 281. Here she is on solid ground, but the slaves also used the word with glowing affection, as seen in the "Run, Nigger, Run" secular. At other times they leaned toward self-laceration but refused to go the whole route: "My name's Ran, I wuks in de sand, I'd rather be a nigger dan a po' white man." Brown, "Folk Expression," p. 51. Some blacks also sang, "It takes a long, lean, black-skinned gal, to make a preacher lay his Bible down." Newman I. White, *American Negro Folk Songs* (Cambridge, 1928), p. 411.

[81]Elkins, who believes Southern white lore on slavery should be taken seriously, does not subject it to serious scrutiny. For a penetrating—and devastating—analysis of "the richest layers of Southern lore" which, according to Elkins, resulted from "an exquisitely rounded collective creativity," see Sterling A. Brown, "A Century of Negro Portraiture in American Literature," *The Massachusetts Review* (Winter, 1966).

[82]Quoted from Archie Epps, "A Negro Separatist Movement," *The Harvard Review*, IV, No. 1 (Summer-Fall, 1956), 75.

But you can't keep de world from moverin' round
Nor Nat Turner from gainin' ground.

And your name it mought be Caesar sure,
And got you cannon can shoot a mile or more,
But you can't keep de world from moverin' round
Nor Nat Turner from gainin' ground.[83]

The introduction of Denmark Vesey, class leader in the
A.M.E. Church, and Nat Turner, slave preacher, serves to
remind us that some slaves and ex-slaves were violent as well
as humble, impatient as well as patient.

It is also well to recall that the religious David Walker,
who had lived close to slavery in North Carolina, and Henry
Highland Garnett, ex-slave and Presbyterian minister, produced two of the most inflammatory, vitriolic and doom-
bespeaking polemics America has yet seen.[84] There was
theological tension here, loudly proclaimed, a tension which
emanated from and was perpetuated by American slavery and
race prejudice. This dimension of ambiguity must be kept
in mind, if for no other reason than to place in bolder relief
the possibility that a great many slaves and free Afro-Americans could have interpreted Christianity in a way quite different from white Christians.

Even those songs which seemed most otherworldly, those
which expressed profound weariness of spirit and even faith
in death, through their unmistakable sadness, were accusatory,
and God was not their object. If one accepts as a given that
some of these appear to be almost wholly escapist, the indictment is no less real. Thomas Wentworth Higginson came
across one—". . . a flower of poetry in that dark soil," he
called it.[85]

I'll walk in de graveyard, I'll walk through de graveyard,
    To lay dis body down.
I'll lie in de grave and stretch out my arms,
    Lay dis body down.

[83]Quoted in William Styron, "This Quiet Dust," *Harpers,* April 1965,
p. 135.
[84]For excerpts from David Walker's *Appeal* and Henry H. Garnett's
Call to Rebellion, see Herbert Aptheker (ed.), *A Documentary History
of the Negro People in the United States.* 2 vols. (New York: Citadel
Press, 1965). Originally published in 1951.
[85]Thomas Wentworth Higginson, *Army Life in a Black Regiment* (New
York: Collier, 1962), p. 199.

Reflecting on "I'll lie in de grave and stretch out my arms," Higginson said that "Never, it seems to me, since man first lived and suffered, was his infinite longing for peace uttered more plaintively than in that line."[86]

There seems to be small doubt that Christianity contributed in large measure to a spirit of patience which militated against open rebellion among the bondsmen. Yet to overemphasize this point leads one to obscure a no less important reality: Christianity, after being reinterpreted and recast by slave bards, also contributed to that spirit of endurance which powered generations of bondsmen, bringing them to that decisive moment when for the first time a real choice was available to sources of thousands of them.

When that moment came, some slaves who were in a position to decide for themselves did so. W. E. B. DuBois recreated their mood and the atmosphere in which they lived.

> There came the slow looming of emancipation.
> Crowds and armies of the unknown, inscrutable,
> unfathomable Yankees; cruelty behind and before;
> rumors of a new slave trade, but slowly,
> continuously, the wild truth, the bitter truth,
> the magic truth, came surging through. There
> was to be a new freedom! And a black nation
> went tramping after the armies no matter what
> it suffered; no matter how it was treated, no
> matter how it died.[87]

The gifted bards, by creating songs with an unmistakable freedom ring, songs which would have been met with swift, brutal repression in the ante-bellum days, probably voiced the sentiments of all but the most degraded and dehumanized. Perhaps not even the incredulous slavemaster could deny the intent of the new lyrics. "In the wake of the Union Army and in the contraband camps," remarked Sterling Brown, "spirituals of freedom sprang up suddenly. . . . Some celebrated the days of Jubilo: 'O Freedom; O Freedom!' and 'Before I'll be a slave, I'll be buried in my grave!' and 'Go home to my lord and be free.' " And there was: " 'No more driver's lash for me. . . . Many thousand go.' "[88]

[86]*Ibid.*
[87]W. E. B. DuBois, *Black Reconstruction* (Philadelphia: Albert Saifer), p. 122. Originally published in 1935 by Harcourt, Brace and Company.
[88]Brown, "Folk Expression," p. 49.

DuBois brought together the insights of the poet and historian to get inside the slaves:

> There was joy in the South. It rose like perfume—like a prayer. Men stood quivering. Slim dark girls, wild and beautiful with wrinkled hair, wept silently; young women, black, tawny, white and golden, lifted shivering hands, and old and broken mothers, black and gray, raised great voices and shouted to God across the fields, and up to the rocks and the mountains.[39]

Some sang:

> Slavery chain done broke at last, broke at last, broke at last,
> Slavery chain done broke at last,
> Going to praise God till I die.
>
> I did tell him how I suffer,
> In de dungeon and de chain,
> *And de days I went with head bowed down,*
> And my broken flesh and pain,
> Slavery chain done broke at last, broke at last, broke at last.[40]

Whatever the nature of the shocks generated by the war, among those vibrations felt were some that had come from Afro-American singing ever since the first Africans were forcibly brought to these shores. DuBois was correct when he said that the new freedom song had not come from Africa, but that "the dark throb and beat of that Ancient of Days was in and through it."[41] Thus, the psyches of those who gave rise to and provided widespread support for folk songs had not been reduced to *tabula rasas* on which a slave-holding society could at pleasure sketch out its wish fulfillment fantasies.

We have already seen the acute degree to which some slaves realized they were being exploited. Their sense of the injustice of slavery made it so much easier for them to act out their aggression against whites (by engaging in various forms of "day to day" resistance) without being overcome by a sense of guilt, or a feeling of being ill-mannered. To call this nihilistic thrashing about would be as erroneous as to refer to their use

[39]DuBois, *Reconstruction*, p. 124.
[40]Quoted in Brown, *Caravan*, pp. 440–41. One of the most tragic scenes of the Civil War period occurred when a group of Sea Island freedmen, told by a brigadier-general that they would not receive land from the government, sang, "Nobody knows the trouble I've seen." DuBois, *Souls*, p. 381.
[41]DuBois, *Reconstruction*, p. 124.

of folklore as esthetic thrashing about.[42] For if they did not regard themselves as the equals of whites in many ways, their folklore indicates that the generality of slaves must have at least felt superior to whites morally. And that, in the context of oppression, could make the difference between a viable human spirit and one crippled by the belief that the interests of the master are those of the slave.

When it is borne in mind that slaves created a large number of extraordinary songs and greatly improved a considerable proportion of the songs of others, it is not at all difficult to believe that they were conscious of the fact that they were leaders in the vital area of art—giving protagonists rather than receiving pawns. And there is some evidence that slaves were aware of the special talent which they brought to music. Higginson has described how reluctantly they sang from hymnals—"even on Sunday"—and how "gladly" they yielded "to the more potent excitement of their own 'spirituals.' "[48] It is highly unlikely that the slaves' preference for

---

[42]If some slavemasters encouraged slaves to steal or simply winked at thefts, then slaves who obliged them were most assuredly *not acting against their own interests,* whatever the motivation of the masters. Had more fruitful options been available to them, then and only then could we say that slaves were playing into the hands of their masters. Whatever the masters thought of slaves who stole from them—and there is little reason to doubt that most slaves considered it almost obligatory to steal from white people—the slaves, it is reasonable to assume, were aware of the unparalleled looting in which masters themselves were engaged. To speak therefore of slaves undermining their sense of self-respect as a result of stealing from whites—and this argument has been advanced by Eugene Genovese—is wide of the mark. Indeed, it appears more likely that those who engaged in stealing were, in the context of an oppressor-oppressed situation, on the way to realizing a larger measure of self-respect. Moreover, Genovese, in charging that certain forms of "day to day" resistance, in the absence of general conditions of rebellion, "amounted to individual and essentially nihilistic thrashing about," fails to recognize that that which was possible, that which conditions permitted, was pursued by slaves in preference to the path which led to passivity or annihilation. Those engaging in "day to day" resistance were moving along meaningful rather than nihilistic lines, for their activities were designed to frustrate the demands of the authority-system. For a very suggestive discussion of the dependency complex engendered by slavery and highly provocative views on the significance of "day to day" resistance among slaves, see Eugene Genovese, "The Legacy of Slavery and the Roots of Black Nationalism," *Studies on the Left,* VI, No. 6 (Nov.–Dec. 1966), especially p. 8. [48]Higginson, *Black Regiment,* p. 212. Alan Lomax reminds us that the slaves sang "in leader-chorus style, with a more relaxed throat than the whites, and in deeper-pitched, mellower voices, which blended richly." "A strong, surging beat underlay most of their American creations . . . words and tunes were intimately and playfully united, and 'sense' was often subordinated to the demands of rhythm and melody." Lomax, *Folk Songs of North America,* Introduction, p. xx.

their own music went unremarked among them, or that this preference did not affect their estimate of themselves. "They soon found," commented Alan Lomax, "that when they sang, the whites recognized their superiority as singers, and listened with respect."[44] He might have added that those antebellum whites who listened probably seldom understood.

What is of pivotal import, however, is that the esthetic realm was the one area in which slaves knew they were not inferior to whites. Small wonder that they borrowed many songs from the larger community, then quickly invested them with their own economy of statement and power of imagery rather than yield to the temptation of merely repeating what they had heard. Since they were essentially group rather than solo performances, the values inherent in and given affirmation by the music served to strengthen bondsmen in a way that solo music could not have done.[45] In a word, slave singing often provided a form of group therapy, a way in which a slave, in concert with others, could fend off some of the debilitating effects of slavery.

The field of inquiry would hardly be complete without some mention of slave tales. Rich in quantity and often subtle in conception, these tales further illumine the inner world of the bondsmen, disclosing moods and interests almost as various as those found in folksongs. That folk tales, like the songs, indicate an African presence, should not astonish; for the telling of tales, closely related to the African griot's vocation of providing oral histories of families and dynasties, was deeply rooted in West African tradition. Hughes and Bontemps have written that the slaves brought to America the "habit of storytelling as pastime, together with a rich bestiary." Moreover, they point out that the folk tales of slaves "were actually projections of personal experiences and hopes and defeats, in terms of symbols," and that this im-

---

[44] Lomax, *Folk Songs*, p. 460.
[45] Commenting on the group nature of much of slave singing, Alan Lomax points out that the majority of the bondsmen "came from West Africa, where music-making was largely a group activity, the creation of a many-voiced, dancing throng. . . . Community songs of labour and worship (in America) and dance songs far outnumbered narrative pieces, and the emotion of the songs was, on the whole, joyfully erotic, deeply tragic, allusive, playful, or ironic rather than nostalgic, withdrawn, factual, or aggressively comic—as among white folk singers." Lomax, *Folk Songs*, pp. xix and xx of Introduction. For treatments of the more technical aspects of Afro-American music, see Courlander, *Negro Folk Music*, especially Chapter II; and Richard A. Waterman, "African Influences on the Music of the Americas," in *Acculturation in the Americas*, edited by Sol Tax.

portant dimension of the tales "appears to have gone un-
noticed."[46]

Possessing a repertoire which ranged over a great many
areas, perhaps the most memorable tales are those of Brer
Rabbit and John.[47] Brer Rabbit, now trickster, ladies' man
and braggart, now wit, joker and glutton, possessed the resourcefulness, despite his size and lack of strength, to out-
smart stronger, larger animals. "To the slave in his condition,"
according to Hughes and Bontemps, "the theme of weakness
overcoming strength through cunning proved endlessly fas-
cinating."[48] John, characterized by a spiritual resilience born
of an ironic sense of life, was a secular high priest of mischief
and guile who delighted in matching wits with Ole Marster,
the "patterollers," Ole Missy, and the devil himself. He was
clever enough to sense the absurdity of his predicament and
that of white people, smart enough to know the limits of his
powers and the boundaries of those of the master class. While
not always victorious, even on the spacious plane of the imagination, he could hardly be described as a slave with an inferiority complex. And in this regard it is important to note
that his varieties of triumphs, though they sometimes included
winning freedom, often realistically cluster about ways of
coping with everyday negatives of the system.[49]

[46]Arna Bontemps and Langston Hughes (ed.), *The Book of Negro Folklore* (New York: Dodd, Mead & Company, 1965), Introduction, p.
viii. Of course if one regards each humorous thrust of the bondsmen
as so much comic nonsense, then there is no basis for understanding,
to use Sterling Brown's phrase, the slave's "laughter out of hell."
Without understanding what humor meant to slaves themselves, one
is not likely to rise above the superficiality of a Stephen Foster or a
Joel Chandler Harris. But once an effort has been made to see the
world from the slave's point of view, then perhaps one can understand
Ralph Ellison's reference to Afro-Americans, in their folklore, "backing
away from the chaos of experience and from ourselves," in order to
"depict the humor as well as the horror of our living." Ralph Ellison,
"A Very Stern Discipline," *Harpers* (March, 1967), p. 80.
[47]For additional discussions of folk tales, see Zora Neale Hurston, *Mules
and Men* (Philadelphia: J. B. Lippincott, 1935); Richard Dorson,
American Negro Folktales (Greenwich, Connecticut: Fawcett, 1967);
and B. A. Botkin, *Lay My Burden Down* (Chicago: University of
Chicago Press, 1945).
[48]Bontemps and Hughes, *Negro Folklore*, Introduction, p. ix.
[49]The fact that slaveowners sometimes took pleasure in being outwitted
by slaves in no way diminishes from the importance of the trickster
tales, for what is essential here is how these tales affected the slave's
attitude toward himself, not whether his thinking or behavior would
impress a society which considered black people little better than
animals. DuBois' words in this regard should never be forgotten:
"Everything Negroes did was wrong. If they fought for freedom, they
were beasts; if they did not fight, they were born slaves. If they cowered

Slaves were adept in the art of storytelling, as at home in this area as they were in the field of music. But further discussion of the scope of folklore would be uneconomical, for we have already seen a depth and variety of thought among bondsmen which embarrasses stereotypical theories of slave personality. Moreover, it should be clear by now that there are no secure grounds on which to erect the old, painfully constricted "Sambo" structure.[50] For the personalities which lay beneath the plastic exteriors which slaves turned on and off for white people were too manifold to be contained by cheerful, childlike images. When it is argued, then, that "too much of the Negro's own lore" has gone into the making of the Sambo picture "to entitle one in good conscience to condemn it as 'conspiracy',"[51] one must rejoin: Only if you strip the masks from black faces while refusing to read the irony and ambiguity and cunning which called the masks into existence. Slave folklore, on balance, decisively repudiates the thesis that Negroes *as a group* had internalized "Sambo" traits, committing them, as it were, to psychological marriage.

III

It is one of the curiosities of American historiography that a people who were as productive esthetically as American slaves could be studied as if they had moved in a cultural cyclotron, continually bombarded by devastating, atomizing forces which denuded them of meaningful Africanisms while destroying any and all impulses toward creativity. One historian, for example, has been tempted to wonder how it was ever possible that *"all* this (West African) native resourcefulness and vitality have been brought to such a point of

---

on the plantation, they loved slavery; if they ran away, they were lazy loafers. If they sang, they were silly; if they scowled, they were impudent. . . . And they were funny, funny—ridiculous baboons, aping men." DuBois, *Reconstruction*, p. 125.

[50]Ralph Ellison offers illuminating insight into the group experience of the slave: "Any people who could endure all of that brutalization and keep together, who could undergo such dismemberment and resuscitate itself, and endure until it could take the initiative in achieving its own freedom is obviously more than the sum of its brutalization. Seen in this perspective, theirs has been one of the great human experiences and one of the great triumphs of the human spirit in modern times, in fact, in the history of the world." Ellison, "A Very Stern Discipline," p. 84.

[51]Elkins sets forth this argument in *Slavery*, p. 84.

utter stultification in America."[52] (Italics added.) This sadly misguided view is, of course, not grounded in any recognition or understanding of the Afro-American dimension of American culture. In any event, there is a great need for students of American slavery to attempt what Gilberto Freyre tried to do for Brazilian civilization—an effort at discovering the contributions of slaves toward the shaping of the Brazilian national character.[53] When such a study has been made of the American slave we shall probably discover that, though he did not rival his Brazilian brother in staging bloody revolutions, the quality and place of art in his life compared favorably. Now this suggests that the humanity of people can be asserted through means other than open and widespread rebellion, a consideration that has not been appreciated in violence-prone America. We would do well to recall the words of F. S. C. Northrop who has observed:

> During the pre-Civil War period shipowners and southern landowners brought to the United States a considerable body of people with a color of skin and cultural values different from those of its other inhabitants. . . . Their values are more emotive, esthetic and intuitive . . . [These] characteristics can become an asset for our culture. For these are values with respect to which Anglo-American culture is weak.[54]

These values were expressed on the highest level in the folklore of slaves. Through their folklore black slaves affirmed their humanity and left a lasting imprint on American culture. No study of the institutional aspects of American slavery can be complete, nor can the larger dimensions of slave personality and style be adequately explored, as long as historians continue to avoid that realm in which, as DuBois has said, "the soul of the black slave spoke to man."[55]

In its nearly two and one half centuries of existence, the grim system of American slavery doubtless broke the spirits of uncounted numbers of slaves. Nevertheless, if we look

[52]*Ibid.*, p. 93.
[53]Gilberto Freyre, *The Masters and the Slaves* (New York: Alfred A. Knopf, 1956). Originally published by Jose Olympio, Rio de Janeiro, Brazil.
[54]F. S. C. Northrop, *The Meeting of East and West* (New York: The Macmillan Co., 1952), pp. 159–60.
[55]DuBois, *Souls*, p. 378. Kenneth M. Stampp in his *The Peculiar Institution* (New York: Alfred A. Knopf, 1956), employs to a limited extent some of the materials of slave folklore. Willie Lee Rose, in *Rehearsal for Reconstruction* (New York: The Bobbs-Merrill Company, 1964), makes brief but highly informed use of folk material.

through the prism of folklore, we can see others transcending their plight, appreciating the tragic irony of their condition, then seizing upon and putting to use those aspects of their experience which sustain in the present and renew in the future. We can see them opposing their own angle of vision to that of their oppressor, fashioning their own techniques of defense and aggression in accordance with their own reading of reality and doing those things well enough to avoid having their sense of humanity destroyed.

Slave folklore, then, affirms the existence of a large number of vital, tough-minded human beings who, though severely limited and abused by slavery, had found a way both to endure and preserve their humanity in the face of insuperable odds. What they learned about handling misfortune was not only a major factor in their survival as a people, but many of the lessons learned and esthetic standards established would be used by future generations of Afro-Americans in coping with a hostile world. What a splendid affirmation of the hopes and dreams of their slave ancestors that some of the songs being sung in antebellum days are the ones Afro-Americans are singing in the freedom movement today: "Michael, row the boat ashore"; "Just like a tree planted by the water, I shall not be moved."

IMAMU AMIRI BARAKA (LeROI JONES) (1934–)

A note on Imamu Amiri Baraka (LeRoi Jones) appears in the poetry section (see p. 207). The following is reprinted from Home *(1966), the first volume of essays by him.*

The Legacy of Malcolm X, and the Coming of the Black Nation

1

The reason Malik was killed (the reasons) is because he was thought dangerous by enough people to allow and sanction it. Black People and white people.

Malcolm X was killed because he was dangerous to America. He had made too great a leap, in his sudden awareness of *direction* and the possibilities he had for influencing people, anywhere.

Malcolm was killed because he wanted to become official, as, say, a statesman. Malcolm wanted an effective form in which to enrage the white man, a practical form. And he had begun to find it.

For one thing, he'd learned that Black Conquest will be a *deal*. That is, it will be achieved through deals as well as violence. (He was beginning through his African statesmanship to make deals with other nations, as statesman from a *nation*. An oppressed Black Nation "laying" in the Western Hemisphere.)

This is one reason he could use the "universal" Islam—to be at peace with all dealers. The idea was to broaden, formalize, and elevate the will of the Black Nation so that it would be able to move a great many people and resources in a direction necessary to *spring* the Black Man.

"The Arabs must send us guns or we will accuse them of having sold us into slavery!" is international, and opens Black America's ports to all comers. When the ports are open, there is an instant *brotherhood of purpose* formed with most of the world.

Malcolm's legacy was his life. What he rose to be and through what channels, *e.g.*, Elijah Muhammad and the Nation of Islam, as separate experiences. Malcolm changed as a minister of Islam: under Elijah's tutelage, he was a different man—the difference being, between a man who is preaching Elijah Muhammad and a man who is preaching political engagement and, finally, national sovereignty. (Elijah Muhammad is now the second man, too.)

The point is that Malcolm had begun to call for Black National Consciousness. And moved this consciousness into the broadest possible arena, operating with it as of now. We do not want a Nation, we are a Nation. We must strengthen and formalize, and play the world's game with what we have, from where we are, as a *truly* separate people. America can give us nothing; all bargaining must be done by mutual agreement. But finally, terms must be given by Black Men *from their own shores*—which is where they live, where we all are, now. The land is literally ours. And we must begin to act like it.

The landscape should belong to the people who see it all the time.

We begin by being Nationalists. But a nation is land, and wars are fought over land. The sovereignty of nations, the sovereignty of culture, the sovereignty of race, the sovereignty of ideas and ways "into" the world.

The world in the twentieth century, and for some centuries before, is, literally, backward. The world can be understood through any idea. And the purely *social* condition of the world in this millennium, as, say, "compared" to other millennia, might show a far greater loss than gain, if this were not balanced by concepts and natural forces. That is, we think ourselves into the balance and ideas are necessarily "advanced" of what is simply here (*what's going on*, so to speak). And there are rockets and super cars. But, again, the loss? What might it have been if my people were turning the switches? I mean, these have been our White Ages, and all learning has suffered.

And so the Nationalist concept is the arrival of conceptual and environmental strength, or the realization of it in its totality by the Black Man in the West, *i.e.*, that he is not of the West, but even so, like the scattered Indians after movie cavalry attacks, must regroup, and return that force on a fat, ignorant, degenerate enemy.

We are a people. We are unconscious captives unless we realize this—that we have always been separate, except in our tranced desire to be the thing that oppressed us, after some generations of having been "programmed" (a word suggested to me by Jim Campbell and Norbert Wiener) into believing that our greatest destiny was to become white people!

2

Malcolm X's greatest contribution, other than to propose a path to internationalism and hence, the entrance of the American Black Man into a world-wide allegiance against the white man (in most recent times he proposed to do it using a certain kind of white liberal as a lever), was to preach Black Consciousness to the Black Man. As a minister for the Nation of Islam, Malcolm talked about a black consciousness that took its form from religion. In his last days he talked of another black consciousness that proposed politics as its moving energy.

But one very important aspect of Malcolm's earlier counsels was his explicit call for a National Consciousness among Black People. And this aspect of Malcolm's philosophy certainly did abide throughout his days. The feeling that somehow the Black Man was different, as being, as a being, and finally, in our own time, as judge. And Malcolm propounded these differences as life anecdote and religious (political) truth and made the consideration of Nationalist ideas significant and powerful in our day.

Another very important aspect of Malcolm's earlier (or the Honorable Elijah Muhammad's) philosophy was the whole concept of land and land-control as central to any talk of "freedom" or "independence." The Muslim tack of asking for land within the continental United States in which Black People could set up their own nation, was given a special appeal by Malcolm, even though the request was seen by most people outside the movement as "just talk" or the amusing howls of a gadfly.

But the whole importance of this insistence on land is just now beginning to be understood. Malcolm said many times that when you speak about revolution you're talking about land—changing the ownership or usership of some specific land which you think is yours. But any talk of Nationalism also must take this concept of land and its primary importance into consideration because, finally, any Nationalism which is not intent on restoring or securing autonomous space for a people, *i.e.*, a nation, is at the very least shortsighted.

Elijah Muhammad has said, "We want our people in America, whose parents or grandparents were descendants from slaves, to be allowed to establish a separate state or territory of their own—either on this continent or elsewhere.

We believe that our former slavemasters are obligated to provide such land and that the area must be fertile and minerally rich." And the Black Muslims seem separate from most Black People because the Muslims have a national consciousness based on their aspirations for land. Most of the Nationalist movements in this country advocate that that land is in Africa, and Black People should return there, or they propose nothing about land at all. It is impossible to be a Nationalist without talking about land. Otherwise, your Nationalism is a misnamed kind of "difficult" opposition to what the white man has done, rather than the advocation of another people becoming the rulers of themselves, and sooner or later the rest of the world.

The Muslims moved from the Back-to-Africa concept of Marcus Garvey (the first large movement by Black People back to a National Consciousness, which was, finally, only viable when the Black Man focused on Africa as literally "back home") to the concept of a Black National Consciousness existing in this land the Black captives had begun to identify as home. (Even in Garvey's time, there was not a very large percentage of Black People who really wanted to leave. Certainly, the newly emerging Black bourgeoisie would have nothing to do with "returning" to Africa. They were already created in the image of white people, as they still are, and wanted nothing to do with Black.

What the Muslims wanted was a profound change. The National Consciousness focused on actual (nonabstract) land, identifying a people, in a land where they lived. Garvey wanted to go back to Jordan. A real one. The Nation of Islam wanted Jordan closer. Before these two thrusts, the Black Man in America, as he was Christianized, believed Jordan was in the sky, like pie, and absolutely supernatural.

Malcolm, then, wanted to give the National Consciousness its political embodiment, and send it out to influence the newly forming third world, in which this consciousness was to be included. The concept of Blackness, the concept of the National Consciousness, the proposal of a political (and diplomatic) form for this aggregate of Black spirit, these are the things given to us by Garvey, through Elijah Muhammad and finally given motion into still another area of Black response by Malcolm X.

Malcolm's legacy to Black People is what he moved toward, as the accretion of his own spiritual learning and the movement of Black People in general, through the natural hope, a rise to social understanding within the new context

of the white nation and its decline under hypocrisy and
natural "oppositeness" which has pushed all of us toward
"new" ideas. We are all the products of national spirit and
worldview. We are drawn by the vibrations of the entire
nation. If there were no bourgeois Negroes, none of us would
be drawn to that image. They, bourgeois Negroes, were
shaped through the purposive actions of a national attitude,
and finally, by the demands of a particular culture.

At which point we must consider what cultural attitudes
are, what culture is, and what National Consciousness has
to do with these, *i.e.*, if we want to understand what Malcolm X was pointing toward, and why the Black Man now
must move in that direction since the world will not let him
move any other way. The Black Man is possessed by the
energies of historic necessity and the bursting into flower
of a National Black Cultural Consciousness, and with that,
in a living future, the shouldering to power of Black culture
and, finally, Black Men . . . and then, Black ideals, which
are different descriptions of a God. A righteous sanctity, out
of which worlds are built.

3

What the Black Man must do now is look down at the
ground upon which he stands, and claim it as his own. It is
not abstract. Look down! Pick up the earth, or jab your
fingernails into the concrete. It is real and it is yours, if you
want it.

But to want it, as our own, is the present direction. To
want what we are and where we are, but rearranged by our
own consciousness. That is why it was necessary first to re-
crystallize national aspirations behind a Garvey. The Africans
who first came here were replaced by Americans, or people
responding to Western stimuli and then Americans. In order
for the Americans to find out that they had come from another place, were, hence, alien, the Garvey times had to
come. Elijah said we must have a place, to be, ourselves.
Malcolm made it contemporarily secular.

So that now we must find the flesh of our spiritual creation.
We must be *conscious*. And to be conscious is to be *cultured*,
processed in specific virtues and genius. We must respond
to this National Consciousness with our souls, and use the
correspondence to come into our own.

The Black Man will always be frustrated until he has
land (A Land!) of his own. All the thought processes and

emotional orientation of "national liberation movements"—from slave uprisings onward—have always given motion to a Black National (and Cultural) Consciousness. These movements proposed that judgments were being made by Black sensibility, and that these judgments were *necessarily* different from those of the white sensibility—different, and after all is said and done, inimical.

Men are what their culture predicts (enforces). Culture is, simply, the way men live. How they have come to live. What they are formed by. Their total experience, and its implications and theories. Its paths.

The Black Man's paths are alien to the white man. Black Culture is alien to the white man. Art and religion are the results and idealized supernumeraries of culture. Culture in this sense, as Sapir said, is "The National Genius," whether it be a way of fixing rice or killing a man.

I said in *Blues People:* "Culture is simply how one lives and is connected to history by habit." Here is a graphic structure of the relationships and total context of culture:

The Axis (context and evoked relationships) of Culture

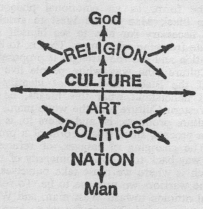

God is man idealized (humanist definition). Religion is the aspiration of man toward an idealized existence. An existence in which the functions of God and man are harmonious, even identical. Art is the movement forward, the understanding progress of man. It is feeling and making. A nation (social order) is made the way people *feel* it should be made. A face is too. Politics is man's aspiration toward an order. Religion is too. Art is an ordering as well. And all these categories are spiritual, but are also the result of the body, at one point, serving as a container of feeling. The soul is no less sensitive.

Nations are races. (In America, white people have become a nation, an identity, a race.) Political integration in America will not work because the Black Man is played on by special forces. His life, from his organs, *i.e.*, the life of the body, what it needs, what it wants, to become, is different— and for this reason racial is biological, finally. We are a different *species*. A species that is evolving to world power and philosophical domination of the world. The world will move the way Black People move!

If we take the teachings of Garvey, Elijah Muhammad and Malcolm X (as well as Frazier, DuBois and Fanon), we know for certain that the solution of the Black Man's problems will come only through Black National Consciousness. We also know that the focus of change will be racial. (If we *feel* differently, we have different *ideas*. Race is feeling. Where the body, and the organs come in. Culture is the preservation of these feelings in superrational to rational form. Art is one method of expressing these feelings and identifying the form, as an emotional phenomenon.) In order for the Black Man in the West to absolutely know himself, it is necessary for him to see himself first as culturally separate from the white man. That is, to be conscious of this separation and use the strength it proposes.

Western Culture (the way white people live and think) is passing. If the Black Man cannot identify himself as separate, and understand what this means, he will perish along with Western Culture and the white man.

What a culture produces, is, and refers to, is an image— a picture of a process, since it is a form of a process; movement seen. The changing of images, of references, is the Black Man's way back to the racial integrity of the captured African, which is where we must take ourselves, in feeling, to be truly the warriors we propose to be. To form an absolutely rational attitude toward West man, and West thought. Which is what is needed. To see the white man as separate and as enemy. To make a fight according to the absolute realities of the world as it is.

Good—Bad, Beautiful—Ugly, are all formed as the result of image. The mores, customs, of a place are the result of experience, and a common reference for defining it—common images. The three white men in the film *Gunga Din* who kill off hundreds of Indians, Greek hero-style, are part of an image of white men. The various black porters, gigglers, ghostchumps and punkish Indians, etc., that inhabit the public image the white man has fashioned to characterize Black Men are references by Black Men to the identity of Black Men in the West, since that's what is run on them each day by white magic, *i.e.*, television, movies, radio, etc. —the Mass Media (the *Daily News* does it with flicks and adjectives).

The song title "A White Man's Heaven Is a Black Man's Hell" describes how complete an image reversal is necessary in the West. Because for many Black People, the white man has succeeded in making this hell seem like heaven. But Black youth are much better off in this regard than their parents. They are the ones who need the least image reversal.

The Black artist, in this context, is desperately needed to change the images his people identify with, by asserting Black feeling, Black mind, Black judgment. The Black intellectual, in this same context, is needed to change the interpretation of facts toward the Black Man's best interests, instead of merely tagging along reciting white judgments of the world.

Art, Religion, and Politics are impressive vectors of a culture. Art describes a culture. Black artists must have an image of what the Black sensibility is in this land. Religion elevates a culture. The Black Man must aspire to Blackness. God is man idealized. The Black Man must idealize himself as Black. And idealize and aspire to that. Politics gives a social order to the culture, *i.e.*, makes relationships within the culture definable for the functioning organism. The Black man must seek a Black politics, an ordering of the world that is beneficial to his culture, to his interiorization and judgment of the world. This is strength. And we are hordes.

4

Black People are a race, a culture, a Nation. The legacy of Malcolm X is that we know we can move from where we are. Our land is where we live. (Even the Muslims have made this statement about Harlem.) If we are a separate Nation, we must make that separateness where we are. There are Black cities all over this white nation. Nations within nations. In order for the Black Man to survive he must not only identify himself as a unique being, but take steps to insure that this being has, what the Germans call

Lebensraum ("living room") literally space in which to exist and develop.

The concepts of National Consciousness and the Black Nation, after the death of Malik, have moved to the point where now some Black People are demanding national sovereignty as well as National (and Cultural) Consciousness. In Harlem, for instance, as director of the Black Arts Repertory Theatre School, I have issued a call for a Black Nation. In Harlem, where 600,000 Black People reside.

The first act must be the nationalization of all properties and resources belonging to white people, within the boundaries of the Black Nation. (All the large concentrations of Black People in the West are already nations. All that is missing is the consciousness of this state of affairs. All that is missing is that the Black Man take control. As Margaret Walker said in her poem "For My People": *A race of men must rise, and take control.*)

Nationalization means that all properties and resources must be harnessed to the needs of the Nation. In the case of the coming Black Nation, all these materials must be harnessed to the needs of Black People. In Harlem, it is almost common knowledge that the Jews, etc., will go the next time there's a large "disturbance," like they say. But there must be machinery set up to transfer the power potential of these retail businesses, small industries, etc., so that they may benefit Black People.

Along with nationalization of foreign-owned businesses (which includes Italian underworld businesses, some of which, like the policy racket, can be transformed into a national lottery, with the monies staying with Black People, or as in the case of heroin-selling, completely abolished) must come the nationalization of all political voices setting up to function within the community/Nation.

No white politicians can be allowed to function within the Nation. Black politicians doing funny servant business for whites, must be eliminated. Black people must have absolute political and economic control. In other words they must have absolute control over their lives and destinies.

These moves are toward the working form of any autonomous nation. And it is this that the Black Man must have. An autonomous Nation. His own forms: treaties, agreements, laws.

These are moves that the conscious Black Man (artist, intellectual, Nationalist, religious thinker, dude with "common sense") must prepare the people for. And the people must be prepared for moves they themselves are already making. And moves they have already made must be explained and analyzed. They, the people, are the bodies. . . . Where are the heads?

And it is *the heads* that are needed for the next move Black People will make. The move to Nationhood. The exact method of transformation is simple logistics.

What we are speaking about again is sovereignty. Sovereignty and independence. And when we speak of these things, we can understand just how far Malik went. The point now is to take ourselves the rest of the way.

Only a united Black Consciousness can save Black People from annihilation at the white man's hands. And no other nation on earth is safe, unless the Black Man in America is safe. Not even the Chinese can be absolutely certain of their continued sovereignty as long as the white man is alive. And there is only one people on the planet who can slay the white man. The people who know him best. His ex-slaves.

VAL FERDINAND (KALAMU YA SALAAM)

The Black arts movement, which has been described by Larry Neal as "the aesthetic and spiritual sister of the Black Power concept," is manifest today in numerous Black cultural organizations and workshops in Black communities throughout the United States. BLKARTSOUTH *is a Black cultural organization in New Orleans and Val Ferdinand is its director. Work by eight* BLKARTSOUTH *poets (see pp. 370–71) concludes the poetry section of this anthology. The following statement was written for* New Black Voices *by Val Ferdinand in response to a request from the editor for information.*

BLKARTSOUTH/get on up!

BLKARTSOUTH started as a community writing and acting workshop under the direction of Tom Dent and Robert "Big Daddy" Costley. The Free Southern Theater had been disbanded for the year and they were the only two left in New O. (our name for New Orleans, Louisiana) to continue on the work of the theater. By that certain inventive process that Black people are famous for possessing the community workshop grew into BLKARTSOUTH without the aid of funds, star attractions, immense programing or anything else that is usually thought of as a prerequisite to developing a theater group. We started in the summer of 68 and by October of the same year we made a vow that we would publish and perform our original material exclusively. Within a year we were performing poetry shows and one-act plays throughout the south; plays and poetry we had written, arranged, directed and produced. In December of 68 NKOMBO's anniversary with a one-hundred page off-set edition that included drawings, poetry, prose, fiction and drama. From the very beginning we were attempting to actualize our purpose which was to develop and perform new/original literary and theatrical material for Black people.

We go deeper now with our purposes. We say that our art is aimed toward building the nation. A nation for Black people. We say that not only do we have to be new/original but that we have to be of some use/have some meaning to Black people in the struggle for liberation. And we mean it. Since we do not operate in a vacuum our motion has created friction and heat. In fact we've burned up some people. But we keep on keepin on just like Shine. BLKARTSOUTH is a whole lot of us striving toward the nation.

What we do, however, ain't mind lunges at paper targets. Our work is instead real spear movements we learned by putting our work out there. Just like the old/our folks used to wash clothes and then hang um out in the sun to dry. Hang um out where every/anybody could see how clean (or unclean) they were. The writing you *see* ain't academic (or un, or anti-academic either) but is some real stuff that's been hanging out in the sun. We are the results of doing/being our poems and stuff. The writing you *see* is not all the writing we are because you ain't seen nothing until you've *heard* us. That's important. That aura of hearing, feeling, seeing; experiencing this kind of writing. Our conclusions are drawn from our experiences and then maybe put down in books. Be aware of that. Be aware that the organization you are reading about is a living, performing group that produces its own material and that the production/performance of this material is an intentional deliberate fusing of technique, content, style and ideology that necessarily gives a total shape to the whole of our work which cannot be realized or appreciated just by reading our writing in books. This does not mean that there is little attention paid to "literary" values per se, rather it means that as far as we are concerned just being "literary" is not and has never been sufficient.

We feel that what we're doing is a relatively new thing in our environment. Our molds aren't quite set yet. Like jazz, what we're doing is constantly moving; the changing same. Right now all we're trying to do is get our work out there and be honest about the things we put out. Maybe two or three years from now we'll be able to set down some standards to judge our work by (real standards and not personal considerations, likes and dislikes, theorizing from "one-eyed" critics). Like what standard was Louis Armstrong blowing by other than what he felt? We can tell now but who could have told then? Maybe not even Satchmo himself. The whole problem centers around the fact that critics invariably want to judge Black artists at their first note. They are afraid to allow the BLKARTS to grow. It took black music less than seventy years to go from Buddy Bolden to Coltrane and beyond. So just as jazz grew, Black writing is going to grow, grow straight from the gutters, from the streets, the people. Grow from our people which is where Louis Armstrong came from with his trumpet playing, his eye opening innovations. He got it all from a culture that accepted, emphasized and respected an African inspired, African-American heritage of music making. We as writers have a similar heritage we must tap, a spoken, verbal art that runs deep and long all the way back to the homeland. Slave narratives, field hollers, shouts, hardluck stories, animal tales, everything. A real heritage which has been systematically crushed, a heritage we have been taught to ignore and belittle, a heritage we must get next to or be like a tree without roots. We must grow to know this heritage and do as it advises us: Sing about what we are in a good strong voice and not get caught up in trying to imitate others or denying the worth of what we are. Sing our own songs.

We at NKOMBO say that our goal is not to put out a magazine full of "little poetic masterpieces," but rather to publish a journal that will serve as an adequate medium of expression for Black artists of the south. We feel that Black writers are ignored (and as a result stunted in their growth) by the traditional publishers both Black, such as they be, and white. Many critics insist that there is very little "quality" Black writing available as an explanation for this exclusion. But the truth is that there is too little Black writing available period, "quality" or not. And furthermore there will never be a large body of so-called "quality" Black writing until there is an even larger grouping of Black writing published irregardless of "quality"; a larger grouping that is written to reach and take in Black people rather than to live up to some vague flat cultured concept of "quality." That sounds cold, defensive and anti-good literature but it's true. It's an unbelievable trip to think that the absence of quality is the cause for the exclusion of Black writers when there is so much garbage being dumped on the heads of people by white publishers. Check it out for yourself. Go to any local bookstand or drugstore and pick out what you consider to be quality writing. After you've done that, look at all the junk that's left. Quality??? Not hardly. And that's what we're out to change. Black writers are not published simply because the publishing industry is for the most part white and doesn't want to or doesn't know how to publish Black writing (that's not meant as a criticism but rather as a realistic assessment of fact and intentions; like we ain't out to publish white writers either). Our policy is that those Black writers who live in our area and participate in our workshops *will* be published, period! We are intent on making sure that any writer who is interested in writing will be able to get at least one of his pieces published in NKOMBO. The future will decide what is of "quality." Let that be taken in, let it remain; throw the rest away.

We've been around for three years now darting in and out of the consciousness of Black people in the south and elsewhere. We feel like we ain't even off the ground yet, still just pecking away at this eggshell environment. But as soon as we break out of this straight jacket society/mind condition . . . we movin on up! We want to move, got to get away. Our art is functional art that's going to help all us Black people find ways to fly. We trying to get Black people together so that we can all consciously make that great migration east.

To quote brother Kush (tom dent), "anyway, our poetry, the beautiful thing about it has to do with making connections with, talking to, grooving with blk people, not with 'poetry' or 'great writing' or being a literary giant, or an ideological father, or any such shit as that. Just making connections giving blk people something they can value and use. This is what we mean by functional writing." If somebody can learn something from it or it draws Black people closer together then our writing has done its do.

We're concerned with surviving and producing and developing. We say first you got to survive. Find ways to stay alive. If you dead you can't do whatever it is you want to do. BLKARTSOUTH started out as a workshop within the Free Southern Theater structure but now FST is dead and we must move on. WE (us Black people and whatever we do) is an ongoing thing. A life process. Survival for us is the constant turning to get next to the sun. A better understanding of who we are, where we are, what are, all are in order to get closer/ next to our brothers and sisters. From the jump the water is over our heads. But we dive in anyway. As a result of our struggles within this tidal wave funky oceanic environment we've learned how to be a little/lot bit of everything. Part deep sea diver, part free style swimmer, part tireless treader and even part water walker; that's what survival motion is all about: Finding ways to stay alive. And it ain't simply about money. It's got more to do with relating to people and our environment. Us relating to Black people as Black people. Our art/organization is invalid if its not about Black people, their lives, the history of their survival in this white water. Invalid. Check it. But just surviving is not enough. Production is our second consideration. By production we mean pushing our work out where people can see it, dig it, use it! In the black light of our sun, sunsss, sons and daughters, our future. Whatever, no matter how many, how well, what we have is and are doing it won't do no good if nobody knows about it. We also mean putting our work over in the best possible manner. Too often we have felt that anything was good enough. WE should not just throw anything at Black people in the name of BLKARTS. A sloppy production is no more useful than a dirty weapon. In fact, a sloppy production is a dirty weapon and is subject to the same malfunctions that might be expected of an unclean rifle or a rusty cannon. Production is the presentation of our work to our people and is also the *how* (or mechanics) of our presentation. That's where the real quality is. We have found that producing our own work is a learning process. The more we work the more we do, the more we do the more we learn. We go stale if we don't work (become old, rusty and slow) and static if we don't learn (be doing the same tired changes over and over and over). Ultimately we learn our most important things from the interaction between us and the Black people we perform for. Dig it. It's all there between us Black people. That's where it's got to happen. That's why it's important that our BLKARTS never be separated from Black people. No matter what we produce, how fine or brilliant it be or whatever, don't care what it is we do, we must always remember that we too are a product. We are a product of the collective history/experiences of Black people and when we divorce ourselves from this reality we replace it (whether consciously or unconsciously) with other realities which other realities become the motor impulses and root of what we do. It is vitally necessary to be aware of this life giving relationship. Irregardless of what we say our art is about, our art is finally all about us. Us. And so for this reason among others we should/must always know what we're about, where we at, what we mean and all that. Be conscious in other words. Got to be conscious of ourselves as Black people. When we present our art we must be for real, be all up in it. And if we call it Black Art then we must live it and get it from the source, Black people themselves. The third consideration is development. Growth is life. If we stop, we're dead. We got to move/grow. Not just jump around up and down but go somewhere, head some place. Fly toward something. Study, seek, search. Be honest, accept, reject. Study, move and study. Study ourselves, our people, who we are, where we came from, where we want to go. In our study we must realize that our people are like the woman in a family, the black earth of our world. We must get closer to our women and work the earth with patience. This is why socalled primitive people often referred to farming as husbandry. All of creation is one. If we choose to develop our art we must understand how all things develop. How the world, our world develops. How our people develop. This is what we must study, must relate to, must understand or else we might as well be jacking off, masturbating for our own self-gratification; either that or be standing out on some corner on the block under the night lights selling our ass for money. All of which ain't really got nothing to do with Black Art except to say we sometimes get confused, mixed up, lost and separated and go in for that kind of living thinking it's hip, thinking we will be successful at it and make it big. Thinking we doing our thang, our weird weird thang. But thinking and perversion ain't where it's at. Once we've studied up and thought some stuff out it be time to get on up. Get on up and act. Time for action. Time to act on them considerations, them conclusions, them thoughts we done thought we had. Go on and make it real. Make us real. Try that for a change—real reality. Making a for real us. Really move. Move in and out, slowly in and out. In and out ourselves, our Black selves and our people. Slowly, faster when we get closer/know where we going, almost reaching it, faster in and out, in and out. In deeper out higher, deeper higher, faster when we really understand what we Black people are all about. Faster when we ready to do something.

It's long slow, hard work but that's OK. We Black people. We got time. We are time, all the time in the world. We are the world! We are. We are most of it (our Black world) gon be all of it and certainly were the beginning of it; we it. You may be laughing now or at least (that is if you're still reading) saying out loud that we're saying bullshit. Ebony hallucinations, slave dreams of ruling empires and conquering the world and bullshit; mostly bullshit. That may or may not be true. But dig, there ain't no bullshit about the fact of what is. WE IS! We is Black people. We have survived. We are doing something real, see; we is Us. Like us or not, understand us or not, be Black or not, nothing you say or do can refute that fact. WE IS! Just dig on the work we're doing, we in this book somewhere . . . in fact quit reading this and look up sister Nayo or brother Kush . . . this ain't nuthin, just an explanation or trying to be an explanation. This is what we ain't. Some of what we are is a little further on (or maybe further back . . . somewhere). Read the real us. Check that out. Read that, read and laugh. HhaaaahhhhaaaaAAAAAA!!! We will survive. We will survive. We will/survive and produce and develop. BLACK PEOPLE CAN DO IT. WE CAN DO THAT, YES WE CAN! GET ON UP!

Nah how bout dat?

PEACE & LIBERATION

ELDRIDGE CLEAVER (1935–)

One of the most widely read revolutionary writers of the Sixties, Eldridge Cleaver was born in Little Rock, Arkansas, and grew up in the ghetto in Los Angeles. He served sentences in the California state prisons of San Quentin, Folsom, and Soledad. Soul on Ice (1968), his first book, has achieved the reputation of a classic of contemporary Black militant expression. It consists of essays and open letters written while he was in prison. After his release from jail he joined the Black Panther Party and was its Minister of Information until 1971 when there was a split in the leadership of the Party. He has also been associated with Ramparts magazine as a contributor and member of its staff and has published articles, stories, and interviews in The Black Panther, Esquire, Black Dialogue, Liberator, Playboy, Mademoiselle, and other publications. In 1968, he was the candidate for President of the Peace and Freedom Party. Threatened with further imprisonment, Cleaver went into exile in 1969 and now lives in Algiers. In the following book review he discusses the significance to "the militants of the black liberation movement in America" of Frantz Fanon and his book The Wretched of the Earth. It is reprinted from Eldridge Cleaver: Post-Prison Writings and Speeches (1969), his second book.

Psychology: The Black Bible

(A Review of *The Wretched of the Earth* by Frantz Fanon)

This book, already recognized around the world as a classic study of the psychology of oppressed peoples, is now known among the militants of the black liberation movement in America as "the Bible."

Written by a black man who was born in Martinique and educated in Paris, who reached the apex of his genius in the crucible of the Algerian Revolution, Fanon's book is itself an historical event. For it marks a very significant moment in the history of the movement of the colonized peoples of the world—in their quest for national liberation, the modernization of their economies, and security against the never-ending intrigues of the imperialist nations.

During a certain stage in the psychological transformation of a subjected people who have begun struggling for their freedom, an impulse to violence develops in the collective unconscious. The oppressed people feel an uncontrollable desire to kill their masters. But the feeling itself gives rise to myriad troubles, for the people, when they first became aware of the desire to strike out against the slavemaster, shrink from this impulse in terror. Violence then turns in upon itself and the oppressed people fight among themselves: they kill each other, and do all the things to each other which they would, in fact, like to do to the master. Intimidated by the superior armed might of the oppressor, the colonial people feel that he is invincible and that it is futile to even dream of confronting him.

When the revolutionary impulse to strike out against the oppressor is stifled, distortions in the personality appear. During the Algerian Revolution, Fanon worked in a hospital in Algeria. A psychiatrist, there he was able to observe carefully Algerians who had caved in psychologically under the pressures of a revolutionary situation. *The Wretched of the Earth* contains an appendix in which Fanon introduces several of these case histories, tracing the revolutionary impulse and attempts to evade it through the psyches of his patients.

Not all of Fanon's patients were Algerian colonial subjects. French policemen who were bothered by the brutality with which they were surrounded and in which they were involved, French soldiers who had inflicted despicable tortures on prisoners, were often confronted with situations in which their rationalizations broke down and they found themselves face to face with their own merciless deeds.

The rare significance of this book is that it contains the voice of a revolutionary black intellectual speaking directly to his own people and showing them the way to harness their forces. Fanon teaches that the key factor is to focus all the hatreds and violence on their true target—the oppressor.

From then on, says Fanon, be implacable. The same point is made by LeRoi Jones in his play, *Dutchman,* when his character, Clay, screams to the white woman who had tormented him, "A little murder will make us all sane again" [Speaking of black people *vis à vis* whites]. What this book does is legitimize the revolutionary impulse to violence. It teaches colonial subjects that it is perfectly normal for them to want to rise up and cut off the heads of the slavemasters, that it is a way to achieve their manhood, and that they must oppose the oppressor in order to experience themselves as men.

In the aftermath of Watts, and all the other uprisings that have set the ghettos of America ablaze, it is obvious that there is very little difference in the way oppressed people feel and react, whether they are oppressed in Algeria by the French, in Kenya by the British, in Angola by the Portuguese, or in Los Angeles by Yankee Doodle.

French philosopher Jean-Paul Sartre wrote an introduction to this book, which, he says, needed no introduction by anyone. Sartre's introduction is itself a masterpiece. Interpreting Fanon's thought for a white audience, Sartre has rendered a valuable service in driving home to the reader that this is a book he dare not pass up.

January 15, 1967

MAULANA RON KARENGA

A leader and ideologist of the contemporary Black cultural nationalism movement in the United States, Maulana Ron Karenga is founder and chairman emeritus of Temple of Kawaida (US) in Los Angeles. Imamu Amiri Baraka (LeRoi Jones), who has been explaining the philosophy of the US organization in lectures and articles, wrote in The Black Scholar *(November, 1969) that "Kawaida, or the doctrine of*

Maulana Karenga" is "a value system" with the initial purpose of Black "Nation building."

The following article is reprinted from Negro Digest, *January, 1968, where it appeared together with an article by the young writer James Cunningham which is the next selection in this anthology. The companion articles by Ron Karenga and James Cunningham were introduced by the following "Editor's Note" in* Negro Digest: *"When Ron Karenga, head of the US Organization (based in Los Angeles) came to Chicago last October at the invitation of the Organization of Black American Culture (OBAC), one of his most attentive listeners was James Cunningham, a young Missouri-born writer who is also a member of the OBAC Writers Workshop. Maulana Karenga spoke on Black Cultural Nationalism (which is the subject of a Karenga book,* The Quotable Karenga), *and it was to that speech that Mr. Cunningham addressed his article. Maulana Karenga's article on the next page, while not specifically about Black Cultural Nationalism, is a response to Mr. Cunningham's criticism of the original Karenga talk on Black Cultural Nationalism." Entitled "Ron Karenga and Black Cultural Nationalism" when this article appeared in* Negro Digest, *the present title was requested with the granting of permission for its publication in this anthology.*

Black Art: Mute Matter Given Force and Function

Black art, like everything else in the Black community, must respond positively to the reality of revolution.

It must become and remain a part of the revolutionary machinery that moves us to change quickly and creatively. We have always said, and continue to say, that the battle we are waging now is the battle for the minds of Black people, and that if we lose this battle, we cannot win the violent one. It becomes very important then, that art plays the role it should play in Black survival and not bog itself down in the meaningless madness of the Western world wasted. In order to avoid this madness, black artists and those who wish to be artists must accept the fact that what is needed is an aesthetic, a Black aesthetic, that is a criteria for judging the validity and/or the beauty of a work of art.

Pursuing this further, we discover that all art can be judged on two levels—on the social level and on the artistic level. In terms of the artistic level, we will be brief in talking about this, because the artistic level involves a consideration of form and feeling, two things which obviously involve more technical consideration and terminology than we have space, time or will to develop adequately here. Let it be enough to say that the artistic consideration, although a necessary part, is not sufficient. What completes the picture is that social criteria for judging art. And it is this criteria that is the most important criteria. For all art must reflect and support the Black Revolution, and any art that does not discuss and contribute to the revolution is invalid, no matter how many lines and spaces are produced in proportion and symmetry and no matter how many sounds are boxed in or blown out and called music.

All we do and create, then, is based on tradition and reason, that is to say, on foundation and movement. For we begin to build on traditional foundation, but it is out of movement, that is experience, that we complete our creation. Tradition teaches us, Leopold Senghor tells us, that all African art has at least three characteristics: that is, it is functional, collective and committing or committed. Since this is traditionally valid, it stands to reason that we should attempt to use it as the foundation for a rational construction to meet our present day needs. And by no mere coincidence we find that the criteria is not only valid, but inspiring. That is why we say that all Black art, irregardless of any technical requirements, must have three basic characteristics which make it revolutionary. In brief, it must be functional, collective and committing. It must be functional, that is *useful,* as we cannot accept the false doctrine of "art for art's sake." For, in fact, there is no such thing as "art for art's sake." All art reflects the value system from which it comes. For if the artist created only for himself and not for others, he would lock himself up somewhere and paint or write or play just for himself. But he does not do that. On the contrary, he invites us over, even *insists* that we come to hear him or to see his work; in a word, he expresses a need for our evaluation and/or appreciation and our evaluation cannot be a favorable one if the work of art is not first functional, that is, useful.

So what, then, is the use of art—our art, Black art? Black art must expose the enemy, praise the people and support the revolution. It must be like LeRoi Jones' poems that are assassins' poems, poems that kill and shoot guns and "wrassle cops into alleys taking their weapons, leaving them dead with tongues pulled out and sent to Ireland." It must be functional like the poem of another revolutionary poet from "US," Clyde Halisi, who described the Master's words as "Sun Genies, dancing through the crowd snatching crosses and St. Christopher's from around niggers' necks and passing the white gapped legs in their minds to Simbas[1] to be disposed of."

Or, in terms of painting, we do not need pictures of oranges in a bowl or trees standing innocently in the midst of a wasteland. If we must paint oranges and trees, let our guerrillas be eating those oranges for strength and using those trees for cover. We need new images, and oranges in a bowl or fat white women smilingly lewdly cannot be those images. All material is mute until the artist gives it a message, and that message must be a message of revolution. Then we have destroyed "art for art's sake," which is of no use anyhow, and have developed art for all our sake, art for Mose the miner, Sammy the shoeshine boy, T.C. the truck driver and K.P. the unwilling soldier.

In conclusion, the real function of art is to make revolution, using its own medium.

The second characteristic of Black art is that it must be collective. In a word, it must be from the people and must be returned to the people in a form more beautiful and colorful than it was in real life. For that is what art is: everyday life given more form and color. And in relationship to that, the Black artist can find no better subject than Black People themselves, and the Black artist who does not choose or develop this subject will find himself unproductive. For no one is any more than the context to which he owes his existence, and if an artist owes his existence to the Afroamerican context, then he also owes his art to that context and therefore must be held accountable to the people of that context. To say that art must be collective, however, raises four questions. Number one, the question of popularization versus elevation; two, personality versus individuality; three, diversity in unity; and four, freedom *to* versus freedom *from*.

The question of popularization versus elevation is an old one; what it really seeks to do is to ask and to answer the question whether or not art should be lowered to the level

[1]Swahili for young lions, the Youth Movement in US Organization.

of the people or the people raised to the level of art. Our contention is that if art is from the people, and for the people, there is no question of raising people to art or lowering art to the people, for they are one and the same thing. As we said previously—art is everyday life given more form and color. And what one seeks to do then is to use art as a means of educating the people, and being educated by them, so that it is a mutual exchange rather than a one-way communication. Art and people must develop at the same time and for the same reason. It must move with the masses and be moved by the masses.

For we should not demand that our people go to school to learn to appreciate art, but that an artist go to school formally or informally to learn new and better techniques of expressing his appreciation for the people and all they represent and his disdain for anything and everything that threatens or hinders their existence. Then and only then can both the artist and the people move forward with a positive pace rooted to the reality of revolution.

The second question raised is the question of personality versus individuality. Now this question is one of how much the emphasis on collective art destroys the individuality of the artist. We say that individualism is a luxury that we cannot afford, moreover, individualism is, in effect, nonexistent. For since no one is any more than the context to which he owes his existence, he has no individuality, only personality. Individuality by definition is "me" in spite of everyone, and personality is "me" in relation to everyone. The one, a useless isolation and the other an important involvement. We have heard it even said that the individual is like an atom, that which can no longer be reduced, or the essence of humanity. However, aside from this being a rather strained analogy, it does not prove that a man who wants to be an individual can stand alone. For the atom itself is a part of a molecule and cannot exist without interdependence, and even then, it is at best a simple theoretical construction for the convenience of conversation. We say that there is no virtue in a false independence, but there is value in a real interdependence.

The third question raised with regard to collective art is an extension of the second one, and that is, does unity preclude diversity? Our answer to that is an emphatic, "NO," for there can be and is unity in diversity, even as there can be diversity in unity. What one seeks, however, is not a standardization of every move or creation, but a framework in which one can create and avoid the European gift of trial and error. One can seek the reality of the concept of diversity in unity or unity in diversity in listening to a Trippin ensemble.[2] In a Trippin ensemble the "leader" sets the pace and others come in, or go out, as it pleases them, but in the end they all come to a very dynamic and overwhelmingly harmonious conclusion. So it is with our dance—two partners dance together the same dance and yet they provide us with a demonstration of that which is unique in each of them. But that is not individuality—that is personality. For it is an expression of uniqueness, not isolation from, but in relation to, each other and the collective experience that they both have shared.

The last question is one of freedom *to* versus freedom *from*. This is really a political question, or social one, and is one that raises contradiction for the artist who rejects the social interpretation of art. However, when he demands freedom to do something or freedom from the restriction that prohibits his doing something, he is asking for a socio-political right, and that, as we said, makes art social first and aesthetic second. Art does not exist in the abstract just like freedom does not exist in the abstract. It is not an independent living thing; it lives through us and through the meaning and message we give it. And an artist may have any freedom to do what he wishes as long as it does not take the freedom from the people to be protected from those images, words and sounds that are negative to their life and development. The people give us the freedom from isolation and alienation and random searching for subject matter and artists, in view of this, must not ask for freedom to deny this, but on the contrary must praise the people for this. In conclusion, the concept of collective art can best be expressed in the African proverb showing the interdependence of all by saying, "One hand washes the other."

The final thing that is characteristic of Black art is that it must be committing. It must commit us to revolution and change. It must commit us to a future that is ours. In a word, it must commit us to all that is US-yesterday, today and the sunrise of tomorrow. It must tell us like Halisi's poem, "Maulana and Word Magic," that we must give up the past or be found out and exposed, "as the notes of a new day come

---

[2]Trippin is our word for what white boys and others call jazz. In line with our obsession with self-determination which demands new definitions and nomenclature, we reject the word jazz, for jazz is taken from the white word, jazzy, i.e. sexy, because that is what he thought our music was. We call it Trippin because that is what we do when we play it or listen to it.

tripping through searching each one's heart for any traces of Peyton Place." It must commit us to the fact that the earth is ours and the fullness thereof. As LeRoi Jones says, "You can't steal nothing from the white man. He's already stole it, he owes you anything you want, even his life." So, "Black People take the shit you want, take their lives if need, but get what you want, what you need. Dance up and down the street, turn all the music up." This is commitment to the struggle, a commitment that includes the artist and the observer. We cannot let each other rest; there is so much to do, and we all know we have done so little. Art will revive us, inspire us, give us enough courage to face another disappointing day. It must not teach us resignation. For all our art must contribute to revolutionary change and if it does not, it is invalid.

Therefore, we say the blues are invalid; for they teach resignation, in a word acceptance of reality—and we have come to change reality. We will not submit to the resignation of our fathers who lost their money, their women, and their lives and sat around wondering "what did they do to be so black and blue." We will say again with Brother LeRoi, "We are lovers and the sons of lovers, and warriors and the sons of warriors." Therefore, we will love—and unwillingly though necessarily, make war, revolutionary war. We will not cry for those things that are gone, but find meaning in those things that remain with us. Perhaps people will object violently to the idea that the blues are invalid, but one should understand that they are not invalid historically. They will always represent a very beautiful, musical and psychological achievement of our people; but today they are not functional because they do not commit us to the struggle of today and tomorrow, but keep us in the past. And whatever we do, we cannot remain in the past, for we have too much at stake in the present. And we find our future much too much rewarding to be rejected.

Let our art remind us of our distaste for the enemy, our love for each other, and our commitment to the revolutionary struggle that will be fought with the rhythmic reality of a permanent revolution.

JAMES CUNNINGHAM

*A young Missouri-born writer, James Cunningham lives in
Chicago and is a member of the* OBAC *Writers Workshop.
He was present when Ron Karenga addressed the organization
and expressed his reactions in an article.*

*The following article was first published together with the
preceding article in this book by Maulana Ron Karenga in*
Negro Digest, *January, 1968. It was introduced by an ex-
planatory editor's note in* Negro Digest *which is reprinted in
this book in the note preceding Mr. Karenga's article.*

Hemlock For The Black Artist: Karenga Style

Maulana Ron Karenga is a spokesman highly endowed not
only with the power to rap in a manner thoroughly Black,
but with a cogency that is severely systematic. This means it
is possible to read a succession of declarations on art, for
instance, that require no more space than three pages, and
gain at the same time a definitive introduction to his thought.
His powers of compression are no less remarkable, and are
eloquently spoken for by the fact that the entire text which
is entitled, *The Quotable Karenga,* and which covers at least
seven major areas, requires no more than thirty pages.

Also, due to close philosophical kinship to both Malcolm X
and to LeRoi Jones, his remarks help to clarify, by their
wealth of implications, far more than his own distinctive
position. That position being: Black cultural nationalism.

Nationalism, be it black or white, must by its very nature
conceive of revolution as a public rather than a personal
event. As a result, individualism is one of its primary objects
of attack, and diversity, one of its first casualties. This initial

attack is prompted by a sincere desire for unity. And reasonably enough public minded movements have never been content to pursue unity without also seeking to control the people they would unify.

Therefore, no one should be surprised that Karenga's opening remark on art is a simple declaration of social control over it: "Black Art must be for the people, by the people, and from the people. That is to say, it must be functional, collective and committing."

This is a very important premise, for the last three words are used at a later point to explain what art must be in order to be revolutionary. In addition, we learn that all art is the reflection of the values of the people. This is understood in such a way as to allow Karenga to dismiss individuality and the concept of art for art's sake.

Now this dismissal of these two concepts is partly explained by a general concern for what might be called "renegade brothers," those who reach for what is thought to be above the heads and interests of the general Black public. Sometimes this reaching out and beyond is hasty, careless and, in a certain sense, self-destructive because of the bland, unexamined values that often support it. And Karenga, like Malcolm and Jones, has a number of penetrating things to say about mixed-up values.

But it should be admitted that part of this singular striving is also due to honest dissent; to bringing one's own values and attitudes, not to mention those of one's community, one's Black community, into serious question. But, more significantly, it is the effort to go one's own way, to follow one's personal bent, one's individual path.

There is a very subtle link between the question of individuality and the notion of art for its own sake. It is taken for granted that there is a relationship between the two. What that relationship is, however, is another matter. It is usually reduced to subjectivism, which is scandalous enough to those critics who insist on defining everything in social terms. Charges of artificiality and decadence are also popular objections.

With regard to the nature of art, Karenga's two key words are "collective" and "functional." And he is being very shrewd in making them so. The first term has to do with origin. Art is seen as the product of the people: "All art should be the product of a creative need and desire in terms of Black people." And again: "all art reflects the value system from which it comes."

It should be noted that function and origin are related, especially when the purpose is said to derive from the needs of a people. Black people, of course, in this case.

Any artist who believes this does considerable violence to his calling. And it would be a very serious matter were it not for the miraculous, wonder-inspiring resilience of art to which the much abused notion of art for art's sake is a very stubborn witness. This notion declares nothing less than the self-determination and the self-sufficiency of art. It is one way of confronting us with the powerful suggestion that what makes us alive and what makes us artists is one and the same force.

It is another way of saying that art makes the artist, rather than the other way around. It does so by allowing him to tap his own inner resources. And one consideration that should be kept in as steady a focus as possible is the meaning of individuality. For there is no better way of calling attention to the irrelevance of bringing up the issue of subjectivity and collectivity, more popularly called "objectivity."

Individuality means wholeness. The sort of indivisibility one associates with the classic notion of an atom. "Collective" and "subjective" refer to the relative point from which reality is to be viewed. Individuality, on the other hand, is concerned with reality itself, and not with the position from which we may view it.

It is a level and an order of reality beyond which one simply cannot go. Like a real atom, it can not be reduced any further. It is a matter of foundation and anchorage. And art itself furnishes the artist with a self. A new self. Just as a guitar or a piano grants new fingers. It makes one conscious of a true and sobering individuality. And its initial work, its initial relationship to the artist reveals itself to be a most rigorous, severe, exacting, sweeping, and delightful as well as thoroughgoing system of a truly radical re-orientation. Both for the artist and for us, the audience.

Ray Charles not only sings the blues, he is also the product of the blues. That is to say, he is the product, the extoller, the champion, the creation of his own art form. And his music, which is also our music without the necessity of regimenting him, allows for a number of things. It allows him to be a man. It does so by allowing him to be a real individual. This it does by not only allowing him to tap his own vocal resources, but also by transforming his blindness, and his whole body as well.

If you really want revolutionary change, here it is. The

spectacle, the drama of a man changed, and charged, and turned into the mysterious power of a vocabulary and a grammar called the blues. A whole language, in fact. "Something's got a hold of me!" It must be art, if it's a musician that's being grabbed.

Art takes care of its own, just as it takes care of us. Administering to the spot where we need to be moved, and stirred. The need which drives Aretha to sing, to moan, to shout is identical in source to what drives us to hear her. Now these are real live needs, and her art attends to hers, no less than to ours. Talk about function! And change! And what do we think puts this art, and these artists, before us as vital resources for us? LIFE!

There are some people who need Coltrane more urgently than a drink. So, Karenga must be mistaken when he suggests that Black artists should go around following the people. The case would almost appear to be the reverse. But not quite. For both artist and audience go around following, pursuing, hungering for what keeps and makes them both alive.

Persons who regard the social aspect of a human's reality as the whole story, or as the most significant part, cannot be blamed for their misguided efforts to apply an external rather than this native function to art. Since it can hardly occur to them that art has its own natural, inherent, built-in reason for being, which is to liberate by being life-giving and life-witnessing: and therefore a reflection of life. Now, if art really went about, as Karenga and Jones insist, simply, docilely following the people, and what they take their needs to be, there would be little chance of liberating them.

The notion that we are merely social beings is part of the chaos from which art has the power to free us. And the notions which people bring to all the vital areas of life are, in reality, part of the deadly folly in which men, black and white, individualists and nationalists, are forever perishing. All people spend endless effort, artists included, in resisting the truth about their lives.

This question of the self-sufficiency of art and its connection with revolution cannot be overstressed. Art is inherently revolutionary. Part of its real force as a criticism of people and society is derived in part from its very diversity.

It is no accident that Karenga harps on the values of the people. He takes pains to do so in such a way as to suggest they are familiar to all, indisputable, and above all, simple. The needs of the people receive the same short-changed treatment in the utterances of Malcolm, Stokely Carmichael, and Jones. Negroes are ruthlessly streamlined and standardized for convenient over-simplification. There's nothing like it for enhancing one's persuasiveness.

But art with its diversity of points of view always manages to reveal people to be far more complex and various than we are otherwise willing to admit or to face. For we seldom know quite what to do with this disturbing complexity, this unneat unpredictableness. Human nature surprises and trips us up.

Both Jones and Karenga stress change and movement. This is central to their understanding of what a revolution should accomplish. This is also central to an artist. Why else is the artist forever talking about freedom. He needs freedom to move. And freedom assumes an order of diversity in art that bewilders even the artist.

But the relevant point is this: art is inherently revolutionary because of the change (not to mention the changes) it requires of the artist himself. And the nature of that change is transformation. It is also essentially personal rather than political. And by being personal it is therefore, at bottom, religious. Which takes us to Karenga's real objection to the blues.

"Our creative motif must be revolution; all art that does not discuss or contribute to revolutionary change is invalid. That is why the blues are invalid, they teach resignation, in a word, acceptance of reality—and we have come to change reality."

This is a very curious position to be backed into. It would surely relieve some of the absurdity if Karenga would only allow just enough individuality to justify accepting so personal an attitude as resignation. Then he wouldn't be forced into the even more untenable position of rejecting so major a part of the people's value system as the blues.

It would certainly behoove him to accept just enough reality to enable his objection to the blues to constitute a real objection. Shouldn't he accept just enough reality to come by some real alternatives to real resignation? But it would never do for a person determined not to accept reality to accept real standards with which to replace the one he really doesn't like.

But of course, Karenga hasn't "real" reality in mind, but simply a social one. That is to say he has only a real part instead of the real whole. So he can perhaps be forgiven.

Nor is it his fault that he rejects his people's past ways and past thinking. A Black nationalist can not escape assuming his people's sense of reality is unreal. How else could he reasonably define as his goal the establishment and the development of a culture for his people without first rejecting as mistaken the stubborn belief that Black people already have a culture, a tradition, of which both the Negro's speech and abundant musical expression are a definitive and irrefutable part?

It is instructive to remember that Karenga's views are no random affair. They are rigorously achieved and arrived at. They form inevitable parts of a system. That system being Black cultural nationalism.

We now come to the third and final element which forms his criteria for an art that would be revolutionary. In addition to being collective and functional, Black art must be "committing." This term turns out to be not a third element at all. Because to insist that art is to be revolutionary is simply another way of saying it is to be committed to revolution.

And knowing that art is to be collective, we can assume that commitment cannot be a matter of personal choice, since Black art is accountable to what is called the people and apparently under their control.

Any art, whether Black nationalist or not, which has the misfortune to be so collective as to allow for no individuality must be totally impersonal as well. And therefore a perfect paternalistic formula and framework for Black slavery and Black suicide.

And by way of conclusion, let us refocus on this element of paternalism, for it is the most characteristic and widespread feature to be found in the rhetoric of all sorts of spokesmen for Black revolution. Not only artists, renegade or otherwise, but the people too who get flattered and burdened with so much tyrannical power are treated in this manner. We all are. We all are looked upon and regarded by our so-called Black liberators as so many sheep.

There is a serious problem here, among these, our own revolutionaries. They seem to have a serious case of shepherd-complex. And it is a tragedy for a people such as we to have produced a generation of youth who seem, on the evidence, so utterly indifferent to what all the fuss has always been about; who no longer remember that revolution is aimed at freedom. Not control, not regimentation, not a mess of Afro-headed robots, but freedom.

And the Black artists who jump into such a constricting bag for the sake of unity have surely placed themselves in a

Black strait-jacket. And with their mouths wide open to swallow a Black man's cup of hemlock.

EMORY DOUGLAS

The drawings of Emory Douglas have appeared in numerous posters issued by the Black Panther Party and in the party's newspaper The Black Panther. *Emory Douglas is Minister of Culture of the Black Panther Party and statements by him on revolutionary art and on revolutionary culture have appeared in* The Black Panther *which has waged sharp polemics against Ron Karenga's philosophy of cultural nationalism. The following statement appeared in* The Black Panther *on a number of different occasions and is reprinted from that newspaper.*

On Revolutionary Culture

ALL POWER TO THE PEOPLE

We, Black people in Babylon, are fighting for liberation from political domination at the hands of the oppressor, from economic exploitation, and from a social system that degrades us as men and women. Out of this struggle comes a new way of life based on the politics of the people's struggle. This new way of life is a struggle for change, a revolutionary struggle involving the masses of people. Just as the liberation struggle brings about new politics, it also brings about a new culture, a revolutionary culture. Born out of the people's desire for change from a corrupt system to a system that serves the people, a system that is free from exploitation of man by man, and meets the desires and needs of the masses of people.

The old culture is a culture based on exploitation and competition whereas revolutionary culture is based on cooperation.

"Breakfast for Children, Free Health Clinics, and Liberation Schools," are just some of the programs implemented that are part of the revolutionary culture. These cultural programs will be carried out throughout the liberation struggle because our children have gone hungry and without proper medical care besides being given misinformation in school for too long at the hands of this oppressive system. Through the new culture, our children receive the nutrients that are needed to develop physically and mentally, so they can survive this corrupt system and build a new one that serves the people.

The cooperation on which the new culture is based is the masses of people working together in the interest of humanity, fighting off a decadent culture, replacing it with a culture that works in the interests of the people. Our new culture being based on the politics of the People's Party can only be implemented through many battles with the pigs of the power structure, the exploiters, since the new culture is free of exploitation. Therefore, self-defense becomes a part of the new culture, manifested in 357 Magnum, Machine Guns, M-15's, Hand Grenades, 12 Gauge Shotguns, and Browning Automatics because the people have accepted the reality of armed self-defense being the only way to liberation.

Also out of the struggle for liberation comes a new literature and art. Based on the people's struggle, this revolutionary art takes on new form. The revolutionary artist begins to arm his talent with steel, as well as learning the art of self-defense, becoming one with the people by going into their midst, not standing aloof, and going into the very thick of practical struggle.

This new born culture is not peculiar to the oppressed Black masses but transcends communities and racial lines because all oppressed people can relate to revolutionary change which is the starting point for developing a revolutionary culture.

SEIZE THE TIME!

JOHNETTA B. COLE

Dr. Johnetta B. Cole is a professor of anthropology and director of Black studies at Washington State University, Pullman. She was born in Jacksonville, Florida, received her B.A. at Oberlin College and her Ph.D. at Northwestern University. The following article is reprinted from The Black Scholar, *June, 1970.*

Culture: Negro, Black and Nigger

One of the many offshoots of the Black Liberation movement is an increased awareness of being black. Black Americans are turning attention to the complexities and glories of Afro-American history, probing the psychology of being black, and seeking the boundaries of black subculture. However, anthropological attention to black subculture remains sparse. When anthropologists, along with sociologists and psychologists, have turned specifically to the study of black subculture, their conclusions (and indeed the very selection of problems) are most often cast in terms of social and cultural pathology or psychological stress: the problem of matrifocality, the dirty dozens as an example of severe role conflict among males, alcoholism and crime in the ghetto.

This paper presents a very basic and exploratory statement on black subculture,

- suggesting components of that subculture,
- identifying soul and style as major expressions in black subculture, and
- describing several life styles.

The data for this paper are drawn from the meager literature, my current research among black university students, and the observations and insights which stem from my own black experience.

This discussion assumes the existence of a black subculture, an assumption held only recently by most scholars. Following the tradition established by E. Franklin Frazier, Charles S. Johnson, Robert Park, and others, the dominant opinion for many years was that the way of life of black folk is no more than an imitation, and a poor one at that, of the mainstream values and actions of white America. Discussions of this position inevitably begin with vivid descriptions of how black Americans were torn from the shores of their African home-land, stripped of their cultural heritage and processed through the severities of slavery. An alternative explanation, best exemplified in the works of Melville J. Herskovits, argues the retention of African cultural traits. Most anthropologists do not accept Herskovits' position, however, on grounds that he over-weighted the influence of Africanisms on Afro-American culture. Whereas we can document certain African retentions in music, folklore, and to some extent in religion, it is difficult and often impossible to establish the persistence of African traits in other areas of black subculture. Regard-less of the difficulty in establishing Africanisms, it is not therefore warranted to conclude that the subculture of black folks is simply a passive receptor for general American traits.

When a people share a learned set of values/attitudes and behavior patterns which are distinctive to them, they possess a culture; when the distinctive patterns are restricted to cer-tain areas, while other patterns are drawn from a mainstream pool, a people possess a subculture. In this sense, black Americans do form a subculture. The term which will be used to describe this way of life is "nigger culture," popular epithet for "Negro culture."

The subculture of black America has three sets of com-ponents: those drawn from mainstream America, those which are shared, in varying proportions, with all oppressed peoples, and those which appear to be peculiar to blacks. We might note a few examples of each. Black Americans share, with mainstream America, many traits of material culture (cars, house types, clothing); values (emphasis on technology and materialism) and behavior patterns (watching TV and voting in terms of interest groups).

Black Americans also share a number of cultural traits with all individuals who are oppressed—Catholics in Northern Ireland, Native Americans, Jews, Chinese Americans. One of these traits is what I call the "minority sense." When a Jew enters a room of gentiles, a Chicano a room of Anglos, a black a room of whites, there is a common reaction, namely, the minority member will attempt to sense out where there is severe hostility and bigotry. Minority subculture teaches that one must detect or at least attempt to detect hostile attitudes and behavior in the interest of self protection—from protection of one's pride and self-esteem to protection of one's life. All oppressed peoples also share degrees of what I call the "denial urge." This is the condemnation of one's status and by extension of one's *self*. It leads 200,000 Asian women each year to undergo operations to reduce the slant of their eyes, it leads Jews to have their noses bobbed, and blacks to suffer through bleaching creams and hair straighteners.

The last set of components of black American subculture, and the ones to which we turn special attention in this paper, are those which we can identify as the essence of blackness. Throughout the literature in anthropology, we do not identify bits of culture which are absolutely confined to a single people. It is in the combination of traits that we see the distinctiveness of a given people; it is in the subtleties associated with universal attributes, the emphasis on certain themes by which we define a people. Using these same requirements with respect to black America, it is suggested here that the consistent and important themes in black American life are soul and style. When blacks refer to "Nigger culture," they often very explicitly speak of soul and style: the way blacks get happy (possessed) in sanctified churches, that's soul; the movement of a black woman's hips when she dances, that's soul; the way a brother bops into a room, especially when he is clean (that is, dressed sharply), that's style; the way a black woman will speak of going to the beauty parlor to get her "kitchen touched up," that's in order to style; the way a young black man says, "I got to go take care of business," that's soul and style. We might focus in more closely on each of these themes.

There is probably no term which is more often used by black folks, and so seldom defined, as soul. By implication, blacks view it as the essence of "nigger culture," the one attribute which is possessed exclusively, or almost exclusively, by Afro-Americans. The explanation is not that it is a genetic phenomenon, but simply that being black in the United States teaches one how to live, feel, and express soul. Anthropologists have only rarely attempted to objectively define soul, and seldom have they recorded folk definitions. On the basis of the limited literature, my own involvement in black communities, and research, currently, among black students, I suggest that soul consists of at least the following three notions:

• One, soul is long suffering. It is the look of weariness on the faces of black folk, weariness with racism and poverty; it is the pathos in a black mother's cry of "Oh Lord, have mercy"; it is the constant presence of the blues. Black Americans cannot claim a monopoly on being long suffering. What is implied, however, is that the type of suffering, the "brand" of weariness which black folks have endured (largely because blacks are so highly and so systematically used as a source of power for white Americans), is what constitutes one part of soul.

• Soul, secondly, is deep emotion. It's the plea, often heard in black churches, "help me Jesus"; it is what a black man feels and expresses when he says, "I just ain't gonna take no more"; it's what James Brown and Aretha Franklin feel and instill in others. A variation on this notion of soul as deep emotion is found in most of the stereotypes which black Americans have of themselves; for blacks (no less than whites) feel that they are better dancers, singers and lovers than whites, because while white Americans perform these acts mechanically, blacks engage in them with deep emotion.

• Finally, soul is the ability to feel oneness with all black people. It is the knowing smile as two blacks, perfect strangers, exchange a glance in the middle of a crowded urban street; it is shucking "the man" (i.e., putting on a white person) while winking at an observing brother or sister; it is the way all black people are tied together because of shared experiences, like being called nigger. Soul then is the theme in black America which minimizes differences in class and political consciousness among Afro-Americans, for it is oneness.

The second major theme in black subculture is style, a theme no less difficult to define and no less important than soul. Style, to define again by example, is when a brother is wearing his gators (alligator shoes), fine vines (clothes), a slick do (process), in the old days, or an "uptight" natural today; style is having a heavy rap (verbal display), like the preacher, the young militant and the pimp (three strong and admired characters in black communities); style is driving an Eldorado; style is standing on a street corner looking cool, hip and ready; style is digging on Yusef Lateef rather than

Johnny Cash; style is the way a black man looks at a woman and says, "Come here with your bad self."

According to the students among whom I work, what constitutes style is the combination of ease and class; among black folks it is the ability to look rich when you are poor, the ability to appear loose when you're uncomfortable or tense; the ability to appear distinctive among many. Style, unlike soul, is not viewed as exclusively black (the students with whom I work say that Ché Guevera had style). Sitting Bull sure had style when he faced Custer and Peter Fonda had it in *Easy Rider*. However, there are clearly black versions of style. The male black students with whom I work feel that Fonda showed style on his chopper, but the black version of style must be in a car (a "hog"). Blackness is best expressed, they argue, when style combines with soul.

All black people, of course, do not express black subculture in the same way. Variation among the members of this subculture is often overlooked, however, in the anthropological literature. The data on black subculture is overwhelmingly that of the street life style—smoking dope, pimping, hustling, and rapping. We have yet to record the variety in the life styles of black people. Again, this paper can only be suggestive, resting on the meager literature, my own limited research, and my personal experiences. Four life styles in nigger culture are the street, down-home, militant and upward bound. Obviously, these are not suggested as rigidly defined and exclusive life styles. Black folk, like any folk, do not live in categories.

The street life style is the cool world, centering around hustling. It is basically the urban world of American blacks. It is here that we see the greatest development of stylized talking, sounding, signifying, shucking and jiving, copping a plea and whupping game (Kochman). This is the world which is best described in the "ethnographies" written by black folk themselves: *The Autobiography of Malcolm X*, *Manchild in the Promised Land* (Claude Brown), *Pimp, the Story of My Life* (Iceberg Slim), *His Eye is on the Sparrow* (Ethel Waters). This is the world of severe poverty for many, hopelessness for most, cool for a few. This life style can be described in many ways, but here I choose to use the medium of a short story from the *Liberator* magazine.

While sitting round in back of the drugstore having our usual taste of Molly Pitcher dark port, our most pleasant conversation was bodily interrupted by the noisy, yelling, arm-waving approach of Little Willie upon the scene. His eyes were mere slits, heavily weighted down by the mellow smoke —light green marijuana. Having the jug in hand and clearly in the sight of Willie, I expected the first four words out of his mouth to be, "Save me the corner," but instead he pleasantly surprised me by screaming, "Big Time is in the poolroom, baby!" Big Time, the magic name that made every young potential pimp, hustler, gamer, mack man, booster or player tremble with excitement, for he represented all the things that they hoped to imitate or possibly even emulate someday. Big Time was it. He was *in* baby—really what was happening. All you had to do was name it and have the proper amount of collateral and Big Time would score for you, or turn you on to someone in the position to do so. He was sharp, cool, untouchable. To quote Brother Cassius, he was "the greatest." Sharp? This man was really sharp. From his nylon underwear to his two hundred dollar imported mohair suit. Cool? No one ever heard him speak above a whisper. Always calm. Never, I mean never in a hurry. Slow and steady. Always seeming to know his next move in advance. Untouchable? He was always a mile further ahead, a pound heavier or a foot taller than anyone he associated with. Like on a pedestal, but always in touch spiritually, you dig?

Down-home life style is the traditional way of black folks. It is basically rural and southern. It centers in the kitchens of black homes, in the church halls for suppers, in the fraternal orders. "Down-home" is a common expression among black Americans, indicating one's point of origin, down south, or the simple, decent way of life. Let me characterize this life style by reading excerpts from the journal of a student, Pamela Smith, in my anthropology/black studies course. She wrote of her first visit south and she entitled it, "Down-home."

The street my grandparents lived on was unpaved, because they lived in the black section of town. The house was kind of shabby but gave off some type of radiant warmth. What really appealed to me was the porch. It had a swing and rocking chair. I found the porch was one of the main facets of the house. If any company came over, it seemed that most of the entertaining was done on the porch. Especially in the evening, the family would gather on the porch to get what little relief they could from the heat . . .

Breakfast at my grandmother's was comparatively big but couldn't compare to what cousin Rosa cooked. My cousin Rosa would start breakfast very early, one usually ate around six-thirty in her home. She would have fresh eggs, homemade biscuits, bacon and ham from their smoke house, homemade applesauce, grits, beans, pork chops, sometimes fish, all sorts of homemade jams, fresh milk, and potato fritters. God, one could hardly move after breakfast. It was puzzling to me why my grandmother didn't have such an enormous breakfast. I found that the reason was cousin Rosa's family worked in the fields and needed a heavy meal to sustain them until lunch . . .

I thought that going to church once a Sunday was enough but my grandma informed me that we were going to get "religion" (we were Catholics and so after mass) . . . we went to the Baptist church . . . After preaching the minister informed the congregation that next Sunday there was to be a dinner in the church to help raise money, and that any women willing to help were to stay after service . . .

Another thing one did not do while down home was to call an elderly lady by her last name. I remember the lady across the street was a Mrs. Brown and I would constantly call her this until one kid confronted me and said "ain't you got any culture, her name is Miss Ann." And naturally I wanted culture so I called her Miss Ann.

The militant life style is the political world, centered today on college campuses, in high school Black Student Unions and in the urban black ghettos. This is the life style of the cultural and revolutionary nationalists—of LeRoi Jones, Ron Karenga, Robert Williams, Eldridge Cleaver and Bobby Seale. Although this life style appears to be new, a product of the 1960's, there have been American blacks of this life style since black folks came to the new world. Gabriel, Denmark Vesey, Nat Turner, Marcus Garvey, Frederick Douglass, are but the most famous of the early militants. This life style is infused with the urgency of changing the plight of black folks; it is the constant search for relief from oppression. To offer only a taste of the fervor of this life style, let me read the opening passage of a speech which Bobby Seale delivered in 1968. The speech was entitled, "Free Huey."

Brothers and Sisters, tonight I want to have the chance to tell you in large mass something about Brother Huey P. Newton; a black man who first introduced me to what black nationalism was all about; a black man that I've been closely associated with for the last three years in the organizing of a black people's party on a level that dealt with black people's problems. To explain to you who Brother Huey P. Newton is in his soul, I've got to explain to you also your soul, your needs, your political desires and needs, because that is Huey's soul . . .

Now look, the Black Panther Party is a revolutionary party. Revolution means that we got to get down to the nitty gritty and change this situation that we're in and don't miss any nits or any grits—that's very very important. (We've got to work at it.) All the time.

Up-ward bound life style is the life style which E. Franklin Frazier characterized in his book, *Black Bourgeoisie*. It is the way that many blacks call high giddy or bourgy. It centers in the "better neighborhoods," in the so-called integrated churches and clubs. It is the way of the black middle class, the teachers, accountants, and other professionals who are trying to move on up. This life style has never been captured more pointedly than in the ironic tone of LeRoi Jones' poem, entitled, *Black Bourgeoisie:*

> has a gold tooth, sits long hours
> on a stool, thinking about money.
> sees white skin in a secret room
> rummages his senses for sense
> dreams about Lincoln(s)
> conks his daughter's hair
> sends his coon to school
> works very hard
> grins politely in restaurants
> has a good word to say
> never says it
> does not hate ofays
> hates, instead, himself
> him black self.

In this exploratory paper, we have looked at some of the dimensions of nigger American culture. We can reach but one conclusion from the very tentative data presented on the components of black subculture, the expressions of soul and style and the variation in life styles. That conclusion is that we need an anthropology of black subculture. Or, to put it in the idiom, when it comes to nigger culture, somebody ain't been takin' care of business.

DARWIN T. TURNER (1931–   )

Educator, poet, critic, and editor, Darwin T. Turner has published numerous critical articles and studies, a volume of poetry, three anthologies of Black American writing, a bibliography of Afro-American writers, and coedited a volume of source materials for college research papers on Images of the Negro in American Literature. *Born and educated in Cincinnati, Ohio, Professor Turner taught in Negro colleges in the South, was president of the College Language Association, served as dean of the Graduate School at North Carolina Agricultural and Technical State University (Greensboro), and is currently professor of English at the University of Michigan. He is chairman of the Committee on Literature of Minority Groups of the National Council of Teachers of English. The following article is reprinted from* College English, *April, 1970.*

The Teaching of Afro-American Literature

Although Afro-Americans have been writing literature in English since 1746 and publishing books in English since 1773, literature by Afro-Americans has become significantly visible in colleges only within the past two years. Three years ago, most of the relevant materials were out of print, including the only anthology adequate for a course in Afro-American literature; few, if any, non-black colleges offered courses in Afro-American literature or even studied Afro-American writers, except possibly Richard Wright, James Baldwin, and Ralph Ellison; and scholarly societies and publishers seemed disinterested in studies about black writers. Today, three major anthologies of Afro-American literature are already in print, and two more are on the way; at least six publishers—Arno, Atheneum, Negro Universities Press, Mnemosyne Press, the U of Michigan and Collier are frantically reprinting books by and about black writers; courses are burgeoning in predominantly white universities, even in Alabama and Mississippi; and almost any meeting of a professional society in literature will include at least one paper related to Afro-American writers. In truth, the frenzy of attention has elevated Afro-American literature (and Afro-American studies) to a pinnacle recently occupied by atomic physics and new mathematics: It is the exciting new concern of the educational world.

I do not propose to discuss here the nature and scope of Afro-American literature itself. Instead, I wish to consider two controversial issues: 1) the place of Afro-American literature in the curriculum, and 2) criteria for teachers and scholars of Afro-American literature.

I will not spend a lot of time endorsing the academic value of Afro-American literature. Already too much time and breath have been wasted on this issue. Those of us who have sat in meetings of curriculum committees know how seldom the members question the academic value of a proposed course. The committee's most frequent worry is, "How much will it cost?" We also know that some institutions entice a professor to them by guaranteeing that he can "work up" any course he wishes to teach—even one narrowly restricted to a study of Washington Irving, Edgar Allan Poe, and James Fenimore Cooper. Few institutions of prestige question the intellectual content of such courses. (Probably they should; but most do not.)

In a discipline which thus continually reaffirms its assumption that any segment of literary heritage is intellectually valid for study in higher education, it is both absurd and hypocritical to raise the question of academic respectability about the study of the literature of an ethnic group composed of people who have been publishing literary works in America for more than 200 years, who have created some of the best-known folktales in America, and who include among their number such distinguished writers as Jean Toomer, Countee Cullen, Richard Wright, Gwendolyn Brooks, Ralph Ellison, James Baldwin, Lorraine Hansberry, and LeRoi Jones. If anyone has doubts about the respectability of this literature, I urge him merely to read Frederick Douglass's *Narrative of a Slave* or Charles W. Chestnutt's *The Conjure Woman* or Jean Toomer's *Cane* or Robert Hayden's *Selected*

Poems or Melvin Tolson's *Rendezvous with America* or *Harlem Gallery* or Margaret Walker's *Jubilee.*

A more significant question to ask is whether these writers should be studied in a separate course or as part of the usual surveys and period courses in American literature. My answer is that they should be studied in both ways.

There is no difficulty about including Afro-American writers in any American literature survey based on aesthetic and thematic criteria. Phillis Wheatley is sometimes praised as the best American neo-classical poet of the 18th century. David Walker's *Appeal* (1828) is as exciting a document as any by Tom Paine. The slave narratives offer interesting parallels with the autobiographies of early white Americans. Any course which wades through James Whitcomb Riley, Thomas Page, and other writers of American dialects can scrutinize Paul Laurence Dunbar. The folktales of Charles Chestnutt furnish intriguing counter-point to the better known tales of Joel Chandler Harris. James Weldon Johnson's *Autobiography of an Ex-Colored Man* (1912) compares favorably with the realistic novels of William Dean Howells. Claude McKay's *Home to Harlem* (1928) vividly depicts a segment of that jazzy, lost generation which found other biographers in Ernest Hemingway and Scott Fitzgerald. In spirit and style Countee Cullen frequently reminds readers of Edna St. Vincent Millay, and Jean Toomer is a logical inclusion in a discussion of the stylistic experiments of Sherwood Anderson and Gertrude Stein. Zora Neale Hurston's *Moses, Man of the Mountain* resembles and perhaps surpasses John Erskine's satires about Helen of Troy and Galahad. And on and on and on. Certainly, if he wishes to, a knowledgeable teacher has no problem fitting Afro-American writers into an American literature survey; for stylistically, black writers often resemble white American authors more closely than they resemble their black contemporaries.

But, for a different reason, Afro-American authors should also be taught in a separate course—not a black "rap" course for revolutionaries, not a watered-down "sop" designed to give three credits to the disadvantaged, but an academically sound course, which may be even more valuable for white students than for black. The reason for such a course is educational or—if you wish—political. Before protesting that our concern is artistic literature not politics, let us remind ourselves that college teachers do teach those documents at the beginnings of most anthologies of American literature—the writings of John Smith and Cotton Mather, the Mayflower

Compact, etc. Let us remember also the courses in New England Writers and Southern Regional Writers. The documents provide a student with awareness of the intellectual and social history of America; the regional courses help him to understand the styles and attitudes of writers who represent a selected population in America. For similar reasons, courses in literature by Afro-American writers must be taught.

As we all know, in a two-term survey of American literature we cannot include all the writers who deserve to be taught: some worthy writers must be omitted. A concerned teacher consoles himself that a student's intellectual growth is not seriously impaired by lack of knowledge of the writers omitted; for, at some point between the first grade and the sixteenth, a student will probably read most of the writers omitted from the survey. Or if he does not read those specific writers, he reads others who offer comparable styles and attitudes: Bret Harte or Mark Twain rather than Riley, Stephen Crane or Edith Wharton rather than Howells, Ernest Hemingway or Edgar Lee Masters rather than Gertrude Stein. Thus, a student learns that literary excellence can be discovered in all regions of America and in all periods of American history. If no writer is included who can be identified as Hungarian or Italian or Polish, neither the teacher nor the student is alarmed; for, in other courses, the student has already learned that intellectual and artistic masterpieces have been produced in all of the countries of Europe.

One cannot, however, regard with such complacency the omission of Afro-American writers from the survey; for, in sixteen years of schooling, a student will probably never read these writers in any other course except a course about Afro-American writers. As I have stated, the reason for concern is not merely an aesthetic issue of whether a student may miss an opportunity for pleasure or art that a black writer may provide. Even more important is the fact that the student lives in a society which, for more than three hundred years, has denigrated the intellectual and cultural capability of black Africans and their descendants. The student has been taught this doctrine of inferiority in books and lectures prepared by respectable professors, in newspapers and magazines, in motion pictures and theater, and even in the church and his home. The only way to repudiate this myth of inferiority is to amass as much evidence to the contrary as possible. But the evidence cannot rest upon two or three black writers since 1940 or 1950: Richard Wright, James Baldwin, and Ralph Ellison, for example. Too easily these few are adjudged the exceptions or are used to exemplify a second myth—that Afro-Americans have developed respectable culture only within the past twenty-five years. The requisite education must study *many* black writers from the eighteenth century to the present —not in a chauvinistic glorification of their effort but in a critical examination of their literary and intellectual merits in relation to the standards, customs, interest, and knowledge which characterized the periods during which they wrote.

A second controversial issue concerns the criteria for selecting a teacher. Conventionally, a teacher's competence to offer a course is determined from evidence of his study and publication in the area. But a serious question has been raised about the competence of a white teacher to teach literature by black writers. Few people of academic background deny that white teachers can learn to teach black literature, just as black teachers can teach white literature. And they realize that, if all colleges were to establish courses in Afro-American literature, the number of courses alone would necessitate the use of white teachers. Nevertheless, many black educators continue to worry that some white teachers will teach the course so badly that they will create more harm than good. Frequently, a black teacher who makes such a statement is accused of racist thinking. Perhaps the accusers are remembering with guilt the fact that, until recently, most white administrators and faculties made little effort to hire qualified black scholars to teach courses in English and American literature. But the black who objects to white teachers is not merely prejudiced; he sees weaknesses which the white teacher must overcome if he wishes to teach Afro-American literature well.

First, some white teachers will teach the course badly because, ignorant of the complexity of the subject matter, they will not take the time to prepare themselves adequately. In the English departments of most universities, a teacher is entrusted with the responsibility for an advanced course, such as one in American Romantics or Victorian Prose, only after years of preparation. In several years of college, he studies the works, critical commentaries about the works, the lives of the authors, and the historical culture in which the works were produced. He not only listens to lectures and reads assigned works; he even conducts independent research in the materials. After such preparation, he is finally permitted to teach a traditional course. In contrast, a teacher may be thrust into a course in Afro-American literature after formal preparation of a summer or even less.

Furthermore, the average white teacher is handicapped by the fact that he has not had the informal or extra-disciplinary experiences which might familiarize him with the material. Consider, in contrast, the manner in which the black teacher of American literature, let us say, is provided, outside the English classroom, with awareness of the materials about which white Americans are writing. He has been forced to read many, many books of history about white Americans; he cannot read a newspaper or magazine without reading factual as well as propagandistic articles about their attitudes, desires, virtues, vices, and living habits. He sees them advertised on the motion picture screen, on television, on billboards. In short, wherever he turns—even within the black community—he is learning about white Americans. The average *white* American, however, has probably known few black people intimately, has read few books by black writers, and until recently has read few presentations about black Americans (and those few have concentrated on the "problem" which the black man poses for America or for himself). Putting it simply, the average white teacher is ignorant about black people and does not even know where to turn for reliable information about such basic matters as the meanings of slang used by blacks, the traditional jokes, and the popular stereotypes of heroes and villains. This individual will teach Afro-American literature ineptly until he learns what he needs to know.

A second failing of the well-intentioned teacher is that, subconsciously, he may be a racist. That is, subconsciously, he may believe that black people actually are innately inferior or that historically they have been made inferior by society. This attitude may cause him to bungle the course in either of two different ways. One, believing that a black writer cannot produce literary work of a quality which would be required of a white writer, the teacher may praise trash because he does not expect anything better from a black writer. Such unconscious patronizing insults black writers. Or, two, a well-meaning humanitarian may become paternalistic. Believing himself securely established in American society and, therefore, superior in judgment to those who are not, he may condemn the philosophy of life which the black author proposes for himself. A teacher has the right to assert that any writer —black or white—has failed to clarify his ideas or has failed to develop them effectively, but only a pompous paternalist will insist that he is better qualified than the writer to determine what the writer should have thought about himself, his race, and his relation to other people. I wish that I were exaggerating these failings, but one sees them too frequently in articles currently published about Afro-American literature.

A third well-intentioned teacher who fails is the one who becomes excessively sentimental about the problems which black people experience in a white-oriented society. Such a teacher may wail about the problems in a frenzy which sickens black students who have learned that tears offer escape not solutions.

These three types of teachers—the unprepared, the subconscious racist, the sentimentalist—can be pitied for their failure. A fourth cannot be. He is the individual who views Afro-American literature as a vehicle for rapid promotion. He is the "instant expert," striving solely for grants and publications.

A final problem for the white teacher is not directly of his own making. Even if he *has* prepared conscientiously, black students may distrust him because their years of living in America have taught them to distrust white men's attitudes towards black culture. They will be looking for the teacher who makes the mistake, if he selects autobiography, of choosing *Manchild in the Promised Land* rather than *The Autobiography of Malcolm X*. They will be waiting for the teacher who does not understand the slang of the black community. In short, they will be looking for the racist or the fool hidden behind a mask. And a lot of valuable course time can be lost while the teacher proves himself to his students.

The white teacher of Afro-American literature must recognize and anticipate these problems and potential failings. But do not let my castigation of white teachers promote false assumptions about the ability of blacks. A black or brown face is not in itself sufficient qualification for teaching Afro-American literature. True, a black man is generally more sensitive to the language, attitudes, and nuances of the black writer; he has the informal, extra-disciplinary knowledge of the subject matter of the writers. But he too must study sufficiently to know Afro-American literature in its historical development, and he must be competent to teach literature.

Literature by Afro-Americans is a new, exciting subject matter for curricula. It needs to be taught, but only by teachers—black or white—who do all the homework which is required.

LANCE JEFFERS (1919–   )

A biographical note on Lance Jeffers appears in the poetry section (see p. 264). The following article is published from manuscript, revised by the author from an earlier version printed in The Black Scholar, *January, 1971.*

Afroamerican Literature: The Conscience of Man

The literature of an oppressed people is the conscience of man, and nowhere is this seen with more intense clarity than in the literature of Afroamerica. An essential element of Afroamerican literature is that the literature as a whole—not the work of occasional authors—is a movement against concrete wickedness. And in Afroamerican literature, accordingly, there is a grief rarely to be found elsewhere in American literature, and frequently a rage rarely to be found in American letters: a rage different in quality, profounder, more towering, more intense—the rage of the oppressed. Whenever an Afroamerican artist picks up pen or horn, his target is likely to be American racism, his subject the suffering of his people, and the core element his own grief and the grief of his people. Almost all of Afroamerican literature carries the burden of this protest, like the virile old masterwork—

> When Israel was in Egypt-land—
> Let my people go.
> Oppressed so hard they could not stand—
> Let my people go.
> Go down, Moses,
> Way down in Egypt-land,

Tell ol' Pharaoh:
Let my people go!

But like "Go Down, Moses" and another old spiritual, Afroamerican literature goes far beyond the protest against injustice and the cry for a people's freedom—

Dis train bound fo Glory
Dis train, Oh Hallelujah
Dis train bound fo Glory
Dis train, Oh Hallelujah
Dis train bound for Glory
Ef yuh ride no need for fret or worry . . .

Dis train don carry no gambler
No fo day creeper or midnight rambler
Dis train, Oh Hallelujah . . .

The cry for freedom and the protest against injustice are a cry for the birth of the New Man, a testament to the New Unknown World (glory) to be discovered, to be created by man. Afroamerican literature is, as a body, a declaration that despite the perversion and sadism that cling like swamproots to the flesh of man's feet, man has unforeclosed options for freedom, for cleanliness, for wholeness, for human harmony, for goodness: for a human world. Like the spirituals that are a part of it, Afroamerican literature is a passionate assertion that man will win freedom. Thus, Afroamerican literature rejects despair and cynicism; it is a literature of realistic hope and life-affirmation. This is not to say that no Afroamerican literary work reflects cynicism or despair, but rather that the basic theme of Afroamerican literature is that man's goodness will prevail.

Afroamerican literature is a statement against death, a statement as to what life should be: life should be vivacious, exuberant, wholesomely uninhibited, sensual, sensuous, constructively antirespectable, life should abound and flourish and laugh, life should be passionately lived and man should be loving: life should be not a sedate waltz or foxtrot but a vigorous Boogaloo; thus when the Afroamerican writer criticizes America for its cruelty, the criticism implies that America is drawn to death and repelled by what should be the human style of life, the human way of living.

Black literature in America is, then, a setting-forth of man's identity and destiny; an investigation of man's iniquity and a statement of belief in his potential godliness; a prodding of man toward exploring and finding deep joy in his humanity.

Paul Lawrence Dunbar's "A Negro Love Song" is an example of the latter: the black Southern-rustic 19th Century lover plunges deeply into the ecstasy of his experience: even in relating it to a listener, he literally jumps back and laughs exuberantly—

> Put my ahm aroun' huh wais',
> Jump back, honey, jump back.
> Raised huh lips an' took a tase,
> Jump back, honey, jump back.
> Love me, honey, love me true?
> Love me well ez I love you?
> An' she answe'd, " 'Cose I do"—
> Jump back, honey, jump back.

We can leap forward in time and find the same exuberant black celebration of life in Sterling Brown's magnificent folk poetry of the 30's; for example—"Southern Road," "The Ballad of Joe Meek," "Slim in Hell"; in Langston Hughes' fiction of the late 20's and 30's: *Not Without Laughter* and *The Ways of White Folks,* and in his innumerable stories of Simple in *Simple Speaks His Mind, Simple Takes a Wife,* and *Simple Stakes a Claim;* and in Ralph Ellison's stories and in his *Invisible Man:* for example, the black farmer in "Flying Home" telling a rich and comical story to the broken-winged black pilot who had come down in an Alabama field, and, in *Invisible Man,* the episode at the Golden Day: the black author prescribing laughter and exuberance of living as the wiser style of life, the more abundant, unbegrudging, and fearless way of living.

Richard Wright's *Native Son,* then, is in its grimness a chronicle of the destruction of joy in the urban hell, and a prophecy of how man, destroyed, will recreate himself and conquer. The protagonist Bigger Thomas is hostile, evil-tempered, sinister, without kindness; borne down and mutilated by the racism of the ghetto North—*Native Son* explicitly condemns the American colonization of the black man in the North—Bigger nevertheless conquers his stuntedness; in prison he grows beyond his moral blindness and crippled feelings; he becomes a superior human being: he understands himself and he accepts himself—both his old self and his new transcendant self; he accepts both of these with the equanimity with which he accepts death; aware, conscious, and fearless, he is a giant, the reborn man, the precursor of the New man.

In Wright's story "Big Boy Leaves Home," man rises above

the perversion that oppresses him to force his unforeclosed option: he symbolically destroys oppression (in the killing of the soldier) and he escapes to the North; but symbolically it is Everyman's "North," not merely Big Boy's, not merely the Southern black man's vision of a "utopia" which he supposed would offer him greater freedom than Mississippi; it is a place where, symbolically, oppression and human sickness no longer exist; "Dis train is bound fo Glory," the four boys sing in "Big Boy Leaves Home" when they hear the train in the distance, "bound fer up Noth." "Glory" is the heaven that, in the eyes of the black author, man has it within his capacity to create. And Big Boy, who is man, is strong enough, resourceful enough, to seize that heaven within his hands despite terrific opposition.

Wright has depicted in "Big Boy leaves Home" the hell that man has created on earth: and the hell is not only the physical oppression of the black man but the mental disease of the white man: the white woman in the swimming hole episode is terrified of four naked black male adolescents who are as terrified of her as she of them—but only their fear is authentic; hers is self-deception. There is profound symbolic significance in the fact that her paranoia brings death to innocent children; the naked black form represents not only her repressed sensuality of which she stands in terror, but also the spiritual growth that frightens her: the possibility that a new world and a new vision of life and a new set of values, valid and different from her own, might force her to grow. Her husband, sharing her paranoia, more stunted by far and far more dangerous than the unrealized Bigger, shoots down two of the boys and is in turn killed; two boys—Bobo and Big Boy—escape, Bobo temporarily, for he is captured by the mob and burned to death.

There is in all of literature no more passionate denunciation of human cruelty than in Wright's description of the burning of Bobo: the burning of the boy who, a few hours before, had been innocently singing vigorous songs of male coarseness and the spiritual that expresses man's longing for freedom and fulfillment:

> Dis train bound fo Glory
> Dis train, Oh Hallelujah . . .

Wright implicitly probes to the meaning behind the external lynching: the burning of Bobo, he implies, stems from a hatred of life itself; the lynchers' hatred of the black man stems from a rejection of the exuberance and sensuosity and richness of life which the black man represents; significantly, the first part of the story is a celebration of life: black boys in the fullness of their adolescence finding enormous delight in life.

In Wright's "Bright and Morning Star," political workers black and white work for social justice in a repressive Southern area; the black man is captured by white defenders of the status quo; he is horribly tortured in his mother's presence in an attempt to force him and his mother to inform; surrounded by armed and hostile whites, she guns down the white informer who had arranged her son's capture, and then she and her son are killed, still unyielding. Man—on the one hand perverse and sadistic, inhuman, conscienceless; on the other hand, the symbol of goodness and strength and potentialities realized. The mother and the son, defying the Southern code, are symbols of the New Man, the New and Unknown World.

In the writing of the Afroamerican author, the blacks attempt often to gain freedom while the whites are often determined not to grant it, and, more significantly, usually determined not to grow, not to see the New Man buried within them. Consciously or unconsciously the black novelist and story-teller and poet see this struggle between good and evil, between God and the Devil, between white and black as the ancient human struggle between the past and the future, between that element in human nature that holds on to the primitive and the superstitious and the inherited and the oppressive, and, on the other hand, that prophetic element in man which seeks to bring to birth the New. Black authors see in this struggle between blacks and whites a struggle between those who wish to perpetuate the Traditional Man and those who wish to bring to birth the New Man.

Indeed, this symbolism of the birth of the New emerges in Langston Hughes' "Cora Unashamed" into a literal struggle which centers about the birth of a child. Cora is a maid for a white family in a small Midwestern town. As a reflection of the neurotic compulsive drive for false status in the town, the family reject their dull daughter and she becomes, emotionally, the daughter of the warm and accepting black maid, Cora. The daughter becomes pregnant in adolescence; she is hustled off to a city for an abortion. After her return, she dies as a result, and, at the funeral, in a display of righteous rage, Cora reveals the truth and condemns the family. She leaves the family's service, for she has lost her child; she has also lost her battle with wickedness; her benign influence, in a crucial test, has been defeated.

But her defeat is not decisive in the framework of the prophetic fervor of the black author, for he is essentially the saviour, the prophet, the obstetrician who presides at the birth of the New Man. Cora foolishly assumed that the family's attitude toward an illegitimate pregnancy would be as humane and broadminded as her own; had she shrewdly managed affairs without informing the family, she might have brought to birth, symbolically, the New Man. Nevertheless, for the black author, the outcome of the war, not the outcome of a skirmish, is crucial—Cora and Simple, in Hughes' vision, will in the long run prevail and bring to birth the New.

Blackness, the black author says, despite his antiracism and despite his belief in the potentialities of man, blackness must not disappear, for it is the counterweight to oppression and stagnation, it is the voice of the future, the black author implies, the instrument of parturition, the element necessary to the birth of the New Man, the New World. Blackness is, moreover, the black man's identity: to give up his blackness would be to castrate his Self. It is noteworthy that in the work of black authors who are integrationists a tacitly separatist or ethnically independent element appears frequently—subtly, like smoke; solidly, like rock.

Therefore, although Cora is defeated in the Hughes story, it is clearly her blackness—her breadth and strength, her humanity—that must bring to birth the New. And although in her story the birth of the New is aborted, the power and perseverance of blackness and the necessity for the existence of blackness are asserted. She leaves the family, not only because she has been defeated, but because to remain would be to destroy her blackness by yielding to the immorality of the family.

The rich white man in Hughes' "A good Job Gone" finds his white mistresses infinitely less attractive than the black mistress upon whom he finally settles; it is not her sexuality that is decisive but the vitality and the character that gives strength to her sexuality, and that vitality and strength find their source in her blackness—in other words, the unique character-formation that has been created by the black man's response to oppression. When the white man discovers that she has a black boy friend, he demands that she cut her ties with the black man. But the black woman literally kicks the white man aside, and he collapses mentally. Hughes implies that the black man must hold on to his racial identity, his racial pride, in order to survive.

Hughes also implies in this story, as in "Cora Unashamed" and as Baldwin has in numerous essays, that white America must recreate its identity in order to survive.

In *Dutchman*, LeRoi Jones (Amiri Baraka) very boldly suggests that black people must hold on to blackness in order to survive; if they do not, he says, they will be destroyed psychologically, perhaps physically. Again the question, on its deepest level, is a question of identity; one endangers one's very life, Baraka says, if one does not accept oneself for what he is; and when one accepts others' versions of oneself, their principles, their criteria (as against one's own wholesome principles and criteria), one commits suicide.

The central character, the "Dutchman," is, like the legendary sailor, homeportless, directionless, without identity; he eagerly accepts the blandishments of a sinister young white woman; he has so completely accepted the white criteria of how to live that he has crippled his perceptions and is blind to the woman's danger. The woman is Death, the symbol of white America, and the "Dutchman's" whole chemistry, in the wake of his having forsaken his black identity, is death-oriented; to be attracted to her, to Death, is suicide. He is so identity-less that only the woman's most extreme insolence rouses, too late, his latent blackness; even then, he is disarmed to her real danger, and she murders him. To be without identity, Baraka says, is to be powerless and suicidal.

Baraka's meaning is clear on several levels. There is the question not only of identity but of dignity, and they are synonymous. In permitting himself to be flattered by the woman's attentions, Baraka says, the "Dutchman" (whose name, significantly, is Clay) has lost his identity, his dignity, has unconsciously accepted the idea that he has less worth than whites. There is the question, finally, of the realization of man's potentialities: the birth of the New Man and the creation of the New World cannot be brought about by men who do not know who they are, who have implicit contempt for their human worth.

In the novel *Autobiography of an Ex-Colored Man*, James Weldon Johnson approaches the question of identity and blackness from a philosophical stance that bears certain strong resemblances to that of Amiri Baraka. Johnson was an integrationist, as indicated by his long leadership in NAACP affairs. Yet he states in the novel that to give up one's ethnic identity, one's blackness, is to disappear as a human being, to lose the humanness that gives one dignity, stature, pride; one loses one's soul if he gives up his identity.

He goes further: he implies not only that it is noble for the oppressed to struggle against oppression, but also that simply enduring oppression bestows nobility on the oppressed, and that to forsake the identity of this nobility is a form of death. Thus, his protagonist, a white-skinned Negro who decides to leave the black race, contemplates at novel's end that he has "sold my birthright for a mess of pottage." His birthright was the nobility of his black heritage, and the nobility that the endurance of oppression bestows.

The black author, then, through his consideration of the questions What is man? and What should man be? and What is man's destiny?—seen from the vantage point of the identity of blackness—raises and answers basic questions on the deepest level of human identity.

ISHMAEL REED (1938–   )

A note on Ishmael Reed appears in the poetry section (see p. 329). The following critical statement by Ishmael Reed, embodying his views on Afro-American literature, appears as the introduction to 19 Necromancers from Now *(1970), an anthology edited by him and published by Doubleday. It is reproduced in its entirety.*

19 Necromancers From Now
Introduction

According to ancient legend the white race results from a nuclear explosion in what is now the Gobi desert some 30,000 years ago. The civilization and techniques which made the explosion possible were wiped out. The only survivors were slaves marginal to the area who had no knowledge of its science or techniques. They became albinos as a result of radiation and scattered in different directions. Some of them went into Persia, northern India, Greece and Turkey. Others moved westward and settled in the caves of Europe. The descendants of the cave dwelling albinos are the present inhabitants of America and Western Europe.

The above is an excerpt from a "story" which appeared in the *Village Voice* on September 12, 1968. It goes on to recount the atrocities committed by the "cave dwelling albinos" and to describe them as "a hideous threat to life on this planet." The story was no narrative of the myth of Yacub, nor was it written by an author who ducked the pigfire in Watts of 1964.

The author of *Astronauts Return* is none other than William Burroughs, a White writer whose grandfather invented the adding machine. This demonstrates the difficulty you encounter when talking of "Black writing," the "Black Aesthetic," or the "Black Experience."

The matter is further complicated when a young "militant" Black poet names a color in a story after a White impressionist painter (Soutine), or another Black writer congratulates a "militant" colleague's outstanding oratory as "Churchillian splendor."

The fact remains that the history of literature is replete with examples of writers not being what their writing represents them to be. In the Western nineteenth-century literature women used male pseudonyms because at the time a female who wrote was considered just a step above the common whore. The category of print is not a racial or sexual category —and when one is reading print; decoding someone else's experience or non-experience, fairy tales, science fiction, fantasy, etc., the author may be a thousand miles away or dead.

In 1967 I went to Berkeley, California, for the purpose of writing a Western. A counselor at Merritt College heard that I was in town and invited me to teach a course in Afro-American literature, but when I told him I could not in good conscience twist the works of Ralph Ellison and Richard Wright to accommodate a viewpoint he at the time believed irresistible, the bureaucrat told me that the job was unavailable.

This counselor, like many people, views Afro-American

culture as something to be exploited for the pursuit of certain political ends. Students who would never think of turning a seminar on Melville into a political rally would not hesitate to dictate to a Black instructor what emphasis should be made, or what works should be covered, in his course. Their unconscious racism is sometimes just as rigid as that of their elders. After all, in this country art is what White people do. All other people are "propagandists." One can see this in the methodology used by certain White and Black critics in investigating Black literature. Form, Technique, Symbology, Imagery are rarely investigated with the same care as Argument, and even here, the Argument must be one that appeals to the critics' prejudices. Novels that don't have the right "message" are cast aside as "pretentious," for it is assumed that the native who goes the way of art is "uppity." He loses his seat in Congress, or is dethroned as Heavyweight Champion of the World.

After my experience with the counselor at Merritt College, I was invited to do a course at the University of California at Berkeley.

Originally, the position of the English Department was that there was no need for a course in Afro-American literature, since no literature had appeared until after World War II—a statement that could be rendered foolish even upon cursory examination. This view, I must say, was not shared by the Department Chairman, James D. Hart, compiler and editor of *The Oxford Companion to American Literature*, who, although Afro-American literature was not his field, solicited materials on the subject, and is now able to hold his own in a discussion with any student of the field. But there were those on the faculty who held this opinion. They confused a fanatical defense of Western religion with "education," just as their counterparts in the critical field confuse this defense with "reviews."

I was to learn that White authors, as well as Afro-American authors, are neglected by the American university. Before I arrived at Berkeley, there was no room in the curriculum for detective novels or Western fiction, even though some of the best contributions to American literature occur in these genres. At another major university, the library did not carry books by William Burroughs, who at least manages to get it up beyond the common, simple, routine narrative that critics become so thrilled about.

I found that some of the students who didn't understand

the language of Chester Himes or Charles Wright were equally at a loss when it came to Horace McCoy or Damon Runyon. I had them translate these works with the same enthusiasm encouraged by the English faculty for explicating a later poem of Yeats. I suspect that the inability of some students to "understand" works written by Afro-American authors is traceable to an inability to understand the American experience as rooted in slang, dialect, vernacular, argot, and all of the other putdown terms the faculty uses for those who have the gall to deviate from the true and proper way of English.

"Slang and colloquial speech have rarely been so creative. It is as if the common man (or his anonymous spokesman) would in his speech assert his humanity against the powers that be, as if the rejection and revolt subdued in the political sphere would burst out in a vocabulary that calls things by their names: 'head-shrinker' and 'egghead', 'boob tube', 'think tank' and 'beat it', 'dig it' and 'gone man gone'," Herbert Marcuse wrote in *The One-Dimensional Man*.

And it may turn out that the great restive underground language rising from the American slums and fringe communities is the real American poetry and prose, that can tell you the way things are happening now. If this is not the case, then it is mighty strange that a whole new generation exploits this language, in what White racist critics call "folk rock lyrics."

Composers of rock lyrics have exploited "Black Talk," and the contemporary "Neo-Slave Narrative" confessional may have revolutionized the essay form. An English writer recently complained that he and his colleagues desired the same freedom as a leading Black exponent of this auto-biographical genre, which dates back as early as *A Narrative of the Uncommon Sufferings and Surprising Deliverance of Britan Hammon, A Negro Man,* published in 1760. Admittedly, there is a frenzy for this kind of writing in publishing circles, and its authors are celebrities on the lecture circuit. At times it seems that the stampede for these books is so great that Afro-American authors who go the route of Art are trampled. Al Young wrote in his book of poems, *Dancing:*

> Dont nobody want no nice nigger no more
> these honkies man that put out
> these books & things
> they want an angry splib
> a furious nigrah
> they dont want no bourgeois woogie
> they want them a militant nigger

> *in a fiji haircut*
> *fresh out of some secret boot camp*
> *with a bad book in one hand*
> *& a molotov cocktail in the other*
> *subject to turn up at one of their conferences*
> *or soirees*
> *& shake the shit out of them*

But. even among the "Neo-Slave Narrative" writers, who somehow confuse their experience with that of thirty million other people, one has to search for the kind of bad writing that typifies the current American "bestseller" scene—a scene that so woefully neglects its own younger White writers: John Harriman, Donald Phelps, Willard Bain—just to mention a few.

What distinguishes the present crop of Afro-American and Black writers from their predecessors is a marked independence from Western form. This holds true even for the authors of the "Neo-Slave Narrative."

The history of Afro-American literature is abundant with examples of writers using other people's literary machinery and mythology in their work. W. E. B. DuBois, in some of his writing, is almost embarrassing in his use of White classical references. And what does one do with a modern writer who terms Egyptians "villains," or equates Babylon with America?

Black writers have in the past written sonnets, iambic pentameter, ballads, every possible Western gentleman's form. They have been neo-classicists, Marxists, existentialists, and infected by every Western disease available. I have a joke I tell friends about a young Black poet who relies upon other people's systems, and does not use his head. He wears sideburns and has seen every French film in New York. While dining at Schrafft's he chokes to death on nut-covered ice cream and dies. He approaches the river Styx and pleads with Charon to ferry him across: "I don't care how often you've used me as a mythological allusion," Charon says. "You're still a nigger—swim!"

One has to return to what some writers would call "dark heathenism" to find original tall tales, and yarns with the kind of originality that some modern writers use as found poetry— the enigmatic street rhymes of some of Ellison's minor characters, or the dozens. I call this neo-hoodooism; a spur to originality, which prompted Julia Jackson, a New Orleans soothsayer, when asked the origin of the amulets, talismans, charms, and potions in her workshop, to say: "I make all my own stuff. It saves me money and it's as good. People who has to buy their stuff ain't using their heads."

Sometimes I feel that the condition of the Afro-American writer in this country is so strange that one has to go to the supernatural for an analogy. Manipulation of the word has always been related in the mind to manipulation of nature. One utters a few words and stones roll aside, the dead are raised and the river beds emptied of their content.

The Afro-American artist is similar to the Necromancer (a word whose etymology is revealing in itself!). He is a conjuror who works JuJu upon his oppressors; a witch doctor who frees his fellow victims from the psychic attack launched by demons of the outer and inner world.

For *The Man* there has always been something spooky about the slave who begins to handle clay or word music, or talks to his fellow victims in what for him are undecipherable codes. One must remember that we live in a country where at one time *literacy for Blacks was a crime*.

Alex Gross, a young White painter, wrote in the *East Village Other*: "The artist is the new preacher, the prophet of the modernist religion. But as soon as a black man appears using the cult words of the religion, the devout begin to feel ill at ease. Why is this? It is because the assumption that art is only white man's work is built into the very culture itself. Art which pays homage to the idea of reaching all of society and influencing it, becomes embarrassed when it is actually expected to do so. . . . The phrases and opinions which seemed like revealed truth when uttered by the white artist have tended to cause doubt and embarrassment when spoken by a black one."

This racism even affects the so-called counter culture—whose scholars write of the Indian and Zen influence, but leave out the Black influence upon those who are seeking to transform the wicked old. Yet the Black influence is pervasive. There were more people doing the boogaloo at Woodstock than chanting, *"Hare krishna hare hare."*

Nevertheless, in certain radical bookstores on the Lower East Side, Berkeley, and other focal points of what is called the "counter culture or the alternative culture," Claude McKay and Robert Hayden are consigned to the Black section, whereas Ezra Pound and Hermann Hesse are in the poetry and fiction sections. And a volume which was audaciously called *The New American Poetry 1945–1960*, edited by

Donald Allen and influenced by Allen Ginsberg, carried the work of only one Black poet.

And if you think that things have changed since 1956, I would direct your attention to *The Young American Poets*, edited by Paul Carroll, and *31 New American Poets*, edited by Ron Schreiber, where the absence of adequate Black representation (they printed three!) was so conspicuous that even a reviewer for the *Village Voice* was called upon to comment.

The exclusionary policy of the traditional American anthology is a mysterious phenomenon. It can't be based upon "inferior quality"—that well-worn private dick the White art world dials when threatened by an invasion of creative gangsters—because many of those Afro-Americans who have chosen to emulate Western form and content excel at their adopted literary devices. Some Afro-American poets can write about flowers, girlfriends and being miserable along with the best of them.

Perhaps those White writers who think American writing is like hunting Big Game (firing from a helicopter while sipping a martini), or going a couple of rounds with a champion boxer have a point.

Perhaps at the roots of American art is a rivalry between the oppressor and the oppressed, with a secret understanding that the oppressor shall always prevail and make off with the prizes, no matter how inferior his art to that of his victims. Art in America may even be related to sexual competition. In the beginning was The Word and The Word is the domain of the White patriarchy. Beware. Women and natives are not to tamper with The Word.

If in Mayan or ancient Egyptian culture writing was considered a royal profession, and the writer a necromancer, soothsayer, priest, prophet; a man who opened doors to the divine, here in America writing is related to bullfighting, or to sports in which men disfigure other men or animals—or sometimes it is compared to wreaking sexual vengeance upon a woman:

"The novel is the great bitch," Norman Mailer said, in *Cannibals and Christians*. "We've all had a piece of her," and he gave a long list of writers who had presumably balled the bitch. Only one Black writer was invited to join the orgy—James Baldwin.

If writing has these *extra-literary* connotations, then it is no surprise when Afro-American writers are treated in the same manner as Afro-American boxers—whatever the arena, they end up giving each other lumps in the semifinals.

Although most of the writers included in this anthology are "cultural independents," some have been involved in important Afro-American or Black writing movements of the 1960s and early '70s.

Umbra magazine, founded by Tom Dent, Calvin Hernton, and David Henderson, began publishing in 1961. Calvin Hernton from Chattanooga, Tennessee, Tom Dent from New Orleans, Louisiana, and David Henderson from the Bronx, New York, established the early workshop in Tom Dent's apartment on Second Street, in the Lower East Side of New York City.

In 1963 *Umbra* was irreparably split over a poem written by Ray Durem. Two of the three editors argued that the poem —which was critical of President Kennedy—was in bad taste, in light of the Kennedy assassination.

Several dissidents held that since the poem had been accepted for publication before the President's murder, and since any poem acceptable for *Umbra* was presumably above any particular historical event, the poem should have been printed. They accused the two editors of timidity, and a very bitter and intense struggle took place whose repercussions were felt throughout the '60s.

The dissidents were promoting a form of "cultural nationalism." They included Askia Muhammad Toure, Charles and William Patterson, and Albert E. Haynes, Jr., who all moved to the Harlem community shortly after the split, where they aided Amiri Baraka in conceptualizing the Black Art Repertory Theater and School.

Like Henderson and Hernton, N. H. Pritchard and Lennox Raphael were members of *Umbra* before the Durem episode. Of these, Raphael, Henderson, and Hernton remained residents of the East Village community, and active in *Umbra*. Tom Dent went to New Orleans, where in 1967 he began the Free Southern Theatre.

Steve Cannon became editor of *Umbra* magazine in 1966, along with poets Joe Johnson, James Thompson, and Lennox Raphael; but the friction resulting from the Durem episode persisted, and under their direction no issue of *Umbra* was published. A very important interview granted *Umbra* by Ralph Ellison was lost to *Harper's* magazine.

In 1965 Calvin Hernton, Lennox Raphael, N. H. Pritchard, and I participated in the American Festival of Negro Art, making AFNA the first major Afro-American cultural organization to ratify what critic-novelist Harold Cruse calls "the new young Negro creative wave."

In 1965 I founded the community newspaper *Advance* in Newark, New Jersey. This newspaper published original material by Cannon, Henderson, poet Allan Katzman, Myrna Bain (who was associate editor), and many other young writers, Black and White. Walter Bowart, a painter, prepared the "dummy" for the first issue, which led him to conceive the *East Village Other*, which I named. Not many people know that a "dummy" prepared for a Negro weekly in Newark gave rise to the powerful underground press syndicate.

Cannon, Pritchard, and Raphael have all at one time or another written for the *East Village Other*, as has critic Wilmer Lucas. Cannon, Lucas, and Raphael have appeared on the masthead.

Clarence Major came to New York from Omaha in 1967, shortly before I left for California, where I came into contact with poet-novelist Al Young, novelist Paul Lofty, painter Glenn Myles, sculptor Doyle Foreman, and critic Adam David Miller. When Clarence Major put together the anthology *The New Black Poetry*, he was able to use some of this West Coast talent, including Glenn Myles and Al Young. *The New Black Poetry* was the cosmic anthology of Afro-American or Black writing of the '60s because it represented work from all movements, and not just those who adhered to a "policy poetry."

Cecil Brown and Ronald Fair have been involved in the Chicago writing scene. Fair, Hoyt Fuller, editor of *Negro Digest*, Don L. Lee, Conrad Kent Rivers, and Gerald A. McWorter set up the Organization of Black Arts and Culture (OBAC) of which Cecil Brown also became a member.

In December of 1967, Cecil Brown went to Berkeley, California, and in 1969 Ronald Fair went to Connecticut, where he became a Fellow at the Wesleyan Center for Advanced Studies.

I met Victor Hernandez Cruz in the winter of 1966, after a friend showed me his first book of poems, *Papo Got His Gun*. It is interesting to note that the book was financed by a collection assembled by his neighbors. Victor Cruz came to *Umbra* magazine during its decline. Later he traveled to the West Coast, where he met the East Bay contributors to this anthology.

William Melvin Kelley, John Williams, Cecil Brown, and

Al Young are world travelers, and the novel *The Life and Loves of Mr. Jiveass Nigger* makes Cecil Brown the youngest Afro-American novelist to have written a book about expatriate life.

Amistad magazine, edited by John A. Williams and Charles F. Harris and first published in 1970, includes three contributors to this anthology. *Amistad* will bring together several generations of Afro-American or Black writers based in many parts of the globe.

The second AFNA conference, held November 21–23, 1969, brought together the younger generation of Afro-American or Black film makers, sculptors, musicians, critics, painters, and writers. Playwright Ronald Pringle presented his film *Alice in Wonderland*, which was one of the highlights of the conference. Reviewing the AFNA event, Walt Sheppard, editor of the *Nickel Review*, which features the brilliant criticism of Ron Welburn, wrote: "No artistic collectives extant today show the excitement about their work that is found among Afro-American artists."

Unlike the Harlem Renaissance, which was pretty much concentrated in the East and Harlem, although Jean Toomer lived in the Village and Chelsea from time to time, and Arna Bontemps later wrote *Black Thunder* in Watts, California, the new Afro-American or Black writing is national in scope, with writers like John A. Williams having international ties. He is in contact with leading writers of the African community. Al Young, who with his wife Arl edits the magazine *Loveletter*, has been published in many South American magazines, and William Melvin Kelley lives in the West Indies.

This anthology is meant to be a sampling of those young artists who are writing in the long forms. There are more poets than you can shake a stick at, and they will be represented in forthcoming anthologies. I know of at least ten that are scheduled for publication in 1970.

I could have published Ralph Ellison, Richard Wright, James Weldon Johnson, Claude McKay, Paul Lawrence Dunbar, James Baldwin, and Langston Hughes, but every list in Afro-American or Black literature has at least some variation on that group. I have also omitted White writers. Examining the many exclusionary American anthologies that flood the market, I somehow feel that they will get by.

My purpose was to make this anthology of Afro-American or Black writing as contemporary as possible, and it is very

important to note that some of the selections that were
originally "from manuscript" are being picked up by astute
publishers. It is also important to note the diversity of style
this anthology represents. Fantasy, Nationalism, the Supernatural, Hoodooism, Realism, Science Fiction, Autobiography,
Satire, Scat, Erotica, Rock, K. C. Blues, International Intrigue,
Jazz—and a few styles and genres that defy definition—are
all here. Harlem, California, East Village, Copenhagen,
Croton-on-Hudson, Mars, Jupiter are all here. Indian People,
Black People, White People, Chinese People, and Blue People
unravel their experiences through its pages.

There are dazzling experiments in content and form, but
what these selections have in common is their originality—
originality even within well-known literary modes. There is as
much experimentation and diversity among these writers as
among any comparable group of writers in the world.

Anyone who told these writers to "stick to [White] verse," as
Max Eastman advised Claude McKay, or to "delete your
Africanism," as well-meaning meddlers advised the "Neo-
Slave Narrative" writers, would have to pick up his teeth.

The new generation of Afro-Americans or Black writers
will not be consigned to the cultural slaves' quarters, as were
our geniuses of the past. They will not allow mediocre men
to sabotage their careers, as Herbert Hill attempted to sabotage the career of the great Chester Himes.

19 Necromancers from Now will certainly not cure everything that ails a moribund literary culture, but hopefully a
younger, more objective generation of Black and White
students will read these pages and learn. And perhaps this
anthology will retire the idea, promoted by various cultural
bandits and opportunists, that Afro-American or Black writing
is conformist, monolithic, and dictated by a Committee.

A man recently told me that he was sick of writing by
Afro-Americans because the writing was "full of raving."
It turned out that he had read only one contemporary Afro-
American writer. He was an ignorant man. There is much
fear, ignorance, and confusion concerning Afro-American or
Black writers, even among those with library privileges, who
should know better.

The readers of this anthology will find that some of us
rave and propagandize extremely well, while others are as
muted as a Miles Davis solo in *Solar*. Some have transcended
print altogether, and are coming very close to what a younger

generation of painters, sculptors, film makers, and musicians are doing in their work.

Afro-American or Black literature is food for a deep, life-time study, not something to be squeezed into a quarter or semester as a concession to student demands, nor a literature to be approached one-dimensionally, as do critics Robert Bone, Edward Margolies, and David Littlejohn. In Bone's case, for example, the categories he uses—Amalgamation, Open Revolt, Separatism, or Back-to-Africa—are not literary categories, but essentially political ones. This is to deprive the student of Black literature of the broad universe the most creative Black authors have painstakingly structured in their work. Black writing requires the same multi-dimensional critical approach that has been traditionally applied to Western literature, and critics Addison Gayle, Adam David Miller, Ron Welburn, Sarah Fabio, Nick Aaron Ford, Darwin Turner, Wilmer Lucas, Elizabeth Postell and Toni Cade are educating serious students of Afro-American or Black literature on these matters.

Marshall McLuhan surveyed—in predictably White scholar-ly fashion—a Western body of literature up to James Joyce, and his conclusions led many students of communications to assume that print had just about run its course. "Words are 'oxcarts' and may disappear sooner than we think," William Burroughs wrote.

If Marshall McLuhan and Burroughs had opened their reading to include the new Afro-American, Indian-American, and Chinese-American writers, they would have found that print and words are not dead at all. To the contrary, they are very much alive and kicking.

ADDISON GAYLE, JR. (1932–   )

Editor of The Black Aesthetic *(1971), an anthology of essays on this subject, and two other anthologies of Black critical and prose writings, Addison Gayle, Jr. is one of the prominent*

*new Black literary critics. He was born in Newport News,
Virginia, attended City College of New York and the University of California, and now lives in New York City where
he is assistant professor of English at Bernard M. Baruch
College of the City University of New York. In his introduction to* The Black Aesthetic *he writes: "The black artist in
the American society who creates without interjecting a note
of anger is creating not as a black man, but as an American.
. . . The serious black artist of today is at war with the American
society as few have been throughout American history. . . .
The problem of the de-Americanization of black people lies
at the heart of the Black Aesthetic." The following selection
is the opening essay in his volume of essays* The Black Situation *(1970), an autobiographical statement which illuminates
the sensibility and consciousness underlying his critical views.*

The Son of My Father

I am compelled to state here, in the beginning, that the
thoughts recorded in this book are mine alone and that I do
not, nor have I attempted, to speak for any other black man
in American Society. I make this statement in the hope of
sparing some other Negro the moments of frustration and
anger which I experience when some "Negro Leader" on television, bright lights illuminating his unscarred countenance,
proceeds to tell America in impassioned tones what I think,
believe, and want.

Such utterances by Negro Leaders have produced severe
traumas for me; causing me to hurl notebook, pen, and
pencil at my television set, shout obscenities at the unhearing
figure before me; and finally, not too long ago, when I had
almost reached the breaking point, I scribbled a note to one
of these leaders asking that on future occasions he preface his
remarks by stating that: "I speak for every Negro in America,
except Addison Gayle." The letter accomplished nothing, for
three weeks ago this same leader was on television again,
informing the public that he, not other Negro Leaders, spoke
for me.

America is at that desperate stage when, feeling the threat
from her long neglected citizenry, she needs some supporting,
sustaining voice to assure her that the neglected are still,
despite all, hopeful, passive, and restrained. Nations, like men,

are wary of truth, for truth is too often not beautiful, as Keats believed, but very painful and very discomforting. It is not comforting to be reminded that those who sow the wind shall reap the whirlwind, not even when the whirlwind appears so visibly, as in frequent summers of discontent when desperate men have belied the vocal protestations of their leaders.

No Negro in America speaks for me; neither do I speak for any one else. It would, perhaps, be too great a shock to find compatibility between my thoughts and those of others; for unlike Narcissus, a mirror image would cause me untold discomfort. I am, I know, a desperate man, a cynical man and, perhaps, according to Freudian psychology which can in no way explain me, a sick man. Some of my friends would add, quickly, a mad man. I do not object. Perhaps to be sane in this society is the best evidence of insanity. To repress all that I know, to keep hidden in my subconscious all that I feel may inevitably force me to those acts of desperation which I am capable of viewing here, frankly and honestly with a certain objective detachment.

This is to say that the very act of recording these thoughts may provide that catharsis which will enable me to retain control of that demon within my breast which allows me no respite in twentieth century America. One wonders what fate might have befallen Dostoyevsky had he not created Raskolnikov or Dimitri? What might Baldwin have become, had he not been capable of traducing Bigger Thomas in print? And Wright, Bigger's creator, what might he have been were not the fearful portrait of Bigger etched upon his subconscious mind, displayed upon that canvas of the psyche in garish, brutal colors?

The end product of writing should be revelation for both the writer and reader. I have no quarrel with those who argue that poetry "should not mean but be": I simply call them liars, and let it go at that. I hold no breach against those who argue that Black literature, in the main, has not conformed to those artistic rules and canons established by the academicians. I know that such tools are important to them. For they are incapable of understanding Black literature without the aid of these instruments of dissection with which they are most dexterous.

Literature, however, and Black literature in particular, should afford revelation and insight into truth when created under conditions favorable to free, honest expression. For the Afro-American, solitude is the most necessary condition; for

Blacks are abominable liars, especially, in those cases where an audience is concerned. This is not to suggest that black writers are not also liars—indeed a great many are the most notorious liars of all. But, alone, secreted only with his thoughts and a desire to honestly record those thoughts, the black writer may, at least, blunder into an awareness of truth.

This truth, then, will come as a revelation; and I have little doubt that mine will—especially to those who, over the years, have professed to "know" me. They will discover, sometimes painfully, that they have not known me at all; yet, this is primarily because I have not known myself. For example, I did not know—or would not admit, which is the same thing—how vehement was my hatred even toward those whom I professed to love most passionately.

If however, those who remember me will recall my unspoken nuances—the quick bowing of my head, the slight raising of my eyebrows, the smile which has never really been a smile, the uncomfortable habit that I have of moving from place to place whenever alone in a room with white people—then they can begin to piece together the puzzle of our relationship, and to make some sense out of what I write here. When I say that I hated, I am uttering my first verbal truth with full cognizance of its import; and if not a revelation to others, this is indeed a revelation to me. This is my first positive statement to white people; and because it is the truth, I do not apologize for it. I only regret that I did not, or could not, make it before.

Perhaps I did not really hate before! Perhaps, despite everything, I retained enough of my mother's Christian preachments to think of love as the universal solvent, the cleansing cream which America need but apply to the ugly, pockmarked blemishes upon its white-hued surface. Perhaps I believed that one could not create a world of hatred because invariably that world became a suspicious one, an isolated one; and, finally, one so infected by disease that life, any life, trapped within it was worthless. Or, perhaps, I was too much of a coward to hate: too timid, too meek.

And this despite the fact that I owe what some people call my success to hatred. Six years ago I worked as a porter at a government establishment in Brooklyn, New York. After four years, I left that job and three days later began to assault the pavements of New York City searching for another. My odyssey began early on a Monday morning, on a dismal, overcast day in May when the streets of New York seemed most indifferent—a day much like those which I had cherished in the Virginia town where I was born.

Long before, on such days, I had searched for jobs in Virginia with less trepidation, with less overt fear than that which plagued me as I searched for employment in New York City. To state for the nth time that the Afro-American's life in the South in comparison with his life in the North is in many ways more comfortable if not more compatible is to state what is general knowledge. For there is comfort in honesty, in knowing that the perils one faces are blatantly visible, not cloaked with the time-honored garb of hypocrisy and deceit. The South is nothing if not honest, and Blacks who hate it the most, grudgingly admit to its honesty.

The indictment against the North, however, stems from its dishonesty, its hypocritical facade which has engendered more frustration in the black intellectual than all the perverted acts perpetrated upon Negroes by those creatures who inhabit the hinterlands of the South. In the South, the Negro is, when visible, merely a Negro, an accursed son of Ham destined, like a mute, to be the stanchion of stubborn support for a romantic, idyllic utopia where class and race are so structured as to allow for a well-ordered society. Here, only the Blacks speak of equality. The whites hurl the correlative word, "place"; for there is a place for the Negro in Southern society: albeit, a place at the bottom of a rotten cesspool—yet a place where being black, though a stigma, is legitimate. The Negroes are still considered as a people and brotherhood means loyalty to one's own race.

In the North, on the other hand, the Negro is conceived of as an instrument, a non-being, the noble savage, who must, in whatever way possible, be civilized; scrubbed clean of his heredity; robbed of his propensitiy for blackness, the last vestige of tribalism erased from his mind. Like the missionary, the Northern white seeks to bring the savage within the confines of Western Civilization with far more potent weapons than guns and bibles: higher horizons programs, civil rights commissions, urban renewal, and cultural centers for black youth.

There is more truth in the South than in the North, more honest feeling in the man who knots the rope about your neck, more honest conviction in the mob which howls for your blood. In the North one falls into that absurd world where impotent men gather unto themselves other men as children, intent on guiding them, on leading them to that coming paradise, that enchanted land of freedom and equality, not withstanding the fact that paradise is only paradise if one finds it himself.

Here in the North, rhetoric and practice come into conflict: It is no surprise that the great rhetoricians of America are Northerners, for here rhetoric is the most celebrated avocation. From the politician in the highest echelons of Government to the freshman college student come the wail of discontent, the table thumping oratory, the endless reports of committees, civil rights groups, civic organizations, all attesting to the deep concern, the great sympathy felt by men of the North, more sophisticated, more liberal, for their fellow citizens who happen to be black.

Such people believe their own rhetoric; and it is their rhetoric which sustains them. They conceive of rhetoric and practice as one and the same. The college chairman who heads a committee to improve conditions in the ghetto, and yet neglects to improve the conditions in his college so that more ghetto residents may attend, is equating rhetoric with practice. The politician who, although voting for civil rights bills, cautions Afro-Americans not to move too fast is equating rhetoric with practice. The college student who demands tolerance from others toward Blacks and neglects to make such demands upon his parents and neighbors is equating rhetoric with practice.

The Negro, therefore, recognizing the conflict, capable of differentiating between rhetoric and practice, yet unable to divine the motives for the great disparities which he knows to exist, is incapable of finding a bearing, a central point in an absurd world where men are victims of their own rhetoric. It is the frustrations engendered by such conflicts which drive black people to acts of frustrations, to acts of violence, ofttimes, as in the case of a friend, to suicide.

The Negro, the world's greatest dissimulator, is unable to survive in a world where dissimulation is the norm, hypocrisy the accustomed and accepted mode of behavior. Better to be entrapped in a web of practicality where men take the word "place" as the God-ordained condition of twenty-five million people than to be enmeshed in a web where men are convinced that their manifest destiny lies in mesmerizing the natives by their spell-binding, hypnotic oratory. The first web can be cut; its strands can be severed; at the least, men never tire of attempting to rip it apart. The second web, however, is non-corporeal, having no body, no structure, no substance. It is impervious to assault, except that of the most violent nature; for the Messiah is incapable of differentiating between rhetoric and practice until such time as those who see truth in men's actions, not in their words, nail him, shamelessly and without guilt, to the cross.

It is not long before the Negro who journeys from South to North is called witness to his moment of truth. Epiphanies are almost daily occurrences. There is so much to be revealed. There are so many thousands of shapes, forms and symbols through which revelation may come. The first epiphany often occurs in the North when the Negro first faces his hoped-for-employer. Contrary to most reports, on first arriving in the North, the Southern Black is not incensed by the ghetto—this comes later—for the Northern ghetto has always held mystical, romantic connotations for him. Here it is that the tenuous tie with the North, perfected through the years by the mass exodus of his ancestors, is most secure. Few Blacks in the South have neither friends nor relatives in Northern ghettoes. Thus, neither the filth and stench of the ghetto, nor its chronic violence can rid the newcomer of that compulsion to dwell among his own in the Harlems, Wattses, Houghs and Bedford Stuyvesants of the North.

Discrimination, northern style, is encountered when the newcomer searches for his first job and is brought face to face with his first northern employer. The encounter is more likely than not to be traumatic, reenforcing the subdued antagonism engendered by the South, intensifying it to the point wherein this antagonism gives way to a hatred which given birth, feeds upon itself like a cancerous cell until the victim is either consumed or miraculously made whole—himself consuming that which would destroy him.

Early in the morning on that dark overcast day, I checked out five jobs, all of which had surreptitiously vanished before I arrived. My sixth stop was the corner of Delancey Street and Broadway, a combination restaurant and newsstand which, according to the New York Times, "Wanted: a man to do light portering, some clerking." It was the "light portering" which caused me to be hopeful, for such job descriptions in the South are usually synonyms for Negroes.

I was met at the door of the shop by a dark-hued white man who, mistaking me for a customer, commented on the state of the weather. Smiling, I proceeded to point out the true nature of my business which was not to buy wares but instead to sell my labor. No sooner had I mentioned the ad than the man abruptly turned his back to me, and walked quickly to the other end of the store, informing me through a running monologue with himself that the job was taken. However, his actions, not his words, convinced me that he was lying. All morning I had been turned away from jobs, always with a smile, a sympathetic murmur of sympathy, unbelievable to be sure, yet unchallengeable on any save intuitive grounds.

This man had made it impossible for me to believe him. I left the store, went across the street to a drugstore, waited a few minutes, and dialed the number listed in the newspaper. The man himself answered the telephone. Mimicking James Mason, I asked if the job listed in the morning paper had been filled. The answer was no. I asked if I could come over to see about the job. I was told to come at once. I went to the store a second time. This time the man met me, rage breathing from every pore of his nostrils, his ugly face contorted into the most weird design.

"Yes?" He growled.

"I came for the job." I announced.

"There ain't no job!" He replied.

"I just called, and you said there was one," I answered, "You said come right over."

Briefly, a flicker of surprise came to his eyes, but he recovered quickly. "You didn't call here," he said; "that's a lie, there ain't no job." He turned on his heels and went to serve a customer who had come in.

I stared after him for a few minutes before finally walking out of the store. There was a big lump in my stomach. My hands shook noticeably. In facing him with what I knew to be the truth, in forcing him to acknowledge his own lie, I had, perhaps, scored a moral victory. Yet I was still without a job because a man who did not know me, had decided *a priori* that I should not have one. The moral victory was far less sustaining than my growing hatred.

Floyd Patterson, in his first fight with Ingemar Johanssen, was knocked to the canvas again and again, only to rise yet another time. Many were awed by the tenacious courage displayed by the champion, the refusal to stay down, to say die. I was not amazed; for I too had learned early to absorb merciless punishment, to pick myself up from the canvas of a ring in which the fight can only end in life or death.

Like the ex-heavyweight champion, I was on my feet searching for another job less that fifteen minutes after absorbing a crushing blow to my psyche. This time I intended to shape the odds nearer to my liking. I decided to buy a job.

The headquarters of the job-buying market is a narrow street at the southern tip of Manhattan, some few feet from the Hudson River. On this narrow street, occupying an entire block, are an assortment of dilapidated office buildings housing numerous agencies which legally traffic in human flesh. Sometimes as many as five agencies are in one single building. Each agency occupies a large room, two at the most, partitioned into two sections. One section, the larger, is usually, though not always, furnished with folding chairs; in the other section, beyond the partition, neat, middle-aged businessmen (white) and their assistants sit at wooden desks surrounded by telephones.

Throughout the day, from opening time at eight o'clock in the morning to closing time at five o'clock at night, people of all races come to these partitioned offices offering themselves as salable commodities. On any given day, one will find a small number of white applicants, a large number of Puerto Rican applicants, and a great number of black applicants.

I chose one of the smaller agencies which had emptied, somewhat, at that hour of the day. A number of people were still present. Some were waiting, I suppose, for clarification of job offers. Some women were checking to see if the prospects for domestic work tomorrow were brighter than prospects today. Standing along the two walls of the agency were older Negro men, in whose faces the tragedy of a people was stenciled in bold, heavy lines, watching each new arrival suspiciously, their ears attuned to the ring of the telephone; they smiled condescendingly each time the eyes of the agent swept their paths; for the agent was their savior, able to reward them with a half day's work, enabling them to fight off the D.T.'s, hunger, or eviction yet a little while longer.

I was met by an assistant, a charming, brownskinned girl of about twenty-one, heavily rouged, her hair in a pompadour, her false eyelashes flickering as if in amusement. We smiled at one another; and she communicated her nervousness by smoking her cigarette almost to the filter, leaving her long fingers stained a deeper brown than her skin. Like me, she too lived at a fever pitch of desperation; though she, like some omniscient spectator of Dante's Hell, watched men, women, and sometimes teen-age children stacked before her eyes, no longer human, but instead objects to be auctioned away for one week's salary—the legal requirements of the agency. She had dwelled among these hollow men and women so long, these mechanical men and women of Kafka's novels, that she had become almost hollow and mechanical herself. I pitied her, even as she pitied me.

She helped me to fill out several forms, and after I had

completed them, she motioned me to a folding chair, took the forms, and deposited them on the desk of a short, fat white man, whose bald head seemed a comic distraction in this place where laughter would have been an unforgivable crime.

Not too long after, I sat in a chair at the desk, staring at the man's bald head, listening to him describe a job recently referred to his agency. The job was located in a restaurant on Broadway, two blocks from City Hall. The prerequisites were for a young man who had some experience at handling a cash register, and who would not balk at long hours. I satisfied the agent that I met all the requirements, after which he brought out a number of papers upon which I scribbled my signature. The assistant gave me a card bearing the agency's letterhead and the name of the man I was to see, and smiled at me knowingly; I quickly left that little room, which smelled like something akin to death.

The restaurant was located in the basement of a large hotel which, at that time, was undergoing alteration. I passed several black workers: plasterers, hod-carriers, and porters, one of whom pointed the way to the manager at the door of the office—he, seeing me approaching, had come from behind a glass enclosure. He was young, blond, his face clean of blemishes, his body thin, athletic in appearance. His movements seemed impetuous, quick, and determined. I handed him the agent's card.

Hardly had he finished reading the card, before, without hesitation, almost as if I were not present, he blurted out: "But why did they send you? We don't hire Negroes."

We recoiled one from the other! He because he had said what he did; I because he had said it so blatantly. He was, I suppose, an honest man, and instinctively, he uttered the truth which needed no supporting rationale. I never thought for a moment that he hated me, nor that he thought much about me at all; this was not necessary to justify the irrefutable statement: "We don't hire Negroes."

It was the look of consternation on my face which made him offer me carfare, which prompted him to tell me that he was sorry. He looked after me with sympathetic eyes, as I, having spurned his offer of carfare, backed away as one fighting to sleep through some horrible nightmare. I walked away, almost in a state of shock. In this shocked state, I telephoned the agency, reported what had happened, hung up the phone, and boarded the "A" train for Brooklyn.

When finally I reached my stop in the heart of Bedford-

Stuyvesant, the ghetto to which I came now for some solace, for some semblance of myself, some testament of myself as a human being, I left the subway, bypassing the bars along the way, where I would find that human misery by which to measure my own. I avoided those who knew me, even at that moment when I wanted their affection the most. I avoided them because I did not want them to see me cry. Crying is an act which one should perform only in private, for crying is a private way of groping for truth. Once inside of my apartment, I removed the phone from the hook, locked my door, fell across the bed, and cried.

On the bed, clawing and clutching at the pillows, my breath coming in quick, short gasps, my nose filled with mucus, my mouth hot, dry. I twisted, shouted, and screamed almost in convulsion; the tears gushing from my eyes; my body burning as if seared by some scorching, burning flame; with my fists I flailed the pillows; with my fingernails I tore at my hair, drew blood from my skin; like some hurt, wounded beast in orgasm. I surrendered my soul to that Faustian devil who hovers over the black male, in pain, in ecstasy, in total to complete, everlasting hatred.

In time I would come to understand that it was not only the acts of discrimination; not only the feelings of rejection; not only the soul-rending words, "We don't hire Negroes"; but, instead, the motivation for the surrender to Mephistopheles was simply that white men had made me cry, had forced me to that point where I would seek a baptism in my own tears; a baptism which would cleanse me of any sense of responsibility to them, any sense of affection for them, any sense of respect for them. The ultimate pain which any man can inflict upon another is to force him to tears.

"God gave Noah the rainbow sign/No more water, the fire next time," chanted a now forgotten black slave. For me the water had come to give birth to that fire which would consume me, almost completely. Sparks from this fire propelled me to college, forced me to attempt, naïvely, to wreak vengeance upon those who had forced me to reveal my soul in all of its nakedness. Instructors who knew me as a conscientious, hardworking student had no cognizance of that demon within which forced me on; nor could they know that the mere sight of them, their whiteness, was enough to trigger that demon into action. Riding the wings of the demon, I pushed my way through curricula foreign to me, spent entire nights writing and rewriting term papers; stood Buddha-like as my instructors attempted to convince me of their dedication to the human spirit.

Some were kind enough to single me out, to invite me to their homes. They questioned me about my hopes, my expectations, and about race relations. Always, I lied to them; partly out of fear, but partly, too, out of the belief that were I to tell them the truth, to relate even one tenth of my truth, they would expel me from school and have me locked up in the nearest hospital for the mentally insane.

Others spoke of me in laudatory terms: They told me that I was the kind of Negro whom they would "not mind living next door to them"; that I should be a "spokesman for my people"; that I was proving that any man with initiative could prosper in this democracy. They refused to see me as other than a phenomenon, a testament to all that their rhetoric had portrayed. I was the emancipated Negro, shrived of the sin of blackness because I had proven that I could absorb the wisdom of Shakespeare, Plato, and Emerson. I was the transformed savage, having been rescued from the jungle of the ghetto and stripped of the ghetto facade; now I was almost human, ready to be welcomed, even if halfheartedly— for the savage can never be completely transformed—into middle class senility, impotence, and death.

Students, on the other hand, were worse than instructors. If the instructors believed me to be intellectually resurrected, the students considered me to be socially resurrected, capable now of association on an almost equal level with them. I was *the Negro* to have at social gatherings. I avoided most of these and went only when I was bored with school work. I was the Negro who talked on their terms, voiced their discontents, and gave words to their frustration.

To them I told as much of the truth as possible, until I discovered that they sought this truth, eagerly, masochistically, as authoritative evidence, facts from the donkey's mouth, with which to substantiate the everchanging tenor of their own rhetoric. To be sure, they dreamed of the new Canaan, but one from which I, as an individual, would be excluded. When I entered their new world, I would enter as mind, as intellect, divested of that corporeal form, body, bedecked by a black skin. Believing in the power of rationality, these students saw me in terms of intellect only; for to them intellect was unlimited. I, however, could not live by intellect and intellect alone; for there was, within my breast, an irrational demon which often propelled me to irrational acts. I could not, therefore, accept their compact, for unfortunately, sometime ago, I had signed the most binding compact of all.

"I fall upon the thorns of life," wrote Shelley, "I bleed!" And sometimes one wishes that the bleeding would be over and done with; and if not this, then that some tourniquet might be applied to stop the flowing blood once and for all. On the other hand, perhaps it would be best if the blood gushed profusely, like a water hose, pushing out the impurities quickly, allowing one only the intoxicating moment of release, an ecstatic descent into a dream world, where there is no life, and thus, no pain.

"*Verweile doch, du bist so schön,*" she called after me. Standing by the plane, tall, slender, deep blue eyes, blonde hair cut short about her neck, tears in her eyes, she watched as I walked slowly, unsteadily up the ramp. The fleeting hour was fleeting all too quickly, and never again would we see one another, never again walk the same sandy beach together; never again share the same world.

Her world had been as strange to me as my world was to her. Few of us, like Malcolm X, make the trip to Mecca where one meets people of different skin color whom one cannot reject outright. Yet many Negroes find their personal Meccas; and there, though color is never irrelevant, there is perhaps something better—one is indifferent to color.

She was my Mecca. Here color was not negated, but simply ignored. Together we found the new Canaan, and yet, I knew that I could not live in it. Too many Blacks were outside, too many Blacks whose tortured faces continued to move before my mind like so many accusing mouths; and we both knew that one day, I would have to acquiesce to the painful utterances of those mouths, desert Canaan, and return to the ghetto not, as my father had hoped, to save the people, but to die with them.

We arrived, therefore, at some definition of our life together, found some way of memorializing all that had been, and we stumbled upon the concept of the fleeting hour (*die fliegende Stunde*).

"*Verweile doch, du bist so schön,*" we chanted night after night together (remain, so fair thou art), for fair those hours were indeed. Two human beings caught in a historic trap, one incapable of destroying a vicious, binding compact, desiring always to be victim, rather than victimizer; two people living for a short span of time in a peace, a serenity to which no words can give form and body; two lovers who, were there some merciful God, would have been allowed to perish then and there.

It was the hour, however, which would perish; not we. Cowards, we would continue to live, to be hurled again and again upon those sharp, jagged thorns which drained us of life-giving blood. Soon the magic of the words, the spell of the incantation, *"verweile doch, du bist so schön,"* would mean little more than an epigram for an essay or a poem. Like Keats, we had spent our allotted time with the nightingale, drunk of hemlock, and tasted of mirth and flora; and yet even such memories were doomed to death in the atmosphere to which I was compelled to return.

The Negro, I have written elsewhere, is timeless; and this is so, for time stopped for us the moment the good ship *Jesus* unloaded its first cargo in the New World. Since that moment, we have sat atop the jagged thorns of life convulsing, like so many tortured animals, from wounds inflicted by weapons as diverse as whips, pistols, ropes and rhetoric. Yet rhetoric is perhaps the most bludgeoning weapon of all. We have been enslaved anew by rhetoric: that of our own prophets as well as that of the missionaries. We fear our own emotions, seek to check them, to subdue them in obedience to some manmade laws which we should neither respect nor honor.

We have chanted love thine enemy, when every fibre of our being has cried "death" to those who despoil us; we have preached forgiveness, when not even the most pious among us can forgive that brutal past from which we sprang; we have sung hymns to a God who, in his infinite mercy, has forsaken us as readily as he forsook his first son; we have dreamed of "a fleeting hour" when even that was not enough to assuage the wounds of the past. Hollow men, we have not dared consider the admonition of Ralph Ellison's invisible man: ". . . maybe freedom lies in hating."

But if not, perhaps freedom lies in realizing that one hates. Perhaps all that is left the black man in America is a revelation, an awareness of himself; and perhaps the key to that conundrum posed by the black poets, the answer to the question of identity, lies in an exploration of one's true emotions, starting at that elementary first principle of denigrated humanity: "I hate."

I begin this book, cognizant of the war which goes on constantly within my soul. It is a fierce war and, no doubt, a destructive one. Yet this war must be fought out to some conclusion before I can begin to wrestle with the problems of men in general. That things which have happened to me, have happened also to others, I have little doubt; yet in happening to me, they have left wounds upon my psyche, and pain others cannot imagine.

I am, I suppose, a stranger; one who has sought a personal truth, hoping to be more enlightened by it than his audience; a stranger, who believes that men live always with some demon within their breasts which can only be exorcised by a dedication to those frightening realities which exist at the moment; a stranger, who has always believed that mankind would be better off today had it accepted as savior the choice of that mob which shouted "Give us Barabbas," instead of accepting one who, from the cross, could only issue his pitiable, feeble moan: "Father forgive them, for they know not what they do."

ADAM DAVID MILLER

A biographical note on Adam David Miller appears in the poetry section (see pp. 300–301). The following essay was written for The Black Aesthetic, *an anthology of criticism edited by Addison Gayle, Jr., and was selected from a manuscript copy received from the author prior to the publication of the book.*

Some Observations on a Black Aesthetic

Just as for the past hundred years blacks have provided the most creative force for dance and music in this country, that is, as the senses of sound and movement in this country have been the creation of Afros, many now feel, I among them, that the seventies will see this Afro creative force ascendant in the other arts. Few can ignore the effects of the cake walk, fox trot, lindy hop, the twist on the movement habits of people in the States. Few, except the issuers of Pulitzer prizes, will doubt that the American sense of music is of Afro origin. A catalogue of names would overrun the page. Today we are seeing fine black filmmakers, painters, sculptors, graphic artists, and craftsmen. And in all fields of literature, the writing aimed at the heart and life of the country is coming increasingly from Afros.

I would like to think of aesthetics as *a way of viewing and sensing and the results of what is viewed and sensed.* Through such thinking, I would like to move the question of aesthetics from "the contemplation of the beautiful" to that of knowing, perception, and feeling. If we take this working definition and apply it to U.S. blacks, we will have to ask how have we blacks seen ourselves, through whose eyes, how do we see ourselves now, and how may we see ourselves? By so doing, we may at least put the question of a black aesthetic in some perspective.

To examine the question of how we have seen ourselves, it would be useful to be reminded of the definitions our former *legal* slavemasters made of us and some of our early responses to them. As early as 1847, Alexis de Tocqueville noted in *Democracy in America:* "To induce the whites to abandon the opinion they have of the moral and intellectual inferiority of their former slaves, the negroes must change, but as long as this opinion subsists, to change is impossible." Note that De Tocqueville states that a change in blacks, not whites, is needed. Being European, De Tocqueville could not see that the masters had no way into the minds of their slaves. The slaves had not only a different language from that of their masters, but also an entirely different view of the world. Thus, having no tools to measure their intellect, most masters found it both convenient and profitable to suppose they had none. Having made this supposition, they proceeded to set up and enforce systems of denial and restriction that had the effective of suppressing the slaves' intellect and directing it so that it was hidden from the masters. And again, as a European, De Tocqueville himself was of such a limited moral sense that he could not understand how preposterous it was that the master should presume to judge the moral condition of his enslaved.

Lawrence Gellert summed it up this way:

> Me an my captain don't agree,
> But he don't know, 'cause he don't ask me;
> He don't know, he don't know my mind,
> When he see me laughing

> Just laughing to keep from crying.
> Got one mind for white folks to see,
> 'Nother for what I know is me; . . .

For generations, then, as slaves and former slaves in this country, we were thought to be morally and intellectually inferior beings. As writers, our responses varied. There was often a discrepancy between what we argued ourselves to be and how we characterized ourselves. For example, see Leon R. Harris:

> . . . When everything's put to the test,
> In spite of our color and features,
> The Negro's the same as the rest.

Meanwhile, Afro writers often used the same stereotypes as white writers when portraying Afros.

What had happened was that the job of conditioning had been so thorough, the intimidation, forced breeding, dispersal, warping, brutalization, so complete, that the values of our former legal owners had become our own, so complete that we saw ourselves as our "masters" saw us; so that while the logic of our lives was clear, the sense of it was not; so that while we could say we were men and equals, we could not imagine ourselves as such. Forced to accept an alien language, alien and hostile gods, and an alien view of the world, our imaginations were shackled to those of our rulers, with the result that we continued for a considerable time the work they had begun in their manner.

Partly because our early writers thought of themselves as spokesmen for the race to outsiders rather than spokesmen to the race, they allowed themselves to use the language of outsiders instead of their own. They felt that if they accepted the standards of white writing, its conventions of language and correctness, its decorum, they and their race would be presented in a better light. With these early writers, language had to be correct, even to the point of stiffness and woodenness; they eschewed "barbarisms," meaning certain characteristic Afro images and usages. Because their speech was "purified," many slave narratives sound as though they could have been written by anyone.

When black writers tried to use dialect to reproduce sounds characteristic of our people, they were told that the only emotions dialect could convey were humor and pathos. We can either laugh at you or be maudlin over you. Our early writers accepted this two-valued orientation, apparently not realizing that this judgment on the possible uses of dialect had nothing to do with dialect, but rather with the only two feelings the arbiters of culture were willing either to show toward us themselves or to allow us to show.

Some writers of the twenties, especially those spoksmen for the "New Negro," attempted to stake out a space for black writing, where black art and culture could flower. In a foreword to his 1925 anthology *The New Negro*, Alain Locke states: "Negro life is not only establishing new centers, it is finding a new soul. There is fresh spiritual and cultural focusing. We have, as the heralding sign, an unusual outburst of creative expression. There is a renewed race-spirit that consciously and proudly sets itself apart."

Out of this "renewed race-spirit" some of the young writers began to present black life as it was lived by the majority of blacks—its vitality, its inventiveness, its strength, its fun, but also its poverty, its bitterness, its squalor. They were misread by both whites and blacks; praised by whites, who hailed them for presenting a new "primitive," and reviled by blacks for presenting "bad" things. Anticipating what was to follow and attempting to prepare the way for it, Langston Hughes issued a manifesto, a declaration of freedom, in "The Negro Artist and the Racial Mountain." He declared himself to be free to write as he chose, for whoever cared to read him. As a writer, he was going to be true to what he saw instead of to some imagined something he ought to see.

Hughes, Wallace Thurman, and others found themselves castigated by that minuscule body of blacks who had successfully copied what they thought were white manners and habits and did not wish their shaky middle place to be disturbed by an awareness of those blacks they knew were "beneath" them. They were so put off by surfaces, that a few years later they were to reject Zora Neale Hurston's *Their Eyes Were Watching God* as a story of black migrant workers, when what Miss Hurston was doing was presenting at eye level two lovers who dared to be happy in a society where happiness was sinful, where work was a duty not a pleasure, and pleasure something other.

Fortunately for us, Hughes, Miss Hurston, and Arna Bontemps (*Black Thunder*) were not dissuaded by indifferent or negative receptions, and as a result we have several works by writers who took the lives of their characters seriously, and rendered them with integrity, clarity, and precision.

In looking at our early writers, we can first see them attempting to shake off the stultifying yoke imposed by their legal masters, then writing in the manner of their masters for a time, hoping thereby to please the more book-educated blacks and not offend whites, and a few of the more courageous seeking to promote a race spirit and to recreate this spirit for their fellows. The writers of the twenties began to feel they should write for black audiences, even with the limitations this task imposed. Many of their readers were still seeing art as "universal," as some of the writers themselves did, and alas still do.

I would like to see the idea of "universal" laid to rest, along with such outmoded usages as *civilization*, as applied to the West; *social protest*, as applied to Afro literature; *pagan* and *fetish*, when applied to non-Christian religions; *primitive*, *barbarian*, and *folk*, as applied to life-styles or as judgments of culture; and *jungle*, as applied to African space. These terms are too-heavily weighted European culture judgments to be of much use.

James Weldon Johnson, writing in 1928 on what was more a dilemma for black writers then than now, that of the double audience—one white, the other black—saw a way out of that dilemma if the black author could make one audience out of what had been formerly two. He said: "The equipped Negro author working at his best in his best-known material can achieve this end; but, standing on his racial foundation, he must fashion something that *rises above race*, and reaches out to the *universal* in *truth* and *beauty*" (emphasis mine), ("The Dilemma of the Negro Author," *The American Mercury*, December 1928). When Johnson says the Afro writer's work must "rise above race" to be important, he anticipates the attempted putdown of Gwendolyn Brooks's work by a white poet: "I am not sure it is possible for a Negro to write well without making us aware he is a Negro; on the other hand, if being a Negro is the only subject, the writing is not important." Something is wrong with being *only* Negro?

Were someone to say to Johnson, "A nigger is a nigger is a nigger," he would probably be questioned about his sanity. But this same man could say, " 'Beauty is truth, truth beauty, —that is all/Ye know on earth, and all ye need to know,' " and Johnson would probably say, "How profound!" Now neither statement says any more about experience than the other, yet because of his cultural conditioning, Johnson imagines "universal in truth and beauty" says something about a standard of aesthetics, when in reality he is talking about cultural judgments, and ultimately the way power is exercised in our society.

Johnson said that we should not ignore whites, because they made up 90 per cent of the population and we were surrounded by them. He might have added, had he dared, that they also control publishing, film, and broadcasting, and make up the largest share of the market for our wares.

Clearly, much of the koash-koash hinges on *universal,* and the value some of us give to it as opposed to the idea of black. Some of us keep feeling that to be black is not to be universal, and to be black is to be limited. Why is black such a limiting idea? Underlying much of the clever words and prolonged agonies is the simple refusal, no matter how sophisticated and learned the attempt at concealment, no matter how much "evidence" is presented for the evasions, the by now complex refusal, to accept the validity of our experience and to give that experience the same credence as any other.

LeRoi Jones said that a man once said to him: "But your experience is weird." Jones replied: "Yes, it *is* weird. Which means it's a weird place we live in." Al Young, black poet and college professor, writes in *Dancing:* "Life *is* more than fun & games/The thought/after all/that either of us is capable of being assassinated/at any moment/for absolutely nothing/ & relatively little/is of course unnerving."

At one point in our history, many U.S. writers made a conscious effort to break with the literatures of Europe. To the extent of taking many of their themes from mainland North America and developing local language, the language founded by Mark Twain, they were successful. They were not successful, though, in eliminating a vertical structure for society, the two-valued orientation, the Platonic ideal, monotheism, and finance capitalism. These were as thoroughly ingrained in the new literature as in the old. What was omitted by the new literature was an attempt to get inside the slave or freedman and inquire: What is it like for *me* in this alien place? Because of this omission, Hughes was prompted to say: "If anybody's gonna write about me, I reckon it'll be/Me myself!"

The black story has not been told. We have written about ourselves neither enough nor well enough. Today's young writers are again attempting to continue the work begun in the twenties, that is, to write out of a central experience of black life in the United States and show that life from their particular racial foundations. That the objections to such a path by our book-educated have not changed much from the earlier time, may be suggested by some reactions to the idea of a black aesthetic.

In a questionnaire to black writers on writers and literary

values, Hoyt W. Fuller asked in the January 1969 *Negro Digest* (now *Black World*): "Do you see any future at all for the school of black writers which seeks to establish 'a black aesthetic'?" This question, partly because of the anxieties it raised, drew some put-offs, some guffaws, and some considered replies. Despite its form, Mr. Fuller has not asked an easy question, as, I think, what follows will amply demonstrate.

Saunders Redding answered: "No. Not in America. Besides, aesthetics has no racial, national, or geographical boundaries. Beauty and truth, the principal components of aesthetics, are universal." Robert Hayden, through implication, shares a point with Redding and asks a question of his own: "It seems to me that a 'black aesthetic' would only be possible in a predominately black culture. Yet not even black African writers subscribe to such an aesthetic. And isn't the so-called 'black aesthetic' simply protest and racist propaganda in a new guise?" An answer with very different implications was Addison Gayle, Jr.'s: "The 'black aesthetic' has always been a part of the lives of black people. To investigate these lives, and the conditions surrounding them, is to reveal an aesthetic inherent in the soul of black people."

What I have been saying is more closely in keeping with Professor Gayle's views. It may be that a black aesthetic is inherent in the black experience, and is rendered when we honestly recreate that experience. No writer "tells it like it is." If he did, we'd probably be bored to sleep. What a writer tells is "it like he needs it to be," in order to make sense out of his experience and the experiences of those whose world he recreates. When we write about ourselves from a point of view that takes black life seriously, that views it in scale, with human dimensions, then we are creating a black aesthetic.

WALT SHEPPERD

Clarence Major, (see note in poetry section, p. 298) and Victor Hernandez Cruz (see note in poetry section, pp. 237–38) were among the writers participating in the Summer Institute on Black Excellence at Cazenovia College in Cazenovia, New York, in 1969. Walt Shepperd, editor of The Nickel Review, *a literary publication which published many contributions by Black writers, published this joint interview with Clarence Major and Victor Hernandez Cruz at this Institute in* The Nickel Review, *September 12, 1969.*

An Interview with Clarence Major and Victor Hernandez Cruz

[SHEPPERD]: Clarence, in your anthology *The New Black Poetry,* are you giving us, by your selection of poets, standards for the definition of a black aesthetic?

MAJOR: What I've had to come to realize is that the question of a black aesthetic is something that's come down to an individual question. It seems to me that if there is a premise in an artist's work, be he black or white, that it comes out of his work, and therefore out of himself. I think that it's also true with the form. It has to be just that subjective. If there is an objective validity for the existence of a black aesthetic I think that it's in a formative stage right now. It hasn't yet been crystallized, and I don't know if it would be legitimate if it *could* be crystallized because there are so many forces at work.

[SHEPPERD]: If we could expand this question to include your book Victor, *Snaps* it seems, is poetry that the cat on the corner, particularly the young, can identify with easily. Do you see the emergence of an aesthetic of the streets, perhaps an aesthetic of the oppressed?

CRUZ: The poems in *Snaps* were written in a period when that was more or less what I was coming out of. I used those experiences just like any poet has done in the past. I don't like to say that my work is a part of a new thing that can be identified or pinpointed so that now I can have an umbrella over me or something, because here I am in Cazenovia and I should be able to write poems about this. I feel that the writer—a black writer or a Puerto Rican writer—should have just as much right to talk about the universe and how it started as any other writer. I think that some of the people who are into this black writing thing really complicate it to the point where you've got to conform to it and if you don't you're supposed to be doing something unnatural. I think a writer should use his total spectrum and no matter what the situation, he should be able to come out with his own thing. I'm Puerto Rican, but when I was on the airplane coming over here there was no Puerto Ricans, there was just me up there in the air, and I could create out of that. I could create out of anything, and I think it's wrong to say that because you're a black or Puerto Rican writer you can't use the whole universe as your field.

MAJOR: That's something that I really began working on with these people in Cazenovia. They're at this conference to try to learn how to put together a Black Studies course, to go back to their black students and teach Black Lit. And like they're sitting there man, really expecting to learn how the black experience and therefore Black Lit is special and different.

They're expecting to be let into some kind of deep dark secret. Like, "tell us what it is . . . we have to know . . . what is this special thing, this experience of yours that we can't penetrate . . . what is it?" They really are so convinced that these problems are real; all this shit is in their minds. They can quote Don Quixote and get through it right away. They never lived in Spain and it would be a very strange place for any of them, and yet they can get through Don Quixote on a human level. And I think they could get through a lot of

Black Lit if they didn't have these social hang-ups that are created by outside forces.

[SHEPPERD]: Let's talk about those forces for a minute. Victor mentioned black writers complicating their own scene. But you've both had experience with the big publishing houses; don't they have rubber stamps for the book jackets that say "bitter," "angry," "oppressed?" Don't the publishing companies really push you into that bag anyway, or at least try to?

CRUZ: Well a woman in *Negro Digest* mentioned that she couldn't understand why my book was published by Random House. But I don't know, publishing seems better than it used to be. Most people who are in publishing seem eager to get black writers. I would have the same approach to the publishers no matter who they were. Today, especially in poetry, one of the most important things is to get it out there. And anybody into poetry knows how hard it is to get it out there.

MAJOR: Along the same line, about the psychology of publishers. I had lunch with an editor not too long ago and she's considering work by a young black poet, one of the poets in my anthology. He had submitted a manuscript of poems and she really dug them. She really thought they were great. But she couldn't possibly consider it or recommend them to her publisher because there's nothing there to indicate that they were written by a black poet. And they can't run a photo of him on each page. She said *that:* "We can't possibly run a photo of him on each page." This is an editor, a person who can make decisions sitting right there and saying that kind of shit.

CRUZ: This is the same kind of thing that happens with a black publishing company. They'll put you in a bag too. It will probably be quite some time before poets can stand on their own worth no matter what they're talking about. I think that Clarence's book *All Night Visitors* is a milestone for a different thing in black writing. In the past some of the black writers have dealt with sex, for example, in a much different way.

MAJOR: In other words, its not a Christian book. That's why a lot of people won't be able to get through it.

CRUZ: It's a book, man, it stands by itself, and you really couldn't go around trying to relate it to a course.

MAJOR: The people at this conference are having a bitch of a time with it, by the way. It's required reading. Before I got here they were all like in the dorm whispering to each other. They were questioning my motives. Some of these people are 60 years old. Two of them are nuns. We finally got into a discussion of *All Night Visitors*. I ran it down and gave them my impression of it and they were really relieved. Some of them said, like, "I'm really glad you told me what you were trying to say because it really puzzled me. I just would never leave this lying around the house where my daughter could find it. And as a teacher I would never consider using it." So then I got into this business about the reason they couldn't get to it. It's because of this whole thing of sex being dirty: because of what St. Paul left to the culture. And the only person who came up to me later and said something about it was a nun. She's not wearing her habit now. She said, "You know, you're right; we are too hung-up."

[SHEPPERD]: Along the line of talking about leaving the books out for the daughters to see them, especially when these days the daughters have probably read them first, Victor's poetry seems to relate directly to what young people can see on the block. Are we reaching a point where we no longer need to append to a page of poetry that it was written by a 14-year-old girl as a rationale for it's not meeting certain aesthetic standards? Are we reaching a point where perhaps a 14-year-old girl in the ghetto can capture in her poetry the images that hit us in the gut perhaps even better than did Langston Hughes with all his aesthetic excellence?

MAJOR: I think those standards should really be questioned. I'm doing it myself. I'm really questioning a lot of accepted standards.

CRUZ: I think that a lot of what's happening in American Literature is that people kind of know what to expect. And if somebody from Harlem writes a book they are expected to be a manchild in the promised land. People only really like something when they know exactly what's coming. But I write what I really *want* to do. I'm dealing more with Puerto Rican music and Puerto Rican rhythm and I'm using a lot of chants. I'm relying a lot on religion, the spiritualism that has always been in Caribbean culture. And I'm dealing with the African gods and how people use them, the whole thing of being possessed by spirits. What I'm getting into is getting away from something you see in a lot of black poetry, the thing it's much more important to get involved in life and what people are experiencing because that will be able to stand a lot longer time than an attack which may be over after a while. Poetry should be creating life instead of using it as some kind of vehicle for some already known object.

MAJOR: Ideally a writer might actually set as a goal the day when he can stop writing.

[SHEPPERD]: Getting back to what you said about being somewhat uncomfortable running down strictly criticism and interpretation, you mentioned that it was a more meaningful experience to read your work. But doesn't the writer run the risk of being put on the shelf as an entertainer?

MAJOR: One person really got to that at the conference. Most of the participants call me Clarence, but she said, "Mr. Major, I sense in you an uneasiness like we're imposing on you, and I don't want to bother you with a whole lot of stupid questions, but I know that somehow all of us are missing the point." And this is what she meant. "I don't want to force you to have to perform, to do something you don't want to do because what's going on in you in terms of yourself as a writer is a very private process." Then just for a moment we were quiet, and I think we really communicated.

I read my work, and that doesn't bother me, but it's afterwards, when people come up to ask dumb questions. Sometimes I can handle it, but I don't like to be nasty. Like when I was at the University of Rhode Island, I read sections of *All Night Visitors*. Afterward a teacher came up and said, "all those four letter words, it's unbelievable in a school situation. But after the shock wore off, it really became functional."

CRUZ: The problem I find is that I go to read my poems, and they want me to predict the future. Like what's going to happen this summer? And how should I know?

MAJOR: What's happening there is that in this society if you've written a book it makes you an authority on everything.

[SHEPPERD]: Isn't this also a very subtle racism? People didn't go to Steinbeck and ask him what was going to happen in the ghetto. Isn't it because the ghetto is supposed to be full of illiterates, minority groups are supposed to be stupid and lazy, and here you both have conformed on the white standard of writing a book and getting it published by a major house? Therefore, you're made the spokesman, just like Richard Wright was made a spokesman, just like Baldwin was made a spokesman, just like Cleaver was made a spokesman.

CRUZ: Right. One cat even asked me about Puerto Ricans in labor unions. They try to make you into something they can understand, then they can go home feeling OK. But with me, they went home without understanding me. And I don't understand myself, because I won't play their game.

[SHEPPERD]: This gets to a point raised in the conference about the balance in a Black Literature course between art and politics. In a time of social change everyone is pushing, and you as writers must get pushed pretty hard. What kind of relationship do you have to work out between art and politics?

MAJOR: Well obviously, art is always neglected. Look at a book like *Cane*, neglected all these years. Even now it's being brought back and revived for the wrong reasons, political rather than aesthetic reasons.

CRUZ: A good example of this is one time I read my poems and I said something about the Puerto Rican flag. Now the flag and all the symbols of the Puerto Rican nationalists are very, very important to them. So afterward one of them came up to me and said, "Hey, what did you have to say that for?" You know, it shows that in a way all these revolutionary nationalist movements are really very conservative. LeRoi Jones said something about this. He said that the *true* revolutionary wants to change the culture.

[SHEPPERD]: In terms of changing the culture, Ishmael Reed seems to be telling us in his work, particularly in his use of Eastern and Egyptian symbolism, that we can participate in this kind of revolution if we change our cultural reference points. What he and Jones before him seem to be saying is that we need a new language. How do you come to grips with this in your work?

MAJOR: I think that we're all suffering from cultural shock. There are a lot of things that won't be clear until we get out of that. The only thing I trust now is my intuition. The American Communist Party has been telling us for generations that all we have to do to get things straight is to eliminate capitalism. But I think we're seeing that it goes way far beyond that. There are, however, some really interesting things happening in Cuba, and I wish I knew more about them.

CRUZ: This is a racist culture, and if you want to eliminate racism, you have to eliminate the whole culture. Even in Cuba they're having problems because they're approaching problems from a European bag. Latin America shouldn't even be called Latin it's really Indo-America.

[SHEPPERD]: Since the novel is a Western invention, do we need a new form to express what the new culture will be?

MAJOR: I don't know if the novel is something worth saving. The word itself is really totally inappropriate.

CRUZ: I'm trying to work a thing into my readings with singing and Caribbean instruments, like the marracas, the cowbell, the cobassa. If you've ever heard Eddie Palmeri or Ray Parreto, you know they have an *after* thing. After one sings, the others come in with something else. It backs you up. This is what I'm trying to do with some people from New York. This, after all, is what Caribbean music is: poetry. In Puerto Rico and Cuba they have street singers who walk the streets singing the blues, or singing about happiness. A lot of Caribbean music is about happiness. Which in a lot of ways is like an Eastern thing. And this is what I want to get into, because this is the way we can tell people to get up and dance. It's the same kind of thing being done by the Temptations. When you get people dancing you can really get people *into* the lyrics, not just listening to them. A big Latin dance in New York is something a very intellectual dude from Harvard can't understand because he can't catch the sensibility of it. Ray Parreto has a song called *Live and Mess Around*. That's what I want to get to in my poetry. It's like a very rhythmic thing. It's like a tradition, like an ongoing thing.

[SHEPPERD]: Are these traditions that have been lost in our culture, or have they been there all the time, in all sectors of American society?

CRUZ: I don't know what the rest of America is doing, but these are things that have been very much kept in black and Puerto Rican neighborhoods, and in the mountains too. It's a music, not a listening music; it's a dance music. If you talked to a group of Puerto Rican teen-agers, they'd be talking about the dance steps and how to do them. And that's really where it's at. It's not something you can sit around and talk about, it's something you've got to get up and do; the invitation to the dance.

[SHEPPERD]: You've both rejected the role of prophets here, saying that you're forced into that role too often, but I'm going to ask you to prophesy just a little. What will we see in the literature of the '70's?

CRUZ: I can only think in terms of what I'm going to be doing. I think that the whole presentation of the writer will be changed. Like the thing about having a book out. I could dig getting more into leaflets. The writer needs to get more into HIS world, what comes out of HIS head: feelings and emotions. Actually the only thing we should keep is words: everything else should break down.

MAJOR: I'd like to pick up on what Victor was saying, particularly about not generalizing. Yesterday Addison Gayle, a consultant to this program, asked me if it bothered me that James Baldwin sees the homosexual crisis as something intrinsic to the black experience. I told him that it didn't bother me because it wasn't *my* problem. What I mean to say with that example is that I wouldn't *dare* to predict the future. In the next ten years I'd really like to do something with the novel. I'd like to do something new with the novel as form, and getting rid of that name would be the first step.

AL YOUNG (1939–   )

A biographical note on Al Young appears in the fiction section (see p. 146), and his poems appear in the poetry section. A lengthy article, based on an interview with Al Young, appeared in the Sunday magazine section of the San Francisco Sunday Examiner & Chronicle, *May 3, 1970. In a letter to Al Young I asked for permission to reprint some of the things he had said in that interview: One thing led to another and finally I received the following statement written for* New Black Voices.

Statement on Aesthetics, Poetics, Kinetics

For me it's touch that matters most. You reach out & you touch someone. Both toucher & the one touched may be changed.

Singing, playing, dancing, painting, sculpting, acting, laughing, crying, winning, hurting, writing—all these are ways of reaching out & they all come back down to that basic touch, a way of seeing, a way of saying: "I live in the world too & this is my way of being here with you." (But *with soul* if it's to have any meaning!)

Sometimes a poem is field enough to contain what I need to say. Sometimes the saying takes the form of an extended solo in prose, a short story, a novel. I don't really have any control over this. It happens as it must. Everything is in process anyway. Love, like electricity or revolution or becoming, is a process (not a thing), a revolving towards, a way things happen. My life happens to revolve around sound (people-talk, language, music) & I express my love of it by writing.

Poems I scribble on scraps of paper which I then stuff

into a desk drawer & may not see again for months. I'm always surprised by what I find. For prose I use a typewriter. What does it matter? Sawing wood, walking the streets or sitting arms folded by an ocean in a dream, I'm writing just the same.

There is now taking place a heady flowering of black genius unlike anything that's been experienced before. Young writers, for example, are emerging who're more concerned with touching other human beings than with titilating the middle-classes; original men & women striving to express & give shape to the unthinkable variety of feeling & thought in the black communities which we weren't allowed to share in the 1960s, say, when Black Anger was all the rage & media made a killing.

This whole business of art as hustle—which seems to be where we've come to at this stage of the interminable 20th Century—has to be challenged. I've always believed the individual human heart to be more revolutionary than any political party or platform.

You cannot wear the word *love* out.

Revolution arises out of need.

Revolution is we need to change our ways of being with one another.

Revolution is we need one another.

Let the revolutions proceed!

4.

Documents

February 21, 1965 the Organization which Malcolm founded

MALCOLM X (1925–1965)

*The great impact of Malcolm X on the contemporary Black
cultural movements is evident in the many poems by Black
poets inspired by Malcolm X and the references to his legacy
in the essays in the Criticism section of this anthology. In
June 1964 Malcolm X announced the formation of the Organization of Afro-American Unity. In a letter that he made
public at that time Malcolm X wrote: "Its purpose is to unite
Afro-Americans and their organizations around a non-religious
and non-sectarian constructive purpose for human rights."
The program of this organization is the final expression of
the views and thinking of Malcolm X and illuminates the
ideological soil in which many of the contemporary Black
arts movements have been nurtured. The "Statement of Basic
Aims and Objectives of the Organization of Afro-American
Unity" was read aloud by Malcolm X on June 28, 1964, at a
rally in the Audubon Ballroom in Harlem.*

In his book The Last Year of Malcolm X, *George Breitman
writes: "The June 'Statement of Basic Aims and Objectives'
was evidently not considered sufficient. On January 17, 1965,
Malcolm announced that an OAAU committee was working
on a program. Early in February he stated that the program,
which was 'designed to galvanize the black masses of Harlem
to become the instruments of their own liberation' and offered
the only 'alternative to violence and bloodshed' would be
presented at an OAAU rally on February 15. This document,
which Malcolm approved and accepted although he did not
write it, was entitled the 'Basic Unity Program.' But Malcolm's
home was bombed on February 14, and the February 15
meeting revolved around a discussion of that event, with
presentation of the program postponed to the next meeting,*

February 21. That was the meeting where Malcolm was shot down, before he could speak about the program or anything else." Following are the two OAAU documents.

Statement of Basic Aims and Objectives of the Organization of Afro-American Unity*

The Organization of Afro-American Unity, organized and structured by a cross-section of the Afro-American people living in the U.S.A., has been patterned after the letter and spirit of the Organization of African Unity established at Addis Ababa, Ethiopia, May, 1963.

We, the members of the Organization of Afro-American Unity gathered together in Harlem, New York:

Convinced that it is the inalienable right of all people to control their own destiny;

Conscious of the fact that freedom, equality, justice and dignity are essential objectives for the achievement of the legitimate aspirations of the people of African descent here in the Western Hemisphere, we will endeavor to build a bridge of understanding and create the basis for Afro-American unity;

Conscious of our responsibility to harness the natural and human resources of our people for their total advancement in all spheres of human endeavor;

Inspired by a common determination to promote understanding among our people and co-operation in all matters pertaining to their survival and advancement, we will support the aspirations of our people for brotherhood and solidarity in a larger unity transcending all organizational differences;

Convinced that, in order to translate this determination into a dynamic force in the cause of human progress, conditions of peace and security must be established and maintained;

Determined to unify the Americans of African descent in their fight for human rights and dignity, and being fully aware that this is not possible in the present atmosphere and condition of oppression, we dedicate ourselves to the building of a political, economic, and social system of justice and peace;

Dedicated to the unification of all people of African descent in this hemisphere and to the utilization of that unity to bring

*Dated June 28, 1964.

into being the organizational structure that will project the black people's contributions to the world;

Persuaded that the Charter of the United . Nations, the Universal Declaration of Human Rights, the Constitution of the U.S.A. and the Bill of Rights are the principles in which we believe and these documents if put into practice represent the essence of mankind's hopes and good intentions;

Desirous that all Afro-American people and organizations should henceforth unite so that the welfare and well-being of our people will be assured;

Resolved to reinforce the common bond of purpose between our people by submerging all of our differences and establishing a non-religious and non-sectarian constructive program for human rights;

Do hereby present this charter.

I. Establishment

The Organization of Afro-American Unity shall include all people of African descent in the Western Hemisphere, as well as our brothers and sisters on the African Continent.

II. Self-Defense

Since self-preservation is the first law of nature, we assert the Afro-American's right of self-defense.

The Constitution of the U.S.A. clearly affirms the right of every American citizen to bear arms. And as Americans, we will not give up a single right guaranteed under the Constitution. The history of the unpunished violence against our people clearly indicates that we must be prepared to defend ourselves or we will continue to be a defenseless people at the mercy of a ruthless and violent racist mob.

We assert that in those areas where the government is either unable or unwilling to protect the lives and property of our people, that our people are within their rights to protect themselves by whatever means necessary. A man with a rifle or club can only be stopped by a person who defends himself with a rifle or club.

Tactics based solely on morality can only succeed when you are dealing with basically moral people or a moral system. A man or system which oppresses a man because of his color is not moral. It is the duty of every Afro-American and every Afro-American community throughout this country to protect its people against mass murderers, bombers, lynchers, floggers, brutalizers and exploiters.

III. Education

Education is an important element in the struggle for human rights. It is the means to help our children and people rediscover their identity and thereby increase self-respect. Education is our passport to the future, for tomorrow belongs to the people who prepare for it today.

Our children are being criminally shortchanged in the public school system of America. The Afro-American schools are the poorest run schools in New York City. Principals and teachers fail to understand the nature of the problems with which they work and as a result they cannot do the job of teaching our children. The textbooks tell our children nothing about the great contributions of Afro-Americans to the growth and development of this country. The Board of Education's integration program is expensive and unworkable; and the organization of principals and supervisors in the New York city school system has refused to support the Board's plan to integrate the schools, thus dooming it to failure.

The Board of Education has said that even with its plan there are ten per cent of the schools in the Harlem–Bedford-Stuyvesant community they cannot improve. This means that the Organization of Afro-American Unity must make the Afro-American community a more potent force for educational self-improvement.

A first step in the program to end the existing system of racist education is to demand that the ten per cent of the schools the Board of Education will not include in its plan be turned over to and run by the Afro-American community. We want Afro-American principals to head these schools. We want Afro-American teachers in these schools. We want textbooks written by Afro-Americans that are acceptable to us to be used in these schools.

The Organization of Afro-American Unity will select and recommend people to serve on local school boards where school policy is made and passed on to the Board of Education.

Through these steps we will make the ten per cent of schools we take over educational showplaces that will attract the attention of people all over the nation.

If these proposals are not met, we will ask Afro-American parents to keep their children out of the present inferior schools they attend. When these schools in our neighborhood are controlled by Afro-Americans, we will return to them.

The Organization of Afro-American Unity recognizes the tremendous importance of the complete involvement of Afro-American parents in every phase of school life. Afro-American parents must be willing and able to go into the schools and see that the job of educating our children is done properly.

We call on all Afro-Americans around the nation to be aware that the conditions that exist in the New York City public school system are as deporable in their cities as they are here. We must unite our effort and spread our program of self-improvement through education to every Afro-American community in America.

We must establish all over the country schools of our own to train our children to become scientists and mathematicians. We must realize the need for adult education and for job retraining programs that will emphasize a changing society in which automation plays the key role. We intend to use the tools of education to help raise our people to an unprecedented level of excellence and self-respect through their own efforts.

IV. Politics—Economics

Basically, there are two kinds of power that count in America: economic and political, with social power deriving from the two. In order for the Afro-Americans to control their destiny, they must be able to control and affect the decisions which control their destiny: economic, political and social. This can only be done through organization.

The Organization of Afro-American Unity will organize the Afro-American community block by block to make the community aware of its power and potential; we will start immediately a voter-registration drive to make every unregistered voter in the Afro-American community an independent voter; we propose to support and/or organize political clubs, to run independent candidates for office, and to support any Afro-American already in office who answers to and is responsible to the Afro-American community.

Economic exploitation in the Afro-American community is the most vicious form practiced on any people in America; twice as much rent for rat-infested, roach-crawling, rotting tenements; the Afro-American pays more for foods, clothing, insurance rates and so forth. The Organization of Afro-American Unity will wage an unrelenting struggle against these evils in our community. There shall be organizers to work with the people to solve these problems, and start a housing self-improvement program. We propose to support rent strikes and other activities designed to better the community.

V. Social

This organization is responsible only to the Afro-American people and community and will function only with their support, both financially and numerically. We believe that our communities must be the sources of their own strength politically, economically, intellectually and culturally in the struggle for human rights and dignity.

The community must reinforce its moral responsibility to rid itself of the effects of years of exploitation, neglect and apathy, and wage an unrelenting struggle against police brutality.

The Afro-American community must accept the responsibility for regaining our people who have lost their place in society. We must declare an all-out war on organized crime in our community; a vice that is controlled by policemen who accept bribes and graft, and who must be exposed. We must establish a clinic, whereby one can get aid and cure for drug addiction; and create meaningful, creative, useful activities for those who were led astray down the avenues of vice.

The people of the Afro-American community must be prepared to help each other in all ways possible; we must establish a place where unwed mothers can get help and advice; a home for the aged in Harlem and an orphanage in Harlem.

We must set up a guardian system that will help our youth who get into trouble and also provide constructive activities for our children. We must set a good example for our children and must teach them to always be ready to accept the responsibilities that are necessary for building good communities and nations. We must teach them that their greatest responsibilities are to themselves, to their families and to their communities.

The Organization of Afro-American Unity believes that the Afro-American community must endeavor to do the major part of all charity work from within the community. Charity, however, does not mean that to which we are legally entitled in the form of government benefits. The Afro-American veteran must be made aware of all the benefits due him and the procedure for obtaining them. These veterans must be encouraged to go into business together, using G.I. loans, etc.

Afro-Americans must unite and work together. We must take pride in the Afro-American community, for it is home and it is power.

What we do here in regaining our self-respect, manhood, dignity and freedom helps all people everywhere who are fighting against oppression.

VI. *Culture*

"A race of people is like an individual man; until it uses its own talent, takes pride in its own history, expresses its own culture, affirms its own selfhood, it can never fulfill itself."

Our history and our culture were completely destroyed when we were forcibly brought to America in chains. And now it is important for us to know that our history did not begin with slavery's scars. We come from Africa, a great continent and a proud and varied people, a land which is the new world and was the cradle of civilization. Our culture and our history are as old as man himself and yet we know almost nothing of it. We must recapture our heritage and our identity if we are ever to liberate ourselves from the bonds of white supremacy. We must launch a cultural revolution to unbrainwash an entire people.

Our cultural revolution must be the means of bringing us closer to our African brothers and sisters. It must begin in the community and be based on community participation. Afro-Americans will be free to create only when they can depend on the Afro-American community for support and Afro-American artists must realize that they depend on the Afro-American for inspiration. We must work toward the establishment of a cultural center in Harlem, which will include people of all ages, and will conduct workshops in all the arts, such as film, creative writing, painting, theater, music, Afro-American history, etc.

This cultural revolution will be the journey to our rediscovery of ourselves. History is a people's memory, and without a memory man is demoted to the lower animals.

Armed with the knowledge of the past, we can with confidence charter a course for our future. Culture is an indispensable weapon in the freedom struggle. We must take hold of it and forge the future with the past.

* * *

When the battle is won, let history be able to say to each one of us: "He was a dedicated patriot: *Dignity* was his country, *Manhood* was his government, and *Freedom* was his land" [from *And Then We heard the Thunder,* by John Oliver Killens].

Basic Unity Program, Organization of Afro-American Unity

Pledging unity . . .
  Promoting justice . . .
  Transcending compromise . . .
  We, Afro-Americans, people who originated in Africa and now reside in America, speak out against the slavery and oppression inflicted upon us by this racist power structure. We offer to downtrodden Afro-American people courses of action that will conquer oppression, relieve suffering and convert meaningless struggle into meaningful action.

Confident that our purpose will be achieved, we Afro-Americans from all walks of life make the following known:

Establishment

Having stated our determination, confidence and resolve, the Organization of Afro-American Unity is hereby established on the 15th day of February, 1965, in the city of New York.

Upon this establishment, we Afro-American people will launch a cultural revolution which will provide the means for restoring our identity that we might rejoin our brothers and sisters on the African continent, culturally, psychologically, economically and share with them the sweet fruits of freedom from oppression and independence of racist governments.

1. The Organization of Afro-American Unity welcomes all persons of African origin to come together and dedicate their ideas, skills and lives to free our people from oppression.

2. Branches of the Organization of Afro-American Unity may be established by people of African descent wherever they may be and whatever their ideology—as long as they be descendants of Africa and dedicated to our one goal: Freedom from oppression.

3. The basic program of the Organization of Afro-American Unity which is now being presented can and will be modified by the membership, taking into consideration national, regional and local conditions that require flexible treatment.

4. The Organization of Afro-American Unity encourages active participation of each member since we feel that each and every Afro-American has something to contribute to our freedom. Thus each member will be encouraged to participate in the committee of his or her choice.

5. Understanding the differences that have been created amongst us by our oppressors in order to keep us divided, the Organization of Afro-American Unity strives to ignore or submerge these artificial divisions by focusing our activities and our loyalties upon our one goal: Freedom from oppression.

Basic Aims and Objectives

Self-determination

We assert that we Afro-Americans have the right to direct and control our lives, our history and our future rather than to have our destinies determined by American racists . . .

We are determined to rediscover our true African culture which was crushed and hidden for over four hundred years in order to enslave us and keep us enslaved up to today . . .

We, Afro-Americans—enslaved, oppressed and denied by a society that proclaims itself the citadel of democracy, are determined to rediscover our history, promote the talents that are suppressed by our racist enslavers, renew the culture that was crushed by a slave government and thereby—to again become a free people.

National Unity

Sincerely believing that the future of Afro-Americans is dependent upon our ability to unite our ideas, skills, organizations and institutions . . .

We, the Organization of Afro-American Unity pledge to join hands and hearts with all people of African origin in a grand alliance by forgetting all the differences that the power structure has created to keep us divided and enslaved. We further pledge to strengthen our common bond and strive toward one goal: Freedom from oppression.

The Basic Unity Program

The program of the Organization of Afro-American Unity shall evolve from five strategic points which are deemed basic and fundamental to our grand alliance. Through our committees we shall proceed in the following general areas:

I. Restoration

In order to enslave the African it was necessary for our enslavers to completely sever our communications with the African continent and the Africans that remained there. In order to free ourselves from the oppression of our enslavers then, it is absolutely necessary for the Afro-American to restore communications with Africa.

The Organization of Afro-American Unity will accomplish this goal by means of independent national and international newspapers, publishing ventures, personal contacts and other available communications media.

We, Afro-Americans, must also communicate to one another the truths about American slavery and the terrible effects it has upon our people. We must study the modern system of slavery in order to free ourselves from it. We must search out all the bare and ugly facts without shame for we are still victims, still slaves—still oppressed. Our only shame is believing falsehood and not seeking the truth.

We must learn all that we can about ourselves. We will have to know the whole story of how we were kidnapped from Africa, how our ancestors were brutalized, dehumanized and murdered and how we are continually kept in a state of slavery for the profit of a system conceived in slavery, built by slaves and dedicated to keeping us enslaved in order to maintain itself.

We must begin to reeducate ourselves and become alert listeners in order to learn as much as we can about the progress of our Motherland—Africa. We must correct in our minds the distorted image that our enslaver has portrayed to us of Africa that he might discourage us from reestablishing communications with her and thus obtain freedom from oppression.

II. Reorientation

In order to *keep* the Afro-American enslaved, it was necessary to limit our thinking to the shores of America—to prevent us from identifying our problems with the problems of other peoples of African origin. This made us consider ourselves an isolated minority without allies anywhere.

The Organization of Afro-American Unity will develop in the Afro-American people a keen awareness of our relationship with the world at large and clarify our roles, rights and responsibilities as human beings. We can accomplish this goal by becoming well informed concerning world affairs and understanding that our struggle is part of a larger world struggle of oppressed peoples against all forms of oppression. We must change the thinking of the Afro-American by liberating our minds through the study of philosophies and psychologies, cultures and languages that did not come from our racist oppressors. Provisions are being made for the study of languages such as Swahili, Hausa and Arabic. These studies will give our people access to ideas and history of mankind at large and thus increase our mental scope.

We can learn much about Africa by reading informative books and by listening to the experiences of those who have traveled there, but many of us can travel to the land of our choice and experience for ourselves. The Organization of Afro-American Unity will encourage the Afro-American to travel to Africa, the Caribbean and to other places where our culture has not been completely crushed by brutality and ruthlessness.

III. Education

After enslaving us, the slavemasters developed a racist educational system which justified to its posterity the evil deeds that had been committed against the African people and their descendants. Too often the slave himself participates so completely in this system that he justifies having been enslaved and oppressed.

The Organization of Afro-American Unity will devise original educational methods and procedures which will liberate the minds of our children from the vicious lies and distortions that are fed to us from the cradle to keep us mentally enslaved. We encourage Afro-Americans themselves to establish experimental institutes and educational workshops, liberation schools and child-care centers in the Afro-American communities.

We will influence the choice of textbooks and equipment used by our children in the public schools while at the same time encouraging qualified Afro-Americans to write and publish the textbooks needed to liberate our minds. Until we completely control our own educational institutions, we must supplement the formal training of our children by educating them at home.

IV. Economic Security

After the Emancipation Proclamation, when the system of slavery changed from chattel slavery to wage slavery, it was realized that the Afro-American constituted the largest homogeneous ethnic group with a common origin and common group experience in the United States and, if allowed to exercise economic or political freedom, would in a short period of time own this country. Therefore racists in this government developed techniques that would keep the Afro-American people economically dependent upon the slavemasters—economically slaves—twentieth century slaves.

The Organization of Afro-American Unity will take measures to free our people from economic slavery. One way of accomplishing this will be to maintain a Technician Pool: that is, a Bank of Technicians. In the same manner that blood banks have been established to furnish blood to those who need it at the time it is needed, we must establish a Technician Bank. We must do this so that the newly independent nations of Africa can turn to us who are their Afro-American brothers for the technicians they will need now and in the future. Thereby, we will be developing an open market for the many skills we possess and at the same time we will be supplying Africa with the skills she can best use. This project will therefore be one of mutual cooperation and mutual benefit.

V. Self-Defense

In order to enslave a people and keep them subjugated, their right to self-defense must be denied. They must be constantly terrorized, brutalized and murdered. These tactics of suppression have been developed to a new high by vicious racists whom the United States government seems unwilling or incapable of dealing with in terms of the law of this land. Before the Emancipation it was the black man who suffered humiliation, torture, castration, and murder. Recently our women and children, more and more, are becoming the victims of savage racists whose appetite for blood increases daily and whose deeds of depravity seem to be openly encouraged by all law enforcement agencies. Over 5,000 Afro-Americans have been lynched since the Emancipation Proclamation and not one murderer has been brought to justice!

The Organization of Afro-American Unity, being aware of the increased violence being visited upon the Afro-American and of the open sanction of this violence and murder by the police departments throughout this country and the federal agencies—do affirm our right and obligation to defend ourselves in order to survive as a people.

We encourage all Afro-Americans to defend themselves against the wanton attacks of racist aggressors whose sole aim is to deny us the guarantees of the United Nations Charter of Human Rights and of the Constitution of the United States.

The Organization of Afro-American Unity will take those private steps that are necessary to insure the survival of the Afro-American people in the face of racist aggression and the defense of our women and children. We are within our rights to see to it that the Afro-American people who fulfill their obligations to the United States government (we pay taxes and serve in the armed forces of this country like American citizens do) also exact from this government the obligations that it owes us as a people, or exact these obligations ourselves. Needless to say, among this number we include protection of certain inalienable rights such as life, liberty and the pursuit of happiness.

In areas where the United States government has shown itself unable and/or unwilling to bring to justice the racist oppressors, murderers, who kill innocent children and adults, the Organization of Afro-American Unity advocates that the Afro-American people insure ourselves that justice is done— whatever the price and *by any means necessary*.

National Concerns

General Terminologies:

We Afro-Americans feel receptive toward all peoples of goodwill. We are not opposed to multi-ethnic associations in any walk of life. In fact, we have had experiences which enable us to understand how unfortunate it is that human beings have been set apart or aside from each other because of characteristics known as "racial" characteristics.

However, Afro-Americans did not create the prejudiced

background and atmosphere in which we live. And we must face the facts. A "racial" society does exist in stark reality, and not with equality for black people; so we who are non-white must meet the problems inherited from centuries of inequalities and deal with the present situations as rationally as we are able.

The exlusive ethnic quality of our unity is necessary for self-preservation. We say this because: Our experiences backed up by history show that African culture and Afro-American culture will not be accurately recognized and reported and cannot be respectably expressed nor be secure in its survival if we remain the divided, and therefore the helpless, victims of an oppressive society.

We appreciate the fact that when the people involved have real equality and justice, ethnic intermingling can be beneficial to all. We must denounce, however, all people who are oppressive through their policies or actions and who are lacking in justice in their dealings with other people, whether the injustices proceed from power, class, or "race." We must be unified in order to be protected from abuse or misuse.

We consider the word "integration" a misleading, false term. It carries with it certain implications to which Afro-Americans cannot subscribe. This terminology has been applied to the current regulation projects which are supposedly "acceptable" to some classes of society. This very "acceptable" implies some inherent superiority or inferiority instead of acknowledging the true source of the inequalities involved.

We have observed that the usage of the term "integration" was designated and promoted by those persons who expect to continue a (nicer) type of ethnic discrimination and who intend to maintain social and economic control of all human contacts by means of imagery, classifications, quotas, and manipulations based on color, national origin, or "racial" background and characteristics.

Careful evaluation of recent experiences shows that "integration" actually describes the process by which a white society is (remains) set in a position to use, whenever it chooses to use and however it chooses to use, the best talents of non-white people. This power-web continues to build a society wherein the best contributions of Afro-Americans, in fact of all non-white people, would continue to be absorbed without note or exploited to benefit a fortunate few while the masses of both white and non-white people would remain unequal and unbenefited.

We are aware that many of us lack sufficient training and are deprived and unprepared as a result of oppression, discrimination, and the resulting discouragement, despair, and resignation. But when we are not qualified, and where we are unprepared, we must help each other and work out plans for bettering our own conditions as Afro-Americans. Then our assertions toward full opportunity can be made on the basis of equality as opposed to the calculated tokens of "integration." Therefore, we must reject this term as one used by all persons who intend to mislead Afro-Americans.

Another term, "negro," is erroneously used and is degrading in the eyes of informed and self-respecting persons of African heritage. It denotes stereotyped and debased traits of character and classifies a whole segment of humanity on the basis of false information. From all intelligent viewpoints, it is a badge of slavery and helps to prolong and perpetuate oppression and discrimination.

Persons who recognize the emotional thrust and plain show of disrespect in the southerner's use of "nigra" and the general use of "nigger" must also realize that all three words are essentially the same. The other two: "nigra" and "nigger" are blunt and undeceptive. The one representing respectability, "negro," is merely the same substance in a polished package and spelled with a capital letter. This refinement is added so that a degrading terminology can be legitimately used in general literature and "polite" conversation without embarrassment.

The term "negro" developed from a word in the Spanish language which is actually an adjective (describing word) meaning "black," that is, the *color* black. In plain English, if someone said or was called *A* "black" or *A* "dark," even a young child would very naturally question: "*A* black what?" or "*A* dark what?" because adjectives do not name, they describe. Please take note that in order to make use of this mechanism, a word was transferred from another language and deceptively changed in function from an adjective to a noun, which is a naming word. Its application in the nominative (naming) sense was intentionally used to portray persons in a position of objects or "things." It stamps the article as being "all alike and all the same." It denotes: a "darkie," a slave, a sub-human, an ex-slave, a *"negro."*

Afro-Americans must re-analyze and particularly question our own use of this term, keeping in mind all the facts. In light of the historical meanings and current implications, all intelligent and informed Afro-Americans and Africans continue to reject its use in the noun form as well as a proper adjective. Its usage shall continue to be considered as unenlightened and objectionable or deliberately offensive whether in speech or writing.

We accept the use of Afro-American, African, and Black Man in reference to persons of African heritage. To every other part of mankind goes this measure of just respect. We do not desire more nor shall we accept less.

General Considerations:

Afro-Americans, like all other people, have human rights which are inalienable. This is, these human rights cannot be legally or justly transferred *to* another. Our human rights belong to us, as to all people, through God, not through the wishes nor according to the whims of other men.

We must consider that fact and other reasons why a Proclamation of "Emancipation" should not be revered as a document of liberation. Any previous acceptance of and faith in such a document was based on sentiment, not on reality. This is a serious matter which we Afro-Americans must continue to re-evaluate.

The original root-meaning of the word *emancipation* is: "To deliver up or make over as property by means of a formal act from a purchaser." We must take note and remember that human beings cannot be *justly* bought or sold nor can their human rights be *legally* or justly taken away.

Slavery was, and still is, a criminal institution, that is: crime en masse. No matter what form it takes: subtle rules and policies, apartheid, etc., slavery and oppression of human rights stand as major crimes against God and humanity, Therefore, to relegate or change the state of such criminal deeds by means of vague legislation and noble euphemisms gives an honor to horrible commitments that is totally inappropriate.

Full implications and concomitant harvests were generally misunderstood by our foreparents and are still misunderstood or avoided by some Afro-Americans today. However, the facts remain; and we, as enlightened Afro-Americans, will not praise and encourage any belief in "emancipation." Afro-Americans everywhere must realize that to retain faith in such an idea means acceptance of being property and, therefore, less than a human being. This matter is a crucial one that Afro-Americans must continue to re-examine.

World-Wide Concerns

The time is past due for us to internationalize the problems of Afro-Americans. We have been too slow in recognizing the link in the fate of Africans with the fate of Afro-Americans. We have been too unknowing to understand and too mis-directed to ask our African brothers and sisters to help us mend the chain of our heritage.

Our African relatives who are in a majority in their own country have found it very difficult to gain independence from a minority: It is that much more difficult for Afro-Americans who are a minority away from the motherland and still oppressed by those who encourage the crushing of our African identity.

We can appreciate the material progress and recognize the opportunities available in the highly industrialized and affluent American society. Yet, we who are non-white face daily miseries resulting directly or indirectly from a systematic discrimination against us because of our God-given colors. These factors cause us to remember that our being born in America was an act of fate stemming from the separation of our foreparents from Africa; not by choice, but by force.

We have for many years been divided among ourselves through deceptions and misunderstandings created by our en-slavers, but we do here and now express our desires and intent to draw closer and be restored in knowledge and spirit through renewed relations and kinships with the African peoples. We further realize that our human rights, so long suppressed, are the rights of all mankind everywhere.

In light of all of our experiences and knowledge of the past, we, as Afro-Americans, declare recognition, sympathy, and admiration for all peoples and nations who are striving, as we are, toward self-realization and complete freedom from oppression!

The Civil Rights Bill is a similarly misleading, misin-terpreted document of legislation. The premise of its design and application is not respectable in the eyes of men who recognize what personal freedom involves and entails. Afro-Americans must answer this question for themselves: What makes this special bill necessary?

The only document that is in order and deserved with regard to the acts perpetuated through slavery and oppression prolonged to this day is a *Declaration of Condemnation*. And the only legislation worthy of consideration or endorsement by

Afro-Americans, the victims of these tragic institutions, is a *Proclamation of Restitution*. We Afro-Americans must keep these facts ever in mind.

We must continue to internationalize our philosophies and contacts toward assuming full human rights which include all the civil rights appertaining thereto. With complete understanding of our heritage as Afro-Americans, we must not do less.

Committees of the Organization of Afro-American Unity

The Cultural Committee
The Economic Committee
The Educational Committee
The Political Committee
The Publications Committee
The Social Committee
The Self-Defense Committee
The Youth Committee

Staff Committees

| Finance | Fund-raising | Legal | Membership |

INSTITUTE OF THE BLACK WORLD

The Institute of the Black World is a community of Black scholars, artists, teachers and organizers who are coming together in Atlanta under the aegis of the Martin Luther King Jr. Memorial Center. (It is also a group of more than two dozen Associates of the Institute who are located in various parts of the hemisphere.)

The Institute of the Black World is a gathering of Black intellectuals who are convinced that the gifts of their minds are meant to be fully used in the service of the Black community. It is, therefore, an experiment with scholarship in the context of struggle.

Among our basic concerns and commitments is the determi-

nation to set our skills to a new understanding of the past, and future condition of the peoples of African descent, wherever they may be found, with an initial emphasis on the American experience. This seems the least that history, or the present—to say nothing of our children—would demand of those persons who lived the Black experience and have developed certain gifts of analysis, creativity and communication.

Statement of Purpose and Program

The Institute of the Black World in Atlanta is the second element of the Martin Luther King Jr. Memorial Center to be brought into being. Its central thrust is towards the creation of an international center for Black Studies, with strong emphasis on research, broadly conceived.

Some persons have requested a statement from the Institute which would present its own rationale and its sense of direction in the creation of such a living institution. Fundamentally, of course, it is also a request for an *apologia* for our particular approach to a very thorny issue. A response to that appropriate request appears below:

Basic Assumptions

The Institute of the Black World approaches the controversial and highly significant issue of Black Studies in America with five basic assumptions. They affect the character of all that we do and all that we plan to do in the arena of Black Studies. These are the assumptions:

1. That Black Studies is really a field still being born—in spite of all the discussion which seems to take for granted the existence of an agreed upon body of thought. This is not to deny the existence of significant, and often unappreciated work related to Black Studies which has already been done, but it does deny the fact that there is any clear understanding of the specific ways in which a profound mining of the black experience challenges and transforms the basic educational structures of the nation.

2. That the establishing and the defining of the field of Black Studies stand logically as a task and a challenge

for black people in America and elsewhere. Others may be called upon for assistance, but the initiative must be ours.

3. That the Institute and its sister institutions of the Martin Luther King, Jr. Center (and the Atlanta University complex) are in an excellent position to play a central role in defining the field and creating some of the models so urgently required. In this task, of course, we must find ways of combining the thought and activities of those black persons throughout the nation who are working at the Black Studies task, often in scattered and isolated situations.

4. That a unified, rather than a conventionally understood academic, discipline-bound approach to the creation of Black Studies is not only desirable but absolutely necessary. Indeed, this unified approach is central to the demands of most thoughtful black student and faculty groups across the country.

5. That a serious building of this field is the task of years and not a make-shift program for a few persons to do in several weeks or months.

Against this background of assumptions, the planning staff of the Institute of the Black World has been working towards tentative models for more than a year (benefiting of course, from the older hopes and dreams of such predecessors in Black Studies as W. E. B. DuBois, Charles S. Johnson, Ralph Bunche and Alain Locke—to mention only a few). Already it has become apparent to us that several elements must be a part of any creative, well-structured approach to Black Studies. We have understandably sought to include them in our own planning. Among these elements are:

1. Serious research in many areas of historical and contemporary black existence which have either been ignored, or only superficially explored (*i.e.*, The Black Church and Its Theology, Comparative Black Urban Development in the New World, Comparative Slavery).

2. The encouragement of those creative artists who are searching for the meaning of a black aesthetic, who are now trying to define and build the basic ground out of which black creativity may flow in the arts. Encounter among these artists on the one hand, and scholars, activists, and students on the other, must be constant, in both formal and informal settings.

3. Continuous research on those contemporary political, economic and social policies which now shape the life

of the black community in America and which determine its future. It is clearly necessary to develop a "think tank" operation which will bring together the many varieties of black approaches to struggle and existence in America. This must be done, of course, in a nonpolemical, unpublicized black setting.

4. Constant experimentation with the meaning of Black Studies for the surrounding black community, and openness to the possible in-put from that community into the creation of Black Studies. The two-wayness of the experience is essential and must be encouraged.

5. The development of new materials for—and new approaches to—the teaching of the black experience, which must grow out of laboratory situations at every grade level.

6. The training of a constantly expanded cadre of persons deeply immersed in the materials, methods and spirit of Black Studies who can help supply the tremendous demands for personnel in a variety of formal and informal teaching environments.

7. The creation of consortium models which will make possible the constant interaction of black students and faculty on northern and southern campuses around certain selected *foci* of Black Studies. This must also expand to the encouragement and development of contacts among black students, scholars, political leaders and artists from various parts of the world. For it is clear that Black Studies cannot really be developed unless we understand more fully both the unique and the common elements of our experiences in the black diaspora.

8. The gathering and consolidation of those library and archival resources which will facilitate the development of Black Studies as it proceeds towards definition.

9. The establishment of a publishing enterprise which will not only make available the results of the experimentation and study of the Institute, but which will also encourage that increasing number of authors and researchers who wish to present their work from the heart of a black matrix.

10. The gathering, cataloging and critical analysis of those black studies programs and personnel which have already developed across the nation, so that we may begin to gain a fuller sense of direction, possibilities and problems. This process began with a summer-long semi-

nar in June, 1969, and will continue—with monthly seminars of Black Studies Directors and several larger working conferences—at least through the summer of 1971.

The Institute of the Black World sees all of these elements as crucial to the development of creative models for the kinds of Black Studies programs which will not be palliatives, but significant pathways to the redefinition of American education and of the Black Experience. These are, therefore, the elements which have guided us so far in the establishment of our own Institute.

THE BLACK WORLD FOUNDATION

The Black World Foundation came into being in 1969. Its president is Nathan Hare (see biographical note in criticism section, page 425). The first issue of its journal, The Black Scholar, was published in November 1969 and declared: "We recognize that we must re-define our lives. We must shape a culture, a politics, an economics, a sense of our past and future history. We must recognize what we have been and what we shall be, retaining that which has been good and discarding that which has been worthless. The Black Scholar shall be the journal for that definition. In its pages, Black ideologies will be examined, debated, disputed and evaluated by the Black intellectual community." Robert Chrisman, editor of The Black Scholar, is vice president of the foundation and Allan Ross is its treasurer.

Program

The Black World Foundation is a non-profit organization for the purpose of creating, publishing and distributing black educational materials.

This is a time of struggle, but there can be no meaningful, sustained black liberation unless there is a research and production center for study, analysis and creation of the necessary materials.

The Black World Foundation has been designed to meet that need.

The overall objective of The Black World Foundation is:

- To provide a forum for extensive research and dialogue for a revolutionary black ideology, the basic premise being that no fundamental change in our society is possible without an ideology that will inspire and lead to revolutionary change.

This objective will be implemented through publication and through special projects.

In publication, The Black World Foundation will:

- Publish *The Black Scholar* on a monthly basis, 10 issues per year.
- Publish basic black books by old and new writers, including booklets, pamphlets, textbooks, poetry, art reproductions, photographic essays, etc.
- Establish extensive apparatus for printing, distribution and promotion of black literature.

The Black World Foundation will establish the following projects:

- A Center for Research, Planning and Statistics, to gather data relevant to this generation of black Americans, its goals, strategy and tactics.
- Symposia and seminars on every phase of black America.
- Dialogue among various liberation groups and progressive factions within the United States, for an effective and creative exchange of information.
- Liaisons with African cultural groups for the purpose of developing a new type of cultural renaissance—from kindergarten to university.

The Black World Foundation recognizes that the condition of black America has always been a revolutionary condition; that 350 years of economic, social and racial oppression have etched this radical fact into the fabric of American life like an acid. The liberation of black America can only be achieved through the development of cultural and ideological materials that will acknowledge this revolutionary black consciousness, that will bring to fruition its new vision of humanity, the new social order toward which black America now struggles and which indeed is the only salvation for all of America.

A black cultural revolution is essential. We must shape

a culture, a politics, an economics, a sense of our past and future history, which will truly liberate. We must develop a new vision, one which is not a carbon copy of the political and cultural system that now exists, or a total rejection of all its tools and instruments, but a vision which retains that which has been good and discards that which has been worthless.

The Black Scholar, journal of black studies and research, was our first instrument for the enhancement of black culture. But much else has been accomplished in the past turbulent twelve months. Numerous booklets and scrolls have been published; many young writers have been encouraged to submit their work for publication. Both the lecture bureau and the essay contest, conducted by *The Black Scholar*, are but the first steps in a cultural and ideological campaign to generate the necessary black cultural revolution.

The Black World Foundation is now entering its second year, with an extensive program to provide analysis, research and symposiums on all the basic issues that concern black America: the economics of labor, land and industry; the control of cities; the police state; the question of genocide; of black education and the arts; of the family, their total health and well-being.

BLACK ACADEMY OF ARTS AND LETTERS

The Black Academy of Arts and Letters was founded in Boston in March, 1969, by fifty Black artists, writers and scholars, with an operational grant of $150,000, for a three-year period, from the Twentieth Century Fund. Its offices were opened and its staff began to function in March, 1970. Mrs. Julia Prettyman, executive director of the Black Academy, informed the editor in a reply to a request for information: "The Academy's programs are still in the developmental process, however, we have established a Hall of Fame and enrolled three persons: Dr. W. E. B. DuBois, Dr. Carter G. Woodson, and Henry O. Tanner. In September, 1971, we *will be enrolling three more persons to the Hall of Fame and hope to announce the establishment of an actual location at that time. We will also present additional honorary citations and monetary awards in Letters and Plastic Arts." The nature and goals of this cultural institution are explained in the following two documents: "Purposes," as defined in the bylaws of the organization, and the founding address, "The Excellence of Soul," by Dr. C. Eric Lincoln, the president of the Academy.*

Purposes

The following are the purposes for which the Black Academy of Arts and Letters has been organized:

1. to define, preserve, cultivate, promote, foster and develop the arts and letters of black people;
2. to promote and encourage public recognition of the universality of the arts and letters of black people;
3. to promote and encourage fellowship and cooperation among black artists, composers, musicians, writers, performers, scholars and all others engaged in artistic and creative endeavors;
4. to promote and encourage the public recognition and honor of its members and such others as it may from time to time choose as being representative of its purposes, goals and objectives;
5. to promote and encourage the dissemination of the arts and letters of black people;
6. to promote and encourage the holding of competitions, exhibits, performances, presentations and showings of the arts and letters of black people;
7. to provide a reference depository accessible to members and others which will depict (through any and all media now known or subsequently developed, including but not limited to photographs, paintings, sketches, carvings, castings, moldings, films, tapes, recordings, engravings and publications) the skills and achievements of black people in the arts and letters;
8. to provide encouragement to and an outlet for the creative expressions and interpretations of black people in the arts and letters;
9. to establish, provide, and grant fellowships, scholarships,

prizes and awards for creative efforts and achievements in the arts and letters of black people.

The Excellence of Soul

The Founding Address, The Black Academy of Arts and Letters, Boston, March 27, 1969
by C. Eric Lincoln

> We have come
> Over a way that with tears has been watered
> We have come
> Treading a path through the blood of the slaughtered
> Out of the gloomy past
> Till now we stand at last
> Where the white gleam
> Of our bright star
> Is cast.*

Look back. Look back, but not in anger. Look back with pride.

There is something happening in America. Something that is new. Something that is refreshing. Something that is beautiful. It is the coming of age of the Blackamerican. It is the maturation of a people. It is the emergence of an indomitable spirit beating strong against the wind and soaring in the sunlight. The chrysalis is broken. We are free.

The Black Academy of Arts and Letters is a sign of that freedom, for if the chrysalis which held us captive was moulded with layers of gossamer gratuitously provided, it was the spittle of our own agonizing uncertainty that glued it together and made it a prison. Freedom is a matter of self-will. It works from the inside out. The true freedom, the self-willed freedom of the Blackamerican is the imprimatur of the Black Academy of Arts and Letters. There can be no other.

Tomorrow an incredulous world will exclaim: "A *Black Academy!* Why a *black* academy?" Tomorrow we will give the world a simple answer for its incredulity: "Yes. A Black Academy because there are black people." A Black Academy of Arts and Letters is one way of coming to terms with reality in a society which has not made up its mind about the

*James Weldon Johnson, *Lift Every Voice.*

significance of color in its evaluations of excellence, and is not at all incredulous about that fact. It will be insisted that there is but one standard of excellence. We agree. We will not ask "whose?" nor will we ask what factors not related to excellence condition the prevailing interpretation and recognition of excellence. We know the answers for they are crystallized in a tradition of parsimony wherever excellence in the black experience has been considered. Let it be said at the outset: the Black Academy of Arts and Letters is not a signification of two standards of excellence. But the existence of the Black Academy may well suggest that we have no comfortable assurance that a judgment of excellence may be taken for granted merely because a common standard may exist. Quite the contrary.

The traditional distribution of accolades in this society has always been drastically influenced by the same traditional conceptualizations which have always determined most of what we do, and why we do it. A Black Academy of Arts and Letters is a way of affirming the existence of creative excellence in places where we are not accustomed to look for it, and recognizing it where it has gone unrecognized. I think the music of Duke Ellington, the painting of Aaron Douglas, the scholarship of Benjamin Quarles, Sinclair Drake, Charles Wesley deserve recognition. The quality of their work is excellent by any standards. If there is but one standard of excellence, show me the man with eyes so dim, ears so encrusted, tastes so mean that he would deny it! Show me the man and I will show you why the Black Academy of Arts and Letters has come into existence.

The Black Academy of Arts and Letters exists for the proper recognition of those who have made a notable contribution to Black America. But there is a more fundamental reason for its existence. It exists as a symbol of the love and concern we have for our children. I intend no cheap and shallow ethnocentric rhetoric when I say that we are a great people. It is time for the world to know it, but more crucial than any other value is that it is time for our children to know it. We are not great because we are black. Color is a physical accident. We are great because for 350 years we have been a latent, silent resource to the developing greatness of America and western civilization. What America is, we helped her to become. There is no aspect of the culture of this nation which has not been touched by the black presence; by what we have said and by what we have done. You will not find the black contribution in the textbooks or in the archives; for that is not in the American tradition. Look rather at the shaping of the law, the development of the economy, the viability of religion, the liveliness and the imaginativeness of the arts and you will feel the black presence. Look at literate, creative, productive, responsible Black America and see what the genius of black educators have produced, *ex nihilo*, as it were, and under the most degraded, demeaning conditions ever known to American education. We are Americans, and properly so. Whatever that destiny may be that shall illustrate the pages of American history, tomorrow, and for whatever tomorrows there are to follow, shall of a certainty bear our impulses. We are Americans. We will remain so. But by some irrevocable accidents of history, we are Blackamericans, and that is our proud and unique distinction. A Black Academy of Arts and Letters recognizes that fact and communicates it to our children. The Academy is the living evidence that black people, people like their own fathers and mothers, and others who comprise their world of significant relationships, do in fact achieve. The Black Academy gives legitimacy to the aspirations of black youth. It gives reality to speculation, solidity to dreams. It insists to the black youth who dares to be creative that somebody cares about your dream, somebody cares about your effort. Somebody cares about you and the shaping of your life, the development of your aspirations.

We shall give the lie to the implication, however inadvertent, that each generation produces its unique, distinctive Negro. One. In the singular. There was Frederick Douglass; there was Booker T. Washington; there was Martin Luther King. A benign, paternalistic society has given honor to these men, each in his time by memorializing them in the names of schools, parks, avenues and the like. Half the universities in the country have Martin Luther King chairs, or fellowships or buildings, or are planning them. Martin Luther King deserves honor—great honor, but when honor is exaggerated in a single individual, a critical judgment is implied on the rest of the group. In the long span of black history in America, was there only Douglass, and Washington, and King? To name a hundred chairs for Martin Luther King is to be contemptuous of the people Martin Luther King gave his life to have recognized. Why are there no Charles Drew or Daniel Hale Williams chairs in medicine? Why no E. Franklin Frazier or Charles S. Johnson chairs in sociology? When will there be a Lewis Latimer chair in physics? When will we have Langston

Hughes fellowships? Ira Aldridge fellowships? Augusta Savage fellowships? Granville Woods fellowships?

Finally, the Black Academy has something to do with soul. Soul is the reaffirmation of the black man's estimate of himself. It is the connective skein that runs through the totality of the black experience, weaving it together and infusing it with meaning. It is the sustaining force which makes endurance possible far beyond the limits of mere physical capacity; it is that which retrieves kinship, and empathy and understanding from the brutalizing atomization of oppression and alienation. Soul is the resuscitated black ego wresting victory from defeat and investing a tragic historical experience with courage, dignity, creativity and determination.

Soul is not art, but it has an artistic expression. It is in the music of Julian Adderly, the canvasses of Vertis Hayes, the choreography of Katherine Dunham, the dancing of Alvin Ailey, the rhetoric of Martin Luther King. Soul is not Letters but it is the empathy that informs with a rare and peculiar distinctiveness the poetry of Langston Hughes, the biographies of Arna Bontemps, the social history of Lerone Bennett. Soul is the essence of blackness. It is the creative genius of the liberated men and women who have come to terms with themselves and with their heritage. If black is beautiful, it is soul that makes it so. If what is black can also be excellent, the Black Academy of Arts and Letters is long overdue.

Second Annual Awards Banquet

(September, 1971)

At its Second Annual Awards Banquet the Academy initiated a policy of honoring the authors of outstanding books published during the preceding year. A special presentation for non-fiction was awarded to George Jackson for his book, *Soledad Brother: The Prison Letters of George Jackson.* Mari Evans received the poetry award for her book, *I Am A Black Woman.* William Melvin Kelley received the fiction award for his novel *Dunfords Travels Everywheres.* Franklin W. Knight received an award for his scholarly study, *Slave Society in Cuba During the 19th Century.*

Three new names were added to the Academy Hall of Fame:
- Frederick Douglass, abolitionist, author, and statesman;

- Ira Aldridge, actor; and
- George Washington Williams, historian.

The Academy regular awards for outstanding and meritorious achievement were presented to:

- Gwendolyn Brooks, poet, "for outstanding achievement in Letters";
- Katherine Dunham, anthropologist, dancer, choreographer, author and teacher, "for outstanding achievement in the Arts"; and
- Edward (Duke) Ellington, musician, "for the Medal of Merit."

BIBLIOGRAPHY

JAMES BALDWIN

FICTION

Go Tell It on the Mountain, New York, Knopf, 1953.
Signet paperback, 1963. Dell paperback, 1965; also
Universal Library. (Novel)

Giovanni's Room, New York, Dial, 1956. Dell paperback, 1964; also Apollo. (Novel)

Another Country, New York, Dial, 1962. Dell paperback, 1963. (Novel)

Going to Meet the Man, New York, Dial, 1965. Dell
paperback, 1966. (Short stories)

Tell Me How Long the Train's Been Gone, New York,
Dial, 1968. Dell paperback, 1969. (Novel)

ESSAYS AND MISCELLANEOUS PROSE

Notes of a Native Son, Boston, Beacon, 1955. Bantam
paperback, 1964; also Beacon.

Nobody Knows My Name, New York, Dial, 1961.
Dell paperback, 1964; also Delta.

The Fire Next Time, New York, Dial, 1963. Dell
paperback, 1964; also Delta.

Nothing Personal, Photographs by Richard Avedon,
New York, Atheneum, 1964. Dell paperback, 1965.

and Margaret Mead, *A Rap on Race*, Philadelphia,
Lippincott, 1971.

DRAMA

Blues for Mister Charlie, New York, Dial, 1964. Dell
paperback, 1964.

The Amen Corner, New York, Dial, 1968.

IMAMU AMIRI BARAKA (LeROI JONES)

POETRY

Preface to a Twenty Volume Suicide Note, New York, Corinth/Citadel, 1961. Totem/Corinth paperback, 1967.

The Dead Lecturer, New York, Grove, 1964. Evergreen paperback.

Black Arts, Newark, N. J., Jihad, 1966, also 1967.

Black Magic: Collected Poetry, 1961-1967, Indianapolis and New York, Bobbs-Merrill, 1969.

It's Nation Time, Chicago, Third World Press, 1970.

DRAMA

Dutchman and The Slave, New York, Morrow, 1964. Apollo paperback.

Baptism and The Toilet, New York, Grove, 1967; also paperback.

Slave Ship, Newark, N. J., Jihad, 1967.

Arm Yourself, or Harm Yourself!, Newark, N. J., Jihad, 1967.

Four Black Revolutionary Plays, Indianapolis and New York, Bobbs-Merrill, 1969.

Jello, Chicago, Third World Press, 1970.

FICTION

System of Dante's Hell, New York, Grove, 1966. Evergreen paperback, 1967. (Novel)

Tales, New York, Grove, 1967. (16 short stories)

CRITICISM

Blues People: Negro Music in White America, New York, Morrow, 1963. Apollo paperback, 1966.

Black Music, New York, Morrow, 1967. Apollo paperback, 1968.

ESSAYS

Home, New York, Morrow, 1966. Apollo paperback, 1967.

and Fundi (Billy Abernathy) photographs. In Our Terribleness: Some Elements and Meaning in Black Style, Indianapolis and New York, Bobbs-Merrill, 1971.

Raise Race Rays Raze: Essays Since 1965, New York, Random House, 1971.

ANTHOLOGIES

Ed., The Moderns: New Fiction in America, New York, Corinth/Citadel, 1963.

Ed., *Four Young Lady Poets*, New York, Corinth/ Citadel, 1964; also paperback.

and Larry Neal, eds., *Black Fire: An Anthology of Afro-American Writing*, New York, Morrow, 1968; also paperback.

GERALD W. BARRAX

POETRY
Another Kind of Rain, Pittsburgh, University of Pittsburgh Press, 1970.

GWENDOLYN BROOKS

POETRY
A Street in Bronzeville, New York, Harper, 1945.

Annie Allen, New York, Harper, 1949.

Bronzeville Boys and Girls, New York, Harper, 1956. (Poems for children)

The Bean Eaters, New York, Harper, 1960.

Selected Poems, New York, Harper and Row paperback, 1963.

In the Mecca, Harper and Row, New York, 1964.

Riot, Detroit, Broadside Press, 1968.

Family Pictures, Detroit, Broadside Press, 1970.

FICTION
Maud Martha, New York, Harper, 1953. Popular Library paperback, 1967. (Novel)

COLLECTED WRITINGS
The World of Gwendolyn Brooks, New York, Harper and Row, 1971. (Incorporates in one volume the following five earlier books: *A Street in Bronzeville, Annie Allen, Maud Martha, The Bean Eaters,* and *In the Mecca.*

ANTHOLOGIES
Ed., *Jump Bad: A New Chicago Anthology*, Detroit, Broadside Press, 1971. (Poems by 12 Black Chicago Poets)

CECIL BROWN

FICTION

> *The Life and Loves of Mr. Jiveass Nigger*, New York, Farrar, Strauss, and Giroux, 1970. Fawcett Crest paperback, 1971. (Novel)

ELDRIDGE CLEAVER

ESSAYS AND MISCELLANEOUS PROSE

> *Soul on Ice*, New York, McGraw-Hill, 1968. Delta paperback, 1968; Dell paperback, 1970.
> *Post-Prison Writings and Speeches*, Ed. by Robert Scheer, New York, Random House, 1969. Vintage paperback, 1969.

INTERVIEW

> by Lee Lockwood. *Conversation With Eldridge Cleaver—Algiers*, New York, Delta paperback, 1970.

CYRUS COLTER

FICTION

> *The Beach Umbrella*, Iowa City, University of Iowa Press, 1970. (14 short stories)

JAYNE CORTEZ

POETRY

> *Pissstained Stairs and the Monkey Man's Wares*, Los Angeles, Phrase Text (n. d.)
> *Festivals and Funerals*, New York, Phrase Text, 1971.

VICTOR HERNANDEZ CRUZ

POETRY

> *Snaps*, New York, Random House, 1969. Vintage paperback, 1969.

TOM DENT

ANTHOLOGIES

and Richard Schechner and Gilbert Moses, eds., *The Free Southern Theater by the Free Southern Theater, A documentary of the South's Radical Black Theater, with journals, letters, poetry, essays and a play written by those who built it*, Indianapolis and New York, Bobbs-Merrill, 1969.

RALPH ELLISON

FICTION

Invisible Man, New York, Random House, 1952. Signet paperback, 1953. (Novel)

ESSAYS

Shadow and Act, New York, Random House, 1964. Signet paperback, 1966.

JAMES A. EMANUEL

POETRY

The Treehouse and Other Poems, Detroit, Broadside Press, 1968.

Panther Man, Detroit, Broadside Press, 1970.

CRITICISM

Langston Hughes, New York, Twayne Publishers, 1967.

ANTHOLOGIES

and Theodore L. Gross, Eds., *Dark Symphony: Negro Literature in America*, New York, Free Press, 1968; also paperback.

MARI EVANS

POETRY

I Am a Black Woman, New York, Morrow, 1970, hardcover and paperback.

RONALD L. FAIR

FICTION

Many Thousand Gone, New York, Harcourt, Brace, and World, 1965. (Novel)

Hog Butcher, New York, Harcourt, Brace, and World, 1966. (Novel)

World of Nothing, New York, Harper and Row, 1970. (2 novellas)

VAL FERDINAND

POETRY

The Blues Merchant, New Orleans, NKOMBO Publications, BLKARTSOUTH, 1969.

RENALDO FERNANDEZ

POETRY

The Impatient Rebel, New Orleans, NKOMBO Publications, BLKARTSOUTH, 1969.

ERNEST J. GAINES

FICTION

Catherine Carmier, New York, Atheneum, 1964. (Novel)

Of Love and Dust, New York, Dial, 1967. Bantam paperback, 1969. (Novel)

Bloodline, New York, Dial, 1968. Bantam paperback, 1970. (Short stories)

The Autobiography of Miss Jane Pittman, New York, Dial, 1971. (Novel)

ADDISON GAYLE, JR.

ANTHOLOGIES

Ed., *Black Expression. Essays by and About Black Americans in the Creative Arts*, New York, Weybright and Talley, 1969; also paperback.

Ed., *The Black Aesthetic*, Garden City, N. Y., 1971.
Ed., *Bondage Freedom and Beyond: The Prose of Black Americans*, New York, Doubleday. Zenith paperback, 1971.

ESSAYS

The Black Situation, New York, Horizon Press, 1970.

NIKKI GIOVANNI

POETRY

Black Judgement, Detroit, Broadside Press, 1968.
Black Feeling Black Talk, Detroit, Broadside Press, 1968.
RE: CREATION, Detroit, Broadside Press, 1970.
Black Feeling, Black Talk, Black Judgement, New York, Morrow, 1970, hardcover and paperback.

ANTHOLOGIES

Ed., *Night Comes Softly: Anthology of Black Female Voices*, New York, Nik Tom Publications, 1971.

NATHAN HARE

SOCIOLOGICAL STUDY

The Black Anglo-Saxons, New York, Marzani and Munsell, 1965.

MICHAEL S. HARPER

POETRY

Dear John, Dear Coltrane, Pittsburgh, University of Pittsburgh Press, 1970.
History is Your Own Heartbeat, Urbana, University of Illinois Press, 1971.

ROBERT HAYDEN

POETRY

Heart-Shape in the Dust, Detroit, Falcon, 1940.
and Myron O'Higgins, *The Lion and the Archer*, published privately, limited ed., 1948.

A Ballad of Remembrance, London, Paul Breman, 1962.

Selected Poems, New York, October House, 1966.

Words in the Mourning Time, New York, October House, 1970.

Anthologies

Ed., *Kaleidoscope: Poems by American Negro Poets*, New York, Harcourt, Brace and World, 1967.

and David J. Burrows, and Frederick R. Lapides, eds., *Afro-American Literature: An Introduction*, New York, Harcourt Brace Jovanovich, 1971.

CHESTER HIMES

Fiction

If He Hollers Let Him Go, New York, Doubleday, Doran, 1945. Signet paperback, 1950; Berkley paperback, 1955. (Novel)

Lonely Crusade, New York, Knopf, 1947. (Novel)

Cast the First Stone, New York, Coward-McCann, 1952. (Novel)

The Third Generation, Cleveland, World, 1954. Signet paperback, 1956 (Novel)

The Primitive, New York, Signet paperback, 1955. (Novel)

A Case of Rape (Une Affaire de Viol), (published only in France, in French translation), Paris, *Editions les Yeux Ouverts*, 1960. (Novel)

Pinktoes, New York, Putnam, 1965; Dell paperback, 1967; Originally published in France, Paris, Olympia Press, 1961. (Novel)

Harlem Detective Series:

For Love of Imabelle, Greenwich, Conn., Fawcett, 1957; Avon paperback retitled *A Rage in Harlem*, 1964. Originally published in France in French translation as *La Reine des Pommes*, 1957 (winner of *"Le Prix du Roman Policier"* for France in 1958).

The Real Cool Killers, New York, Avon paperback, 1959; Berkley paperback, 1966. Originally published in France in French translation as *Il Pleut des Cours Durs*, 1958.

The Crazy Kill, New York, Avon paperback, 1960; Berkley paperback, 1966. Originally published as

Couche dans le Pain in France in French translation, 1958.

Run Man Run, New York, Putnam, 1968; Dell paperback, 1969. Originally published as *Dare Dare* in France in French translation, 1959.

The Big Gold Dream, New York, Avon paperback, 1960; Berkley paperback, 1966. Originally published in France in French translation as *Tout pour Plaire,* 1959.

All Shot Up, New York, Avon paperback, 1962; Berkley paperback, 1966. Originally published in France in French translation as *Imbroglio Négro,* 1960.

The Heat's On, New York, Putnam, 1967; Dell paperback, 1968. Originally published in France in French translation as *Ne Nous Everons Pas,* 1961.

Cotton Comes to Harlem, New York, Putnam, 1966; Dell paperback, 1967. Originally published in France in French translation as *Retour en Afrique,* 1963.

Blind Man With a Pistol, New York, Morrow, 1969; Dell paperback retitled *Hot Day Hot Night,* 1969.

EVERETT HOAGLAND

POETRY

Black Velvet, Detroit, Broadside Press, 1970.

LANCE JEFFERS

POETRY

My Blackness is the Beauty of This Land, Detroit, Broadside Press, 1970.

NORMAN JORDAN

POETRY

Destination: Ashes, Cleveland, Vibration Press, 1969.

MAULANA RON KARENGA

The Quotable Karenga, Los Angeles, United States Organization, 1967. (Mimeographed)

BOB KAUFMAN

POETRY

> *Solitudes Crowded With Loneliness*, New York, New
> Directions, 1965. ("The Abomunist Manifesto,"
> "Second April," and "Does the Secret Mind Whis-
> per," included in this selection, were originally pub-
> lished separately as Broadsides by City Lights, San
> Francisco, in 1959 and 1960.)
> *Golden Sardine*, San Francisco, City Lights Books,
> 1967.

WILLIAM MELVIN KELLEY

FICTION

> *A Different Drummer*, Garden City, N. Y., Double-
> day, 1962. Bantam paperback, 1964, and Doubleday.
> (Novel)
> *Dancers on the Shore*, Garden City, N. Y., Double-
> day, 1964. (Short stories)
> *A Drop of Patience*, Garden City, N. Y., Doubleday,
> 1965. (Novel)
> *dem*, New York, Doubleday, 1967. (Novel)
> *Dunfords Travels Everywhere*, Garden City, N. Y.,
> Doubleday, 1970. (Novel)

JOHN OLIVER KILLENS

FICTION

> *Youngblood*, New York, Dial, 1954. (Novel)
> *And Then We Heard the Thunder*, New York, Knopf,
> 1963. Pocket Books paperback, 1963. (Novel)
> *'Sippi*, New York, Trident, 1967. (Novel)
> *The Cotillion, or One Good Bull is Half the Herd*,
> New York, Trident, 1971. (Novel)

ESSAYS

> *Black Man's Burden*, New York, Trident, 1965.

ETHERIDGE KNIGHT

POETRY

> *Poems From Prison*, Detroit, Broadside Press, 1968.

ANTHOLOGIES

    Ed., *Black Voices from Prison*, New York, Pathfinder Press, 1970.

OLIVER LaGRONE

POETRY

    Footfalls: Poetry from America's Becoming, Detroit, Darel Press, 1949.

    They Speak of Dawns: A duo-poem narrating the journeys of the Astronaut and the Freedom rider. Detroit, Leatherman Printers, 1963. Third printing revised with additions, 1970.

DON L. LEE

POETRY

    Think Black! Chicago, Nu-Ace Social Printers, 1967.

    Black Pride, Detroit, Broadside Press, 1968.

    for black people (and negroes too) a poetic statement on black existence in america with a view of tomorrow, Chicago, Third World Press, 1968.

    Don't Cry, Scream, Detroit, Broadside Press, 1969.

    We Walk the Way of the New World, Detroit, Broadside Press, 1970.

    Directionscore: Selected and New Poems, Detroit, Broadside Press, 1971.

CRITICISM

    Dynamite Voices I: Black Poets of the 1960's, Detroit, Broadside Press, 1971.

RICHARD A. LONG

ANTHOLOGIES

    Ed., with Albert H. Berrian, *Négritude: Essays and Studies*, Hampton, Virginia, Hampton Institute Press, 1967.

AUDRE LORDE

POETRY

    The First Cities, New York, Poets Press, 1968.

Cables to Rage, London, Paul Breman (Heritage Series), 1970.

JAMES ALAN McPHERSON

FICTION

Hue and Cry, Boston, Little Brown, 1969. Fawcett Crest paperback, 1970. (10 short stories)

NAOMI LONG MADGETT

POETRY

Songs to a Phantom Nightingale, New York, Fortuny's, 1941. (Published under the name of Naomi Cornelia Long.)

One and the Many, New York, Exposition Press, 1956.

Star by Star, Detroit, Harlo Press, 1965. Revised edition, 1970.

CLARENCE MAJOR

POETRY

The Fires That Burn in Heaven, Privately printed, 1954.

Love Poems of a Black Man, Omaha, Nebraska, Coercion Press, 1964.

Human Juices, Omaha, Nebraska, Coercion Press, 1965.

Swallow the Lake, Middletown, Conn., Wesleyan University Press, 1970.

FICTION

All-Night Visitors, New York, Olympia Press, 1969.

ANTHOLOGIES

Ed., *The New Black Poetry*, New York, International Publishers, 1969.

DICTIONARY

Dictionary of Afro-American Slang, New York, International Publishers, 1970.

MALCOLM X

AUTOBIOGRAPHY

with assistance of Alex Haley, *The Autobiography of Malcolm X*, New York, Grove, 1965; also paperback, 1966.

SPEECHES AND INTERVIEWS

Ed., George Breitman, *Malcolm X Speaks: Selected Speeches and Statements*, New York, Merit, 1965. Grove paperback.

Two Speeches by Malcolm X, New York, Pioneer Publishers paperback original, 1967.

Malcolm X on Afro-American History, New York, Merit paperback original, 1967. Expanded and illustrated edition, 1970.

The Speeches of Malcolm X at Harvard, Ed., Archie Epps, New York, Morrow, 1968.

Malcolm X Speaks to Young People, New York, Young Socialist Alliance (distributed by Merit), 1969.

Two Speeches by Malcolm X, New York, Merit paperback original, 1969.

The End of White World Supremacy: Four Speeches, Ed. Benjamin Goodman, New York, Monthly Review Press, 1971 (hardcover and paper).

ADAM DAVID MILLER

ANTHOLOGY

Ed., *Dices or Black Bones: Black Voices of the Seventies*, Boston, Houghton Mifflin, 1970.

NAYO (BARBARA MALCOM)

POETRY

I Want Me a Home, New Orleans, NKOMBO Publications, BLKARTSOUTH, 1969.

LARRY NEAL

POETRY
> *Black Boogaloo, (Notes on Black Liberation)*, San Francisco, Journal of Black Poetry Press, 1969.

ANTHOLOGY
> Ed. with LeRoi Jones, *Black Fire*, New York, Morrow, 1968; Apollo paperback, 1969.

TEJUMOLA OLOGBONI (ROCKIE D. TAYLOR)

POETRY
> *Drum Song*, Privately printed, Milwaukee, 1969.

RAYMOND R. PATTERSON

POETRY
> *26 Ways of Looking at a Black Man*, New York, Award Books, paperback original, 1969.

ROBERT DEANE PHARR

FICTION
> *The Book of Numbers*, Garden City, N. Y., Doubleday, 1969; Avon paperback, 1970. (Novel)
> *S.R.O.*, Garden City, N. Y., Doubleday, 1971. (Novel)

N. H. PRITCHARD

POETRY
> *The Matrix. Poems 1960–1970*, Garden City, N. Y., Doubleday, 1970, hardcover and paperback.

DUDLEY RANDALL

POETRY
> with Margaret Danner, *Poem Counterpoem*, Detroit, Broadside Press, 1966.
> *Cities Burning*, Detroit, Broadside Press, 1968.

Love You, London, Paul Breman, Heritage Series, 1970.

More to Remember, Chicago, Third World Press, 1971.

ANTHOLOGIES

and Margaret G. Burroughs, Eds., *For Malcolm,* Detroit, Broadside Press, 1967. (Poems on the life and death of Malcolm X)

Ed., *Black Poetry, A Supplement to Anthologies Which Exclude Black Poets,* Detroit, Broadside Press, 1969.

EUGENE REDMOND

POETRY

A Tale of Two Toms, n.p., East St. Louis, Ill., 1968.
A Tale of Time and Toilet Tissue, n.p., East St. Louis, Ill., 1969.
Sentry of the Four Golden Pillars, n.p., 1970.

ANTHOLOGIES

Ed., *Sides of the River: A Mini-Anthology of Black Writings,* n.p., 1969.

ISHMAEL REED

POETRY

catechism of d neoamerican hoodoo church, London, Paul Breman (Heritage Series), 1970.

FICTION

The Free-Lance Pall Bearers, Garden City, N. Y., Doubleday, 1967. Bantam paperback, 1969. (Novel)
Yellow Back Radio Broke-Down, Garden City, N. Y., Doubleday, 1969, hardcover and paperback. (Novel)

ANTHOLOGIES

Ed., *19 Necromancers from Now,* Garden City, N. Y., Doubleday, 1970, hardcover and paperback.

ED ROBERSON

POETRY

When thy King is a Boy, Pittsburgh, University of Pittsburgh Press, 1970.

SONIA SANCHEZ

POETRY

Homecoming, Detroit, Broadside Press, 1969.
We A BaddDDD People, Detroit, Broadside Press, 1970.
It's a New Day (poems for young brothers and sisters), Detroit, Broadside Press, 1971.

STEPHANY

POETRY

Moving Deep, Detroit, Broadside Press, 1969.

SOTÈRE TORREGIAN

POETRY

The Golden Palomino Bites the Clock, New York, Angel Hair, 1966.
The Wounded Mattress, (Poems 1965), Berkeley, Calif., Oyez, 1971.

QUINCY TROUPE

ANTHOLOGIES

Ed., *Watts Poets: A Book of New Poetry and Essays,* Los Angeles, House of Respect, 1968.

DARWIN T. TURNER

POETRY

Katharsis, Wellesley, Mass., Wellesley Press, 1964.

ANTHOLOGIES

with Jean M. Bright, Eds., *Images of the Negro in America: Selected Source Materials for College Research Papers,* Boston, Heath, 1965.
Ed., *Black American Literature Fiction,* Columbus, Ohio, Merrill, 1969.

Ed., *Black American Literature Essays*, Columbus, Ohio, Merrill, 1969.

Ed., *Black American Literature Poetry*, Columbus, Ohio, Merrill, 1969.

BIBLIOGRAPHY

Afro-American Writers, New York, Appleton-Century-Crofts, 1970.

MARGARET WALKER

POETRY

For My People, New Haven, Conn., Yale University Press, 1942. Yale paperback, 1969.

Prophets for a New Day, Detroit, Broadside Press, 1970.

FICTION

Jubilee, Boston, Houghton Mifflin, 1966. Bantam paperback, 1967. (Novel)

RAYMOND WASHINGTON

POETRY

Vision from the Ghetto, New Orleans, NKOMBO Publications, BLKARTSOUTH, 1969.

TOM WEATHERLY

POETRY

Maumau American Cantos, New York, Corinth Books, 1970.

ANTHOLOGIES

and Ted Wilentz, Eds., *Natural Process: An Anthology of New Black Poetry*, New York, Hill and Wang, 1971.

JAY WRIGHT

POETRY

The Home Coming Singer, New York, Corinth Books, 1971.

AL YOUNG

POETRY
> *Dancing,* New York, Corinth Books, 1969.
> *The Song Turning Back into Itself,* New York, Holt,
> Rinehart, and Winston, 1971.

FICTION
> *Snakes,* New York, Holt, Rinehart, and Winston,
> 1970. London, Sidgwick and Jackson, 1971. (Novel)

MENTOR   Ⓢ **SIGNET**   (0451)

AFRICAN AMERICAN STUDIES

☐ **AFRICANS AND THEIR HISTORY by Joseph E. Harris.** A landmark reevaluation of African cultures by a leading black historian. "A major brief summary of the history of Africa."—Elliot P. Skinner, *Columbia University* (625560—$4.99)

☐ **THE CLASSIC SLAVE NARRATIVES edited by Henry Louis Gates, Jr.** One of America's foremost experts in black studies, presents a volume of four classic slave narratives that illustrate the real nature of the black experience with the horrors of bondage and servitude. (627261—$5.99)

☐ **BEFORE FREEDOM edited and with an Introduction by Belinda Hurmence.** The oral history of American slavery in the powerful words of former slaves. Including the two volumes *Before Freedom, When I Can Just Remember* and *My Folks Don't Want Me to Talk About Slavery.* "Eloquent . . . historically valuable."—*Los Angeles Times Book Review* (627814—$4.99)

☐ **BLACK LIKE ME by John Howard Griffin.** The startling, penetrating, first-hand account of a white man who learned what it is like to live as a black in the South. Winner of the *Saturday Review* Anisfield-Wolf Award. (163176—$4.99)

☐ **THE SOULS OF BLACK FOLK by W.E.B. DuBois.** A passionate evaluation of the blacks' bitter struggle for survival and self-respect, and a classic in the literature of the civil rights movement. Introduction by Nathan Hare and Alvin F. Poussaint. (523970—$4.95)

Prices slightly higher in Canada.

Buy them at your local bookstore or use this convenient coupon for ordering.

PENGUIN USA
P.O. Box 999 – Dept. #17109
Bergenfield, New Jersey 07621

Please send me the books I have checked above.
I am enclosing $_____ (please add $2.00 to cover postage and handling).
Send check or money order (no cash or C.O.D.'s) or charge by Mastercard or VISA (with a $15.00 minimum). Prices and numbers are subject to change without notice.

Card #_____ Exp. Date _____
Signature_____
Name_____
Address_____
City _____ State _____ Zip Code _____

For faster service when ordering by credit card call **1-800-253-6476**

Allow a minimum of 4-6 weeks for delivery. This offer is subject to change without notice.

By the year 2000, 2 out of 3 Americans could be illiterate.

It's true.

Today, 75 million adults...about one American in three, can't read adequately. And by the year 2000, U.S. News & World Report envisions an America with a literacy rate of only 30%.

Before that America comes to be, you can stop it...by joining the fight against illiteracy today.

Call the Coalition for Literacy at toll-free **1-800-228-8813** and volunteer.

Volunteer Against Illiteracy. The only degree you need is a degree of caring.